The UNEXPECTED KING

Volume Two of
The Raspero Chronicles

A. J. McMAHON

The Unexpected King: Volume Two of the Raspero Chronicles

A.J. McMahon

Published by Silverbird Publishing

First published 2020

978-0-6487561-6-3 (pbk)

978-0-6487561-7-0 (ebook)

Designer / typesetter: Working Type Studio (www.workingtype.com.au)

Printed by Lightning Source.

 A catalogue record for this book is available from the National Library of Australia

CONTENTS

CHAPTER ONE

I saw you once.
I knew you through myself.
Frankie the Villain

8:45 AM, Monday 13 April 1882 A. F. (After the Fall)

The path twisted and turned through the large oak and sycamore trees spreading their branches overhead, burrowing through islands of green ferns as it deftly threaded its way through the forest. The forest was deep and dark and cool, lit by bright slanting lines of golden light which fell like arrows through gaps in the tree tops onto clumps of pale-yellow primroses, lavender-blue bluebells and golden-yellow daffodils that lay here and there as if scattered by a generous hand. At times the forest fell back from the path into clearings which opened up to the bright dome of the sky with its white clouds floating in the blue; at other times the forest crowded the path as if meaning to swallow it whole; and all while the existence of the path attracted the continued tread of feet which kept it in existence.

A man walked along this path on this fine April morning. It was the day after his twenty-second birthday. He was of medium height, black-haired and grey eyed, dressed in plain light blue robes belted with a weapons belt carrying a wand and disc and bolts, his leather boots laced up to his knees, his loose red trousers concealing yet more hidden weapons strapped around his upper thighs. A deer munching with delicate lips on a shrub gave a nervous look at him walking past, tense and ready to flee;

1

a bee droning past fell silent as it crawled happily up into a bluebell; birds perched on branches overhead, their heads turning from side to side as they stepped here and there, their movements as indecipherable as hieroglyphs. He jumped lightly over a tree-trunk fallen across the forest path, as cheerful as the day.

Matthias Raspero was on his way to work. He worked at the Ministry of Transport in one of thirty identical cubicles filled with other men and women engaged in the many and varying tasks associated with the transport of goods and people and livestock between Anglashia and the wider world. He was known as Ryan Grangeshield to his fellow workers, which was a false name he had acquired via his genuine relatives. Although his working day was filled with mundane tasks, his job was not yet tedious as he found that living in exile with a price on his head helped him to appreciate the simpler things in life.

He emerged from the forest into the Park of Regana. The park was laid out with ponds and trees, ornamental rock gardens and sculptures, fountains and flower-bordered walkways. Various people were making their way along these walkways to the Ministry, which stood at one side of the park. The Ministry was a large mansion with a square tower in the centre. Once the highly-polished pride of a duke, the Regana Palace was now the well-worn seat of bureaucrats and politicians and workers, all bowed down by the tedium of their employment.

There was one notable difference, today, however to the usual work-day: to one side of the open gates of the Ministry there stood a delegation of Westrigonian noblemen, awkwardly aware of the curious looks they were attracting from the Anglashian Ministry of Transport employees, because of their foreign clothes and equally foreign wide-brimmed hats decked with the even more foreign regalia of their still yet more foreign offices. The Westrigonian delegation had been waiting since dawn. They were stiff and cold and hungry, and tired from lack of sleep; yet the importance of their mission kept them standing to attention on that April morning.

As Matthias approached, they kneeled before him and said in a chorus: 'Good morning, Your Majesty.'

Matthias considered them for a moment, his face carefully impassive.

'Arise, good subjects,' he said eventually, with a lofty wave of his hand, looking a little amused; but he waved them to their feet with his left hand, while his right hand stayed casually by the hilt of his wand.

The Westrigonians clambered to their feet a little stiffly, the cold of their early morning arrival lingering a little still in their bones.

'Greetings to you, Lord Camdenshall,' Matthias said politely to one of the delegation.

Lord Camdenshall bowed deeply, sweeping his plumed hat low to the ground. 'I am at your service, Your Majesty,' he said.

'It's a pleasure to meet you again, Lord Shyester,' Matthias said as politely as before.

Lord Shyester and his hat also bowed deeply. 'Your Majesty is too kind.'

'Cavalier Lyttleton,' Matthias said, nodding to the next man along.

'Your Majesty!' The Cavalier bowed so deeply he nearly overbalanced.

'You look familiar,' Matthias said to the young man standing beside the Cavalier.

'Alaric Niedbala, Your Majesty,' Alaric said with the required deep bow.

'Of course! Now I remember! Honourable Niedbala. And I remember you from the Vidaldmeet,' Matthias continued, looking at a short man with a large black beard.

'Sigdale Rayerfeld, Your Majesty,' said blackbeard and bowed.

'Ah, of course, the Baron of Rayerfeld. Greetings to you, Lord Rayerfeld. And you are?'

'Emmerich Waldemar, Your Majesty.'

'Greetings, Counsellor Waldemar,' Matthias said, as if reading his title from his insignia. He raised his eyebrows at the next man along.

'Akseli Englebert, Your Majesty.'

'Greetings, Counsellor Engelbert.'

'Anastasius Annora, Your Majesty.'

'Keeper Annora, greetings to you. Well met to you all, and welcome to Anglashia.'

There was a pause during which no-one seemed inclined to say anything. Matthias looked impassively at his Westrigonian visitors, while they gazed impassively back at him.

'So what's all this with addressing me as *Your Majesty*?' Matthias asked eventually, addressing his question to Lord Camdenshall.

'The Vidaldmeet has elected you King of Westrigonia, Your Majesty.'

'Have they indeed? And when did this happen?'

'Yesterday, Sire, at three o'clock in the afternoon.'

Matthias thought about this, again looking at the Westrigonians, while they in turn again considered him. 'You'd better come with me and tell me all about it,' he said at last.

He led them off to the side where a number of stone chairs and benches stood in front of a rock garden ruled by a statue of the Lord of the North which loomed overhead. Matthias sat down and waved his fellow Westrigonians to their seats.

'So why was I elected King?' Matthias asked with a smile. 'Apart from my obvious monarchical qualities?'

'As I am sure you are aware, Your Majesty, our beloved homeland has been invaded by the Baalbabakans and Melisendiens,' Lord Camdenshall replied. He paused while Matthias nodded to confirm that he had indeed heard of this invasion, and then continued: 'The Baalbabakans and Melisendiens have divided our country between them. Westrigonia is now under foreign occupation. King Frederick is a prisoner in Rozneft and the price of his freedom is to grant the Baalbabakans sovereignty over the province of Steynrad and to give the Melisendiens the province of Prosstogne, in addition to a number of concessions concerning trade routes. King Frederick has agreed to these demands. The Vidaldmeet were allowed by these occupiers to meet yesterday to approve his decision as required by the constitution. However, we decided instead to depose Frederick and elect you, Your Majesty, as King in order that these concessions made by Frederick should be rendered null and void. Frederick's capitulation to the demands of his captors is no longer the capitulation of the monarch of Westrigonia but the agreement of a person without the authority to make such decisions.'

'So you needed someone other than Frederick to be King, but why me?' Matthias asked.

'Your name is known from one end of Westrigonia to another, Sire.

Your fame is unrivalled,' Camdenshall observed, as reverently as if this explained everything. 'This is necessary in order for the common people as well as the nobility and those of the third force to accept you as King. It makes such a change politically feasible.'

'You're a Westrigonian nobleman,' Rayerfeld added emphatically, leaning forward as if to fire his words into Matthias from a closer range. 'It is time for a Westrigonian monarch to arise. For too long have we been ruled by these foreign usurpers, these Zoller-Abstein intruders, these Zoller-Abstein foreigners, these Zoller-Abstein auctioneers. Let a Westrigonian ascend to the throne of Krastienst! I say a Westrigonian nobleman is worth more than the Protector and his whole crowd! Let us have a Westrigonian monarch once again!'

'This is all very well,' Matthias said calmly, 'but as I am not of the royal houses I cannot be a candidate under the Constitution.'

'The recent revocation of the Changeling Laws by which the Protector D'Asterides himself was enabled to be elected has changed the status of the Barony of Raspero into a cadet royal House of Harentain,' said Councillor Waldemar. 'Alyssa, the first Baroness of Raspero, was declared a Changeling, as you yourself of course will know; but as the existence of Changelings has been legally revoked, her status has reverted to that of the royal house of Harentain as her father was a Duke of that house. As her direct descendant, you are now eligible under the Constitution to be a candidate for the throne of Westrigonia.'

'So where is my Letter of Declaration?' Matthias asked.

Everyone looked at Camdenshall, who looked a little uncertain of what to say. 'I can only humbly apologise, Your Majesty, but the Letter was still being signed as we departed. We were obliged to make such haste to the portal that there was no time to wait for all due formalities to be completed. The Letter has undoubtedly been completed by now. It shall in due time be presented to you.'

'Perhaps you could tell me about the vote, then?' Matthias said.

'Certainly, Sire,' Rayerfeld said eagerly, as if it were a tale that warmed his heart. 'There were proxy votes as not everyone could make it due to the occupation. Seventeen of us voted for you to be King, the traitorous

Zoller-Absteins voted fifteen against, the Speaker nominated proxy votes according to province, nine proxy votes went to the Zoller-Absteins, six proxy votes from absent Zoller-Absteins fell to me; a further two absentee Zoller-Absteins votes fell to Camdenshall, which brought our total to twenty-five votes in favour to twenty-four against. Thus were you elected King of Westrigonia, Sire!'

'Where is Queen Yolande and the rest of the Royal Family?'

'They are very likely at the Palace of Krastienst, Sire. The exit Portal was burned out in an act of treachery by a departing Baalbabakan delegation.'

Matthias looked directly at Camdenshall. 'What is he talking about?'

'The day before the invasion a visiting Baalbabakan delegation came to discuss peace talks, and as Baron Rayerfeld has said, they burned out the exit Portal of the palace on their departure. Thus Queen Yolande was unable to leave when the invasion took place.'

'Queen Yolande. What about Princess Eleanor?'

'She is with Yolande in the Palace.'

'Why did they not leave through the public Portal?'

'I believe that the defences of the city were overcome in a much shorter time than anyone had anticipated. Probably Yolande thought she had plenty of time to make such an arrangement if necessary.'

Matthias was silent for a short while, as if he had run out of questions to ask, then said: 'I hope later historians will excuse me for failing to come up with a memorable quotation on this historic occasion, but I must admit that I can't think of anything to say! I'm speechless! And you can quote me! Hopefully that's a good omen.'

'It is your destiny to be King, your Majesty,' said Lord Rayerfeld excitedly.

'Destiny?' asked Matthias, a little warily.

'Do you not believe in destiny, your Majesty?' asked Shyester.

'Ever since the beginning of the world, men and women have been subject to various tricks of Fortuna,' said Matthias.

'Is that a quote?' Lyttleton asked.

'Probably,' said Matthias. 'Anyway, destiny or not, we have our decisions to make. So what happens next?'

'There is only one course of action that is practicable at present, Sire,' said Camdenshall. 'We must proceed to the Embassy of Westrigonia, from where we shall inform the Anglashian government that the King of Westrigonia is currently in exile and on Anglashian soil. From here you can convey to the Baalbabakans and Melisendiens your refusal of their demands. You can set up a government-in-exile here in Anglashia.'

Matthias fell silent, plunged deep in thought for five or six minutes or so. While Matthias thought things over, the members of the Westrigonian delegation took this opportunity to contemplate their new king. He was undeniably handsome, the regular features of his face forming a pleasing harmony which reconciled the gothic disjunction of his jet black hair and pale white skin like a ripple of piano keys. His grey eyes were observant and intelligent. The folded hands on which he was resting his chin were long-fingered and elegant. His strong nose formed a striking profile that evoked comparison with the haughtiest of the ancient nobles. It had to be said that he would look good stamped on a coin.

Yet there was not one of the Westrigonian delegation present on that day who was unaware of the reputation of Matthias Raspero. He was said to have more tricks up his sleeve than a barrelful of monkeys, and that was not counting the tricks he had already played up to that date. This was the *unrivalled fame* to which Camdenshall had earlier referred.

Matthias roused himself and stated very clearly, as if dictating a speech for transcription: 'There are so many things wrong with your policy that I don't know where to begin pointing them all out. Never mind. It is simpler instead for me to tell you in plain language what we are going to do. If I'm to be King, I'll return to Westrigonia and lead the war of liberation from there. We are going to travel from here to the portal of the Royal Palace of Krastienst right now, without delay.' He looked around at everyone present. 'Spare me your protests. I am not interested. Let's go.'

With that Matthias rose to his feet and set off towards the Ministry of Transport. The members of the Westrigonian delegation looked around at each other as they stood up and followed him in some disarray.

'Your Majesty,' Camdenshall protested as he trotted after his sovereign, 'you will be arrested immediately on arrival and –'

Matthias sighed, halted then spun to face Camdenshall so abruptly that Camdenshall reared back on his heels. 'Which part of the phrase *spare me your protests* did you fail to understand?' Matthias asked belligerently.

'But surely you do not understand the situation, Your Majesty,' Shyester protested. 'As the exit portal is burned out, it is a one-way journey into the Palace through the entry portal. It is only a matter of time before the Palace is taken by the enemy, you will fall into the hands of either the Baalbabakans or the Melisendiens and forced to surrender to their demands or be killed. You must stay here in Anglashia in order to form a government-in-exile that will preserve our beloved homeland in the face of this existential threat. It is an abdication of your responsibility to take such a reckless action as this.' Shyester, having been a prosecutor, knew how to send his words flying though the air like throwing knives, the word *abdication* especially being an implicit threat, as what the Vidaldmeet had given, namely the throne, the Vidaldmeet could take away.

Matthias then showed he could utter threats of his own. 'Before you choose not to follow me, take a good look around you at Anglashia, as this will be your home for the rest of your miserable lives. I will personally see to it that you pay for your treason with the loss of your lands, your titles and everything you hold dear in this earthly realm. Now: make your choice but stop bothering me with your whining!' Matthias was pleased to note, from the thunderous silence that followed, that no-one dared say anything. He was well on his way to being a king in more than just name, he reflected to himself.

With that, Matthias turned on his heel and walked off towards the Ministry. Alaric followed him without hesitation, then came Rayerfeld, who was so excited that he was tugging at his beard, then came the others one by one, hesitant but trapped into going along by the prospect of making a life-time enemy of their new king.

9:30 AM, Monday 13 April 1882 A. F.

The group of outlandishly attired foreigners, striding purposefully along with Matthias at their head, drew plenty of looks from the Anglashians as they proceeded along their historic path towards the Ministry of Transport. Matthias led his uneasily-bound-together-for-the-moment band along the main driveway of the Ministry between the pillars of the front gate towards the front doors. Up the stone steps and into the stone-flagged courtyard they marched.

Matthias then led his little group into the entrance hall of the Regana Palace, long familiar to him as his workplace and also familiar to him in other terms. Matthias knew various arcane details of Anglashian history of which by then only the most erudite of contemporary historians could tell, and one of these obscure details was that the Regana Palace had been at one time hired out as a vehicle of dreams several centuries ago. One of these dreams was the dream of the forthcoming marriage, and here it was that Sir Nicholas Grangeshield and his Lady Isabel had held their engagement party more than three centuries ago, in the same building where they had first been introduced. Sir Nicholas was a direct ancestor of Matthias Raspero, and Matthias could not help but think, wherever he looked, that the same sight had once been present to Nicholas's eyes in an earlier layer of historical time.

The entrance hall of the Regana Palace had a large domed ceiling with twelve separate quadrangular frescoes of the agricultural seasons of different months of the year, with a glorious sun and moon in the centre of it all with attendant stars in the deep dark blue in which they floated. It was stunningly beautiful, and hardly anyone trudging to work ever gave it a single look. Ahead was a flight of stairs leading to a corridor which itself led to further depths of the ducal palace. At the top of the stairs was a plinth surmounted by the statue of a naked discus thrower. A large vase of flowers was discreetly positioned in front of this statue.

Matthias led his little group past this statue and took them to the right, down some stairs, through a courtyard, and then into the Waiting Room of the Portal itself.

If function is value, then everything but the Portal could have been scrapped and no-one could have cared less about the loss of the intellectual and artistic heritage of antiquity. The Portal was money. This was what people really came here for. Never mind the rest of the Ministry of Transport. That was just the window dressing of the Portal.

More than three centuries ago, in Trentland, an experimenter by the name of Marmaduke Baxter Presley Hartwin had set forth in a slightly manic way with his disheveled appearance and chatterbox mannerisms to spend the entirety of his inheritance upon the funding of experiments which only a madman could have countenanced for a moment. By an unwitting combination of magnetized metals and an utterly fallacious sequence of reasoning, Chevalier Hartwin had transported an object between two positions through space at that same instant of time. Not a single person had believed a single word he had said concerning his discovery. What he had claimed to have achieved was, after all, impossible, or at least unknown to the knowledgeable people of the day, which came to the same thing. Where was the mechanism by which this process took place? What forces of nature could be said to be at work? It was all utterly absurd and beside the point and in any case, it hadn't even happened because it could not.

Hartwin was undaunted by this opposition but then Hartwin, even by the most sympathetic account of his most adoring biographers, was a little bit mad. He challenged his chief opponent, Aniketos, to a bet: if he, Hartwin, could achieve this feat then he, Aniketos, would have to pay Hartwin the sum of one million strada, if not, then vice versa. Never mind that neither he nor Aniketos had a million strada to bet. The challenge was its own money, to be paid by the grovelling apologies by the loser, and cashed in by the gracious, condescending and damning forgiveness of the winner.

It was a cunning ploy. Those unwilling to credit Hartwin with genius in two separate fields later credited the authorship of this move to his childhood friend Lady Alvis Caramia Sable; but be that as it may, Aniketos's immediate and lofty refusal of this challenge went nowhere. What Hartwin (or Sable) had instinctively understood was that the desire of onlookers to witness a fight was greater than the desire of onlookers to witness the truth. Hartwin could either do what he claimed or he could not; Aniketos could say what he wanted; but still, a million strada was a million strada! That was a lot of money. And just to keep the pot simmering, there was the ever-insistent mutterings of the mutterers that a wandfighting challenge could be issued, whether to Hartwin or

Aniketos or anyone who happened to be passing by. The interest and amusement was mounting almost to lustful argumentation, with each lash of logic being its own moment of exultation.

In a drunken moment of feeling greater than this vexing debate which had come to seem smaller than the clothes of yesteryear, Counsellor Callahan Palmer Burkhard Aniketos finally agreed to the challenge and history was made. The venue was selected, the judges were appointed, the conditions were set, the observers took their positions, the audience took their seats with many a laugh and outspoken comments, the bets had all been made with outlandishly improbable odds concerning Hartwin making good, and in the midst of all this, to the utter disbelief of all present and with an insouciance that did him credit, Hartwin succeeded in the sight of all present in transporting an object (a pen) from one table in the Exhibition Hall to another table in the same hall. No-one believed what they had just seen. It was all some kind of trickery, they protested. It was done by mirrors or some kind of conjuring. Hartwin was required to perform his portal transportation all over again, this time monitored by people who took him seriously, and stood looking over his shoulder; but even that was not enough.

On that historic day, Hartwin had to perform the feat over and over again before his claim was finally believed. Aniketos made his grovelling apology, Hartwin let him off paying the million strada, and then, surrounded by his newly made admirers (which included Aniketos), Hartwin explained his great discovery and was finally listened to by all those present. Every word Hartwin spoke was attended to as that of a pronouncement by the emissary of a god, which Hartwin had in fact become in the minds of many of those present.

And now this was all history. Portals had been established all around the world and had superseded even flying carriages. People and their goods could be transported anywhere in the world between portals in an instant. No-one really understood how portals worked, but an elaborate terminology based on the materials and procedures involved had produced an illusion of understanding by which the experts could "explain" things to the public.

One thing remained constant, however, over time: portals were expensive to build and maintain. The Portal of the Ministry of Transport of Anglashia charged high fees to transport people and goods, these fees being carefully calibrated to be less than all alternative means of transport. This was a successful business model, given that politics could be used to make money which in turn made more politics. Everyone was happy, except those who mistrusted on principle the idea of changes being made to how the world worked.

9:40 AM, Monday 13 April 1882 A. F.

Leaving his followers standing to one side, Matthias walked straight across the Waiting Room to where a wide-set, balding man stood stooped over a desk on which were spread various papers. This man was Markel Baldassare, the Officer in Charge of Portal Access. Baldassare was known far and wide (but never to his face) as Baldy.

'<Good morning, Mr Baldassare>,' Matthias said, speaking in Anglashian. He spoke very loudly, so Baldy, who had his head bent over the afore-mentioned papers, couldn't pretend not to have heard him. Baldy didn't like foreigners, and Matthias was always stamped as a foreigner by every heavily-accented word that he spoke in his broken Anglashian. (By the end of this day, Baldy would have thoroughly been confirmed in his prejudices against foreigners, given the string of illegal acts which Matthias had committed by then.)

Baldy grudgingly half-looked up, as if he only had a moment to spare, and not even that.

'<It is that we are to go Krastienst today>,' Matthias declared as loudly as before, the loudness of his voice compelling Baldy's attention. '<So it is please make Portal ready. It is priority access.>'

Baldy's nostrils flared, as if Matthias was a bad smell. '<Paperwork?>'

Matthias appeared to be astonished. '<It is not the paperwork already for you? Then it is the slip-up.>'

'<No paperwork, no access,>' Baldy stated baldly, already turning away from Matthias.

'<Then it is the paperwork from this very moment!>' Matthias said as loudly as before, and then turned away.

A later inquiry was to establish that this apparently inconclusive exchange of views had in fact laid the foundation for Baldy's later acceptance of Matthias's forged paperwork because it had implanted the idea of already-existing paperwork into the mind of the Officer in Charge of Portal Access. It had been a matter of subliminal imprinting. But by then it was much too late to do anything other than write a government report as Matthias himself, as a foreign head of state, was beyond extradition. The lawyers charged their fees, nonetheless.

Matthias led his Westrigonian delegation to one side with a wave of his hand into the neighbouring Annexe to the Waiting Room for the Portal. 'Wait here,' he told them briefly, already as preoccupied with the shuffling thoughts of his latest plans as a riverside gambler shuffling the cards of his loaded deck. 'Honourable Niedbala, come with me please.'

Matthias led Alaric to the stairs at the back of the Annexe to the Waiting Room, stairs that had led upwards, at one time in a much more romantic past, to the bedchamber of the Duke's mistress, but which led now to the much less attractive figure of the Chief Cleric of the Portal Records, Messire Bertrand Andromeda.

'Honourable Niedbala,' Matthias said as they walked along, 'say nothing, do what I tell you, and never stop moving. Got that?'

'Yes, Matthias,' Alaric said obediently, but as if he hadn't really listened to a word of what Matthias had said.

'And don't call me Matthias. We're supposed to barely know each other.'

'Yes, Matthias,' Alaric said as automatically as before.

Matthias shook his head and groaned out loud, but at the same time he was nearly grinning.

Messire Andromeda's head was bent over his desk as they walked into his office. He did not look up as they walked in, raising his left hand in the air to forestall any attempt on their part to interrupt his work, given that he was busily writing something.

'<It is that I am to have the day off, friend Andromeda, and it is from you the paperwork for this,>' Matthias said loudly.

Andromeda was caught between his upraised left hand and the interruption which it supposedly forbade, not to mention having been addressed as *friend Andromeda,* which unconventionality had momentarily unfocussed his attention, but he was not left in this interregnum for long.

'<It is from you the swift reaction at this moment,>' Matthias said as loudly as before.

Andromeda lowered his hand as if in surrender. '<The day off?>' he queried, as if trying to place this concept.

Matthias, however, had only been having his little joke. '<It is that we are to have Priority Access paperwork for Portal without this delay of any moment, not even for the important reason,>' Matthias said peremptorily. '<This is straight of the Minister so it is not from you the least delay.>'

'<The Minister?>' Andromeda said cautiously. He was always cautious when there was mention of *the Minister.* He did however look more attentively than before at Matthias.

But Matthias, not so much restless as ever-aware of the precise value of each passing moment in the grand scheme of things vis-à-vis his ever-unfolding plans, now shifted gear. He pulled his wand, and with the motion of pulling the wand, rotated through the air in a swirl of arms and legs; Andromeda was bound and gagged and the door locked and every desk and filing cabinet in the office flung open. This all happened in a few moments. Alaric, standing to one side nervously chewing his thumbnail, and Andromeda, astonished at finding himself bound and gagged, together observed Matthias rifling thorough the papers of a particular filing cabinet with the air of a practiced thief; they each felt like spectators of a play in a theatre, watching from a distance, spared themselves from the labour of the pretence of labour by the cost of their tickets. But for Alaric it was all nerves and for Andromeda it was a feeling of dislocation from having been bound and gagged with no idea at all of what was going on. Ryan Grangeshield (for as such he saw Matthias) appeared to have gone mad, or worse.

The skill with a wand as evidenced by Matthias added to the dangerousness of his behavior as apprehended by his supposed superior.

Andromeda trembled at the sight of his wayward employee. Madmen in general are troubling, but brilliant madmen are especially so. Matthias was tearing through all of the Ministry of Transport's extensive (and expensive) security as if it wasn't there at all. He had inherited from his ancestor Sir Nicholas Grangeshield, the most famed wand-fighter of his own sixteen-century day, far more than the eyes through which he saw the world. He had inherited secrets of wandlore that went back to the days of Daniel, the first Baron of Raspero.

Wandlore by now had passed through several lifetimes. In the early days it had lived the life of a simple rustic, plainspoken and straight to the point. What wands could do was the main point, and all else was mere embroidery. What the wand-user could do with wands was move objects through the air by the power of focused thoughts combined with bodily movements. The objects that were moved in this way needed to either be made of magnetized metal or to contain such magnetized metal as a certain proportion of their over-all mass. But wand-use had a further, apparently unconnected, area of operations. By the activation of a particular form of cognition, arduously developed over several years, wands could be used to provide the wand-user with an image of the surrounding world in their minds even if their eyes were actually closed at the time, and this kind of wand-use was called macchato.

Wands were formed of a thin rectangular wooden casing containing a soft silvery-grey metal called magneterium; the wooden casing of the wand was open at one end at its hilt, so that the magneterium itself could press directly against the palm of the wand-wielder. This contact between the magneterium and the skin of the wand-wielder produced a slightly tingling sensation all over the body from the top of the head to the soles of the feet, and it was in this energized state that use of the wand was possible.

The best attested history of wands could only trace their first appearance to some five or six centuries after the Fall, and the first incarnation of wandlore had lasted from this time to about the tenth century. This wandlore, classical and austere in its approach, was by Matthias's day often referred to as *the real wandlore* by those who felt disenchanted by their own times. Categories relating to focused thoughts and bodily movements and their combinations had been developed, training techniques had been devised, and voluminous manuals had been written which explained everything down to the last dotted i and crossed t. Macchato had been discussed with only the briefest reference to the question of why such a wildly different kind of wand use should be possible, and how the two kinds of wand use could arise from the same contact with magneterium.

But then the question of what it all meant had arisen, and attention had turned to the metaphysics necessary to explain why all this should be. Who had invented wands in the first place anyway? It had probably been the Herakrim, but no-one seemed to know for certain, and as what the Herakrim knew they liked to keep to themselves, the mysteries continued; theoretical frameworks were developed and the mysteries multiplied. This was the second phase of wandlore, and it ended with the sixteenth-century rebellion against the world of the Herakrim, who by then were already extinct, or at least apparently so. The third phase of wandlore lasted about two centuries, following from a wide-spread rejection of Herakrim beliefs, leading to the fourth phase, which was still continuing by Matthias's day, and which consisted largely of a rejection of metaphysics.

But from the day of the first appearance of wands to this, mastery of the use of the wand was recognized as ability in the use of the wand, no matter the beliefs involved, and it was this mastery that Matthias was demonstrating before his audience of Andromeda and Alaric by so expertly breaking and entering into all the bureaucratic cabinets of the office of the Chief Cleric of the Portal Records. All the locks Matthias encountered simply flew open with a wave of his wand.

The aforementioned government inquiry was to note in passing the swiftness of Matthias's breaches of Ministry security, and was further to suggest, as tentatively as deemed appropriate, that some degree of preparation must have gone into all these depredations. In fact they were perfectly correct: Matthias had spent some months in various burglaries and briberies in preparing the grounds for the seemingly careless, even nonchalant, manner in which he committed felonies one after another like a conjurer pulling rabbits out of a hat.

Matthias, with an air of triumph, came over to Andromeda's desk bearing several pieces of paper, swept the said desk clear with an abrupt motion of his wand directing sundry metallic items across the plane of its surface, and laid the papers out on the desk's surface, inviting Alaric to step forward with a wave of his newly royal hand.

Alaric, as nervously as a student facing the all-important final examination, stepped forward and looked down at the desk and stared at the papers Matthias had laid there.

'Get this wrong and you're dead,' Matthias said helpfully.

Andromeda had not understood this sentence, as it was spoken in Westrigonian, but Alaric understood more than the words that had been spoken. He was being told that he was not to take it all so seriously as there were back-up plans if this went wrong. Besides it was not going to go wrong because he had rehearsed it so exhaustively. Alaric found his nerves receding and he was remembering to breathe again. He took out his pen with a studied air, and bent over the papers and set to work. He used the old forger's trick of copying signatures upside down in order to reproduce Andromeda's signature with a flourishing perfection which the closely watching Andromeda, despite himself, could not help but admire. It was a perfect forgery. Having done the more difficult task first, Alaric set about filling in the remainder of the Priority Access paperwork in the Anglashian language which he did not understand but did not need to in order to achieve his goal. Everything was now in place except the Minister's signature. The bulging eyes of the bound and gagged Andromeda, loyal as ever to his boss the Minister, showed that his thoughts had reached this very conclusion at the same time as Alaric's pen.

Leaving Andromeda at his desk, and locking the door behind them with his own special combinations so Andromeda would remain undiscovered for at least the time that was necessary for his plan, Matthias led Alaric out of the office of the Chief Cleric of the Portal Records and onward up the stairs. They took a special short-cut (which Matthias had discovered on one of his burglaries) to the Minister's office at the very top of the square tower which surmounted the Regana Palace. This short-cut avoided all prying eyes and had been installed by a long-ago duke for a nefarious purpose. It led Matthias and Alaric directly to the corridor outside the Minister's office on the other side of the Reception Area through which the visitors to the Minster's office normally passed. Matthias and Alaric, however, were not normal visitors.

Thus undetected by guards and receptionists, Matthias and Alaric entered the office of the Minister of Transport in search of the one remaining signature which would complete their forged document.

10:00 AM, Monday 13 April 1882 A. F.

His Excellency the Minister of Transport, Sir Rafferty Hammond, Knight Peregrine of the Ninth Level, Crown-Bearer of the Second Order and Honorary Member of the Reserve Council, was sitting behind his enormously expansive desk and staring vacantly out of the window as Matthias entered with his personal forger in tow. To all external appearances, His Excellency was day-dreaming, but in actual fact, the Minister's brain was teeming with his latest political scheming. It was excellent scheming, full of salacious detail and black-guarded skullduggery, but it was about to be interrupted by another even more outrageous imposition.

'<It is from you at this time the direct co-operation,>' Matthias said peremptorily, coming to a standstill before Sir Rafferty's desk and fixing his boss with a direct gaze. '<So wakey, wakey, Minister, it is the time to go to work of now.>'

Sir Rafferty came out of his reveries, which had just reached the point at which he was explaining to the Secretary of the Treasury certain budgetary changes which he, Sir Rafferty, had deemed necessary.

'<What?>' asked His Excellency the Minister of Transport.

Matthias rapped sternly on the desk with his knuckles. '<It is from you the co-operation of now without the imbecile hesitation of the Minister without the clue.>'

'<Who the devil are you?>' asked Sir Rafferty Hammond, Knight Peregrine of the Ninth Level.

'<Silence!>' Matthias shouted and slapped the desk with the palm of his hand. '<From you it is only the signature of this document. Come!>' He waved his left hand vaguely in the air, prompting Alaric to step forward and lay the Priority Access to Portal Travel document on the desk before the Minster of Transport.

Sir Rafferty looked not at the document but across the room at the closed door beyond which were his receptionists and his guards. His right hand reached out in a blindly groping fashion to take up his wand in order to send a signal for outside intervention. Matthias was having none of this, and in the blink of an eye Matthias's right hand was upraised holding his own wand while the wand of the Minister flew through the air to be neatly caught by Matthias's left hand.

'<What the devil is going on?>' asked Sir Rafferty, frowning fiercely at Matthias.

'<Silence!>' Matthias shouted again, pointing the Minister's own wand at him. '<From you it is only the signature of Priority Access and it is the silence of such the insolent questions from you!>'

Sir Rafferty's mouth fell open briefly, but the Minister recovered sufficiently to close his mouth, straighten up in his chair, and place both hands down before him spread out palms down on his desktop preparatory to rising to his feet. He could have been posing for a painting entitled: *Sir Rafferty Arises!* but Matthias was having none of this either. With a motion of his wand he rose into the air while four mobile karns shot out of various recesses of his robe and fastened onto the wrists and ankles of Sir Rafferty and bound them to the armrests and legs of his chair, by which time Matthias had landed adroitly behind Sir Rafferty's shoulder, sweeping the Minister's desk clear of all else but the Priority Access document with another wave of his wand. The Minister's mouth opened again, but Matthias was as always one step ahead of his employer, with another mobile karn appearing on the instant, this one of the gagging kind that neatly slotted into the Minister's mouth, latching onto his teeth and lips and wrapping around his head in order to incapacitate the great man's speaking faculties. There was a slit in the gag which charitably (and as required by law) allowed a modicum of space for breathing through the mouth.

The Minister was breathing heavily through this slit as his indignation climbed the ladder of his outrage.

Karns were artefacts made of leather which had magnetized metal embedded in them. Wandfighters wore karns as bracelets around their wrists and ankles, and by the use of their wands they could bring forces to bear on these karns that could enable their bodies to move through the air extremely fast and with breath-taking agility; if they could achieve control over the bracelet karns of their opponents in a wandfight, they could move the bodies of these opponents in any way they chose to whatever ends, including the ends of grievous bodily harm and death. This required breaking the bond between the wand and karns of the opponent. Wandfighters also carried about their person mobile karns, which could be brought out and attached to the bodies of their opponents in order to control them. It was these mobile karns which Matthias had used in order to bind and gag his employer. The Minister clearly would have spoken sharply about his treatment if he had not been gagged, judging from the inchoate sounds, obviously of a protesting nature, which emanated from him.

Matthias ignored his newly-acquired prisoner, and briskly opened the drawers of Sir Rafferty's desk, stooping over them and shuffling through the papers inside until he had found what he was looking for: a document with a specimen of Sir Rafferty's signature. This he threw onto the desktop with an expansive gesture designed to draw Alaric into the proceedings.

Alaric stepped forward with the air of a figure entering a sporting contest on which the hopes of a nation rested: grave and composed, austere and fully present in this moment and no other. He was ready. Producing his pen and ink jar with the air of a conjuror, he set about his task. The Minister's angry growls subsided as he watched his own signature being reproduced with a degree of exactness in which the spirit and letter of the law were one. A watchful look fell over him like a silken veil, as if he had come to realize that he was in the hands of crooks who knew what they were doing. Sir Rafferty was starting to take this situation seriously, but the questions being formulated in his mind would remain, for at least the next seventy-three minutes, unspoken.

'<It is to you all these thanks of this the passing moment, and it is never again such the service from you,>' Matthias said in a friendly fashion as he collected the by-now-fully-forged Priority Access document from the surface of Sir Rafferty's desk and rolled it up into a scroll. '<You are the gentleman and the scholar, not to mention the champion Minister.>' With a slightly mocking bow, Matthias departed the room, with Alaric following, nervously chewing his fingernails again, afflicted by another bout of nerves.

10:15 AM, Monday 13 April 1882 A. F.

Matthias and Alaric strolled back into the Annexe to the Waiting Room of the Portal. Matthias waved to the Westrigonian delegation to rise to their feet and follow him into the Waiting Room itself. Shyester hurried forward to speak with Matthias.

'Might I respectfully ask Your Majesty if such a policy as you advocate may be momentarily delayed in order to be briefly discussed?' he asked in his most-reasonable-tone-of-voice.

Matthias paused, as if to summon meaning from the very air around him into his pursuant words: 'I am going to the Royal Palace of Krastienst. It is my royal command that you follow. If you disobey, then you are guilty of treason.'

'Naturally that is so, Sire,' Shyester agreed, with a bow of his head to show how *naturally so* it all was. 'My obedience to your royal command can be assumed without assumption. It was the merest concern on my part that we might in the swiftest of passing comments inform the Anglashian authorities of our diplomatic presence before we leave, thus perhaps even gaining a certain measure of assistance from those who we have thus made our allies.' At the back of Shyester's mind was a vague hope that the Anglashian government could be persuaded to detain Matthias for the time being, either in prison or under some kind of house arrest, in order that this insane idea of going immediately to Krastienst could be locked up with Matthias.

If Matthias guessed Shyester's thoughts (which he probably did) he gave no outward sign of it. 'Absolutely not. I depart this country under the same false name by which I entered it. End of discussion.'

Shyester nodded understandingly. 'It is clear to me that you seek to delegate such an undertaking to one whose status is not of your own luminous eminence. May I ask if I can have such an honour –'

'Shut up, Shyester, and stop prattling,' Matthias ordered brusquely.

By now they had reached Baldy's desk. Matthias threw the Priority Access document in front of Baldy and spoke to the Officer in Charge of Portal Access with a certain deliberate rudeness that was apparent even to the watching Westrigonians, who could not speak a word of Anglashian between them, not even Alaric, who had been Matthias's companion in many a law-breaking undertaking.

Baldy scrutinized the forged document with a scowl, but its apparent authenticity could not be faulted by the most critical observer. Reluctantly, Baldy set the wheels in motion: the approval for the connection had just come through from Krastienst, the Portal happened to be available for use at that moment, and there was nothing to be done but to send Matthias and his companions from the Portal of the Anglashian Ministry of Transport to the Portal of the Palace of Krastienst. The lengthiest interrogations by sundry government inquiries could not shake this basic scenario. Only conspiracy theorists were later to doubt Baldy's innocence.

So it came to be that His Majesty Matthias the Fourth and his loyal band of Westrigonian retainers entered the Portal in order to travel to the Royal Palace of Krastienst.

The entrance to the Portal was shaped like a doorway, with a lintel made of cobalt, surmounted on two pillars, one made of lodestone and the other of pyrrhotite. At the base of this doorway were steps leading down into a courtyard surrounded by walls which were layered by magnesium, while the floor was a layer of iron over glazed brick. The roof was gadolinium, which was raised over the walls by regularly spaced copper inserts which left gaps to permit air inflow. The overall impression given by the Portal was that of a silvery-greyness which flickered to the eyes, being difficult for the eye to focus on, as if the near and the far were impossibly combined on its shimmering grey surface. It was all a grey shimmer, a floaty unearthly grey.

If paradox could be a colour, it would be this particular but universal grey.

10:30 AM, Monday 13 April 1882 A. F.

The protocols were observed, the paperwork filed and the connection established. Only the travellers standing in the Portal understood that history was being made as they departed for the Royal Palace of Krastienst in Westrigonia. But none of them, not even Matthias the Fourth himself, could possibly have understood just how much history was going to be made in the times that would follow. They were all going to live in interesting times.

Excerpt from The Life and Times of Matthias the Fourth, otherwise known as Matthias the Just, being by the hand of Gahariet Octavian Iahonnes Pamphilos, Esquire of Taavetti, published in September 2370 A. F. as this the only truthful account of our most noble and just sovereign of old:

And it came to pass, on the thirteenth day of April in the year 1882 After the Fall, that these Westrigonian gallants, esteemed even to their shoe buckles, did arrive in the land of Anglashia and came unto the place of employment of His Majesty Matthias the Fourth, living as he was in the deepest anonymity, hunted by his enemies far and wide; and there they paused, at a loss to perceive amidst the teeming multitudes wherein lay their quarry. And as they besearched the throng, lo and behold, a shaft of sunlight pierced the air and fell on the figure of a man standing in the midst of all those around. Whereupon these gallants, may the buttons on their hats be ever polished anew, understood immediately that this was a sign from on high, given by the Lord of Hosts himself to single out such a one who was in this manner singular, and so they went forthwith and fell to their knees before this man and gave praise to His Majesty. And so Matthias, for such was he on whom fell the shaft of sunlight, made great surprise to hear that the Vidaldmeet had elected him King, such was the enormous humility of that fair and just sovereign; and besides that he was yet startled to be so uncovered after all the precautions betaken by this our gracious sovereign of old to hide his identity secret inwithdst the tumult of the world. And yet all those present besides, on hearing that such a man as they had befriended as a common man, even as one of them to his everyday neckwear, were yet astonished to hear that such a man was now become sovereign of a great kingdom over the seas, and they made such cheer that those orderers of the workplace wherein the sovereign perspired, made swift show to satisfy their reckonings as to what had caused such commotion. And the chiefest of them, the great knight Sir Rafferty, was begladdened in his heart of hearts to hear such news, that such a man, of his own lowly workers, was become far greater even than he, such a knight as Sir Rafferty himself in all his bedecked and resplendent gloriousness of the noontime day. And yet doubting all the while that such a man, ranked amongst the highest, had been treated in accordance with his natural sensibilities while in his lowly state, Sir Rafferty was enjoyened to be betokened on the instant by his fair and noble interlocutor that the workers beholden to Sir Rafferty had, no doubt impelled by a natural awe beyond their own understanding, takenest to their fellow worker with such courtesy and kindness as would befitten the gentlest of souls. By all accounts satisfied, the generality of those present formed such a procession as to please the sternest admirer of pageantry, for impromptu and heartfelt as such was known, there it was that Matthias the Fourth, newly discovered, and his loyal followers the Westrigonian gallants who had come so far to find him, proceeded on their way with the shouts of their new friends ringing in their ears, entered the Portal and thereby departed for the Portal of the Palace of Krastienst in the Kingdom of Westrigonia. And following this great advent is the task of many volumes to record, such are the mighty consequences to have followed from such a day, faithfully written down by my own hand as the wholly accurate story beknownst to all who have steadfastly preserved the memory of those far-flung days of the long-distant past. This I have written here is the truth of the matter.

CHAPTER TWO

The nobles want to be robbers.
So let them be robbers.
Frankie the Villain

The walled city of Krastienst looked in the distance like a crown, its circular wall being surmounted by a crenellated design of square merlons. The circular wall was in fact not quite circular; in fact, it was a figurative arm's distance from the perfectly circular, being elliptical in shape, with the Royal Palace at one foci of the ellipse and the Vidaldmeet at the other. This had been designed and laid in place by the leading mathematicians of the day as a geometrical expression of the distribution of powers as codified by the Constitution of Westrigonia. The city wall itself was intended to be as much military as architectural, as in theory it was supposed to withstand a besieging enemy by unleashing forcible blows on the said enemy from above by the defenders of the city.

The theoretical nature of the city wall as a defensive line had not on this occasion of the invasion of the country actually been put to much of a test. A series of blunders had left the country's armies misplaced on the military map, so the city was barely defended at the time the Baalbabakan and Melisendien armies attacked on the fourth day of April 1882. The flying carriages of the invading armies were thick in the air overhead like flocks of large wooden wingless birds lumbering through the skies on that sunny spring day. They entered the air-space above the city without hindrance as the aerial shields around the city entirely failed to repel them, and seized the gates from above, opening the city to the invading soldiers. These gates were five in number, and through all five poured the Baalbabakan and Melisendien soldiers; they foamed and splashed along the narrow cobblestoned streets, gushing through the city like turbulent water sloshing along canals. How the defenses of the city's walls and gates could have been so quickly over-run was a mystery best left to posterity given that such questions were the last thing on anyone's mind at that moment in time. Westrigonian soldiers fought as best they could, hopelessly outnumbered by the invading forces while the statues of the city looked on helplessly. The foreign soldiers systematically took control of the city, the red and green of the Baalbabakans keeping separate from the purple and red of the Melisendiens as they assumed command of their respective zones; civilians ran screaming; people hid where they could; the Palace closed its gates and marshaled its forces. Captain Romano, commander of the Palace Guard, saw to it that the Palace defences held. The flying carriages were beaten back, the magnetic force-fields of the Palace proving to be invisible walls that did not permit passage; the doors held, and in fact it was only before the Palace walls that the invading armies suffered any casualties at all. Before the sun had gone down on that day, the whole of the capital was in the hands of the invaders except the Royal Palace of Krastienst.

8:45 AM, Monday 13 April 1882 A. F.

Her Royal Highness the Crown Princess Eleanor of Westrigonia sat despondently in her elegantly carved wooden chair before the five-petalled rose window of her Palace Chambers. Melisendien and Baalbabakan soldiers had set up checkpoints all around the Palace, but they had no-one to stop and checkpoint on as the streets were completely deserted. They were in full combat readiness, nonetheless, as they played their part in probing the defences of the Palace. There was the occasional shout of an attacking or defending soldier, the thud or whizz of weaponry in play and a general continuous tension in the air like a thunder-storm crouched over the city.

Eleanor's ladies-in-waiting kept her company in her chambers, sitting here and there about the room as despondently as their patroness. They were three in number. Lady Nina Delwyn was Eleanor's favourite because she was the most loyal and devoted of them; in actual fact, she was the only one who was devoted at all. (Loyalty could always, rightly or wrongly, be assumed in Westrigonia.) She loved being Eleanor's lady-in-waiting and idealised the Crown Princess of Westrigonia as the embodiment of romantic sensibility. As for the others: Lady Marica Philokrates, known as Mitzi, barely disguised her resentment at her position, with her habitual facial expression being a permanently frozen disguised sneer, while Lady Georgette Marjolaine seemed largely indifferent to whatever was going on around her, being as tall and dark-wild-haired as a legendary female warrior of the forests. Eleanor had in the past, with many a roll of her delicate long fingers on the armrests of her chair, brooded over their many failings and contemplated their replacements, but the time had never come to pass. But now she had far more weighty things to ponder as she sat in her chair.

Like many a heroine of fable Eleanor was now in considerable personal danger. It had been brought to her attention by her Chief Attender Astrudel that certain measures had been enacted on the part of Westrigionia's invaders that concerned her personally as the Crown Princess of Westrigonia. If Astrudel had not told her of these matters then no-one would have, and Astrudel herself had made this plain. (This was in order to emphasize how indispensable she was, and how Eleanor would not be able to get by without her.) The lamentable facts of the unspeakable pronouncements issuing forth from Astrudel's red-rimmed mouth were these: the Baalbabakan army and the Melisendien army had each separately, presumably by consultation, held a lottery whose winning prize would be the pleasure of spending a night in the intimate and unrestricted company of Her Royal Highness the Princess Eleanor, Crown Princess of Westrigonia and the Jewel of Krastienst. Whichever army captured her first would deliver her to their lottery winner, and then hand her over to the other army's lottery winner, after which there would be *further consultations* in the words of officialdom. Such were the times in which Eleanor lived.

Not only did the profits of the two lotteries help to pay the costs of the invasion of Westrigonia, but the morale of the Westrigonians was undermined by such an insult to their national honour. It might have made them fight with doubled vigour if they had managed to fight at all, but the staggering ineptitude of the Westrigonian military strategy meant that Westrigonia had become occupied without actually fighting at all.

And thus matters stood for the beleaguered Crown Princess of Westrigonia. The thought of the conscripted armies of thugs holding their lottery tickets in their diseased hands, with a winning ticket somewhere amidst the quivering mass of corrupted flesh, was enough to make anyone shudder, let alone a refined lady of distinction. But Eleanor was not one to do nothing in the face of such a challenge. She had taken action.

Eleanor had affected an outward indifference to the news of this behaviour on the part of her country's invaders. She regarded them as so vastly her inferiors that they could hardly be said to have anything more than a material existence, but nevertheless she had pursued the acquisition of suicide pills via Astrudel and had distributed them to herself and her ladies-in-waiting. These suicide pills, dramatically evil-looking and expensive, were in fact flour pills, blackened by fire and coated in wood polish, and they couldn't have harmed a fly; the pragmatic Astrudel, entirely failing to see that things were *that* bad, justified the deception in terms of her unflagging service and took the money on the very reasonable grounds that everyone, including Astrudel, had to live after all. (Astrudel had by now buried three husbands and five boyfriends by the road of her forceful journey through life.) And it was this Astrudel, formerly the Nanny to Her Royal Highness the Crown Princess Eleanor, and now Chief Attender to Her Royal Highness the Crown Princess Eleanor, who came bustling into the Chambers of the Crown Princess, with her usual bursting-through-doors with a sway of her voluminous skirts, her shirt sleeves rolled up to her elbows, her cheeks reddened from the flames of the kitchen and the sharp eyes in that rounded face missing nothing.

'Greetings to you all,' Astrudel said with her everyday cheerfulness.

No-one said anything in reply. All those present were plunged into their own thoughts.

'So the same to me,' Astrudel said as cheerfully as always. 'I don't mind saying it myself, if you're busy.' Astrudel busied herself with changing the water in the flower vases, straightening up this and that and generally spiraling around the room. With the slap of a table and an occasional bang, Astrudel went about her merry task-making, ignored by Eleanor and her ladies-in-waiting.

The Palace was besieged and the end was near. Food was running low. Absolutely no-one showed the least inclination to come to Westrigonia's assistance. It was times like this that showed the value of friendship. No-one cared that Westrigonia was invaded, that its Crown Princess had become a lottery prize, that its treasures would be removed to foreign storehouses, that its culture and language would be eradicated from the surface of the earth and that all it was would come to not be.

In all fairness, if the same fate were to befall any place else, what would Westrigonia care? What did it mean to care, after all? What were the bonds of friendship, of kinship, of caring? Religion, politics, the family fireplace, these are all a roll-of-the-eye in the dark, for self-interest governs all.

Astrudel, who bore news worth dying for, spoke eventually. She had waited her moment. Her calculation was that in time it would pay her well.

'Your boyfriend's in the news again, Your Royal Highness,' said Astrudel.

The ladies-in-waiting looked back and forth between them in perplexity. Eleanor had a boyfriend? Since when? What boyfriend? Heads would roll, quite literally. This was a deadly serious matter. It was news to the ladies-in-waiting that Eleanor had a boyfriend, but needless to say, it was very interesting news, very interesting indeed. The Palace Chambers of the Crown Princess had all of a sudden become Gossip City Central. The ladies-in-waiting leaned forward as one in order to eagerly follow this conversation.

These words reached through to Eleanor after a while, some time after they had registered with her ladies-in-waiting. She was sunk deep in her own very personal gloom. She roused herself and said: 'Matthias? What's he gone and done now?'

'He's gone and got himself elected King of Westrigonia, that's what he's gone and done,' replied Astrudel.

'Matthias? King? But he can't be. He's not from a royal house. He's only a Baron.'

The ladies-in-waiting leaned forward further in their seats, as if leaning forward would help them hear everything better.

'Don't ask me to explain the mighty deliberations of the Vidaldmeet, Your Royal Highness,' Astrudel said with a delicate and deliberate absence of sarcasm.

'Are you serious, Nanny?' Eleanor asked. She was incredulous but hopeful.

'Oh yes, Princess, everyone's talking about it,' Astrudel said insistently. 'It's all over town, believe me.'

'But that means he'll come here!' Eleanor exclaimed.

'I wouldn't count on it, Princess, what with us being under occupation and everything,' Astrudel said, shaking her head.

'But he has to if he's King! Anyway, you don't know Matthias. If he's been elected King he'll come straight here. And the Baalbabakans and Melisendiens had better watch out! Matthias is very clever.'

'Aye, that must be it, your Royal Highness,' Astrudel said, disguising her skepticism with a smooth tone of voice. She knew too much about the fatal nature of the politics of Westrigonia to believe that Matthias would come anytime soon; but Eleanor knew Matthias too well to doubt that he would come immediately.

There was a silence in the Chambers of the Crown Princess.

'Is Lord Raspero really your boyfriend?' Nina asked.

'No, he is most certainly *not* my boyfriend,' Eleanor stated emphatically. 'He is merely the Baron of Raspero and even that is too much absurdity for this modern world to bear. He is utterly unfit for … *anything*, anything at all!'

Eleanor's vehemence was such as to make the ladies-in-waiting wonder. Eleanor was as a rule detached and aloof. It was not like her to lose her cool.

For a short while all those present contemplated their individual path in life.

'Matthias will come here today,' Eleanor declared imperiously. She leaned back in her chair and declared even more imperiously than before: 'Nina, go to my jewel box and fetch me the blue case.'

Nina brought Eleanor the blue case, happy as always to serve. Eleanor opened the case and took out a gold bracelet. She handed the blue case back to Nina with a wave of her hand which instructed Nina to return the case to the jewel box, and contemplated the bracelet for a while, turning it round and round in her hand. Then she fastened it around her left wrist.

The memories came back without hesitation. It was rarely that she allowed herself the indulgence of recalling these times past. Her future had long been one of nothing but an arranged marriage and a dutiful obedience to a planned life. The recent invasion had offered an alternative scenario: an honourable death as opposed to various versions of a celebrated but tedious life, which was at least some kind of variety. Her earlier oceanic dissatisfaction had come to seem vastly tenuous in the light of her recent days of being threatened by the brutish hordes of Baalbabak and Melisende. But now Matthias was about to return. Matthias . . . she closed her eyes and fell backwards in time, ten years or so, ten years ago in this very place, when she had seen an intruder in the Palace, a boy about the same age as her, strolling boldly through the Reception Room as if he owned all its furnishings . . .

10:30 AM, Tuesday 12 July 1872 A. F.

The boy was very composed, perhaps about twelve years old, with black hair and grey eyes. He was wandering through the Reception Room looking about him with great interest. He was well dressed, with a large R on his chest. The R was shaped like three or four R-shaped figures interlaced amongst themselves.

'<Stop, thief!>' the girl shouted, running towards him. '<What are you doing here?>' She spoke in Anglashian.

'<And you are . . . ?>' the boy replied haughtily in the same language.

The girl was also about twelve years old, very pretty, with jet black hair lying loosely around her shoulders. She wore a green velvet dress with red trimmings, and a jewel encrusted ribbon was tied around her neck like a necklace. Her eyes were a shining green. She said nothing but stared at the boy suspiciously.

'<Ah, I see it is that you are ashamed of who you are so it is that you do

not speak. Go, leave me!>' the boy said with a dismissive wave of his hand and turned away.

The girl reached for her wand in a moment of anger but before she could pull it clear the boy had spun around, his wand instantly in his hand and pointed at her. Thus it was that in a flash her arms were trapped by her sides, unable to move. His grey eyes were cold and hard like glass and as she looked into them she felt a moment's fear.

'<It is that you do not pull the wand on me again ever!>' the boy said softly but with a grim tone to the softness of his voice that made a soft voice more threatening than a raised voice would have been. Then he raised his wand and let go of her, saying: '<If it is that you are not the ashamed of who you are, tell me this! Otherwise go your way.>' And the boy put his own wand away and waited, staring at her with an implacable edge to his imperious stance.

The girl's fear disappeared and her anger returned. '<I am Her Royal Highness the Crown Princess Eleanor!>' she snapped with all the regal disdain she could muster.

The boy looked surprised as if he was pretending to be surprised, his eyebrows raised. '<Then you are the important one!>' he said with great seriousness. '<I am Matthias Raspero, second son of the thirty-sixth Baron of Raspero.>' He moved his wand hand forward, bowed and said: '<At your service!>'

'<What are you doing here?>' Eleanor asked severely. '<Are you allowed to be here?>'

Matthias leaned toward her and said in a low conspiratorial tone: '<There was the door that was little bit locked so I little bit unlocked door.>' He looked about him in a guilty fashion.

'<So you are not allowed to be here. You are a thief!>' Eleanor cried triumphantly.

Matthias shook his head. '<No, this is not the true saying for me. I am come for only to make the quick gaze upon the Palace. This is all. I give to you my word for this matter.>' And he bowed again.

'<You must leave immediately!>' Eleanor commanded. She was delighted to have someone on whom to take out her bad mood.

Matthias shook his head again and gazed at her with a look of amusement in his eyes. '<It is the choice for you, Your Royal Highness. If you are stay with me and keep the eye on my walkings then you are the hero and everyone praises you and you are give what you want. But if you go and tell guard *Oh, there is boy in Palace* then you are in much the trouble because they will say you have leave boy without to be watching what he does because as you go to tell guard I am not to be watched for you. So: this is your choice! Now, I continue. You will make this choice.>'

With that Matthias seemed to feel that the matter had been dealt with. He turned away and started walking to the door into the Purple Room of Blessings. Eleanor watched him walk away, thinking about what he had said. The prospect of being a hero and being given whatever she wanted was too tempting for her to refuse, however. She felt entirely ignored and was never able to have anything she wanted (or so it seemed to her). And if she left him alone what might he get up to? He was an intruder, in her own home. He had blatantly confessed to this without the least embarrassment or apparent sense of wrong-doing. So she would keep an eye on him and be a hero and then she would get whatever she asked for. Everyone would pay attention to her, for once.

She started after him with a fierce glint in her eye. Wherever he went she stalked beside him glaring at him. She felt no fear of him. Somehow she understood that he would not harm her as long as she didn't pull a wand on him.

Matthias stopped and looked eagerly at a large painting on the wall. '<The battle of Cadell!>' he exclaimed excitedly. '<My ancestor was fighted in this battle!>' He pointed at the painting. '<There! You see! It is seventh Baron of Raspero!>'

Eleanor looked where he was pointing and saw a wand-fighter with a large intricate R on his chest, the same R as Matthias was wearing. '<It is a very bad painting,>' Eleanor remarked disdainfully.

Matthias ignored her negative vibes. '<He is close for Prince Wallrem, you see, they are the good friends for that time. Later Prince Wallrem is having seventh Baron executed, so they are not such the good friends later.>'

'<Why did he have the Baron executed?>' Eleanor asked, interested despite herself in this tale of family history.

'<I do not know,>' Matthias said with a sigh. '<It is that I am not told why this was happened. Isn't it so very much the annoying time when the grownups do not answer the questions we are asking of them?>'

'<All my questions are always answered!>' Eleanor declared loftily.

Matthias looked at her with a smile. '<How nice for you!>' he said, his eyebrows raised in astonished praise.

'<Yes it is,>' Eleanor said, pretending not to notice his sarcastic skepticism. '<It is very nice for me and it is very sad for you that your questions are not answered but I suspect it is because you deserve not to have your questions answered because you are unworthy of being treated any better than you are because you are a thief who breaks into other people's homes and that is the kind of boy you are!>'

Matthias nodded as seriously at this as if he was trying not to smile again. '<How do you like Westrigonia, Your Royal Highness?>' he asked politely.

'<I hate it here!>' Eleanor burst out. '<It is such a horrible place to be. I hate this country and I hate everyone here and I hate everything about this whole country and I hate you as well!>'

'<Where were you before?>' Matthias asked.

Eleanor said nothing but glared at him as if to say: *How dare you question me?*

'<Oh, it is that you are ashamed of this. You are in the inferior place so you are not say where it is you are been before.>' Matthias turned away with a dismissive wave of his hand.

Eleanor took the bait. '<I was in Troderent before and it's a much nicer place than this and it's civilized and this is a barbarian country.>'

'<Ah, I understand,>' Matthias said and nodded. '<You are the home sick. Yes, I am also once the home sick. But it is alright, it is that the home sick is passing before not long.>'

'<Home sick? What do you mean?>'

'<It is that you are missing everything about Troderent, your friends, the house where you are lived in before, and because of this you are hated

where you are being now here in Westrigonia. It is that you are the home sick. Yes, this is so,>' Matthias said, nodding gravely in approval of his own diagnosis. '<But it is not to be worry for it is pass away after not too long.>'

'<When were you home sick?>' Eleanor asked.

'<It is when I am first go to school in Anglashia, this is last year, and I am missing Raspero very much, my room in castle, my friends, all the places I am go to, even my brother Stefan, yes, this is how home sick I am being then, and I am hating everything about Anglashia, I feel it here,>' Matthias said, putting his hand on his stomach, '<it is that I am empty in the stomach, you understand, I am very much the home sick.>'

'<And how did you get better?>'

Matthias shrugged. '<It is no reason for this for get better. I am meeting the new people, it is being interesting where I am, in this Anglashian school, it is very different from Westrigonia, and it is one day it is alright for me be there and I am not the home sick any more.>'

These words struck Eleanor like a revelation. She felt that her eyes had been opened to a great truth that changed everything about her new circumstances. So that was what was going on! At last she understood. She was home sick! That was all that was wrong. She missed everything about Troderent, just as Matthias had missed everything about Raspero. She felt her stomach empty as well. And somehow understanding what the problem was had solved it! Her homesickness was gone and in its place was a sense of interest in standing here talking to Matthias. It was at that moment that she started to feel at home in Westrigonia.

Matthias was already moving on. He was gazing at the next painting along, like a sightseer. '<And that is Radbertin of Trissal,>' Matthias said, pointing at the painting. '<Later he is to be ask by king of going the journey Mountains of Weiden; he is say, "oh no, this is not the journey for me," so king is say, "yes, I understand, clearly there is the limit to the duty of you," so he is the ashamed one and he is go Mountains of Weiden and he is been killed there.>' Eleanor considered this story and said nothing. '<It is the good time for him, this death,>' Matthias continued, '<because he was walked down this road of command of king. Before this death is taken him, this death is bowing low to him because he is make death bow to duty.>'

Eleanor understood, as if she had already become linked to Matthias, that he was doing more than merely tell a story. He was telling her something of how things were in Westrigonia.

'<Where it is this stairs are go to?>' Matthais asked, gesturing to a staircase at the side that wound around out of sight.

'<We're not allowed to go up there,>' Eleanor said sternly.

'<I am not allowed for be here at all!>' Matthias laughed out loud suddenly at this and Eleanor had to catch herself not to instinctively laugh in reply. '<Come on, you are watch me, you are remember this?>' Without waiting for her to reply Matthias started lightly up the stairs.

Eleanor chased after him. As she came out onto the balcony she saw Matthias take his wand and effortlessly whisk a nearby bench over to the balcony wall. She was impressed by the casual skill with which he used his wand, as if wand use was so easy he didn't have to think about it. She herself was struggling with the simplest commands. As she came to the bench Matthias took hold of her around the waist and lifted her to stand on the bench.

'<How dare you lay hands on me?>' Her Royal Highness snapped.

Matthias climbed onto the bench beside her and looked down at her in amusement. '<Are you always like this?>' he asked.

He turned away and looked over the top of the wall. Eleanor came beside him and they looked around them.

The city of Krastienst was located on a plateau surrounded by escarpments sloping downwards in all directions. The Palace and the Vidaldmeet were the tallest buildings in Krastienst, being each exactly the same height as the other. It followed therefore that the two children had from their vantage point high on the Palace walls a stunning view southwards and westwards. On their right, across the Park of Venusar, they could see the Vidaldmeet. All below them were the red and black roofs of the houses of the city of Krastienst. They were facing south, and could easily see clear over the city wall to where the River Ostralunaco glinted on the far horizon like a silver snake. The fertile plain stretching south before and after the river was farming country, and was covered with farms and small towns joined by a network of roads. Far to the west were the Mountains of Salrautor, whose grey-green-blue contours folded into each other like endlessly flexing fingers.

The Palace walls beneath Matthias's outstretched hands were extremely wide; they were the length of a man's body laid out flat, which was in fact how they had been measured, the man in question being a lamentably unlucky prisoner of war of unusual height whose blood had been sprinkled all around the foundations of the walls in order to keep them strong, this being an expression of the beliefs of those long ago times. (Architectural procedures had since changed but bloodthirstiness itself had only moved on to other domains.) The walls were made of a mixture of white limestone, red sandstone and black granite (as were also the walls of the Vidaldmeet).

'<These walls they are being so thick,>' Matthias commented, impressed. '<Of course, it is for defended against the enemies in the war if they are march against King, so walls are thick.>'

'<We don't have enemies,>' Eleanor declared, taking care that her voice did not tremble.

Matthias looked at her. '<Of course not, not your family, it is not the enemies for you.>' He said this so promptly that Eleanor felt that she could believe it. She allowed herself to believe it. But she had seen, with the perspective of a small child who is overlooked, the hatred of her mother and father from many of the Westrigonian nobles. This enmity was veiled by bows and translated phrases extolling the new monarchs of Westrigonia but she could see their hatred more clearly perhaps because she could not understand a word of Westrigonian.

'<But of course everyone has enemies,>' Eleanor declared, unable to let go of her fears. '<You are very foolish if you do not know that yourself.>'

Matthias hesitated a moment. '<You have the strong defences here,>' he said carefully. '<You are much the safe.>'

Eleanor sensed his evasions and grew angry. '<What do you know?>' she snapped scornfully. '<You can't even speak Anglashian properly!>'

'<If you want we are speak Westrigonian,>' Matthias offered with a hint of amusement that suggested he knew full well she could not speak a word of Westrigonian.

'<I prefer not to speak in such a barbarian language!>' Eleanor snapped with her nose lifted high in the air.

Matthias looked at her for a moment. Then he said: '<Your Royal Highness, I answer the question from you, but you are make promise that you will not say you are hear this from me. Come, make promise and I speak.>'

Eleanor nearly blazed away at him for his insolence in setting conditions in telling her what it was her right to know, but she swallowed back the words before they emerged. '<Very well, I promise,>' she agreed casually as if this entire conversation meant nothing to her and she was only being polite.

'<The secret of politics it is this,>' Matthias said, leaning over to her and talking in a low voice. '<It is factions, you understand? So, it is that there is faction in Westrigonia that is say, *Oh, we have King and Queen that is Westrigonian*, then there is faction that is say, *Oh we have King and Queen from Zoller-Abstein House*. So it is the parents of you are Duke and Duchess of Leland and you are come here from Troderent to be Royal House for Westrigonia after death of Jugold because of this faction, and this faction is the more strong for these two so it is that they have this outcome. But it is know that Zoller-Abstein are very powerful, so it is faction that is against Zoller-Abstein that is not raise hand against you. And so it is that your family are safe because of this power of Zoller-Abstein family, which is your family.>'

'<I see,>' the former Honourable Eleanor Leland said thoughtfully, and she did see. Much of what had been going on suddenly made sense to her, as if coming close to frosted glass had made it clear by a trick of the light.

Matthias stiffened, his hand on his wand. '<It is time for go now your Royal Highness. Come!>' He jumped down from the bench, took hold of Eleanor before she could protest and lifted her down to the ground. With a whisk of his wand he sent the bench back to the side, took Eleanor's hand in his and started for the stairs.

Somehow Eleanor didn't feel like protesting. It felt comforting to have her hand in his. She decided to put up with this behaviour only for the time being because even though it was outrageously unacceptable it really wasn't too unpleasant.

As they neared the bottom of the stairs Astrudel came tearing into the room. 'Your Royal Highness!' she exclaimed. 'Where have you been? And who's your boyfriend?' she asked, looking at Matthias.

Matthias drew himself up and declared haughtily: 'I am Matthias Raspero, second son of the thirty-sixth Baron of Raspero.'

'How nice for you!' Astrudel said admiringly with a deliberate absence of sarcasm.

Matthias looked at her for a moment as if to make a point of letting it go then turned to Eleanor. '<I am leave now, your Royal Highness. Soon we meet again.>' He stooped unexpectedly and kissed her hand. It was yet another unprecedented experience for Eleanor since meeting Matthias.

Matthias took his wand in his hand and flipped himself over the room, covering thirty feet in one elegant motion. He looked back at Eleanor from the door, bowed and disappeared from view.

'Come on, your Royal Highness,' Astrudel fussed, taking Eleanor's hand and pulling her towards the door. 'You don't want to be late for the ceremony. Oh, you've got a Raspero as a boyfriend, have you? Well, that's something. They're one of the oldest families in Westrigonia. That's a famous name, Raspero. You're a fast worker, you are. Only been in the country five minutes and already you've snagged yourself a Raspero. I'd better keep an eye on you.'

Eleanor couldn't understand a word of what her nanny was saying, but she caught the name Raspero and knew that her nanny was saying something about Matthias in an approving tone of voice.

And it was at that moment that she resolved to learn the Westrigonian language.

11:25 AM, Wednesday 13 July 1872 A. F.

The Coronation of Frederick and Yolande as King and Queen of Westrigonia had taken place the day before, and so it was now time for the Ceremony of Recognition. This basically involved all the nobles of

Westrigonia being presented to the new monarchs, who would formally declare that they *recognized* the nobles which meant that they were confirmed in their titles and possessions. If they did not recognize them, the nobles were dispossessed of their titles and possessions on the spot which as a rule required instant beheading. In times past, Ceremonies of Recognition had been bloodbaths, and it was not always clear to a noble setting forth to be *recognized* whether or not he would return home alive. Yet the noble had to go, or automatically forfeit his lands and title. The Coronation Regiment, a specially handpicked military unit that surrounded the Throne Room where the ceremony took place, were nowadays a largely symbolic presence, but they had not always been so.

The newly crowned monarchs Frederick and Yolande sat on their thrones in the Throne Room with their son Jason, the new Crown Prince, and their daughter Eleanor, the new Crown Princess, seated on ornately carved chairs by the sides of the thrones. The nobles and their families came forth one by one in descending order of importance, kneeled before their sovereigns and pledged allegiance; in response, Frederick declared in Anglashian that he recognized them, the translator translated this statement into Westrigonian, and the noble and his family would depart with many a bow. It was later on in the ceremony that the Baronial order appeared; the Rasperos, being the oldest Baronial family in Westrigonia, came first. The short and plump Baron Adelmar Raspero walked sedately along, accompanied by his taller wife the Baroness Jimena Raspero, followed by their three children Stefan, Matthias and Lena. They kneeled before Frederick and Yolande, who paid them no special attention while going through the formalities of recognition; only Eleanor of the Royal Family noted every detail of their demeanour. Matthias for once seemed in awe of his circumstances, his eyes downcast and his face set in a serious cast; or so Eleanor thought until he looked up at her for the briefest of instants and for a moment more imagined than real he winked at her. Eleanor wrinkled her nose at him in disdain; and then the Rasperos were departing, walking backwards with the prescribed number of steps, pausing to bow, and repeating these formalities the required number of times. Then they were gone, and the next family were being presented to Their Majesties. And so the afternoon proceeded. Frederick and Yolande, schooled in diplomacy and etiquette, played their roles equably; Jason had never been so bored and felt that it was the longest afternoon of his life; Eleanor was fascinated by every moment of the ceremony, and it could have gone on all week as far as she was concerned. But the Ceremony of Recognition came to an end eventually as do all things, good or bad, under the sun.

7:00 PM, Thursday 14 July 1872 A. F.

The Ball Room of the Palace of Krastienst was decorated with flags, lanterns, banners, strips of coloured cloths and glowing masks. A multitude of candelabras overhead lit up the celebrations with the light of several thousand or so candles; tables and chairs were placed around the walls, with more tables and chairs outside in the courtyard. It was the occasion of the Coronation Ball, which by tradition completed the three days of the Coronation. In times past, those who were still alive by this stage had good reason to celebrate. Even in these more modern times, there was a general sense of relief that everything had been done, and now it was nearly time for everyone to go home and begin this new historical era.

Eleanor sat in her place by the side watching everything that went on. In theory she should not have been able to complain at her treatment for she had her very own chair and table with drinks and nuts to nibble, and a good view over the proceedings; but complaints are not so easily avoided as all that. Eleanor counted herself as being alone, she seemed to herself to be abandoned, she was bored, and she felt pretty left out.

Every now and then she looked over at Matthias on the far side of the Ball Room. Matthias seemed to always be at the centre of attention of a group of boys and girls. They were laughing and talking and having fun. This annoyed Eleanor. She did not see why Matthias and his friends should be having fun when she herself was not, especially given her own saintly forbearance with regard to Matthias's misbehavior.

In the end, Eleanor had not reported Matthias's incursion into the

Palace to her parents. Young as she was, she was aware that however Matthias had pulled off his burglary, it was something that would be deemed unacceptable, and so everyone involved would get blamed, including no doubt her. She was in two minds about whether she wanted to see Matthias get into trouble or not. There was no doubt that he deserved some form of punishment after his behavior, but still, she was tied up by her doubts. She felt that at some level of understanding she should be the one to punish him. And that punishment would be severe, of that there could be no doubt. But it would have to be a punishment determined by her. So she had let it go.

But in the meantime, Eleanor felt lonely. No-one spoke a word to her. She was completely ignored. Her mother and father had opened the Coronation Ball with the first dance, and now they were circulating around the room, talking to the guests.

Eleanor saw Matthias start to make his way over to her, in the slightly apprehensive way of a young boy in a room full of adults. He dodged his way around legs and wine glasses while traversing the room in her direction.

'<Good evening, your Royal Highness,>' Matthias said, turning up at her side.

Eleanor looked away and pretended not to have heard him. She was outraged by his impertinence. How dare he disturb her solitude when she had so much been enjoying it!

People were starting to move into position for the next dance.

'<It is very much the interesting ball, is it not, yes?>' Matthias said, persisting in his attempts to converse with her.

Eleanor simply ignored him. It was as if he did not exist.

'<I say this, your Royal Highness,>' Matthias said firmly, '<it is that even if you are give me the royal command that I am dance with you I refuse dance with you! This I tell you now so you know it!>'

With that Matthias started to walk away. Eleanor was furious at his insolence.

'<Stop!>' she shouted, leaping to her feet. Matthias stopped and turned around to look at her. Various people standing nearby turned to look at them. '<You will dance with me! It is a royal command and you will not refuse!>'

Matthias looked startled, but he also looked trapped. He had been caught out. All the guests in the radii of this drama were staring at the quarrelling children.

Matthias bowed with enormous courtesy. '<Of course I dance with you as royal command is not be refuse!>' he declared loudly so that everyone nearby could hear him. He stepped up to her and held out his arm. She graciously put her hand on his arm, just as she had seen the grand ladies do, and allowed Matthias to escort her onto the dance floor.

There was a murmur of talk around them, laughter, and then the normal hubbub of sound resumed. And so Matthias and Eleanor danced, watched in silent envy by all the other children, who were banned from dancing themselves. The very spectacle of how Matthias and Eleanor had entered the dance floor had conferred a legitimacy to the two children dancing. The young princess had shouted at the child of a noble that it was her royal command that he dance with her, and so it came to be that no-one thought to stop them dancing. It was a matter of the appearance of monarchical authority, with the attendant baronial trickery well hidden.

After the dance Matthias escorted Eleanor back to her seat, bowed stiffly, and said: '<If you are give me royal command to make introduce for you to my friends, I refuse this!>'

Once again Eleanor took the bait. '<You will introduce me to your friends. It is my royal command!>' she said grandly.

Matthias looked startled. '<Again you are have the better of me!>' he complained. '<Very well, so it is to be so!>'

He offered her his arm and escorted her over to his friends. With a mixture of Westrigonian and Anglashian he introduced Eleanor to: his sister Lena; Haris Olander; Alaric Niedbala; Marica Philokrates, known as Mitzi; Acteon Quattroy; Fionola Uaithne and Hyder Treasach. As children do the world over, they looked shifty and uncertain while in fact noting every detail of their new companion. Eleanor returned their scrutiny with her own and the children all settled into their seats around the table they had commandeered at the side of the Ballroom.

A prophet would have cast a knowingly sardonic eye over the particular children seated around that table as it was quite a gathering for someone who could see the future. The stellar accomplishments, larger-than-life lifestyles, impeachment scandals, royal pardons and endless gossip that would swirl around the figures at that table and their friends and lovers and associates would keep a bevy of biographers in business for an age or two. But there were not only prophets casting their sardonic eyes over those card-playing children. Historians and painters also joined in. At one time this would be a fashionable topic among painters, and the celebrated painter Ueli Kallikrates caused a storm of controversy by endorsing the historian Nadege Sakina's theory of the seating arrangements at the table in his masterpiece *Card-Players at the Coronation Ball*, as by that time there had arisen a heated (and possibly pointless) debate on the historical significance of who was sitting where.

7:40 PM, Thursday 14 July 1872 A. F.

By the time everyone was settled in their seats, Haris had already fished out two decks of playing cards from the pockets of his red velvet jacket, and began shuffling them together.

Eleanor was sitting beside Matthias. '<You are know of this game Piccolet?>' Matthias asked.

Eleanor had never heard of it. '<Of course. But I would prefer not to play as this game is beneath my dignity given my social rank, which is so much superior to your own.>'

Matthias understood her perfectly. '<You are sit here and I am show you game.>'

They used two decks of cards, given the number of players. The decks of cards were cut and dealt and the children played a round, Matthias explaining the rules to Eleanor as they went along. The cards were of the twelve types of the astrological signs, with each type numbering seven cards showing different professions which were the courtesan, the wandfighter, the Herakrim priest, the banker, the story-teller, the farmer and the artisan. Each card had a numerical value depending on which other cards in the player's hand could be related to it, and these shifting numerical values added up to winning or losing totals. Body posture, details of clothing, the presence or absence of personal items and symbols placed in the corners all had their significances. Matthias explained to Eleanor how the Capricorn Courtesan, which had been worth eleven points at the beginning of the game due to such and such a set of circumstances, had its value changed to seven points after the addition to his hand of the Gemini Courtesan due to another set of complicated circumstances, only to have the value of three points by the end of the round once the Gemini Courtesan had been paired with the Leo Wandfighter.

Eleanor's initial reaction was one of alarm: she did not want to seem stupid in her new country by failing to understand the rules of this bewildering game, especially as the other children seemed to think nothing of the detailed and complex calculations called for by the changing fortunes of the succeeding hands of the game. But her concern at feeling inadequate was mixed with puzzlement at the disjunction between what she had been told about Westrigonia being a backward country and her own personal experience of a country that seemed highly sophisticated in its own terms.

Haris Olander was getting edgy at the delays in the game caused by Matthias explaining things to Eleanor, and seeing this, Matthias commented: 'We shouldn't be too keen to play a game so much associated with gambling. After all, look what happened to my ancestor, the twenty-ninth baron of Raspero.'

'What happened to him?' Alaric asked.

'Who cares what happened to him?' Haris snarled. 'Are we playing cards or what?' Haris's hero was the professional gambler, living by his wits and his crooked card-playing, with a throwing knife up one sleeve and seven cards up the other, surrounded by danger and large-breasted women. As Haris was the heir to the Keephouse of Diya, this was all just a pipe dream.

'My ancestor, the twenty-ninth Baron of Raspero,' Matthias began, with a warning look at Haris not to interrupt, '<it is that my ancestor, who

is twenty-ninth Baron of Raspero>,' Matthias added for Eleanor's benefit, 'was taken a cup of hot chocolate by his sister one night, <he is have this hot chocolate from sister for the night-time drink>, and he was found the next morning completely stone dead, <the next morning he is the dead one>, and needless to say it remains a mystery to this day how he died, <it is the great mystery how it is that he is dead at this time>, but it was just as well that he did die, given that he had gambled away half the estates of Raspero and was well on his way to gambling away the remainder of the barony, <it is the good luck he is the dead one because he is gambler losing much of Raspero fortune>, and it was not until Oliver that the Raspero estates were restored to their former extent, <it is Oliver who is later rescue Raspero barony>, and so the moral of the story is we should beware of gambling too much, <so moral of story is it is the great danger of gambling>.'

'No, it isn't,' Haris said. 'The moral of the story is not to drink your sister's hot chocolate late at night.'

The children laughed.

'Oh ho, what have we here?' a voice intoned from above, 'miscreants up to no good, I'll be bound. And who's your new friend?'

'Get lost, Stefan, before I re-arrange your face,' Matthias said pleasantly.

'Oh yeah, you and whose army?'

'You want to see my army?' Matthias said with a grin. 'Please let me oblige. Hey, Master-of-the-Tables,' Matthias shouted out, waving his left arm in the air, 'could you come over here please?'

The Master-of-the-Tables, a melancholy-looking man who worried about everything at the best of times (and this was the occasion of an historical coronation, no less!) came over promptly, almost on the run. He had noted earlier that the Crown Princess had gone with a child of a noble to sit at a table full of the children of nobles, and no-one else in authority seemed to have noticed this. He, the Master-of-the-Tables, was alone in his observation of this event and thus alone in being in possession of the knowledge of this event. But what was he to do? Should he do something, or should he do nothing? Matthias, who had eyes in the back of his head, had already noted the nervous twitches of this troubled man. The Master-of-the-Tables could think of no reason to interfere, but nor could he entirely feel relaxed about what might or might not be proper etiquette. He was anxious and ready to lash out, and Matthias knew exactly how to harness all this pent-up energy.

'Master-of-the-Tables,' Matthias said in a commanding manner, 'as you can see, the Crown Princess of Westrigonia is our honoured guest at this table. But her peace of mind is under attack from these young gentlemen,' Matthias indicated Stefan and all his friends standing to the side of the table with a vague wave of his left hand, 'so could you please be of service to our beloved monarchy and see to it that these young gentlemen are made to go away before the Princess is upset and names you as having failed to perform your duty? Or should I ask someone else?'

The hand of the Master-of-the-Tables closed around the wand at his belt and he turned on Stefan and his friends with a set expression to his face. Everything had now become clear to him. 'Out!' he barked, raising his left forefinger as if to point in the direction of Out. Given that there was no Out, it was all a bit absurd. He really should have said "Away!" But it was done, and in any case, it was all clear enough.

'We'll settle accounts later, *miscreant*,' Stefan said as he turned away.

The Master-of-the-Tables watched his newly acquired foes depart the scene of battle with a sense of having settled something.

'Well done, Master-of-the-Tables,' Matthias said approvingly. 'Now, if you can see to it that we are brought grape juice, apple juice, bowls of nuts and raisins and potato chunks, the Crown Princess and her friends can enjoy this historic evening. And please also see to it that we are not again disturbed by ruffians such as that lot. How did they even get in here? I know I can appeal to your sense of duty in this matter.'

'Very well, Your Royal Highness,' the Master-of-the-Tables said with a brief bow to Eleanor, 'I shall see to it.' The Master-of-the-Tables now had peace of mind. Everything was clear. If no-one troubled the Princess while she sat with her friends, then all was as it should be. And he saw that the food and drink was sent over as promised, thus saving the children the trouble of actually having to walk over the room to fetch them for themselves.

'<But what is going on?>' Eleanor asked.

'<It is that Stefan is the trouble-maker,>' Matthias said and lightly slapped the table-top with his hand. '<But now it is alright once again.>'

'<Stefan is your brother, isn't he?>' Eleanor said, turning her head to look at the departing teenagers. She remembered Matthias mentioning Stefan before. She had a good memory.

'<Unfortunately yes,>' Matthias said a little glumly. '<But what it is that I can do?>'

Eleanor, who had a vexed relationship with her own older brother Jason, understood this comment perfectly.

'Are we playing cards or what?' Haris asked. 'I mean, hello, wakey, wakey, someone start dealing.' Haris, who was good-looking in a surly, fat-cheeked kind of way, spoke gruffly to conceal his admiration of Matthias. His feelings towards Matthias were a mixture of envy at the stunts Matthias pulled off, and a genuine admiration of these stunts. Haris wanted to do the same himself but couldn't think-on-his-feet in quite the same way. But even that wasn't the real issue. Matthias's great-great-uncle was widely suspected of having fathered Haris's great-grandfather, and this insult to Haris's family, namely the seduction of Haris's great-great-grandmother, an insult which Haris felt keenly to this day, was confused by the shared blood which now flowed through their veins and which made them family (if this seduction had really happened, which it might not have done). But besides, when all was said and done, Haris liked and respected and admired Matthias and wanted to be like him in every way, but his envy told him that this could never be. This was all too complicated, leaving Haris to yearn for the simplicities of a life of deceit and skullduggery as a professional gambler far from the duties of the family home.

Matthias started shuffling the cards, giving Haris an oblique look that was in itself a measure of their difficult friendship, but stopped as something across the room caught his eye. The children all turned to look to see what was up. Eleanor was struck by the sudden tension in the air. Even Haris forgot to look cynical.

Everyone (and not only the card-playing children) seemed to be mainly looking at a man dressed all in white, who had led out onto the floor an elegantly dressed woman. Eleanor noticed that the other dancers on the dance floor kept well away from them, as if they had a contagious disease. When the man in white smiled, it was like the baring of fangs.

'<Who is that man?>' Eleanor asked Matthias.

'<He is Chief of Necessaries, this is State Bureau of Security, Chevalier Phelan is name, very the danger, he is killed these many people, men, women, children, he is hungry demon arrive here from below the ground.>' Matthias leaned toward her to say all this in a low voice, as if he was being careful not to be overheard. Even the normally unflappable Matthias seemed a little bit scared.

Eleanor wasn't sure if Matthias was speaking literally or metaphorically, and her uncertainty sent a delicious shiver down her spine. She felt for a moment far from home; but with the feeling came the recognition that this was now her home and she was in it. There was a sense of a double vision sliding into the single focus of where she was now, as if she was only now transitioning into Westrigonia; but she was already here, and the past was far behind her.

Eleanor looked about her as Matthias finished shuffling and gave the cards to Mitzi, who cut the deck and dealt the next round of cards, and unexpectedly, like an ocean-wave of pure sun-warmth surging over her and singing through her blood, Eleanor knew-all-at-once that she belonged here: these were her friends, her new Westrigonian friends, and she was the Crown Princess of Westrigonia. It was at that moment that Eleanor accepted her new life without reservation. Everything was different now, and from this moment onwards, there would never be any turning back. The Anglashian daughter of the Duke and Duchess of Leland was now a Westrigonian Princess.

She bent her head over the hand of cards Matthias was unfolding before them, determined now to understand everything, absolutely everything, about this game of Piccolet, so that she would be just as Westrigonian as anyone else in the future, because that future was already now.

10:15 AM, Friday 15 July 1872 A. F.

And now Eleanor arrived at her last memory of speaking to Matthias in person. She was standing with Matthias in the Rose Garden, with her uncle Lord Caerwyn Sakesheld observing them from the side.

'<It is that I am come for say goodbye for you, Your Royal Highness,>' Matthias said.

'<Very well.>' Eleanor lifted her nose high into the air and looked disdainfully at Matthias. '<Goodbye.>' She was in fact upset that her only friend in Westrigonia was leaving her to be all alone again.

'<But first I have the present for you.>' Matthias unbuckled a bracelet from his wrist, took her hand in his and buckled it around her own wrist. The bracelet was made of solid heavy gold and it was still warm from having been on Matthias's own wrist moments before. '<It is from Royal Treasury of Sashkind. It is that my great-etc-uncle General Willselm Raspero was took bracelet for the victory in the war. Before this it is worn by Queens of Sashkind for many centuries. And now I give to you.>'

Eleanor turned the bracelet around on her wrist, studying its mysterious markings. It looked very old and very valuable.

'<But it is that it is very important that you are not tell anyone it is present from me, you understand,>' Matthias continued, taking her chin in his hand and tilting her head up to look at him directly. '<Then it is that bracelet is taken away from you if you are tell of me given it for you as present. So it is the secret present.>' Matthias leaned forward and kissed her full on her lips. Then he let go of her and stood back.

Eleanor looked at him, saying nothing, the feeling of his kiss still on her lips.

Matthias stepped back, bowed formally with his wand hand extended forward, and said: '<I bid you farewell, Your Royal Highness. May it be that soon we meet again.>'

He turned away then and walked off to where Lord Sakesheld was standing, gazing over at them with a benign smile. He spoke briefly to Lord Sakesheld, bowed to him and left.

At the gate to the Rose Garden Matthias stopped, turned around and looked at her, bowed and smiled, then left with a practiced grace.

Eleanor, still traipsing about her memories, smiled as well, caught up in that moment, but her smile was only as brief as that moment, given that

Matthias had never come back to see her again; nor had he even bothered to write to her. Eleanor had kept his bracelet as *the secret present,* ever mindful that it would be taken away from her if she told anyone about it, but she had grown angrier and angrier with Matthias as time went by and she did not hear from him, until she had come to believe that she would never hear from him again, and so she had turned against him.

By one measure she had become opposed to Matthias, who in her own mind was one incarnation of Westrigonia; but there were other measures of her relations with Westrigonia. In any case, she was marching day by day further and further into her brand new, yet immeasurably old, Westrigonian home. It was not long before she was so far from her origins that Troderent was barely remembered. Yet in the land of Westrigonia as the saying goes *the past isn't even past* and so it went for the young Crown Princess as the sun continued in its never-ending procession as the monarch of the heavens, unfolding the time of today from the eternal now.

CHAPTER THREE

True love is never clothed,
While all skill is forgotten in a fight.
A woman's eyes are soldiers in ambush.
Frankie the Villain

3:45 PM, Friday 15 July 1872 A. F.

Flying carriages were built of a large hoop of magnetized metal, surrounded by interacting component parts of a mechanism that both kept the metal magnetized and connected to a rod of magneterium that was used by the pilot of the carriage to activate the magnetized hoop which lifted it into the air. Around this mechanism and fastened on to it was the wooden body of the flying carriage itself.

The flying carriage of the Barony of Raspero was of the Reffari model, purchased by Oliver, the thirty-fourth Baron of Raspero; it was old-fashioned now but still one of the most luxurious of all flying carriages. The interior was of dark red cherry wood, with polished bronze fittings and crystal chandeliers. The Raspero family sat in their respective places as they returned home after the coronation. Baroness Jimena Raspero sat calmly dealing out cards on the table. She was either playing a solitary card game, or reading the future. Lena, the youngest, was gazing into space, rapt in all her memories of the coronation; the dresses, the dancing, the palace, the royal procession . . . There was a fund of memories that would keep her young and girlish mind occupied for weeks to come. It would be some time before the real world could claim her attention once again.

The Baron himself was gazing onto an interior landscape with an enclosed look on his face.

Matthias was pretending to read a volume of wandlore while every now and then stealing looks across the carriage at his older brother Stefan, who for his part was reading a novel full of action and mayhem, with twists and turns and unexpected outcomes, his very favourite kind of novel. Stefan might be unaware of Matthias's covert surveillance, but this was unlikely. There was trouble ahead for Matthias at Stefan's hands, and they both knew it. Stefan would have revenge for his treatment by Matthias when Matthias had sent him flying at the hands of the Master-of-the-Tables, and it was only a question of when and how that revenge would come.

Stefan laid down his novel and stretched with a slight yawn. It all might have been as innocent as it seemed, but Matthias tensed slightly while he continued to pretend to read.

'You had a good time, little brother, didn't you?' Stefan said in his most friendly manner.

Matthias looked up as if he had really been reading and was just now re-focusing his attention. 'What? Oh, yeah, I suppose.'

'No, I have to admit, I'm impressed by your boldness. It is just that I am concerned about the family. I hope that you have not endangered the Raspero family by your behavior. You see, little brother, we are members of the Raspero family, and we must never forget this no matter how much fun we want to have.'

Both the boys registered that the Baron's distraction had faltered, as if these words had pierced through the cloud of thoughts which enshrouded him.

'That is quite true, Stefan, and I thank you for your guidance,' Matthias said in a friendly fashion. 'Didn't you have fun yourself at the coronation? It would have looked very strange if you had no fun at all.'

'I did have fun, little brother,' Stefan conceded, 'but not such fun as to endanger the Raspero family and our public standing.'

The Baron stirred at this and his attention came back fully to the present moment. Papa turned his heavy-lidded gaze on his innocent-looking younger son.

'It's good to hear that you didn't have *that* kind of fun,' Matthias said approvingly, as if only too well aware that Stefan was capable of far worse, 'but neither did I so it's good that we are both in the clear on this issue.' He spoke with a serene confidence.

'What trick did you play on the child of our latest monarchs, may I ask?' Stefan asked with an admiring grin. 'Children under the age of seventeen, such as myself, for example, were strictly forbidden to dance which is why, in case you didn't notice, I, unlike you, didn't dance. It was a clear breach of palace protocol for you to lead Her Royal Highness the Princess Eleanor out onto the dance floor with her hand in yours. So how did you pull that one off?'

'Her Royal Highness shouted at me that it was her royal command that I should dance with her. Given that many of those present heard her say this, I was obliged to dance with her. Or are you suggesting that I should have refused this royal command?'

Stefan shook his head as if giving up on Matthias. 'Well, of course you didn't provoke her into making that royal command. But that is not the point. Can you even guess at what the point is?'

'Yes, Stefan, I can,' Matthias said as if becoming impatient with this whole conversation. 'You are being eaten alive with your jealousy that I danced at the Coronation Ball and you did not.'

'We may feel about our new monarchs as we wish,' Stefan said as sternly as if hinting that Matthias was an enemy of the state, 'but it is reckless of you to take our newly arrived Crown Princess as your girlfriend.'

The Baroness looked over at Matthias, open-mouthed. Lena remained in her own private little world.

'Shall I say that you are lying, Stefan?' Matthias said. He was as grim-faced as if ready to fight a duel. 'Or just that you are stupid? Princess Eleanor is not my girlfriend. What craziness is this on your part?'

Stefan leaned forward now, grim-faced in his turn. 'If you say that I am lying, Matthias Raspero, I will know what steps I have to take.'

'Be silent, both of you,' the Baron commanded, lifting one pudgy forefinger into the air like a tentacle-eye spying the landscape. 'You will both guard your tongues.'

The boys fell silent on the instant.

There was silence in the carriage. The tension was such that even Lena was waking up to the fact that something was going on. She blinked around at the others as if just waking up. The Baron let the silence drag on as if to impress upon his boys that they would only speak at his discretion; then he said: 'What do you mean by this, Stefan?'

'At the Coronation Ball, Matthias danced with the Crown Princess Eleanor, and then took her back with him to his table where she spent the remainder of the evening playing piccolet with him and his friends. It was a public display that I have to say was, well, let me say, incautious, given, well, given the political sensitivities of the moment. I hope that I am the only one saying that Princess Eleanor is the girlfriend of Matthias Raspero.'

The Baron's heavy-lidded gaze turned back to Matthias. 'Is this true?'

'Yes, Papa, it is true,' Matthias said promptly without hesitation. 'And I am sure that it is also true that only Stefan is talking such nonsense as this about girlfriends and the like. It wasn't like that at all.'

The Baron's upraised finger warned the boys to be silent. After some moments thinking all this over, the Baron said: 'Matthias, you will stay away from that girl. If I catch you near her again, I'll cut your balls off.'

'Then I will most certainly stay away from Her Royal Highness,' Matthias said immediately.

So came the end of Matthias's first-ever romance. Eleanor would now wait in vain to hear from him again. The kiss in the Rose Garden would be all the passion of their youthful romance, and the love-token in the form of a bracelet would be the only tangible reminder of that moment. The world itself in the form of the Baron of Raspero had separated them from each other, and like sundered lovers throughout history they now only had their memories of the time they had shared. A cold malevolence in the form of Stefan's envy had struck at their newfound warmth.

The Baron's heavy-lidded gaze appraised the youngest son, then he turned back to his private thoughts. Matthias turned back to his volume of wandlore, inwardly furious. Lena looked back and forth between Stefan and Matthias, wide-eyed. Stefan picked up his novel again.

Matthias tapped his bookmark down on the table-top next to him. The sound of the tap said very clearly: *Stefan, you will pay for this. I will get you and I will get you good, no matter how long I have to wait!*

Stefan shifted in his chair, and drummed his fingers on his thigh. The drumming of his fingers said: *Relax, little brother, take it easy.*

Matthias turned over a page with a sudden motion that said: *You miserable excuse for a rat disguised as a human being, I will get you! Just you wait!*

The Baroness set her glass back down on the table with a clunking sound that said: *Take it easy, boys! Enough!*

Matthias didn't move, and his stillness proclaimed very clearly: *For now!*

The dynamics had now shifted and it was Stefan who was aware that he had become the target. And so the Raspero family carriage flew onward through the gathering twilight, a noble and ancient family in some ways, but very young and freshly energised in others. Apart from their noble status, they were like many another family, constricted in their petty grudges and loosened by their large hopes. Some things never change in any family at any time of history. But as they prepared to leave the carriage at the end of their journey, Stefan threw an arm around Matthias's shoulders. Matthias stiffened and nearly wriggled away; but then stood still and accepted the peace offering. So it was that the warring brothers were once again at peace with each other.

9: 40 AM, Monday 12 April 1860 A. F.

On the day that Matthias was born a raven had come to perch on the windowsill of the open window to gaze upon the mother and newborn child. The large black bird had refused all hints to move on, shuffling up and down the windowsill while an elderly servant had fearfully tried to shoo the dangerous-looking bird away from the vicinity of her mistress. Eventually a broom shoved into its body brought about the departure of the visitor, which flew away with a loud and aggrieved squawk.

Matthias had been born into a life of wealth and privilege as the second son of the thirty-sixth Baron of Raspero. The Raspero family, which had had its ups and downs over the millennia of its existence, including near-ruination, had some time ago been saved by Oliver, the thirty-fourth Baron, and put back in business as a going concern. One hundred days after Matthias's birth, the traditional celebration of his survival for that length of time was held, given the custom that a baby that had lived one hundred days was now more likely than not to live to adulthood. Among the multitude that attended this celebration were twenty-seven families who wished to arrange a future marriage between the infant Raspero boy and their own eligible infant daughters; the Baron received them all kindly and wrote down their names in a ceremonial fashion. Custom and tradition were still observed across the length and breadth of Westrigonia as they always had been.

For the first seven years of his life, Matthias had been allowed to enjoy his childhood. His only formal education had been to learn his letters and numbers, but apart from that he had been allowed to play and have fun. All that changed on his seventh birthday. After having been given his wand in a ceremony attended by a multitude of family and friends and townsfolk, his instruction had begun.

First of all, his father had taken him aside and there told him: '*Your noble birth is a bright lamp which makes everything you do visible to the whole world. Never imagine you can do anything in secret that the whole world does not see. But hidden in you is a seed which if you nurture to full growth will carry you along to the destination which awaits you. Never forget that Fortuna rules everything that happens in this world.*'

Later in life, Matthias would wonder if his father had said these things to him for him to believe or for him to think critically about.

Next, Matthias had been required to sit inside a circle made of white paint on the stone-flagged floor in the dungeons for thirty-six hours without leaving the circle; food and drink had been brought to him, his washing and toiletries had been carried in and out from the circle by servants who were allowed to come and go while Matthias had been obliged to remain where he was, until the time came when he was allowed to rejoin the outside world. The point of his incarceration was to impress upon him that he was never, *never*, to reveal those secrets of the Rasperos which he would receive to any person, either living or dead. Alarming tales of the terrifying and miserable fates of those who broke such injunctions were read to him by his father who sat outside the circle while his son sat inside, separated from each other by the geometry of time and space that the circle constituted; and in the night-time, by the flickering flames of his candles, the dungeon walls glistened with the candle-flame shadows of the demonic terrors of the night who came up from the darkness below the world to gaze upon the world in the form of the boy encircled before them. His only protection against these demons was his innocence, which made of this circle an impassable barrier; but without his innocence he would have been defenceless. Over and over, in an almost hypnotic repetition of cadentic phrases, the Baron of Raspero impressed upon his son that he was never to reveal those secrets of the Rasperos which he would learn to others; and throughout this entire ordeal, Matthias was not allowed to speak a single word to anyone. His father had drawn the dull edge of a sharp knife across the back of Matthias's tongue, with the warning that his tongue would be cut off if he spoke a single word in the time of his trial to follow; after which this very same knife, turned around so as to use the sharp edge, had been used to cut off the tongue of a slaughtered calf in the courtyard while Matthias watched. Silent for thirty-six hours in the presence of demons in the dungeons, Matthias had kept his counsel and waited.

After this initiation, Matthias had begun his instruction in the use of the wand. He began with simple commands and by the age of nine was allowed to have his own bodily karns, and by eleven his own mobile karns. Until the age of twelve, his education was largely in the hands of the Raspero private tutor, Master Dalmalym Kashopol. Matthias was a dutiful and obedient boy. Other boys might be rebellious, but not him. He placed a trust in his elders and betters that was in essence a logical conclusion that they had to know better than he did given their comparative circumstances. Matthias therefore meekly obeyed his father in all that he was told to do. He paid attention to everything his father said, including his father's casual endorsement one day, in a passing comment that could easily have been overlooked, of *stolen knowledge.*

'And so it was,' said the Baron, 'that Samstride Celestyn took that knowledge which had not been given to him, and it was stolen knowledge by that token; and in that way the glass-maker prospered.'

Matthias had concluded, logically, that if the chance came for him to steal knowledge, that is what he should do. And so he began, with the utmost caution, to borrow without permission books from his father's library, and also to return those books in a fashion equally undetected. And so his education proceeded.

In the meantime, Stefan was as rebellious as Matthias was dutiful. He fidgeted constantly during their shared lessons, which he skived off whenever he could, paying little attention to his education while it was underway and evading it as best he could the rest of the time. While Matthias studied his runes and the mathematical basis of music, Stefan had fun. While Matthias stole books on wandlore from his father's library, Stefan had fun. While Matthias studied the framework of the cosmos, Stefan had fun. Until the day came when the two boys clashed and the eleven-year-old Mathias thrashed the fourteen-year-old Stefan in a wandfight with an ease that shocked Stefan into paying attention to his studies. By then however, despite having begun studying under Kashopol three years before Matthias, Stefan found himself unable to catch up with his younger brother. Stefan found himself reduced to continually reminding Matthias that he, Stefan, would be the next Baron of Raspero while Matthias would be obliged to shift for himself and beg for scraps from Stefan's table.

9:45 AM, Saturday 16 July 1872 A. F.

Matthias sat at the desk in his room, gazing out through the window at the world outside while trying to decide what to do. Stefan had gone off with friends to have fun, and Matthias's only consolation on being left behind was that the day was overcast; being stuck indoors on a sunny day would have been too much. Even so, Matthias groaned at the thought of having to do his homework. For once, even a dutiful student like Matthias wasn't in the mood for study. But all of a sudden, a thought occurred to him and his eyes glinted in recognition that he could have a different kind of fun to Stefan's.

He promptly slid off his chair and sauntered out the door and up some stairs and along a corridor and up some more stairs and along another corridor and up some more stairs and along the corridor to his father's study. The long corridor was paved with polished marble slabs gleaming with their red and white and black veins of variegated colours, while the walls were of solid stone slabs, the ceiling being of varnished panelled oak. Ever since Oliver had renovated Castle Raspero, it had become renowned as one of the most luxurious castles in Westrigonia. There were many who sought invitations just to gaze in admiration at the symphony of colours and textures backed up by the solid stone foundation and walls of the nine-hundred-year old castle. Everyone was always impressed.

Matthias knocked at the door of his father's study and was invited to enter.

His father's study was at the top right corner of the castle and overlooked the town below, the river running through the town and the valley all the way to the Rohesia mountains in the distance. It had remained largely unchanged over the centuries, as Oliver had chosen to leave everything just as it always had been. (The only other room he had left unchanged was the Master Bedroom.) The oak beams crossing overhead were often a haven for spiders, but as no-one but the Baron and his sons and daughter and wife were ever allowed to set foot inside the study, even the Steward being forbidden from entering on any occasion whatsoever, the oak-beam ceiling was cleaned only rarely, when the Baron himself could be bothered to take wand and cleaning brushes in hand. As he had a high tolerance threshold for spiders, whose cleverness and industry he admired, not to mention his recognition that they kept the population of flies and insects down, it was only rarely that the Baron turned house cleaner. The stone walls were largely unchanged from Daniel's time: the painting of the first baron Daniel himself on the wall dated from Daniel's own time, being of oil paints on wood and was in remarkably good condition. Beside it was a painting of Etienne, the eleventh Baron of Raspero. An eighteenth century oil painting of Oliver, Matthias's great grandfather, took up much of another wall. That was all the decoration the study had to offer. Along the walls were bookshelves of varying woods, made at different times by different carpenters of Raspero: whether these furnishings made an aesthetic ensemble was perhaps a matter for debate. But what was not a matter for debate was the quality of the books they held. By consensus opinion, there were fifty-five Great Libraries in the whole wide world, and the Raspero Library was one of them.

The books were in the forms of scrolls, of leather-bound volumes, of clumsily- tied-together sheets of loose paper, some mass-printed, others handwritten, ornately illustrated, personalized productions of ancestral Rasperos and friends of the family over the centuries, eccentric and brilliant views of historical cycles and the astrological nature of the universe, extensive reference works on the noble families of Westrigonia, the genealogies and personal histories and financial assets of said families, collections of now-unread correspondence dating back centuries, files of scandalous information on prominent people which could be used for blackmail, most (but not all!) of which was now out-of-date and hence no longer potent, extensive reference material on a variety of subjects from agriculture to finance to geography to politics, the great philosophical works of history, works on languages, linguistics, logic, mathematics, music, astronomy, biographies, folk-tales, mythologies, religious work, dictionaries, novels, collected poems, travelogues, but above all else, supremely above all else, was the thorough and extensive collections of writings on wandlore, and subjects related to wandlore, which in the hands of an imaginative thinker could be subjects about absolutely anything. It was writings on wandlore that largely made up the claim of a Great Library to be Great. It was not just that knowledge of wandlore was power, but also that knowledge of wandlore was held to relate, however tangentially, to every subject under the sun.

Matthias entered his father's study, closing the door behind him by hand, as no-one but the Baron was allowed to pull out a wand in the Great Library; he turned to face his father, who was sitting behind his desk in the corner, bowed deeply as required and approached the desk, hooking his thumbs casually in his belt as he came closer. This casual thumb-hooking brought the edge of his right hand close to the hilt of his wand, which had worked loose of the sheath it was in and become pushed to the left by means of a wire pulled by the big toe of Matthias's right foot, all of which was concealed by the overhanging folds of Matthias's robe.

The Baron looked up with a distracted air from the papers before him on his desk. As it happened, he had a right to appear distracted. The web he was spinning was as fine and delicate as anything ever spun by a spider, but if it broke the fall it would engender would be colossal. The Baron was playing a very dangerous game.

'Father, I wonder if I might borrow a book on wandlore,' Matthias said, coming straight to the point as he could see the impatience written over the paternal countenance, and followed his words with a bow, which served the purpose of being extremely courteous while concealing the contact his right hand was now making with the hilt of his wand. The magneterium ripples of consciousness spread through him on the instant.

'What is it you are after?' his father asked brusquely.

'Am I old enough for instruction in macchato?'

'No.'

'What about some preliminary reading in macchato?'

'No.'

'What would you advise me to study at this time, father?'

The Baron took a deep breath and sighed heavily. With an upraised hand, he instructed Matthias to stay where he was while he laboriously stood up and beetled his way across the room, straightening up to loosen his stiff back as he went.

In a flash Matthias drew his wand, sent two karns flying across the room to grab a volume from a shelf on the wall behind his father's desk, stuffed the volume out of sight into his robes and put his wand away, all in time to present a patiently-waiting-face to his father as the Baron turned around and shuffled back across the room, carrying a book in his hand, which he handed to Matthias with an impatient gesture which all by itself said: *My good nature has been troubled enough, now get going!*

With a bow Matthias was gone.

The thirty-sixth Baron of Raspero, heir to a great lineage but also a father with the paternal headaches of any father, briefly glanced at the shelf with the missing book, smiled as briefly at the sight, and returned to his desk to resume his labours. He was far from smiling as he leaned over the papers on his desk.

10:05 AM, Saturday 16 July 1872 A. F.

Matthias returned to his room and eagerly examined his prize. It was a Sixteenth-Century treatise on the relationship between wandlore and geometry as expressed in ratios, which promised to be fascinating. Matthias carefully stored the stolen book away from all prying eyes, especially Stefan's, and returned with a sigh of resignation to his homework, which he could no longer postpone.

The lower-fourth subject of *Truth and Meaning* required an essay from the holidaying schoolboy on any one of the following questions:

1) It has been said that even the devils of hell do not lie to each other. Can you imagine a society where no-one told the truth, and would such a society manage to function?

2) Ibtisam says that 'Lying always requires an explanation while telling the truth does not.' Why should this be? Extra marks are given for thinking of an occasion where telling the truth does require an explanation.

(Matthias saw the logical trap of Question 2 as answering the Question would require explaining his presumably truthful statement, so his own homework would be such an occasion. In his mind's eye he could see Mr Kimball Marzio, his *Truth and Meaning* teacher, rubbing his hands together with glee while he explained to the class why they were such fools as to have failed to have seen through his game. It was an easy way to get bonus points, but where was the challenge?)

3) 'All's fair in love and war.' Is lying justified in these two domains of

human activity and not justified elsewhere? Argue your case with reference to at least 5 real-life examples.

4) Consider a society in which no-one ever lies, and everyone always tells the truth; consider another society in which no one ever tells the truth, and everyone always lies; in which ways can these societies be said to be equivalent?

(Matthias contemplated this question. Marzio wanted to know if people had done all their reading and could therefore discuss the theory of Proportionality, by which truth and lies were required to exist in a particular numerical proportion to each other, this ratio being that of the irrational number phi. Matthias marked down this question as a possibility.)

5) Is lying with mental reservations no longer a form of lying? For example, if someone asks you: 'Did you break the window?' and you say: 'No', while thinking silently to yourself, 'not today,' does your mental reservation nullify the moral act of lying?

6) If a robber asks you if you have money, and you lie by saying: 'No', is this lying justified? And if it is, is this justification a form of mental reservation?

Matthias settled on the fourth question, given that the Theory of Proportionality was something that he wanted to study in any case. He bowed his head over his desk and set to work. The day passed by, Stefan came in, pestered him for a while then went out, there was lunch, more interruptions from Stefan, an attendance at a courtyard function to honour a retiring servant, and finally in the late afternoon Matthias finished his essay and sat back with a sigh. It was done. It was much later in the day that Matthias turned to his real study of the day, eagerly opening his stolen book on the relationship between wandlore and geometry. Like every other boy of his generation, Matthias yearned above all things to be a great wandfighter.

12:40 PM, Tuesday 19 July 1872 A. F.

'I feel sorry for Matthias having to go to school in Anglashia,' Stefan declared loudly, dipping his bread roll in an eggplant dip and taking a bite.

'Oliver went to school in Anglashia,' Matthias countered promptly.

'Yes, but he laid down the rule that the *second* son should go to school in Anglashia, not the *eldest* son, the heir, the son who would be the next Baron. Which is me, not you, by the way, in case you've forgotten.'

'How could I forget when you remind me every day?' Matthias countered again with the smile of a saint-in-training. 'Anyway, perhaps it is my destiny to go traipsing around the world having adventures while you do your duty here at home.'

'Yes, you'll wind up in a cannibal's pot being cooked for dinner in the Mountains of Weiden,' Stefan commented and took another bite of his bread roll.

Matthias was silent. The fact was, Stefan was frightened that his brilliant younger brother would overtake him and leave him far behind, if he had not already done so, and their difference in schooling fed into this fear. Oliver had decreed that the second son should go to school in Anglashia, and Stefan was insistent that this meant that Matthias's schooling at Vientae in Anglashia was inferior to his own Westrigonian schooling at the school of Ramhart. In Stefan's view, the important son stayed in Westrigonia, which made Matthias the less important son. He was very keen for Matthias to understand this as clearly as he did. Also, it was necessary for everyone to be aware of the dangers of an Anglashian association.

'I am concerned that you will become an Anglashian in your outlook on life. This is surely a concern for you as well, little brother. It is just that the Anglashians are so interested in change. By now you must be infected with this mania yourself. Change is a disease.'

'Only absolute stillness never changes, and absolute stillness is immaterial. Surely you must regret neglecting your education.'

'The Anglashians are bringing back usury. Perhaps you support this innovation. Or does the concept of absolute stillness somehow make it all irrelevant?'

'This is nothing but the wildest gossip. But how unlucky for you that you are unable to speak Anglashian yourself. You can only hear about Anglashian gossip in Westrigonian! But don't let me lecture you, not when you have such a superior education to my own, even if it leaves you speaking fewer languages!'

'Boys, enough!' said the Baron. 'Eat.'

Matthias managed in taking a bite of his bread roll to make an unmistakably rude signal with his middle finger in Stefan's direction. Stefan's eyes glinted, and he wrenched his bread roll into two pieces as if he was wringing someone's neck. Matthias smiled scornfully as he chewed his mouthful. Lena giggled helplessly over her plate of food. Their mother rolled her eyes. The baron was oblivious to all this, already one hundred and thirty miles away in the midst of his cogitations. Another family dinner proceeded to its harmonious end.

And so Matthias happily powered on, ensconced in his childhood, which enwrapped him in multifarious layers that glittered like all the stars in all the galaxies of the universe. He had all the time in the world, which was all his remaining life, held in his hand like an enormous fortune which he had not yet got around to even begin to spend. There is nothing like having everything.

But paradise would be far from eternal; in point of fact, it would not last longer than another three years. The childhood of Matthias Raspero would end on 11 July 1875 A.F., the day that the secret police came to arrest him.

CHAPTER FOUR

The mind is a castle.
I built it myself.
Frankie the Villain

The Royal Palace of Krastienst was the shape of a cube, the same as the Vidaldmeet, except where the Vidaldmeet had a domed top, the Palace was crowned by a square tower. Internally, however, the two buildings were as vastly different as were the roles played by their residents in the public life of Westrigonia. Where the Vidaldmeet was quadrangular and mapped out in floors with rooms of a square or rectangular design, and connected by corridors of a conventional design, the Palace was very different. For a start, the concept of "floors" per se, did not apply exactly, as the architectural design of the palace was not structured in terms of "floors". The Palace was not divided from top to bottom by horizontal planes; rather, the internal geometry formed a dizzyingly complex, interlocking arrangement of rooms, anterooms, conservatories, nooks, dining rooms, personal chambers, reception rooms, hallways, concourses, corridors, stairs, L-shaped half-stairs leading to L-shaped corridors leading to L-shaped rooms, ramps and abrupt dead-ends. It was all too easy to get lost in the Palace if you did not know your way around.

The Palace was divided up into four parts. These were known as the North, East, South and West Quarters as the corners of the palace walls were precisely aligned to the points of the compass. However, these names were misleading. What was called the North Quarter in fact stretched from the northern point of the compass to the eastern, and so on around the compass. In short, the mid-point of the North Quarter was not due north but due north-east. The North Quarter was known as the Royal Quarter, and here were to be found the private residential rooms of all the members of the Royal Family. This was so that all the royal chambers could have the advantage of the morning sun. The other Quarters of the Palace had to do with the public life of Westrigonia, while to the East side of the Palace were the Palace Gardens, where members of the royal family and other residents of the court could commune with the spirits of nature, with access from the North and East Quarters and protected from trespassers by high walls. Next to the Gardens was the Park of Venusar, and after that came the Vidaldmeet, the other centre of the fabled city of Krastienst.

7:00 AM, Thursday 20 September 1874 A. F. (After the Fall)

Eleanor's day now always had the same beginning. At the moment of dawn, as the first arc of the sun appeared and was cut by the horizon, there was a sharp double-rap on the door, a clearly spoken phrase: 'It is dawn, Your Royal Highness!', and another double-rap on the door. The maid-servant would then silently retire.

Eleanor would yawn, stretch, sit up, and jump out of bed, full of an immediate energy. She was most definitely a morning person. With her wand in hand, she would go to the bathroom-annexe of her ensuite palace bedroom, activate the shower controls with a wave of her wand, disrobe and dive into the falling water without hesitation.

The plumbing system of the Palace of Krastienst was of a composite nature of the archaic, the modern and the innovative. The acrylstyre butanite piping was of the most modern design and manufacture, thus ensuring the most efficient distribution of the water, while the aeratorial admittance augurian water-flow valves dated back to the sixteenth-century with a design that remained to be improved upon; the encasing-heating rods embedded in their blowdown bonnet compression flange heated the water in such a way as to fire up the rotating wheel of the impeller manifold that pumped the water through the piping; the flex coupling of the gate diverter distributed the pressure evenly throughout the plumbing system while the diffuser diaphragm fitting modulated the mixture of the hot and cold water flowing though the shower heads and bath and sink taps. The result was not always reliable, to the bafflement of every engineer ever consulted on the matter. The hot water coming through the pipes could, on occasion, suddenly turn cold, with the result that the innocent recipient of this water, having done nothing wrong, and not deserving in the least of such treatment, would be blasted by cold water with no warning whatsoever; on other occasions the water could become striped hot and cold, which was apparently not impossible. Royal curses would arise into the air. King Frederick, who disliked surprises, took to only having baths.

Eleanor had decided to accept any outcome as the right one, and for this reason was never thrown off balance by her morning shower. Having showered, she would towel herself dry and return to her bedroom, by now nicely heated by warm air arising through the floor vents, and pull the cord for her maid-servants to attend her. Once having dressed, she would sit herself at her desk for her early morning studies.

Over two years had passed since Eleanor had arrived in Westrigonia, and she was no longer the same Anglashian girl who had left Troderent clutching her best friend Freddie the Teddy Bear in her arms. Freddie still had a distinguished place in her bedchambers, but the truth to tell was that he was neglected of late. Eleanor was moving on beyond teddy bears. If Freddie could have spoken, he would have reproached her.

During the days that had followed the coronation, Eleanor had determined, through observation and introspection, on her plan of action and set out to implement it. Like a struck match flaring in a dark cavern, her decision to become Westrigonian was a tiny point of light that faintly illumined the interior space of her whole life.

Clearly priority number one was for her to learn the Westrigonian language, and by a polite but unflagging insistence Eleanor was eventually granted her wish, a private royal tutor in the Westrigonian language. The hapless pedagogue in question, the Honourable Horatio Hottentotenheim, glad enough to receive any employment at all, being generally hopeless at worldly matters, and sensible enough of the honour of such a royal association as this, was soon enough reduced to doing what the eleven-year-old Princess demanded of him. Eleanor kept Hottentotenheim on his toes by first of all grilling him continuously, never letting him slack off for a single moment, and secondly by the occasional threat. She would wide-eyed wonder out loud in her fragmented Westrigonian if she would get him dismissed from his employment if she complained about his lack of due diligence, and then ask Hottentotenheim if she had expressed all that correctly in the proper grammatical forms. Hottentotenheim would correct her grammar while feeling his stomach tie itself up into knots at the thought of losing this employment on which he and his family so desperately relied. None of Hottentotenheim's anguish escaped the sharp-eyed girl. But on the plus side, Hottentotenheim could not have wished for a harder-working pupil: Eleanor would not rest until she had attained a complete mastery of the Westrigonian language. Even late at night, when she was long supposed to be asleep, she would walk in her bare feet over the Ramudien carpets of her palace bedroom, dressed only in her nightie, a lantern in one hand and a grammatical primer in the other, memorizing out loud the sixteen conjugated verbs of action related to movement, or the nineteen cases of personal nouns as related to verbs of growth, immobility and rotation. There were seven different prepositions, four of which could be taken as full verbs in seventeen different kinds of clausal constructions, three of these four verbs becoming gerunds when forming compound nouns associated with verbs in the future tense. The Westrigonian word that meant <for> in Anglashian could mean <of> when in the <second degree of possession> but it could mean <for> in the sense of <purpose> when preceding <an action of intent>. The word <for> could never be used in the <first degree of possession> but if used in the <third degree of possession> it meant the direction <towards> as in, for example, a journey.

The young princess soon enough soaked up the Westrigonian language like a sponge, and not long after turning twelve was speaking it as if she had spoken nothing else her whole life. Next she set her sights on learning High Westrigonian. High Westrigonian was a language that was now more honoured than spoken, existing largely in written forms and in ceremonial occasions. Low Westrigonian, or more simply, Westrigonian, was the national language of Westrigonia as it existed for its native speakers. High Westrigonian in its purest form was the Westrigonian language as it had existed five centuries or so ago, although the times before and after that time had constituted earlier and later forms of the language, less pure, but still nonetheless High; and this had been so until the advent of the modern form of the language. If normal everyday Westrigonian seemed complicated to the native Anglashian speaker, High Westrigonian was complicated even for the Westrigonians. Eleanor's imperious nature naturally gravitated towards High Westrigonian, the mastery of which would be a sign of her superiority over everyone else. Before long, she was even correcting the grammar of high-up officials in the Westrigonian court, and it was said that courtiers trembled when their Crown Princess passed by. The fierce figure with her glittering eyes and black-haired beauty was becoming a presence in the Palace of Krastienst.

Eleanor next turned her attention to the subjects of history, metaphysics, religion, politics, and the constitution. These were all so inter-related in Westrigonia as to constitute a singular subject of endless complexity. Everything started with the *Book of the Herakrim*.

The Herakrim had passed through several incarnations over the nearly two millennia of their existence. Founded directly after the Fall, they had preserved the secrets of the ancients. It was said they could call down fire from heaven, could look into a box and see what was happening on the other side of the world, could call forth any knowledge from that same box, see through the surface of the earth all the way to its centre with special spectacles, wield the power of life and death with a weapon no bigger than a fountain pen, and so on. Of course, only children and the credulous believed such tales.

There were so many myths and legends and semi-historical and historical (and hysterical!) accounts of the Herakrim, either truthful or not or mixed, that no-one could tell what the truth was anymore. As the saying went, *those who know do not speak, those who speak do not know.*

But the following account of how the Herakrim had come to be was as widespread as any other.

The story of the Herakrim by Magister Kacey Sabia as written in the year 1298 A.F.

Immediately after the Fall, a number of men and women gathered to discuss their changed circumstances. In their gathering, they gathered their shared beliefs and disbeliefs, and from that tumultuous agitation came forth many things, of which many different recollections have been preserved. (Yet the destruction of "heretical" documents at the Council of Purging Heresies in 325 A. F. have forever removed from public knowledge many of these recollections differing from approved orthodoxy.) The primary objective of their gathering was to objectively appraise the many and varied causes of their misfortune, with a view to finding a way forward.

Let us here bring forth what many have believed from the beginning, although it was later proclaimed a heresy, the so-called "Alphinian heresy", namely that the original Herakrim were all atheists. They believed that the Fall was due to religion, and that the attraction of religion for humanity because of all its weaknesses had been the cause of the Fall. They therefore devised the following remedy: they would invent a new religion which would hoodwink the masses into obedience while becoming thereby the masters of these masses, and the masters of all the destructive tendencies of religion which had been manifest in the Fall. So their plan went, at any rate, in the beginning of the heaven and earth as according to the Book of the Herakrim.

But what the Herakrim in their wisdom, or in their unwisdom, as the case might be, failed to understand was that time is its own master. Time passed, and with that passing, went one generation of Herakrim to be replaced by another, in turn to be in their turn replaced, and so it went on, generation after generation after generation. And as their original beliefs were handed down and re-formulated and adjusted to the changing circumstances of an ever-changing world, the Herakrim came to be divided between two factions, those who believed that God could be Named and those who believed that God was essentially Nameless. (The original atheism of the Herakrim, namely that God did not exist at all, had long since died out with the execution of the last such believers.) The Herakrim had come to believe that their own creation, namely their made-up account of the Creator and the Creation, was objectively true, and violence took the place of dialogue as it always does in such circumstances. After all, that is the way of the world. The Fall itself proves the truth of this.

And so the Herakrim rolled along, with one faction after another dominating, dividing, devastating regions and towns. And so today what can we say in answer to the question: who are the Herakrim? There are so many answers available that the questioner is left none the wiser. There are some who say that as for births, deaths and marriages, the Herakrim still provide a reasonable service for a moderate fee, and that is all that can now be said on the matter. There are others who say that the Herakrim are far from finished, and whatever the precise nature of their ignoble birth, they are a force to be reckoned with who will still come good. And so the debate continues, each eruption like the next wave of an endless sea washing onto the shore.

Eleanor was already familiar, of course, with the *Book of the Herakrim*, which had first appeared in 63 or 64 A.F.; or to be more accurate, she knew of its existence, and something of its contents, but the study of this book had long been neglected in her home country of Trentland, where it was considered to have been superseded by later developments. This holy text began with an account of the creation of the world and human beings; then followed with an account of the nature of God, the nature of the world and the nature of human beings; and the set of inter-relationships between these three. This constituted Volume One, and was followed by two more volumes. Eleanor began the study of runes in order to read the *Book of the Herakrim* in its original version.

Eleanor read in the *Book of the Herakrim*: "*There is only one infinity. If there were more than one infinity, each would limit the other; but infinity is without limits, therefore there can be only one.*" Eleanor understood that part, but the following paragraph soon got so complicated that she had difficulty following it all.

Hottentotenheim gave her as a thirteenth birthday present the *Principles of Metaphysics* by Etienne da Silva, which proved enlightening.

In Verse 5, lines 33 – 37, of the *Book of the Herakrim* was the following passage: *And God brought forth his right hand and in it was the heaven, and in the heaven was (a man); and God brought forth his left hand, and in it was the earth, and in the earth was (a woman); and for seventy two days and nights God fashioned the human being with his hands.* The commentary by da Silva explained that this was why men had precedence over women, as heaven had appeared first; also that each day and night stood for a thousand years, so this was really a period of seventy-two thousand years; and also that the human being thus fashioned was not material as it was both male and female, which was why the terms *man* and *woman* were in brackets.

Eleanor would never forget reading this commentary seated at her desk in her Palace Chambers, with the sunlight streaming in through the windows and falling across her desk and the red leather of the chair in which she sat. She was struck by the revelation that social conduct was governed by writings such as this one. Up till then, the social arrangements of the world had seemed as fixed and given as compass directions; they were just there of their own accord, dependent on nothing but their own being. Now she had come to see that things were how they were because of beliefs such as these, and by understanding these beliefs she could understand her world.

Eleanor continued reading, fascinated by every line of da Silva's book: all identity is oppositional, because heaven is opposite earth, and everything created is intermediate between these two. Because every existing thing is between heaven and earth, all of life is in terms of polarities. All existing things carry heaven on their backs and carry earth in their arms, and between the two comes the middle world in which we live. The interaction of the male and female principles pervades all levels of existence and creates all existing things, while all of the material and the immaterial constitutes the sheer oneness without limits that is the infinite.

Eleanor felt like an explorer who had travelled so far afield as to find herself approaching the origin of the universe. This was where everything had begun.

The Heart is the House of Being (Eleanor read). It is not sentimentality, although it can be; it is not the mathematical dispositions by which the universe is arranged, although it is not different from these; it is not good or evil, even when it is; it is the central place in the human being where all that is turns and returns, goes back and forth, changes by flipping over to its opposite; it is what the universe turns around, as it turns around itself, going forward and coming back; it is all that we are, and in its centre is the infinite itself.

The time came when Eleanor's studies had progressed to the point where she needed to start using the Library of the Palace of Krastienst. Given her rank as Crown Princess, she was one of the very few people in the world who had access by right to this Library. Her first visit to the Library had been memorable. Hottentotenheim had not been able to come with her, forbidden as he was from entry himself, so she had gone there alone, walking down the corridors in between the statues and benches and suits of armour and paintings and tables set with ornaments and pitchers of water, until she had come at last to the wooden double doors of the library itself. These doors were themselves forbidding, bound with iron and inset with runes made of black and white precious stones, and through these doors she passed, to wander through rooms lined with stone-and-wood bookcases crammed full of ancient books until she came across the Librarian, Hadamard, a stooped old bald man, carefully examining some ancient volumes in the Geography Room. Hadamard ignored her presence, so she waited patiently, sensing that his rudeness was not the real obstacle she faced in this place.

Hadamard eventually chose to acknowledge her presence by turning his head and looking at her.

'You will take me to the *Wendell Commentaries on Metaphysics*,' Eleanor pronounced grandly.

'If you wish, Your Royal Highness,' Hadamard said obediently. 'Yet I do not go there myself. It is said that the books in that room are booby-trapped, with poisons, flying knives, jumping spiders and I do not know what else. If you insist on seeing these books, I cannot come with you.'

These invented scenarios were very real terrors for the young girl.

Hadamard the librarian, who had raised children of his own, understood this well.

Eleanor hesitated. 'I understand. I will open them myself. Clearly there is a limit to your duty.'

The librarian considered this, his head to one side like a bird, looking steadily at her with black unfathomable eyes, almost smiling. Then he bowed to her (for the first time) and said: 'That was well spoken, your Royal Highness.'

'It is not for you to judge me!' Eleanor snapped. 'How dare you be so insolent!'

'If I am insolent to you, I will be dismissed from my employment and thrown into prison.'

'Then do you dare to be insolent?'

'Only if there were no limit to my duty,' the librarian said, still almost smiling as he considered the intense thirteen-year-old girl standing rigidly before him.

'You will do as I command!' Eleanor snapped.

Her condescending elitist arrogance delighted Hadamard, who was very far from being egalitarian. The librarian bowed again, much lower this time. 'I never thought to see a Crown Princess of Westrigonia come here from abroad, your Royal Highness the Princess Eleanor.'

And so Eleanor's studies continued. After some time, Eleanor began to encounter principles such as those of sympathetic magic, by which power over other people could be acquired. A variety of techniques were suggested in well-worn books that had obviously been much read, about how, for example, by synchronizing one's breathing with those of another and thinking certain deeply intimate thoughts while expressing a certain sequence of sounds buried in normal spoken phrases, their passion could be awoken and their minds bound by desire. Incantations, spells, and recipes for a variety of brews could be found in some of the books of the Great Library of Krastienst. All of these followed as applications, in some sense and often very indirectly, of ideas from the *Book of the Herakrim* and all its commentaries.

Eleanor didn't know it yet, but with her black hair and pale skin and the air of ancient knowledge that was beginning to enshroud her, she was starting to acquire the nick-name of *The Witch of Trentland.* And then something happened that caused this nick-name to become widely known.

3:35 PM, Thursday 20 September 1874 A. F. (After the Fall)

The campaign to succeed Lord Stanley Deasun, the First Protector, had begun even while he was still alive, given that his increasing infirmity increasingly pointed in the direction of the ultimate. While his friends and intimates were, naturally, beside themselves with grief at the thought of his passing into the beyond, they were also, equally naturally, out of an empathy for those trapped in this vale of tears which is called the land of the living, minded to contemplate the precise details of his succession. Such was this concern that the legend arose that his nearest and dearest had forgotten even to attend his funeral: but this was a vile calumny perpetrated by wicked tongues. What had actually happened, as meticulous historians were to demonstrate, in elaborate detail, was as follows.

Deasun had died, not unexpectedly, and indeed after dragging out his deathbed scene more than was considered considerate to the feelings of others, on 2 September 1874 at 5:20 in the afternoon, after which the Supreme Council of the Protectorate had gone into emergency meeting to discuss the succession. So deeply felt was the concern of those august personages for the safety and well-being of the citizens of the Protectorate that Deasun's funeral wound up being forgotten; one week later, the increasingly irate personnel charged with this matter of the funeral, not to mention his widow and children and other beneficiaries of his will, simply went ahead in the absence of further consultations with the Supreme Council of the Protectorate. Deasun was buried on the ninth day of September at eleven in the morning; his widow, sniffing on a crushed onion concealed in her black-gloved fist in order to assist with her tears, and Deasun's children and various relatives and other beneficiaries of his will, did attend Deasun's funeral, as historians were later to attest;

but those caught up in the drama of the details of the succession were not present at the interment of the casket. So much for the funeral of Deasun.

There still remained, however, the question of the succession. Who would next become the First Protector of the Protectorate? Five candidates had emerged even before Deasun had lain down on his death bed, and they had formalized their candidacies before his body was even cold. They were: Faonarom, Hadriadst, Machthreld, Ramvert, and De'Asterides.

The speculation as to who would be the next First Protector was feverish; it was the number one topic of conversation throughout the Anglashian circles of Westrigonia, if not anywhere else in Westrigonia, at the time, and this must be understood in order to make sense of what Eleanor did. An older and wiser head might have judged her action foolhardy; had her ex-boyfriend Matthias Raspero been consulted by the Princess he would have advised her to keep her own counsel in this matter; but rightly or wrongly, Eleanor charged head-first into this matter with an excess of enthusiasm that she was later to regret. What happened was this.

The Crown Princess of Westrigonia had recently encountered the lore of divination known as Dagrun, much believed in at one time, which involved combining letters and numerical values in a tree-like structure in such a way as to come up with a definitive value matched to an interpretation. In short, the future could be read by this means. The results of Eleanor's calculations were clear. Braeden De'Asterides would win the election and become the First Protector.

The Crown Princess very proudly informed her parents of the results of her deliberations. The mockery of Cadwalader was merciless. Jason joined in gleefully and Eleanor was publicly humiliated. It was one of the most miserable experiences of her life. So crushed did she feel that even when Braeden De'Asterides was elected First Protector on Tuesday 25 September 1874 (an historic date which future generations of schoolchildren would be made to memorize by their teachers), she made no reference to the fact that she had been right all along. Cadwalader and Jason even made use of the correctness of her prediction as the basis of further mockery. The Witch of Trentland learned the value and function of discretion. From now on, she would guard what she knew. She understood now what Perchuhi had said: *the world wants to be ignorant, so let it be ignorant.* The truth was not to be shared with everyone.

The only person who was impressed by what Eleanor had done was Astrudel, who tried to engage Eleanor in a discussion of such matters as foreseeing the future by means of divinations such as Dagrun. Eleanor played dumb, having by now given up talking to others about these things and withdrawing into a protective shell of simulated incomprehension. Astrudel, who would have taken her infant grandson gurgling from his cot and skinned him alive in exchange for these dark powers, had to give up on her questions. She retreated into a cloudy silence. Life returned, not to what it had been before, but to what it could only be now in these changed circumstances.

Eleanor was growing up, with all the pains attendant upon this irreversible process.

2:25 PM, *Thursday 12 October 1874 A. F.*

Eleanor underwent her Ceremony of Recognition on her fourteenth birthday on 12 October 1874. Strictly speaking, she did not have to undergo this process but she insisted on it as part of her journey towards becoming fully Westrigonian. The Ceremony of Recognition, which confusingly had the same name as the presentation of the nobles to newly coronated monarchs, was a question-and-answer session between a panel of scholars and the son or daughter of a member of the Vidaldmeet, who constituted the elite fifty noble families of Westrigonia, concerning the understanding of the child with regard to the Constitution of Westrigonia. The child was usually twelve years old at the time of the Ceremony of Recognition, but it was allowed for children to take the test up till the age of fifteen. No child could take their place in later life amongst the Vidaldmeet nobility without passing this test. Without being recognized, the child was officially nameless and thus technically did not exist. Over time, the other noble families of Westrigonia had adopted the practice of submitting their children to this trial, although strictly speaking their performance had no legal standing under the Constitution, and the panel of scholars were not officially appointed. Eleanor passed her test with ease, even lecturing a member of the panel on the correct pronunciation of certain terms of High Westrigonian, a fact which was duly noted in certain Westrigonian circles, although her own parents barely registered this development themselves. They had little idea of what the Ceremony of Recognition was about. It was yet another ritual of the bafflingly foreign country of which they were the imported monarchs.

Eleanor now began to turn her attention at this stage of her studies towards politics and the history of Westrigonia. She began by reading about the controversy over sinecures that had raged three hundred years ago. Sinecures were when someone was given a job for which they were paid despite not having to do any work. Some people said there was nothing wrong with sinecures because everyone needed money but not everyone wanted to work. Other people said that sinecures were wrong because everyone needed to work in order to get the money which they all needed and it wasn't fair for some people to get money for doing nothing when other people had to be working. There had been a great battle to abolish sinecures.

After due consideration, Eleanor came to the conclusion that she couldn't see anything wrong with sinecures. There were people who got paid for doing nothing. So what? It was all part of the grand tapestry of life.

Eleanor's next reading was of Simplesarchus, who expressed the heretical view that God was not necessarily entirely good. After having been brutally tortured to the point of death, his last words were: 'You have made my point far better than I ever did.' Enraged by his lack of rage, his captors broke his neck on hearing such indifference to their violence, which was all that they had to offer to the debate he had engendered.

Occasionally in her reading the name Raspero would appear; and so it was that Eleanor read of Daniel, the first baron, and of the Anglashian Baron Oliver, and of the devious genius Etienne, much admired from that day to this for being so clever. Cleverness was greatly admired in Westrigonia, when it was not being condemned. In a country which hero-worshipped the ancient, the Rasperos could lay claim to being ancient.

CHAPTER FIVE

Oh, he was a fine king, a paragon.
He sailed on a raft of skulls.
The waves lapped at his feet,
As if he were a god, but deep down,
The sea was afraid of him.
Frankie the Villain

11:00 AM, Thursday 11 July 1875 A. F.

The student of Politics and Human Nature is required to write an essay of not less than 3000 words on the following topic: Contingent enmity arises from a contingent cause and can be changed; natural enmity arises from the natures of the enemies involved and cannot be changed. Discuss the difference between contingent and natural enmity with particular reference to the trade dispute between Anglashia and Pashtunvale and the subsequent war between these countries.

The secondary school subject of *Politics and Human Nature* had dealt with the topic concerning the *rules of statesmanship* in Matthias's last term at school, and it was this topic which Matthias's holiday homework was today concerned. There were five sections of the rules of statesmanship: the formulation of policy; the identification and evaluation of resources; time and space as political concepts; counter-measures; and bringing things to completion.

Counter-measures involved such things as how to recognize treachery, when executions were appropriate and whether they were to be public or private, the nature of enmity and a variety of other related perspectives. The course of counter-measures had been extremely popular with the students at Matthias's school. They would debate these matters on their own at great length, and did all the extra readings required. The students eagerly discussed the conditions under which they would order the executions of traitors and how those executions would be carried out. Some of the means of execution were actually quite imaginative, which is to say that they were as imaginative as they were gruesome, and they were often extremely gruesome. Everyone's homework on these topics was always done on time, and the standard of scholarship was generally high. Their teachers told them in a tone of lamentation that if they always applied themselves like this to every subject they would all be geniuses. Their students gazed silently back and kept their own counsel. This was one of the constants of history, as unchanged as the Great Eye of Jupiter.

Matthias was hard at work on his essay when a loud rap at his door brought him to turn around with his pen poised in the air. The Steward of Raspero, Dacre Rachelle, entered his room without being invited to do so, a breach of courtesy that made Matthias pause more than his pen. Breaches of courtesy did not happen in the Castle of Raspero.

The Steward came to a stop in the middle of the room and stood there inscrutably.

'Greetings, Steward,' Matthias said affably, laying his pen down on the table. 'I would invite you to enter, but you have already done so.'

'Your father commands your attendance,' said the Steward with a certain brusqueness.

Matthias leaned back in his chair. It was not so much what he had been told that he was paying attention to but the manner in which he had been told it. Rachelle was trying to warn him of something without actually saying anything.

'Then I will come immediately without delay,' Matthias said without moving a muscle. 'After all, you did not delay a moment yourself.'

'I was not asked to delay,' the Steward replied, as brusquely as before.

In all this time, Rachelle still had not addressed Matthias by name. By now, Matthias was starting to wonder just how serious this was, but he was not too worried. For once, he had a clear conscience. Matthias got out of his chair and stretched lazily. 'What is this about?' he asked with a half-yawn.

He had little hope of getting an answer to his question. The Steward's loyalty was to the Baron, not the Baron's second son. He was asking more for the sake of making conversation than anything else. But on this occasion he was surprised both by being answered and by the answer itself.

'The secret police have come to arrest you,' said Dacre Rachelle, the Steward of Raspero.

'But why?'

'The charge is treason.'

Matthias stopped in the middle of his room, trying to catch up with everything that was happening. For once the quick-witted boy was at a loss. 'Does Papa want me to run for it?' he asked, almost as if thinking aloud.

'It is not my place to say,' said the Steward, whose face was unreadable.

Matthias took a deep breath and then resumed walking towards the door. 'Treason, did you say? Well, of *that* charge I'm innocent,' he said as cheerfully as he could manage, as if glad that he didn't have to face the charge of which he *was* guilty. But it was nothing more than hollow bravado. No-one in Westrigonia could be anything but half-dead from nerves at the prospect of being arrested by the secret police.

Matthias kept his cool as he neared the Room of the Globe, which served as the reception room of Castle Raspero; or to be more accurate, he tried to keep his cool, while his head floated along somewhere behind his somehow-walking-along body. As he entered the Room of the Globe it was with a rush of impressions: he noted that Stefan was white-faced with fear, not knowing that he himself was white-faced with terror; he noted that his mother was sitting in her usual high-winged chair with a certain self-imposed calm, with Lena clinging to her knee, almost sitting in her lap; while his father was on his feet as indifferent as ever, keeping even a drama such as this like an importunate beggar at a baronial arm's length; and it was Phelan himself, Matthias observed, who was standing there waiting by the side, his head lowered as if he were a bull about to charge.

'I have come in response to your summons, Papa,' Matthias said as calmly as he could.

'Chevalier Phelan is here to take you with him to the headquarters of the State Bureau of Security,' said the Baron.

'May I ask why, father?'

'He has some questions to ask you. I suggest you answer them all as truthfully as you can.'

'Of course, father.'

'I shall come along to see you tomorrow morning. By then, I am sure that this matter will be concluded.'

'Yes, father.'

'It will be a matter for the Bureau to decide when this matter is concluded, Lord Raspero.' Phelan spoke for the first time. Neither of the boys had ever heard him speak before, and they noticed with fascination that the voice of this demon from below the ground was low and deep and gravelly.

The Baron turned to face Phelan with a host's disdain for the guest who presumed too much. 'I shall be granted an audience with His Majesty tomorrow, not to mention my old school friend Grystoalfyr, and so I assure you, Chevalier, that this matter, such as it is, will be concluded tomorrow.'

Phelan didn't look the least bit intimidated by all these implied threats. 'I have already had my audience with His Majesty this morning, and he is in full agreement with his humble servant that this matter must be looked into properly.'

'But of course it must be. If I have to convene the Vidaldmeet in full, then that is what I will do, if that is what it takes to look into this matter properly.'

'That is excellent, Lord Raspero! How glad I am that we see eye to eye on this matter. This matter must be looked into . . . properly. And now I must be off. Time presses. Honourable Matthias, you may now say your goodbyes.'

Matthias and Stefan held their breath as one. The Baron's face flushed. This had been a deliberate insult on Phelan's part, to usurp the Baron's authority in his own home by telling Matthias to say his goodbyes. Yet the deadly threat implied by the reference to goodbyes escaped no-one. The Baron swallowed the insult, turned to Matthias and nodded briefly.

It was then that Matthias understood what was going on. His father was Phelan's real target, and his second son was being arrested as a way of putting pressure on him. It was not his eldest son and heir, but the second son, the spare heir, who was being taken into custody. This was like a knight move in a chess game.

Matthias said his goodbyes and left with Phelan. He looked back briefly as he went through the door, and nodded in farewell.

He would never see his father and brother alive again.

11:25 AM, Thursday 11 July 1875 A. F.

Phelan's flying carriage rose into the air from the castle courtyard into the blue skies of that beautiful July day. It occurred to Matthias that really the day should have been thundery and rainy, with dramatic flashes of lightning overhead; that was how he would have staged the drama. Blue skies and sunshine did not match his mood at that moment in time.

Justin the Second had founded in the early days of his reign a secret police by which to safeguard his person and enforce his rule. The official title of this secret police was *The Office of the Security of the National Integrity of the State of the Kingdom of Westrigonia*. Of the five sections of this organization, the section entitled the *State Bureau of Security* was the one that actually arrested people, and so the whole organization was informally referred to under this name. The motto of the State Bureau was *The Necessity of Duty*, and for this reason they had been nicknamed *the Necessaries*. They were much feared, and for several very good reasons: they were ruthless; they were violent when necessary and also when not necessary; they were torturers by choice; but above all else they were highly organized. Nothing escaped them, nothing distracted them and nothing slowed them down. They were like some red-eyed machine that would get you in the end no matter what you did. There was some talk after the overthrow of Good King Justin to the effect that the Necessaries were no longer necessary, but by then they had become too useful to be discarded. They were kept on after having been supposedly reformed, but a sharp steel blade cannot be "reformed". It can only be changed by being broken; and so the Necessaries continued, as a power behind the throne that perhaps rivalled the throne itself. It was even said that an alternative history of Westrigonia from Justin's time could follow the reigns of the State Bureau chiefs from Dejan to Phelan, rather than the reigns of the Kings and Queens of Westrigonia from Good King Justin and Malia to Frederick and Yolande.

Phelan had sat Matthias opposite him in his flying carriage to be a seated figure in the full glare of Phelan's unremitting stare, like a waxwork in a museum. Matthias bore this unendingly silent scrutiny with a composure bordering on indifference. It was not bravado or the bravaduro of ignorance: it was rather a sense of disconnectedness from what was happening. His head was floating somewhere in the air above his torso. He was being taken to the Ankalybu, and everyone knew about the Ankalybu. Furthermore, he was not being taken there by just anyone: he was being taken there by Phelan himself.

Chevalier Phelan always dressed in white robes, of which he had numerous identical copies. His face was large and flat and square. His black hair lay on his scalp in clumps. His eyes were the darkest of browns, almost black. There was something solid and heavy about Phelan, as if he had risen up out of the earth. This was a man who had no compassion, no fellow-feeling for his humans, if he was even human himself, which many doubted. Matthias told himself that everything would be fine, and worked hard at getting himself to believe it.

5:35 PM, *Thursday 11 July 1875 A. F.*

The infamous headquarters of the State Bureau of Security was called the Ankalybu and was situated in Karsten street, towards the southern quarters of Krastienst. It was a tall rectangular building of five levels. The bottom level was made of large shiny pure-black blocks of marble so cleverly fitted together that to the casual eye it seemed like an unbroken wall of stone; there were no doors or windows anywhere in this lowest level. This bottom level, next to the street itself, was the top level of the three levels where prisoners were detained, the other two levels being below the ground, and it was these three levels that made the Ankalybu infamous.

The higher four levels looked ordinary enough, with windows and windowsills inset in sandstone archways running along their lengths all around the building. The very top level, the fifth floor, was in fact called the first floor and the floor at street level was the fifth, from a tradition that stretched back to Justin the Good himself, who had personally overseen the building of the Ankabylu when he founded the State Bureau of Security in the early years of his reign.

On the left hand side of the Ankabylu was a rampway that ascended to the second level (that was called the fourth floor) and provided the only entry point to the building. The rampway was large and wide, with a landing spot for flying carriages by the front doors.

Hardly anyone except State Bureau agents ever walked along Karsten street, although on occasion an ordinary Westrigonian might walk past the Ankalybu to show off their bravery and gain a boastful tale or two, or a visitor to the city might pass by all unknowing. But where crowds thronged the other streets of the capital, Karsten street was largely deserted, as pedestrians simply walked the long way around to avoid ever passing by the Ankalybu.

Matthias was not walking anywhere on this occasion, however, as he was being taken to the Ankalybu in the flying carriage of the Director-General himself. The carriage settled down by the front doors and Matthias exited from the flying carriage behind Phelan. The front doors were large oaken double doors that stood wide open during daylight hours and were closed at night, at which time a small door set to one side provided access to and from the building. On this occasion, the double doors had been left open past sunset.

No Westrigonian could feel anything but the deepest unease at walking in through those doors. Matthias could feel a cold stone settle in the midst of his gut, a stone which had acquired a movement of its own volition, in strict disagreement with all the beliefs of philosophers concerning the nature of volition and the nature of stones. Stones could not move by themselves in theory, but this one was the soul of its own agitation. Matthias focused on his breathing, and called to mind all the various techniques of self-control he had been taught, eventually settling on the one that involved counting a complicated passage of time in terms of a wheel turning around a cross.

It was in this spirit of calm contemplation that Matthias viewed the Entrance Hall of the Ankalybu. It was impressive in an austere fashion. Polished black and white marble slabs like a chequerboard formed the floor, while numerous large chandeliers hung overhead from a ceiling of panelled mahogany. Along the left was a large counter staffed by State Bureau of Security agents, all standing stiffly to attention like flagpoles as the Chevalier passed by. Other agents stood here and there, also standing to attention. Straight ahead was a marble staircase, again of alternating black and white marble, and it was toward this staircase that the Chevalier directed his footsteps, ignoring all his flagpole subordinates. Matthias gained the clear impression of a world that had been totally flattened by the will of a single being, the Chevalier Phelan; it was as if Phelan and Matthias were the only three dimensional beings in a two dimensional world.

As they mounted the staircase, going ever upwards, Matthias felt that he was ascending beyond the reach of gravity, and that soon he would start floating away. The alert and sceptical mind of the fifteen-year-old boy couldn't help but wondering if this was all purely imaginary, or whether or not chemicals undetectable by the olfactory senses were entering his brain via his nostrils; and at that thought, he stiffened and tried not to breathe too deeply. And ever onward beside him marched the silent Chevalier, the absolute ruler of this deathly cold world.

At the very top of the stairs on the fifth floor, which was the first level, Matthias marched alongside the Chevalier Phelan into a large reception room with more Security agents standing stiffly to attention, and onwards into the room beyond, which was the Office of the Director-General of the State Bureau of Security itself.

Phelan's office was a long rectangular room with large windows overlooking the inner courtyard of the Ankalybu. The oaken floorboards were stained a dark brown and the curtains were the deepest reddest hue of scarlet, but what struck Matthias's attention on first entering was the enormous portrait over the desk at the far end of the room. He was so astonished that he stopped dead where he was and his mouth fell open.

The portrait was ten feet high and five feet wide. It was of Winstan Leygerard, the infamous leader of the Levellers of the 18th Century.

Phelan appeared not to have noticed Matthias's consternation, for the Director-General carried on walking forwards, seating himself behind his desk, and waving for Matthias to take the seat before this very desk.

Matthias sat down reluctantly, as if coming to a stop would end more than just the forward motion of his feet.

Phelan said nothing but stared at Matthias with almost a mocking air; but Matthias had enough self-control to deal with this challenge. Without being in the least rude, in a polite, deferential yet reserved manner, Matthias sat there in complete silence, neither staring back at Phelan nor staring away, but simply waiting, as if to acknowledge that it was not his place to do anything else but sit there.

Phelan shifted in his seat, as if to acknowledge the end of round one, and then spoke: 'You seemed interested in the portrait on the wall behind me.'

'I am sure you have your reasons for putting this painting of such a man in such a place of honour,' Matthias said in his most conversational manner.

'Do I? And what reasons would they be?' Phelan asked in a friendly fashion, as if inviting Matthias to incriminate himself now and get it all over with to save them all time.

'I could only guess,' Matthias prevaricated, 'but if you were to instruct me in this matter, I would pay the most careful attention.'

'Go ahead and guess,' Phelan ordered flatly, interlocking his hands and turning his gaze onto his now-twiddling thumbs. 'I am all ears.'

'Whether or not visitors to this room are against or in favour of this man is a central preoccupation of your approach to your work.'

Phelan paid Matthias the compliment of saying nothing for a moment or two. Then he asked: 'Are you in favour of this man yourself?'

Without hesitation Matthias replied: 'Certainly not. He is utter scum. He is beneath contempt. The only thing to be done with a man like Leygerard is to stamp on him.'

'He happens to be a personal hero of mine,' Phelan stated categorically, 'which is why I have his portrait in such a place of honour.'

Matthias contemplated this statement for a moment or so, then said: 'If the King, the Vidaldmeet, the Chief Justices, were to hear you make such a comment, you would wind up in very hot water indeed.'

Phelan raised his eyebrows. 'But how on earth would they ever hear me make such a comment? Do you have any intentions to be a tale-bearer, a tattle-tale, about such a matter as this, which we have not even been discussing except in your imagination?'

'Absolutely not. I am only pointing out what you know that I know.'

There was another silence, which Matthias again bore without flinching. It was Phelan who, once again, moved on from their impasse. 'We are both nobles and so I understand your feelings well. But you must consider the course of history. You must understand that the logic of events is towards Liberty, Fraternity and Equality.'

'That is entirely antithetical to everything that I stand for.'

'That is your misfortune. You might be surprised to learn how easily and quickly fortunes can change.'

'Not at all. Look at what happened to Justin himself. The lord of the realm at one moment, down in the gutter the next.'

'And those who are down in the gutter today will rule tomorrow.'

'If Fortuna decrees it to be so, then it will be so.'

Phelan laughed his crunching-gravel laugh. 'Such superstition. Like your belief in the social hierarchy, which is equally superstitious. All distinctions of rank are illusory. Do you really believe you were born with your baronial chains already attached?'

'I was born into my world.'

'Yes, and those baronial chains were fastened onto your limbs *after* that birth on day one.'

'You are expressing a point of view with which some would agree.'

'How polite you are.'

'*It is necessary to be courteous on occasion.*'

'*And it is especially necessary when receiving the necessaries,*' Phelan promptly added.

Matthias calmly noted Phelan's vanity for despite the fear that gripped his throat he was alert to the nature of his enemy. The Chevalier wanted to be known as a man who could complete a poetry quotation.

'I would not have expected leading members of the government to have read Frankie the Villain,' Matthias commented in order to flatter his captor.

'I had that miserable excuse for a human being sitting just where you are now, in that very chair,' Phelan said with his bared-teeth snarl-grin. 'Later on he begged me not to hurt him anymore.'

'I am sure that his agonized pleas were in the form of rhyming couplets.'

Phelan laughed and then kept on laughing, almost helplessly. It seemed that Matthias had found the kind of joke that amused him. 'You're a bright spark, young Raspero,' he said once his laughter had subsided enough that he could speak once again. 'And the second son, too. No, no, you are very far from the mark. When that miscreant poet screamed when put to the question, he did not scream in rhyme. Trust me!'

There was a silence then, which Matthias again bore without flinching. Phelan eventually rose to his feet saying: 'It is time, young Raspero. Let us go.'

Matthias rose to his feet as calmly as he could. He was more frightened at that moment in time than he had ever been in his whole life, or would ever be again. The sentence *it is time* rang in his ears as if it had been spoken by a hanging judge. Whatever dark fate lay ahead of him was less of a concern to him than his worry that he would dishonour the family name of Raspero by failing to meet this fate in a dignified manner. He steeled himself to be equal to any challenge.

CHAPTER SIX

A beggar won't give you a single strada.
Only a strong arm can give you justice.
Frankie the Villain

6:25 PM, Thursday 11 July 1875 A. F.

Eleanor made her way into the Green Room of Oaken Leaves to await dinner. She sat by the side trying to ignore the nearby figure of her older brother Jason, who looked bored. Jason came over to sit beside her, and she noted that he *was* bored, and hence truculent and hence looking for trouble and hence, in short, ready to be a nuisance. She groaned inwardly and braced herself for whatever deliberately provocative thing he might say.

'<And how are you, sister of mine?>' Jason asked pleasantly.

'<I am very well, Jason. Thank you for asking. And how are you?>'

'<Well, let me see,>' Jason said reflectively, looking up at the ceiling with its gold-painted cherubs flying overhead, '<after yet another day living in this open toilet that is called Westrigonia, I am as well as can be expected.>'

Eleanor made a point of not looking at a passing Westrigonian servant, who might well have understood something of Anglashian, placing a bowl of fruit on a nearby table. But Jason, with a sibling's instinct, understood the stiffened muscles in her neck.

'<Oh no, I keep on forgetting, you've gone native. You're Westrigonian now, aren't you? Yes, yes, this is what I keep on forgetting. You had that,

93

what was it, the Cerumonnayee of Reconstitution a while ago, so you've been, what, Reconstituted, is that right?>'

Eleanor understood perfectly well that Jason knew the correct term for the Ceremony of Recognition, and so side-stepped this argument. '<You continually misunderstand the nature of my interest in Westrigonian history and culture, Jason. I have noted that I may be Queen of Westrigonia one day. I am surprised that you show so little interest yourself. You are, after all, the Crown Prince of Westrigonia. You might become King one day. After all, one of us will be the monarch of this country eventually.>'

'<Do you know what they call you, sister of mine?>' Jason said with a little smile. He was not going to be deflected from his goal of ruining her mood. '<The Witch of Trentland. Do you note the geographical reference? *Trentland*. No-one is fooled by all your Westrigonian foolery, least of all the Westrigonians.>' Jason knew about this from his Westrigonian sycophants, who shared with him all the gossip he would never have learned otherwise.

Eleanor kept a strict hold of her temper. Jason knew exactly how to provoke her. '<I hope the day never comes when you need to know the least thing about Westrigonia, Jason. What you will do on that day, I do not know. Perhaps you will come to me and ask for help.>'

The gong for dinner rang at that very moment and so Eleanor jumped to her feet with a disdainful look at Jason, who for his part looked pleased with himself. He knew full well that he had at least damaged her mood.

At the dinner table, Sakesheld asked Eleanor what she had been up to that day.

Eleanor's latest project was studying *Westrigonian Folk Tales, Popular Beliefs and Commonplace Sayings* by an eccentric Westrigonian nobleman called Cedomir Helladius. So she replied to her uncle: '<Today I was reading the folk tale about Neil of the Strong Arm and his voyage to the moon.>'

'<Oh, give me a break,>' Jason said rudely, having been listening in on their conversation. '<Neil of the Strong Arm never went on a boat to the moon. Let me put this matter simply, sister of mine. Boats float on water.

Stop me if this principle escapes you. You've understood this, right? Boats float on water. But there *is* no water between here and the moon. Therefore Neil of the Strong Arm never went to the moon on a boat. I don't care how strong his arm was.>'

The Honourable Kliment, one of Jason's Westrigonian hangers-on, chuckled sycophantically on hearing this witticism.

Jason looked pleased with himself.

Eleanor could have cheerfully broken a nearby pitcher of water over her brother's black-haired head.

'<We must not be too literal minded about these things,>' Sakesheld told his nephew in a tone of mild rebuke. '<Folk tales are metaphorical in nature. In this particular instance, it is clear that the moon represents the feminine nature, and Neil, who is a man, is going to the moon by voyaging there in a boat, which is symbolic of the material vessel in which we journey through life. In other words, the tale is a metaphor for a man contacting his feminine nature through feeling the presence of his own body, which contains both the male and the female.>'

Jason looked profoundly unimpressed by this interpretation, but he said nothing. He wanted to stay on the good side of Sakesheld for a number of self-serving reasons.

'<I am sure that Jason is being idealistic,>' Eleanor observed, remembering that Sakesheld had of late been very critical of idealism. Her chance foray was immediately rewarded.

'<Young people are more apparently idealistic than oldsters such as myself,>' Lord Sakesheld remarked, '<because their egoism has expanded to such an extent that life can only be experienced as it returns to them from the outside. They are so completely preoccupied with their own being that it seems to them that their subjective feelings are objective facts. Hence their endless whining about what they see as right and wrong.>'

Jason's fingers whitened on his cutlery, as if the Crown Prince was holding back what he wanted to say. Seeing a chance to annoy her annoying brother Eleanor asked innocently: '<Does that mean that young people are in the wrong, Uncle?>'

Sakesheld's eyes twinkled at his favourite niece. He was delighted to be asked to say more. '<No, not at all, Eleanor, far from it. We only observe in the case of idealistic young people that their head is too far up their own posterior to see that their head is up their own posterior.>'

Jason swallowed his food the wrong way and had a coughing fit.

Eleanor retired into silence with a satisfied smirk.

8:30 PM, Thursday 11 July 1875 A. F.

Eleanor would shortly retire to bed, so she sat close to her father in the Room of Opinions, so named because of the paintings of philosophers on the walls. Despite these paintings Eleanor knew enough not to mention anything of her philosophical interests to her father.

Frederick the Fifth had had a very bad couple of hours the day before his coronation when, as part of a crash course in everything Westrigonian, he had been instructed in traditional metaphysics by The Keeper of Keys. He had not understood a word of what he was told. Lord Sakesheld, who had invited himself to sit in on the meeting, had greatly enjoyed the exposition of The Keeper of Keys while wildly misunderstanding everything their tutor was saying. The *oneness* that is in every existing thing without being part of the *otherness* of every existing thing was to Sakesheld a statement concerning the soul of the world, which Frederick could tell just from the expression on The Keeper of Keys's face was a hopelessly misconceived reading of a very simple matter. The Keeper of Keys explained patiently that the *oneness* of everything, being *immaterial,* could not be a part of the *otherness* which is necessarily *material,* as the *otherness* which cannot achieve the precision of *identity* is everything *other* than *oneness.* This is why *oneness,* which is always *equal to itself,* does not change while *otherness,* which can never be *equal to itself,* is subject to change and death. Sakesheld was delighted by this, which to him was a statement which so clearly expressed the growth of the inner being through the transformational processes of seeking the transcendental. The increasingly apprehensive Frederick watched The Keeper of Keys's face grow steadily more impassive at what was clearly, to him, the most wanton and irresponsible of misinterpretations. The Keeper of Keys explained that *oneness*, being *identity*, could alone achieve *precision* whilst *otherness*, partaking of the *oneness* by which it existed, could never achieve *precision* because of its separation from the *oneness* that was its true being. By now Frederick was reduced to the helpless status of a young child in a world suddenly become much too large, repeating what he was told to show he had heard it while trying to read from the body language and facial expression of The Keeper of Keys if he was in the clear or not. The future monarch of Westrigonia, who had never really wanted to be King in the first place, struggled through to the end of that nightmare meeting and resolutely ever after avoided anything to do with traditional metaphysics. (The Keeper of Keys, for his part, resolutely avoided the company of the ever-cheerful and friendly Sakesheld, and had been known to even run to get out of the way of an approaching Sakesheld on occasion.) Everyone had played their part in what no-one saw as a comedy.

Eleanor herself by now would have understood every single word that the Keeper of Keys had spoken, which after all was fairly straightforward once the basics were properly grasped. But she also understood by this time, three years after becoming the Crown Princess of Westrigonia, that she was alone in her family in having any affinity for Westrigonian metaphysics.

Despite their differences, Eleanor felt an enormous affection for her father, who was always kind to her, if not always helpful. In his own way Frederick tried, when he remembered, to be a father. There was, for example, the time just last month when he had instructed Eleanor and Jason to walk along slowly, each with a glass of water balanced on their head. The three of them had walked along the length of the Throne Room with glasses of water balanced on their heads, a feat which Frederick had carried off with aplomb. In this particular matter, he obviously knew what he was about. Frederick explained how the regular practise of this exercise would lead to a long and healthy life. Eleanor shot sideways looks at her brother, whose face showed such a multitude of exasperations as to cheer Eleanor up for the whole of the rest of that day.

Whether or not Frederick himself really believed that the regular exercise of walking along with a glass of water balanced on one's head would lead to a long and healthy life was not entirely clear to Eleanor, who often observed that her father liked, in his own ponderous way, to have fun. For example, he once signalled to a servant to fill up his wine glass with wine, after which he said to a dinner guest that he was drinking grape juice; Frederick then laughed his spluttering laugh and his dinner guest laughed as well. Eleanor could see that her father was having fun in the lumbering way in which grown-ups had fun; but she had often observed nonetheless that grown-ups did not properly understand how to have fun. To make the palace guards wear pink dresses every Tuesday would be fun. This was what grown-ups failed to understand. They lacked the appropriate sensibility. She often had occasion to observe that grown-ups were generally hopeless, but of course any given child understands far more about the business of having fun than any given adult. Fun is their special province.

'<And how are your studies proceeding?>' Frederick asked his daughter. This was all that he knew of her life.

'<Very well, thank you, father,>' Eleanor replied. '<But what is happening with Lord De'Asterides and our Library?>'

Eleanor knew something of the titanic clash taking place over her head which was so studiously bowed over the books of the Royal Library of Krastienst. For the First Protector had requested, no, demanded, that all the books of the Great Library of the Royal Palace of Krastienst be sent to Perntharborg, where they would be copied and then the originals returned to Westrigonia. Frederick and Yolande had at first shrugged and been about to agree, indifferent to the demand itself and reluctant to quarrel with the Protector given an already strained relationship with him; but Frederick and Yolande had soon enough been forced to backtrack, given that the Westrigonian opposition to this plan seemed on the verge of snowballing overnight into a nationwide insurrection. Nationalist forces sprung into action: fiery speeches were made in the Vidaldmeet and on street corners, after which pamphlets appeared which pulled no punches in advocating the speedy departure from Westrigonia of the

Zoller-Abstein monarchs, who should not have come to Westrigonia in the first place. Frederick and Yolande informed De'Asterides that the books of the Great Library of Krastienst would not be made available to him for copying. The Protector was not at all pleased but seemingly accepted his defeat.

Eleanor continued her reading in the Library of Krastienst, aware that she sat where the most powerful man in the world could not. Thus it was that she addressed her question to her father.

Frederick looked displeased at being placed in the position of having to answer such a question. '<Oh, everything is being arranged in all such matters,>' he said vaguely. The truth of the matter was that he knew little more himself, and had even less interest. Eleanor read all this on her father's face in a moment, so she changed the subject.

'<I was reading the other day about the Melanton Oath, father,>' she confided. '<The Chevalier Melanton was a prisoner of the Delarians and he was released from captivity in order to go home to raise the ransom for his release only after giving his word of honour to return. After walking down the road for a while, he came back and claimed that he had forgotten something in his tent; he went to his tent, then emerged and left again. Once he got home, he claimed that he had honoured his promise to return to his captivity, because he had already returned, and that therefore he didn't have to go back again. Was he right? What do you think, father?>'

Frederick contemplated all these complexities. '<He sounds like a clever man to me,>' he said eventually. Given the moral ambiguity of a word like *clever*, this was a highly evasive response.

'<His own son bound him hand and foot and took him back to captivity, in order to preserve the family honour, although some said it was really in order to get his father out of the way for his own purposes. Anyway, the Melanton Oath to this day stands for this kind of trickery.>'

Frederick said nothing, gazing down at the floor as if he was thinking nothing as well. Eleanor leaned over to kiss her father on the cheek and said: '<Good night, father,>' and departed for the Chambers of the Crown Princess.

8:50 PM, Thursday 11 July 1875 A. F.

The Chambers of the Crown Princess of Westrigonia were located high up on the east side of the Palace of Krastienst overlooking the Palace Gardens. The large double doors were made of thick oak beams reinforced with cast iron, with inlaid black fulgurite glass and polished bronze letters which spelled out in High Westrigonian: The Chambers of the Crown Princess of Westrigonia.

Eleanor pulled out her wand and waved the necessary combination, causing the massively heavy doors to open effortlessly on their well-oiled hinges. Only Eleanor, her maid-servants, her parents, Astrudel and the Steward of the Palace could open those doors. Even Romano, Captain of the Palace Guard, was not allowed to know this combination. Eleanor stepped through the doors onto the black flag-stones of the Entrance Hallway, waving the doors closed and locked behind her. Ahead of her on the facing wall was a large mural by the great master Queralt showing Yadira, the charioteer of the gods, driving his chariot between the Pillars of Knowledge into the Abyss. The ceiling and walls of the Entrance Hallway were paneled with a richly varnished walnut wood that had been carved into complicated patterns and gilded with gold-leaf to catch the light from a chandelier of highly polished bronze which hung down from the high ceiling to throw its shining-white radiance to be scattered and reflected in an effect like waves of light moving around the room.

To the left was a door leading into the Morning Room, also known as the Room of the Sun, whose large windows overlooked the Central Courtyard and faced east, thus flooding the room with bright sunlight during the morning. The high ceiling contained a fresco by the famous Farrukh, which had a sun at its centre streaming resplendent light down over bare-breasted females clad in swirling clouds who represented the Virtues, whilst to one side fierce warriors battled fang-toothed serpents on the side of a mountain below an invisible peak. From the centre of the sun hung a large chandelier made of a semi-transparent rock crystal which took the light of its own candle flames and refracted them around the room with delicate shadings. Richly patterned Ramudien carpets of blue and red and green and orange colours covered the red cherry floorboards, while numerous tables and chairs and sofas of the most elegant design were positioned about the room in a geometrically harmonious arrangement. Lamps of intricately-patterned coloured glass were fixed on the walls, which were lined with an oak panelling. Paintings by the acclaimed masters Rainard, Jannah and Davena hung here and there about the room, while the wide cornice was covered with a gilded floral arrangement over a white background.

To the right of the Entrance Hallway was the Drawing Room, also known as the Room of the Rose. This was the largest room in Eleanor's Chambers, being about forty feet wide and ninety feet long with the ceiling being about fifteen feet high. This ceiling was covered by a fresco made by the great master Vohegn, the theme of the fresco being the Seven Ages of the Human Being, from infancy to schoolhood to youth to adulthood to middle age to old age to senility, the cornice being made of lozenge-shaped figures of lapis lazuli inset in layers of black fulgurite glass frosted with gold dust. This ceiling fresco was one of the greatest works of art in the world, and it was reserved exclusively for the occupant of these Chambers, to Eleanor's private exultation. (A princess deserved no less!) The enormous rose window overlooking Dejan Street gave the room its name, and had been installed by the master Goyelle over five hundred years ago, and before this window, in pride of place, was Eleanor's high-backed elegantly carved winged oaken chair, made comfortable by red velvet cushions embroidered with gold thread. Five large bronze and solid silver chandeliers hung from the ceiling, while the floor was a mosaic of black and red marble so highly polished as to almost be a mirror, covered in elegant tables and chairs and sofas and more Ramudien carpets, with a piano in one corner and a coffee table with chairs in another. At the far wall was a small door set into the wall in such a way that it could not be seen: this door led to the rooms of Eleanor's two maid-servants, and would be the rooms of her three ladies-in-waiting at a later time.

A door set in the left wall of the Room of the Rose led into Eleanor's Dressing Room, and a door from there led into Eleanor's Bed Room.

Eleanor's bed was an enormous four-poster with richly woven curtains embroidered with scenes from various animal fables: here a tortoise listened to a deceptive fox, while there a rabbit carrying a bag made its way into town. Overhead was a large vaulted ceiling with a fresco showing the glittering star-strewn night-time sky, the phosphorescent-painted stars embedded with real white gemstones that captured the faintest of light and glowed in the near-dark; there were faintly painted amongst the starry sky the nine circles of angels which intricately interacted with the ambiguous flowing lines of brilliant white and black. When viewed sleepily from bed late at night, the fresco became a three-dimensional night-scape through which the mind could wander, journeying amongst the stars and the angels until sleep fully came.

The door to the bathroom was on one side, while embedded in another side was the door which led into the maid-servants quarters, while opposite that was a door leading to Eleanor's Study, which was also her personal library. A large red leather chair in front of a large scroll-topped writing desk dominated the room, while stone-and-wood bookcases lined the walls. One of Eleanor's predecessors had had a passion for romance novels, which took up all of three shelves of a bookcase; Eleanor's favourite recreation was reading her way through these novels. Apart from that the study was used for work. Eleanor was perhaps the first Crown Princess in history to study history and metaphysics in her free time out of choice.

Sometimes at night Eleanor saw ghosts pass through her Chambers. They could only be seen by looking obliquely as they were formed of the shadows and the angles of the walls, the slant of a shelf or the reflected moonlight off a mirror. They looked at her and at each other and spoke in soft tones she could not distinguish as words but whose sounds were made up of the night-time creakings and shiftings of the floorboards and window-frames and furniture. Eleanor had no fear of them. She was there by right as the Crown Princess of Westrigonia. Even the dark bowed to her authority. The stone walls themselves were her friends and would defend her. Nothing of the palace could harm her; here she was protected by a royal status that gave her the power of command even over the things of the dark. Eleanor knew there were unseen creatures in the darkness, but all they ever did was bow to the Crown Princess of Westrigonia as she passed by.

And those were the days of Eleanor's childhood. She did not realize it at the time, but she was happy. She was the crown princess of an ancient mystical kingdom; she had a place in the world. The Palace of Krastienst was more than a royal residence. It was her home.

9:30 AM, Friday 12 July 1875 A. F.

Eleanor was sitting reading in the Rose Room when Astrudel came in and wandered about with a feather duster, dusting (unnecessarily) a Melisendien vase on a side table, and a ceramic owl nearby, all the while darting sideways glances at Eleanor. Eventually she spoke.

'Your boyfriend's in the news.'

Eleanor knew immediately, of course, that by *your boyfriend* Astrudel meant Matthias Raspero. It had been a long-running joke on Astrudel's part that he was Eleanor's boyfriend. It had been an equally long-running emphatic denial of this assertion on Eleanor's part.

'But who do you mean by *my boyfriend*?' Eleanor asked as if puzzled. 'I don't have a boyfriend. Who on earth can you be talking about?'

'Matthias Raspero,' Astrudel said sternly, as if to imply that Eleanor really should remember this kind of thing without prompting, because after all a boyfriend should not be so readily forgotten as all that!

'He is *not*,' Eleanor said with all the severity she could muster, 'my boyfriend.'

Astrudel ignored Eleanor's severity, as she always did, which somehow made the said severity not very severe or even said. This infuriated Eleanor, but she had not yet figured out what she could do about it, given Astrudel's endlessly self-assertive energy.

'Oh, did you break up? Was it a quarrel?' Astrudel asked with an entirely feigned concern. They had had this conversation several times before, but at some salivating level of her malicious being Astrudel enjoyed its every repetition.

Eleanor raised the book she was reading (on the philosophical implications of international law, written in Sixteenth Century Westrigonian) to screen out her annoying nanny. Astrudel knew full well that Matthias meant nothing to her now, if he had ever meant anything to her before, which he hadn't because, well, because he hadn't, contrary indications at the time notwithstanding.

There was silence on the other side of her upraised book, a silence that continued alongside her pretended reading.

Eleanor sighed and conceded defeat. She lowered her book and asked: 'What has Matthias been up to now?'

Astrudel paused just long enough to make it plain that she could choose not to answer; then said: 'He's been arrested.'

'Arrested? What for?'

'What for?' Astrudel shrugged. 'Does it matter?'

'Well, of course it matters,' Eleanor said with some heat. 'What are the charges which have been brought against him?'

'I haven't a clue,' Astrudel said, flapping her feather duster against the bust of Antonio the Younger. 'Anyway, whatever it is, it'll be about something else.'

The Crown Princess of Westrigonia knew enough about her own country to understand this cryptic remark. But even so, her heart was pounding in a way that surprised her. It made no sense to her that she was so upset. It was a puzzle, especially because Matthias meant nothing to her now, nothing at all. She reasoned to herself that it was simply the abrupt nature by which the news had been brought to her. Anyone would be startled by the way Astrudel went about things. It was all Astrudel's fault. Astrudel was a living menace. But what was going to happen to Matthias?

'Well, where is he now?' Eleanor tried to keep her voice steady.

Astrudel looked at her sideways, those eyes in that puffy face missing nothing. 'The Ankalybu, from what I heard.'

'The Ankalybu!' Eleanor gasped. 'Goodness!'

'You don't want to go there,' Astrudel agreed with a sadist's smile, 'not where the only paint on the walls is the dried blood of those what have died screaming in the direst of pain. Not where -'

'Yes, Nanny, I get it!' Eleanor snapped. 'That is more than enough.'

The continued flapping of Astrudel's feather duster was the only movement in the room for some time, and then there was not even that: Astrudel, with a narrowed gaze and after a prolonged calculation, withdrew from the room, leaving a silence behind her that would in due time, she felt sure, prove profitable. Astrudel knew how to wait until the strada fell into her opened hand like ripe fruit from a tree.

Eleanor sat in her sudden isolation surrounded by fallen thoughts that lay strewn all around her. What these thoughts were exactly she could not have said, given that they disintegrated into puffs of smoke upon inspection. She was upset, though; that much was clear. The stupidity of the world in general, infuriating as it was in the general terms of being the never-ending never-ending, had become unbearably particular in this instance as the news of the arrest of Matthias Raspero.

Eleanor had no objection, in a principled sense, to the prospect of Matthias being crushed into a painful oblivion. He deserved no better, given that he had never troubled to even write her a letter after having kissed her in the Rose Garden. It was only now that she was older that she found that she could fully comprehend the enormity of his misbehavior on that occasion. The kiss he had taken, or more properly, stolen, had by now become a large heavy object whose imagined weight could shift the Earth if properly leveraged. Eleanor wanted that kiss back! That ruffian Raspero should never have taken it in the first place, and by rights he should be punished. It was just that he should be punished by being incinerated by the ice-white blinding glare of the truth turning him into ashes. The dull fleshy incarceration of the Ankalybu was not the same and would not do at all as a substitute. And besides Eleanor wanted him, Matthias the-second-son-of-the-Baron Raspero, to be in such pain and torment as only she, Princess Eleanor, his social superior, could release him from as an act of mercy within her power alone. She wanted Matthias to beg her to forgive him for having kissed her and also for having never contacted her again; and once having released him from the chains of his torment, she wanted him to be aware that it was to her that he owed his deliverance so that he could be properly grateful and suitably submissive.

But for Matthias to suffer at the hands of the State Bureau was not at all the same thing as for Matthias to suffer at the hands of the Crown Princess.

Eleanor's concern for Matthias became all-of-a-sudden a heavy bowling ball rolling to a painful stop in the midst of her intestines. She stood up and paced about the room to dislodge this swollen feeling of distended unease. She ran through a sequence of breathing exercises, followed by intense visualisation of complexities closely connected to the esoteric universe of Westrigonian metaphysics, but nothing helped. She was too upset. After a while, she gave up and left her rooms in search of something to distract her. To start with, she went in search of her parents, in part because they were her parents and she was still, all her bluster notwithstanding, only fifteen years old; but also because they were the monarchs of Westrigonia who would surely know the secrets of state concerning the arrest of Matthias Raspero.

CHAPTER SEVEN

The necessaries are the emissaries of necessity.
Frankie the Villain

6:25 PM, Thursday 11 July 1875 A. F.

Matthias walked beside Phelan all the way back down the stairs to the Entrance Hall and then continued down the stairs leading to the fifth floor of the Ankalybu, the one at street-level whose outer walls were of shiny black marble. Phelan took the stairs going down to the next floor down, the one below street level, and then the stairs leading down to the floor below that, the lowest level of all, the seventh floor, the deepest darkest part of the Ankalybu. As they descended the stairs into the lowest level of the Ankalybu, everything became darker. No sunlight ever reached down here. The only lighting came from gas lamps in their wall fixtures, not all of which were alight, and many of which sputtered as if being choked by their guttering blue-tinged yellow flames. Matthias felt that his surroundings were becoming so cold that his breath should be frosty, but noting that this wasn't so, he decided that the coldness was an illusion. Yet he could feel the clammy coldness, illusory or not, settling on his skin like a second skin, stifling his pores and shivering his hams. He kept calm by keeping his hand unobtrusively on his wand and exploring this new world by using more than his eyes and ears. It was this exercise of his wandlore that kept his fighting spirits up. He had noted to his surprise on the way down that there was a Portal here in the Ankalybu, on the seventh level, which was something that was certainly not public knowledge. He observed as they passed that the entrance looked merely like the door of a cupboard. He made a mental note to tell his father when they next met. Even his father probably did not know this.

Phelan was striding along the corridors of the seventh level of the Ankalybu with a measured stride. The walls were so claustrophobically close together that Matthias was unable to walk at Phelan's side but had to follow along behind. The floor was of pink and white sandstone slabs that were encrusted with dirt and blood stains. It seemed as if no one ever cleaned down here. The air stank of urine and stale sweat. The whole place was deathly silent, due no doubt to the enormous thickness of the walls blocking out all sound. The walls were coated with a pale green plaster that was cracked and peeling in numerous places. At regular intervals along the walls on either side, these intervals being three of Phelan's strides, were grey painted iron doors splotched with rust, with ancient blackened bolts holding the doors in place. Matthias guessed that these must be holding cells for the prisoners of the State Bureau. As Phelan turned to his right and began walking down another corridor, the doors, while still grey painted and rust-splotched, became more widely spaced, with rickety latches as door handles. Matthias guessed that these were the interrogation rooms, or torture chambers, of the Ankalybu, where the real work of this place got done.

A State Security agent, grinning idiotically to himself, the dark-blue shirt-front of his uniform splatted all over with fresh red bloodstains, came out of a side door. Seeing Phelan he snapped to an immediate attention. The agent was tall and lanky, with a mop-top of hair sticking up and a small square moustache. Despite being taller than Phelan, he somehow managed to convey the impression of gazing upward adoringly at his boss.

'Chevalier!' he said with an enormous depth of feeling.

'At ease, Alfonso,' Phelan said genially. 'And what are you up to?'

'I'm off home, Chevalier,' Alfonso said with the utmost seriousness, as if this was yet more important business of the state. 'My shift is over.'

'And how is life at home these days?'

'Wonderful, Chevalier, wonderful. My little Charlotte is three now. She is an angel. I've promised to bring her some gingerbread biscuits today.'

'It is very important to have a good family life. We can't work all the time. All work and no play makes Alfonso a dull boy.'

'How true that is, Chevalier! But –' And here Alfonso giggled out loud with a sudden shiver as if he was being tickled, 'when I cut off Gregorio's fingers with a pair of shears one by one, how he howled!' Alfonso gestured with his chin over his shoulder to the room he had just exited. 'He's still howling. There are times when work is a lot of play, Chevalier, I can tell you that for nothing!'

'You should pay us to work here!' Phelan roared with laughter.

Alfonso roared with laughter as well, but then made haste to say: 'Oh, there's work as well being done here, Chevalier, let me assure you. It's not all fun and games. But it's the best job in the world.' Alfonso's eyes shone as if being unable to express all his devotion to the Chevalier through words alone had reduced him to communicating through the ardent adoration of his glistening eyes.

'You're a good boy, Alfonso.' Phelan reached up and patted his subordinate's shoulder. 'Well, off home now.'

'Yes, Chevalier.' Alfonso snapped to attention again and then raced off down the corridor.

Phelan and Matthias resumed their stroll down the corridor. Several steps later Phelan looked down at Matthias and said: 'Do you know why my job is on occasion a heavy burden to bear, young Raspero?'

'Because you feel sorry for the sufferings of those in your custody,' Matthias replied promptly. He said this in all sincerity, being careful not to allow the least trace of sarcasm to become apparent.

Phelan considered this reply as if a little surprised by this suggestion, then shook his head decisively. 'No, not at all, I am doing to them what they wish to be done to them. They wish to be cleansed of their guilt. It is what I would wish for myself in their place. Their sufferings grant them atonement. Dead or alive, they leave here as innocent as the day they were born. No, my concern today is that my young friend Alfonso, eager and hard-working though he is, loyal to a fault, an exemplary employee in all respects, will be tortured and shot next week on my orders.'

'But why?' Matthias asked, genuinely surprised. 'If he's such a good employee, why kill him?'

'I am offended by the fact that he complained about his pay to my very face. That was insolence of the highest order. You heard him yourself.'

'That can't be the real reason.'

'You don't know anything about the government of men and women, do you, young Raspero? And why should you? Well, suffice it to say that if an employee is executed for being a bad employee, for being a good employee, for being too tall, for being too short, for being too fat, for being too thin, for laughing too loudly, for not laughing at all, then you have all your employees in such a state of terror and confusion that they are as obedient as you could ever wish.'

'Until you no longer have any employees at all.'

'You are young, young Raspero. The State Bureau of Security will always have employees. That is quite simply a fact of life. We have a hundred applicants for every place at training school. We can take our pick. And do you know why?'

'People defecate in their pants when a necessary walks by.'

Phelan frowned, as if Matthias had said the wrong thing; then his brow cleared, as if he had seen what the problem was. 'Yes, astutely observed, young Raspero, but to serve the State Bureau of Security is the highest calling in the land. We serve and protect.'

'But why not just punish the bad employees and leave the good employees alone?'

'Ah, because people can bear any hardship except that of random suffering. If there is a reason, any reason at all, for their suffering, they can stand tall and look the world in the eye. Only the fear of complete meaninglessness will bring them to their knees. Only that will break their spirits and give you total power over them. They never know how and for what reason the blow will fall, or if it will not fall, and this and this alone keeps them permanently cowed, this alone brings them to their knees in pure terror.'

'But how can anyone act according to chance?' Matthias asked, feeling as if he were in a classroom, albeit a macabre one. 'Actions must be coherent, yet chance is incoherent by definition.'

'Ha!' Phelan slapped his thigh approvingly. 'That is a great secret, young Raspero, one of the greatest of all secrets. You surely don't expect me to just tell you, do you?'

'You have arrested me to put pressure on my father. This is not random.'

'But you are not under arrest, my young friend. And your father is up to his neck in matters about which you know nothing. But you are quite correct, nonetheless. Your presence here is not random.'

'Then what is the point of my presence here?'

'I could tell you, my good friend, but then I would have to kill you to stop you telling anyone else.' Phelan laughed at his own joke, and then continued laughing almost helplessly as if his own witticism was just too much for his sobriety to bear.

Matthias said nothing and let the man laugh. Despite his revulsion at Phelan and everything that he stood for, he could not help but feel a certain fascination for this monster and his doings. The revulsion was somehow the fascination; yet he wished nonetheless to be far away from this place and this company. Phelan seemed to be a being who knew totally what he was about. He appeared to lack all doubt; there was a calm still darkness about even his movements that stamped them as issuing from a subterranean cavern that had never known sunlight, or even the light of phosphorescence.

Matthias waited until Phelan's laughter had come to an end and then spoke very precisely: 'As I know nothing about what you are about by your own admission, it is only my presence here by which you seek to profit, nothing else.'

'I had hoped for more   intelligence from the second son of the thirty-sixth Baron of Raspero than this.'

'Then I am sorry to have disappointed you.'

'You are clever, young Raspero, but what will all your cleverness avail you, here in the depths of the Ankalybu?'

'Cleverness alone is of limited help,' Matthias said carefully. He was making sure that all his statements were at least partially truthful, but strictly limited in that partiality. He wished that he understood something of the danger he was in on that circumstantial evening.

'But you are clever, are you not, my brilliant little schoolboy of Vientae. Continued high distinctions in all your subjects, except Anglashian, which you have never bothered to properly learn, what is it your teacher said, um, let me remember, something like, <Matthias is a bright and attentive pupil but he needs to work harder>.'

Matthias understood that Phelan was trying to impress him with the extent of his spy network. 'All teachers say that their pupils have to work harder,' he said casually. 'It is their universal complaint. But I understand what you are saying. Your eyes and ears are everywhere. You cannot be escaped.'

Phelan's nostrils flared and his eyes narrowed in a deep, almost exultant satisfaction on hearing these words. 'How truly you have spoken, my young friend. How truly you have spoken! I am pleased with your acumen. Yet despite your cleverness, here you are in the Ankalybu!'

'Clearly I have a lot to learn,' Matthias said in a neutral tone of voice.

Phelan laughed his crunching-gravel laugh and clapped Matthias on the shoulder. 'You *are* a bright spark, young Raspero. Have you ever considered a career in the State Bureau yourself?'

'No, Chevalier, I haven't, as it happens,' Matthias said in his politest tone of voice. 'Do you think I would be suited for such a line of work?'

Phelan stopped dead in his tracks and peered closely at Matthias. 'We never know what we're capable of until the time comes,' said the Chevalier in a meaningful-tone-of-voice. It was as if he wanted Matthias to remember this moment for the rest of his life.

'That is certainly something to think about,' Mathias said as steadily as possible.

Phelan nodded to show that this had been the correct answer, and the two resumed their journey through the bowels of the Ankalybu.

Matthias wondered whether to comment that a form of employment where survival is a matter of chance was not necessarily in his estimation the most attractive form of employment, but then decided against it. But it was as if Phelan could read his mind.

'Do you plan to live, young Raspero, a life that is never subject to chance?'

'Definitely!' Matthias said defiantly.

Phelan laughed. 'Good luck with that! Of course, *luck* is another name for *chance*.'

Matthias had been taught to maintain self-control by focusing on his breathing and he was practicing this technique now. He nodded slowly as if he was thinking about what Phelan had said.

They had by now returned to the bottom of the stairs down which they had earlier passed, and here Phelan stopped and looked down at Matthias. 'The time may come, my young friend, when you shall return here. If that day should ever dawn, we will speak again on the other side of one of those doors which you have passed today, here on the lowest level of the Ankalybu.'

'That is understood, Chevalier Phelan,' Matthias said calmly.

Phelan looked down at his prey with an unblinking gaze for an age or so, then turned away and set off up the stairs. Matthias followed him to the Entrance Hall, where a squad of Defence of the Realm militia were awkwardly waiting, obviously and abjectly terrified by their Ankalybu surroundings. Matthias recognized them by their blue-and-red uniforms. He had only seen these uniforms before in illustrations.

Phelan surveyed the militia with a slight smile, inhaling their fear through his nostrils as another man might sniff a glass of Rehunda wine. The State Bureau agents standing around the place breathed in through their own nostrils as if wanting to share this moment with their boss. Matthias felt, yet again, as if he was in a weird dream. The militia bravely tried not to tremble.

'Who is in charge here?' Phelan asked peremptorily.

The officer in charge stepped forward and saluted briskly. 'Lieutenant Burkhard, commanding officer, Chevalier Phelan.'

'Young Raspero here is to be taken for trial in the Star Chamber. If he is found innocent, bring him back here. If he is found guilty, take him to Cayetano Prison.'

'Yes, sir,' Lieutenant Burkhard said and saluted again, as briskly as before. It was as if the precision of his salute was his defence against accusations of impropriety.

The rest of the militia merely trembled, their bravery having evaporated in the meantime.

Phelan surveyed the militia as if disappointed by their servility, looked down at Matthias with an appraising look, then set off for the stairs leading back to his own office and his painting of Leygerard the Leveller.

At a nod from Lieutenant Burkhard, two soldiers grabbed Matthias by the arms and hustled him out of there, in haste themselves to be away from that nightmare building, the Ankalybu. Matthias found himself bundled into a flying carriage, where he sat jammed in a corner while the militia piled in and the flying carriage lifted up immediately into the air as if everyone involved wanted to get as far away from the Ankalybu as quickly as possible.

'So that was Phelan,' said one of the militia with a laugh that shook on the vowels of his speech-sounds.

'Nice chap,' said another with his own erratic laugh.

Matthias tried to dislike his new captors but it was impossible. They were human beings, like him, and they were all in the same real world that he had known all his life. He could not help but feel a certain kinship of humanity with his new companions. 'Phelan is my boss, so mind your language,' Matthias said. 'I will have to report to him about everything that happens tonight, including your conduct.'

'That's enough talk!' Lieutenant Burkhard said sharply.

They flew on in a silence that Matthias appreciated, for it helped him to think. His invented scenario of being Phelan's employee had been a flippant way of agitating his latest captors. The second son of the Baron of Raspero was the picture of indifference as he gazed out of the window at the rooftops passing below, but beneath that studied calm he was thinking very intently. And the focal point of his intense thinking, a focal point as hot and bright as that formed by rays of sunlight falling through a magnifying glass and being drawn together on the surface of a flammable material, was the parting instruction of Phelan to Lieutenant Burkhard: *If young Raspero is found innocent, bring him back here. If he is found guilty, take him to Cayetano Prison.*

Matthias had no intention, no intention at all, either in this life or the next, of being taken back to the Ankalybu. Once had been more than enough.

This mean that if he were found innocent, he would have to run for it; but how? Would they take his wand from him before the trial? How could he fight without his wand, given the odds against him? Should he run for it before the trial?

Or should he plead *guilty* in order to be found guilty and be taken to Cayetano prison? That way he would avoid being taken back to the Ankalybu. It was not possible to escape from Cayetano prison, but his father would come for him soon enough and get him released. (Presumably.) But had Phelan been trying to spook him into pleading guilty at his forthcoming trial by what he had said to Lieutenant Burkhard? In which case, if he pleaded guilty, he was being stampeded into foolishness, or even a dishonourable cowardice. Perhaps he should keep his nerve and plead *innocent*.

But what *were* the charges he would face in the Star Chamber? That was obviously a key point in all this, although, as Matthias understood very well, not *the* key point. Still, he certainly could not plead guilty to anything that would detract from the Raspero family honour.

But then a new idea occurred to him, born of his earlier flippant comment. Matthias wondered briefly at the nature of inspiration. How had he come to make a comment, purely as a joke in passing, that now had come to be the seed-crystal of a rapidly expanding network of declarative statements couched in the form of the algebra of formal logic? Such a mysteriousness made one wonder about the role of Fortuna in human life. It was as if Fortuna could speak through you without you even realizing.

And so Matthias's thoughts continued down the decision tree of his speculations, branching hither and thither like an ever-expanding network of molecules in a theoretical space.

11:35 PM, Thursday 11 July 1875 A. F.

They had kept Matthias waiting all this time in the anteroom to the Star

Chamber, chained to the wall in an uncomfortable fashion, and only now, as the clocks ticked their way towards midnight, dragged him out into the Star Chamber itself.

The Star Chamber was so called because it was in the shape of a pentagon, with an inner pentagram inscribed in pure gold lines inset into the black marble floor. Overhead was a huge vaulted ceiling with all the twelve Labours of Hercules represented in frescos made by the master Cedric Frankenvinge. Twelve gas-flame chandeliers made of silver and bronze hung below the twelve frescos to light up the cavernous chamber. The accused entered the Star Chamber through a door set into the south side of the pentagon; the judges entered through a door in the north-east side. The accused was taken by the guards to stand in the exact centre of the room and was chained to an iron pillar standing there, after which the guards left the chamber; the judges took their seats on raised chairs before a bench set along the northern side of the pentagon formed inside the inscribed pentagram. Along the south-western side of this same pentagon was a bench where two Clerks of the Court were seated who wrote down everything that was said: one Clerk wrote down everything the accused said while the other wrote down everything the Justices said, with their composite records providing the transcript of the proceedings as a whole.

Legend had it that a globe-trotting Westrigonian of the long-distant past had brought back a starfish from a country where the starfish was the emblem of truth, and this starfish served as the architectural inspiration of the Star Chamber.

Another legend had it that one of the framers of the Westrigonian Constitution in the thirteenth Century had been inspired to create the Star Chamber by a dream he had had that had been so numinous as to ensure its own provenance.

Whatever its origin, it was understood that the geometry of the Star Chamber was so designed as to always produce justice. Corruption could not enter the realm of such a sacred inner space. All the judgements of the Star Chamber were therefore necessarily infallible.

The Justices of the Star Chamber, who were, of course, five in number, entered one by one and took their places. They were Ibtisamade, Deemer, Yakimire, Zhirayr and Abbey. They paid Matthias no attention as they settled down in their chairs and shuffled papers about on the bench top in front of them, and exchanged comments about various topics of the day. They looked like giant birds to Matthias, who was reminded that the slang term for judges was *beaks.*

After some time, Chief Justice Yakimire looked towards Matthias and spoke.

'Honourable Matthias Raspero, you stand here today charged with treason, namely a wilful attempt to undermine the authority of the state. How do you plead?'

'Not guilty, my Lord.'

The judges all looked dubious on hearing this plea.

Justice Zhirayr now took over the questioning.

'Such defiance will avail you little in this place, Honourable Matthias. I ask you again, and I urge you to consider carefully your circumstances: how do you plead?'

'Definitely not guilty, my Lord. I am totally innocent.'

This continued defiance produced muttering and headshakes amongst the assembled judges. They all seemed to be wondering for how much longer they would have to put up with this trouble-maker.

Justice Abbey now spoke.

'Given that we have already found you guilty, Honourable Matthias, due to the enormity of the evidence against you, there is little point in being so defiant. If you throw yourself upon our mercy, it may prove to be to your advantage. I ask you again, for the third and last time: how do you plead?'

'Not guilty, my Lord.'

Chief Justice Yakimire sighed heavily, and shook his head. 'Very well, Honourable Matthias. On your own head be it. You have no-one to blame but yourself for the consequences which will follow from your deliberate defiance of this court. We have extended you the possibility of mercy, and you have thrown this mercy back in our faces. So be it. Let it be entered into the record that a plea of *Not Guilty* has been made.'

After a silence which no-one seemed especially inclined to break, Justice Ibtisamade cleared his throat, coughed in a self-important manner, and said: 'It has been reported to this court that on the eight day of September in the year 1862, you did maliciously and with premeditation begin protracted negotiations with two persons, whose names are at present withheld, over a period of several months, concerning a conspiracy against the lawful rule of His Majesty King Jugold. Do you confess to wilfully and with malice aforethought taking part in said conspiracy?'

'I would have been two years old then, my Lord. At the age of two I would have been unable to participate in a conspiracy due to still being a toddler.'

'Miscreant Raspero, to produce tautologies in your defence does not augur well for your future. Mark your words more carefully or this court will find you in contempt.'

'I thank you for your guidance in these matters,' Matthias said courteously. 'I must re-phrase my response. At the age of two, being a toddler, I had not yet developed such faculties of the mind and body such as the use of reason and language sufficient to participate in such a conspiracy as the one you describe.'

'You are quite sure of this?'

'Beyond any doubt.'

The judges looked skeptical but they let the matter go.

Justice Deemer now spoke. 'Can you declare to this courtroom that you accept Frederick and Yolande as our lawful sovereigns, and do you regret any seditious behaviour on your behalf at these past times of which the numerous testimonies of reliable witnesses have convicted you in the eyes of all reasonable persons?'

'I most certainly accept Frederick and Yolande as our lawful sovereigns, and as there has been no such seditious behavior of the sort which you describe I cannot regret what has never existed.'

'Sophistry is not tolerated in this courtroom,' Justice Abbey shouted. 'Your continual evasion of our questions, your dissembling, your general shiftiness, does not stand in your favour, young man.'

Justice Abbey addressed Matthias as *young man*, as if he were still a toddler of two.

'I steadfastly maintain my innocence,' Matthias said as steadfastly as he could manage. 'I did not conspire in the manner you allege.'

Justice Deemer pounced on the form of words of this statement. 'Hah! But you did conspire! Just not in the manner in which we have alleged.'

'I did not conspire in any way at all,' Matthias replied calmly, shaking his head emphatically. 'This is the truth of the matter.'

Chief Justice Yakimire intervened at this point. 'Lies and evasions, I have never seen anything like this performance by such a crook as this one. I have never in my life ever seen anyone as guilty as this miscreant! His guilt is plain. You only have to look at him to see it! He is a gargoyle of guilt!'

The other Justices of the Star Chamber all nodded in agreement, gazing at Matthias with an air of loathing as if his very appearance made them shudder with horror. Matthias maintained a calm and composed demeanour, gazing back at their esteemed Justices in a respectful and reserved manner without appearing to look at any one judge in particular.

Chief Justice Yakimire then read out aloud from an already written document laid out on the bench top in front of him. It was as if he wanted to emphasize that Justice Abbey had not been joking earlier when he said that Matthias had already been found guilty before the trial had even begun. 'Miscreant Raspero, you have been found guilty of treason and you are hereby sentenced to be taken from this place and confined in Cayetano Prison for an indefinite period of time until Their Majesties should see fit to release you.' Chief Justice Yakimire raised his gavel and rapped lightly to declare that sentence had been passed.

The judges then stood up one by one and filed out of the Star Chamber, not looking back as they departed.

Deep down Matthias was relieved to hear his guilty verdict, given that it meant that Lieutenant Burkhard would not be taking him back to the Ankalybu. Being incarcerated in Cayetano Prison would be no picnic, but at least people were not tortured there. And besides, Matthias was more and more convinced that all this was some ploy to put pressure on his father for whatever reason. He was merely a pawn in a larger game, and thus would soon be free to return home.

Matthias did not know at that time that his father was already dead.

CHAPTER EIGHT

I only ask this:
Please do not smile or speak,
About what you brought here.
Please do not take away,
My possessions.
Obey me, I beg you.
Frankie the Villain

11:00 AM, Friday 12 July 1875 A. F.

Eleanor had spent the past week studying the turbulent period of Westrigonian history starting in the 1750s and culminating in the coronation of Justin the Second in 1789 AF. No group had marked this period more than the Levellers, and so it was this group which had attracted most of her attention.

She was now reading the account of the Levellers by Achaikos Ruzenadana, the Tetrarch of Anderlapia, and she had arrived at this passage.

The error of Erdagest

And so it was that Ergardest the Erroneus proclaimed his belief in the egalitarian doctrine of the Brotherhood of the Level, into which he had been initiated while still a youth. For the Levellers believed that all should be equal, and that there should be no distinctions of social rank between people, nor that a hierarchy of any kind should exist in any form of human society.

Eleanor was always shocked on reading of this belief of the Levellers. No matter how many times she encountered this profession of equality, she could hardly believe her eyes. If there were no distinctions of social rank, then her own position as Crown Princess would no longer exist, because it was the very personification of social hierarchy. This shook her to her very core. She was reminded of that day not even so very long ago when, with the sunlight streaming in through her windows, she had come to understand that the social world in which she lived was based on the metaphysical beliefs of the ages; and now it was borne in upon her with a sense of dread that if those beliefs changed then so would the world itself change, and become a world in which she might no longer be a princess. She forced herself to carry on reading, holding her book as if it had become a venomous snake.

As proof of these unbelievable contentions, Egardest declared the Golden Rule as the summation of the egalitarian doctrine. The Golden Rule states that we must treat others in the same way as we should wish them to treat us. The Keeper of the Keys subjected him to the most searching cross-examination, during which time the utter fallacy of this so-called Golden Rule was made clear to all right-thinking subjects of the monarchs of Westrigonia, yet Egardest stubbornly refused to recant his error. So it was that his bodily organs, internal and external, were crushed like grapes in a grape-press in order to subject him to a death whose pain would be so proportionate to the duration of the last agonized moments of his life as to send his soul back to the inferno from whence it had originated.

Eleanor relaxed and breathed in relief on learning of the end of Ergardest the Erroneus. The evil which he had represented had been stamped upon in his very own misbegotten person. Danger had been averted. But what had happened to this Golden Rule in which these Levellers believed?

And thus it is that from that day to this we can rejoice that the Levellers have been driven from the lights of civilisation and kept at bay. Yet the danger will never be past while misguided men and women are still foolish enough to fall for their evil doctrines. And so to guard against the return of the great evil of the Levellers we must strengthen our minds and hearts by learning these four major arguments by which the fallacy of the Golden Rule is most clearly apparent.

Firstly, there is the hatred and enmity of diversity as established by the Golden Rule. For the Levellers would like, as they have said, to have everyone hatched from the same egg. Of diversity there are two kinds. There is the diversity between the higher and the lower, and secondly the diversity between individuals. The diversity between the higher and the lower is the basis of hierarchical distinctions, and without hierarchy it is not possible to have civilisation. This truth has been extensively proven by many authorities. This distinction is not empirical and so can only be perceived by the intellect. The diversity between individuals is the other pillar of civilization, and makes possible, for example, the division of labour upon which the functioning of society depends. For who would wish to live in a society where everyone lacked musical ability or in a society where everyone possessed it?

Diversity is attacked further as follows. The Golden Rule states that we must do unto others as we would have them do unto us. Yet suppose that there is a bereaved person, and this bereaved person is grieving. Now there comes upon this grieving person a Leveller. Now if that Leveller is a person who would wish to be left alone while grieving, the Leveller will say: "I would wish to be left alone while grieving, therefore I will leave this person alone." This Leveller thus departs. Yet along comes another Leveller who says: "I would wish to be comforted while grieving, therefore I will sit beside this person and grant them the solace of my company." Which of the two is right? Neither of them has considered the grieving person as being different from themselves, because for the Levellers it is their own feelings which are paramount over all others. What is this but the most arrant egoism? A man who is most shocked by sexual behavior, a woman who is most shocked by lack of public manners, will judge others accordingly, yet their judgement will only be that of their own feelings on the matter. If the feelings of an individual are to be paramount in deciding conduct, then what is right for that individual is right for the whole world, according to the Levellers. And so it is that by failing to acknowledge that people are different, the Levellers proclaim the so-called Golden Rule by which the ego alone of one particular individual rules supreme and all else is eclipsed. Given the obvious problems when two egos clash, force alone must prevail until all distinctions are abolished, all people are the same, and there are no longer any differences of opinion or sentiment. The last opinion standing will be the only opinion in existence. In the end, there can only be one point of view in a world shaped by this hatred of diversity.

Secondly, the Golden Rule is not even the opposite to what the Levellers claim for it, unless the particular can be said to be opposite to the universal. They claim that it is a universal moral principle, yet it is a particular principle that is not a moral principle at all. Morality always acknowledges that there is something higher than the human. This understanding is the basis of all moral perspective. Given that this our human life is constituted of varying matters and sentiments and thoughts and feelings and memories and imaginations and so forth, it cannot be so that a moral arbitration can proceed from any component factor of our lives, because what is measured cannot itself be that measure. If a person should wish to either perform one action or its opposite, their choice, if it is moral, must refer to another standard against which their actions are measured. The Golden Rule is the supreme statement of egoism by nominating human sentiment as the only standard of morality, in consequence of which this sentiment is expected to measure itself. Indeed, the height of absurdity was reached by the Leveller Jynee who argued that to attack the Golden Rule was to hurt the feelings of its advocates, and so therefore such attacks should not be allowed because no-one would like their own feelings to be hurt by others. This circular reasoning is the inevitable result of taking sentimentality alone to be the basis of morality. The consequence of this is to cut through the root of morality itself, for this root lies in a higher world to that of the merely human. In this way, the doctrine that "do what thou wilt shall be the whole of the law" is established as the basis of human conduct. This is because the Golden Rule is founded entirely on the assumption that one point of view, namely that of the Leveller, is necessarily the same point of view of everyone else and therefore can be imposed on everyone else. Here there is nothing higher than the human, and of the human there is nothing higher than the ego itself. The abolition of hierarchy enforces uniformity.

Thirdly, if sentimentality becomes the basis of morality, then moral laws can only be determined by majority decision because logic and reason are no longer involved. This is the position of the sophists, long exposed as frauds. The sophist will say that if the majority of one state has decided on a moral law, such as that the death penalty is right and proper, then it is so because of this majority decision; yet if the majority of a neighbouring state has decided the opposite, that the death penalty should not be allowed, then this opposite contradictory law is also correct because for the sophists moral laws are determined by majority decision. No more need be said about this fallacy.

Fourthly, the Golden Rule is put to such a use as to become socially divisive because of its assumption that other people are the same as the person applying the Golden Rule. The sage Arktos the Wanderer puts the matter simply as follows: "Never assume that another person's feelings or responses are the same as your own." For example, it often happens that a person will say something apparently as a joke which another person finds offensive. When the offended person complains of their treatment, they will be accused of taking things too seriously by their supposed tormentor, who will claim that they did not mean it in that way. Who can judge between them? The Golden Rule assumes that the feelings and responses of other people are the same as your own, and yet this is self-evidently not true. The Golden Rule is the basis of all harassment.

It can be seen from an inspection of the historical records that the Golden Rule becomes more widely cited the more that it happens that true religion recedes from human affairs. Only atheists love the Golden Rule. The periods of history where true religion was at its height are those periods where the Golden Rule is hardly ever referred to, while those times of evil strife and corruption are those times when the Golden Rule becomes pandemic.

There followed a long and fairly tedious list of all the scholars who had written against the Golden Rule, which Eleanor skimmed until she came to the following:

But we need not look only to those great scholars who wrote so movingly before the advent of the Levellers in Baalbabak. For there in that greatly unlucky country has it been so that the Golden Rule has been applied, and all opposition to this principle destroyed. For in Yiannisberg, the ancient capital of Epona, over the town gates had stood the inscription "In the beginning were the heavens and the earth" which the Levellers changed to "Do unto others as you would have them do unto you shall be the whole of the law". With what result? We see in unfortunate Baalbabak how the rise to power of the Levellers has resulted in the greatest tyranny ever known to history, and how the unfortunate Baalbabakans suffer to this day under this tyranny. The Baalbabakans claim that they are the only people to have ever implemented the Golden Rule in their daily life; this is, alas for the Baalbabakans, all too true, and thus none of those who flee Baalbabak, who are many, have any patience with those who do anything less than perform the most necessary and utter condemnation of that Golden Rule which is the foundation stone of the edifice under which their lives were crushed. For always we see how those who most loudly proclaim that they are the friends of humanity are those who wish most ardently to stamp out all traces of humanity, and those who claim to be the defenders of human freedom attack that freedom at its core. If we are to be human, we must place the eternal first in our lives, and only in this way can we be truly our temporal selves. The Golden Rule places humans first and makes no mention of the eternal at all. This is the ultimate source of its fallacy.

The Levellers had grown in numbers during the reign of King Hariwald, and of this reign Eleanor read as follows:

In the days of Hariwald

When the nobles of the land looked upon King Hariwald, and beheld that he was a kind and good man, sweet-tempered and honest, fair-minded and honourable, they began to break the oaths they had sworn to him, one by one, even though they became dishonoured thereby in their treachery, and each turned to his own choice. They would force honest men and women to their designs without regard to law; virtuous maidens were snatched from the streets and treated abominably without regard to decency; they placed their hands on those who had money and made foul tortures of them until they had surrendered their wealth; none dared oppose them. The land cried out with the agonies of the people, heaven turned its face away so as not to see such horrors, and the nobles cared nothing for any reckoning of their crimes, for they were too powerful to be brought to trial, and they did not believe in the afterlife. And so in all the land there was no justice.

Yet one man there was in whose breast still burned a human flame. Justin he was by name, and he was of the army, and of royal descent. He gathered about his person those who were of his mind and for the law and he opposed the lawlessness of the nobles. When he defeated their armies, the cowards came to him and flattered him and made him King, hoping thereby to return to their earlier ways, yet always Justin upheld the law, never would he turn even a step from upholding the law. Those who broke the law were punished severely, to those who were wronged came justice. The people loved Justin, and he was their king. And such justice came to Westrigonia as had never been there before. For if a man laid his goods down in the street and departed, they were there untouched when he returned. None dared steal for they knew King Justin would most severely punish them. The innocent prospered, the virtuous were protected and justice was done.

But always the cowards hankered after the return of the days of lawlessness, when depravity had been all their good and darkness had covered their sins. They said that Justin was a tyrant because he upheld the law. And so they plotted the downfall of Good King Justin.

CHAPTER NINE

Fate can find its own way well enough.
We're the ones who get lost.
Frankie the Villain

Cayetano Prison was built in the days of Good King Justin on the panopticon design as proposed by Berenth Jeymam. A circular five-storeyed building with one hundred cells in each storey faced inwards towards a central watch-tower. The front of each cell was made of a clear unbreakable artificial-crystal door on titanium-glazed iron hinges, so the occupant of the cell could be observed at all times. The central watch-tower was manned by a guard with optical instruments who might or might not be watching any given prisoner at any given time. The prisoners were required to propel a treadmill with their feet for eight hours of every day, which had the effect of turning the machinery of five flour mills located outside the prison. There was an automatic mechanism for monitoring the five hundred treadmills of Cayetano Prison, and any failure of an individual quota was punished by ways too obvious and tedious to list. The idea was that they had to work for their bread and board. After all, why should an innocent citizen pay for their upkeep? Given that the use of the treadmill was counted as exercise, the prisoners were let out of their cells into the exercise yard only once a week. Berenth Jeymam was later exposed as a secret Leveller, but not before his prison had been built and put into operation by the State Bureau of Security. Cayetano Prison was a monument to humanity's inhumanity. It was famous above all for one thing. No prisoner had ever escaped from there. This prison was escape-proof.

It was Cayetano Prison where Lieutenant Burkhard and his men now took Matthias, whose life had of late become so extraordinarily interesting, or perhaps cursed. It was on the way there that a story, or perhaps more accurately a series of stories, began that would be told for several decades, if not centuries, in some confusion. While the actual truth of what happened was simple enough, it was never to be told faithfully enough to be discerned with clarity. The competing versions of these events, contradictory and incoherent as they often were, collided with each other like out-of-control flying carriages into a kaleidoscopic narrative of complementary inconclusiveness. The participants wound up too greatly falsifying too much of their own parts of the drama for the whole of the truth to ever be recovered. It is often said that *truth is the first casualty of war,* but it is not always added that it is factions that are to blame for this. Burkhard himself was the first to falsify his own account of what had happened, by insisting that he and his men had disarmed Matthias of his wand while they had been escorting the prisoner to Cayetano Prison. It followed from this that the wand which had appeared in Matthias's hand at the critical moment must have been provided for him by some means or other after his arrival at Cayetano prison. It was this re-alignment of the facts that sent the story off the rails to begin with, but everyone else was later to pile in and add their own falsifications. The truth was never to recover.

Let it be stated clearly for the record what actually happened during that fateful night.

12:35 AM, Friday 12 July 1875 A. F.

Lieutenant Burkhard and his Defence of the Realm Militia were waiting at the main doors of the building which housed the Star Chamber. Matthias was taken to them by the guards of the Star Chamber, who handed the prisoner over to Burkhard and his men with the letter of cachet detailing the sentence of imprisonment in Cayetano Prison as handed down by the infallible Justices of the Star Chamber. Burkhad and his militia escorted Matthias forcibly to their flying carriage, at which point the herald of history ducked behind an opaque curtain as Burkhard uttered these everyday words.

'Search him and disarm him.'

This was standard practice. His men could do this in their sleep, and no artefact that could possibly be weaponised would escape their attention. They were highly trained. They were, after all, Defence of the Realm militia.

Matthias tensed, clenched his muscles and shouted: 'No!'

Given that Matthias had been calm and co-operative up to that moment, everyone was so startled by this abrupt action as to give Matthias a chance to speak. They were paying attention to what he said, and his shout had stimulated their adrenal glands and made them fearful, which was to say potentially angry. They were momentarily not themselves.

'The Chevalier Phelan made plain to you that I was to be taken back to the Ankalybu if found innocent. This is because I am working for the State Bureau of Security, and my mission is to infiltrate Cayetano Prison. If you disarm me, you will be going against what Chevalier Phelan himself told you, and the heavens help you then. Therefore you will not disarm me, given that you will make an enemy of Chevalier Phelan himself by doing so.'

This was wild talk from Matthias, which made no real sense. Yet Burkhard's fear of Phelan was such as to set him thinking, which is to say that he did not immediately reject Matthias's argument as the nonsense which it was.

'The Chevalier Phelan made no mention of any such arrangement,' Burkhard pointed out.

'The Chevalier Phelan made a very specific mention of precisely this arrangement when he said to you that you were to bring me back to the Anklalybu if I was found innocent. What do you think he meant by that instruction? He said no more than that because no more needed to be said. If you disarm me now, Director-General Phelan's plan will come to nothing and you will be taken to the seventh level of the Ankalybu, and there you will be asked to explain yourselves, all of you.' Matthias indicated the other members of the militia with a circular movement of his chin.

The other members of the militia stepped back as if Matthias's chin was spraying the plague at them. Burkhard said nothing, but he looked too doubtful for Matthias's peace of mind.

Matthias kept on. 'I have been chosen for this mission by Chevalier Phelan precisely because no-one could possibly suspect me of what I am about, which is in service to the highest ideals of our beloved Kingdom of Westrigonia. What are you in service to? In any case, once we are at Cayetano Prison, I will be searched again, will I not? All prisoners entering Cayetano prison are stripped of all their belongings, including their clothing, which is replaced by regulation prison-wear. If I have my wand on me at that point, it will be taken off me. And that is the key point of this matter. It is the whole point of my undercover mission. If my wand is not on me, then my whole mission has become pointless. Why do you think Chevalier Phelan uttered the instruction to you that he did? Have you ever in the past been instructed to return a prisoner to the Ankalybu if found innocent? Well? The Director-General never makes unnecessary comments. He told you all that you need to know. If you disarm me now you will be directly disobeying Phelan's instructions. Now why don't we get a move on, bird-brain, before we grow old standing around here?'

It so happened that Burkhard had never been to the Ankalybu before, and had never met Phelan before, and so had no idea whether or not Phelan had ever given such an instruction as this on any past occasion. That was key to the decision he then made. It was not that he believed Matthias, necessarily; it was more that he did not dare to disbelieve him. If Burkhard had ever been asked to explain himself, he would have said all this in his own defence. But his later falsification of what had happened meant that he was never asked to explain himself.

Additionally, Burkhard had no reason to believe that Matthias would be able to make trouble when in the custody of the guards of Cayetano Prison. The fifteen year-old would be searched and disarmed in any case, whatever Burkhard did. If he was lying about Phelan, the heavens help him then because he would have to answer to the State Bureau of Security, which took such misrepresentation very seriously. In any case,

Burkhard could not be faulted for having bowed to what he had perceived as Phelan's wishes.

The last factor that tilted Burkhard's decision was as much subliminal as anything. Burkhard had seen Matthias walking beside Phelan in such a way as to influence him into believing now that Matthias was indeed working for Phelan. There had seemed to be a rapport between the two. Matthias's earlier flippant comment about being Phelan's employee also had had its effect.

'Alright, let's go,' Burkhard said and turned towards the flying carriage. His men obeyed him with a certain sense of relief evident in their postures. They did not want to do anything that might lead them to be questioned later by the State Bureau of Security. And in any case, they were also thinking that Matthias, who after all was only fifteen years old, would be searched later anyway. Nothing could go wrong whatever happened.

They were all later to lie about what had happened, given their general stupidity in having failed to follow the elementary rules of their profession.

1:55 AM, Friday 12 July 1875 A. F.

The flying carriage bearing Burkhard's party set down in the landing area adjacent to the Admissions Hall of Cayetano Prison. The door opened, spilling bright light out into the night-time as Burkhard and his men escorted Matthias towards the Hall.

'Not a word about anything out of the ordinary,' Matthias instructed his captors as they approached the open door where his new captors were waiting for him. 'Hand over the bag to them as always. This prison is under investigation, and it begins now. I will not be the only one answerable to the Chevalier if you speak out of turn at this point.'

Burkhard handed over the letter of cachet to Chief Jailor Bronimir with a brief nod, in addition to the yellow bag supposedly containing the prisoner's wands and weapons. Bronimir, roused from his sleep twenty minutes earlier, took this paperwork and the bag with his own brief nod of acknowledgement. Burkhard and his men saluted, turned on their heels and walked off into the night.

Bronimir and two other jailors escorted Matthias through the Admissions Hall, which was a cavernous room with a vaulted ceiling, through a door at the far end, along a corridor, up some stone steps, along another corridor, and into the Governor's Office.

Governor Ariston Warrick was a tall thin man whose sunken cheeks and dark-shadowed eyes made him seem like an animated corpse. He said nothing as Matthias was brought to a stop in front of him, but inspected the prisoner with an air of malicious amusement. Matthias in the meantime, his hand resting on the hilt of his wand (which was well out of sight), gazed levelly ahead of him at the puffed white striping of Warrick's robes, while he conducted his own inspection of his surroundings in two ways. One was with his senses, taking account of his surrounding by what he could see and hear. The other was with his wand by means of macchato. Macchato was a use of the wand that produced an image of the surrounding world in the wand-user's mind that did not depend directly on the senses. Matthias took stock of his surroundings as follows: He had three guards standing behind him, plus the Governor in front. He noted their casual assumption of total control over these proceedings from the way they were standing. They had done this many, many times before, and they knew exactly what they were doing.

'Prisoner Raspero, I am Governor Warrick. You will find that we are gentle and kind with those who are obedient and willing to reform their characters and gain the forgiveness of society. But should you choose to be anything other than submissive and obedient, we will instruct you thoroughly in the error of your ways. Do you understand what I have just said to you?'

'Governor Warrick,' Matthias said steadily, 'my father is a member of the Vidaldmeet. It follows therefore that my imprisonment in this place will be under an immediate inspection of the highest authorities in the land. You yourself would therefore be well advised to choose your own steps with the greatest of care. Do you understand what I have just said to you?'

It was then that Governor Warrick, provoked by Matthias's insolence in not being fearful, made a strategic blunder. 'Your father is in no position to do anything,' he said with a sneer.

Matthias flipped, pulling his wand as he somersaulted backwards and pulling out all four of his mobile karns while still cartwheeling through the air. One and one-eighth seconds had passed by the time his feet hit the ground again, and Warrick and his jailors had not moved. They were still registering what was going on. Matthias had Bronimir directly ahead of him, with his deputy jailors standing one to each side. Matthias grabbed both ankles of the jailor on the left with two mobile karns and upended him and threw him to the right, bringing him onto Bronimir with such force as to send both of them flying into the jailor on the side, bringing him down as well. The three jailors were now a tangle of limbs and swear words. Another two and one-seventh seconds had passed and Warrick's mouth falling open had been his only movement to date. Matthias, judging Warrick to be his least formidable opponent in the fight, and wanting his mobile karns for the jailors, used the direct forward kick of savarate, the unarmed combat he had been taught in physical education at school, to kick Warrick at full force in the stomach and send him flying backwards, doubled up and breathless. Matthias could now forget about Warrick for the next minute or two. Whisking back his mobile karns from the jailor's ankles with a wand movement, Matthias turned back to the jailors, who he judged to be his real opponents at this time; and time had now become everything.

All three of the jailors were rising to their feet. Sending out three mobile karns to grasp three ankles and upending all three jailors again, Matthias used his fourth mobile karn to grasp the wrist of one jailor and tie it to one of his ankles; he repeated this process on the other deputy jailor and then on Bromimir himself, who Matthias had left till last because he had seemed older and fatter than the others, even if meaner. Matthias had one mobile karn left, which he used on Warrick, who was still lying on the ground and had not yet even begun to start breathing again.

The fight had come to an end, nine and five-eighths seconds after it had begun. Matthias was, truth to tell, a little embarrassed by the sloppiness of his performance, but he reminded himself that real life fights were always held to be much messier than the competition fights in the ring. Had this been a competition fight he would now be placed last; but in real life he was still standing, and that was all that counted.

Matthias stripped Warrick of his robe, the puffed white striping of which he had earlier found annoying, and cut the robe into strips using his disc as a knife. (The wandfighter's disc was a circular steel object, slightly oblate, meaning that it was thicker in the middle, with razor sharp sides, that was used to kill or maim in a wand fight.) Matthias then used the strips of Warrick's robes to tie the ankles and wrists of his prisoners. He took his time doing all this, so by the time he had finished Warrick was managing to drag in laboured breaths of air, with groaning sounds out of all proportion to the skinny frame of his underwear clad body. Matthias retrieved his mobile karns and stowed them away, and then stood to one side and waited with a patient air, as if overlooking Warrick's failings. He quelled the protests of Bronimir and his jailors with an upraised wand and such a fierce look that they fell silent. The son of a baron, raised from birth to defend his position, was not in a mood to listen to protests from his would-be jailors. Bronimir had, for example, earlier addressed the newest arrival to Cayetano Prison as "sunshine". Matthias had been deeply unimpressed by Bronimir's form of address. It was one thing to be unfairly imprisoned; it was another thing entirely to be called *sunshine* by a man to whom he had never been introduced.

When Warrick's breathing had steadied somewhat, Matthias used two mobile karns to grab the Governor's head and tilt it upwards, while he stood over Warrick and looked down at him. 'What did you mean, Warrick, by what you just said about my father not being in a position to do anything?'

Warrick glared back at his interrogator with a furious look. 'Your behaviour, Prisoner Raspero, will without doubt-'

Matthias slapped a gagging karn on the Governor and stepped backwards. He looked across at Bronimir and the jailors, who for their part were gazing at Matthias with looks that were far from fearful. Despite their predicament, they saw it as only being a matter of time before the approved order of things was restored. Nor could Matthias think of any way to entirely refute their conclusion. He had reacted to what Warrick had said rather than having had any kind of plan about what to do next.

He had, however, regained his freedom for the first time in over fifteen hours, and he closed his eyes and breathed deeply as if to treasure the moment. He opened them again and took another look at his prisoners. It was obvious that Warrick, even with his gagging karn removed, was not going to say anything. It was at that moment that Matthias decided upon his plan. It was a simple one. He was going home. His father would have to decide what would happen next. Perhaps Matthias would have to become a fugitive from justice, perhaps he would have to return here to Cayetano Prison, or even to the seventh level of the Ankalybu, but at any rate, it would be his father who would pronounce his fate, not these strangers. Matthias immediately felt better, more centred, more decisive and optimistic, about having made a plan and actually having some idea of what to do next. He even started to look forward to telling Stefan in great detail about all his adventures, with the clear implication in everything he said that Stefan would not have handled things nearly so well. Stefan, of course, would scoff at this and scornfully point out all of Matthias's mistakes, and rebuke his little brother; and for the first time in his life Matthias would welcome Stefan's patronising condescension. He even looked forward to it, such was the distance he felt towards his normal life at that moment, standing in Cayetano Prison with his prisoners at his feet.

Matthias took back his gagging karn, and exited the room, ignoring Warrick's continuing complaints. His plan to go home required certain intermediate steps to be implemented, which he now turned his mind to.

2:45 AM, Friday 12 July 1875 A. F.

Matthias exited the Governor's office, turned right and walked along a corridor. He was like a falcon with its feathers all puffed up. He was like a hunter in a hall of mirrors. He was like a cobra on a tight-rope far above the gorge below. He was like an executioner of old pacing along with his axe in his hand, the shouts of the excited multitude echoing in his ears. He was the second son of the thirty-sixth Baron of Raspero with his wand in his hand in the midst of his enemies.

There were lanterns here and there along his journey which lit his way. Matthias turned right and left repeatedly until he came to an exit which led to a pathway sloping downward. This pathway led from the complex of buildings constituting the administration of the prison to the panopticon itself by going along a tunnel and then rising up above ground again. Matthias found himself on a pathway leading to the centre of the panopticon, where the watch-tower was placed. Without hesitation (for if he had hesitated he was lost) Matthias set forth towards this watch-tower, placing his hand holding his wand behind his back.

Wands were forbidden inside the prison. The guards were not allowed the possession or use of wands. This was part of the security arrangements that had made Cayetano Prison so renowned as being escape-proof. If a prisoner had seized a wand from a guard, control might have been compromised. If there were no such wand to be seized, such a development could not occur. Given that the longer a prisoner had been in Cayetano Prison, the less sentience they had, it followed that muscle alone could rule. And so muscle ruled in Warwick's domain.

Whether or not the guard in the watchtower was observing Matthias's approach was not clear. The black-tinted windows all around reflected light like a mirror without allowing anyone to see inside. Matthias could see himself approach in the mirror-like window facing him, and he fashioned his features into something resembling a friendly smile. It looked like a hideous grimace, but he left it in place anyway. In a certain light, and from a distance, it might be mistaken as a smile, and Matthias was already feeling a little light-headed from all this promenading towards the watchtower in any case. He arrived at the watchtower, stepping as lightly as a shadow all the while, without any incident occurring.

It was possible that the guard had been looking the other way all this while but the truth of the matter was the guard was sound asleep. This was not unusual. The watchtower guards slept during the night-time hours as a general rule. They always got away with it for the simple reason that the doors to the watch-tower could not be opened from the outside, having no external handles. Therefore anyone seeking admittance had to bang on the door from the outside, which meant that the guards could never be caught napping.

Having arrived at the door without being challenged, Matthias used his wand to flip himself onto the roof of the watchtower, landing as lightly as a mouse on its small feet, leaned over the eave and banged once on the door with his hand.

The sleepy-headed guard could not fathom why he could see no-one standing outside when he had been awoken up by what he seemed to remember as a bang on the door. What was going on? Perhaps nothing, but he had better check. Had he pulled on the cord to activate the alarm, things might have been very different. Matthias would have been trapped beyond all hope of escape. But had it been a false alarm, the guard would have had a lot of explaining to do. Besides, he had no reason to pull the alarm. Something had awoken him, and he was sure it had been a bang on the door. But no-one was standing outside. And nothing untoward ever happened in Cayetano Prison, and no-one ever expected it to. The mistake he therefore made was Matthias's good luck. After a minute or so, the door opened cautiously as the guard opened the door that could not be opened from the outside. Matthias instantly grabbed the opportunity that arose, swooping down from above and into the room, wand in hand and mobile karns flying. He used all four of his mobile karns on the guard, and slapped his gagging karn on him to boot. Matthias was fired up.

Closing the door behind him, Matthias took stock of his surroundings. The watchtower was hexagonal in shape, surrounded by the circular sweep of the prison cells. A handheld telescope lying on the table in the centre of the watchtower could be used to examine any prisoner through the clear artificial-crystal doors of their cell. Matthias picked up this telescope and looked through it, but at this time of night everyone was sound asleep. Matthias looked thoughtfully at the keys in his hands which he had removed from the possession of Bronimir, the Chief Jailor. He had already confirmed earlier while walking along what everyone knew, namely that wands could not be used here as the hinges of the doors were not magnetised.

Matthias was wondering to himself just how far he could go with his law-breaking activities. Clearly he was already in so much legal trouble that a little more of the same would not notably add to the scope of his felonies. He decided, therefore, to throw all the guards of the prison into all the vacant prison cells. He ruminated over whether to free all the prisoners in order to aid his own escape in the general confusion, but decided not to given that he did not know for what reason they had all been imprisoned. It would be on his conscience if any of them committed a further crime against an innocent. Taking one of the six paths leading from the watchtower to the prison cells, he dragged the watchtower guard behind him by using his wand acting on the mobile karns fastened on the guard, who was protesting his treatment in a muffled manner furiously through his gagging karn. The five-storeys of prison cells ascended in a stepwise fashion, with a walkway passing along before the doors of the cells. The first four storeys of cells were all occupied, and half of the fifth storey also, but the remainder were all empty. Matthias took his prisoner up the stone steps to the fifth storey, picked out a master-key from Bronimir's bunch of keys, and opened the cell door. He threw his prisoner inside the cell, retrieved his karns and locked the door under a hailstorm of profanities from the guard, who threw himself shouting against the cell door, but Matthias was already moving away.

Matthias retraced his steps and made his way through the complex of buildings that made up the administration area, methodically taking prisoner all the guards who had been up to that moment enjoying their sleep. There were six of them, which meant that Matthias had a total of ten guards as prisoners, plus Governor Warrick himself making an eleventh. Matthias threw them all into the cells, taking them three at a time and so managing it all in no more than four trips back and forth. He let them make all the noise they wanted, quite sure by now that there was no-one left in the vicinity to come to their rescue. He left Warrick until the last, and asked him once more what he had meant by what he had said about his father, but Warrick's only response was to threaten Matthias with such future punishment as to make him wish he had never been born. Matthias shrugged and departed, commenting to Warrick that the next person who would be asking him questions would be Phelan.

5:40 AM, Friday 12 July 1875 A. F.

The skies were brightening in the east as Matthias exited the Admissions Hall through the same door to which Burkhard had taken him at what seemed like a century ago. There were four flying carriages lined up next to the landing area. Matthias chose the first one to hand and entered it.

Matthias had never actually flown a flying carriage, but like every boy of his generation he knew how it was done in theory. Stefan had often boasted of his illegal exploits in flying carriages with his friends. These stories were undoubtedly made-up, but their commentaries on how flying carriages were operated were based on what everyone knew. Matthias soon enough mastered the controls and looked about him as he lifted up into the air. As he came to the force-field surrounding the prison, he spelled out via the communication console the code from the book he had taken from Bronimir's office. The code was accepted and he was let through.

5:40 AM, Friday 12 July 1875 A. F.

Governor Warrick and the guards of Cayetano Prison were not unduly worried by their current confinement. They knew it was only a matter of time before they were freed. What did worry Warrick, however, was Matthias's parting comment that he would be interrogated by the State Bureau of Security. He knew that this was all too probable.

It seemed to Warrick, therefore, that he had to somehow look better than he did in the eyes of the State Bureau. To say that a fifteen-year-old boy had single-handedly overcome the governor and all ten of his burly guards somehow made the governor and said guards seem less than completely impressive servants of the state. To be perfectly frank, it made them look utterly stupid. It therefore seemed necessary to change the story as it stood into a version that was more Warrick-friendly. The Governor of Cayetano Prison decided, therefore, to lie through his teeth about the whole business. After some thought, he settled on a story in which twenty or so masked and wand-wielding assailants had appeared from nowhere and snatched Raspero from his grasp. This was the story he told when he was freed from his cell, making sure that his guards overheard him, and this was the story which all the other guards also agreed upon.

Needless to say, it was impossible for Cayetano Prison to be stormed in this way given the external circumstances in which it was placed. All incoming traffic, whether flying carriages or more earth-bound vehicles or people on foot, was subject to inspection. While a flying carriage had been recorded as having departed that morning, it was of a size that could not carry more than four or five people. Nothing seemed to make sense.

The truth of what had happened was now lost beyond all recovery.

2:35 PM, Friday 12 July 1875 A. F.

Matthias brought the flying carriage to the border of Castle Raspero's force fields, and spelled out his name via communication console. He was given permission to enter, and he brought the flying carriage down into the courtyard.

Steward Rachelle came over to the carriage almost on the run, looking like a man who had been through a much harder time even than Matthias. Behind him came Lady Raspero and Lena, their faces drawn with tension. Matthias wondered to himself, a little dully, what more bad news he had to put up with now.

His mother and Lena fell on him, crying and kissing him and stroking his hair as if they had feared never seeing him again. Matthias bore their attentions a little impatiently.

'Enough!' he said, pushing them away and stepping back. 'I have to see Papa.'

After a moment, his mother, fighting back another wave of tears, said: 'Matthias, your father is dead.'

'Stefan too!' Lena wailed, and burst into tears.

Dacre Rachelle fought back his own tears. By now the courtyard was filling up with members of the Raspero household. Matthias learned that on the day he had been taken away by Phelan, his father and Stefan had left by portal to go to Krastienst. While leaving the public portal at Krastienst and making their way along Calogera Street, they had been attacked by assassins and killed. The assassins had fled, taking only the wand of Baron Raspero with them. Nothing more was known.

Matthias made his way to the Great Hall, where his father and Stefan lay in open coffins before the door leading down to the family crypt.

Matthias was struck by the surprised look on Stefan's face, who looked as if he were about to make a witty comment. But Stefan would never speak again, never laugh or make fun of the world again. What Stefan had been was ended. Matthias's father looked as impassive in death as he had in life. His paternal authority had now become something fixed, no longer a living reality but something stone-like carved with historical markings.

Matthias bowed his head over their dead bodies and closed his eyes. It was only a moment before his tears began to flow, hot and heavy as if gushing from a geyser.

Matthias wept for some time. It was the end of his childhood.

CHAPTER TEN

Nothing ever stands on its own,
Because it can't because,
Everything is interdependent.
Can't you see how it is your
Understanding of me,
That is me?
Frankie the Villain

The Throne Room was located in the north-east corner of the Palace of Krastienst. It was shaped like a square chest with a curved lid, with each side of the room measuring one hundred feet. The east side of the room was made up of panels of stained glass windows set in an elaborate iron framework, these windows representing various rural scenes of medieval Westrigonia. Opposite on the west side were mirrors and paintings and various priceless ornaments of an historical nature on mahogany shelves supported by bronze brackets. The Thrones of the King and Queen were located on the north side facing south. Each Throne was a massive oaken chair with inlaid gold and silver spelling out runic inscriptions. The King sat with the Queen on his left. The south side of the room was a large archway through which the monarchs could look down along the Corridor of Approaching with a polished marble floor that stretched for two hundred feet. The floor of the Throne Room itself was made of irregular black and green slabs of granite fitted together so neatly that the joins could not be detected.

There were three steps leading up to the Thrones formed of white, red and black sandstone.

Before the Thrones was an enormous carpet with three overlapping ellipses representing the Three Worlds. Its delicate black and gold and red tracings mapped out the entire cosmos. The curved ceiling above had a fresco showing the sun and moon encircled by a snake swallowing its own tail.

The Throne Room was mainly used for government proclamations and reports to the monarchs. Once a week, at ten o'clock on Wednesday morning, the Royal Councillor made a report concerning the business of government to the King and Queen. Receptions for foreign dignitaries, the investiture of important officials, and sundry other ceremonies were held in the Throne Room. Emergency meetings could be held here. As with every other public activity in Westrigonia, the Constitution decreed what could and what could not be done in this sphere.

10:15 AM, Saturday 13 July 1875 A. F.

Eleanor sat in the Throne Room next to her parents, who were sitting on their respective Thrones waiting for Cadwalader, the Royal Councillor, to make an important report which their Majesties had been especially summoned to hear. Frederick did not bother to conceal his boredom. Courtiers and hangers-on stood around gossiping and discussing government policy, occasionally including the young princess in their acerbic exchanges.

Eleanor's extensive studies of everything connected to being a Westrigonian princess had uncovered archaic but still valid rules concerning life in the palace. An important policy (*important* in Eleanor's opinion) which dated back to the time of Otway the Impetuous (reigned 1535 – 1540 AF) concerned the access of the Crown Prince or Crown Princess to matters of state. King Otway, who had himself been frustrated as a teenager by being excluded from discussions of all the important things he wished to know, such as briefings to the monarchs about what was going on in the wider world around, had issued a royal decree in

1535 AF that from the age of thirteen onwards the Crown Princess or Crown Prince were to be granted access to the Throne Room at all times. Otway's short reign had meant that the impetuous king, who might have reconsidered the matter at a later date when dealing with his own rebellious teenagers, and even possibly revoked his own decree, had died before reconsidering anything. So the decree still stood, having never been revoked. Eleanor was the first royal child for over three hundred years to have found this rule, and applied it.

On her thirteenth birthday, she explained the situation to her parents. Frederick was not impressed. 'Was there ever such a country as this one for absurd and archaic rules?' he complained.

Yolande was also inclined to oppose the implementation of this rule, which could, after all, be reversed by another royal decree. But Jason, for once in his life, helped Eleanor out by taking her side in the family debate. In the end, Frederick and Yolande, who deep down did not care one way or the other, decided to accept this situation, and so it was that the attentive fierceness of the delicate figure of the Crown Princess of Westrigonia, always beautifully dressed, was often to be found seated at the side of her parents' thrones during discussions of matters of state. Jason, who found these meetings as tedious as his parents did, soon gave up attending; but Eleanor, who found them fascinating, was so often present as to be overlooked by all those present. She was, in effect, an invisible watcher, who observed the often deliberate mistranslations by which her parents were misled in order to further the interests of one Westrigonian faction or another. Armed with Matthias's dictum that all politics is factions Eleanor was able to decipher the labyrinth of Westrigonian politics and see which thread of the web led where. She especially noted the role played by Lord Augustus Cadwalader, the Royal Councillor of Westrigonia.

Cadwalader was enormously fat, even more so than Frederick, which had played some part in his appointment as Royal Councillor. Frederick wanted another fatty about the place. Until his coronation as King, he had never paid too much attention to his girth; but now Frederick found his rotundity the subject of continual and unwanted attention. For example, when cartoonists drew a pear-shaped object with human facial features, it was widely understood what they were about. Frederick's courtiers pretended that this was a demonstration of the affection of his subjects for their king, and Frederick pretended to believe them.

Cadwalader was by now nearing the end of a career of public service which had spanned some forty-seven years (the starting point having been aged twenty-one when he had been the personal secretary to Lord Katica). The Royal Councillor was a large, fleshy man with a round cherubic face. Married twice, the father of five, Cadwalader had done his duty to society, and more: in his own feeble-bodied way Cadwalader was a womaniser. Like a bloated jelly-fish he spread his flabby body over the bodies of his unfortunate conquests. He was not particularly bright. He had no strong passions, no viciousness, no kindness. Yet Fortuna favoured him, for reasons known only to the deity. He had been an ambassador to Trentland, a regional governor, a holder at one time or another of the four most important offices of state after the Royal Councillorship itself, amongst many other achievements too numerous to mention. He had been personally acquainted with all of the movers and shakers of his era, and his wit and judgement were renowned on all five continents of the world political. In short, he was widely regarded as one of the most significant political figures of his generation, not least by Cadwalader himself. Cadwalader was a man fully aware of his own importance. He had taken care throughout his life to keep hold of every scrap of paper that had ever passed through his hands and which would be of interest to future historians, ranging from flying carriage tickets to letters to numerous diaries which meticulously detailed his conversations with important personages. By now there were 761 boxes of these records, and in these days his mind often turned to the arrangements which needed to be made with regard to preserving his historical legacy. After all, 761 boxes were a lot of boxes, and their importance, which was his own importance, was such that they had to be handled just right. They could not be placed in the hands of clowns who would fail to treat them with the appropriate white-gloved respect. Fortunately, Cadwalader had by now vastly amplified the already considerable wealth into which he had been born (by no more than the usual corruption of public office) and so he could purchase the services of those who would do the right thing. There would, no doubt, even be a dogfight amongst the canine academics competing to be Cadwalader's literary curators and executors, given the immediate importance of such a position, and Cadwalader knew exactly how to play all this up, given that he had, after all, been in this business for a long time.

But alas, alack, calamity and misfortune, how capricious is Fortuna, how whimsically affectionate, how cruel even to her own favourites. The truth of the matter of what would happen would be as follows: by the passage of a century or two after his death, no-one would have heard of Cadwalader. An obscure historical footnote here and there would be all that would remain of his whole career as told in all the detail of those 761 boxes of slavishly kept documents. No-one would care about anything he had done or said, no-one would be interested about how he had lived his life, and in the end only specialist historians, such as those who know how many horses pulled the carriage of King Daumantas at his ceremonial entry into Aamina, would have even heard of the name of Cadwalader. It would be as if he had never lived. So much for all Cadwalader's commemorative labours, which were pointless given that he was destined to be by and large forgotten by history. (But it can be said, to salve the bruised feelings of those who feel sorry for the unfortunate Cadwalader, that the man himself went to his grave still fully believing in his importance, and passed into the beyond in this state of mind. He was mercifully spared the brutal truth of his ultimate unimportance in the judgement of posterity.)

10:35 AM, Saturday 13 July 1875 A. F.

Cadwalader stepped before the Thrones of Westrigonia, cleared his throat loudly, and waited for a perfect hush to descend over the Throne Room. Awaiting his moment to begin, Cadwalader struck a pose as if for a painting, which would be entitled *Cadwalader Speaks!*

'Your Majesties, it is with an indefinable trepidation that I utter historic words which may by this time tomorrow prove to have been in error. Yet I cannot avoid my duty. Therefore let me say this: the Honourable Matthias Raspero, arrested for treason and convicted of the same by the Justices of the Star Chamber, appears to have escaped from Cayetano Prison.'

Eleanor immediately saw the significance of this, and also saw why Cadwalader was using the word *appears*, even hedged around as it already was by provisional diffidence. It was considered impossible to escape from Cayetano Prison, and governments everywhere disliked their subjects doing what was considered impossible. (It put ideas into people's heads where no ideas had been before.)

Frederick and Yolande looked as if they had never heard of Cayetano Prison. They sat there looking baffled long after the translator had finished. (Cadwalader, who spoke fluent Anglashian, had long ago pretended to their Majesties that he was required by protocol to make these formal reports in Westrigonian. In fact, he was really appeasing Westrigonian nationalism by so doing. Cadwalader had found in his political career that such little things can often make a big difference.)

Everyone else present muttered excitedly amongst themselves on hearing the confirmation that the rumours were indeed true.

Cadwalader waited his moment to speak again, as if he were a professional actor on the stage. 'A reward of twenty thousand strada for the apprehension of Honourable Matthias Raspero has already been publicly offered by the State Bureau of Security, subject only to the approval of your Majesties. I await any questions from your august personages.'

When Frederick was annoyed, and he was annoyed now, he could be quite blunt. '<I have this question, Cadwalader. Why on earth are you telling us all this? What is your point?>'

'My point is that the escape of Matthias Raspero from Cayetano Prison has political implications. There will be an immediate question in the minds of many people as to the number of collaborators he must have had in order to do this. Is there a conspiracy? If so, how dangerous is this conspiracy to the safety and well-being of our beloved Kingdom? Chevalier Phelan himself is taking charge of this investigation.'

Eleanor noted what Cadwalader was *not* saying. This investigation might prove to be the perfect cover to settle a lot of issues to the advantage of those empowered to investigate. Hidden agendas would already be in motion all over the country by that moment in time, and who could tell what would be the outcome of all this once the dust had settled? Anyone who could be named as a conspirator would be in big trouble, which meant that big profits could be made by those in a position to do such naming.

'<And I am being told about this for what reason?>' Frederick said petulantly, feeling that his original complaint had by no means been addressed by all this talk of conspiracies. Lady Gabija had been very chatty, with a distinct look in her eye, when he had been called away from her company by this urgent message regarding an important report by Cadwalader. Frederick strongly suspected that when he next met Lady Gabija, there would be a distance between the two of them as measured by the requirements of propriety, and the moment would have been lost. He felt robbed.

Cadwalader knew exactly what to say to his boss. 'It is at times like this that the gaze of the whole country turns to their king. Men admire his courage and dignity and women lean on his strength and manliness.'

Frederick's suddenly still posture showed that these words had not been without their intended effect, while Yolande's thinning lips showed that she, too, was aware of why Cadwalader had phrased things this way.

'<Absolutely!>' Frederick said with an air of decisiveness, as if bracing himself to be leaned on by women. '<So, ah, this fellow, Raspero, escaped from this prison? Is that what you said?>'

'He is a rebel and a renegade, a traitor to the kingdom and a miscreant before the law!' thundered Cadwalader. As soon as this had been translated, he thundered on: 'Let the Kingdom of Westrigonia observe the steadfastness, the fury of the righteous, of their monarchs faced with such effrontery as this. You can only be praised, sire, for your leadership in these times of peril.'

'<Peril?>' Frederick queried cautiously. '<What kind of peril? Exactly?>'

'None to yourself or Queen Yolande,' Cadwalader immediately assured the uneasy monarch. 'The peril is only to Raspero and his conspirators.'

'<What conspirators are these?>'

'That is exactly what our investigation shall uncover, sire.'

'<And this, ah, conspiracy, was behind the prison escape of this, ah, Raspero fellow?>'

'Very likely, your Majesty, we can only surmise and conjecture at these uncertain times. Indeed, we do not even know if Raspero actually escaped from Cayetano Prison. This must be decided upon by further evaluation of the information forthcoming from the careful and –'

'<Wait a minute!>' Frederick interrupted, a little exasperatedly. '<Is this fellow in custody or is he not? If not, then how did he leave custody? Well>?'

'He is not in custody, having left custody unlawfully. So by this criterion, he escaped. But was he actually a prisoner of Cayetano Prison in the sense of being in a cell, being in striped pyjamas behind a crystal door, or did he, so to speak, make a run for it at the door on his arrival? In which case, did he actually escape from Cayetano Prison, or did he escape before the doors of Cayetano Prison? Or did he leave the lawful custody of Cayetano Prison as a result of an armed intervention from outside that broke the prison's restraints, in which case it was not an escape but a liberation, or a removal, so to speak. These are the crucial questions that need to be answered as soon as possible in the interest of good government. He was never in striped pyjamas, so was he ever actually a prisoner? Did he get away *before* becoming a prisoner? Can someone who is not a prisoner be said to have escaped?'

Cadwalader had fairly succinctly summarized the debate over this issue that was to rage for several decades without resolution.

Frederick held his hand politely over his yawn, before saying, in a tone of monumental indifference: '<Is that everything you have to tell me? Or is there anything more of this very important issue?>' Frederick yawned again, less politely this time, as if to emphasize his sarcasm.

Cadwalader knew an exit sign when he saw one. He bowed deeply with a flourish of his hand and said: 'I will keep you informed of further developments as they occur.'

'<Please do,>' Frederick said as he stood up, yawning even more widely than before. '<Till then, Cadwalader, till then.>'

Yolande stood up as well, everyone present bowed deeply, and the meeting was over.

Eleanor went straight back to her Chambers in order to summon Astrudel. She wanted to find out everything she could about what was going on. What had Matthias been up to?

And what would he do next?

10:35 AM, Sunday 14 July 1875 A. F.

It was at times like these that Eleanor felt her Anglashian foreignness weigh upon her acquired Westrigonian being. She dreaded the thought that Jason might be right after all, and that her attempt to become Westrigonian was doomed to fail. She felt like the sage who had dreamed of being a butterfly, and on waking, wondered if he was now a butterfly dreaming of being a man.

She had been careful to phrase her defense of Matthias in a considered fashion. She began by condemning his general unlawfulness. Her Westrigonian friends nodded in agreement. Then she proceeded to criticize the precise formulation of the charges against Matthias. For example, she pointed out the absurdity of supposing that Matthias could have conspired against the State at the age of two. She felt that the self-evident falsity of the accusation weakened the case against Matthias and undermined everything else. Her Westrigonian friends nodded again, but in a baffled fashion. They obviously could not understand what she was on about. It was this that troubled Eleanor. She had read the transcript of the trial of Matthias in the Star Chamber with a certain amount of disbelief, only to find that no-one else seemed to share in her perspective on things. Her parents merely shrugged and the palace officials, courtiers, general hangers-on and sundry personages, looked wary, as if she was attempting to entrap them into taking sides against the Kingdom. She could see that even those who agreed with her were only pretending to agree with her in order to get themselves into her good books.

She tried to explain to the others that it was justice itself that she was advocating, but nothing helped her make her argument. She understood at an intellectual level what the problem was. The problem was that for the Westrigonians nothing could be appraised in isolation from everything else. Justice was bound up with morality which was bound up with tradition which was bound up with your hope for preferment. To behave with farcical absurdity could even be a point of pride if it furthered your ambition and made people laugh in the right way. The obvious falsity of an accusation was not always directly relevant to the verdict of a Westrigonian court. Only foreign barbarians thought that things were so simple. Life was more complicated than that, and justice involved the whole of life. Yet there were lines that could not be crossed, and every Westrigonian knew what they were. It was just that logic and truth did not form those lines. But none of this intellectual understanding helped Eleanor. It was one thing to think these things, it was another to feel them. And where did such feelings come from? Was she hopelessly Anglashian after all? If Eleanor's fist had been the size of a mountain, she would have brought it down on everyone in a way that would have knocked sense into them all, that was for sure! But the fourteen-year-old girl could only feel foolishly foreign.

Another part of the problem was the general uncertainty as to whether Matthias had escaped from Cayetano Prison or not. He had been taken there in chains by the Defence of the Realm militia and handed over to the prison guards. He had apparently been rescued by twenty or so assailants who had appeared from nowhere and overpowered the Governor and his guards. Yet given that it was impossible for armed assailants to have suddenly turned up, it followed therefore that some other explanation must be sought for. Yet it had been the team bringing the prison's supplies who had discovered the Governor and his guards in the prison cells, and their report was definitive and unanimous. All of the prison staff who had been taken prisoner and locked up in their own cells had been locked up from the outside. It was impossible for them to have locked themselves up. Even if one of them had locked the others up, there was still the question of how the last one would have locked *himself* up. Therefore an outside agency had locked them up. And as a flying carriage had been logged leaving the prison premises that morning carrying at least Matthias Raspero himself, given that Matthias Raspero had gone, it followed that there was a logical explanation for the departure of this outside agency. Yet as this carriage could not have carried twenty people, it left unanswered the question of where the extra assailants could have disappeared to given that they were neither in the prison premises nor in the departed flying carriage. Mysteries abounded, and everyone loved discussing them.

But still Eleanor was faced with the question of how the kingdom of Westrigonia had treated the prisoner Matthias Raspero.

By now Eleanor felt that all the facts were in and she could arrive at a considered appraisal of the respective nations of Trentland and Westrigonia. The two countries had plenty in common, such as certain proverbs. *The dogs still bark at flying carriages* – this proverb existed in Westrigonia, just as it did in her native Trentland.

Eleanor had found that Westrigonians often talked in code. A reference to silver, for example, might be a reference to the Silver Rule (that *all people are different*), or to the moon, or to something else, depending on the context. "Silver can be more valuable than gold on occasion," Eleanor had been told, "the fortune-tellers seem to believe so." So a statement such as "I paid her in silver" could have a variety of interpretations, any one of which depended entirely on context.

The concept of having precedence was central to everything in Westrigonian society. While the Anglashians were also hierarchical, there was a pretended egalitarianism which had originated in the famous humility of Hundayi, the first of the First Protectors. The Westrigonians had no time at all for any form of egalitarianism. Only the dead were equal to each other, and not even them. Yet the very rigidity of the Westrigonian view of hierarchy had its own function which followed from this formula. Someone who was raised in social rank was accepted completely as being of that new rank. It did not matter what they had been before. Their new social rank belonged to them as much as to those who had been born with it.

This differed from the Trentlandians. Eleanor often noticed how those raised in rank in Trentland were all too often not fully accepted by their peers. They were mocked behind their backs as being of *new money* or of being defective in some other way. The person raised in social rank was never really accepted; they had only a legal status, and would always be looked down on as continuing to be inferior. The well-bred and the low-born would always be different. The pretended egalitarianism of the Trentlandians was just that: *pretended*. Your birth fixed you for life.

Another difference between the two were the signs used to denote rank in Westrigonia. Clothes, ornaments, even hairstyles, were used to signify key details of a person's social rank. A brooch of a silver heron, for example, meant that an ancestor had been present in King Hatchijo's court in the early Sixteenth Century AF, which meant that the person in question was entitled to certain privileges (though not, in these modern progressive times, that of inherited sinecures). There was nothing like this in Trentland, apart from such things as military medals and the like.

Then there was the matter of religion. Lachina the Sage had observed, on visiting Westrigonia in the Fifteenth Century, that: *Religion is everything in Westrigonia. It is the air they breathe.* The Trentlandians were much more dismissive of religion. While not yet daring to advocate outright atheism, the Protectorate as a whole was known for its lack of enthusiasm in religious matters. For the Westrigonians, as devout followers of the Herakrim, the Creator was known through the Creation, which meant that the Cosmos was the focus of their devotions. The year was divided up by the solstices and equinoxes into four parts, and these four parts were halved again to form the eight parts of the year of approximately forty-five days each, usually represented iconically as a wheel with eight spokes. The zodiac signs, lunar phases, seasons of the year and the cycles of plants and animals were all combined into interlocking patterns that comprised the metaphysical framework of Westrigonian public and private life.

For the Westrigonians everyone had the same culture. The nobles and peasantry enjoyed by and large the same poetry, the same music, the same dances, the same festivals, the same stories and fairy-tales. The Trentlandians had differing cultures for the nobles and the peasantry. The nobles enjoyed opera, the peasantry bawdy songs and doggerel; the nobles enjoyed certain elevated kinds of poetry, the peasantry passion plays; the nobles and peasantry danced different dances, listened to different stories and in general enjoyed different entertainments. They lived in different worlds.

The Trentlandians were superficially more egalitarian, yet Eleanor wondered if deep down they were in fact more divided. The Westrigonians were irredeemably hierarchical, and yet formed an unbreakable unity nonetheless.

Eleanor's heart and mind had long since been given over entirely to Westrigonia. Her Anglashian origins had by now receded so far into the distance as to barely be perceptible. Her visits to Trentland evoked dissonant feelings in her. On the one hand, the sights and sounds of her native land were still familiar to her; on the other hand, she felt at a certain distance from them. The jokes that all the Trentlandians laughed at did not seem to her to be funny, so she had to pretend to laugh along with everyone else. The dramas of day-to-day life in Trentland seemed to her like a puppet show for children that she had long ago outgrown. But the imprisonment of Matthias Raspero, not to mention the murder of his father and brother, shocked Eleanor in a way that seemed Anglashian rather than Westrigonian.

At times like these, Eleanor felt like a migrating bird blown way off course.

CHAPTER ELEVEN

They ordered me to take up arms to defend my country.
I said: of course, but please give me one minute,
While I write a poem to make our country worth defending.
They jailed me for saying that, which goes to show.
I'll write that poem tomorrow, or the day after,
When I'm feeling more patriotic than I am today.
Frankie the Villain

1:30 PM, Sunday 14 July 1875 A. F.

It was two days since Matthias had returned home. His first priority, once he had mourned his father and brother, had been to formally have himself recognized as the thirty-seventh Baron of Raspero. To this end, he had contacted Justice Narek Deemer, one of the justices of the Star Chamber and also his cousin, who he had last seen during his recent trial, in order to contract Deemer to supervise the formal Ceremony of Proclamation by which Matthias became legally Baron of Raspero. This ceremony had just taken place that morning. Matthias then busied himself with making funeral arrangements for his father and brother. There were no more tears now. Matthias understood that he was now answerable to nothing less than the past, present and future of his family and the threat it was now under. He was in a state of shock, even if he did not realize it himself, but his mind was functioning like a perfectly-ordered machine.

Naturally enough, it soon became common knowledge that Matthias

Raspero had returned home and was openly living in Castle Raspero, and even more naturally, this news came to the ears of Chevalier Phelan.

Phelan had noted that Phelan did not know what was going on, and Phelan did not like to be in such a position. Action had to be taken. He had therefore assembled a show of force and set forth to arrest Matthias.

When reports reached Matthias that seventy or so flying carriages were approaching the town of Raspero carrying one thousand soldiers under the command of General Kefirez, who was himself under the authority of Councillor of State Chevalier Phelan, the Baron of Raspero made his plans accordingly.

As the flying carriages came towards Raspero in their trapezoid formation, Matthias stood in the town square, surrounded by his servants and the townsfolk of Raspero, his mother and sister and Justice Deemer standing by his side. The invading army settled to the ground and emerged and formed their military ranks, the white suited Phelan looking on, surrounded by State Bureau of Security agents. When all was ready, Phelan marched towards the waiting Matthias, followed by his agents and Kefirez and his soldiers. The townsfolk of Raspero watched the show avidly. This was the drama of their lives, and they knew that they would be telling the story of this day for many years to come. Nothing escaped their many-eyed attention.

Chevalier Phelan came to a standstill about twenty feet from Matthias and said loudly, so that everyone could hear: 'By the authority of His Majesty King Frederick, I hereby place under arrest the Honourable Matthias Raspero, miscreant, rebel and renegade, charged with unlawful sedition and the wrongful prosecution of public office, misuse of public funds and general misconduct in matters which will be fully explained in a court of law.' Phelan finished reading out loud his arrest warrant and rolled it up into a scroll, staring fixedly at Matthias.

'I insist on being able to inspect the arrest warrant for myself in accordance with the law. If need be, Chevalier Phelan, we can refer to Justice Deemer as to whether or not I am within my rights to request this inspection.'

Phelan's stone face moved into the semblance of a grin. His exposed teeth seemed somehow to be made of white-coloured iron. 'There is no need of that, Honourable Matthias. I am well aware of the law. I do enforce it, after all.' He uttered a sound that could have been a laugh if it hadn't been so much like a grunt. Nonetheless, the State Bureau agents standing all around laughed out loud. It clearly was supposed to be a laugh.

The warrant was brought to Matthias, who inspected it carefully, then declared loudly, so that everyone could hear: 'This arrest warrant is invalid. It is made out for the arrest of *Honourable* Matthias Raspero, yet I am *Baron* Matthias Raspero.' Matthias looked levelly at Phelan. 'You may ask Justice Deemer, who has just supervised the Ceremony of Proclamation, which has been carried out in full accordance with constitutional law, if you need confirmation of this. The mistaken use of my title renders the warrant invalid. If you are as well aware of the law as you claim, you will be aware of this legal distinction. If you are not, however, you have only to ask me and I will explain to you in great detail why this is so.'

As it happened, Matthias was not bluffing. He would have been able, if challenged, to back up his assertion with a detailed legal argument. Phelan, who could smell a man's testimony as other men could smell the weather, chose not to betray his own ignorance of this matter. No-one had ever challenged the validity of an arrest warrant held in Phelan's hand in his whole career in the State Bureau. Phelan was in uncharted territory.

'I will have that arrest warrant returned to me,' Phelan said, holding up his hand.

The Steward looked enquiringly at Matthias, who nodded his approval and waved his hand holding the warrant in a "return-the-warrant" gesture. The Steward came forward to take the warrant from Matthias's hand and carried the offendingly false document over to the Chevalier Phelan.

Phelan took out his pen, gazing steadily at Matthias while taking the arrest warrant in his other hand. A neighbouring State Bureau officer bent over so that Phelan could use his back as a writing table. Phelan scribbled away for a moment, then turned around to face Matthias.

'Here is an arrest warrant for Baron Matthias Raspero,' the

Director-General declared loudly, holding the newly-amended document high into the air.

'May I see the warrant?' Matthias asked meekly. 'My request being in accordance with the law, as you have already claimed to know yourself.'

Phelan thrust the warrant towards the Steward of Raspero, his face a sneering mask. Soon Matthias would be in his custody and at his mercy and Phelan's fury was such that he was nearly quivering. He did not like to be thwarted, and Matthias had thwarted him once already, which was one too many times. Unluckily for Phelan's temper, which was about to become even more inflamed, Matthias hadn't yet finished being difficult.

After having inspected the arrest warrant with a serious air, Matthias declared as loudly as before: 'This arrest warrant is invalid.' He looked across at Phelan with a set expression to his face, like someone who was looking for a fight. 'You have crossed out the word "Honourable" and written "Baron" in its place. This warrant is now for the arrest of Baron Matthias Raspero. At the bottom of the warrant is the signature of Chevalier Phelan. While this signature would suffice for the arrest of the Honourable Matthias Raspero, it does not suffice for the arrest of Baron Matthias Raspero. This is because Baron Matthias Raspero is a member of the Vidaldmeet, and only the King's or Queen's signature can be at the bottom of an arrest warrant for a member of the Vidaldmeet. This is a clear point of law. But I defer to Justice Deemer with regard to points of law.' Matthias turned to face Deemer and held the arrest warrant out in his direction saying: 'Steward, would you be so good as to bring the Justice this document for his inspection?'

After Deemer had inspected the arrest warrant and confirmed that it was invalid, Matthias turned and pointed straight at Phelan with an accusing finger and said loudly: 'You have put your signature in the place of the King. This is to usurp the monarch's authority. This is treason! Your guilt in this matter is plain. I say to General Latta Kefirez that he is now duty bound to place you, Chevalier Phelan, under arrest. No warrant is necessary for this, ask Justice Deemer. Well, General Kefirez? What do you say? Will you do your duty and arrest Chevalier Phelan?'

It was clear from the expression on General Kefirez's face, and from the way he was standing, that he had no intention, either in this life or the next, of doing any such thing.

Phelan's face grew murderous. 'You are opposing an officer of the King in the exercise of his duty. If you continue to defy the King then the consequences will be on your own head. Beware, Raspero!'

'If you fail to act according to the law then the consequences will be on *your* head, Phelan. If you act unlawfully against a member of the Vidaldmeet then I am entitled to give you a lesson in the limits of your authority. I say to you: beware!'

Phelan's face was now something to behold. It was as if the human skin was stretched by inner forces that were not human. His face was a mask of fury that seemed about to melt from the molten blood bubbling beneath. It was then that Matthias did something truly extraordinary that made him a legend across the Kingdom of Westrigonia. No-one who was present would ever forget what they had themselves witnessed with their own eyes. He drew his wand in a leisurely fashion, a mobile karn arose from under his robes, and with this mobile karn he slapped Phelan hard across the face. The silence that followed this slap was the silence of a multitude of people all simultaneously holding their breath and not daring to move a muscle.

After the tick of a clock, it was as if the world had shifted back into gear and started moving again. Phelan drew his own wand as if in a blood-hazed daze, the State Bureau agents present drew theirs, the soldiers of General Kefirez readied for battle, as did also the hopelessly outnumbered Guard of the Castle of Raspero.

'If you give the order to attack, Phelan, let it be known across this our land that you have usurped the monarch's authority, and acted on your behalf, not his. You will have taken the law into your own hands and you will not have acted in accordance with the Constitution of Westrigonia. Now, Phelan, give the order to attack and let this be your last mistake, the error of your undoing. You will pay for this mistake with your own life.'

Matthias's disc came out of his robes and lay in front of him, hanging in the air six inches above the ground. He was going to send that disc directly into Phelan's throat when the time came.

At the sight of the disc, and the deadly look in Matthias's eyes, Phelan backtracked. He put his wand away and waved down his troops. He was calm again, and his anger had simply disappeared. It was as if a switch had been flipped in his brain. 'I will return to Krastienst, Miscreant Raspero, and acquire an arrest warrant for Baron Matthias Raspero signed by His Majesty King Frederick, after which I shall return here to Raspero. If you are not here, your lands shall become forfeit and you shall be stripped of all you possess, including your name itself. If you are here, I shall take you into custody, and you shall wish in time, in the fullness of time, that you had never been born.'

Matthias still had his wand in his hand, and he promptly raised his wand and slapped Phelan across the face again. He caught his returning mobile karn in his left hand with a casual gesture and said loudly, so that everyone could hear: 'For one thousand years, the Barons of Raspero have held this ground. I will not stand here in my own domains and be threatened by a man who is nothing better than a thug. Hold your tongue, Phelan! You talk to the Baron of Raspero in Raspero itself. Show some respect, or you will not leave here alive. I could have my disc in your throat before your men have even grasped the concept of what has happened. I pledge on my word of honour as the Baron of Raspero that I will kill you here and now if it becomes necessary. From Daniel to the present day, no-one has threatened the Baron of Raspero in the way you have done today. I say to you again, back off or you will not leave here alive. Is there anything about these very simple statements I have made which you fail to understand?' Matthias concluded these comments by waving his wand and raising his disc to eye level. As he had given his word of honour to kill Phelan, it was understood by all present that Matthias's disc would be in Phelan's throat before Phelan had even blinked if the legendary wand-fighting ability of the Barons of Raspero, attested to by the one thousand years to which Matthias had alluded, held good today. Matthias's implicit threat had now become explicit. If Phelan moved now against Matthias, he would be a dead man. So would Matthias himself, who had placed his own life on the line with an implacability that was its own surety.

Phelan's hand was on his wand, which he had not drawn again. There was a stillness about his posture as if he had turned into a statue. But Phelan knew above all else how to safeguard his own life, and so he let go of his wand as if letting go of everything else and said in a measured manner: 'There is no need for either of us to resort to threats or to take the law into our own hands. The law will be applied in due time. We are each of us subject to law, to the dictates of the King, to the constitution of this our land. The law is on your side today. But this day will pass, and another day will come.'

'Get out of here, Phelan, before I slap you again.' Matthias's face was a mask of implacability. 'The Baron of Raspero has had enough of your presence, which is unwanted.'

Phelan gazed at Matthias slightly too long. His attempt to save face backfired as Matthias slapped him for the third and last time on that day. There was almost a growl, a movement among the State Bureau of Security agents present like a wind moving through the ears of corn in a cornfield. It was as if the repeated occurrence of the unthinkable was having an effect on their minds that was itself undefined. It was probably this more than anything that prompted Phelan into withdrawing from the battlefield with any further delay. With an abrupt turnaround and a wave of his hand to instruct his followers to follow, he walked back towards his flying carriage. Matthias watched him go, the State Bureau of Security agents watched Matthias, and the soldiers of General Kefirez stirred uneasily and looked about; the guards of the Castle of Raspero held their positions, and everyone else eagerly watched the waning moments of this drama, which they would remember to their dying day.

It was dawning on the Bureau agents that their boss had departed, and one by one they started to move away, throwing hostile looks of pure venomous fury at the Baron of Raspero as they went their way like slithering snakes. General Kefirez waved his soldiers to depart, and before he turned to leave, looked briefly at Matthias. For a moment, perhaps as much imagined as real, he bowed his head to the Baron of Raspero as if to pay his respects, and then he turned and walked away, followed by his soldiers. There were furtive smiles among these soldiers, and furtive admiring looks, as if Matthias had just become their hero. But truth to tell, not one of them believed that Matthias would live longer than them. Matthias would become an ideal that no-one could ever live up to, and so life would roll on as always before. But nonetheless they kept looking back at Matthias, as if they could not believe their eyes to see him standing there. Matthias stood there, wand in hand, and watched them all leave.

The thirty-seventh Baron of Raspero felt at that moment that he could take his place in the afterlife among his peers without regrets. It was true that he would have failed in his duty to propagate his line; but the cadet branch of the family issuing from Oliver's second son would supply the thirty-eighth Baron and the barony of Raspero would continue. Stefan would no doubt reproach him in the after-life, and say that he, Stefan, could have done better; but no-one could fault what he had done. He had shown that a man could act without fear of those who could do him harm, and what else was the essence of barony but this? The thirty-seventh Baron of Raspero would be one to remember.

Justice Deemer was seventy-eight years old. He had seen much in his long and illustrious career. No-one would remember him for long, for in the years to come (eight more years, as it would happen) he would die, be moderately and appropriately praised by friends and surviving family members, be buried with all due process; and as such would leave untied all those loose ends that had their own ends. In short, he was not unaware of what he had just witnessed. He came across to Matthias then and spoke as follows: 'The Chevalier Phelan did not speak in vain. He will return just as he . . . threatened.'

Matthias looked up at Deemer with a certain affection. He gazed at the white hair, the lined face, the legal eagle bound and tethered by the laws of organic life, and said in the friendliest of fashions: 'Believe it or not, Justice Deemer, I already know what I am going to do next. And what I will do after that. And after that. And trust me, Phelan is never going to get his hands on me. Before I am done, Phelan will be begging me to forgive him so that he can enter my service. You may believe me or not as you choose, and I assure you, on my honour, I bear you no ill will if you do not.'

Deemer was a picture of age as he looked at Matthias, but in those warm brown eyes there was a heart that beat steadily. 'I do believe you, my lord Raspero, and I will tell you something more. You could have given Daniel himself a run for his money. And that is saying something.'

Matthias laughed merrily. His tension was dissipating, and his laughter was that of a man who has just escaped being hanged. 'Daniel was the first baron. And I will not be the last. But I thank you for your praise.'

'You have done all that merits such praise,' Deemer said, thus revealing, even if inadvertently, that he didn't really believe Matthias would get away with his defiance of Phelan. It was as if his defiance of Phelan could come to nothing, just as the actions of a man shouting against the waxing of the moon could come to nothing. In other words, there would be no more praise to give, so it was all being given now.

'No, I haven't,' Matthias said a little sharply, shaking his head disapprovingly. 'If I keep the barony then it might be that some will say that I am the equal of Daniel himself. But all I have done today is to show that I have honour.'

'That is exactly what I said,' Deemer replied, who as a lawyer had debate as his second nature. '*You have done all that merits such praise.*'

It was one of the many reasons for his successful legal career that Deemer could always remember the exact phrasing of his earlier comments.

Matthias may have only been fifteen years old, but he knew enough not to argue this point. 'Ah, yes, your point is clearer now. But I thank you, Justice Deemer, cousin though you may be, for all you have done. I shall always be in your debt.'

'Not at all,' Deemer replied as a matter of form, but looking pleased nonetheless. 'I merely provided those legal services which my client requested.'

'And which he shall pay for. Don't forget to get your bill to me in the next few days while I can still pay it. The game is afoot.'

'I have never,' Deemer declared, like a man about to say something witty, 'been advised on the speed with which to present my bill by a client before this day.'

'You have never had a client like me before,' Matthias riposted, entering into the spirit of things.

'That is true,' Deemer acknowledged with a bow of his head. 'You have slapped the Director-General of the State Bureau of Security in public. That is . . . unique.'

'Unprecedented also begins with the letter "u", does it not?' Matthias commented. He knew how lawyers loved to play with words.

Deemer chuckled as if Matthias was being brilliantly witty. 'The letter "u" turns up everywhere, being so ubiquitous.' He chuckled again, as if he was being brilliantly witty himself.

'An enquiry should be made into this letter "u".' Matthias was growing tired of this conversation.

Deemer laughed merrily. 'It shall be chaired by Mr Undertable.'

Matthias laughed again, and bowed. 'Please forgive me, Cousin Deemer, for making my departure. I have much to be getting on with.'

With that, Matthias bowed again and was on his way, waving imperiously for the Castle Guard to escort him back to the Castle. He was already planning his next move against Phelan.

2:40 PM, Sunday 14 July 1875 A. F.

Chevalier Deimos Phelan was from the Salrautor region of Westrigonia. This mountainous region was populated by hardy men and women with leathery faces who drank strong spirits and lived to be a hundred. Their propensity for revenge and violence and law-breaking was legendary. One of the role models of Salrautor was Deimos Terenti. Having once been offended by another man over some comparatively trivial matter, he had stood waiting on a street-corner for ten years, disguised as a painted statue, until eventually this other man passed by, whereupon he promptly stabbed his enemy in the back, killing him outright.

This was the man who Chevalier Deimos Phelan had been named after. As Phelan flew back to Krastienst in his flying carriage, his thoughts about the insult done him by Matthias would have done the people of the Salrautor region proud. Phelan did not, however, have to wait ten years for his revenge. The next day would be enough.

Chevalier Phelan was not a man with much of an imagination or with any poetic sensibilities at all. Yet in so far as the master of the Ankalybu was capable of daydreaming, he was daydreaming now of what he would do to Matthias when he next had the chance.

Unhappily for the distinguished member of the Council of State, Matthias was already giving his instructions to his baronial staff while he prepared to make a journey whose sole purpose was to thwart the Chevalier's hopes.

Matthias had not misled Deemer. He knew exactly what move he would make next, and it would not be an action unworthy of the thirty-seventh Baron of Raspero. Daniel himself would have approved. Actually, all preceding thirty-six barons of Raspero, even the drunk ones, would have approved.

CHAPTER TWELVE

You take her body,
She takes your soul.
It's a fair exchange,
If you ask me,
Or maybe it's unfair.
Frankie the Villain

3:15 PM, Sunday 14 July 1875 A. F.

Matthias entered the Raspero Portal and exited at the Krastienst Portal. He had logged his journey, made by the Special Priority which was a privilege of members of the Vidaldmeet and other select personages, under the name of "National Considerations", which meant that his name would not be registered as a Portal traveller. The most wanted man in Westrigonia was trying to keep a low profile as he arrived in the capital itself.

It would have been beneath his baronial dignity to skulk along, so Matthias exited the Portal with a bold air, his head flung back and his robes billowing in the air as he strode forth (albeit with a scarf around his face). No-one challenged him, so he sailed through the Krastienst Portal facing nothing more than curious looks, and set off immediately for the Vidaldmeet.

The Vidaldmeet was the shape of a cube with a domed top. The front entrance faced onto Wafiwade Square, and consisted of large oaken double-doors situated at the top of a long flight of forty-nine stone steps.

The Vidaldmeet was one of the twin centres of the ellipse of the walled city of Krastienst, the other centre being the Palace. Each building had been designed to be the same height and floor area as the other, but the Palace, due to its underground crypt for royal burials was one-fiftieth larger in volume than the Vidaldmeet. The two buildings, the centre of all political life in Westrigonia, faced each other across Venusar Park.

No-one seemed to be about as Matthias climbed briskly up the black stone steps to the Vidaldmeet front doors, skipping them two steps at a time, such was his energy and determination to charge into this building, which was his latest battlefield. He walked through the open front door with a confident energy, and into the Hall of Reception. This room was built largely of sandstone, with an enormous vaulted ceiling covered with frescoes depicting various scenes from mythology and supported by stone pillars that had foliage carved around their sides. There were a variety of alcoves containing statues of people, animals and mythological deities. Chairs and tables were set here and there. There was absolutely no-one about except for a wizened old man called Master Boyan Conrad seated behind the reception desk, which was a long mahogany counter at the far end of the room. Matthias marched straight up to the reception desk and unwound the scarf from his face.

'I am Baron Matthias Raspero, member of the Vidaldmeet. I demand entrance to this building as by right. Furthermore, as a member of the Vidaldmeet, I demand that my visit on this day and at this time shall be incognito by reference to Rule 17 of the Vidaldmeet Charter. This means that you cannot, by reference to any other law or ordinance which may apply, mention my presence here to any other person, including law enforcement personnel. Now, I will speak with the Speaker of the Vidaldmeet if he is present. If not, I will explain to you what is then to be done. Now, what have you to say, Master Conrad?'

Master Conrad sat there like a tortoise with its head out of its shell, immobile, and either aware or unaware of its surroundings.

Matthias waited patiently. He knew that even a Baron of Raspero, in this place, had to watch his step. The Vidaldmeet, although younger in its founding, had powers even more ancient than the Barony of Raspero, given the provenance of its founders. For this very reason, however, they were even more bound by protocol than anyone else, except perhaps the monarchy. But protocol alone bound them. If Matthias were to draw his wand, he would be lucky to get out of there alive. So Matthias waited, patiently.

Master Conrad eventually turned his head towards Matthias and spoke. 'Your case is known to us, Lord Raspero,' he said in a manner neither welcoming nor unfriendly. 'The Speaker of the Vidaldmeet is present. Whether he shall receive you or not, it is not for me to say.'

'He will receive me,' Matthias said as if fate had ordained this matter from the beginning of time. 'I am here on important business.'

Master Conrad contemplated the young baron in an almost friendly fashion. 'Very well. Please wait here.'

Master Conrad arose to his feet in a painfully arthritic fashion and shuffled away as if this took up all the energy he had. He made a simple matter like walking to a nearby room seem like an epic voyage to pluck the golden apples at the ends of the earth. Matthias watched him depart and then stood where he was in the silence of the Vidaldmeet Hall of Reception. The silence of ancient buildings is made of layers of sounds long gone. The absence of these sounds can be felt. *Life was once here, but now only we remember it,* said the stone walls around Matthias. *Just as we will remember you when you are gone.* Matthias tried not to groan in exasperation. He was not in the mood for a lecture from the wise at that time. He had too much to be getting on with.

Master Conrad returned with his usual agonising slowness and sat down. 'The Speaker of the Vidaldmeet will see you now,' he said.

Matthias bowed with a peremptory politeness and set off along the corridors along which Master Conrad had voyaged. He stepped briskly, as if to nullify all perceptions of ageing. Although he had never been here before, he had in fact followed Master Conrad's voyage with his hand on his wand by a special form of macchato discovered by Daniel himself, so he proceeded along this route which he had memorised until he came to an ornate wooden door with a bronze plaque reading: *The Office of the Speaker of the Vidaldmeet.* Matthias knocked, and was bade to enter.

He turned the handle of the door by hand, careful not to use his wand, and entered the room, closing the door behind him. He found himself in a large room with a high ceiling painted with starry constellations of the night-time sky in the form of various animals and sea serpents. There were Ramudien carpets of ornate designs on the polished wooden floorboards, a large fireplace, a variety of furnishings and at the end of the long room an enormously large green-leather-topped desk behind which sat Lord Timur Zelimir, the Speaker of the Vidaldmeet.

Lord Zelimir was a white-haired man of nondescript appearance. His pale blue eyes regarded Matthias with a patrician disdain, while his stiff old hands fumbled with stuffing his pipe full of tobacco. Matthias took this as a compliment. Lord Zelimir saw the visit of the Baron of Raspero as an occasion worthy of a puff of smoke or two. Smokers do not realise, when they reach for their smokes, how much they give away of their inner feelings.

With a deliberate arrogance, Matthias drew his wand, set forth a chair before the Speaker's desk, snatched a cushion to place on the chair so he would be seated at eye-level with the Speaker, replaced his wand, and then sat down with an elaborate stateliness.

Lord Zelimir, whose pipe filling had paused in astonishment during these shenanigans, returned to the task of tamping down the tobacco and flicking the gas lighter and puffing on the flame. Aromatic smoke filled the air as Lord Zelimir puffed away, inhaling the odd lungful of smoke or two, and then settling back into his chair with a sigh of pleasure as a cloud of blue smoke rose into the air.

Matthias waited without moving. Lord Zelimir puffed on his pipe again. Time passed. Lord Zelimir stared at the ceiling.

Eventually Lord Zelimir brought his eyes down to look at Matthias and said: 'You have come to see me on important business, I believe.'

Matthias nodded. 'Yes, Lord Zelimir. I have indeed. Just how important will become apparent to you in due course.'

Lord Zelimir puffed three mouthfuls of smoke and then very gently, as if measuring out silk in the form of blue air, inhaled a light lungful of tobacco smoke, which he exhaled with an appreciative sigh. 'And what is this important business?'

'There are two parts to this important business. The first is how I shall depart the Vidaldmeet at our next meeting. This shall be by the Sinners Door, by your own order as Speaker. This is because I will publicly insult you in front of all those present. Although this is chronologically second, I mention this first because it is, in effect, first in order of importance.'

There followed a long silence after which the Speaker puffed on his pipe, which by now had gone out, and relit it.

Matthias resumed speaking. 'But as to the second part of this important business, which comes first, I am here to inform you, Speaker, in all formality and by means of this document' – here Matthias fished out a scroll from beneath his robes – 'that I enforce and enact a motion in accordance with Clause Seven of the Constitution on the fitness of the monarchs of Westrigonia to continue in their role as monarchs. In short, I move a motion of no confidence in our monarchs Frederick and Yolande.'

This statement took hold of the Speaker's full attention. He stared at Matthias for so long that by the time he next puffed on his pipe, it had gone out again and he had to relight it all over again.

Matthias waited, his eyes half-closed like a cat crouched outside a mouse-hole.

'Clause Seven?' Lord Zelimir queried eventually. 'On what grounds?'

'Clause Seven is its own grounds,' Matthias replied promptly, 'as of course you are only too well aware. As a member of the Vidaldmeet, I am authorised to enforce and enact this motion, am I not?'

'You are very young,' Lord Zelimir commented, gazing at Matthias as if he had only just realised how young Matthias was.

'Justice Deemer presided over the ceremony of proclamation by which I was formally recognised and installed as the thirty-seventh Baron of Raspero,' Matthias countered promptly. 'I am the same age as Daniel when he became Daniel of Sacramento. In any case, I am a member of the Vidaldmeet with all the appropriate rights and privileges.'

'Clause Seven,' Lord Zelimir repeated. 'That is a drastic step to take, young Matthias.'

Matthias ignored the patronising disrespectfulness of being

addressed as *young Matthias*, and said firmly: 'Drastic or not, it is the step I am taking.'

Lord Zelimir contemplated matters for a while, rapping his pipe stem against his teeth. After a while he decreed: 'I must refuse your suit, young Matthias. This cannot proceed.'

'It is not for you to refuse my motion,' Matthias protested. 'It is my right as a member of the Vidaldmeet to make this motion.'

'This matter is closed, Honourable Matthias. You may leave.'

The Speaker of the Vidaldmeet had made his position plain. Nothing more needed to be said. But Matthias did not move from his chair.

Matthias looked Lord Zelimir in the eye and said: 'Your father knew a certain lady named Melete, did he not? You are only too familiar with the details of their relationship, are you not? If the full story should emerge about this relationship, certain questions would arise as to your conduct in the year 1843 with regard to the legal declarations which you made then concerning your right to inherit the estate of Torbven. If certain other parties should hear of these matters, and I mention no names, and certainly not those of Chevre, Lettvriad and Otway, there would undoubtedly be certain consequences which would fall directly on your head, resulting in prosecution and imprisonment. If I were to make public what I know, you would go to jail, Speaker Zelimir.'

'Are you blackmailing me, young Matthias?'

'Definitely,' Matthias said firmly. 'And listen to me, bozo. If you still have the sense you were born with, you will address me as Lord Raspero.'

Lord Zelimir considered this statement with a mulish expression on his face, like a young child refusing to drink his milk. 'Young Matthias, your behaviour is unacceptable. Blackmail is an offence punishable by imprisonment.'

'So is false representation, illicit gains and perjury,' Matthias said loudly. 'All of which you are guilty of yourself. Now, old Zelimir, or ancient toothless Zelimir, if you prefer. Do you really want to make an issue of this, you decrepit old fool? Be my guest. But you may not find prison congenial at your advanced age. Prison is of course not congenial at any age, but for someone as aged and feeble as yourself, it may prove especially unfriendly. I am already wanted by the law, bozo, so you cannot threaten me with the advent of something that already exists. But what about you, old Zelimir? How ready are you for prison? Because that is where you are going to, you stupid old fool, if you defy me on this matter.'

There was a silence. Zelimir's forgotten pipe remained between his fingers, while Zelimir's pale blue eyes gazed at Matthias as if Zelimir was trying to remember what Matthias was doing there.

After a while Matthias resumed speaking. 'So, Zelimir, or moron, whichever name you deem to be most appropriate. My motion is now before the Vidaldmeet.' Matthias laid down his scroll on the Speaker's desk in a ceremonial fashion. 'You will publicise this matter in the appropriate manner before the end of today. But now we come to the second matter of our meeting. You do not, I am sure, want me to fall into the hands of the authorities, given what I can tell them of your own past. You have enemies, do you not, Zelimir? Of course you do. So it follows, therefore, that when I leave the Vidaldmeet, I will insult you, and you will be so justly offended by my insult that you will punish me by sending me out by the Sinners Door. In this way I will evade arrest by the forces of Phelan, who will be waiting for me outside the front door of the Vidaldmeet. If I fall into Phelan's hands, Zelimir, then the State Bureau of Security will know exactly what they need to know to move against you with perfect legality. After passing through the Ankalybu, you will be good for little else than prison, if you can even manage that by then. Now, Zelimir, can you grasp everything that I have said, or are you so enfeebled in mind that you cannot follow any of this?'

Matthias fixed Lord Zelimir in a cold-eyed steely glare. At that moment in time, Matthias was quite prepared to watch Lord Zelimir being escorted to the seventh circle of hell by a troop of demons. His implacable hostility to the Speaker of the Vidaldmeet was evident.

Lord Zelimir said after a while: 'Young Matthias –'

'*Silence!*' Matthias shouted and rose to his feet. 'You will address me as Lord Raspero or I will leave this room right now. Do you understand this very simple statement I have just made, bozo, or are you so far gone that there is no point in talking to you any more?'

The two scions of Westrigonian nobility stared at each other. Lord Zelimir said nothing; but the hostility with which he regarded his visitor made everything plain. Matthias turned on his heel and strode to the door. With a deliberate rudeness, he drew his wand and threw the door open as he approached, and slammed it behind him as he passed through.

3:45 PM, Sunday 14 July 1875 A. F.

Everything had gone as well as Matthias could have hoped for.

Or to put it another way: everything had gone according to Matthias's hare-brained plan, which is to say that it had all gone much better than it could have done. Zelimir had entirely failed to notice the one fatal flaw in Matthias's strategy, which was that as Matthias had not yet sworn his oath of membership to the Vidaldmeet, he was not technically in a position to move motions. Nor did the pipe-smoking Zelimir, afloat in his clouds of blue tobacco smoke, look likely to make such an observation any time soon.

Once again, Matthias had lucked out.

CHAPTER THIRTEEN

I have been wise,
And I have been in love,
But not at the same time.
That would be impossible.
Frankie the Villain

11:00 AM, Monday 15 July 1875 A. F.

As he had promised he would, Phelan came back the next day. He again brought Kefirez and his thousand soldiers. The lumbering wooden birds of all their flying carriages landed lightly on the ground before the town square of Raspero.

Matthias stood where he had stood before, his castle guard around him, the townsfolk of Raspero around them, with his mother and sister and Justice Deemer standing to one side. Everyone had come to watch the drama.

There was a space around Matthias, as if all those present to watch the drama were being careful not to be seen to be associated with him. Phelan was going to grab Matthias today, and they did not want to be taken along with him.

Phelan marched along towards Matthias. There was a stately, measured air of triumph to his progress, while beside him marched the agents of the State Bureau of Security, who all had the same gleam of triumph in their eyes, like identical glossy black beads on a necklace reflecting the same point of light.

'Miscreant Raspero, Baron Matthias Raspero, you are under arrest, and here in my hand is an arrest warrant signed by His Majesty King Frederick the First. The legality of this document, which has been inspected by the finest legal minds of our country, is beyond dispute. If you wish, you may inspect this document, as is your right under law, but I assure you, it will avail you nothing. Your fate is sealed on this day. Now, I say again: you are under arrest and I am your arresting officer. Give yourself up, Raspero, or suffer the consequence of non-compliance with the law of the land.'

'There is no need for me to inspect your arrest warrant,' Matthias said loudly. Continuing as loudly as before, he said: 'Your arrest warrant is invalid, Phelan. You are the one who needs to contemplate the consequences of your actions.'

Phelan had spent decades watching people desperately try to wriggle out of being arrested. He always enjoyed the spectacle. He raised his eyebrows on hearing Matthias's defiant proclamation, after which his face moved into a grimace that was a semblance of a smile. 'You say that this arrest warrant is invalid? This arrest warrant, that has been inspected by the finest legal minds in the country, and which you have not even yet seen? Perhaps you might care to explain yourself.'

'Certainly,' said Matthias calmly. 'And I will explain myself in such simple terms that even the biggest moron in the world, who might be present here today, can understand what I have said.'

As Matthias had said the words *the biggest moron in the world* he had raised his left hand (while his right hand rested casually on the hilt of his wand) and pointed the forefinger of that left hand directly at Phelan, thus making his identification of Phelan plain if unspoken. Everyone present understood that Matthias was adopting the principle that you might as well be *hanged for a sheep as for a lamb*, given that Phelan was obviously going to torture him to death anyway.

Still confident that he would have Matthias in his power and screaming in pain before the sun went down on that day, Phelan inclined his head, and said: 'Very well, then explain yourself, miscreant Raspero, before I lose patience and order my troops into action.'

'In the castle behind me,' Matthias said, waving his left hand in the air to point vaguely behind him (while his right hand remained resting casually on the hilt of his wand), 'there once lived the eleventh Baron of Raspero, Etienne, who contemplated the nature and the limits of monarchical authority while discussing the clauses of the forthcoming Constitution of Westrigonia with his friends, Xanthe, Zahra, Yermolai, Uffe, Hartmut, among others. They all agreed that if the Vidaldmeet should need to discuss the monarchy of Westrigonia, then that meeting should take place without duress. Are you understanding everything I am saying, Phelan, or are you failing to grasp these simple statements? I only ask because you are obviously a moron.'

Phelan had stiffened, as if his confidence was fading, but he said nothing.

'They therefore put a clause into the Constitution, Clause Seven, which said that if a member of the Vidaldmeet should table a motion for a debate on the conduct of the monarchy with regard to the continuance of that monarchy, that member of the Vidaldmeet should be immune from any form of impediment, including arrest, until that debate was concluded. Are you still managing to follow my very simple statements, Phelan? Or are you such a moron that you fail to comprehend what I am saying?'

Phelan continued to say nothing, but the dawning comprehension on his face was eloquent enough.

'Yesterday, I went to the Vidaldmeet, and tabled this motion. The debate is going to be held later this month. Until then, you cannot arrest me. It therefore follows, Phelan, that your arrest warrant is invalid. If there is anything about my argument that you fail to understand, say so now.'

Matthias and Phelan locked eyes while the silence grew all around them. Matthias was perfectly content to wait. He understood that this time belonged to him. It was clear even to Phelan that the longer this silence continued, the more apparent it was that he, the Chevalier Phelan, Director-General of the State Bureau of Security, had nothing to say with regard to his attempted arrest of Matthias. He was starting to look like a beaten man in the eyes of those watching, and it was this impression which Phelan now had to deal with.

Phelan made his calculations. If he challenged Matthias on this point, and it was indeed the clause of constitutional law which Matthias claimed, then he would look foolish, and to look foolish for a man like Phelan was to be one step away from the grave. But on the other hand, he could not be defeated on any grounds other than the law. Phelan reached his conclusion at the exact moment which the watching Matthias anticipated.

'The written evidence for my statement now follows,' Matthias said loudly just as Phelan was opening his mouth to request this very evidence. By taking the words out of Phelan's mouth in this manner, Matthias was demonstrating his command of the situation. 'Steward, take this document over to this officer of the law.' Matthias used the document which he was holding in his left hand to gesture towards Phelan.

The Steward of Raspero carried the document over to Phelan and withdrew, trembling slightly. A lifetime of service to the barony of Raspero gave him the backbone to stand by his master's side in his defiance of Phelan, but Dacre Rachelle was a nervous wreck nonetheless. Everyone knew who Phelan was.

Phelan read through the document briefly. It was indeed a Clause Seven motion on the conduct of the monarchy, counter-signed by the Speaker of the Vidaldmeet. Phelan was trapped.

'It would follow from this, miscreant Raspero, that if you fail to turn up for this debate at the Vidaldmeet, your lands and title are forfeit,' Phelan said grimly, trying to save face by being threatening.

The more intelligent observers of this drama uttered a collective (but silent!) sigh of tension released upon recognition of the true meaning of Phelan's statement, which was in effect an acknowledgement of defeat. No matter how grimly he spoke, Phelan was not going to arrest Matthias today. He had accepted that this arrest now lay in the future. Phelan had been beaten again.

'I will turn up for this debate,' Matthias said serenely, like a saint who had placed his faith in a power greater than the temporal. 'I will be there, Phelan, but you will not be. You are not a member of the Vidaldmeet, are you?'

'I will be waiting for you outside the Vidaldmeet,' Phelan said as grimly as before. 'Trust me.' The Director-General of the State Bureau of

Security had a fixed staring look on his face as he looked at Matthias. 'And it is there that I will finally arrest you, miscreant Raspero. You cannot run away from me forever.'

'Time will tell,' Matthias said in a relaxed manner. 'Now, Phelan, you are standing in the presence of the Baron of Raspero in Raspero itself, and the Baron of Raspero has this to say to you. Get out of my domains!'

Once again there was silence, and once again it was Matthias who was the master of this silence and Phelan who was its subject. All the clocks in the world ticked away.

'Before I slap you,' Matthias added pleasantly, drawing his wand slowly but meaningfully.

The State Bureau of Security agents drew their wands as one man.

All the clocks in the world stopped ticking.

'The day will come, miscreant Raspero, when you will be asked to answer for everything you have said and done,' Phelan said in an almost casual tone, as if this matter had now become settled beyond debate. 'The heavens help you then.'

Phelan turned away, Matthias didn't move, all the clocks in the world started ticking again and one by one and two by twos and three by threes, the State Bureau of Security agents turned away to follow their master.

Phelan strode away towards his flying carriage, his face a mask of impassive impersonality, as if the stone blocks that made up his cheeks and lips were grinding each other into immobility. The Baron of Raspero was proving to be a slippery eel, but Phelan told himself that he could wait. He had waited before, and he had always gained his goal. This time would be no different, the Chevalier told himself.

But time itself was running out for Phelan, if he had but known how to read the future. But who can read the future?

3:20 PM, Tuesday 16 July 1875 A. F

General Kefirez had finished giving his account of his second visit to the barony of Raspero to Their Majesties Frederick and Yolande. The Chevalier Phelan stood to one side, his face impassive.

Eleanor listened to Kefirez's account in a whirlwind of emotion. She understood the significance of what Matthias had done far more quickly than her parents. Her parents had never heard of Clause Seven of the Constitution. Eleanor felt betrayed by Matthias. An attack on her parents' claim to the throne was an attack on Eleanor's status as Crown Princess. Eleanor felt that nothing would ever be the same again.

'<But how can this Raspero simply move a motion of no confidence like this? Surely it cannot be allowed. What are his grounds for acting thus? This is simply absurd,>' Frederick complained.

'<Unfortunately, it is a legitimate tactic for Raspero to employ,>' Cadwalader observed. '<But it would seem on the face of it to be a stalling tactic intended merely to evade arrest. Raspero himself must know that nothing can come of it.>'

'<So by now he has run for it, I presume,>' Frederick said indifferently.

'<Oh no, Sire, far from it. If he runs for it his lands and title are forfeit. No, he will turn up for the Vidaldmeet debate. He has no choice.>'

'<Well, he *could* choose not to come,>' Frederick insisted. '<He could run for it and save his skin.>'

'<He will not run, Sire. Trust me. He will come for the debate which he has nominated.>'

'<You will excuse me, I am sure, if I insist on a point of logic,>' Frederick said obstinately. '<He *could* choose not to come.>'

'<Ah, now I understand the point made by your Majesty. Yes, it is a logical possibility that he *could* choose not to come. But it will not happen. He *will* come for the debate. It is an *actual* impossibility that he does not come.>'

Frederick grunted in exasperation at never being able to understand these impossible Westrigonians.

'And after this debate, as he leaves the Vidaldmeet building, I will place him under arrest,' Kefirez said confidently. 'He cannot dodge me forever.'

'<He has dodged you so far,>' Frederick commented.

'He is a monkey, no doubt about it,' Kefirez conceded, as if being a monkey was a good thing, 'but his luck will run out.'

Phelan remained silent, a fact noticed by no-one except Eleanor and Kefirez.

'<And when he is arrested, what then?>' Frederick wanted to know.

'<He must be questioned closely concerning his role in his father's plot against your royal persons,>' Cadwalader pronounced, '<followed by a swift execution immediately after being found guilty. Matters like this can't be allowed to fester. Examples must be made for the purpose of deterrence, and the drama brought to an end with a satisfyingly definitive conclusion. No conclusion to an affair like this is more satisfying and definitive than a headless body lying on the ground with its formerly attached head standing next to it impaled on a stake. This is like the end of the third act of a play. Dramatic conventions apply in circumstances like this, in politics as much as the stage.>'

'<Exactly!>' Frederick agreed enthusiastically. '<That is well observed. *Very* well observed.>'

Cadwalader made a little bow. '<I thank your Royal Personage for such praise, poorly merited though it is by my humble self.>'

'<Yes,>' Frederick said absently, '<but, um, we are quite sure about the, ah, thorough integrity of such a policy as this.>'

'<Oh, indeed, beyond doubt. I assure Your Majesty that there will be no backlash, no consequences, no complications of any kind. This matter will be done and dusted in a matter of weeks, and will not return to trouble us again. We are only nearly out of patience. Raspero is nearly out of time.>'

Eleanor felt conflicted emotions on hearing this. She could not see how Matthias could possibly come to the Vidaldmeet and escape arrest yet again. Yet she knew as well as Cadwalader that Matthias would come. It was a matter of honour for him not to forfeit his lands and title. He literally had no choice. The entire weight of history, which constituted the entire mass of the universe, directed him along this path. If Matthias failed to come, he would never be able to live with himself afterwards. Not to come was simply unthinkable. He could no more not come than a man could lift up a mountain on his own. He would come. Only those of an Anglashian mentality, like her parents, could fail to see this.

It would be the end of Matthias. His death was certain. Eleanor steeled herself to face the next few weeks. Despite everything Matthias had done to offend her, she found that the prospect of his imminent death made her tremble inwardly.

11:00 AM, Monday 29 July 1875 A. F

The day was blue-sky sunny with white puffy clouds overhead. Matthias departed for his Vidaldmeet meeting with a sense as of a life determined by fate. Whatever would be would be. Fortuna ruled all.

Matthias arrived in the Krastienst Portal in very different circumstances to his last journey. While booking his trip through the Portal under Special Priority as before but this time under his own name, he found on this occasion that General Kefirez, Chevalier Phelan, and a number of other Westrigonian officials were waiting for him in the Waiting Room of the Portal.

Matthias acknowledged their presence with a raised eyebrow as he stepped out of the Portal, his right hand resting casually on the hilt of his wand.

'Greetings, Lord Raspero,' General Kefirez said calmly. 'I see you are a man of your word.'

'Did you really expect me to be anything but?' Matthias replied in an unsmiling manner. He was drawing attention to the implicit insult of Kefirez's praise. He was ready to slap Kefirez for what he had said.

Phelan made haste to move things along without distractions. 'None of us expected anything else from the Baron of Raspero,' Phelan said loudly so that everyone present could hear him. Phelan was as happy as a spider whose web had just trembled under the impact of its latest arrival. Phelan had no doubt now that he would have Matthias in his custody before the sun had set on this day, and in this way Phelan would resolve this matter, which had become a loose end in danger of becoming its own end. A man as tidy as the Chevalier did not like loose ends for this very reason.

'The day will come, Phelan, when you will not dare to speak to me except when asked to do so. But perhaps you will whine that I have not slapped you yet.'

Matthias glared at Phelan and Phelan glared at Matthias. No-one dared to say anything.

'Get out of my way, Phelan, or I will slap you until you beg me to remind you of what your name once was.'

With this belligerent statement, Matthias set forth for the exit, almost shouldering Phelan aside as he left. Phelan was left staring after the departing Matthias with a face buckled with fury. Yet by reminding himself that he would have Matthias in his custody before the day was done, Phelan swallowed even this latest insult and set forth after his latest enemy with a determined step. Kefirez and the others followed.

Matthias exited the Portal and strolled along Calogera Street, the same route along which his father and brother had been assassinated. The entire street had been cordoned off, and throngs of excited onlookers observed the young baron as he walked along. Matthias eyed them askance as he made his baronial passage towards the Vidaldmeet, feeling that they were being impertinent by continually staring at him, but otherwise he ignored them. Kefirez and Phelan and the other officials followed Matthias close behind. As Matthias approached Wafiwade Square, and came to where Calogera Street entered the Square, he came to a halt.

Wafiwade Square was filled with the army of Kefirez, aligned in a phalanx outside the front entrance of the Vidaldmeet. The very regimentation of this multitude could have inspired dread in many an onlooker, but Matthias burst out laughing.

Kefirez and Phelan came abreast of the Baron of Raspero.

'You are amused, Lord Raspero?' Kefirez said pleasantly.

'What are all these soldiers for?' Matthias asked.

'They are here to arrest you, Lord Raspero,' Kefirez said, as pleasantly as before.

Matthias laughed again, almost too merrily. 'There are way too many of them to arrest me, General Kefirez. By the end of this day, you will understand this. But by then, you will face your own arrest on charges of treason.'

Matthias turned to face General Kefirez, and there was no humour or good will in his expression as he locked eyes with his opponent. 'But perhaps you feel, General Kefirez, that your failure to arrest me on this day, by your own bungling, will be overlooked by those who will seek to find someone to blame for what has gone wrong.'

Kefirez said nothing in reply to this in-your-face statement. He was, truth to say, a little astonished.

Phelan watched this human drama with his usual detachment, making his usual calculations. If the cold-blooded creature that was Phelan was ever amused, he was amused then.

Matthias turned away and set forth for the Vidaldmeet along the open path between the ranked soldiers.

Kefirez followed, his mind set upon how to entrench the ranks of his soldiers so that nothing and no-one could get through.

It was this which was exactly what Matthias wanted him to think.

Phelan was thinking that he was going to leave everything concerning the arrest of Matthias to Kefirez, after which Phelan would take custody of Matthias after a handover from Kefirez to Phelan. Given everything that had gone wrong so far, Kefirez could take full responsibility for this matter, and as far as Phelan was concerned, his best policy was to stay in the background and do nothing for the time being while others played their roles. Phelan thought it best to wait.

It was this which was exactly what Matthias wanted him to think.

11:55 AM, Monday 29 July 1875 A. F

The Debating Hall of the Vidaldmeet was the heart of the building. It was this hall that people thought of when they referred to *the Vidaldmeet*. The Vidaldmeet as a whole comprised a large assemblage of rooms, hallways, amenities, libraries, reading rooms, study halls and administration offices, but at the very centre of the building was the Debating Hall.

The vaulted ceiling above the chamber was a smaller-scale reproduction of the domed top of the building. The fresco on the ceiling represented the night-time sky at midnight of the 30 June 1267, which was the national day of Westrigonia, the day of its founding. The chamber was circular in shape, and divided in two halves. Along the diameter of this dividing line was a wooden mahogany wall made of panelled sections, and in the centre of this wall was raised the podium at which sat the Speaker. To either side of the Speaker were scribes and experts in constitutional law. In the semi-circle before the Speaker were arcs of curved benches, with bronze plaques inset at regularly spaced intervals on the benches. These plaques displayed the family names of the members of the Vidaldmeet. There were fifty plaques for the fifty members of the Vidaldmeet, but one seat was always vacant. This was because the Speaker was drawn from the ranks of the Vidaldmeet. He was chosen by lot, the lottery in question being that every member of the Vidaldmeet had to draw a ball from a barrel in which there were forty-nine black balls and one white ball. The member who drew the white ball had to be Speaker, unless he declined the honour, in which case the lottery was held again. (If the same member drew the white ball again, he was put to death. This had never yet happened in the whole of recorded history.) Once accepted, the Speakership was held until death or the incapacity to discharge the necessary duties.

Along the walls all around the circular chamber were alcoves with inset statues of various distinguished Westrigonian personages of the past. Etienne, Matthias's ancestor, the eleventh Baron of Raspero, was one of them. The other semi-circle of the chamber, behind the Speaker's back, was deliberately and ostentatiously empty. There was nothing to be seen but a polished stone floor below the empty air. The statues continued around the sides. There were three hundred and sixty of them equally spaced around the whole chamber, and before them on the ground was a strip of polished black obsidian which could be walked along in a reverential manner, which took place when a newly inducted member of the Vidaldmeet swore his oath of loyalty to the Vidaldmeet, an oath which bound him for life and from which only death could release him.

Directly below the Speaker was the lectern from which the Vidaldmeet was addressed. Only members were allowed to speak at sessions of the Vidaldmeet. Once everyone had settled down and the hubbub of muttering conversations was at the level of the background drone of a multitude of bees, the Speaker called forth the Baron of Raspero to speak. An immediate hush descended on the chamber.

Matthias strode confidently to the lectern. The concerted gaze of the full session of the Vidaldmeet was fodder for the fires of his egoism on that day and in that place. He felt like a hero, and what hero did not want their heroism acknowledged by the admiring multitude? Indeed, what was the point of a heroic act that was not sung about, let alone even witnessed? If a tree falls down in the forest and no-one sees it fall, did it ever really fall?

'My fellow members of the Vidaldmeet,' Matthias said loudly, making sure that everyone could hear him, including those who were elderly and a little hard of hearing. 'I am the thirty-seventh Baron of Raspero, and a Westrigonian patriot. I move a motion for the due consideration of the conduct of the monarchs of Westrigonia. Should they continue as they are? I say not. I say that the Vidaldmeet shall vote today to depose Frederick and Yolande.'

There was a collective shudder, almost a silent groan, from all those present on hearing these words. Everyone had known this was coming, indeed that was why the Vidaldmeet was so unusually full to capacity, but to actually hear the words of doom proclaimed was something else. History had been made, and everyone present had witnessed it being made. They all had their money's worth right then and there. What was done was done.

Matthias settled into a long-winded, fairly dull speech extolling the virtues of Westrigonia, interspersed with references to the distinguished history of his own family, and ending with a platitudinous vision of the future. He gave no reason to depose Frederick and Yolande, nor did he present the Vidaldmeet with anything remotely resembling a rationale for his own motion. But he was understood with perfect clarity by everyone present. This whole business of the vote of no confidence was a dodge to escape the claws of Phelan, who was even then waiting outside the Vidaldmeet to arrest Matthias. They had, like the country as a whole, been following the story of Matthias's stand-off with Phelan with fascination. From the moment Matthias had left Cayetano Prison and become wanted by the authorities, he had become a national figure, but from the moment he had slapped Phelan, he had become a legend. Everyone knew that Matthias had made plans to leave Raspero and go into exile, leaving the Steward of Raspero as caretaker of the barony; but everyone also knew that he had to get out of the Vidaldmeet and get back to Raspero first in order to go into this arranged exile. This was like a sporting contest which had the audience on the edge of their seats. Indeed, there were even bets on the outcome, and Matthias's chances of escaping were, sad to say, judged to be not better than 73 to 1 by those with their tables of calculation laid out on the table-top before them.

There was little drama in the ensuing proceedings. Various members of the Vidaldmeet stood up to declare entirely predictable decisions on whether they supported or opposed the motion. Baron Rayerfeld excitedly supported Matthias, but few others did. The vote went against Matthias in a manner that the bookmakers could have (and in fact already had) predicted to a money-making precision. It was 45 votes against, 4 in favour.

Matthias arose to his feet once the Speaker had declared this outcome and said loudly: 'I claim by right to speak in conclusion on this matter.' He promptly strode to the lectern, looking far more confident than he in fact felt.

Everything (*everything!*) now hinged on his earlier blackmail of the Speaker. If Lord Zelimir sent Matthias out of the Sinners Door, Matthias had won, but if Lord Zelimir did not, Matthias would find himself in Phelan's cold and clammy embrace before the sun went down on that day. Rationally, in a logical sense, Matthias felt that Lord Zelimir would consider it prudent to obey his blackmailer; but logic did not always win through.

'And so the vote is cast and the day is done!' Matthias shouted. 'And who is to blame? It is this man, this creature, this offspring of a dog and a donkey, who is to blame.' He raised his left hand in the air with his forefinger pointing straight behind him at Lord Zelimir while uttering the phrase *this offspring of a dog and a donkey,* so as to make his intended meaning unspeakably plain. 'He has sat there on his fat posterior with his grinning monkey face,' Matthias continued, mixing not so much his metaphors as his animal species, 'with his jibber-jabber yellowed teeth and his noxious smell, his insufferable stupidity and his unbelievable, utterly unbelievable, craven spineless capitulation to the forces of imbecility marching up his throat and around the cracked bowl of his cranium. It is this miserable misbegotten spawn of a rat in a drainpipe who can be held fairly and squarely to blame for this day's debacle, this miserable misbegotten Speaker of the Vidaldmeet' – Matthias pointed with a dramatic flourish of his forefinger directly at Lord Zelimir again – 'who I bring forth to your notice as a creature beyond even the stupidity of the multitude of this day or any day. I stand here, with a heart pure and free of darkness, an innocent man unjustly pursued by the forces of darkness incarnate here and now in this day and in this place by this grotesque gargoyle of a Speaker who is come from those of his ilk among the denizens of the infernal regions. I stand here today an innocent man, free of sin, while this clown, this muckraked miscreant who has arisen from the depths of his own self-administered pleasure, sits there on his seat of imbecility like a vomited up knob of a hyena's intestinal tract. Let this be understood in this time and place by all who are present. I have spoken so that you shall all know the truth of this matter. I now leave this place with my head held high in the sight of all.' Having fired out all this fighting talk, Matthias turned around and looked directly at Zelimir, perched in his eyrie above the lectern.

Matthias and Lord Zelimir locked eyes. The members of the Vidaldmeet, taken aback by Matthias's unexpected tirade, looked back and forth between the two figures as if they were duelling wandfighters. There was a silence throughout the venerable and august debating chamber of the Vidaldmeet. Even the statues along the sides held their breath and did not dare to move.

Behind the line of sight of the members of the Vidaldmeet, at an oblique angle to the plane of their shared cognition, there took place an exchanged understanding between Matthias and the Speaker. The scroll which Matthias had laid on the Speaker's desk two weeks ago had in fact been made up of two sheets of paper, the one being the necessary legal submission for the motion of no confidence in the Vidaldmeet, the other being a letter (the genuine original, not a copy) written by the Speaker's father Lord Zelimir to a certain lady of the day (or night) which referred to another letter written by this lady to Lord Zelimir (the father, not the son) which had certain statements in ink which were unmistakably plain to any legal mind enthroned over a court of law. Matthias had proven that his blackmail could be backed up by written evidence, and this evidence could destroy Lord Zelimir. This was the basis of Matthias's rationally calculated confidence that the Speaker would play along with Matthias's scheme.

But there was always the unexplainable, however it could not be explained, to be prepared for by those wary of the sudden twisting and turning of the accustomed and normal ways of the world. What if the Speaker, for no apparent reason at all, should decide to throw Matthias to the wolves of Phelan regardless of the personal consequences? Who was to say that this could not happen, or would not happen?

It was this possibility which the Speaker's silence spoke of as he gazed at Matthias. "Do not *ever* try this again!" his silent gaze said, "or I will pull down the pillars of the world so that the sky will fall upon both of us and it will be the last thing you ever perceive in this world. You may blackmail me, but it will only be for this one time."

Matthias's gaze in return said: "Think what you want to think. I will keep my counsel."

The stand-off was complete. There was no give, no take, no movement, only an implacable opposition between the two.

Had Matthias given any other answer, he would have lost everything even then and there, on the brink of victory. But honour was satisfied. Each understood that their personal survival was secondary to other considerations, and for this reason, and for this reason alone, the Speaker could safeguard his personal survival by giving way to Matthias's blackmail.

'Baron Matthias Raspero,' the Speaker intoned with an ascending octavial progression, like a figure in an opera about to launch into an aria, 'you are so far from sinless that you will leave here by the Sinners Door.' The Speaker pointed, with a dramatic flourish of his forefinger that was an exact mirror image of Matthias's earlier finger-flourishing, to the other side of the chamber behind Matthias, and said: 'Now, be gone from my sight, sinner that you are.'

This was the standard formula by which the Speaker of the Vidaldmeet sent out a member of the Vidaldmeet through the Sinners Door. It was so rarely used that hardly anyone ever even thought of it. No-one within living memory had ever heard this sentence passed. Matthias had dug up one of the Vidaldmeet's most obscure procedures. No-one had been sent out of the Sinners Door for one hundred and twenty-three years, so it was an exit more referred to jokingly than actually used.

Matthias said defiantly, with a sneer, 'I see that you do not dare to send me hence in a *shamed silence*. No doubt you are fearful lest your voice should quake as you make such a demand. No, you will sit there shaking from head to toe while you declare your timid decree.'

'Baron Matthias Raspero,' the Speaker intoned as operatically as before, 'you shall leave this place by the Sinners Door in a shamed silence. I am the Speaker and I have spoken. Let all hear and obey, for in this place the Speaker's word is law.'

Matthias bowed his head as if overwhelmed by the force of this occasion of his public downfall. The implications of what was happening were spreading through the brains of the members of the Vidaldmeet like an electrical storm through a forest of lightning conductors. People were catching on. If Matthias left through the Sinners Door, he was leaving the building on the other side to where Kefirez and his men were waiting to arrest him. But had Kefirez thought to put troops outside the Sinners Door? That was the key point. No-one knew because no-one had thought to check.

Lord Camdenshall, shifting in his seat as if he had ants in his pants, was trying to catch the Speaker's eye, but with no luck. (As it happened, the Speaker was deliberately not letting anyone catch his eye.) Lord Camdenshall was eager-beaver to race through the front door of the Vidaldmeet to tell General Kefirez that Matthias Raspero was leaving through the back door. But the *shamed silence* which the Speaker had declared meant that no-one could say anything until Matthias had departed.

Matthias turned away from the lectern with a suitably composed face and walked sedately, with his head bowed as required by tradition, towards the Sinners Door, which was an unobtrusive door sandwiched between the statues of Ogden the Virtuous and Katell the Indecisive. The Speaker flourished his wand to open the Sinners Door as Matthias approached, and flourished it again to close the door as Matthias went through it out of sight.

Camdenshall was on his feet at that very instant. 'I leave this assembly without delay!' he shouted and ran, *ran*, for the exit to the Hall of Reception. A general laugh rose into the air behind his departing back, followed by a hubbub of noise as everyone present turned to talk to their neighbour about what they had just witnessed. Most people now thought that Matthias would get away from Phelan. By now, everyone felt that they had more than their money's worth. They all felt ahead of the game. All that remained now was to go home and wait for the next news item as to whether Matthias had gotten away or not.

The Speaker sat where he was, his hand holding his gavel, waiting to declare these proceedings closed. His role in these proceedings would be speculated over, but nothing would ever be proved. The Speaker would go to his peaceful grave many many years hence without hindrance, for the truth would not emerge for a century or so. The Speaker could live with the cloud of suspicion that would hang over him, for not even Phelan would dare move against a figure as powerful as the Speaker without clear evidence of wrongdoing. After all, perhaps the Speaker had really been so foolish as to fall for Matthias's ploy; who could say?

'I declare these proceedings closed!' the Speaker declared and brought down his gavel with a dramatic *bang!* He rose to his feet, followed by all those present; the Speaker bowed to the assembly, the assembly bowed back, and the day was done, at least for the Vidaldmeet.

Matthias's day was far from over. He had a world of escaping still to do.

CHAPTER FOURTEEN

A jiggle and a higgle and a miggle,
That is how a woman's cleavage,
Turns about itself on its own axis.
Don't go there, my friend.
Once you're in, there's no way out.
Frankie the Villain

11:00 AM, Monday 29 July 1875 A. F

Eleanor had made a special point of visiting her Westrigonian friend Honourable Filippa Lacey, who lived with her parents in a large spacious well-appointed apartment on Wafiwade Square, one of the most desirable and prestigious places to live in the city of Krastienst, and which also just happened to have a commanding view of one of the most eagerly sought after events of the day, the arrival of Baron Matthias Raspero at the Vidaldmeet. Eleanor was not alone amongst Filippa's friends in having realized the excellence of the vantage point provided by her parent's long wide balcony with its ornate iron railings and superb view over Wafiwade Square. Numerous other fourteen and fifteen-year-old girls had turned up, dressed in such a variety of reds and blues and greens and yellows that it looked as though the Lacey's balcony had been over-run by a flock of brightly coloured birds. There was a party atmosphere in the air, a bubbling of voices, cheerful looks and lots of jostling for a good position at the railing from which to see the show.

No-one jostled Eleanor. Being the Crown Princess had its privileges. Eleanor had a Yadria telescope with her, the kind that was only the length of a fountain pen, and with this telescope she was able to see Matthias on his arrival as if he was standing right next to her. She had not seen him for three years, and while she remembered him well, she felt that she was seeing him with such new eyes as to be seeing him for the first time. She felt that she had not realized before how good looking he was. She was almost forcibly struck by this perception. She had half-forgotten his personal charm and manner of talking, but she was reminded now of the time in the Rose Garden when Matthias had kissed her as if it was only yesterday as she watched Matthias laughing and then making a comment of some kind to the nearby figure of General Kefirez. The Witch of Trentland knew then intuitively that Matthias had already made his plans to escape his would-be captors, and she knew further, as if the dispositions of the soldiers in the square had become a living Dagrun block of letters and numbers, that Matthias would succeed in escaping.

All around her she heard the other girls cooing and clucking over how good-looking the Baron of Raspero was, only to fall silent in a step-wise fashion. Eleanor did not need to lower her telescope and look in order to identify the nature of this sideways-looking silence. Everyone would be nudging each other and gesturing in her direction in order to point out that praise, even of something as ostensibly non-political as good looks, was inadvisable given that the Baron of Raspero was calling for Eleanor's parents to be dethroned.

The problem was now, as at other times, that of Eleanor's status as a Zoller-Abstein princess in Westrigonia. There were those Westrigonian families of the nobility who had aligned themselves with the new dispensation, such as the Lacey family; there were nationalists who detested anything and everything to do with foreigners in general and the Zoller-Abstein Protectorate in particular; and there was besides a cornucopia of differing political views that were bewildering in their kaleidoscopic configurations. But whatever the full complexities of the politics of Westrigonia, there was always for Eleanor the never-ending sense of feeling like a foreigner in a country which she had chosen as her own.

No matter how often she was in this position, Eleanor could never get entirely accustomed to it. There were a variety of strategies with which she had responded in the past, ranging from a direct engagement with the issues involved, which never properly worked out, to a resolute ignoring of the situation as if it did not exist, which never worked out either. Direct arguments, indirect arguments, arguments alternating between direct and indirect comments and arguments which were deliberately nonsensical went nowhere, although at times she wondered if the nonsensical arguments might have made the most impact.

Seeing Matthias in the distance had affected Eleanor emotionally in some way which she could not define, leaving her unmotivated to be accommodating and understanding. She was in no mood to be pointed out as a foreigner who did not belong in Westrigonia. She was ready to hit someone.

'What do you think, Your Royal Highness?' Filippa asked after a while during which no-one was saying anything. The silence had come to seem uncomfortable. She had not wanted to speak. She felt obliged to be the one to say something given that her parents were hosting this gathering.

'He's not bad looking for a rebel,' Eleanor said as if conceding this point grudgingly. 'What do you think, Filippa?'

'Oh, the same,' Filippa said immediately in reply.

Eleanor could see in her peripheral vision a slight stiffening of posture as if of a stifling of giggles amongst some of the girls behind her to the right, and given a knowledge of the limited repertoire of witticisms of those in her peer group, she deduced that someone had silently mouthed *the same* in order to mock Filippa's response. Eleanor turned around quite calmly, and by inspecting the postures of the girls as a physicist inspects the ripples of a pond made by a falling stone, she identified the girl at the centre of all this attention as Honourable Mallory Everfall. Eleanor looked directly at Mallory, who tried to look innocent.

'What do you think, Mallory? Is it,' Eleanor silently mouthed the words *the same,* 'or is it something . . . *different?*'

Mallory's bravado fled. Mockers are never courageous. It is why they are mockers. She looked about her for help, but no-one seemed disposed to come to her assistance.

'What's the matter, Mallory?' Eleanor asked acidly. 'Cat got your tongue?'

Mallory stood there in a frozen posture. Eleanor quite deliberately turned her back on her enemy and looked back over the Wafiwade square.

The other girls would have laughed if they haven't felt so nervous. There was the silence of people not laughing out of fear which Filippa's mother sought to charm away by saying: 'I will now bring you all some refreshments.'

The girls all muttered their appreciation.

The awkward silence returned.

Eleanor knew that later, with her courage returned, Mallory would be saying that there was *no way* Eleanor could have seen her mouth those words, with everyone eagerly agreeing. The rumour that Eleanor was a witch would grow larger.

Filippa's mother came with her servants and trays of refreshments. The girls all helped themselves, and tried to chatter, but the earlier festive atmosphere was gone.

'Will you be staying for lunch, Your Royal Highness?' Filippa's mother asked with an air of false kindness.

'No, thank you, Lady Lacey,' Eleanor replied. 'I will stay to watch the Baron of Raspero's escape, and then I will return to the Palace.'

'Oh,' Filippa's mother said, 'well, ah, how very, yes, very charming.'

'Isn't it?' Eleanor said with a falsely pleased smile.

Filippa's mother turned and fled.

'What do you mean, Your Royal Highness?' asked Honourable Hadia Cadence. 'Will the Baron of Raspero really escape?'

'Didn't you see him laugh earlier?' Eleanor said impatiently. 'What did you think that was about?'

'What was it about?' Honourable Dafina Hanga asked eagerly.

'Let us wait and see,' Eleanor asked with an air of finality, and turned back to the railing and gazed out over Wafiwade Square. She ignored all further attempts to engage her in conversation until those attempts died away.

Time passed. Eleanor ignored everything said to her, even by Filippa's mother, and so was left alone by everyone, who began slowly to chatter amongst themselves once more. Then came the moment that Eleanor had been waiting for all this time: the figure of Lord Camdenshall, long familiar to her from his visits to the Palace, came running out of the large front doors of the Vidaldmeet and down the steps, gesticulating wildly and talking, from the looks of things, even more wildly; and there followed, like a ballet conducted by arthritic dancers, the slow, tortuous unwinding of the soldiers locked-in to their formations in order to be sent hither and thither by an agitated Kefirez.

Eleanor knew then that Matthias had indeed escaped, just as she had known he would. Almost dispassionately, as if she were watching herself through her own inner telescope, she could not help but note an enormous cheerfulness flood the heart of her being like a room with large windows is flooded with warm sunlight.

Eleanor made her departure shortly afterwards, and returned to the Palace.

6:30 PM, Monday 29 July 1875 A. F

Eleanor sat at the side in the Throne Room, chatting to the occasional courtier passing-by, until her parents came in, having been summoned to hear the latest urgent matter of state.

Cadwalader was delighted to inform Their Majesties that Matthias's motion of no confidence in their rule had been crushed in the Vidaldmeet 45-4. He made much of this show of support for the Zoller-Abstein monarchs of Westrigonia. He spoke at some length about the complete and utter devastation of the hopes of Westrigonian nationalism by the outcome of this vote. He made it sound as if peace would now rule throughout the whole universe forever until the end of time as a result of this tremendous victory over this impertinent insubordination of a member of the baronial order. Eleanor enjoyed the show Cadwalader put on, given that it was at least in part intended to defer having to discuss the next obvious point of order. But that could not be put off indefinitely.

'<I now leave this briefing to be continued by General Kefirez,>' Cadwalader said, '<who was entrusted, as of course we all recall, with the arrest of Baron Matthias Raspero.>' With a bow, Cadwalader retired.

Eleanor noted Cadwalader's skill as a politician. She detested the man as a person. For some reason, the physical presence of Cadwalader always made her skin crawl. However, she noted, as a job well done, how Cadwalader had made a favourable impression upon the monarchs of Westrigonia by flattering them over the great victory which they had won, without actually having troubled to lift a finger themselves, while leaving the bad news to be brought to their ears by someone else, who Cadwalader had already made plain was responsible for what had happened. Cadwalader was left smelling of roses, while Kefirez would be left smelling of what made the roses grow.

Like the soldier that he was, General Kefirez bit the bullet without hesitation.

'It is with the utmost regret,' Kefirez said gloomily, 'that I must inform your Majesties that the Baron of Raspero has escaped arrest.'

This gloomy statement was translated from Westrigonian into Anglashian by the translator. Eleanor subjected the translation with her usual critical eye, and concluded, as she had done so often before, that she could have done a better job herself. Still, the point was clear enough.

'<What, again?>' asked Frederick.

'I am afraid so, Sire.'

'<And how did that happen?>'

'It turned out that there was an exit from the Vidaldmeet in addition to the four exits of which we were informed. Our soldiers were stationed at these exits, but not at the additional secret exit by means of which Raspero left the building and got past our soldiers.'

'The Baron of Raspero got past *your* soldiers,' Phelan said loudly.

Kefirez's eyes shifted uneasily about the room as the corrected possessive pronoun was translated to Their Majesties.

'<Well, where is Raspero now?>' Frederick asked in a petulant tone of sullen exasperation. He was fed up with this entire business. He had been promised a headless body worthy of the final act of an opera, only to be let down. But even that disappointment was not Frederick's main complaint. The most annoying part of all this were the seemingly endless interruptions to his normal daily routine. Day in and day out, he found himself summoned to the Throne Room for an emergency briefing on the Raspero affair. For example, he was supposed at this moment in time right now to be getting ready to go to a performance of Mozart's Horn Concertos. And was he doing this? No, far from it, he was spending his time on matters of governance, an obligation which he found tedious at the best of times, let alone when he found himself missing a musical performance which he had been looking forward to all week.

'As he cannot have left Krastienst by a portal, as both the public portal and the palace portal were inaccessible to him, and these are the only portals in the capital, we can be sure that he must either still be here in Krastienst or en route to a hiding place. We are looking for him everywhere.'

'<You might well be looking for him everywhere, but will you succeed in finding him?>'

'We are doing our very best,' Kefirez replied, avoiding making any such promises such as that of ever finding Raspero.

'<*You are doing your very best,*>' Frederick repeated nastily once Kefirez's reply had been translated, for once to Eleanor's satisfaction. '<How very reassuring! The matter is as good as settled, isn't it? All we have to do now is just wait for you to come up with the goods. And how long will that take?>'

'Might I suggest that we recommend to the First Protector that a reward of five million strada be offered for the apprehension of Baron Matthias Raspero?' Phelan asked. 'This will both increase the chances of Raspero being captured, and also make plain that this is an international affair, given that Raspero will almost certainly go abroad, either to Anglashia itself, where he attended school, or to a country with which the Raspero family has connections, of which there are several. He also must take care of his mother and sister, who will have to flee with him into exile. One way or another, a price on his head of such a magnitude is greatly to our advantage.'

'<Five million strada? De'Asterides might well find such a sum excessive.>'

'The Barony of Raspero is considered to have a fortune of ten million strada or so. The capture of Matthias Raspero would result in these funds being seized by the state. If the First Protector finds that he has to pay such a reward, he will be repaid double his expenditure; if he does not have to pay this reward, he has lost nothing.'

Frederick nodded. He could see the logic of Phelan's argument. '<I shall raise the matter with De'Asterides. But what else is to be done?>'

'I will raise this matter at the next meeting of the Council of State. I shall launch special investigations. And I shall take into the custody of the State Bureau all those whose conduct has been at the least suspicious. Raspero might well have had accomplices.'

Kefirez licked his dry lips, which only Phelan and Eleanor noticed.

'<Alright.>' Frederick took out his pocket watch and inspected the time. His temper was not improved by noting that he was far too late to have any hope at all of attending Mozart's Horn Concerto now. This blasted business of being a king had got in the way of his social life yet again. '<I take it that we are finished for the day?>'

Everyone bowed as Frederick and Yolande and Eleanor stood up and departed the Throne Room. A grim-faced Phelan went on his way accompanied by a white-faced Kefirez. Hope was now all that Kefirez possessed in the whole wide world.

Eleanor returned to her Chambers feeling so happy she could have skipped all the way. She had to give Matthias full credit, yet again, for being so clever. As the Westrigonian saying went, *his shadow was in the shape of a corkscrew.* Despite her best efforts to remain aloof, Eleanor could not help but feel proud of her ex-boyfriend. He had run rings around everybody yet again.

CHAPTER FIFTEEN

When Amaterasu said of Odsetseg that
He was born of the Wind to follow the Sun,
Tatienne asked: What does that even mean?
I have my answer ready for you,
If you are ready for it.
Ready?
Here it is:
It doesn't mean anything at all.
It just sounds good.
Frankie the Villain

2:20 PM, Monday 29 July 1875 A. F

Matthias wasted no time in leaving the Vidaldmeet. From the moment he stepped through the Sinners Door, he found himself in a narrow tunnel shaped corridor, crudely shaped by the architect Saranna (known for his sense of the dramatic) as if the "tunnel" was a natural rock formation leading out of a cave. Matthias drew his wand and sent himself flying along, reaching the door opening out onto Leudagar Street long before Camdenshall's feet had propelled himself halfway to the Vidaldmeet hallway.

Kefirez, who had never heard of such an obscure detail of architecture as the Sinners Door, had set his men outside the four exits of the Vidaldmeet that he did know about: the exits to Wafiwade Square, Leudagar Street, Goyathlay Street and Delara Street. Each exit was situated in the exact middle of the exact square that constituted the Vidaldmeet building. The Sinners Door was not listed in the public records, any more than wrong-doing was listed in the achievements of the nation. The exit of Matthias at this location was, therefore, not something for which the distinguished general had prepared any form of impediment. Stepping through this Sinners Door with a casual air, Matthias found himself near the corner of Leudagar Street and Goyathlay street. To his left was a large contingent of Kefirez's men, one hundred strong, under the command of Major Gerulf Finnguala, who had the main exit onto Leudagar Street completely surrounded. The soldiers were arranged in a complex series of overlapping and interlocking geometrical patterns rigidly fixed on this exit. Neither a mouse nor history's greatest wand-fighter could have gotten past them. Kefirez had come over to inspect Major Finnguala's arrangements, and found them satisfactory, and gone back to Wafiwade Square, but not before impressing upon Major Finnguala the absolute necessity of guarding this exit in a thoroughly professional manner. Major Finnguala and his men were thus highly motivated to guard the exit. They thought of nothing else. The sudden appearance of Matthias through a non-existent door caught them by surprise. Saranna, with many a chuckle, had disguised the outward appearance of the Sinners Door so as to look like the surrounding wall in which it was embedded, and so it seemed to the hapless Major Finnguala and his men as if Matthias had somehow emerged from the wall of the Vidaldmeet itself. This was already confusing. Nor did it help matters that Matthias gave the soldiers an indifferent look before calmly turning to his right and walking around the corner for all the world as if he was a normal person just like anyone else. This appearance of normality had the effect of further paralysing Major Finnguala's men. A guilty look and a sudden run for it would have galvanised them, but Matthias's calmness was itself calming. Even Major Finnguala, who after all was in charge of the military situation, took a moment to register what was going on and another moment to make his military decisions. Orders were shouted by Major Finnguala to pursue the fugitive, who by now had disappeared from view, but it took time for the soldiers to unlock themselves from their rigidly regimented positions guarding the door and begin the pursuit, given the fixedness of their initial formation. The amount of time given thereby to the fugitive was almost ridiculously generous, given the capabilities of the fugitive in question. Matthias, having gone around the corner, then strolled across the street in a relaxed manner, glancing across to his right to observe the soldiers guarding the Vidaldmeet's exit onto Goyathlay Street, as he walked towards the narrow cobblestoned alley leading down a sloping hill to Uladzimir Plaza. The soldiers, fixated as they were on guarding the Vidaldmeet exit onto Goyathlay Street, barely gave Matthias a look, not having seen him emerge from the Vidaldmeet and not at all realising who he was. The crowds of people thronging the street along the pavements, having come along to watch the show, made room for Matthias to step through them and enter the alley. They also had no idea who this wandering youth might be and paid him no attention, having come along to try to catch a glimpse of the legendary Baron of Raspero. The fugitive was already out of sight as the first of Major Finnguala's men came charging around the corner, which delayed their understanding of where to direct their pursuit. Eventually everyone worked out what was going on, but by then it was already much too late, because by the time the forces of law and order entered the alley where he had last been seen, the thirty-seventh Baron of Raspero was nowhere to be found.

Kefirez frantically sent his forces in all directions to shut down the entire city, which was pointless given that the entire city was *already* shut down. He already had the public Portal under guard, but he sent more men there anyway. He re-deployed the men under his command surrounding the Vidaldmeet to surround the entire city of Krastienst, especially the city exits, which were already guarded, but which would now be doubly guarded. He sent more men to places where he already had men and sent for more reinforcements to report for duty in order to have even more men to send out wherever he could. (He cursed out loud as well, which was something that he never did normally. Kefirez avoided cursing as a general rule, but not today.) Kefirez understood full well that Matthias now had to get out of Krastienst, and the fugitive's options were strictly limited. Matthias could leave through the public Portal, through the Portal at the Palace, or through the city gates, or via the flying carriages, whether public or private. There were no other options but these. Kefirez set forth to shut down every one of these options. The Baron of Raspero was not going to escape Kefirez's grasp here in Krastienst. Kefirez was determined upon that, for a number of reasons. Not least amongst them was the utterly silent figure of Chevalier Phelan standing by his side.

2:45 PM, Monday 29 July 1875 A. F

It might have been one hundred and twenty-three years before anyone had been sent through the Sinners Door, but it would only be eighty-one years before the secret of Matthias's escape from Krastienst would become a matter of public record. It happened this way.

Matthias walked briskly through the streets of Krastienst, heading southwards towards the most unlikely destination imaginable. It was the last place on earth that Kefirez would ever have thought of sending his soldiers, but that was not why Matthias was going there. Matthias was going to the Ankalybu because there was a Portal there.

Matthias had never been directly instructed in such matters as the means of detecting Portals, but he had long ago deduced how to do such things by reasoning from first principles. Phelan himself would have been unaware that such a thing was possible, but Phelan knew more of human nature than he did of wandlore. Phelan was also very likely unaware of just how much of the security arrangements of the Ankalybu Matthias had identified during his visit, with his hand unobtrusively resting on the hilt of his wand, having no idea at all the degree of expertise in wandlore which Matthias had mastered even at such a young age. In point of fact, it had only been the knowledge of how he could take down Phelan at any time which had kept Matthias's spirits up during his time with Phelan in the Ankalybu. Without his wandlore mastery Matthias would have felt as helpless as anyone else in such circumstances.

Matthias approached the Ankalybu, which was to all appearances completely deserted, and walked up the stairs to the second level where the entrance door was located. The large double doors were standing wide open, and Matthias walked boldly through these doors as if he came this way every day of his life. This was one reason why his attack succeeded.

Another reason was that no-one in the Ankalybu could ever have suspected that anyone, anyone at all, would ever dare to attack the Ankalybu. The State Bureau was much too feared. Matthias was alone, he was a youngster of fifteen or so, he was walking towards the Reception Desk apparently without a care in the world, and no-one recognised him as the Baron of Raspero who had slapped Phelan in public. The staff on duty at this point of the daily roster were not those who had been on duty when Matthias had come here before in Phelan's company. Matthias's phenomenal luck was holding yet again.

There were nine agents present in the Entrance Hall. There were two present standing on either side of the stairs leading down to the subterranean levels of the Ankalybu. There were three behind the Reception Desk. There were two agents by the front doors, one on each side. Finally, there were two agents by the stairs leading upwards to the higher floors.

Matthias was by now halfway towards the Reception Desk, with everyone present watching his progress in a relaxed, almost sleepy fashion, such was the everydayness of all this, when Matthias sprang into action. Pulling his wand, he flung himself like a forcefully-thrown projectile towards the Reception Desk, seizing hold simultaneously of all twelve karns around the wrists and ankles of the three agents behind the desk, each of whom was now flung violently through the air towards the three pairs of guards standing around the Entrance Hall as soon as Matthias had his feet planted on the wall behind the desk, standing there in an impossibly horizontal fashion before launching himself back towards the guards by the large double front doors. There were yells flying through the air along with the flying bodies, but the agents behind the Desk were now separated from the alarms systems they could have activated, and their wands were now securely held in Matthias's left hand. Step one was done.

All six guards standing around the Entrance Hall were both pulling their wands and being bowled over by the bodies slamming into them while Matthias was already taking hold of the wands from the guards by the doors, who were separately already flying through the air towards their comrades, who were knocked down again while struggling to their feet. The door to one of the rooms by the side of the Entrance Hall was opened while someone came in to see what all the fuss was about. He had his wand in hand, but only as a matter of form, and in a moment his wand was gone and in Matthias's hand while he flew through the air to join the others, and by this time Matthias had grabbed hold of all the wands of all the agents in the Entrance Hall. Step two could now be ticked off. With his special form of macchato, Matthias could tell that there were three more wands in the room from which the latest agent had exited, and so he plucked three agents from the floor and threw them into this room at the exact locations where these wands were located, following them in order to pluck the wands from the hand of these agents, after which he threw them out into the Entrance Hall.

There was a good deal of noise by this time, which Matthias did not find at all helpful. Throwing agents hither and thither against whatever surrounding walls seemed a convenient way of passing the time while Matthias waited for more agents to come, which only one did, rushing down the stairs only to be taken captive. Matthias busied himself binding and gagging his fourteen captives, lining them up along a wall. He then used his special macchato to scan the building he was in and identify the location of all the other wands that were present, but there was no movement that he could detect that presented a potential problem. The third step was now completed. All seemed well. Matthias's direct assault in the Ankalybu, being both unexpected and masterfully executed, had succeeded.

Matthias used his wand to thrown his captives one by one down the stairs leading to the sixth level of the Ankalybu, not sparing any of them multiple bruises and repeating this process to take everyone down to the seventh level, after which he threw each bound and gagged agent into a separate holding cell and bolted them in. Now came the critical moment on which everything depended. Matthias walked to the Portal, threw open the door, and inspected the interior. As he had suspected, it was a Portal which could transport two people at a time, the minimum size for a Portal. Matthias activated the controls with his wand, dialled in the number for the Raspero Portal, and pressed Send.

A Baron of Raspero expects his orders to be obeyed, but even so, Matthias was relived to see the switch acknowledging Receipt slide into place. Two minutes later, Peregrine Fusun and Odovacar Leofstan were standing by his side at the seventh level of the Ankalybu.

They looked cheerful and eager to take part in this adventure. Young Peregrine, eighteen years old, who had just proudly become a member of the Castle Guard, was caught up in a tense race with manly rivals to win the hand of Cara, the nubile daughter of Ualan, the inn-keeper who kept the premises of The Laughing Lion in Raspero. Anything that helped him look impressive was welcome to him, and that was what he hoped to achieve by being here today. (He could casually tell Cara how he and the young baron were like *that*.) His best friend Odovacar, following in his father's footsteps to become Master of the Raspero Portal, dreamed of going abroad to make his fortune in Trentland. Matthias had taken them to one side the day before, explained to them that he would pay them one thousand strada each to help him out in a special and highly confidential venture, ordered the Master of the Raspero Portal to follow certain instructions concerning the operation of the Portal on the following day, and in this way had laid his plans which were now coming to fruition.

'You will send me back to Raspero, after which you will leave this place,' Matthias ordered them. 'You will go directly to Oberon Street and take the flying carriage to Katia, where you will spend the night, after which you will make your way to Raspero. Here is one hundred strada for your travel expenses.' Matthias placed a bag containing money into the hand of Peregrine. 'Now, let us proceed.' Matthias promptly stepped into the Portal and waved imperiously for his servants to activate the Portal to send him back to Raspero.

'What is this place, my Lord?' Odovacar asked while studying the controls of the Portal.

Matthias decided to be less than completely forthcoming. He did not want Peregrine and Odovacar to be so paralysed with terror as to be unable to send him back to Raspero. 'It is a government building in Krastienst,' he told them. 'As you know, I have, regrettably, been involved in some less than perfectly harmonious dealings with the forces of law and order in our beloved country. It therefore follows that my departure is slightly unauthorised. This is why, as you will recall, I am paying you one thousand strada each for your services today. In order for you to receive this money, you must send me promptly to Raspero, and then leave this place without delay. I repeat, do not hang around or the authorities will detain you. Get straight out of here as soon as I am gone. Now, let's get moving.'

Matthias concluded his comments with a distinctly baronial tone of authority. Peregrine and Odovacar, accustomed as they were since birth to obey the orders of their social superiors, made haste to comply with the instructions of their Baron. In a moment, Matthias was gone, and the signal showed a successful transport to Raspero. Peregrine and Odovacar closed up the Portal, as per the instructions Matthias had given them yesterday, and set forth to make their way out of that building. Matthias had told them to go up two sets of stairs and exit the double doors standing open, go down the stairs to the street, and then follow the left-and-right, etc. directions which he had written down for them and which would take them to the Departure station for public flying carriages. They were never, in the end, to follow Matthias's carefully written instructions.

A student of experimental psychology would have been fascinated by the experiences of Peregrine and Odovacar in the Ankalybu. Despite having no idea of where they were, a chill entered their bones as they set forth along the claustrophobic corridors of the seventh floor of the Ankalybu, as something of the nightmarish quality of that place became present to their perceptions in a non-empirical manner. (Empiricism had been refuted then and there!) They began to almost run along the corridors, until they came to the stairs Matthias had mentioned and began to run up them. Their heart beat had increased, their palms were sweaty and they were breathing heavily, even though absolutely nothing had happened to them yet. Coming up into the Entrance Hall they found no-one about and headed straight for the double doors. Still there was no-one about as they exited the building, and after a moment of confusion, found the stairs leading down to street level. And it was there that they saw, on the plaque embedded into the wall by the stairs at street level, the following inscription: *The Office of the Security of the National Integrity of the State of the Kingdom of Westrigonia.*

Peregrine and Odovacar looked at each other for a moment of pure terror, and then they turned and they *ran*. All thought was lost, except for the knowledge of each other's company as they hurtled their way around street corners and across public parks and city squares. At some point in their mad flight, Kefirez's soldiers stopped them, but they were let go given their incoherence, which no-one in authority wanted to be troubled by at that moment in time given their quest for the fugitive Baron Raspero. So it was that Peregrine and Odovacar eventually found the Departure station for flying carriages and bought their tickets out of there.

They were thoroughly and emphatically agreed upon one thing. Matthias should have promised them a lot more money than a mere one thousand strada each. What had seemed like a large sum yesterday now seemed like a grotesque underpayment. With nervous laughter and shaking hands they poured themselves drinks and commented in aggrieved tones about how Matthias had advised them *not to hang around* in the Ankalybu, which was a joke that was not a joke.

In fairness to the gallant baronial servants of Raspero, when they got merrily drunk that evening in an inn at Katia on their journey home, their exploits that day seemed to them like the heroic doings of myth, so extraordinary that no-one would ever believe them. All was well in the golden glow of their drunken happiness, fuelled by their memories, which by now had expanded to explain how they had walked away from the Ankalybu like the coolest of cucumbers and talked their way past roadblocks of soldiers as if they had not a care in the world. They snapped their fingers at Phelan and his agents, just as they had, in their memories, snapped their fingers at him earlier that day. Matthias was now the best baron in the world, and they no longer had any complaints about their pay for that day's work, which meant less to them than their remembered heroism.

11:45 PM, Monday 29 July 1875 A. F

During the two weeks from when he had registered his motion of no confidence in the monarchs of Westrigonia, till the day of reckoning itself, Matthias had been busier than he had ever been before, or would ever be since. Sleeping three to four hours a night, cat-napping when possible, writing letters, organising things, researching and fact-finding and packing and directing sundry affairs: all these constituted a maelstrom of daily activities that threatened on occasion to drown the young Baron. Memories of Phelan and the Ankalybu, of his dead father and dead brother stretched out in their coffins, of the need to take care of his mother and sister, were never far from his waking consciousness, and served to drive him onward whenever he felt like a rest. It was all a whirlwind. Fear and anger became his daily companions and the clock was always ticking loudly in his ears day in and day out. All of the Library, the valuables, everything that was movable, had been packed and sent abroad or stored in nearby caves.

Matthias had read through the papers in his father's desk, skimming quickly with an eye to anything particularly noteworthy. It was not easy to tell what his father had been up to. Journal entries, letters and brief notes were often cryptic, mnemonics to jog the memory as much as anything. Doodles were interspersed with acronyms and poetry quotations without the least surface indication of an ulterior meaning. Matthias could find nothing to make sense of Phelan's comment that *your father is up to his neck in matters of which you know nothing.* The only thing that was clear was that there was nothing that was overtly incriminating in his father's papers. But then, that was only to be expected. What did not have to be written down would be memorised. Like every educated person of the age, Matthias's father understood how to use mnemonics to memorise vast tracts of data.

One key point which Matthias had to deal with was what would happen after the Vidaldmeet vote. If Phelan laid hands on him, that would the end of Matthias Raspero. Matthias would be glad to see death when it finally came. It would also be the end of everything Matthias knew about, which was why he had made sure that he himself did not know where his mother and sister (under the false names of Faina and Margaretha Faramund) would be hiding. If he escaped Phelan, they would contact him at a prearranged place; if he did not escape, they would open a sealed envelope he had left with them which told them where the money was, and how to transfer it away from where Phelan could grab it once he had made Matthias talk.

But escaping from the Vidaldmeet trap was not the only trick which Matthias had to pull off. There was one more crucial item to deal with before Matthias could sit back and have a rest. Matthias now turned his attention to this matter.

CHAPTER SIXTEEN

There is the legend of the sage,
Who saw the bull eating the valuable barley crop,
Of a destitute family unable to drive the bull away,
One sunny summer's day long ago when the sky was blue,
And the world was young.
The sage went and whispered in the bull's ear,
With the result that the bull immediately went away,
And never ate barley again.
I say to all those who believe that this really happened:
Please step forward.
Frankie the Villain

10:20 AM, Tuesday 30 July 1875 A. F

Phelan's rage was titanic, but contained within his rib-cage. Those of his circle who knew him well trembled to the marrow of their bones at the sight of his face. His least wish was granted even faster than usual, which is to say with even more abject grovelling than usual. The very air itself inside the Ankalybu trembled as if incubating a thunderstorm; and that thunderstorm was brewing, of that there could be no doubt.

Phelan had deferred his revenge, had swallowed all the insults which that unbelievably insolent ape Raspero had thrown at him, and had waited for his time to come, which it always did. Phelan knew how to wait. Raspero had slapped him in public! This was not only literally unheard of, but an insult that Phelan had not yet lived down. It was an insult that swanned about as if enjoying a life of luxury, skulking its narrow-hipped feline arrogance all around the vaulted ceiling painted with the sufferings of the innocent that constituted the inside of Phelan's skull. It was an insult that banged like a drum inside Phelan's sense of self, beating out a rhythm that spelled out in a biological code Phelan's inner anguish at having had the whole world in the township of Raspero look at him as at a man who had been slapped in public. Phelan groaned out loud, then looked quickly about his office to check that he was alone. He was indeed alone, loner than alone, more alone than a loner could be when alone. Solitude was the essence of his very being.

Phelan aimlessly shuffled papers around his desk, trying to gather his scattered thoughts together. The escape of Matthias Raspero from the Vidaldmeet had shaken Phelan. He was a man who liked order, who liked things to be under control, and who now had to face the following question: how had he overlooked the Sinners Door?

Phelan had no real intention of properly facing this question. Someone else was to blame, and that someone was General Kefirez, who was at present on the seventh level of the Ankalybu profoundly regretting that he had ever been born. Kefirez was learning of the intimacy of physical pain. Phelan was baffled as to how a simple matter like the Sinners Door could have been overlooked by that moron Kefirez, and he had instructed his interrogators to probe so deeply inside Kefirez's mind as to identify what cog of that mind had slipped its gear. If things were to be properly under control, nothing could be overlooked. Everything had to be taken into account. Systems of logic had to be developed that governed databases, information theory had to be applied, human nature had to be accounted for, and when all was said and done, the final report that landed on the desk of the Director-General would be one of the very finality that gave it the status of being the final report. Incompleteness gave Phelan the shivers.

Enough! Phelan brushed aside all recriminations, all doubts and second-guesses and personal feelings, and turned his mind onto addressing what had to be be done now. He had just received information that Matthias Raspero had left the barony of Raspero after having given a farewell address to the townsfolk. He had left the affairs of the barony in the hands of the Steward. It was clear to Phelan that it was no use attempting to have his enemy stripped of his title and lands in these circumstances. The Vidaldmeet would not stand for it. Matthias had beaten his enemies fair and square, and it was implicitly understood by all concerned that exile, with a distant but ever-present hope of return, was a sufficient punishment for the fugitive baron.

But that did not mean that nothing at all could be done. Within certain limits, Phelan could vent his destructive fury on the innocent townsfolk of Raspero. In a moment, Phelan felt better, more himself, more the Chevalier Phelan, Director-General of the State Bureau of Security, as a feeling of his own personal power flooded into his renewed sense of self. He had no power over the past, but over the present . . . well, that was a very different matter. He had more power than the King, more power even than the First Protector, in his narrowly limited sphere of things. Where Phelan ruled, he ruled as an absolute monarch.

Phelan considered this matter. As a Minister of the Crown, he had the authority to commandeer any regiment he wanted. As it happened, the regiment commanded by General Tola had certain advantages to Phelan's way of thinking. The main advantage was that General Tola had been named as a co-conspirator of Baron Adelmar Raspero. It followed therefore that he could be obliged to be present while the town of Raspero was . . . disciplined. Phelan tingled inwardly at the prospect of inflicting such degradation on General Tola, the descendant of such a noble family.

Phelan knew that by now Matthias Raspero would be long gone. He would be over the border in hiding in his self-imposed exile and there would be no catching him now. But the town of Raspero which he had left behind was a very different matter. There was no running and hiding for them. Phelan took a deep breath, held it for a moment, and then let it out slowly. There was atonement to be done, and the town of Raspero was ready and ripe for such atonement.

Phelan took pen and paper in hand and began sketching out his early ideas. He would approach the town of Raspero with overwhelming force. He would seize hold of the town. And then he would teach the people of Raspero to respect and fear the name of the Chevalier Phelan. They would not think of him again as the man who Matthias Raspero had slapped in public, or if they did, they would curse the day Matthias Raspero was born. And when Matthias Raspero, wherever he was now, heard of the destruction that had fallen on his Barony of Raspero, he would bitterly regret the day he had ever offended Phelan. He would realise that he now had no barony to return to, that all that he had once been lord over was now rubble and desolation.

Phelan looked over the whole situation from every perspective, being careful not to overlook anything. Kefirez had overlooked the Sinners Door. Phelan would not overlook anything.

The Vidaldmeet would do nothing. Usually so solicitous over the fate of one of its members, on this occasion they would be unable to act without being marked as sympathisers of rebels. Besides, by the time they had held their committee meetings and debates, everything would have been done and dusted and it would long be time to move on to other things. Phelan would not directly challenge Matthias's claim to his title and lands, which alone would provoke the Vidaldmeet into action, given their own sensitivities.

Frederick and Yolande would do nothing. The Barony of Raspero had already been marked as a place of rebellion against the monarchs by the reports of the State Bureau of Security, and the motion of no confidence which Matthias had moved in the Vidaldmeet had only cemented that reputation. The Crown Prince Jason would not care now or later, being entirely indifferent to Westrigonian matters; if he ever became King, he would not pay attention to the survivors' tales of what had happened in Raspero. As for the Crown Princess Eleanor, so interested in her adopted country of Westrigonia, she would have no reason to care for the sufferings of the people of Raspero either.

The Barony of Raspero had no allies who would come to its aid. Baron Adelmar's co-conspirators would wish for nothing more than to lie low and not draw attention to themselves.

The people, as always, would do nothing. Without leadership they could, as always, be discounted.

The more he contemplated the situation, the more Phelan realised that he had a clear field. He could do what he wanted. There was no-one to stop him. He could make of the Barony of Raspero a large punctuation mark over a place where the spirit had once been. And he, the Chevalier Phelan, would be feared as no man had ever been feared in the history of Westrigonia. Not even Good King Justin would have done anything on the scale of what Phelan planned to do. This would be, Phelan mused to himself, the beginnings of a new order. After all, the Council of State of the Kingdom of Westrigonia at some point needed be put under the rulership of one man, who could govern the kingdom in the names of the monarchs as an absolute monarch himself; and Phelan would be that man, and the destruction of the town of Raspero would be a stepping stone to that goal.

Like the returning tide of the sea rushing in to all the hollows and reefs and salt flats of the sea shore, Phelan's sense of self was filling up with all the rushing waters of his thoughts. And the more his water-thoughts teemed and bubbled in the landscape of his brain, the more elated Phelan became in his own mind, expanding his own perceptions as he became increasingly aware that he was ten feet tall and would be obeyed automatically by everyone he encountered. He would answer to no-one except the First Protector, with whom he was already on the best of terms.

4:20 PM, Tuesday 30 July 1875 A. F

Phelan stood on the deck of his flying carriage, feeling himself to be the master of the world.

Around him there were four hundred and thirty two flying carriages, carrying his State Bureau subordinates, and ten thousand soldiers of the regiment under the command of General Tola. This huge flotilla filled the space around Phelan, filled his sense of self, filled the sky over the town of Raspero.

As his flotilla landed, and Phelan stepped down onto the ground, he strode forward like a conqueror over his newly conquered terrain. He made his demands for the Baron of Raspero to come forward, half-listened to the legal explanation from the Steward of Raspero to the effect that Baron Matthias Raspero had gone into exile, leaving the Steward with the said deputed authorities of etc-etc-etc. Phelan was barely listening now as the Steward descended into the legal psycho-babble of his office. Phelan was paying more attention to those perceptions in which he excelled. He noted from the craven attitude of the Steward that the Steward was terrified of him. Good! Phelan noted this approvingly. This was as it should be. He also noted from the way people were standing a long way away from the Steward that everyone present could be divided and ruled.

'Enough, Steward!' Phelan held up his hand.

Dacre fell silent as if a switch in his brain had been turned.

'There is the matter of accommodation and provisions for my men while the matter of the insurgency of Raspero is looked into. And there is also the matter of accommodation and provision for the men of General Tola.'

Dacre closed his eyes. Matthias had been very specific on his instructions to Dacre about what he should say at this point. Dacre trembled inwardly at saying anything contrary to the will of the State Bureau of Security, but by focusing on how he could lay this all on the shoulders on the departed Matthias, he nerved himself sufficiently to open his eyes and say: 'I have been instructed by Baron Matthias to say that the castle is sealed and no-one at all is permitted to enter its domains.' At the sight of Phelan's face becoming grim, Dacre hastily added: 'I was ordered to say this. Please excuse me, Chevalier, for merely being obedient to what I was ordered to say but-'

Phelan held up his hand: Dacre silent. Phelan dropped his hand, and turned around with a stage actor's showy deliberation to look up at Castle Raspero looming overhead. Tilting his head as if mulling things over, Phelan narrowed his eyes, widened them, and then turned back to the Steward of Raspero and declared: 'Myself and the agents of the State Bureau of Security who accompany me will reside in the Castle Raspero for the duration of our stay in this town.'

Dacre immediately bowed his head in agreement. 'Of course, Chevalier. It shall be as you have directed.'

Matthias had ordered him to say this in response to Phelan's predictable command.

Phelan, inwardly crowing over his victory, and looking around him triumphantly at the adoring faces of his followers, would not have heard any alarm bells even if they had ben ringing in his ears at that time, such was the enormity of his elation at this, his moment of victory over the insolent Matthias Raspero.

But those alarm bells were, nonetheless, ringing insistently, even if the Chevalier Phelan couldn't hear them.

10:40 PM, Tuesday 30 July 1875 A. F

Phelan paced around the Master Bedroom of Castle Raspero, which he had, of course, taken as his own personal room. It was somewhat bare, as indeed was the whole castle, having been stripped by Matthias of everything which he could carry away. But it was, nonetheless, the master bedroom of the castle, and Phelan was sleeping in it. Phelan, who had been raised in a poor family far from that of the status of chevaliers, felt as always a sense of triumph at grinding down the rich and powerful into the dust. There was both a rightness and a sense of expansion whenever this happened. The end-point of history was on his side. The past may have belonged to these people, and some of the present, but the rest of the present and all of the future belonged to Phelan and his kind.

Phelan undressed slowly, laying his white robes carefully over a nearby chair. His spare white robes, all identical, were folded neatly in his suitcases. Now dressed in a silk shirt and silk shorts, Phelan climbed into bed, clicked off the lamp with a wave of his wand, which he laid on the bedside table, and closed his eyes in the dark. He fell asleep thinking pleasurably of all the terrible things which he would begin doing tomorrow.

1:20 AM, Wednesday 31 July 1875 A. F

Phelan awoke groggily to find the lamp on, his bedclothes stripped away, his wrists and ankles bound with karns and a gagging karn even now being applied to his mouth. Matthias Raspero was standing over his bed, his wand in his hand, looking down on him.

Phelan tried to speak, but was unable to. He tried to move his hands and feet, but again without result. He writhed about the bed in a fury. It was not just that his hands and feet were bound, but also that a looping chain held his whole body secured to the pillars of the four-poster bed in which he lay. Matthias stood and watched all this without moving.

Eventually Phelan came to an end of his pointless labours. He lay there, breathing heavily through his gagging karn, looking up at the expressionless Matthias.

'For someone who styles himself as the incarnation of chance, Phelan, you are very predictable.' Matthias turned away and walked around the room for a while, watched by the captive Phelan, then resumed speaking: 'When we last met, Phelan, you had much to say about chance. It is now my turn to speak. It is not possible for a human being to simulate chance. The best anyone can do is to produce choices which are known as *pseudo-chance*, choices which are generated by formulas which, while complex, are nonetheless formulas. No human agency can produce pure chance. If you had received a proper education, Phelan, you would have known this. But you are ignorant. You have never been anything but ignorant.'

Matthias paused, as if courteously allowing Phelan a chance to respond; but such courtesy only drew attention to the gag behind which Phelan was placed. Matthias resumed speaking. 'Your over-confidence is one cause of your downfall, Phelan. It was extremely foolish of you to let slip that you are a Leveller. The weakness of the Leveller is to assume that everyone else is the same as them. You believed that I would go into hiding and abandon the people of Raspero to your tender mercies because that is what you would have done yourself. You are incapable of understanding that I could not abandon the people who I have known all my life long, and who have always been loyal to the barony. I love them, and men like you do not understand love. Thus you failed to take proper precautions. This was utterly predictable, and indeed my presence here as your captor is proof positive that I predicted it. But tell me again, Phelan, how you are the possessor of the great secret of chance.'

Phelan breathed stentoriously through his gag, his fury evident. Matthias waited a moment, then continued: 'As I'm sure you have noted, I've taken a leaf out of your book, Phelan. You like to arrest people in the middle of the night, don't you? Ostensibly because people have their defences down, they're half-asleep, weakened and feeble, groggily waking up to find you and your men standing all around them. But that is mere happenstance, is it not? What is really going on is mythology, is it not? The associations with a night-time visit are endless, aren't they? Have they really woken, or is what is happening really a nightmare? And the darkness of the night from which you and your men emerge, and into which you take your victims, why, it is cosmic in its scope. So it is fitting then, Phelan, that I have come to take *you* in the middle of the night. I have emerged out of the night, into which I shall subsequently take you.'

Phelan made indistinguishable sounds through his gag.

Matthias paced around the room for a while. 'This was my parent's bedroom. I was conceived in this room, but I have never been allowed to set foot in it all my life while my father lived. And here you come, as bold as brass, and march into this very room, a room that has such sensitivity for me, a room where my parents slept together in the same bed, the very bed wherein I was conceived, and shall I claim to be shocked by your behaviour? Well, I am as much as relieved as anything, given that I predicted that you would do precisely this out of sheer malevolence, but your presence nonetheless offends me. You played a role in the scheme of things that led to the deaths of my father and brother, Phelan, and for this you must pay. But I have one regret. It is that my life has become linked to yours in this way. You are a monster, Phelan, and I feel that your presence here today is a familiarity which I cannot easily wash away. You are a dirty stain, and your very presence makes everything you touch dirty.'

Matthias turned to contemplate Phelan tied up on the bed. He waved his wand, using karns to strip Phelan of his short and shirt, and turn

Phelan around so he was awkwardly suspended in the air, bent over in an uncomfortable position with his head facing his knees.

'Do you recognise your current circumstances, Phelan?' Matthias asked in a friendly fashion. 'Of course you do. An expert like you! It is called *Opening the Gates of Doubt*. A full description of this interrogation technique is to be found in section 2.3.7 of the Data System Manual volume 5, is it not? Straight out of the State Bureau textbook! So how do you find it yourself? No doubt you are already using your knowledge of what this is about to guard yourself against being broken by this interrogation, which you must understand is only beginning.'

Phelan made indistinguishable sounds.

'We will talk again later, Chevalier. I will now leave you to your thoughts. By the way,' and here Matthias's tone of voice became noticeably grimmer, 'you would be very well advised to start contemplating the matter of the deaths of my father and my brother, because I expect you to fully enlighten me on this matter tonight.'

Matthias turned away and walked to the door, stepped through it and was gone.

4:30 PM, Monday 15 July 1875 A. F

Two weeks earlier, Matthias had prepared for this day of reckoning. He had sat down at his father's desk in his father's study, which he still could not get used to now being his own desk in his own study, taken pen and paper in hand and began roughing out his ideas.

Matthias had known that Phelan would want revenge on Matthias for the humiliation of being slapped in public; and if Phelan could not lay his hands on Matthias himself, he could at least lay hands on the township of Raspero and the people who lived there. Phelan would come to Raspero in force and wreak vengeance upon its citizens.

Matthias could not allow this to happen. He was bound as baron to protect his people. He could not abandon them to Phelan. He had to save them, whether or not they deserved it. He therefore laid plans to deal with Phelan's forthcoming scheme of destruction, which Matthias had no doubt Phelan planned to implement. Some conclusions, even if inferred, are too certain to doubt.

Matthias found the secret passage in Castle Raspero which all castles possessed; but in the blueprint in his father's study he also found the second secret passage, so cunningly hidden that even Phelan's men, highly trained though they were, would not find it. Even Matthias would not have found it without these directions.

Matthias laid his plans, made his preparations accordingly, and set everything into motion. On returning to Raspero after departing the Vidaldmeet through the Sinners Door, Matthias had summoned the townsfolk of Raspero to the town square and, standing on the same place on the wall where Oliver had stood to first address the people of Raspero long ago, Matthias informed his dependents that he was going into exile and that he was leaving the Steward to be caretaker of the barony. There was much wailing and lamentation, and loud pleas for Matthias to stay. Matthias said that everything would continue exactly as before, that all public employment would remain unchanged, all legalities would be properly observed, and that no-one would lose out by this change coming into effect. There was more wailing and lamentation, and more loud pleas for Matthias to stay. Matthias said that wherever he went, the barony would remain in his heart as a guiding light to him through the darkness of the world, and that one day he would return to Raspero to once again live with the best and most wonderful people in the world. There continued more wailing and lamentations, and loud pleas for Matthias to stay. Matthias jumped down from the wall and moved through the assembled gathering, speaking briefly to those present, making light-hearted comments and trying to sound as if nothing very bad was happening. Some of the tears being shed were perfectly genuine. Matthias's own grief, still close to his own throat, was itself far from over, yet the young baron maintained an iron control over himself. There was too much remaining to be done, and he had not at all told the people of Raspero the danger remaining of Phelan's vengeance.

Lady Raspero and Lena left through the Portal for Anglashia. They would then go to Yusravakia, where arrangements had been made for them to live under false names. Matthias would visit them when he could. Matthias himself would go to Filataltar, from where he would make his way to Anglashia. He had already gone to see the Master of Grangeshield House, a descendant of Sir Nicholas and Lady Isabel and therefore Matthias's very distant cousin. On the basis of being family, plus a tidy contribution from Matthias of the sum of two hundred and fifty thousand strada, the false name of Ryan Grangeshield and the prospect of future employment had been supplied to the fugitive, in addition to false identities for Lena and Lady Raspero, including a place to live in Yusravakia, and schooling for Lena. It was pricy, but the quality of such protection, being almost that of a government, could hardly be bettered. Matthias and his family would be well hidden from pursuit.

10:20 AM, Tuesday 30 July 1875 A. F

As portal traffic from Raspero would be being monitored, Matthias departed Raspero in his baronial flying carriage, with two attendant flying carriages containing the Castle Guard of Raspero, plus a hooded figure. This hooded figure was Alaric Niedbala. Alaric's parents believed he was on a hiking holiday in the mountains with his older cousin, learning about geology and plants and such things. (It had been decided by everyone involved that what Alaric's parents didn't know wouldn't hurt them.) Alaric's cousin was playing along in return for the princely sum of ten thousand strada which the wealthy Baron of Raspero was paying him for his services. Alaric, for his part, would always do whatever Matthias wanted him to do. High into the air they went and past the Mountains of Lochfric, watched by the townsfolk of Raspero waving their goodbyes.

Once out of sight, the carriages made a sharp right and flew into the Mountains of Lochfric. They flew low through the valleys and passes and gullies until they came into the Forest of Cadeyrn, and landed in a clearing.

Alaric took off his hooded cloak to reveal himself as being already attired in some spare clothes of Matthias. He then, with four Castle guards attending him, left in the baronial flying carriage for the town of

Lentiagestes. There he would leave for Iahsalt through the public portal there under the name of Fedlimid. The necessary bribes had already been paid to the transportation officials involved, including bribes paid for it to later be disclosed that Fedlimid had in reality been the fugitive Baron Matthias Raspero. A second false trail had already been laid by which Alaric would return to Westrigonia and meet up again with his cousin in the mountains.

4:20 PM, Tuesday 30 July 1875 A. F

Matthias paced up and down in the clearing of the Forest of Cadeyrn, looking up into the sky. What was due to happen next was vital to his plans.

At one side of the clearing there was a strange rock formation, cleft in two as if struck by a divine axe, with a pond at its base fed by a little stream of clear water. The clearing was formed of largely bare rocks and bracken surrounded by yew trees. A barely discernible mound of rocks, so long ago overlaid with moss as to be barely distinguishable, lay on the eastern side of the clearing. It was the length and size of a grave (which in fact, long ago, it had been. A famous bandit of the forests had been killed in this place and buried in that grave.) The main part of the clearing was windswept bare rock, open to the sky. It was a forbidding place and haunted by ghosts, chosen by Matthias from a memory of having been brought here by his father as a child.

Two flying carriages appeared. Ten Baalbabakan men dressed in peasant clothing, but with a measured way of moving that suggested military training, descended to the ground. With them was Paderau, who Matthias had taken with him to Rozneft, the capital of Baalbabak. Matthias had gone there in secret through the Raspero town portal. Also with them was Cacilio, the Baalbabakan translator Matthias had hired. Matthias talked to the Baalbabakans through this translator, while his Castle Guard looked on and tried to figure out as best they could what was going on. Matthias had fires lit and food and drink brought out while night fell, and they all sat down in the clearing lit up by the firelight and ate and drank. Everyone was feeling cheerful for no reason at all, unless it was the wine and the festive atmosphere. The fires were like miniature suns, with their yellow light shining forth among the green leaves and the brown trunks of the surrounding trees: the golden flames of the fires washed over them like waves of an ethereal phosphorescent sea lighting up the craggy promontories of a sea-shore.

Musical instruments suddenly appeared, due entirely to Matthias's foresight, and the Westrigonians played and sang for the benefit of the Baalbabakans, who watched with expressionless faces. At the invitation of Matthias, the Baalbabakans played and sang while the Westrigonians, who felt that the performance they had witnessed was awful, and was not even musical in the least, politely clapped and pretended to enjoy the Baalbabakan discordance. It was a night that no-one who was present would ever forget. Even the stars looked down on them all like a massed audience crouched above a stage, as if eternity itself was enjoying a diversion like this one from the serious business of the universe.

Mathias brought the proceedings to an end. Going over the route to be taken again with Radboud, Captain of the Castle Guard, with the translator Cacilio in attendance explaining to the Baalbabakans what was going on, Matthias stated the details of the plan that was to unfold that night with such clarity that everyone understood everything perfectly.

Matthias then stepped onto a contraption that looked like skis lashed together by a basket-weaving arrangement of straps. It was a flying sled. Waving his wand, he fastened his feet onto this device, waved his wand again, and took off vertically into the air, and then southwards. His Castle Guard and the Baalbabakans got into their flying carriages and flew along low to the ground in the same direction as Matthias.

That direction was where Castle Raspero was located.

The game was afoot.

CHAPTER SEVENTEEN

My friend wrote passionately about potatoes.
His name was Radomir.
I have never loved potatoes.
I have only ever eaten them.
Frankie the Villain

12:05 AM, Wednesday 31 July 1875 A. F

Matthias had flown so high into the air on his flying sled that Castle Raspero, gleaming in the moonlight below, looked like a child's toy that he could cover with the palm of his hand stretched out. He descended onto the roof of the castle from above. The guards posted on the roof were not looking into the air above their heads, and in fact were half-asleep. Matthias captured and gagged all four of them with ease. The sounds made thereby were passing and unmemorable. Even the owls hardly noticed. All was well so far. This was stage one of the night's proceedings. Matthias gave himself top marks so far. He was doing well. Had this night's proceedings been a course at school, his teachers would have been pleased. But of course, in taking State Bureau of Security agents captive, he had passed far beyond a normal school's curriculum.

Matthias knew (he *knew!*) that Phelan would have wanted to demonstrate his command of the situation by taking the Master Bedroom as his own personal accommodation. Matthias went directly there, and took the Director-General of the State Bureau of Security as his prisoner. Stage two was done. All was well.

1:30 AM, Wednesday 31 July 1875 A. F

Matthias drifted down through the corridors of the castle, barely touching the floor with his floating feet, like a ghost in the night. He went down to the Great Hall, capturing the five guards on duty there with a minimum of noise and fuss. Going down to the crypt from the Great Hall on the spiral staircase, he stopped a certain distance down the staircase and waved his wand to open up a panel in the wall (that looked exactly like the surrounding wall), uncovering a passage leading downwards. Unhooking a lamp from the wall and lighting it, Matthias set forth along the passage. At the far end, he opened up another panel, to let in the Castle Guard waiting on the other side. The Baalbabakans were not present, having been instructed to remain on the other side of the gully neighbouring the castle. It was not for outsiders such as them to know of such secrets as this second secret passage into the castle. Matthias was reluctant for even his own Castle Guard to know, but sacrifices had to be made to the exigencies of the moment.

The Castle Guard entered Castle Raspero through the secret passage, and the battle began. They were in their own home ground, under the expert direction of the Baron of Raspero himself, who held the wandlore secrets of a thousand years in his hand, and the agents of the State Bureau of Security didn't stand a chance. It was not long before Castle Raspero was back in the hands of its rightful owner. The Castle Guard then departed through the second secret passage with their forty-nine prisoners in tow, after which they went to their rendezvous with the Baalbabakans, and handed their prisoners over.

Matthias had arranged to have the State Bureau of Security agents sent to Baalbabak. There they would be enslaved and put to work as beasts of burden, all in accordance with the Levellers principles which Phelan professed.

Matthias felt that there was something poetic in the justice which he had meted out. But the justice being meted out was far from done. There was the Chevalier Phelan himself who remained to be dealt with. Everything that had happened so far had been merely a prelude to this, the main event.

2:50 AM, Wednesday 31 July 1875 A. F

Chevalier Phelan, the Director-General of the State Bureau of Security and one of the most powerful men in Westrigonia, if not *the* most powerful man, found himself contemplating more than his own uncomfortable situation. The *Opening of the Gates of Doubt* to which Matthias had referred was such an effective interrogation technique that Phelan did not realise the extent to which his own introspection was a result of the physical posture in which he had been placed, as to have one's naked body in an upside-down V-shaped position with one's bare posterior sticking up into the air was to be placed in such a confluence of vulnerabilities and indignities that anyone at all would feel a consequent disintegration of their earlier presumptions. The gates of doubt could not but be opened thereby. Phelan was plagued by uncertainties which were being newly formed of old materials. His circumstances, and the extent of his utterly thorough strategic beating at the hands of Matthias, who had proved himself to be the master of gamesmanship, were forcing Phelan to re-think his options.

On the one hand, he had the entire apparatus of the machinery of state on his side. On the other hand, he was the captive of a baron who had shown himself so far to be without fear of Phelan.

Now that Phelan came to think about it, which was obviously, being *now*, much too late, Matthias had not been abject with fear from the beginning. Phelan had overlooked this, in part because of a personal delight in the rare pleasure of for once being able to talk with someone who was not hyper-ventilating with fear at being in the same room as the dreaded Director-General of the State Bureau of Security, and in part because it had not been necessary to throw a scare into young Matthias. It was the boy's father who had to be intimidated by what was happening. Phelan was struck yet again with having overlooked something. He had assumed that time was on his side, that young Raspero would return to the Ankalybu if it proved necessary, and that if it should not prove to be necessary there would be nothing left to contemplate in any case, everything having been settled. He had not realised at the time that

Matthias's lack of grovelling showed him to be such a threat, but how could he have? How could anyone? No-one –

Phelan abruptly pulled himself out of the self-excusing meander of his thoughts. Acquitting himself of all blame was a luxury that would have to wait till later. The thirty-seventh Baron of Raspero, having re-entered the Master Bedroom, was coming towards him.

3:00 AM, Wednesday 31 July 1875 A. F

The Chevalier Phelan found himself taken out of the Master Bedroom and thrown along the corridor. Along corridors and down stairs he was taken, bound and gagged and as naked as the day he was born, thrown hither and thither like a sack of potatoes. At some level of his being he understood all the theoretical dimensions of his treatment, the humiliation, the discomfort, the disrespect, all bound up with the threat of more, much more unhappiness to come, yet this theoretical understanding helped him not at all. His anger arose of its own volition, despite his knowledge that this anger was in these circumstances a weakness that undermined his later capacity to fight back. Anger now would turn to fear later which would turn on its own source in its own turn. Phelan knew all this well, yet he could not help but be angry now. And as he tried not to become angry, he felt anger at having to not feel anger, as if his mind had become a Moebius strip with only one side to it. He had watched his own men, schooled in the techniques of the Bureau, crumble under the impact of being subject to those very same techniques when tortured by their own former colleagues. Fore-warned was not fore-armed in these circumstances. Knowledge was swamped by experience every time. There was nothing to be done when fear began to consume your very being, nothing at all.

Phelan was left alone in a room in the dungeons, bound to a chair by a table in a room of bare stone walls and floor with an oak ceiling overhead while Matthias went off somewhere. By now he was more bruised than angry. His thoughts turned to his men, who could save him from these indignities if they came along. It was this turn of his thoughts that brought another dimension of suffering into his circumstances as experienced by his capacity for sensation. The emptiness of an empty building is perceived by being felt as much as heard or seen. Phelan began to understood that Castle Raspero, somehow, mysteriously, was completely empty. He was alone with Matthias in an empty castle. Phelan by now was in a heightened extremity of awareness. He did not know how Matthias had done what he had done, but he did know that he would have to watch his step carefully. Phelan was beginning to feel far from all-powerful.

Matthias returned and stood across the room, looking at his prisoner with an expression of ice-cold disdain on his face.

'It's just as you said, Phelan,' Matthias commented. 'We meet again on the other side of a closed door. Spooky, isn't it? How did you know?'

'We meet again in regrettable circumstances, my Lord Raspero,' Phelan replied, forsaking his usual superior demeanour. 'I fully understand that you must wish to avoid having to go into exile, and I have no doubt that as reasonable men we can arrive at an accommodation with regard to this matter.'

'Chevalier Phelan,' Matthias said loudly, 'I name you as being involved in the deaths of my father and my brother. For this reason, I say that you have given me offence. The satisfaction of this offence which you have given me I name here and now. I demand satisfaction in final combat.'

'My Lord Raspero,' Phelan said as pleasantly as he could manage, 'I can assure you that I had no involvement whatsoever in the lamentable deaths of your illustrious father, and your noble brother who had such a brilliant future ahead of him.'

'How polite you are.'

'*It is necessary to be courteous on occasion.*'

'I am not a necessary, Phelan. But you have received me, nonetheless. But you have not replied to my challenge. I demand satisfaction. How do you answer?'

'Duels of combat are illegal, my Lord Raspero. I must refuse your challenge. I am sworn to uphold the law. I cannot myself break it.'

'And what did you plan to do in Raspero, Chevalier, during your visit here? Well?'

'My purpose was to search for you, and then return to Krastienst.'

'And what of all the torture instruments which you brought with you? To what use were they to be put?'

'None at all. They were merely for show.'

'Phelan, I ask you for the third and final time. I demand satisfaction for the offence you have caused me. What do you reply?'

'My Lord Raspero, duels of combat have been forbidden by law for many years now. I cannot accept your challenge. I am an official sworn to uphold the law.'

'The law?' Matthias made a scoffing noise. The tension in the air was such that even he couldn't laugh at this moment in time. 'This is a matter of honour, Phelan. I am referring to the ancient code by which your life is forfeit by the blood of those other lives you have helped to take. If you have honour, Phelan, you must accept my challenge.'

'This ancient code is no longer relevant in the modern era, Lord Raspero. The reforms of the Zoller-Abstein Protectorate have outlawed all duels, especially duels of final combat, and personal vengeance is now illegal. These are our modern times, not the dark times of savagery of our long distant past. If you have a grievance, you must pursue the matter through the courts.'

'The dark times of savagery to which you refer blaze like beacons of civilization compared to the darkness of our modern Ankalybu. You're a fine one to talk about savagery. The fact is, Phelan, you are a coward and you are hiding behind legalisms. My challenge stands, Phelan. Answer me!'

'I refer you again to the law,' Phelan said carefully, 'and to the courts. If you have a complaint, there you must take it. You can no longer take the law into your own hands in these modern times.'

'Tonight we are outside the law, Phelan. You are in my ancestral castle, where the bodies of my father and brother lie recently interred in the family crypt. This is a matter of justice. That is why you are here tonight. I give you the chance of a fair fight.'

'You have the wand-lore secrets of a thousand years in your hand, I do not. This is not *a fair fight*. If you want a fair fight, take me to court.'

'There are no modern legalisms in the afterlife, Phelan, and that is where you are going. Do you really wish to make this journey with lies upon your lips?'

'Lord Raspero, it seems that you are in a position from which you may bargain. State your demands, and I will listen to them.'

'I have only one demand, Phelan, and this is it. And I still await your third and final answer.'

'Your demand is illegal, Lord Raspero. And foolish. I say again to you that I am prepared to go to trial.'

'You are a coward, Phelan.'

'You do not know that I am guilty of the offence of which you accuse me. You are behaving unjustly in finding me guilty of a matter of which you know nothing.'

Phelan had actually made a telling point, and Matthias's ensuing silence acknowledged this. In the end, Matthias shifted his feet and ignored Phelan's argument. 'Do you accept my challenge, Phelan? Yes or no?'

Feeling more confident than before, Phelan said definitively: 'I refuse your challenge, Lord Raspero.'

Matthias breathed heavily and said: 'So be it.'

Matthias said nothing further for a moment or two. It was a standard technique, straight from the State Bureau textbook, to have long pauses in the dialogue between captor and captive. Matthias had not broken off eye-contact even once since beginning to speak, and in his eyes were a hatred and fury that were not feigned. He was capable of doing anything, anything at all, to Phelan and he was making sure that Phelan knew it. Matthias resumed speaking: 'Listen to me, Phelan. The time has come to speak of many things. You will speak and I will listen and judge. But you will tell me of your involvement in the deaths of my father and my brother, and you will tell me now. But now: talk to me, Phelan.'

'My Lord Raspero, as I have already said, I had no involvement in these tragic and unnecessary deaths. My only role in this affair were to detain you. I repeat: my orders, which I received directly from His Majesty King Frederick, were to detain you and do nothing more. This was my entire role in the matter. I was deeply shocked and sorrowed to hear of the tragic events which followed.'

'Yes, you must have been. I can see the picture in my mind's eye. *Phelan shocked and sorrowed.* It could be the subject of a painting.'

'It is Frederick who holds the answers you seek.'

'Frederick's only interests are his mistresses and the opera. He signs those documents which are placed before him by his ministers, such as you. It is those like you who make policy. Now, tell me of this particular policy.'

Phelan felt like a man obliged by circumstances to throw meat to the wolves. 'Your father planned to put your older brother Stefan on the throne of Westrigonia.'

Matthias grunted without humour. 'That is impossible. We are not of the Royal Houses.'

'Lord De'Asterides campaigned to have the Changeling Laws revoked in order for himself to become a candidate in the election for First Protector. In consequence, your ancestor Alyssa became once again the legitimate daughter of the Duke of Harentain.'

Matthias paused to consider this. 'You said nothing of this to me before.' It was a weak response but even Matthias, accustomed as he was to living on his wits, especially in the past few weeks, could think of nothing else to say at this moment in time. A whole new vista had opened up for him, revealing to him something that he had never before suspected. He was a newly minted royal person! Phelan had partially blown his mind.

Phelan's eyes glinted at noting Matthias in retreat. He followed up his initial foray with the never-failing appeal to self-interest. 'You are now the heir to more than the Barony of Raspero. You are now the heir to your father's plot. You are now eligible to be King. All you have to do is remove Frederick and Yolande.'

'And how is that to be done?'

'We did not penetrate sufficiently into this conspiracy to uncover every detail. There is much that we still do not know.'

'Why should I believe a word of this?'

'Why should you not?'

'And so this is why you were part of the network that killed my father and my brother?'

Phelan stiffened on hearing this accusation. His life swung by the rope woven of these words over an abyss. 'I had nothing whatsoever to do with their deaths. I learned of their deaths as much as you did, by surprise. This I can swear to you on my honour.'

'You will tell me the full truth, Phelan. This I can guarantee. And do you know how I can be so sure?'

There followed the kind of pivotal silence that exists between two crucial chess moves. Matthias took out his pocket watch, inspected its face and declared: 'I know this because there are still two more hours of darkness in this night.' He then replaced the watch in its pocket in his robes, rummaged around and fetched forth a bottle, which he stepped forward and placed on the table. His cryptic comment about *two hours of darkness* was still hanging in the air, but now it was hanging over this bottle on the table, and in its presence its cryptic nature entirely dissipated and became crystal clear. Two hours of darkness was equivalent to the remaining length of the life of a sane mind during which all secrets would be told.

The bottle on the table was made of a black ebony wood with silver inlaid markings, and those markings were of a skull next to a tree and a star. The bottle contained the Sweet Drink.

3:30 AM, Wednesday 31 July 1875 A. F

The Sixth Century AF, sometimes called the axial age due to the number of key developments which occurred during that era, was seen by many as a magical and mysterious time when the supernatural was commonplace. One of the most mysterious groups of that mystery-shrouded century was the heretical branch of the Herakrim called the Wayfarers. A sub-branch of these heretics known as the Ladies of Light and made up entirely of women came to acquire a legendary status in the annals of history. Their fame was largely due to their skill in brewing potions capable of producing a variety of effects such as mental confusion, compulsive dancing, derangement of the senses, an extremity of carnal lust, hallucinations, blind unthinking terror and loss of memory. These Herakrim women were naked when they picked the herbs for these potions in the varying appropriate phases of the moon, and it was said that wild animals would tear apart any mortals who happened to encounter them at such times, such was their power over the phenomenal world. Out of these potions came the Sweet Drink which was first referred to as such in the Ninth Century, by which time it had already gained its fearsome reputation.

The Sweet Drink was so called because it was believed to be extremely bitter, the bitterest of all beverages, judging from the shuddering responses of those unfortunates who came to swallow it. The ensuing state of mind of those who had imbibed the Sweet Drink very rapidly passed into a condition of terror in which they became extremely receptive to any suggestion that they could be rescued from their terror if they obeyed the instructions they were given, such as for example giving truthful answers to any questions put to them. This state of affairs only lasted for about twenty minutes or so, after which the unfortunate victim descended into a state of complete madness, which could last for a year or two, or longer, or for the remainder of his or her natural life. Even those who eventually recovered were never the same again. It was said that a saint could swallow a good mouthful of the Sweet Drink and enjoy a good night's sleep, while the inner darkness of those who were not saints was the true source of the potion's potency. It was also said that the tiniest drop of the Sweet Drink caused the secrets of heaven and earth to be revealed to the seeker for knowledge, but at the risk of losing their sanity. How, or even if, it continued to be made even into modern times was so obscured that some said that it was a myth that it even existed or had ever existed.

Phelan was not one to try to take comfort in such a notion. He knew that the Sweet Drink existed for two reasons: firstly, he had used it himself on others; and secondly, the bottle of the Sweet Drink which Matthias had placed on the table before him was Phelan's own bottle, taken from his belongings which he had unpacked the night before. Phelan cursed himself for having brought it along.

'I am waiting, Phelan,' Matthias said with a bleak and implacable look to his face.

Phelan began to talk, prodded every step of the way by Matthias.

Matthias heard him out, questioned him some more, and then set forth to establish the truth of the matter beyond any doubt. He poured a good mouthful of the Sweet Drink down Phelan's throat, and made the Director-General of the State Bureau of Security answer the same questions all over again.

4:40 AM, Wednesday 31 July 1875 A. F

Matthias left the roof of Castle Raspero on his flying sled. Dawn was not far away, but the stars still ruled the world as if there would be no tomorrow. He rose straight up into the air and headed north towards the Mountains of Lochfric. Returning to the forest clearing, he found his Castle Guard waiting for him there. He walked around, saying goodbye to each of his Castle Guard and thanking them personally for their loyal service. But being well aware that thanks is as well-received in other forms, he gave each a bag containing one thousand strada. To the Captain, two thousand. And to the Steward, no money at all – but Matthias took him to one side and conferred with him out of earshot of the others. Matthias took to his flying sled, lifted a hand in goodbye to his baronial subjects, and flew towards the north. It was in this way and on this day that the thirty-seventh Baron of Raspero left his homeland to go into exile.

CHAPTER EIGHTEEN

The wise man explained to me,
Everything that would happen,
And charged me a reasonable fee,
Which I had to pay in advance,
For his sterling silver service.
Nothing of any of it came true.
The uneducated fool told me,
Everything that would happen,
And all of what he said came true.
I still refuse to pay him a single strada,
Because it all would have happened anyway.
Frankie the Villain

10:00 AM Thursday 1 August 1875 A. F

The disappearance into thin air of the mind of the State Bureau of Security chieftain and the physical beings of his forty-nine subordinates caused a sensation all across Westrigonia. No-one was talking of anything else. The facts were these.

Chevalier Phelan and forty-nine agents of the State Bureau of Security had taken up residence in the empty castle of Raspero. All forty-nine agents had disappeared during the night without a sound being made, while Chevalier Phelan had been found the next morning by General Tola crouched in the castle courtyard, completely naked and as mad as a hatter. No sense whatsoever could be made of his incoherent statements, which did not appear to be in a known language and so might not even be statements; yet curiously, his speech sounds did sound as if they might be a form of garbled Baalbabakan.

Castle Raspero itself was completely empty. All of the belongings of the State Bureau agents had disappeared along with their bodies. The secret passage of Castle Raspero was located, and explored. The passage itself was shrouded in cobwebs of many years standing, and the ground outside this passage was completely unmarked, thus incontrovertibly indicating that no-one had entered or departed this passage on the night in question. There was no other secret passage, as all the experts testified.

Enquiries made in the town of Lentiagestes had brought forth the information that the Baron of Raspero had arrived with his men at four o'clock, travelling under a false name, and the Baron of Raspero had departed Lentiagestes through the public portal under the same false name, after which the Castle Guard had returned to the town of Raspero the following day. Enquiries were on-going into how the fugitive could have left the country, but given that he *had* left the country, it was clear that he could have had nothing to do with the mysterious goings-on at Castle Raspero, as it would have been physically impossible for him to have returned to Raspero in time.

General Tola could confirm that no-one had approached the castle. His sentries, stationed all about the town, had seen and heard nothing all night long.

The disappearance of Phelan's mind and all his men had the makings of a classic ghost story. Only supernatural agencies could have effected such an outcome as this. It soon enough came to be widely believed, even by people normally sceptical of such things, that demons from hell had taken the Bureau agents bodily and whole, but had only taken Phelan's mind for arcane reasons known only to those inhabitants of the underworld region of the three worlds.

The more people scratched their heads about this mystery, the more impenetrable the mystery became. As the legend grew, parents would hush their misbehaving children by saying, 'Be quiet, or you'll spend the night in Castle Raspero.'

11:00 AM Thursday 1 August 1875 A. F

The Witch of Trentland was entirely unmoved by the tales of supernatural horror being bandied about even in the Palace of Krastienst. The human all-too-human trickery of the Baron of Raspero seemed sufficient to account for what had happened. Eleanor's eyes glinted as she contemplated Matthias's latest misdemeanours. She looked as if she were trying not to smile.

She acknowledged to herself that secretly she was glad that Matthias had overcome his enemies and escaped. It was not that she was on Matthias's side, or even that she liked him one little bit. Far from it: Matthias had moved a vote of no confidence against her parents in the Vidaldmeet, and such effrontery could not be forgiven. But it was just that, in an obscure sense which she could not properly define, Matthias was in her mind Westrigonia itself. His success was an endorsement of the choice she had made in turning her back on her own country in order to become Westrigonian. His defeat would have been in this sense a personal defeat for the Crown Princess herself. But he had not been defeated. He had been victorious. It followed from this that Eleanor had made the right choice.

She would never see Matthias again. The fugitive baron would never return to his estates, let alone Westrigonia, but he would laugh yet while he enjoyed his freedom, and that somehow meant something.

9:20 AM Friday 2 August 1875 A. F

A rumour had started to spread that Phelan's mind, improbably contained in a casket, and his missing men were in fact holed up in the Ankalybu. In consequence of this rumour, the Speaker of the Vidaldmeet raided the Ankalybu. Say what you would about the tobacco-fiend Lord

Zelimir, but he was in fact one of the few men in Westrigonia with the guts to do this.

The real story behind this latest development, unknown to historians for the next seventy-eight years, was as follows.

The letter of Matthias Raspero to General Tola

The day after his arrival in the barony of Raspero, General Tola found under the pot of tea on his breakfast tray a letter from Matthias Raspero that went as follows:

"My dear General Tola, the fondest of greetings to you, and I trust that you are greatly enjoying your stay in my barony. I wish I could be there myself in order to properly entertain you as a host entertains his guest. I have no doubt that you understand that my absence is no disrespect to your highly esteemed personage. I have had to run for it, like the hero of an opera! One last thing. The State Bureau of Security will undoubtedly blame you personally for what has happened to Phelan. You will have to shift yourself to avoid ending up on the seventh level of the Ankalybu. I have written to the Speaker of the Vidaldmeet, informing him of what I now inform you, namely that there is a portrait of Leygerard hanging on the wall of the office of the Director-General of the State Bureau of Security. Enjoy your breakfast! Matthias Raspero."

Historians would enjoy commenting at a later date, with scholarly smiles, that General Tola was hardly likely to enjoy his breakfast after having read a letter like that! The letter to Zelimir referred to by Matthias was never found, but its existence was all too likely, given the raid on the Ankalybu which Zelimir led personally, and which did indeed uncover the portrait of Leygerard in the Director-General's office. The scandal was so immense that the State Bureau of Security never recovered. While it continued to exist, it existed in name only, being so scrutinised from day to day that it never managed to recover its earlier prestige. Nor did the figure of Phelan help in this matter.

Phelan was never to recover the use of his reason, and his bodily form continued for another twenty-three years. Sad to say, his remaining physical form was mocked and slapped about by those who had done nothing but grovel to him before while his mind had still been resident. Phelan was led around like a large baby being bathed and fed until the time came to bury him in a modest graveyard in the region of Salrautor from where he had originated. His grave was tended only by being urinated upon, and was soon enough overgrown. Whether or not he ever rested in peace is a question that no mortal can answer. It would seem unlikely on the face of it, after all that Phelan had done during his time on earth.

11:20 AM Monday 5 August 1875 A. F

Sensing that the Matthias Raspero saga had ended for the time being, Eleanor returned to her studies. The recent scandal about the portrait of Leygerard being found in Phelan's office reminded her about the Levellers, and so she took the time to have another look at them (holding her nose all the while).

The abolition of humanity

The abolition of humanity is long over due, said Leygerard. "Humanity" is the pretence that humans are different from animals. To "humanity" we say good riddance. The human is no different to any other animal. This means that all properties of living beings such as strength, speed, intelligence and so on, vary by quantity and magnitude. There is no other variation but this kind of variation. In short, there is no difference of quality, only of quantity. If people vary amongst themselves by in these quantitative ways, then it is this variation by which they must be ordered. Once humanity has been abolished, social distinctions must also cease to exist, and the community that remains will be organised by those variations that are relevant to the functioning of the community. The strongest therefore rule as only might can be right. There is no hierarchy for the Leveller, therefore, but there is an ordering of affairs by rational and empirical considerations such as these.

Eleanor shook her head in disbelief. Where did all this leave civilisation? No wonder Baalbabak, the only Leveller state in history, no longer produced anything worth anything. The Crown Princess of Westrigonia turned to the wisdom of the sage Arktos the Wanderer.

The human soul

A person is human by virtue of having a human soul, but no one individual has more of a soul than anyone else. It follows that no-one can be more human than anyone else, which means that we are all equally human. This is the only true equality that exists. Being human, we all have the same requirements of food and shelter and other necessities. We can only fulfil all these needs by banding together in a community, yet the formation of that community automatically gives rise to the requirement that it be ordered, which order can only be provided by a hierarchy. It follows from this that hierarchy is the most basic necessity of life to humanity as it is the necessity upon which all the other necessities of life are based. Therefore, hierarchy is necessary to protect the humanity which everyone possesses. This humanity is the basis of all our knowledge, because all the things that we know are made up not of the things themselves but by our own nature by which we apprehend them.

Eleanor picked up her pen and started to take notes.

10:00 AM Thursday 1 August 1875 A. F

It so happened that five days before the mysterious goings-on at Castle Raspero, Lord Zemfira departed this earthly realm. Naturally, his loved ones were grief-stricken, and equally naturally, their minds were already turning to the reading of his will. The long days and the slow hours passed in their own time, while the funeral was held, eulogies were solemnly given, and the casket containing Lord Zemfira's corpse was lowered into the ground on the same day as the naked figure of Chevalier Phelan was found by General Tola in the grounds of Castle Raspero, crouched on all fours like a wild animal and raving mad. These were interesting times to live in Westrigonia, as subsequent events would show.

The will of Lord Zemfira was read out the next day. By and large, those who had expected to receive his venom did so, while others received in their turn their expected portion of his estate. There was, however, one unexpected bequest that set the town of Rayton talking. Lady Acantha Godelric was left 70,000 strada in his will for her "conversation". Everyone in Rayton rolled about laughing, given that it had been hitherto unheard of to have *conversation* valued at such remuneration.

Lady Godelric took the point of this mockery, but she also took the money.

10:00 AM Saturday 4 May 1852 A. F.

When does a story begin? Should the story of Lady Godelric begin with her birth on 4 May 1852 AF as the only daughter of a prosperous merchant, Messire Taalay Samara, who purchased for her the title of "Mamselle" as a birthday gift for her fifteenth year, or with her engagement to Lord Fenton Godelric, or at some other time?

Her engagement to Godelric may as well serve as the starting point, as the image of Lord Godelric on one knee proffering a diamond ring for the consideration of his beloved has at least all the romantic promises of such a moment, which is at least cheerful.

Mamselle Acantha Samara was aged seventeen when she became engaged to Lord Fenton Godelric in August 1869 AF. At this point there arises a version of events whose provenance was never established, but which came to be widely believed.

The seduction of Mamselle Acantha Samara by Lord Godelric's secretary

The secretary entrusted with making all the practical arrangements for the wedding of Lord Godelric and Mamselle Samara became so entranced with the beauty of the young bride-to-be that he completely lost his head and pretended to her that she was required to rehearse her wedding night with him. The young lady, whose father had been overly protective, was so naïve as to believe him. The secretary then called in a Restorer to return her virginity to her in the form of a sac of chicken's blood attached by needle and thread to the appropriate place. A secretary is one who knows secrets (hence the name secret-ary), and thus did Lady Godelric's marriage begin, with a deeply buried secret.

Lord Fenton Godelric was handsome, young, virile, kind, intelligent, witty and sophisticated. He was also enormously wealthy. All the girls were mad about him. He adored his "Adorable Acantha" and loved to leave her notes in the shape of a heart addressed to "My One and Only." The wedding was a grand affair. Gifts were showered on the happy couple. The Chevalier Lachlann Cadence gave the bride a wedding gift of 180 wine glasses, thirty sets of six glasses, each set suited for a different kind of wine, to symbolize the sumptuous pleasures that lay ahead.

Soon Lady Godelric was pregnant, and the Godelric household, the ancient, wealthy seat of Castle Godelric, was blessed with a healthy baby boy, Cadfael.

Lady Godelric had everything, but having everything was not enough for her. Lady Godelric wanted more, far more, than her perfect life. And so she began an affair with the Chevalier Cadence, Lord Godelric's best friend and the giver of all those wine glasses. Lord Godelric found out about this affair and divorced her. His faith in morality, the afterlife, humanity and anything beyond the material was destroyed. The worst of his agony was that he remained besotted with his dazzlingly beautiful but promiscuous ex-wife. The second worst of his agony was that he now doubted the paternity of young Cadfael. In his depth of these agonies he sent the boy into the custody of Lady Godelric, refusing to have anything more to do with him.

So far, so ordinary: but now Lady Godelric's life spread wings and flew into the level of opera. She moved to the town of Rayton with Cadence, where she set up court with Cadence's money. A year and a half later, she gave birth to (presumably) Cadence's child. A year and a half after that, she was bequeathed 70,000 strada by Lord Zemfira for her "conversation".

12:15 AM Friday 2 August 1875 A. F

Chevalier Cadence was beside himself. Wild with jealousy, he roamed around the town looking for a fight with someone, anyone, and only a serried array of angels marshaled in the skies overhead saved him that night, such was his recklessness. But even angels can only do so much, and the time came when Cadence led a drunken band of campaigners converted to his cause to the Rayton graveyard, where they dug up the recently-interred body of Lord Zemfira to the accompaniment of a variety of popular songs, the percussion being bottles smashed on tombstones, the wind instruments being the necks of empty bottles being blown upon and the vocals being provided by those who knew the words while the others shouted inanities at inappropriate moments. The body of Lord Zemfira having been dug up, his corpse was propped up against a nearby tombstone, after which Lord Zemfira was put on trial for *malicious slander*, the graveyard itself serving as an impromptu courtroom.

Tales can become tangled in the telling (due no doubt to factions) and so it was unclear whether or not Lord Zemfira's corpse was indeed as claimed dressed in a night-shirt with a night-cap on his head, given the improbable appearance of such accessories at such a time, despite the sworn testimonies of eye-witnesses. What was beyond dispute was that Cadence, a rum bottle in one hand and a scimitar in the other, set forth to prosecute Lord Zemfira for the malicious slander of having claimed to have conversed with Lady Acantha Godelric. The case of the prosecution was that Lord Zemfira had never even exchanged a single "word" with Lady Godelric, let alone an entire "conversation". Chevalier Cadence claimed, his scimitar held over the corpse of Lord Zemfira, that Zemfira's motivation in making such a false claim was to go into the after-life with such kudos as these, gained by lying in order that the living should think him more of a man in death than he had ever been in life.

The painting of Daedalusine of this graveyard scene, long esteemed a classic and destined to hang in the Palace of Krastienst (no less!), shows this wild scene: the graveyard lit by candles stuck on tombs and lanterns in various drunken hands, the wild figure of Cadence surrounded by the disheveled and diseased human detritus of Rayton, the centre-piece of the painting being the figure of Lord Zemfira in his night-shirt and night-cap propped up against a tombstone, obscuring all but the first name of the deceased as written on the tomb-stone (this first name being "Acantha").

Cadence concluded his ranting speech of the prosecution by calling for the death penalty to be applied against Lord Zemfira for his crime, after which Cadence, seeming all of a sudden to lose all his energy, wandered here and there while looking in all directions as if hoping to see something that wasn't in fact there, and then sat down with his back leaning against a tombstone and went straight off to sleep.

All the others present, after various muttering conversational exchanges, and having lost the motive force of their revelries, departed one by one and two by twos and three by threes until there were only the two figures remaining at that time and place: Cadence and Zemfira, the one asleep and the other dead. Now *that* was the theme of the painting as chosen by Fedelej, judged by many authorities to be by far the superior painting of that wild night.

The authorities, realizing that they had to prosecute Cadence for *something*, but unable to find a law against digging up a body for no sane reason, settled on "public misconduct". The term *misconduct* could be applied to just about anything, and on this occasion it applied to Cadence's drunken night out.

For whatever reason, all this had caught the public's attention, and no-one was talking of anything else. Even the sober transcripts of the court-hearings could not but inflame the popular imagination yet more. Cadence's hangover had been succeeded by this trial, which was surrounded by a publicity circus, and Cadence's personal torments were amplified by all this attention. Chevalier Cadence now wanted only to disown his son, who he no longer believed to be his own, and retire far away from the world into a monastery where he would do nothing but contemplate God, his faith having been strengthened by his personal suffering.

But the publicity circus called for nothing less than the appearance of Lady Godelric at his trial. Scandals were her decoration and an appealing smile her only make-up as she wafted into court, fragrance in her wake and the world of men at her feet. According to Frankie the Villain, the poet who attended the court hearings, she had *the face of an angel, the body of a goddess and the soul of a whore*; in short, all the madness now made sense. The judge fell over himself to see that she was treated respectfully, over-ruling the mildest of questions from anyone who had the temerity to do anything other than to ask Lady Godelric if she was alright and if they could get her anything.

Troubles are said to come in threes, and Lady Godelric was not one to go against a popular superstition. The wealthy and powerful Lord Temur Katar took her away with him to Stayrint, his country estate near Waybridge, like a knight of old carrying her away from danger on his horse; there on his country estate she reputedly became his mistress. It seemed that every man who gained the apparent affection of Lady Godelric came to make the fatal mistake of believing that he was the one who would win her heart and gain her undying affection; in short, that he was the One. Some months later Katar was found dead with a knife in his heart, and the authorities launched an investigation.

11:15 AM Thursday 19 March 1876 AF

The authorities turned up in the person of Chief Investigator Justice Pepe Sabas, dressed in black legal robes and followed by assistants carrying his books, writing materials and personal belongings sufficient to maintain his legal presence for the span of one week or so. The good man, armed with warrants and official documents, and with the power of summary arrest and closed-door interrogation, arrived at Katar's country estate in full battle array. Justice Sabas was a stern-looking man with thin lips and a metallic glare to his eyes. Notaries and criminals trembled equally in his presence, given that his very being was a sharp instrument in the service of the law. He was incorruptible, with a mind like a steel-trap. Against this formidable adversary was a frail and slender woman.

Lady Godelric greeted him still dressed in mourning black, with bare shoulders barely visible under her flimsy silken veil, seemingly helpless in the depths of her grief, and agreed without hesitation to all his demands with regard to the pursuit of his investigation. There came a time when she insisted on speaking to him alone while they had tea together. This tea had been brewed by Lady Godelric herself, and Justice Sabas was a thoughtful man that night as he returned to his rooms. Soon their regular meetings took place in rooms in which the curtains had been drawn, and Justice Sabas would not emerge until the morning. Three weeks had passed and then the following dramatic denouement leaped forth: Justice Sabas identified the murderer of Lord Katar as the assistant second gardener. This unfortunate fellow, almost certainly innocent, was arrested and taken forth to be tried and, ultimately, such was the force of Sabas's finding, hanged by the neck until dead.

Now the learned Judge turned his attention to the claims of Lady Godelric on Katar's estate. Katar's will had left everything, absolutely everything, without equivocation or qualification, to Lady Godelric. Katar's estranged wife and children had challenged this will, claiming that it had clearly been forged. Soon Sabas begged to disagree. The will by which Lady Godelric had been bequeathed Katar's estate was, in his view, undoubtedly and with an astonishing exactness and correctness, legally valid beyond all dispute. Lady Godelric was the lawful possessor of all that Katar had once possessed, and the law, in the person of Justice Sabas, said so in impeccable legalese. Five weeks had now passed since Justice Sabas had arrived at Katar's, now Lady Godelric's, country estates.

Justice Sabas ventured forth to Rayton to emplace his depositions in the required interstices of the judicial nebula, thus formalizing and finalizing all legalities, after which he returned to Lady Godelric's country estates in order to continue his enjoyment of the company of the lady who he had come to call Acantha. But on his arrival, he was beaten by the servants of Lady Godelric and thrown back into his flying carriage. Justice Sabas left the estates of Lady Godelric a broken man. His hair had turned white and he never practiced law again. He died a few months later of a bodily infection. The last words he spoke on his deathbed were, *'Hell is empty and all the devils are here.'*

11:15 AM Wednesday 15 April 1876 AF

The public paid little attention to the tribulations of Justice Sabas. They had by this time moved on and turned the fickle affections of their ardent attentions elsewhere. No-one spoke of anything else but the story of the drinking men of Gennaro. This story was as follows.

The drinking men of Gennaro

What had happened was that a group of men had been drinking in a tavern when something in what they were drinking drove them mad. They came to believe that they were in a ship at sea whose safe passage was endangered by a storm. So they threw the goods of the tavern such as its furniture and wine barrels out of the windows into the street outside, believing that they were throwing it into the sea, thus lightening the ship and making it more likely that they would survive their time on the storm-tossed waves. The protests of the tavern-keeper and his family were to no avail, as the only response of these raving madmen was to throw these innocent (and sane!) personages out of the windows as well. (The members of this innocent family landed safely on the ground outside, being only bruised and shaken by their experiences, as everyone was greatly relieved to hear. The inn-keeper, however, took up another profession, having conceived an aversion to the drinking of alcohol.) The question on everyone's lips was whether or not these drunkards were guilty of wrong-doing or whether they were themselves the victim of whatever strange brew had been in the barrels from which they had drunk. It was a vexed question, and arguments over the matter grew heated. In the end, they received suspended prison sentences of three months each, and were bound to good behavior. Nothing more was ever heard from them, and they disappear from the pages of history from that time on.

6:40 AM Sunday 11 June 1878 AF

Lady Godelric's third child, another boy, was born with her latest paramour, Lord Fiete, striding up and down impatiently in the next room like an anxious father-to-be, even though the child was very likely not his. The paternity of this child was by now impossible to ascertain by any means of discernment other than that of occult divination.

Lady Godelric had retained ownership of Katar's estates, had been granted large payouts from the Godelric and Cadence estates in compensation for her suffering at their hands, and continued to receive a stream of gifts from her numerous admirers. She lived like a queen in the midst of the abundance of her overflowing prosperity, her daily life a lesson in luxury and opulence.

Such was the power of her beauty, which achieved greater things than the most brutal of bandit gangs could have done.

CHAPTER NINETEEN

Poverty alone makes a man a thief.
But poverty is never alone.
Frankie the Villain

2:15 PM Tuesday 10 February 1876 A. F

Six months had passed since Matthias had questioned Phelan, and Lord Lennard Camdenshall was now in his hands. It had taken Matthias some time to engineer, but all things, even the secrets of the universe, come to those who know how to wait.

Matthias and Camdenshall were in a cabin on the shores of Lake Capricia in the country of Melisende. Camdenshall had been lured there in a fashion involving forged letters and bribed intermediaries, and was now bound hand and foot in a chair on the bare wooden floorboards of the log cabin. Matthias had taken off his mask and revealed himself to his captive. Lord Camdenshall had not been able to avoid an instinctive flinching on recognising the face of his captor, and Camdenshall had known that Matthias had observed both this flinching and the meaning of the flinching. Much of what was already known did not need to be said. Camdenshall was an intelligent man.

'Your name was told to me as the man who engineered the deaths of my father and my brother,' Matthias said in a companionable fashion, as if making a comment on the means by which the weather was being forecast in these, the most modern of times. 'I have therefore brought you here in order to ask you, as a man with his heart in the right place on the left side of his chest, to tell me more of what this whole business was all about. You cannot deny me this knowledge, given that we are talking about my father and my brother. I am also a Baron and a member of the Vidaldmeet. Even if these moral and legal justifications do not suffice, let me make it plain that you will suffer greatly if you do not oblige me in this matter. Now: tell me what you know.'

'I assure you that you have been greatly misinformed. May I ask you how it is that you have come to grasp such misconceptions as these?'

'Phelan told me, both before and after I poured the Sweet Drink down his throat.'

As proof of this contention, Matthias produced a bottle of the Sweet Drink and gently placed it on the table by the side of the chair where Camdenshall was bound hand and foot.

Camdenshall turned red and broke out into a sweat. Matthias said nothing, but his eyes were cold and his face looked mean. Circumstances had made Matthias far more ruthless than the impish schoolboy he had once been. He was ready to do to Camdenshall what he had already done to Phelan.

As it so happened, Camdenshall had visited the incarcerated Phelan, and seen the mindless hulk of the man who had once been so feared across the length and breadth of Westrigonia. The experience had left a profound impression on him. His racing mind was making all the calculations necessary for its own survival. He did not want to end up like Phelan, yet he knew that Matthias had not idly produced the bottle of the Sweet Drink while making threats about how Camdenshall might *suffer greatly*. Camdenshall fully understood the danger he was in on that sunny late winter's day on the shores of Lake Capricia. He knew enough to say nothing for the time being.

'Does the earth go around the sun or does the sun go around the earth?' Matthias asked, after some time had elapsed.

'Sometimes one, and sometimes the other,' Camdenshall replied with a knowing smile. It was an urbane witticism intended to invoke shared associations that could be turned into an affectionate rapport between questioner and questioned, but Matthias was having none of it.

'Which one, Camdenshall?'

Camdenshall's smile faded. 'The earth goes around the sun,' he said reluctantly, dragged despite his best intentions into earth-bound factuality.

'That is a start. In a moment, I will pour the Sweet Drink down your throat. But first, you may beg for mercy.'

'Surely there is no need for such unpleasantness. Whatever questions you have, I will answer. Whatever-'

Matthias gagged him on the instant, uncorked the bottle containing the Sweet Drink, and came over to stand by the figure of Camdenshall. He forced Camdenshall's head back, made as if to pour the Sweet Drink down Camdenshall's throat, then hesitated and ungagged his prisoner. The only sound in the room was the harsh laboured sound of Camdenshall gasping for breath.

Matthias was in fact bluffing. There was no Sweet Drink left in the bottle, as he had used all of its remaining contents on the unfortunate Chevalier Phelan. But he had by now sufficiently terrified Camdenshall, and Matthias pressed this advantage all the way.

'I am about to pour this Sweet Drink down your throat. You have one last chance to persuade me not to do this. Now: take that last chance or do not. It is up to you.'

'I would much prefer if you were not to do this,' Camdenshall said in a calm and measured manner. He had measured his calmness so as not to plead, for he was a proud man, yet he was indeed measuring his calmness. Camdenshall faced a fate worse than death.

'I'm sure you wouldn't,' Matthias said with an entirely humourless chuckle. 'Perhaps you would appeal to the Golden Rule to stay my hand?'

'I am no Leveller,' Camdenshall declared with the appropriate distaste of a nobleman born, 'yet we are of the same culture, journeymen of an ancient way of life, and so I would yet seek an alternative road to this.'

Matthias leaned forward and looked into Camdenshall's eyes from a distance of six inches. 'Well, then, brother Camdenshall, tell me, what does our culture prescribe to me today, with my father and brother dead and buried and yet unavenged?'

'That you shall seek justice for their deaths, and that there is always more than one road up the mountain.'

Matthias straightened up, turned and walked away, taking the infernal bottle of the Sweet Drink with him, to Camdenshall's immeasurable relief. Matthias gently pushed the cork back into the little bottle, treating it as gently as if it had been a living venomous snake, and lightly placed the bottle on the table-top. Then he sat down, stretched out his feet, and said, almost with a yawn, 'Go on. I'm listening.'

'I can give you my word of honour that I will answer all your questions truthfully, so that there is no need to pour that potion down my throat.'

'To promise to answer my questions truthfully by no means guarantees that you will tell me the truth which I require from you. Why don't you try again?'

Matthias's eyes were so cold that Camdenshall could not help but feel a shiver. He was reminded that his great-grandfather Erasted, whose urine was said to be as cold and clear as a mountain stream, had faced the laughing demon Good King Justin at the same age as Matthias was now. Camdenshall composed himself.

'How should I address you, may I ask?'

'I have come into my estates, and we are not friends. You shall address me accordingly.'

'Very well, Lord Raspero. I am prepared to pledge upon my honour to tell you the truth as far as I know it. But I shall require from you a pledge that you will not pour that infernal potion down my throat. Are we agreed?'

'No. But I tell you what. You tell me the truth, and I will decide whether or not to pour this infernal potion down your throat. And you would do well to remember that I may choose to remove your head from your shoulders and use it as a football before leaving these your premises in any case no matter whether you tell me the truth or not. Now start talking. I said: Now!'

'My lord, while there is – '

Matthias moved with the speed and ferocity of a striking snake. Camdenshall's head was forced back and the bottle of the Sweet Drink, still corked, pushed into his open mouth. Matthias's face was pinched white with an ugly fury. Camdenshall felt both anger and fear; and then he felt shame at feeling these emotions.

'You have one more chance, Camdenshall, before I lose patience. Just start talking. I am not going to tell you again. Why I am being so kind I do not know.'

Matthias sat down with a deliberate staginess, stretched out his feet as before, and said: 'I am listening.'

Every story has multiple origins, but for the sake of convenience, the story which Matthias had requested on pain of death or the worse fate of insanity, could be said for the sake of argument to have begun with the summons Lord Camdenshall had received to Pentharborg, the seat of the First Protector, Lord Braeden De'Asterides.

4:20 PM Saturday 23 March 1875 AF

The Camdenshalls had been of the Zoller-Abstein party ever since the days of Erasted, and so Camdenshall thought little of this summons at the time. Whatever it was about would be fitted into the scheme of things that was the new order of the new First Protector, and that would be that. Camdenshall was later to reflect on the phrase that ignorance is bliss.

Lord De'Asterides was expansive and charming, as a great man should be. He was tall and thin with a commanding presence. He was an impatient man whose leadership qualities had been evident from when he was young. He had always been hungry for personal glory, and the flatterers who had surrounded him for much of his life had done nothing but feed this hunger as a fire is fed by logs. There were dimples in his cheeks when he smiled, and light-brown curls clustered around his scalp like a tangle of weeds. Some women found him attractive, while others found that he gave them the creeps for no apparent reason. He enjoyed company and maintained a network of friends and relations. His parties were infamous for their depravity among those privileged enough to be invited. No-one was afraid of De'Asterides and that was his curse; or rather, one of his curses. There were numerous encyclopedia entries connected to his name, and a knowledge of his career could always be counted on to score points in answering trivia questions in late night dinner games.

'<My good friend Lennard,>' De'Asterides said after embracing the Westrigonian noble. '<I had so hoped that you would come.>'

'<How could I not?>' Camdenshall replied courteously. '<Your invitations are as eagerly received as they are beautifully worded.>'

'<I never word my own invitations,>' De'Asterides said with a laugh. '<I leave that to my secretary.>'

'<My own secretary is as equally invaluable to my own humble self,>' Camdenshall said with his own laugh, '<but I did read your invitation myself with the greatest of care.>'

'<Walk with me in the garden,>' De'Asterides said abruptly.

'<I am greatly honoured by your invitation.>'

'<Your words are more true than you yourself know. These are my private gardens for my exclusive use. But today it is my pleasure to invite you along with me, Lennard.>'

Camdenshall guessed (correctly) that De'Asterides said this to everyone he invited into his private garden. '<In which case I am now properly sensible of the truly significant honour which is being paid to my humble self.>'

De'Asterides nodded absently, his thoughts already elsewhere. After a few more briskly taken paces along the carefully tended grass, he said: '<You are Westrigonian, are you not?>'

'<Indeed, my lord. Yet I am also an internationally minded person. I am a citizen of the world.>'

'<How nice for you!>' the First Protector said a little rudely. He did not want the scope of things widened at that time. '<I had hoped to speak to a Westrigonian at this point in time. You are Westrigonian, are you not?>'

'<Born and bred, my lord. To the bone.>'

Silence ensued. The two men were walking along between flower-beds strewn with brave white snowdrops, flirtatious purple wood violets, cheerful yellow daffodils, attention-seeking primroses with their yellow hearts and white bodies, dignified yellow cowslips and the lady of them all, gracious lilies-of-the-valley. The borders of De'Asterides private gardens were hedgerows laid out in an octagonal pattern. In the centre was a pond with a fountain depicting a wand-fighter from whose upraised wand jetted the water of the fountain. A pair of regal-looking swans floated in the water, snobbishly ignoring the cheerful ducks paddling about them. A short distance away was a weeping willow next to a small orchard of pomegranate trees. The garden was criss-crossed by paths forming tessellated triangles among the flower-beds and trees. Horse chestnut, apple, elm and almond trees were stationed around the garden at harmonious and geometrically determined intervals.

'<Tell me, Camdenshall,>' De'Asterides asked with his customary abruptness, forgetting that he was supposed to be calling his latest best friend "Lennard", '<What would you say if I told you I wanted, as First Protector, to have my own Paladins?>'

'<Paladins?>'

'<Yes, Paladins-Paladins-Paladins. You do know what the Paladins were, don't you?>'

'<Only what the legends say. That they were fighters without parallel who were never defeated.>'

'<Never defeated,>' De'Asterides repeated. '<That's something, isn't it?>'

'<Indeed.>'

'<Do you understand the position I am in, Camdenshall, ah, Lennard?>'

'<I am afraid that I am not always up to date in political matters.>'

'<Oh for God's sake, Camdenshall, that's what I hear every day from people who think about nothing else. Are you anything but stupid? You are here because the First Protector has invited you to be here. Do you have any idea, any idea at all, of how much this visit could benefit you? Or are you stupid?>'

'<You have asked if I understand the position you are in. Very well. My understanding is that you have gained your position is such a fashion as to require it to be established as a fact in the eyes of your many enemies.>'

'<That's not badly put,>' De'Asterides agreed with a shrug and a smile. '<But it is bold of you to speak of my *many enemies*. Everyone else assures me I have no enemies.>'

'<If you have no enemies, then you have no need of Paladins.>'

'<Hah!>' De'Asterides slapped his thigh. '<You're a sharp one, Camden-, ah, Lennard, Lennard, ah, yes, Lennard. I should have you here with me permanently. What position would you like? Take your pick, you would have my ear on a daily basis, trust me you would prosper mightily. Money, women, power, I like you, Lennard, you have my favour. What do you say? Would you like to have a position here at Pentharborg daily at my side?>'

Dear God in Heaven! No! Camdenshall screamed silently to himself. Maintaining his face as blank as a blank wall, and his demeanour as nothing but a courteous inclination into the most willing of servitudes, he ventured to say to the most powerful man in the world: '<Nothing would please me more greatly. My commitments are innumerable, my appointments as manifold as the sands by the sea, yet . . . >' Camdenshall trailed off as if pondering a bewildering array of choices.

De'Asterides nodded understandingly. '<Of course, of course, yet my offer remains open. You have only to remind me of it and the deal is done.>'

Camdenshall realised to his enormous relief that De'Asterides had only been going through the motions of trying to grab a closer hold of his subordinate. There was no embrace to be wriggled out of in the immediate future. Yet clearly De'Asterides wanted something from him, Lord Camdenshall, or Lennard-ah-yes-Lennard. And Camdenshall could also see that the blundering De'Asterides was nearing the point of actually requesting of Camdenshall what it was that he, De'Asterides, wanted from his invited guest. Camdenshall braced himself for the moment of truth.

The silence lengthened. After a while De'Asterides asked, with a barely concealed smirk that showed that he was deliberately dissembling: '<Where were we, Lennard? I have completely forgotten.>'

'<Paladins.>'

'<Ah, yes, of course, Paladins. What do you know of them, ah, friend Lennard?>'

'<They were the legendary regiment of half-animal half-human soldiers

who were the personal bodyguard of the self-styled Emperor Cayden of Lentia.>'

'<Go on.>'

'<The secret to making such hybrid creatures was lost in the Fall.>'

'<Bah! Stuff and nonsense! There may have been a Fall, but there never was such a secret. These Paladins have never existed outside of tales believed only by children and the credulous. Which are you, Camden-, ah, Lennard, eh, which are you? Are you credulous or are you a child?>'

'<I am credulous, my noble lord,>' Camdenshall confessed.

He made his confession with a smile to show that he was joking.

He was desperate by then to get out of the time and place where he was.

De'Asterides laughed a little too loudly. The man had a certain manic energy that was like hair sticking up frenziedly into the air. '<Well, then believe this, Camden-Lennard. Hah! Camdenlennard! Not a bad nickname, is it?>'

Camdenshall laughed with a pretended amusement. '<It is excellent, my lord. You have a gift for such things.>'

'<No, no, no, no, no!>' De'Asterides emphasized his stream of negatives with a pursed-up hand pecking the air like a woodpecker. '<No flattery, friend Lennard, no flattery. I liked you better before you started grovelling.>'

'<I am in the company of the great Lord De'Asterides, the greatest man of the age! Nothing I could say could possibly be flattery! Superlatives themselves tremble in your presence!>'

'<Hah! Good man, Camden-, ah, Camdenlennard! I see what you're about. Yes, clever. Irony, that's what everyone's calling for today, isn't it? It's the very latest thing. I like you even better than before, Camdenlennard.>'

'<I like myself even better than before as well, my lord. Your affection inspires my own.>'

'<I found a nickname for you. No-one ever found a nickname for me.>' De'Asterides said this as if confiding a profound intimacy.

Camdenshall nodded and looked thoughtful, as if this was a confidence which he was receiving in all earnestness. Privately, however, he couldn't help but feel that it wouldn't be hard to come up with a nickname for

De'Asterides. There were plenty of derogatory terms that started with the letter "D", for a start, while to combine the letters "D" and "A" was to be spoilt for choice.

'<Where were we, Camdenlennard?>'

'<I had to believe what you were about to tell me with regard to your project concerning Paladins.>'

'<Believe this, Camdenlennard! I am going to make a personal regiment of shock troops that will be invincible. Invincible! You know what the word *invincible* means, Camdenlennard?>'

'<Not able to be defeated, my lord.>'

'<And how should such a regiment be created? Well?>'

Camdenshall was genuinely stumped. '<I have no idea, my Lord De'Asterides.>'

'<Let us start with a simpler question, Camdenlennard. Shouldn't the First Protector have such a personal regiment under his personal command, answerable to him alone?>'

'<Are you asking me to speak for myself, my lord, or from the hypothetical point of view of the Supreme Council of the Protectorate?>'

De'Asterides came to a standstill and gazed intently at Camdenshall. '<Why do you think we are having this conversation alone in my private garden, Camdenlennard?>'

'<Ah! Because it is not happening at all, my lord.>'

'<Good man. Leave legalities to me. Trust me, there's nothing to worry about. We are talking under a rosebush at this very moment, so we are sub rosa. Do you know what it means to be *sub rosa*, Camdenlennard?>'

'<It means that I am not to speak of this conversation to anyone else.>'

'<When I have my Paladins,>' De'Asterides said reflectively, reaching out his hand to grasp the ankle of a nearby statue of a cherub, '<then it will not matter who knows about this. I will be invulnerable. Do you know what the word *invulnerable* means, Camdenlennard?>'

'<Yes, my lord, I do,>' Camdenshall said briefly, restraining his temper. He was fed up with De'Asterides's endless badgering of him with regard to the meaning of words. But more than this, his surprise at De'Asterides's naivety was combined with a certain dread of being sucked into a situation that probably would not end well. How on earth had De'Asterides become First Protector? Camdenshall asked himself. De'Asterides's belief that an invincible bodyguard would make him invulnerable was the thinking of a child. '<I grow increasingly curious as to what service it is that I am to provide you with in order for you to have your Paladins.>'

'<Hah, now we are coming to it!>' De'Asterides said enthusiastically. '<But first tell me, friend Camdenlennard, what is the source of all power?>'

'<The sun?>' The newly nicknamed Camdenlennard spoke cautiously so as to deflect any suspicion of sarcasm, although he was in fact being sarcastic. '<The source of all heat and light, the prince of the metaphysical heavens, the manifestation ->'

'<Bah! Stuff and nonsense! Metaphysical nonsense! Knowledge, man, knowledge! Knowledge is power! And where do we find knowledge?>'

'<The wisdom of the ages?>' Camdenshall suggested even more cautiously than ever, hoping to offend De'Asterides even more than before. But he was out of luck. He had given what De'Asterides considered to be the correct answer.

'<Good man! And where do we find the wisdom of the ages?>'

'<Ah! Mythology and metaphysics in the fairy tales of the people,>' Camdenshall pronounced with an authoritative air, as if he was sure about this one. '<Not to mention through tutorial lineages, instruction in dreams, the interpretation of omens and, ah ... >' Camdenshall trailed off as if trying to remember the rest of it. His current thinking was to push De'Asterides's buttons until the imbecile gave up on his plan to employ Camdenshall to help further his bizarre policies. He wanted De'Asterides to see him as too big a fool to bother with any more.

De'Asterides did in fact give him a strange look; but then simply shook his head and said briskly, '<The libraries! And what is the highest form of knowledge? Wandlore! Now do you see what I am about, Camden, ah, Camdenlennard?>'

'<Not really,>' Camdenshall confessed. He was not thinking clearly because in part he did not want to know.

'<What do troops do, Camdenlennard? They fight. How do they fight? With weapons directed by wands. How are wands used? By knowledge of wandlore and the requisite training thereof. And where is the highest, the deepest, the most profound and extensive expositions of wandlore? Well, Camdenlennard?>'

Camdenshall couldn't play dumb on this one. '<The Great Libraries, my lord.>'

'<And what are the Great Libraries? Name them!>'

Camdenshall gathered his thoughts together to prepare an answer. '<The fifty-five Great Libraries, my lord, around the world, starting in->'

'<Only in Westrigonia, Camdenlennard. Never mind around the world. What are the Great Libraries of Westrigonia?>'

'<Well, Krastienst, obviously, Quinlan, Dacre, Raspero, Walburga. By repute, of course. Who knows what they really contain or whether other libraries are better? It's like the hidden compartment paradox.>'

'<The what?>'

'<A carpenter once entered a cabinet making competition. He put a hidden compartment into his cabinet that was so cleverly hidden that the judges couldn't find it. They did find the hidden compartment in the cabinet of another carpenter's entry, and they were so impressed that they awarded him the first prize in the competition. Hence the paradox. The one who deserved to win didn't win precisely *because* he deserved to win. The best Great Library might be unknown precisely because its owners have the knowledge to keep it secret.>'

'<Keep your paradoxes to yourself, Camdenshall,>' De'Asterides said rudely. '<I'm not interested. Now, the five libraries you mentioned, yes, I have heard those names put forward for Westrigonia. I want all five of those libraries, and I want you to get them for me.>'

'<I beg your pardon, my lord? I do not follow you.>'

'<I want all five of those libraries, and I want you to get them for me.>'

'<And how am I supposed to do that?>'

De'Asterides sighed. '<By using your initiative, man. Money, blackmail, murder, theft, I really don't care. I am prepared to spend twenty million strada on this project. That money is yours. Anything left over can be

your own personal money, to be kept for your own use. And they keep the originals. All the books are brought here, they are copied, the originals are returned to Westrigonia, I keep the copies, I have a Great Library which has all the books in all the Great Libraries of Westrigonia, and in fact of the whole world. I shall make the Great Library of all Great Libraries, Camdenlennard, and with the knowledge of that library I will have troops instructed in combat to such a degree of skill that they will be invincible, and in that way I will have my Paladins.>'

'<The whole world, my lord?>'

'<This will wind up costing me three hundred million strada,>' De'Asterides said casually, as if it was his own money and not that of the public treasury, '<but look at the result, Camdenlennard! Think of the library I will have at the end of it all!>'

Now that Camdenlennard understood everything of what the First Protector was about, he felt emotions of a mingled nature: a grudging acknowledgement of the not entirely trivial character of the enterprise being embarked upon, along with an instinctive desire to be gone without any further personal involvement on his part. There are times when it is obvious that something will end badly, and this was one of those times.

'<It is a bold project,>' Camdenshall said perfectly truthfully, '<but it is possibly deeply flawed, my lord. I would counsel you against such a policy. You may make enemies capable of assassinating you, thus bringing upon your head the fate you have set out to avoid. The books may not be all that you hope they are, and the wandlore you have amassed may be of much less value than the price you have paid for it. The scale of such an enterprise cannot be kept secret in ->'

'<This project has already been up and running for seven months and what have you heard of it?>' De'Asterides interrupted brusquely.

'<Seven months, my lord?>'

'<It takes time to get around to a backwater like Westrigonia,>' De'Asterides said with a certain affable contempt, '<but here you are and your time has slouched around at last. I will give you twelve months to complete this project.>'

'<Twelve months, my lord, is not ->'

'<Twelve months, my lord, is all you get,>' De'Asterides pronounced definitively. '<Go and see Queralt to make arrangements concerning the funds.>'

Camdenshall noted that he was not actually being asked if he agreed to take the project on but, instead, his agreement being taken for granted, he was being directed in how to proceed. He felt as if the noose had already been placed around his neck on the gallows as a sign that his time had run out. It was perfectly obvious to him that De'Asterides would have him killed within the hour if he refused this employment. There was more than one aspect of being a guest in De'Asterides's private garden. He was being given no choice because he really had no choice.

And so it began for Camdenshall. He had set out to gain the five Great Libraries of Westrigonia for Lord De'Asterides. He had offered Baron Adelmar two million strada in return for being allowed to copy all the contents of the Great Library of Raspero. Baron Adelmar had refused. Camdenshall had increased his offer to three million, four million, and then the final offer of five million strada. Baron Adelmar had made plain that he would not accept any offer whatsoever. Camdenshall had therefore conferred with Phelan, who had already been taken into the First Protector's confidence with regard to this project, and in consequence the two had put the following strategy into play. Matthias would be arrested and imprisoned in Cayetano Prison in order to put pressure on his father. It was anticipated that Baron Adelmar would immediately go that very day to the Vidaldmeet to respond to this development, and arrangements had been made to have him assassinated by five corrupt members of the Defence of the Realm militia as he exited the Portal and walked along Calogera Street. The assassination of the Baron had been Phelan's idea, and Camdenshall had gone along with it to the extent of Phelan receiving one million strada of De'Asterides's money in return for his participation in this business. With the Baron out of the way, plans would be made to deal with his much less formidable successor, the youngster Stefan, with his younger brother Matthias still in Cayetano Prison. It was thought that a way would be found to get at the Great Library of Raspero in the future, but the precise plan had remained to be formulated. As it happened, Baron Adelmar had taken Stefan with him and his assassins had bungled the job and killed both of them. That was the first thing to have gone wrong. Phelan's men had later that same day killed the militia assassins and gotten rid of the bodies in order to cover the tracks of the conspiracy. The second thing to go wrong was that Matthias had somehow escaped from Cayetano Prison. Given that he could only have done this by means of a large conspiracy acting on his behalf, Phelan and Camdenshall had conferred and agreed that it was vital to take hold of Matthias and make him talk about this conspiracy. No-one knew what was going on. Phelan had therefore gone to arrest Matthias to regain control over a course of events that had gone haywire.

The rest, as the saying goes, is history.

3:45 PM Tuesday 10 February 1876 A. F

Matthias had listened carefully to Camdenshall's story, his head tilted carelessly back. Everything he had heard had dovetailed perfectly with what Phelan had already told him. There was nothing in what Camdenshall had said that seemed out of place or false. Matthias was satisfied that Camdenshall had told the truth. Camdenshall appeared to know nothing of Baron Adelmar's plot to put Stefan on the throne.

'I will talk very simply, Camdenshall, and you will listen. If at the end of all this, you still do not understand why it is that you should do as I have requested, I will pour the Sweet Drink down your throat, question you again, and leave you in the same condition in which I left Phelan. But perhaps you will protest that I have not given sufficient weight to your whining. Well? Is this to be your complaint?'

Matthias could have given the Grim Reaper lessons in looking grim about reaping as he stared coldly at Camdenshall, who by now had no doubt whatsoever about the very real prospect of having the Sweet Drink poured down his throat. In short, Matthias had Camdenshall exactly where he wanted him: on the edge of the edge of terror, which is the sharpest place to be in all of existence.

'My Lord Raspero,' Camdenshall began to say in his most friendly manner, but Matthias was having none of it.

'I have not finished speaking, bird brain,' Matthias said coldly. 'I will lay down the conditions for the survival of what you laughingly call your brain, in the face of the Sweet Drink which will end this laughter. Point One: you have offended me, my family, and the honour of the Rasperos. Do you dispute this?'

Camdenshall was not given time to answer this question. Matthias was already moving on.

'Point Two: I am entitled thereby to destroy what you value most, namely, your sense of self and memory even of the history of your being by pouring the Sweet Drink down your throat. Do you dispute this? Point Three: given that I accept that you have honour, being noble born, we can make peace here and now on one condition, namely that you pledge your word of honour to whatever agreement we reach. What have you to say?'

Like a sheep terrified by snapping teeth into running into a pen, Camdenshall found himself saying: 'I am naturally suitably cognisant of your position, my Lord Raspero. But it would be dishonourable on your part to pour the Sweet Drink down my throat merely in order to assuage your sense of honour impaired.'

'Absolutely!' Matthias agreed, with an encouraging emphasis on his immediate agreement. Matthias had carefully read the DSM (the Data System Manual) vol. 5 edition of the State Bureau of Security and his encouragement here of Camdenshall's eagerness to co-operate was straight out of Phelan's own textbook. 'Well spoken! There are times, Lord Camdenshall, when I think that you are the kind of man who I can do business with.'

'Absolutely!' Camdenshall agreed emphatically. 'We can do business together, my Lord Raspero.'

'Then here is the deal,' Matthias stated peremptorily. He was timing everything straight from Phelan's textbook. 'You will swear *temporary fealty* to me or I will pour the Sweet Drink down your throat or challenge you to a duel of Final Combat which you will be honour bound to accept and which you might well lose. I haven't decided yet what your fate will be. Now: make your choice!'

'Temporary fealty?' Camdenshall queried. He understood the concept, but was running from the twin fates of death or madness. He was playing for time, even though he had none nor could he gain any in these circumstances. But what else could he do?

'*Temporary fealty in jurisdiction tertiary,*' Matthias explained.

'Ah!' Camdenshall nodded. He was keen to keep talking, given that the direction of their conversation was pointed away from the fearsome Sweet Drink. 'On what terms?'

'That you accept my directions in all matters regarding my return to my estates provided that these directions do not impinge on your sense of honour, or the well-being of you and your family. That you are always free to challenge me to a duel of Final Combat, as I am always free to challenge you in such a manner. That our agreement shall last until either I am returned to my estates or one of us is dead, whichever comes the sooner. And of course, I may never threaten you with the Sweet Drink again. Are we agreed?'

Camdenshall looked as if he were contemplating his options, but the truth was that he felt he had none. The bottle of the Sweet Drink had sprouted a hundred eyes all over its rough leather exterior and was staring at him in a terrifying manner. He had never felt so frightened in his whole life. He was ready to agree to anything. Additionally, given that he had been involved to some extent in the deaths of Matthias's father and brother, he did have considerable amends to make to the injured Baron of Raspero. Logically, Camdenshall had to acknowledge his own guilt. He was therefore, all things considered, in no condition to put up any kind of fight.

'We are agreed,' he said.

'Pledge on your honour that you accept all the conditions I have stated. Repeat those conditions.'

Camdenshall pledged on his honour to observe all the conditions which Matthias had stated that were to constitute their agreement, while Matthias pledged in his turn on his own honour to also be bound by the same agreement.

The time came when the deal was done. Matthias set Camdenshall free from his bonds, pocketed the bottle of Sweet Drink, and said: 'Here is my first direction to you, friend Camdenshall. You will go to see the First Protector and inform him that you wish to devote all your energies to the pursuit and capture of Matthias Raspero and the subsequent delivery of his Great Library to the First Protector. You therefore wish to be personally put in charge of everything concerning this matter in order that the job is done thoroughly and properly. Once your request has been granted, and I trust that you will see to it that you do not fail to win the approval of De'Asterides, you will keep me informed of all developments. Do you accept this direction?'

'Yes, Lord Raspero,' Camdenshall agreed.

Matthias threw a letter onto the table. 'Here are all the relevant instructions concerning how we are to communicate with each other. Memorise these pages, and then burn them. Got that?'

'Yes, Lord Raspero,' Camdenshall said meekly. Although not a blow had been laid on him, he felt as disoriented as someone who had been slapped around.

By now Matthias was at the door. All of a sudden he threw back his head and laughed merrily. 'It's a funny old world, friend Camdenshall, isn't it? I will soon be in charge of the hunt for Matthias Raspero, directing all the resources which the Protectorate has pledged to this task. You've got to laugh, wouldn't you agree?'

'Yes, Lord Raspero,' Camdenshall agreed gloomily. 'It is indeed extremely funny.'

Matthias threw back his head and laughed again as merrily as before. He disappeared through the door while his laughter flowed back into the room and faded away like soap bubbles popping in the air. Some time passed before Camdenshall bestirred himself, picked up the letter and left the room to go his own way.

Much later in another country, back at home on his own country estates in Westrigonia, seated in his own study, with a glass of Rehunda wine in his hand, Camdenshall did in fact, reluctantly at first, and then with an accelerating tempo, find himself laughing as merrily as had

Matthias, if even perhaps a little hysterically. It took some time before his laughter subsided and he was himself again.

He raised his glass to the portrait of Erasted on the wall and guzzled down the remainder of his wine. At one level of understanding Camdenshall felt like a packhorse who has been loaded up as a beast of burden at the behest of the man with the whip. His life would not be fully his own again until the Baron of Raspero had returned to his estates. Grudgingly, Camdenshall had to acknowledge that Matthias had played his hand skilfully. At least the young baron was not a fool.

That made a change from dealing with De'Asterides.

Camdenshall leaned back, closed his eyes, and began to plan out his next moves. Twenty seconds later, the exhausted earl was fast asleep.

CHAPTER TWENTY

I told my best friend,
All my most secret plans.
He laughed so hard,
He died upon my knife.
Tell me again what they all say,
That laughter is the best medicine.
Frankie the Villain

7:00 PM Friday 5 November 1877 A. F

Beauty does not grow in straight lines. Eleanor had been a very pretty girl, but there was no guarantee that her looks would continue along a projected pathway. Pretty girls sometimes became plain adults, while plain girls sometimes became pretty adults. Eleanor was a pretty girl who grew into a beautiful teenager who grew into a dazzlingly beautiful young woman.

While Eleanor was still a beautiful teenager, shortly after her seventeenth birthday, a Ball was held at Pentharborg, the ancient castle seat of the Earls of Penthar that was now the modern seat of the First Protector, to commemorate the tradition of the Fire of the Personage. A fire was kindled at sunset and rapidly enlarged into a bonfire whose flames reached into the sky, after which an effigy, as in a likeness of a human person, was thrown into the flames. The origin of this ritual were so obscured that some scholars had suggested that it dated to before the Fall itself. But who by now could say for sure?

The Ballroom at Pentharborg was the largest ballroom in the world. Each side of the Ballroom was five hundred and four feet long. The flooring was of red cherry wood parquetry, while the ceiling was of glass panes in steel brackets in a vaulted iron framework built on the designs of suspension bridges to lift high into the air. Weather permitting, the glass panes could be opened out onto the starry sky overhead. On this particular Fire of the Personage it rained continually, so the glass ceiling ran with swirling flows of water lit up by the chandeliers which were fastened to the iron framework of the ceiling, these chandeliers being the size of small flying carriages. Two sides of the Ballroom had large archways providing access to the gardens outside. The other two sides had matching archways providing access to the enormous neighbouring rooms. Tables laden with buffet-style food and a variety of drinks were spread out in these neighbouring rooms and outside in the gardens under large umbrellas. Several hundred servants attended the guests, many of them bearing silver trays with more food and drink. Four thousand guests made merry in these festivities, splendidly dressed and cheerfully swirling in their varied configurations as they danced the night away.

Amongst these guests was Her Royal Highness the Crown Princess Eleanor of Westrigonia, who was the centre of more male attention, both overt and covert, than any other personage of the evening, including the unfortunate effigy thrown into the flames.

Eleanor was, it had to be said, a sight to behold. The long black tresses of her hair had been braided and coiled and studded with so many sparkling emeralds and diamonds as to enhance her elegant neck, her arched eyebrows, her high cheekbones, her sparkling green eyes under their long eyelashes, and her long and slender white arms. While all this was going on, she was stylishly dressed in a dazzling white ball gown that wrapped around the upper body leaving her bare shoulders exposed to view and displaying a cleavage as modest as her budding potential. Queues formed of young men eager to dance with her, while duels were fought out of sight of the ballroom between those who were thought to have disagreed about the extent of her beauty. Such were the passions engendered on that bonfire night.

It was then and there that Eleanor gained her nickname of the Jewel of Krastienst.

3:00 PM Sunday 7 November 1877 A. F

Yolande had decided that it was time to have a mother's talk with her daughter, who had seemed at times dangerously naïve during the ball, requiring Yolande's constant supervision. Eleanor's only knowledge of romance came from her romance novels (or so Yolande thought, not knowing of the kiss Matthias had given her in the Rose Garden). The time had come for instruction, or, failing that, at least the giving of orders. Consequently, upon their return to Krastienst, Yolande had summoned Eleanor to the Pearl Room of the Queen's Chambers to enlighten Eleanor on dark matters.

The Queen's Chambers had a different layout to that of her daughter. The King's Chambers and Queen's Chambers overlapped in having the same Bedroom, which was located in the square tower surmounting the Palace. To one side of the Bedroom was the Queen's Chamber, to the other side the King's, which in layout were mirror images of each other.

The Pearl Room was immediately to the left of the Entrance to the Queen's Chambers. Seventy feet long and fifty feet wide, it had an oaken parquetry flooring covered in Ramudien carpets of varying sizes and designs. The twenty-foot-high vaulted ceiling had a fresco by the master Ferko showing the bottom of the sea where varying imaginative stages of the growth of pearls as symbolized by different scenes of human life were taking shape, these scenes being presided over by bare-chested muscular men and equally clothes-free curly-haired women, whose presence no doubt bore some relevance to the growth of pearls. Bronze chandeliers hung over luxurious chairs and tables and musical instruments. The east side of the room was made up of windows in an elaborate iron scroll-work, stretching from knee-height to well above head height.

Yolande received Eleanor at a coffee table at the side. Above her was a large painting of the banker Scroundel surrounded by tables on which money was being counted out by apprentices under the watchful gaze of supervisors. Yolande had personally commandeered that painting from a downstairs room and had it transferred to her private quarters, considering it to be a painting of the greatest refinement. The two Fifteenth Century oaken chairs with their green chintz upholstery positioned on opposite sides of the coffee table were reserved by Yolande for occasions such as one-on-one family discussions of a serious nature. Jason or Eleanor knew immediately upon being summoned to the Pearl Room that an important meeting had been appointed to them whether they liked it or not.

Yolande began this important meeting by vague and meandering comments that included her maternal concern about Eleanor's trusting nature and her innocence without actually specifying what she was about. Eleanor's bewilderment was too plain to be pretended, so after a while Yolande came to a stop, and then made a second start.

'<You must beware of seasoned seducers,>' said the Queen of Westrigonia.

Eleanor giggled suddenly. The image that had come to her mind was that of a man coated in salt and pepper.

'<This is not a matter for laughter,>' Yolande said sternly. '<This is of the utmost importance for your future conduct, your future safety. Why do you laugh?>'

'<I was wondering how their *seasoning* was acquired, Mother,>' Eleanor said in her most dutiful-tone-of-voice.

Yolande contemplated this nearly-meaningless question, and sighed in exasperation. '<Never mind that,>' she snapped. '<The point is that there are men who know what they are about. They are predators, and you are prey. Do you understand?>'

'<Yes, Mother.>'

'<In fact, just to be sure that you get things right, simply keep all men at arms length except that one man, and that one man alone, whom has been chosen to be your husband by myself and your father.>'

'<Could I help to choose that man, Mother? Can I not be consulted?>'

'<It is out of the question. You are not old enough.>'

'<Surely being old enough to take on the burden of marriage is being old enough to help to define that burden.>'

'<Not at all,'> Yolande said immediately and with a confidence she did not feel, because she often felt that her brilliant daughter put her on the back-foot. She wondered where Eleanor had gotten her brains from, because it was certainly not from Yolande or Frederick. Her own mother, Eleanor's grandmother, had been exceptionally bright, Yolande remembered. Perhaps this grandmother's intelligence had somehow made its way across the barriers of time and space like a magical octopus. '<You are entirely misunderstanding everything, and that is more than enough! You will be silent and you will be obedient! Is that clear?>'

'<Yes, Mother,> Eleanor said in her most dutiful-tone-of-voice.

Yolande scrutinized her daughter with her most searching gaze, which was the gaze of a mother who suspects malfeasance in her young, but Eleanor's demeanour was as uninformative as a blank wall.

3:10 PM Thursday 25 November 1877 A. F

All of a sudden, from one day to the next, Eleanor's world was turned upside down. She was summoned to the Pearl Room and informed that she was betrothed in marriage to Kayeld of Carnovia. The wedding was planned for the following October, immediately after her eighteenth birthday.

Eleanor had to rack her memory for the entry in her brain for this personage. Then it all came back to her. A fat old man, crouched like a toad, his face mottled with age, had persistently followed her around all evening during the Ball at Pentharborg, shuffling his feet as he walked as if incapable of lifting them off the ground. Out of politeness (and her mother's insistence!) she had danced with the old gentleman, only to find herself fending off his very unwelcome advances and pretending not to understand his insinuating comments. She had eventually escaped his company.

The interest of Kayeld of Carnovia in the Jewel of Krastienst was only inflamed by all this running away on the part of his quarry. Age and decrepitude had increased the fund of lust that constituted all of Kayeld's regrets about a life partly unlived. He had set his heart on possessing this ethereal beauty who had lit up the Ball of the Fire of the Personage, and had entered into marriage negotiations the very next day with Yolande.

'<That toad of a man!>' Eleanor protested. '<I have to marry *him*? Well, I will not. I refuse! It is unacceptable. It is out of the question. It is preposterous. I refuse and that is all that needs to be said.>'

Yolande smiled understandingly. It was a smile that always infuriated her daughter, given that her mother had no understanding.

'<It is natural for a young girl such as yourself to be apprehensive about such a matter as being given away in marriage.>'

'<Your sentence is incomplete, mother. It must end: *being given away in marriage to a toad.*>'

Yolande smiled even more understandingly, which made everything even worse. '<There are advantages to this alliance that outweigh any shortcomings such as those of mere physical appearance. You must look beyond these superficial matters. Think of the fairytale in which the beast is really a handsome prince! What is truly important is the enormous wealth which Kayeld of Carnovia possesses. That wealth has more value than any fairytale ever told.>' Yolande stopped there with an encouraging smile, as if to invite Eleanor to complete her argument.

'<I am not marrying a toad like that no matter how rich he is.>'

Yolande was no longer being understanding. Her face had become businesslike and impersonal. '<Let me make this whole matter clearer. Kayeld of Carnovia is eighty-four years old. Now do you understand?>'

'<Do you understand, mother, that I am not marrying him, whatever his age? I will run away. I will jump out of the window. I refuse to marry him. That is all I have to say about this absurd proposition.>'

Yolande's face hardened further.

'<I can offer you two pieces of advice that will cheer you up, but first of all, let me remind you, Eleanor, that selfishness is only to be condemned. We have birthed you, raised you, clothed and fed you and given you all the advantages in life that you possess. It is not for you now to turn around and refuse to be liable for all that you have taken. A selfish and ungrateful daughter is an utterly unworthy human being. You owe us all that you are.

'<But now to your good fortune. It is entirely possible, even perhaps probable, that a man of such an advanced age will be unable to perform the, ah, act of consummation in which case you will be spared what is, I

am well aware, an event of some foreboding to a young girl. But if such is not the case, look on the bright side: he will be puffing and out of breath in thirty seconds, and thirty seconds of unpleasantness is easily borne. Furthermore, even if the novelty of having a young wife stirs his blood to such vigour as this, that novelty will wear off in weeks if not days, and so you may calmly contemplate a continued married life with no such obligations on your part. You can, in short, live the life of a nun under the guise of a married woman. If as time passes and you mature as a woman and you should choose, due to, shall we say, those temptations of the flesh to which we are all subject, to take a lover, then for heaven's sake retain the sense you were born with and be discreet about the business. So much for your duties as a married woman. Now look at the rewards to come, which is my second piece of advice. Do you have any idea, any idea at all, how many seventeen year-old girls around the world right now are on their knees praying for an eighty-four-year-old husband with such a fortune? Did you just giggle? You laugh, do you, daughter, you laugh? I will repeat what I just said, and I dare you to laugh again. Do you know how lucky you are, as a seventeen-year-old girl, to be betrothed in marriage to a wealthy eighty-four-year old man? Ah, you do not laugh now. Pay attention to what I am saying. Your husband will not live long, and we have made it a condition of the marriage contract that you are to be the sole inheritor of everything. *Everything*, his estates, his money, his assets, everything. It is only a matter of some years before you will be a wealthy widow, and even if the old man shall linger on, he will be in such an infirm state that you may rule his domain by your own hand under his name, and you may well find, by the time he finally falls off his perch, that you miss the convenience of his nominal presence. You will then be in a position to marry for love, if that is your choice, but consider then your circumstances. A girl of your natural beauty, but with your royal background *and* your immense wealth can take her pick of the best suitors available. You will have the world at your feet. Do you not see how much you have to gain from this marriage? Athletes willingly forego years of their lives while they train blindly, forsaking all else, to achieve a momentary glory that will cast its golden glow on all the rest of their lives. Think of this marriage in these terms and you will see how much you have to gain for what is really, when all is said and done, a paltry loss on your part. Such is your choice.>'

Yolande's eyes had sparkled while saying all this. She was delighted to be the bearer of such good news and it was clear that she regarded Eleanor's objections as merely the result of an imperfect reasoning that her maternal wisdom had now straightened out.

'<My choice, mother, if left to me, is to make an advantageous marriage now that does not involve my skin crawling in horror and my body shuddering from head to toe.>'

'<Oh, stuff and nonsense!>' snapped Yolande, her good humour jolted to a sudden stop and her cheerfulness in an equally sudden disarray. '<Your head is clouded by false ideals, no doubt gleaned from those romance novels for which you have such an affection. Very well, if you have not yet grown up, no matter. Time will deal with that. Time deals with the stupidities of youth in quite a sharp and effective manner, I assure you. You will find out for yourself that the lord of time does not carry a sickle for nothing.>'

'<The lord of death also carries a sickle,>' said Eleanor, who by now was feeling morbid.

'<Lord of death, lord of time, it is all yabbadabberoo in any case,>' Yolande said briefly with a dismissive wave of her hand, betraying momentarily her atheistic tendencies.

'<I understand that your own marital happiness has come about by strategies such as these,>' Eleanor said in her most unstudied manner, looking across the room away from her mother and biting her lower lip as if deep in reflection and speaking her thoughts out loud. '<But perhaps my own marital happiness lies along a different path?>'

'<Marital happiness?>' Yolande snapped. This was like waving a red flag in front of a bull. She was very far from being happily married, as her sharp-eyed daughter knew full well. '<When will you get it into your head, child, that marriage has nothing to do with happiness? It is all about advantage, advantage in alliances, in money, in property, in titles, in all sorts of things of a purely worldly, even mercenary, character. You are a

child and so you think as a child, but you will find, daughter of mine, that as you shall become an adult you will think and speak as an adult. Until then you must do as you are told. There is really nothing more to add.>'

And nothing more had been added.

The remainder of Eleanor's day was full of her sense of the loss of her future.

7:10 PM Friday 26 November 1877 A. F

'<You seem thoughtful, sister of mine,>' Jason said with a smile as he sat down next to her in the Zovartovian Room of the Palace of Krastienst. A recital of chamber music was being given that evening, and Eleanor was surprised to see Jason turn up. But a slight stiffness in his neck indicating a deliberate decision not to look in the direction of Lady Ameris and her bosomy daughter Bellina gave Eleanor a clue as to Jason's sudden interest in chamber music.

'<I am preparing myself for the musical recital to come. Surely you are about to do the same.>' Eleanor was dropping a big hint that she was not in the mood for conversation at that moment in time. Jason ignored her hint.

'<I am already prepared, sister of mine. So! Shall I offer you my congratulations?>'

'<If you wish.>'

'<Such a good match! And he's only, what, eighty-nine?>'

'<Something like that.>'

'<So he'll be dead before long, leaving you with a life of perfect freedom ahead of you.>' Jason sighed in an exaggerated fashion. '<Some people have all the luck.>'

'<Yes,>' Eleanor said in a composed fashion. She was determined not to be dragged into further discussion of her happiness but Jason, his eyes glinting, had other ideas.

'<It rules out becoming Queen of this dump, though, doesn't it? And after all the work you've put into getting ready, like learning the language and all that. What a waste of time.>' Jason shook his head, as if commiserating with her over the harshness of fate. '<You must feel as sick as a dog.>'

'<No, far from it,>' Eleanor said evenly. '<But I do agree with you that it looks as if you will become King after all, despite having made no preparations whatsoever for the role.>'

'<Oh, I wouldn't say that,>' Jason replied with a slight yawn. '<I've seen Mother and Father on the throne, doing their thing. That's given me all the preparation I need. Just delegate everything, sign the decrees of government, turn up now and then and give a public speech, and that's pretty much it. I think I can handle all that without losing any sleep. I think I could even do it *in* my sleep.>'

'<Good for you,>' Eleanor said in the most indifferent tone of voice she could assume. '<It's all settled then.>'

'<You can't be exactly over the moon about marrying such an old codger,>' Jason said with a pretended sympathy. '<I mean, he won't make your heart beat faster as you walk down the aisle toward him standing by the altar. If he even manages to stand. They'll probably have to provide him with a chair to sit down in while he waits for you to come along. Your wedding won't exactly be Romance City, will it? And will he carry you over the threshold? Hah! That's a laugh! He couldn't lift up a folded blanket in his arms, let alone a whole human being. Still, *them's the breaks*, as the saying goes. If I was required to go off to war, I'd just have to go, wouldn't I? You have to do your duty. We all have to do our duty.>'

The problem with Jason's argument from Eleanor's point of view is that she could not imagine Jason ever going off to war. She said nothing along these lines, however, in order to keep the peace. Jason could become hysterical at the slightest personal criticism.

There were times, mind you, when Eleanor was fed up to the back teeth of having to be understanding of everyone else's shortcomings, with not a single moment being spared by anyone else to pay attention to her own feelings. Eleanor felt beleaguered, with her back against the wall, surrounded by baying wolves; and did anyone care? No, far from it. Eleanor's future looked bleak, but the young princess raised her chin and readied herself to look the future in the eye and damn the beast to do its worst.

5:40 PM Wednesday 2 February 1878 A. F

After months of wedding preparations, Fortuna suddenly changed course like a dancer spinning on a toe. Kayeld of Carnovia went off the rails and the engagement followed. Eleanor was spared the fate that had so troubled her.

What had happened was that Kayeld of Carnovia had become infatuated with a music hall dancer by the name of Emmeline the Magnificent. The bare limbs of her scantily clad body had provided alternative roads for Kayeld of Carnovia to travel down other than the straight and narrow road of his honourable duty, and so he had forsaken his forthcoming marriage to Eleanor for the sake of this dalliance, even becoming engaged to the erotic dancer, despite already *being* engaged. Yolande had been prepared to overlook this misbehavior, which after all was neither here nor there, if it could all have been hushed up but the scandal had become public knowledge. This entry into the light of day had made of the scandal an unsurmountable obstacle, and so Yolande had no choice but to call off the marriage.

Yolande therefore summoned Eleanor to the Pearl Room and told her the sad news. Her daughter had ruined the entire occasion of mourning this disaster by rejoicing over it as good news, which Yolande found exasperating, given all the care she had taken over the legal contract by which Eleanor would have become unbelievably wealthy on the death of her husband Kayeld of Carnovia. Yolande had employed no fewer than fourteen lawyers to scrutinise the wedding contract, while spending much time herself over all the details of all its one hundred and seventeen clauses, only to find her own daughter failing to lament her loss. Yolande brooded over her inability to understand this disobedient and impractical younger generation, while her daughter hammered home her joy at being released from what she saw as marital imprisonment. Mother and daughter parted company on the worst of terms, each considering the other insufferably ignorant.

5:40 PM Saturday 26 February 1878 A. F

The entry of the Jewel of Krastienst into the marriage market had not taken place unnoticed. Yolande found herself besieged by offers, the majority of which she could ignore, but the remainder of which did indeed require her undivided attention. So it was that she summoned Eleanor back to the Pearl Room three weeks later.

'<I have good news for you, my beloved child,>' Yolande declared. She made her declaration a little cautiously given the baffling propensity for her wayward daughter to fail to see her good fortune even when it was presented in the plainest of terms. '<I have found a husband for you.>'

'<I am perfectly content to continue at present without any such accompaniment as a husband.>'

'<How lucky you are that this is exactly what will follow! You cannot complain on this occasion that your wishes are not being respected. The marriage will not take place for four years, given that your fiancé Lord Fulton Engelbert is at this time only twelve years old. So all is well!>'

Eleanor said nothing, but unfolded her fan and looked towards the window as if to say she would jump out of that very same window in four years' time. Yolande rolled her eyes at the melodramatic propensities of the young.

Eleanor's diffidence did not save her from being obliged to travel to Port Loberainton the very next week to meet her future husband.

11:00 AM Wednesday 2 March 1878 A. F

Lord Fulton Engelbert was strawberry blond with a thick scattering of freckles that were so prominent as to give him the appearance of having just emerged from a mud-storm. His eyebrows were so pale as to seem non-existent, giving his large pale blue eyes the illusory sense of floating in space. He spoke in a very precise and didactic fashion, and went directly to the point on the occasion when he and Eleanor were alone together for the first time (alone in the sense of being observed by a chaperone on the other side of the living-room who was too far away to hear what they were saying to each other. This form of chaperoning was considered quite daring in some circles, given the seductive powers of the spoken word, but it had been allowed on this occasion by Yolande due to Fulton's extreme youth.)

Fulton made clear a number of conditions that Eleanor was to observe as his wife during the time of their marital happiness to come. Point Number One: If Eleanor wished to visit his room, she was to submit a request in writing by sliding a letter under the door. This letter-sliding action was to be followed by a discreet double-knock, and all this was to take place no less than one hour before the designated time of the requested visit. Point Number Two: Eleanor would arrange all of her husband's clothes precisely in the manner specified by him without discussion. Point Number Three: if Fulton chose not to sit up straight at dinner, that was entirely his business, and Eleanor would do well to remember that if she knew what was good for her. Point Number Four: all finances were to be in Fulton's hands, and Eleanor would be fully required to justify any requests for pocket money that she might make. Point Number Five: Fulton could make all the noise he wanted, day and night, and Eleanor was forbidden to complain about it. Point Number Six: Eleanor was not to speak to her husband until spoken to by the same. Point Number Seven: Eleanor had to agree with any opinion on any subject whatsoever voiced by Fulton. She was never to have a contrary opinion. Point Number Eight: Eleanor was never to lay hands on Fulton's toy soldiers, under any circumstances. The severest consequences would follow from the breaking of this rule. Point Number Nine: if Fulton chose to feed his pet dog Alfher under the table, Eleanor would pretend not to notice. Point Number Ten: if Fulton chose to send Eleanor away from the dinner table, Eleanor would obey without question. Point Number Eleven: Eleanor would learn to play any musical instrument as selected by Fulton, and play this instrument at any time, day or night, as Fulton should direct her.

Eleanor expressed her opinion of Fulton's conditions in such a succinct and forthright fashion that Fulton refused to speak another word to her for the rest of the day, which suited Eleanor just fine.

Yolande was delighted by their quarrel, because it prompted in her mind the following syllogism: taking her major premise as *true love never runs smooth* and her minor premise as *Fulton and Eleanor have quarreled*, she arrived at the conclusion that *therefore they will get married.*

The next day, with a forced politeness, the two love-birds said farewell to each other. Eleanor retuned to Krastienst and Fulton went back to his toy soldiers, who did what they were told to do without any back talk. And as their respective families laid plans for the wedding, to be held in four years time, and for mutually profitable financial ventures, to be held imminently, Fortuna changed course like a hurricane swerving aside onto a newly chosen hapless city. The Engelbert family fortune was wiped out in the Gellertide financial disaster and they lost everything and became poor overnight. This happened early the following year.

Yolande dropped Fulton like a hot potato.

Eleanor bore the news of becoming disengaged with a stoic fortitude bordering on indifference. (Truth to tell, it *was* actually indifference.) She had never taken any of this nonsense seriously to begin with, especially given that her Achorat system of divination had prognosticated that this marriage would never take place. (Eleanor had by now given up on the Dagrun system of divination, which had proved to be too often unreliable.) She sighed with relief to herself, glad once again to not be betrothed.

Her newfound happiness did not last long. Fortuna was having too much fun playing with her life to stop now.

CHAPTER TWENTY ONE

I know when to tell the truth,
And I know when not to tell the truth.
Which of you can say more?
Frankie the Villain

2:15 PM Monday 19 June 1879 A. F

'<We have found you a husband, Eleanor,>' Yolande declared. '<Isn't that good news?>'

'<Another one? How many of them are there?>'

'<Yes, very droll. You will be pleased to know that your earlier complaints do not apply. Earl Lanzo Farran is twenty-four years old, which is an excellent age for a husband, is it not? He is handsome, intelligent, manly, courteous and educated. He has set many a female heart a-flutter, and without a single scandal resulting, which means that he has always observed the utmost propriety in his dealings with his innumerable female admirers. He is a splendid match. You may thank me if you wish.>'

'<Is there anything else I must know?>' Eleanor asked, skipping her thanks as if already thoroughly bored by this entire conversation.

'<We are going to Kasimirton next week. You will meet his family, who will become your family in due course. The wedding will be in November. May I be the first to congratulate you on your happiness?>'

'<No, you may *not!*>' Eleanor replied with a flash of temper. '<Why on earth can I not be a party to this matter of selecting my husband? If I am old enough to marry, then I am old enough to help make this decision.>'

'<We have been over this before,>' Yolande said patiently, '<and I really am losing patience with your endless complaints about a matter which you entirely fail to properly understand. You are too young now to participate in choosing your husband, but when the wedding takes place later you will be of age to become a wife. For now, you must accept your fate. After all, that is what everyone else has to do.>'

Eleanor shot back instantly with this rebuttal: '<I am of the same age now as when I was going to be married to Kayeld of Carnovia. Therefore if I am old enough to have been married to Kayeld of Carnovia at this time, I am now old enough to become a wife, in which case I am old enough to help choose my husband.>'

'<Oh, enough of this!>' shouted Yolande, and banged the table with her fist. She was not at all happy to have been so swiftly beaten in this argument. '<This endless argumentation must cease! You will do as you are told!>' She breathed heavily in her fury, and then brought herself under control in order to say as calmly as she could manage: '<Our discussion is ended. You may now leave the room>.'

Eleanor made sure to slam the door on her way out.

9:45 AM Monday 26 June 1879 A. F

Lanzo was everything Yolande had said that he was. Eleanor treated him coolly. None of his qualities, no matter how estimable, could make up for his chief failing, which was that she had played no role in choosing him. Lanzo's cheerful attentiveness never wavered, even when Eleanor became quite deliberately rude. Eleanor pointed out that his wardrobe was highly deficient, which suggested to her that he had no taste in clothes. She asked him his opinion on matters pertaining to literature, the arts and philosophy, only to observe from his replies that his education had been deficient; although perhaps, Eleanor suggested after some further reflection, it had not been the fault of his schooling but the fault of his mentally subnormal intelligence.

Lanzo took all these provocations with unfailing good humour. His white teeth flashed as he smiled charmingly at his fractious fiancé while running his fingers through the brown curls of his handsome head of hair. His urbane demeanour seemed to flinch slightly only when his close friend Neasa, who often accompanied them on their outings, attempted to defend Lanzo against these attacks. Eleanor's response to this was to raise the temperature of the debate by attacking Neasa as well. Neasa's comments became as much snarls as anything, while Eleanor's icy insults became all the more pointed. Lanzo would try to smooth over the resulting friction as best he could.

Two days of their visit had passed and Astrudel, who had not been idle all this time, stepped into the fray. She was accompanying Eleanor through the arched walkway connecting the Eldon House, which was being used as a royal guest house, to the Sandalio mansion, the ancestral seat of the Earls of Farran, on the morning of the third and last day of their visit, when she pronounced to the princess the following.

'My good friend Udane told me something of great interest to your personal situation what you have told me yourself about this marriage. You want the goods on Lord Farran, my mistress? I got the goods on him for you. But I want to help you something rotten I do, but you gotta understand that Udane doesn't give out nothing for free, you get me. Even though she's such a good friend of mine. She's something mercenary she is, Udane, it's shocking, but it's how it is, Princess, what can I do?'

Astrudel had met Udane for the first time two days ago. Given that Udane was kindly, chatty, friendly and endlessly helpful to all those in need, Astrudel could not help but despise her a little. The wily, battle-scarred servant of the Crown Princes of Westrigonia had found Udane useful enough, though, in terms of information about her mistress's latest fiancé.

'How much will it cost?' Eleanor asked bluntly. She knew this rigmarole already. She had been here before.

'Two thousand strada.'

'*Two thousand strada!*' Eleanor gasped. 'That is a preposterous sum of money for a servant's gossip.'

'It's something shocking what she can ask for such a preposs-, ah, what-you-said, sum of money. But it's more than just gossip. It's what is seen and known about by everyone here and is knowledge pure and simple. It's knowledge like what the earth is round, round like a ball, which is not gossip, my mistress, but it's the matter is this plain. When you marry Lord Farran, it's you what will have the whip hand over him from knowing this. Trust me, mistress. It's not that Udane is asking too much money, like what you said. It's cheap at this rate, you get this dirt cheap, it's a give-away.'

Udane had no idea how she was being misrepresented on this occasion. The entirety of the two thousand strada was going straight into Astrudel's pocket. Udane would never know a thing about it. Indeed, out of a sympathetic concern for Eleanor's feelings, Udane would have made sure that Eleanor would never have heard the truth about her fiancé. But Astrudel had seen that there was money to be made.

Eleanor pondered the situation. Astrudel had never asked for this much money before. And if this information really had the value which Astrudel claimed for it, then Eleanor simply had to purchase it.

'Very well, Nanny. What is this information?'

Astrudel leaned in close to whisper the following into Eleanor's ear: 'It's that Lord Farran's already got himself a wife, what with him and that friend of his who like to wrestle with each other.'

'I see,' Eleanor said coolly. 'Now that *is* interesting.'

As far as Eleanor was concerned she had gotten her money's worth.

7:00 PM Wednesday 28 June 1879 A. F

Eleanor had decided to make a scene at the dinner table that evening. This meant that she could spend the day fattening up Lanzo like a calf about to be slaughtered. She accordingly treated Lanzo and his close friend Neasa with much more warmth than formerly. All three of them laughed and passed the day in pleasant pursuits, closely attended by their chaperones who themselves laughed as well. Everyone was cheerful and in good spirits. Lanzo and Neasa started to relax as if the worst was over and they could all now be friends. From what they could see, Eleanor seemed to be coming around to accepting the fact of her arranged marriage. They knew too little of the deceptiveness of a scheming princess of Westrigonia to be on guard against her apparent friendliness.

If Lanzo's ears had been attuned to the sounds of his approaching fate, he would have trembled at the sound of the dinner gong. Instead, he tugged at the folds of his robes with his usual cheerfulness, and urged Neasa to hurry up so they would not be late. (Little did he know what was in store for him. If he had known, he would have wanted to be late!)

The Little Dining Room of Sandalio, so-called because it was a lot smaller than the Main Dining Room, was a long rectangular room ninety feet long, with a ceiling fifteen feet high with a fresco depicting the wedding of the first Earl Farran to Lady Lancing of Sterrenby. The five-foot-wide cornice was decorated with gilded swirling leaf-like shapes, while along the cornice at intervals were positioned large circular portraits of men and women from the Farran family's long and distinguished past. The walls were hung with large paintings with gilded fames and here and there were alcoves with pedestals supporting vases or other precious objects such as the silver brooch worn by Queen Lean of Trentland herself. Gilded chandeliers bearing blazing white candles hung down in a pattern designed in accordance with the constellation Taurus, while the highly-polished parquet floor had been designed by the master Faddey himself.

The seventy-foot long dining table was covered in a gleaming white table-cloth. Plates and glasses and cutlery were laid out neatly, and the guests were guided to their places by white-gloved servants.

Soup was served. Eleanor bided her time like an assassin waiting to plunge in the knife. She smiled at Lanzo, she smiled at Neasa and she politely nodded at the inanities of Yemelyan of Raiden. Every now and then, she unfolded her fan and held it over her bare shoulders as a way of suggesting to Yemelyan of Raiden that he need not stare at her cleavage quite so insistently as all that. Yemelyan of Raiden seemed never to grasp the hint she was dropping.

The main course was served. Everyone chatted animatedly to their neighbours, entirely unaware that they were on a ship that was about to go down beneath the unforgiving waves. The dinner guests were all having fun like there would indeed be a tomorrow.

Desserts were served, along with coffee and liquor drinks and a variety of sweets swamped in luscious strawberry and chocolate sauces. It was then, while everyone, including Lanzo, was at their most relaxed, that Eleanor struck.

Eleanor tapped her knife on her wine glass in order to create a ringing sound that brought about a hush as its concentric sonic ripples spread. Before everyone knew what they were about, they were all looking in silence at the Witch of Trentland casting her spell.

'<I have a question to put to my fiancé, Lanzo Farran, before all of you as witnesses to both my question and his answer. I ask you all to pay careful attention. Please be silent for the moment.>'

Eleanor paused. She waited while the tension built up. Even Yemelyan of Raiden forgot to stare at her cleavage.

'<Lanzo,>' Eleanor said, turning to her fiancé, '<please answer me this. How can you prepare to take me as your wife when you already have a wife? I refer, of course, to your wrestling partner, Neasa.>'

Lanzo's good humour looked as if it had missed a step while going down the stairs and taken a tumble. Trying desperately to recover, Lanzo reached for his wine glass, knocked it over, picked it up with a forced laugh and set it back upright while waving for it to be refilled by a nearby servant. '<Oh no,>' he said, '<this is entirely not so, and, um, I am not sure what you mean? What do you mean, ah, my beloved Eleanor?>'

'<She means what she said,>' Neasa said with a set expression to his face. '<And she's not exactly your beloved if she's, well, as you see.>' The wave of Neasa's hand through the air was so expressive as to render this last comment far more eloquent than it might have seemed otherwise.

'<Perhaps *you* are his beloved,>' Eleanor suggested, putting the boot in while her opponent was down.

Lanzo spoke hastily before the intemperate Neasa might say the wrong thing before witnesses. '<Not at all, we are only good friends, I am surprised to learn that, um, people are putting such a wrong spin on what is the most innocent of friendships. Really, what is the quote of that poet, how does it go, *you turn around*, and, ah, something?>'

'<There are many quotes of many poets,>' Eleanor said acidly, '<which would not do you the least good. Poets will not help you now, Lanzo. Far from it. You need a wandfighter's disc.>'

Eleanor's oblique reference to duels of final combat, at which death was the fate of the losing combatant, was not lost on any of those present. Duels of final combat had been banned by the progressive agenda of the Protectorate, but the Jewel of Krastienst might well be able to call upon male admirers who still retained the mentality of an earlier age, especially in a backward country like Westrigonia. Eleanor had made a veiled, but nonetheless deadly, threat.

By now Lanzo's glass of wine had been re-filled, but while trying to sip from it in an elegant fashion, Lanzo's hand trembled so much as to spill red wine all over his puffed white collars. This did not look good.

King Frederick the First groaned out loud. Things had gone so far that he had no choice now but to take part in these proceedings. '<Oh great,>' said the father of the bride-to-be, '<so Lanzo has Gresham's disease.>'

'<Surely we are not so barbaric as to speak in such terms,>' Lady Farran, Lanzo's mother, said loftily.

'<What is Gresham's disease?>' asked Eleanor, pretending not to know. She knew perfectly well what the term meant, but this was her way of stirring the pot.

'<It is historically –>' Lord Sakesheld began to say. He was obviously preparing to supply an academically precise and irreversibly unambiguous definition of this term, but Lady Farran was having none of it.

'<Yes it is, Lord Sakesheld!>' she shouted, holding up her hands. '<And that will do! As I was saying, we do not speak in such barbaric terms at this table!>'

Lord Sakesheld looked about him, trying to figure out what was going on and fumbling his way to the insight that it might be best for him to drop this topic of conversation.

'<No, but we are barbaric enough to consider our public image,>' Frederick replied. '<Anyway, the Westrigonians are dead set against this kind of thing.>'

'<Westrigonia is such a primitive country.>'

'<That may be, but I'm King of that primitive country, in accordance with the decree of Fortuna. The future King of Westrigonia can't be a lover of other men.>'

'<I'm sure past kings have been.>'

'<Yes, Stantaur the Deviant who died by having a red hot poker inserted into a bodily orifice judged relevant to his punishment.>'

'<Well, that was then. This is now.>'

'<Now is also then in Westrigonia. Even time itself can't move a muscle there. Nothing ever changes in Westrigonia. Trust me, you don't know the blasted place.>'

'<Which is highly commendable in its own way,>' commented the irrepressible Lord Sakesheld, who was able to see the good in everything. '<There is continuity in this approach to life, a sense of the transcendent in the everyday.>'

'<Exactly!>' Frederick said hastily, agreeing at top speed in order to move the conversation along. He had no time for his brother-in-law's endless esotericism. '<It's continuous and everything, which is all good. But I'm afraid Lanzo's engagement to Eleanor is at an end.>'

And so that was the end of that suitor.

3:20 PM Wednesday 27 December 1879 A. F

After the debacle at Kasimirton, Yolande had icily refused to speak a single word to Eleanor for six months. Even when Eleanor was standing right next to her, Yolande would make a point of instructing someone nearby to relay anything she had to say to Eleanor, and Eleanor's reply would have to be relayed through an intermediary before Yolande could hear it. Yolande had never in all her life been so angry. Eleanor made sure to hide her amusement, knowing that this would only have made everything worse.

But it seemed now that finally everything had blown over. Yolande had decided to return to being on speaking terms with her impossible daughter. Eleanor had been summoned to her Chambers. After exchanging meaningless pleasantries, the Queen of Westrigonia said: '<I am sure, my beloved daughter, that your natural interest in who will be your husband cannot have been checked by the lamentable run of bad luck which you have had to date.>'

'<My interest in who will be my husband is exactly proportionate to the role I have to play in choosing him.>'

'<Whatever,>' Yolande replied with a dismissive wave of her hand. '<But now to business. We have pledged your hand in marriage to Honourable Yorgos Yolst. He is a youth of fourteen, which is why the marriage will be held in two years time. I am sure that you have many questions to put to me, do you not?>'

'<Not really,>' Eleanor replied, holding her hand over her mouth so as to cover up a slight yawn. '<I wouldn't say that I have *many* questions, but I do have one. How long is this farce of an engagement due to last this time?>'

'<You are being very rude, Eleanor,>' Yolande said rudely, '<and very ungrateful, given all that I have done for you.>'

'<Do you know why all your attempts to arrange my marriage fail, mother? It is because you never involve my participation in the decision making. That is why. When will you grasp this basic point?>'

'<Oh, stuff and nonsense! When will you grow up, daughter of mine? I grow tired of your endless childishness.>'

'<Well, I grow tired of your endless insensitivity. Nothing matters except what *you* want, does it? Never mind what *I* want. That doesn't count, does it?>'

'<I am taking the welfare of *everyone* into account,>' Yolande snapped, '<while all you can do is think of yourself. Your marriage is not about you. When will *you* grasp this basic point?>'

'<Probably *never*,>' Eleanor observed icily. '<But does it matter what I think?>'

'<No, Eleanor, it does *not* matter what you think,>' her mother pronounced with a deliberate harshness. '<It only suffices that you do as you are told.>'

'<Then I will tell myself this,>' Eleanor said, rising to her feet like a boxer who has heard the bell ring. '<I will tell myself to leave this room immediately. Please observe, mother, how readily I do as I am told.>'

Eleanor made sure to slam the door on her way out.

10:45 AM Wednesday 9 January 1880 A. F

Eleanor's engagement to Honourable Yorgos Yolst had been publicly announced on Monday, the seventh day of January. Two days later, Yolande summoned Eleanor to her Chambers.

'<Your engagement to Honourable Yorgos Yolst is at an end,>' Yolande said abruptly. '<I am letting you know this so that you, well, so that you know.>'

There was a silence.

'<And why has this engagement ended, mother?>' Eleanor asked.

'<Never mind that,>' Yolande said brusquely, waving her hand as if to forestall all further questions on the matter. '<It just has, that's all.>'

'<But why?>'

'<That will be all.>'

'<You cannot possibly leave me in the dark as to why this development has occurred. Why has this engagement ended? I insist on knowing.>'

'<You may leave this room, Eleanor.>'

There was another silence. Eleanor stared at her mother, who looked implacably back at her daughter.

'<If I were *ever*,>' Eleanor told her mother, her voice trembling in fury, '<to treat you as you have treated me, you would understand why I despise you as I do.>'

'<If I *ever*,>' Yolande replied, '<have to repeat the simplest instruction to you again, you will understand the meaning of obedience. Now *get out!*>'

And that was the end of that. Not even Astrudel could find out why this engagement had been called off, given that no-one at all knew anything about it. This did not mean that no-one was saying anything about it. Lamentably when people cannot find out the true story, they will make one up. (Of course, if the true story is not to their liking, they will make one up anyway.) A variety of stories abounded throughout the drawing rooms of the Kingdom of Westrigonia, some vastly more improbable than others, ranging from madness to abduction to secret ancestries being uncovered. But no-one could say for certain. It would always remain one of life's mysteries.

By now, of course, the Witch of Trentland was spoken of as being cursed.

10:45 AM Tuesday 21 May 1880 A. F

Yolande had decided to play it safe. She chose Justice Felicjan Gennadios of Vaclavszjdom to become Eleanor's husband, given that he was the epitome of respectable dullness, in addition to (it went without saying) being extremely wealthy. (Being extremely wealthy was necessary to even get onto Yolande's match-making short-list. It was the condition without which not.) Felicjan was a Justice of the Fifth Circuit of Vaclavszjdom, whose family were nobles of five centuries standing. He would end his days on the ruling Council of Vaclavszjdom or in the higher circles of the Protectorate. He was forty-seven years old, with fat jowls and a double chin; there was plenty of middle-aged spread about the middle of his body. When Eleanor took his outstretched hand in hers, she felt that it was like taking hold of a large warm flabby fish. Dressed in dark blue robes with red velvet collars, his bulbous red nose supporting half-moon glasses over which his piggy eyes peered at his fiance, he seemed so solid as to seem immoveable. Yolande felt that here was a fiancé who would last the distance to the marriage altar. Fortuna's winds would not lightly blow down such a heavy-weight figure as this.

But Fortuna was not to be so easily disregarded. In August of that year, three months before the wedding was due to take place, Felicjan choked to death on a fishbone. Yolande was outraged as much by the manner of his death as the death itself.

'<Who on earth chokes to death on a fishbone?>' she complained. '<This is utterly absurd. I feel at times that I am in an opera! But even in an opera, the composer would stop short of such a level of absurdity as this. The audience would lose all sympathy. They would not return to their seats after the interval. I ask again: who on earth chokes to death on a fishbone?>'

Yolande's mood was not helped by those who answered her question in the negative. According to them, no-one choked to death on a fishbone, as the passage of air was impeded but not entirely blocked. Others, however, pointed out that if a sizeable globule of fatty food had fastened onto the fishbone in question, such an outcome might then be possible.

Alas for the heartlessness of the human race! Some people even laughed during the discussion of this question.

But there were those who did not laugh, and who whispered of darker forces at work. This was now the fifth fiancé of the Crown Princess of Westrigonia to have failed to get to the altar. The Witch of Trentland found that many eyed her askance as if suspecting her of engineering the death of her latest fiancé by the practice of black magic. Eleanor bore the scrutiny attendant upon these comments by pretending not to notice the stares being directed at her. Even Astrudel spoke to her mistress with a deferential respect for a while.

The rumours of Eleanor's witchcraft became pronounced enough so as to come to Yolande's ears, but the Queen of Westrigonia impatiently dismissed such talk, given that she did not believe in such things. Yolande and Eleanor attended Felicjan's funeral, shrouded in black veils. They stood next to the children from his first marriage during the funeral service, but were not invited to attend the reading of the will which was to be held the following day. Yolande had ended up with nothing, despite all her scheming.

Yolande put everything down to bad luck. Eleanor put everything down to experience. Others formed their own conclusions. Everyone moved on with their own lives, which after all was all that really matters to anyone when it comes down to it. In the end, who could care less about Felicjan's end?

2:45 PM Friday 14 March 1881 A. F

Yolande summoned Eleanor to her Chambers. The dazzlingly beautiful Crown Princess of Westrigonia walked in twirling her fan through the air as if she had not a care in the world. The Queen of Westrigonia bore herself with a determined set to her posture as if to say that matters were settled this time beyond all doubt. Frederick was also there. Frederick had become involved as Yolande's failure to date to arrange a marriage for Eleanor was starting to raise questions even at the highest levels of the Protectorate. Eleanor learned of her latest betrothal with a smirk, which she concealed behind an unfolded fan.

Her fiancé was Prince Vahan of Gadarstan, who was politically well-connected and widely spoken of as a high-flyer even at the age of thirty-two. While he was not due to inherit the throne of Gadarstan, being the third of five sons, he was spoken of as a possible future First Protector, which would be even better. Frederick had known Vahan from his boyhood, which was another point in his favour. Frederick disliked new things (except when it came to his mistresses or the opera). Yolande had no objections. The twenty-year-old Crown Princess of Westrigonia bided her time and said little, other than to voice the usual platitudes. Yolande observed this apparent acquiescence with some skepticism, but said nothing; she, too, was biding her time.

The wedding was scheduled for September, and for a while people spoke of little else. But then along came the affair of the Forged Will of Yngvar Mamuka, and public attention shifted elsewhere.

11:45 AM Friday 25 July 1881 A. F

The entry of Sarkis Pasquale into Baalbabak at just before noon of the last Friday in July via the Public Portal of Rozneft, the capital of Baalbabak, was duly noted by the customs officials at the time. It was not, however, noted by these estimable functionaries that he was importing a controversy that was to eventually enshroud much of the continent in war. It was the beginning of a story that would come to be known as the Tale of the Forged Will. Heads would roll, countries would be invaded, and destinies changed forever, and all because of a scroll amongst Sarkis's possessions which was, supposedly, the last will and testament of Yngvar Mamuka. In order to understand the importance of this will, it must be understood that Yngvar was the late owner of the Kader of Dalibor.

The Kader of Dalibor was a vast sprawling estate which was mapped, spider-like, as a bulbous body surrounded by outflung and wandering strips of land that formed its legs. It contained townships, artisan communities and hotels on the tops of mountains; vast orchards of apples with attendant breweries where the famed alcoholic beverage of Joyace was brought forth from those self-same juicy and nutritious apples; and riverside walks with plenty of benches for philosophers to sit down and contemplate the meaning of life. Egg producers, vegetable growers using the rich black soil of those parts, clear rivers filled with fish and ducks and delicate, beautiful river-plants, all flown over by flocks of happily chirping birds, formed the daily contemplations of poets and painters. Horse-breeding stations and numerous sheep farmsteads and honey-bee producers jostled each other merrily amidst the general fecundity of the Kader of Dalibor. The milk of that region was so nutritious as to restore anyone who drank only one glass to good health instantly. This might have been because the milk was pulled from the udders of happy laughing cows by the capable hands of the buxom rosy-cheeked milk-maids of that region, especially as the lives of these buxom rosy-cheeked milk-maids were so carefully nurtured and sheltered by the protective landscape all around as to imbue their daily singing with such a resonance with the meadows in which they worked as to give rise to the legends that the milk itself vibrated with sounds. And let it be further noted that that same milk was turned into Beata cheese, which after all was only one of the most famous cheeses in the world.

It can be seen, then, that to be the owner of the Kader of Dalibor was such a fabulous fate as to make anyone straightaway into the happiest person in the world. From such goodness, however, can come the darkest of outcomes, given the clashing of desires that can thereby arise. After all, everyone wants to be the happiest person in the world, and many people will do anything, even dark deeds, to have a happy life. But nothing dark ever happened in the Kader of Dalibor, until Sarkis came along.

Legend said that the skies darkened unnaturally in 7 November 1850 AF on the birth of Sarkis Pasquale in the Kader of Dalibor (although some said that this legend might well have been planted at a later date in order to cast Sarkis in a bad light. Others said that the darkening of the skies on the day in question was due to a recent volcanic eruption.) What can be said for certain is that the Master of the Kader of Dalibor at that time, its owner by rightful inheritance, was Yngvar Mamuka, who had come into his inheritance some ten years earlier; and being long-lived, enjoyed every day of his life in the happiest of continually pleasing situations until sunrise of the last Friday in July 1881, at which time he died after a peaceful and gently lingering illness, surrounded by his family and loved ones and faithful servants. He had lived the happiest of lives, and died the happiest of deaths, and would no doubt have been as greatly surprised as everyone else at what was to follow. Lord Camdenshall, who had been staying in the Kader of Dalibor for some time in order to recuperate from a chest infection, was amongst those to visit Yngvar during his last days, and also to console Filize, who was due to inherit his father's estates any time now. Camdenshall was even seen talking with Sarkis, who was later to be so infamous.

From his apprenticeship in 1866 until the time of his master's death, Sarkis had steadily risen through the clerical ranks of the administration of the Kader of Dalibor to the position of personal secretary to Yngvar himself. Dutiful and hard-working, he had attracted no attention out of the ordinary during all that time, other than acquiring the unusual nickname of *the Seven-Eyed*. But on the death of his employer, Sarkis did something remarkable.

Sarkis the Seven-Eyed went to Baalbabak to formally lodge a will which he claimed had been given to him in the following manner.

The Handing over of the Last Will and Testament of Yngvar to his servant Sarkis as told by the self-same Sarkis

Yngvar Mamuka called to his deathbed his dearly-beloved personal servant Sarkis Pasquale, and gave to him his last will and testament, and requested that it be lodged in a Baalbabakan court. The document in question, splashed by the freely-falling tears of the heart-broken Sarkis, had promptly been taken to Baalbabak and formally submitted to a Baalbabakan court, which had accepted the lodging of this will, and ruled it as valid. By this will, Yngvar's whole estate, the Kader of Dalibor, had been bequeathed to Sarkis, leaving his wife and children penniless.

Yngvar's son and heir Filize and the rest of his family ignored the communication from the Baalbabakan courts to the effect that they were required to hand over the estate of the Kader of Dalibor to Sarkis. It seems that they did not even bother to have the letter translated into Westrigonian. Filize's family entirely failed to recognise the seriousness of the claims submitted thereby. They did not even honour the Baalbabakan letter with a reply.

It might even be, given that the Baalbakanian writing script is different to the Westrigonian, that the Mamuka family did not even recognize the scroll *as* a letter.

The young, ambitious seven-eyed servant of Yngvar had then gone to Rozneft, the capital of Baalbabak, and sank down ceremoniously on his knees to the Great Cadfan, the ruler of Baalbaka, to plead for justice in this matter. After delivering his petition, Sarkis banged his head on the floor with a satisfyingly loud thump. Cadfan agreed that Sarkis was now the sole possessor of Yngvar's estate.

A greatly distinguished Baalbabakan delegation, consisting of the highest of the high, then visited Frederick and Yolande. They ceremoniously handed over a letter from the Great Cadfan, emphatically insisting that the claim of Sarkis to inherit the Kader of Dalibor must be honoured by the Westrigonian authorities.

What had started out as farce was becoming serious. A foreign head of state was now involved. Yngvar's family was told of these diplomatic developments. They promptly rushed to a Westrigonian court of law to submit their own claim to Yngvar's estate. They pointed out that Yngvar had never mentioned anything about such a change of heart as this supposed will. They pointed out, furthermore, that as a Westrigonian, Yngvar's estate could not be judged upon by a Baalbabakan court.

It was this last point that was, of course, key to the whole affair. Yngvar's estate was located in the Steynrad province of Westrigonia, which lay on the border with Baalbabak. At a time before Westrigonia even existed,

Steynrad had been part of the kingdom of Epona, which had ceased to exist long ago. However, the Kingdom of Epona was considered by Baalbabak to be a forerunner of the Glorious Egalitarian Paradise of Baalbabak, and so they had long claimed nominal sovereignty over Steynrad.

There were further complications. Last wills and testaments formed a branch of law all of its own in Baalbabak, given that there was no such thing as private property in Baalbabak. Now, the five justices of Baalbabak who ruled over such matters as last wills and testaments had themselves been named as beneficiaries of Yngvar's will, and had formally submitted their claims to the bequests thereby nominated. Nor was this the extent of Yngvar's generosity to Baalbabakans who he had never personally seen. He had also granted the ownership of Joyace in the form of all its breweries and its attendant apple orchards to the Great Cadfan, the ruler of Baalbabak, and Cadfan was himself insisting that this bequest be honoured. This made Yngvar's will into a national matter of honour for the Baalbabakans. Cadfan was as absolute a ruler as history could show, which meant that a personal slight to him was a matter of life and death to everyone in the country.

Westrigonian public opinion was outraged by the chicanery of the Baalbabakans. The scholars led the charge of the thundering hooves of the masses. Everyone united in complaining about the conflict of interests faced by the Baalbabakan justices, and the Great Cadfan. Of course they found in their own favour! That was precisely why they should not have been allowed to pass judgement in the first place. There were rules against this kind of thing in Westrigonia. (There were also, in theory, rules against conflict of interests in Baalbabak as well, but on this occasion, for whatever reason, they had been bypassed.) No-one believed a word of anything the Baalbabakans had to say. The will of the seven-eyed servant was the stolen inheritance as engineered by outrageous perfidy. The Baalbabakans for their part, instructed by their leaders to engage in mass protests, complained loudly and bitterly at the failure of the Westrigonian to honour the law. After all, Steynrad was part of Baalbabak, so the will of Yngvar was valid. Camdenshall spoke to Frederick and Yolande and then went off to consult with the First Protector.

Attitudes hardened on all sides when De'Asterides, surprisingly, adopted what he called a fair-minded approach to the issue, calling for a negotiated settlement. This encouraged the Baalbabakans and outraged the Westrigonians. As far as they were concerned, there was nothing to negotiate about. The Baalbabakan demand was simply unacceptable, and that was all that there was to be said about the matter. Frederick and Yolande found themselves in the uncomfortable position of facing a Westrigonia united even between normally disputing factions on behalf of an issue about which the Protectorate itself was being equivocal. A Council of State had been convened in Krastienst, the decision had been taken to refuse the Baalbabakan demand, and Frederick had no choice but to sign the decree placed before him. The Baalbabakan delegate who came to take a letter from Frederick to Cadfan took off his shoe and banged it on the table in front of Frederick's startled gaze.

Already, there was talk of war.

1:25 PM Monday 1 September 1881 A. F

Prince Vahan of Gadarstan's engagement to Princess Eleanor now became a matter of controversy in Gadarstan itself. Should the marriage go ahead as planned, and should war later break out between Baalbabak and Westrigonia, Gadarstan would necessarily have to go to war on Westrigonia's behalf given that this marriage would have formalized such an alliance. But the network of alliances and treaties and trading agreements to which Gadarstan was already subject made such an outcome deeply problematic. To put it bluntly, Gadarstan stood to lose a lot of money in terms of a loss of trade. Furthermore, neutrality in the advent of war looked to be a lot more profitable to the Gadarstanians, as well as much more popular with public opinion. Eleanor's rumoured practice of witchcraft was brought to the attention of the Gadarstanian people, who had a horror of such matters. The decision was taken, to general acclaim, to call off the engagement between Eleanor and Prince Vahan.

Yolande summoned Eleanor to her Chambers and told her the news. Eleanor nodded and said how she hoped that this would all be for the best in the long term. Yolande's fingers whitened on her fan, but she did no more than to briefly agree with this platitude. Yolande was, truth to tell, completely fed up with this endless saga of arranging Eleanor's marriage, and Eleanor's barely concealed gloating was making Yolande feel sick to her stomach. Mother and daughter parted in the icy politeness of frozen smiles and empty phrases. Eleanor would always remember walking away from the Queen's Chambers through the corridors of the Palace with the autumnal sun shining through the windows and lighting up the floors and furnishings with an ambient golden glow. She had weathered the storms of six engagements, and she felt like a soldier returning from the wars in an optimistic mood. The Crown Princess of Westrigonia was at peace with the world.

11:00 AM Tuesday 11 November 1881 A. F

The peace conference began at Pentharborg under the auspices of the First Protector himself. Baalbabak had sent its delegation, and after some prodding, Westrigonia had reluctantly responded by sending its own delegation. Public opinion in Westrigonia was firmly against granting the Baalbabak case even this measure of legitimacy, but Frederick and Yolande had been given no choice by their own patron, the First Protector, whose requests they could only oppose up to a point. Camdenshall had been placed in charge of the Westrigonian delegation, given that he had long been acquainted with Baalbabak, having even been granted the highly unusual privilege of private audiences with Cadfan prior to the eruption of this whole matter of the Forged Will. It was thought that if anyone could persuade the Baalbabakans to withdraw their suit, it would be Camdenshall.

But by now, things were already more complicated than even a seven-eyed servant's many-fingered trickery. The Tale of the Forged Will, like a great river being divided up by a sprawling landscape into numerous new rivers, had become an impossibly complicated matter of many more political issues which were now everywhere being heatedly debated, even though they were often only tangentially connected to the original crisis.

Dispossessed and exiled Baalbabakan nobility of past times had emerged to press their own claims on the Kader of Dalibor, and other estates besides, including many in Baalbabak proper which had been overrun by the Levellers revolution there. A self-styled Earl of Steynrad had emerged in Gadarstan, Steynrad being the region of Westrigonia which was claimed by the Baalbabakans due to its being part of the long-lost Kingdom of Epona; and all while a self-styled King of Epona, complete with his own royal family, had emerged in the city-state of Pacifica. Even the established political parties of mainstream politics, normally held to be more responsible than the fringe parties of politics, were incorporating into their policy platforms ideas intended to take advantage of these changing circumstances for their own vested interests, no matter how idiosyncratic these ideas might appear. It seemed that numerous agendas, hidden or otherwise, had seized on the Tale of the Forged Will as the perfect excuse to advance their own, often absurd, claims. Factions were dividing and merging and multiplying like a bacterial plague of historic proportions.

There were no fewer than nine peace conferences being held in five capital cities. Everything seemed to be spinning out of control. There was a succession of clumsy decisions by the First Protector, which, while intended to improve the situation, in fact made everything worse. (Conspiracy theorists said that this clumsiness was deliberate.) Armies were going through peace-time manoeuvres that were falsely claimed to have been scheduled long ago. Demagogues were whipping up public sentiment in their respective countries. Learned scholars were lending their names to unlearned nonsense. Historians were later to comment that 1881 was one of those years in which Fortuna shed her guise and showed her face openly, as if to remind humans of who was in charge around here. When the use of free will appears to make no difference to the outcome of events, Fortuna is left as the only explanation of what then happens.

As 1881 turned to 1882, things began to quieten down. It was as if the drunken revelers at a party began to sober up and become aware that they were dancing half-naked in the light of the rising sun. There was a plague outbreak at Ganbaatar, which reminded people that countries could fight opponents other than each other. Demagogues began to give reflective speeches extolling philosophical contemplation. Camdenshall was sent by the First Protector to Melisende to conduct high-level discussions with the Melisendiens, whose own demands had lately become increasingly insistent, and this visit by Camdenshall was seen by many as a turning-of-the-corner, finally, away from the road to war. By the end of February, the general feeling was that the crisis was nearly averted.

Then everything flared up again, like a dying fire experiencing a resurgent blaze from one of its knots of wood. On the first day of March an official flying carriage of the Kingdom of Westrigonia carrying King Frederick the First himself, summoned to Pentharborg by the First Protector, was hijacked by the Baalbabakans while travelling through Baalbabakan airspace and Frederick was taken prisoner. Westrigonia was outraged. The First Protector sent Camdenshall to Rozneft to negotiate. The crisis was back, bigger and badder than ever.

6:25 AM Saturday 4 April 1882 A. F

The Baalbabakan and Melisendien armies attacked Westrigonia at daybreak under the cover of the latest peace proposal from the First Protector. This took Westrigonia by surprise, for although it had mobilized its army to deal with a logically possible invasion, it was believed that because its international security was supposedly guaranteed by its membership of the Protectorate, such an invasion was theoretically out of the question. The most powerful coalition of countries in the world, the Protectorate, was slow to come to Westrigonia's aid, while the ineptness of the military strategy of the Westrigonian Marechal meant that Westrigonia was rapidly over-run and the bulk of her army taken prisoner.

The Westrigonian people were left abandoned by everything except their own dark suspicions. They noted that the Baalbabakan general was called Styrast and the Melisendien general was called Asteorl. As both these names were seven letters long, and one name ended with the same three letters that the other name began with, people wondered how long this invasion had been in the planning, given that each general had been appointed to his position long before even the Tale of the Forged Will. Above all else, however, there spread amongst the people of Westrigonia a widespread hostility to the Protectorate, which had so spectacularly failed to protect them against invasion; and this hostility to the Protectorate extended to the Zoller-Absteins in general, and their own royal family in particular. People said that Frederick, who was still a prisoner in Rozneft, might as well stay there and rot; and Yolande and Eleanor, holed up in the Palace of Krastienst, dependent now entirely on the loyalty of their palace guard, could meet the worst of all fates for all that their subjects cared.

9:25 AM, Monday 13 April 1882 A. F.

Eleanor came back to the present moment. By virtue of the dreamlike telescoping of time, the many years of her lengthy trip down memory lane had taken only a few minutes of real world time, and so her return to the present was not long after she had learned from Astrudel of the Vidaldmeet's latest Act of its potency.

Matthias had been elected King!

One thing was clear to Eleanor. Matthias would come to his new kingdom without a moment's delay. Eleanor would have to look sharp so as not to be left behind.

Eleanor stood up and inspected herself in the mirror, pulling on long red velvet gloves so as to conceal her bracelet. 'We are leaving immediately for the Queen's Chamber,' she informed her ladies-in-waiting. 'Come.'

Eleanor stepped briskly for the front door of her Chambers. The Crown Princess of Westrigonia felt at that moment that the future lay at her feet, and all would be well.

CHAPTER TWENTY TWO

Where there are two Westrigonians gathered together,
There are three separate plots being hatched.
Frankie the Villain

9:30 AM, Monday 13 April 1882 A. F.

Eleanor set forth for the Piccolet Room, where she knew her mother would be found at that time. With her ladies-in-waiting in tow, she proceeded to her destination, overcoming all obstacles in her way by the simple expedient of marching onwards. The guards who were positioned so as to prevent any such incursion as hers would have had to physically lay hands on the Crown Princess in order to impede her progress, and this they did not dare to do. Eleanor consequently forged forward.

Yolande was anything but busy, being plunged into her own gloom. The Royal Councillor, Lord Cadwalader, was present, along with two or three other advisors. Eleanor barged into the Piccolet Room and declaimed: '<You must excuse me, Mother, and I thank you for doing so.>' She promptly went to the side and sat down, gesturing to her ladies-in-waiting to dispose themselves appropriately.

Eleanor at this point did not know if she was before her mother in hearing the news of Matthias's ascension to the Throne of Westrigonia, so she said nothing for the moment while she unfolded her fan and composedly settled herself down.

The Piccolet Room was square-shaped in its bottom half, and dome-shaped in its top half, with a circular band of stone carvings representing plants and animals joining the two halves together. Each side of the room was fifty feet long, and the central point of the dome was forty-nine feet high. Seven gold-and-silver plated chandeliers were suspended from the domed ceiling. The walls were covered in paintings and tapestries representing various of the Piccolet cards, while the dome was covered in an elaborate geometrical configuration of abstract patterns made of red-and-gold-and-blue tiling with black-and-white lines running through them. (It was said that a mathematician who spent too long gazing at the domed ceiling would fall over backwards and need to be carried away on a stretcher, but no-one knew if this was really true or not.) The floor was made of alternating black and white marble slabs, covered with a variety of Ramudien carpets made of traditional designs that were thousands of years old, predating the Fall itself. In the centre of the room was a circular mahogany cabinet containing packs of Piccolet cards, other kinds of playing cards and a variety of board games. All around the room were scattered tables and chairs for the playing of games. The Piccolet Room had witnessed the highs and lows of civilization over the centuries, ranging from the excesses of past gamblers such as monarchs and nobles to public suicides to declarations of love and proposals of marriage. Wives and daughters and sons and husbands had been gambled away at these tables. The historical collection of anecdotes entitled *Stories from the Piccolet Room* had been banned immediately after publication, given that its scandalous and scurrilous contents were all completely true.

Yolande, who had a passion for the board game Rahmong, was often to be found in the Piccolet Room. Since the Palace had come under siege, Yolande had turned the Piccolet Room into an impromptu centre of government. It was here that she waited to receive the latest news, as the only way she could keep up her spirits in these gloomy times was to be reminded of the past times when she had had fun. Yolande sat at the side with a crystal glass and a jug of water and a bowl of nuts in front of her, and a disconsolate expression on her face.

'<What news of Lord Raspero, Mother?>' Eleanor asked abruptly.

There was a shudder all around, even from the Piccolet Room itself, accustomed though it had become over the centuries to high drama.

Yolande did not speak, though she was gazing at Eleanor with the expression of a mother trying to identify the nature of a transgression.

'<Lord Raspero will of course immediately come here to the Palace to press his absurd claim,>' Eleanor observed with a detached air, '<so it is a matter obviously of the highest import to have a strategy in place to deal with this imminent arrival.>'

'<Your Royal Highness,>' Cadwalader said with an open-mouthed exasperation while quite openly rolling his eyes, '<it might well be in your interest to desist from such speculations given their mental infirmness. The last thing the Baron of Raspero will do will be to come here to the Palace. He will remain in the safety of Anglashia attempting to form a monarchy-in-exile while the Anglashians consider their best interests. But in any case, I do not know why we are even discussing this matter, which is so far beyond your comprehension.>'

'<No doubt you are already planning a diplomatic approach to the Anglashians which will result in the apprehension and extradition of Lord Raspero, who is after all a fugitive from Westrigonian justice. This is one of the two reasons why Lord Raspero will not remain in Anglashia. He will not trust the Vidaldmeet, who after all are only using him as a pawn; he will not trust the Anglashians, who will seek their own interests first; so therefore he will come here to the Palace without delay in order to secure his own position.>'

Eleanor had completely ignored Cadwalader and addressed these remarks directly to her mother. Cadwalader looked in consequence more annoyed than ever.

'<Whatever your esoteric deliberations may have told you in the enormous wisdom of those fakery illusions,>' Cadwalader said with all the sarcasm he could muster, '<this is the world of reality. Hello, Princess, wakey, wakey, Raspero is a rebel and a rascal, but he is at least not a fool with a woman's brain. Pardon me, ma'am,>' Cadwalader said, turning to Yolande with a forced smile, '<but the stupidity of your daughter's comments is driving me into making the observation of the common man in the street. It is – >'

'<The *common man in the street* knows nothing worth repeating,>'

Eleanor snapped, leaning forward with a hand upraised into the air, '<and so that is no excuse for referring to this source of information. I say again that Lord Raspero is already on his way here to this Palace and we must have a plan of action if we are to deal with his arrival.>'

Cadwalader now had the expression on his face of a saintly man who has simply had enough. '<Your Majesty, I fear I must leave further discussion of this matter to be that of a mother with her daughter. My business is that of politics, not the remedial nature of wayward children.>'

'<Thank God for that!>' Eleanor stated, half-closing her long-lashed eyes and breathing in through her flared nostrils. She knew full well that she was amplifying the white-bosomed expanse of her womanly beauty by doing this. '<I may now speak directly with you, Mother, which is all I have sought from the beginning.>'

'<How much longer is this going on?>' Cadwalader groaned. '<Your Majesty, please send your daughter away. We have too much on our plate at the present moment.>'

'<Not now, Eleanor,>' Yolande said briefly.

Eleanor said nothing but flared open her fan while gazing directly at her mother. It was a gesture that said more clearly than words could express that Her Royal Highness the Princess Eleanor would *say nothing more*, and that this was all the fault of her mother.

The silence which had reigned in the room prior to Eleanor's arrival returned. Before long, there was a peremptory knock on the door and Keeper of the Royal Portal Perun Wright entered without waiting for permission, such was the urgency of the message he carried.

'Your Majesty,' Keeper Wright said, bowing deeply, 'we have received a most unusual request from abroad.'

Eleanor's grip tightened on her fan.

Yolande's translator muttered into her ear.

'<Well?>' Yolande snapped at Wright, whose morose appearance made it clear that he was the unwilling bearer of bad news. Yolande didn't look happy at the prospect of receiving more bad news.

'I have received, um, well, as it happens, what is termed an order, in fact a Royal Order, so called, but of course it is not, but there are rumours, the

Vidaldmeet, what has supposedly happened, and there is of course the authority of the Vidaldmeet, naturally, which is not doubted, but even so, but this so-called Royal Order, forgive me Your Majesty, but it is from a certain Lord Raspero, who claims, please forgive me, Your Majesty, but there are rumours, the Vidaldmeet, supposedly, otherwise of course a madman, but there are rumours, so this order, from Lord Raspero, well, he claims as King of Westrigonia, he has given me orders, supposedly so he says, that he is coming to the Palace within the hour and to make ready the Portal for his arrival.'

The translator cut Wright's verbiage down to sixteen Anglashian words, by which time Cadwalader had his policy advice all prepared.

'<Lord Raspero is most certainly not to be allowed to come here!>' Yolande declared. '<He is nothing more than an imposter, and I will not grant his vanity the satisfaction of having his so-called Royal Order obeyed by the Keeper of the Portal!>'

'<If I may advise Your Majesty in this matter,>' Cadwalader began in his most self-important manner, '<we must allow Raspero to come to the Palace, whereupon we may have Romano arrest him. With Raspero in our custody, we will have a key advantage in our dealings with the Vidaldmeet.>'

Yolande considered this advice, tapping her folded fan on her knee restlessly. After a while she said: '<It must be understood that if Lord Raspero comes here, the Royal Order to open the Portal will be mine, not his.>'

'<But of course, Your Majesty,>' Cadwalader agreed with a little bow. '<So are we agreed on my suggestion?>'

'<May I ask what you are doing, Mother>?' Eleanor asked quietly, but with sufficient emphasis to be heard.

Yolande might have not have heard her, so busily was she thinking about the advice of her Royal Counsellor.

Eleanor leaned forward and said loudly: '<*May I ask what you are doing, Mother*>?'

Yolande turned around with a distracted mother's air of exasperation. '<Not now, Eleanor.>'

'Do you know anything at all about Westrigonia?' Eleanor asked in Westrigonian. '<Oh excuse me,>' she corrected herself by continuing in Anglashian, '<of course, you don't understand Westrigonian, do you? What I asked was: do you know anything at all about Westrigonia?>'

Yolande turned away with an exasperated sigh.

'<If we welcome Lord Raspero as our guest, then he is bound by the laws of hospitality to respect us as his hosts. If we attack him on his arrival, then he is not bound by anything.>'

Yolande did not appear to be listening.

Eleanor tried again. '<Listen to me, Mother. Lord Raspero will not come here without a plan to turn the tables on you. To attack him is to invite a reversal of fortune that will place you in the weaker position. He expects you to attack him. If you welcome him as your guest, he cannot act against you.>'

Lord Cadwalader stepped in at this point, seeing that Yolande was nothing but vexed by Eleanor's incessant babbling. 'Your presence here is merely as an observer, Your Royal Highness, although it has never been clear, to me at any rate, what exactly it is that you hope to observe. Be that as it may, perhaps you might oblige us by ceasing to prattle about matters of which you know nothing.'

Cadwalader had spoken in Westrigonian, but like Eleanor, he was equally fluent in both languages, so Eleanor replied in Anglashian. '<I was also an observer on those many occasions when the Baron of Raspero ran rings around my father's administration. On this occasion, I see yet again that the conduct of matters is in the hands of those like yourself who simply don't have a clue. You are a fool, Cadwalader.>'

Cadwalader flushed with anger on hearing this. '<I must protest at your rudeness, Your Royal Highness. I wonder why it is that your mother has so graciously allowed you to be present.>'

Yolande turned around and snapped: '<You will be silent, Eleanor, or I will require you to return to your room.>'

Cadwalader's fat face creased in a rubbery-lipped grin, so Eleanor unfolded her fan and held it high to shield herself from this grotesque sight. She said nothing further, but it was yet another of the innumerable slights that she would always remember and brood over. Yet on reflection, she would have to admit to herself later that on this occasion at least, it was just as well that her advice had not been heeded. She was the only one who had known how to stop Matthias, and she would have been best advised to have said nothing at all to anybody.

10:15 AM, Monday 13 April 1882 A. F

Yolande had taken her place in the Waiting Room of the Palace Portal, with her Anglashian-Westrigonian translator discreetly to one side. This Waiting Room had once been nicknamed, a little sarcastically, as the Room of Accomplishments, although its official title had been the Room of Green Oaken Leaves. The nickname had arisen due to the hunting exploits of a past Westrigonian king. All around the walls of the Portal Waiting Room hung the antlered heads of stags who had all been hunted and killed by the same enthusiastic King of Westrigonia, Leonidas the Quick. The invention of portals had presented the Steward of the Palace of Krastienst with a problem. Clearly the Palace had to have its own portal, in order to keep up with the changing times, but where was this portal to be placed? A committee was appointed by the Vidaldmeet, who chose to interfere in this matter, only to be ignored by the monarchy which appointed its *own* committee to investigate this matter. Years passed, the politicians bickered, the Public Portal was established before the Palace one, which was seen as a blameworthy matter for which there seemed to be no-one to blame; but eventually, in the fullness of time after the rising and setting of numerous political suns, the Palace finally got its own Portal. This Portal was situated in the Room of Green Oaken Leaves, otherwise known as the Room of Accomplishments. All of the hunting paraphernalia and memorabilia was taken away except for the antlered heads of the stags on the walls, which remained behind due as much to indifference as anything else, given that they weren't in anyone's way and no-one could be bothered with the extra work of removing them. Some kind of bureaucratic excuse was invented for their retention and the matter was done.

The portal itself took up half the room. There were a variety of sizes of portals as portals could be constructed of any size or capacity. The Palace Portal was one of the larger kinds. The remaining half of the room was designated as the Waiting Room of the Portal, where chairs and small tables were scattered about in a similar fashion to a Public Portal. On this occasion of the imminent arrival of Matthias Raspero, the thirty-seventh Baron of Raspero, the tables had been cleared away to one side with some of the chairs placed on top of them, while the members of the court took their seats on the remaining chairs, which were all lined up in three rows facing the Portal. Eleanor quite deliberately, with an authoritarian wave of her fan, instructed Palace servants to set her seat and those of her ladies-in-waiting to one side, with a slight space between them and the rest of the court. Strictly speaking, according to Palace protocol, Eleanor was supposed to be seated next to her mother, but Eleanor was flouting all such rules with a complete disregard for anything other than her own plans for this particular moment. Yolande did not notice her daughter's wilfulness, being caught up in her own thoughts, but Cadwalader did, and looked as if he might intervene. Eleanor gave him such a venomous look that even the Royal Councillor decided that the game was not worth the candle, and gave it up. Whether or not others noted this little drama was unclear. Sideways looking is commonplace in a palace, and what people see they very often keep to themselves, at least for the time being. All behaviour is supposedly determined by calculations of rational gain in the corridors of power.

Keeper Perun Wright had a ticklish throat, which plagued him with a cough he repeatedly held back by swallowing or, when that didn't work, tried to get rid of by discreet half-coughs, but that didn't work either. It seemed that his hay-fever, normally in full bloom with the pollens of summer, was happening today out of season due no doubt to the stress he was under. Sweat trickled down from his temples, which he ineffectually dabbed away. Perhaps no-one noticed, or perhaps everyone did; who could say? But time ticked by and Keeper Wright busied himself with all the tasks with which he was charged by his role in life. It was seemingly inevitable that the time should come when the controls were set and the levers turned for travellers to arrive in the Palace Portal.

Keeper Wright turned to the assembled gathering. He sought out Her Majesty Queen Yolande and said directly to her, 'Lord Raspero is to arrive.' Then he turned away and pulled the lever marked Receive. Greyness flooded through the Portal, an opaqueness that shimmered and then cleared. Nine figures stood in the Portal. At their centre stood Matthias Raspero, the newly-elected King of Westrigonia, clad in Anglashian garb, with four Westrigonian noblemen to each side. The noblemen standing in the Portal looked out at the court sitting in the Waiting Room, and the court looked back at them. The stage was set and the curtain had arisen. It was time for Captain Aedan Romano of the Palace Guard to step forward.

10:25 AM, Monday 13 April 1882 A. F

Captain Romano was a tall burly man with a scar on his right cheek. (The scar had been left from a disc which had nearly killed him in an illegal duel of final combat. Romano was still alive, which meant that he had killed his opponent on that occasion.) The large domed skull of the shaven-headed Romano was his other striking feature. He was well aware that his very presence filled people with trembling. He had long ago given up on any hope of being friendly with his fellow human beings as, no matter how nice he was, other people shrank away from him or gave him the bare minimum of human interaction. Something about him scared people, and he had long ago accepted his fate in life and given up trying not to be scary. Only his social superiors, such as the members of the Royal Family, or his military superiors, seemed unaware of his fearsomeness. Romano had decided therefore to be Romano, which was to say, the Captain of the Palace Guard accountable to no-one but Their Majesties and the kingdom of Westrigonia as manifested in the proper authorities. Everyone else could tremble for all he cared.

Romano had received his orders, made his plans, and arranged his guards accordingly. Given that the maximum number of passengers that the Portal could transport was twenty, he had selected forty of his Palace Guard to be there on that occasion, giving him two-to-one odds if

Raspero and his companions resisted arrest. These forty Palace Guards were the best of the best, and given that the Palace Guard already was the elite, being among the most prestigious and best-paid jobs in the military, this meant that the caliber of the men under his command was all that a commander could desire. The guards were spread out in a tessellated pattern just as the textbook required. Romano's orders were to arrest Lord Matthias Raspero and his companions immediately upon arrival. Now that they had arrived, Romano surveyed his opponents with an experienced eye, and his observations were such as to set his mind at rest, or as nearly at rest as anyone could be on the edge of a fight. Raspero's companions were obviously not fighters, being by and large to all appearances pampered noblemen who had never been in a fight in their lives. Raspero himself, who had his wand drawn, and another nobleman of his own age (Alaric) who also had his wand drawn, looked as if they would put up a fight. It now looked as if the odds were twenty-to-one. From what Romano could see, there would be a brief scuffle, followed by a lengthy lording over the defeated. Romano looked forward to that. This would be as much a pleasure as a duty. He didn't like rebels.

Romano stepped forward. 'Drop your wand, Raspero!' he shouted. 'You're under arrest!'

'Under arrest?' repeated Matthias questioningly. 'What for? And who are you?'

'Drop your wand, Raspero!' Romano shouted again. 'Do it now!'

'There is no need to shout,' Matthias replied peaceably. 'I have perfectly good hearing. Do you have an arrest warrant? If so, where is it?'

'Alright, take them down!' Romano shouted to his guards.

This was where things became mathematical. An analytical eye, surveying the unfolding sequence of actions, would have duly noted its coherent nature. It all had to happen as it did, given all the particular parts it was made up of in order to form the whole.

Alaric, his wand in hand, launched himself into the fray without hesitation. Having been in numerous fights before with Matthias, he was ready to play his usual role in such affairs, but he had never encountered foes of such fighting qualities as the Palace Guard of Krastienst before.

Alaric's foray into the fight lasted two and seven-eights seconds, being ended by mobile karns binding his hands and ankles and his wand being snatched from his hand. Rayerfeld and Lyttleton fared no better, being taken down pretty much on the spot without having moved forward at least one yard. (Alaric had travelled seven feet, and parried twelve blows from five opponents.) The other companions of the King, who had not even bothered to reach for their wands, given that they did not see themselves as having any kind of fighting roles to play in these proceedings, found nonetheless that the indignities of forcible restraint were being imposed on their persons forthwith by the soldiers of the Palace Guard, whose eyes were gleaming in a maniacal way as they took down their social superiors. Everyone except Matthias was now prisoner, but that did leave Matthias still at large, and a Baron of Raspero is never to be discounted in a wand-fight.

Yolande and her court made themselves ready to watch the fight between Matthias, who was on his own, and forty Palace guards and their fearsome Captain.

Eleanor was perfectly correct in having warned her mother that Matthias would not have come visiting in such an innocent manner had he not laid plans in advance that were far from innocent. The most idle observer of Matthias's career could have concluded by now that the thirty-seventh Baron of Raspero was no fool, and it followed therefore that Matthias's decision to come to the Palace of Krastienst was a calculated one. Just how calculated was now to become clear.

Immediately upon Romano's command, Matthias rose into the air, wand upraised, Romano's eyes fixed upon him. By the textbook procedures which Romano was following (and which Matthias had also studied attentively), Romano was charged with arresting Matthias. Certain specified guards in the tessellated pattern in which the guards had been arranged were designated to assist Romano in this priority activity, and Matthias knew who these guards were as well as Romano did. That is the danger of textbooks. Anyone can read them.

Matthias, by now fifteen feet in the air, threw himself directly at Romano, his wand pointed straight at the leader of his enemies. One second and three-eights had passed since Romano had issued his call to battle, and Romano threw all four of his mobile karns into the air at his opponent while rolling to his left while the precisely designated guards, five in number, who were his back-up threw all their mobile karns, twenty in number, through the air at the figure of Matthias hurtling through the air, all according to plan. But things now became so interesting that conspiracy theorists were later to enter into the picture. How had Matthias been able to do what he did at that time? No inquiry was later held into how Matthias Raspero had managed to subvert the defences of the Palace on this occasion. Unofficially, however, from the informal discussion of those wandlore experts who pondered such matters over their glasses of mead, certain things became clear. Wandlore experts were unanimous in their diagnosis of the basis of his strategy. Matthias could only have used a Sabahudin Energy Structure, and such a set-up could only be established by a geometrically arranged pattern of magnesium flanked by particular separations of pyrrhotite and lodestone and at a carefully measured distance from four bars of gadolinium. An experienced wand-user who knew of such an arrangement could activate its energies in such a way as to overcome any enemies in a wandfight, but that left the question of how such a Sabahudin Energy Structure could have been in place for Matthias to have activated at that time in the first place, as its emplacement would have required an infiltration of the Palace at some time prior to Matthias's arrival. The entire set-up could have been concealed in the antlered heads on the walls of the Waiting Room of the Palace Portal, but how did it get there?

As it happened, there had been a review of Palace security in December of the previous year on the instructions of the First Protector, and that review had been overseen by Lord Camdenshall, again on the instructions of the First Protector. Camdenshall and his men had sealed off the Portal, allowing no-one in while they thoroughly examined everything, after which Camdenshall had pronounced the Portal clear of anything which might compromise its security, and that had been that. If anything had been laid in place to compromise the Portal's security, therefore, it must have happened after Camdenshall's inspection. But all this retrospective reasoning was too late to influence the outcome of the fight between the Palace Guards of Krastienst and the Baron of Raspero.

Matthias took hold of Romano's four mobile karns, flying through the air toward his own royal person, plus *all* the other karns of the five other guards (twenty in number) and threw all twenty-four mobile karns back through the air in *seven-eights of a second!* Romano and his five guards were taken down on the spot, their wands all flying into Matthias's scooping-up left hand as the newly-minted King of Westrigonia hit the ground and rolled onto his feet and flew back into the air. There were still thirty-five guards to fight, and there was everything still to play for, in theory. But given the Sabahudin Energy Structure upon which Matthias was drawing, it was a very uneven battle-ground. Matthias had every advantage, and his opponents, despite their numerical superiority, had not a chance. It is said that *they also serve, who only stand and wait,* and in this sense Matthias's companions had helped him out by taking up the attention of the fifteen guards who had gone into action against them, while the remaining twenty guards had stayed out of the action as a reserve fighting force. However, seeing Romano and the other five guards taken down, these reserve guards flew at Matthias in a trapezoid formation, just as their training and instructions dictated, while the other guards were securing their prisoners and establishing their ground, just as *their* training and instructions dictated. The problem for the forces of officialdom was that Matthias had planned for precisely the battle he was now in, while his opponents had not. Matthias had even rehearsed his seemingly spontaneous moves, while leaving himself with a multiple choice of improvised responses. The result was a masterpiece which wandfighting enthusiasts around the world would have thoroughly applauded.

Matthias moved with such speed, drawing on the Sabahudin Energy Structure, that he became a blur. The four guards at the vertices of the trapezoid were flung towards each other simultaneously while the other sixteen guards were thrown against each other in a sequence that enabled Matthias to circle behind them and start throwing them one by one against the other guards, who by now were turning away from their newly acquired prisoners and seeking to take part in this continuing fight only to find themselves bowled over onto the ground by the guards falling onto them from above. Still Matthias was moving so fast that he was a blur, and still the wands of his opponents were flying through the air into his left hand, so many by now that he had to use a mobile karn to make a bundle out of them and throw it to one side. One guard after another was thrown this way and that, colliding with other guards in a chaotic jumble of limbs and karns and wands. The air was filled with the shouts of the guards, still falling to the ground onto the other guards like gigantic hail-stones. The Baron of Raspero fought with a precision and a ferocity that was itself unnerving, and when coupled with the the sheer power of the Sabahudin Energy Structure, the guards found themselves constantly trying to catch up. Their textbook had long ago ceased to be relevant, and it was all they could do to still manage to think. Matthias was turning the sheer numbers of his opponents against themselves, as they kept on getting tangled up with each other, while Matthias kept on moving. Three and a half minutes after the battle had commenced, it was over. Matthias was the only one standing.

Matthias surveyed his fallen opponents, and turned and surveyed the Queen and her court. They sat immobile, not quite sure what would happen now. Matthias stepped forward, fixed Yolande with a hard look, and quite deliberately, but in an almost gentle fashion, bound her wrists to the arms of the chair in which she sat with mobile karns. He extended his hard look to all the members of her court, paused in an exaggerated way, and then turned around and walked back to the Portal in a casual manner.

It was delicately done. Yolande alone had been taken prisoner. Everyone else of her party were technically at liberty to fight or try to escape. However, their fates might or might not be bound to Yolande's. They could, after all, defect. The effect of all this was that everyone sat where they were as peaceable as lambs, waiting to see what would happen next. They were as restrained as if they had been bound, while being theoretically free to move.

Matthias freed his companions from their binding karns. The distinguished noblemen regained their feet with a flood of complaints about their treatment, except for Alaric, who got back his wand in a calm manner and went and stood beside Matthias, and Lyttleton and Rayerfeld, who also found their wands and looked about grim-faced. Matthias held up a hand in order to command their silence and asked conversationally: 'Would any of you gentlemen care to explain to me what is going on here?'

'Her Majesty is guilty of treason!' shouted Lord Rayerfeld, tugging angrily at his full black beard.

Matthias laughed out loud. 'That's an interesting sentence,' he said in a tone of amusement. '*Her Majesty is guilty of treason.* However, I would like to start with something more simple than a paradox.'

'The Zoller-Absteins will oppose your accession to the throne, Your Majesty,' Lord Camdenshall said. 'It is only to be expected. As you recall, we advised against your coming here precisely because of the danger of this manner of reception.'

Matthias sighed. 'Factions!' he observed. 'Where there's politics, there are factions.'

'Indeed that is very true, Your Majesty,' Lord Camdenshall agreed with a slight bow.

'Who is this anyway?' Matthias asked Camdenshall, waving to Romano. He was in fact pretending not to know in order to mislead observers as to the extent of his spy network. He knew full well who Romano was.

'This is Captain Romano of the Royal Palace Guard.'

Matthias whisked Romano across the room with a gesture of his wand and brought the captive Captain to a standstill in front of his own newly royal personage.

'Captain Romano,' Matthias said coldly, 'you are not to address me as *Raspero* but as *Lord Raspero*. You will not make this same mistake again if you still have the sense that you were born with. Now tell me what it is that you are about. What is all this talk of being under arrest and dropping wands? What is the meaning of your behaviour? Explain yourself.'

'You are under arrest, Lord Raspero,' Romano said forlornly. He was now only going through the motions. He was in no position to arrest anyone now.

'Do you have an arrest warrant?' Matthias asked.

'I do not need an arrest warrant when in the presence of Her Majesty Queen Yolande,' Romano replied. 'That is the law.'

'True,' Matthias said approvingly, 'but the situation is complicated slightly by the fact that I have been elected King of Westrigonia by the Vidaldmeet. Which means that in order to arrest me as King you require an Orstredun Document as authorized by a plenary vote of the Vidaldmeet. Do you have such authorization?'

Romano was silent.

'Answer me, Romano!' Matthias snapped. 'Yes or no?'

'No, Lord Raspero,' Romano replied.

'Then you can't arrest me, can you?' Matthias observed.

Romano made no reply to this observation.

Matthias lifted Romano into the air, and hung him by the strapping around his shoulders and chest from the antlers of a nearby stag's head on the wall. Surprisingly, the antlers and the head both took the weight. Matthias then started to work his way through all the captured guards, lifting them through the air and hanging them one by one from an antlered head. There were more than enough antlered heads for everyone. The Palace Guard, hung on the walls all around like children's toy accessories to sporting trophies, dangling awkwardly from the antlers in all the red-and-purple splendor of their Palace Guard costumes.

'Camdenshall,' Matthias said in a friendly fashion, 'perhaps you could be so good as to introduce me to Queen Yolande and her court.'

Lord Camdenshall bowed. 'I would be honoured to be of service in this way,' he said with stiff formality. 'Your Majesty, may I present His Majesty Matthias the Fourth, King of Westrigonia by election of the Vidaldmeet. Your Majesty, may I present Her Majesty Queen Yolande the First, former Queen of Westrigonia.'

Matthias extended his wand hand and bowed slightly as to an esteemed equal. 'It is an honour to meet you again, Yolande,' he said, with the lightest of emphasis on his use of her first name. 'I was presented to you on the day of your coronation ten years ago and we were all very proud on that day to have you and your family here as our royal house.

Times have changed but our affection for you has not. We are well met again.' He bowed again as before.

Yolande said nothing in reply. She seemed frozen in her posture, her eyes gazing off into the distance as if not aware of the presence of Matthias. Yet it was clear that she was listening to her translator mutter his translation of Matthias's comments into her ear.

Matthias nodded to Camdenshall to continue.

'Your Majesty, may I present Her Royal Highness the Princess Eleanor. Your Royal Highness, may I present His Majesty Matthias the Fourth, King of Westrigonia by election of the Vidaldmeet.' Camdenshall was three-quarters a politician, so he kept on referring to the Vidaldmeet's decision during his introductions, to make it clear that he was only relaying what others had decided, even though he had voted in favour himself.

Matthias looked then directly at Eleanor for the first time since his arrival. The Jewel of Krastienst sat regally straight-backed, with her left arm raised so that her fingers touched her jawline, the golden bracelet on her left wrist catching the light, her right hand holding her fan half-unfolded in her lap over her red gloves. Her pose was that of the classically striking pose of Princess Oleksandra in the painting *The Diamond Necklace* by Zubin. Her black hair was drawn back and tied in an elaborate gemstone-studded spiral bun. The raised white arm brought the golden bracelet on its wrist to the viewers' attention, just as the diamond necklace in the raised hand of Princess Oleksandra in Zubin's painting was the focus of attention of its audience.

Matthias looked briefly at the bracelet and then back at Eleanor, his very impassivity showing that he had registered the point she was making; and just at that moment, Eleanor lowered her left arm and casually moved her fan to lie over it, hiding it from sight. This all happened while Camdenshall was making his introductions, and only Matthias, Eleanor, and Eleanor's ladies-in-waiting observed this silent speaking of the bracelet. No-one else noticed a thing.

'Greetings, Eleanor,' Matthias said with the faintest inclination of his head.

Eleanor drew herself up and with the straightest of backs and the stiffest of necks said: 'You have addressed me incorrectly, Lord Raspero.'

'How should I address you?' Matthias asked.

'I am to be addressed as Her Royal Highness the Princess Eleanor,' Eleanor said grandly.

'No, that's too complicated for a simple person like me,' Matthias replied. 'I'll just call you Eleanor.'

'That is unacceptable, Lord Raspero,' Eleanor said frostily.

'I'm the King of Westrigonia, Eleanor. I can call you what I like.'

'No, you are not the King of Westrigonia,' Eleanor snapped. 'You are nothing but a barbarian who has barged in to where he does not belong.'

Matthias considered this assessment with a slight smile on his face and then sighed audibly. 'You haven't changed.'

'Neither have you,' Eleanor riposted without hesitation.

Matthias sighed again. 'Next!' he ordered Camdenshall and the introductions continued. They followed the strict sequence of precedence as dictated by Westrigonian hierarchy through courtiers and ladies-in-waiting and Councillors and regional governors and others. Matthias memorized all the people to whom he was being introduced with his mnemonics system, while they in their turn stared with fascination at the legendary Baron of Raspero, who was now, supposedly, the King of Westrigonia.

Eventually the introductions came to an end. Matthias waved his wand and used his mobile karns to pull over a nearby chair, and sat down opposite Yolande, gesturing with a wave of his royal hand for his followers to do likewise. There was a clattering of furniture all around until everything came to a silence that was a pause-on-the-edge-of-a-cliff silence.

Matthias then spoke, somewhat grimly, as follows: 'I came here, Yolande, in all peace and with empty hands, blown by the winds of abroad to your abode as the guest who seeks shelter from all the storms of the world within the hands of a gracious and kindly hostess. In violation of all the norms of civilized behavior, you have assaulted me most violently with no cause whatsoever, even though I came here in peace as a guest comes to a sanctuary where he seeks shelter. There are some, of course, who will say that you are a foreigner who does not understand the sacred bonds of hospitality. In any case, whatever the state of your ignorance on these matters, I am in consequence freed of the bonds of civility which would normally bind the hands of a guest. You have declared yourself my enemy, and now you are in my hands. I say this so that you know it. But now we move on to the purpose of this my visit.'

Yolande's translator muttered into her ear. After he had finished, there was a silence in the Waiting Room of the Portal. Matthias sat there like a cat crouched outside a mouse-hole. Eleanor's eyes had never left Matthias for all this time. The Witch of Trentland was like another cat crouched outside another mouse-hole. Yolande sat there and said nothing in reply. And there matters stood for an immortal moment, as captured in the painting *Antagonists in the Waiting Room* by the master Iagan.

The story of Westrigonia stood at a crossroads. Two monarchs faced each other, surrounded by two armies of occupation. Eternity itself peeked down through its fingers at them, like a child gripped by a bed-time story. Matthias sat calmly with his arms stretched along the arm-rests of his chair, like an imperial figure presiding over proceedings, totally in control. Eleanor waited as calmly as the newly arrived King of Westrigonia, equally alert to the demands of the moment.

And there matters rested for the time being.

CHAPTER TWENTY THREE

Nursery rhymes are coded political messages.
Believe me or not as you choose.
Frankie the Villain

10:45 AM, Monday 13 April 1882 A. F.

The silence in the Waiting Room of the Portal was peopled by living statues that did not dare to move. Even the soldiers hanging from the antlers overhead tried to cope with their uncomfortable situation by becoming as immobile as the heads from which they dangled. Eleanor passed the time by contemplating the thirty-seventh Baron of Raspero, and in this she was not alone. The baron-turned-monarch was the observed of all the observers of Yolande's court on this occasion.

Matthias allowed the silence to stretch as long as the fish that got away and no longer, before he began to speak. 'Perhaps I might begin our conversation, Yolande. I was on my way to work this morning when I encountered a delegation of Westrigonian gentlemen who informed me that I have been elected King of Westrigonia. I came here immediately, of course, only to find that you wished to place me under arrest. So that's been my day so far. How has your day been?'

There was a silence after Yolande's translator had finished. It was not clear whether Yolande planned to say anything or not in reply. She seemed paralysed.

Matthias said nothing further to break the silence. He simply gazed directly at Yolande, his face courteously impassive, leaning back in his chair as if politely waiting for her to reply. But it was clear to everyone that he was deliberately taking charge of the situation by remaining silent in order to dominate the course of events by a subtle form of intimidation.

The silence dragged on, gaining an imagined weight that oppressed the company. Some of those present breathed as silently as they could, holding themselves rigid as if braced against forces that would push them into swaying in the air.

'You are enjoying this, aren't you, Lord Raspero?' Eleanor asked coolly, completely unaffected by the tension in the room.

Matthias looked over at her. 'Up to a point,' he said briefly.

'Yes, up to the point where your vicious and evil character enjoys playing cat and mouse.'

'Cat and mouse? What are you talking about?'

'We know exactly what you plan to do with us,' Eleanor continued evenly. 'So it's no use pretending.'

'What, you mean like torture you and everything?' Matthias said with a grin, looking her up and down meaningfully. 'Yes, I look forward to torturing *you* later.'

'No, I mean that we know that you will hand us over to the Baalbabakans and Melisendiens,' Eleanor pronounced calmly, as if the imminent fate of rape and imprisonment at the hands of their enemies was merely one option amongst others.

'Of course I won't!' Matthias said without hesitation.

'That's what I mean by cat and mouse!' Eleanor cried out triumphantly.

Matthias growled and rolled his eyes in exasperation. 'Eleanor,' he said emphatically, looking her directly in the eyes, 'I will not hand over you or your mother or any of the members of the court to the Baalbabakans or the Melisendiens. I give you my word of honour on the matter.'

While this was being translated to Yolande the Westrigonian delegation stirred in consternation, looking amongst each other as if to somehow find a refutation of this shocking development. Lord Rayerfeld shouted: 'Such generosity of spirit . . . ' but his voice trailed away as if uncertain of what to say next. Yolande said in Anglashian, '<I am sure Lord Raspero understands the nature of this commitment.>'

A gentleman's word of honour was a guarantee of such an absolute nature that Yolande and the rest of her court could have complete peace of mind that they were safe from this danger at least. Even the soldiers of the palace guard hanging on the antlers overhead stirred in recognition of this sudden good news, making it seem as if a wind was blowing through the antlered heads on the walls.

The unfeigned shock on the part of Matthias's companions showed Yolande's court that he had thrown away this bargaining point without consulting them, and it seemed to show an impulsiveness on his part that came from a lack of experience in high matters of state. Matthias's companions brooded over the loss of a negotiating advantage so abruptly thrown away, while Yolande's court rejoiced over this sudden gift. But Matthias was already moving on.

Matthias didn't wait for the translator to translate Yolande's assertion into Westrigonian but promptly replied: 'Yolande, I fully understand the exact nature of the commitment I have just given. Lord Rayerfeld, generosity of spirit has nothing to do with this decision. I am motivated by two considerations. Firstly, a former monarch of Westrigonia is not handed over to our enemies under any circumstances. Secondly, the armies of Baalbabak and Melisende will leave Westrigonia empty-handed. They will gain nothing from their invasion of our country, no material benefit of any kind at all. This had best be understood by everyone now, because this topic of conversation is closed.'

Turning back to Yolande, Matthias continued: 'However, it is possible that you will have to go into exile. If this development should occur, I will of course grant you the liberty of choosing your own destination to be your place of exile.'

'I am not going into exile!' Eleanor snapped.

'If you need any advice on the matter of going into exile, Eleanor,' Matthias said, giving her a hard look, 'then I can give you plenty of tips based on my own personal experience.'

Eleanor said nothing but raised her chin and gave Matthias a defiant look.

'Yolande,' Matthias continued, turning back to Yolande, 'let us deal now with those things which can be dealt with now, leaving other matters to their appropriate time. Can we agree at least on this?'

'<Certainly, Lord Raspero,>' Yolande replied. She seemed restored to life now that she had learned that she would not be handed over to the invaders.

'The first matter to be dealt with is the liberation of Westrigonia from foreign occupation. This must be the priority because until this is dealt with there is no future of Westrigonia because there is no Westrigonia. Now I would like to make the following proposal. As the elected King of Westrigonia I will appoint myself Marechal. If you agree to publicly recognize my appointment as Marechal, then I will agree in turn to be bound by the outcome of a second meeting of the Vidaldmeet with regard to the question of the monarchy. Let there be a second Vidaldmeet to elect the monarch of Westrigonia, whether it is you or me or whoever. What do you say to this?'

'Your proposal is unclear in certain key respects, Lord Raspero,' Lord Cadwalader, the Royal Councillor, enunciated with a cool deliberation while this was being translated to Yolande. 'Of what value will Her Majesty's endorsement of your appointment as Marechal be when you claim that she is not the monarch of Westrigonia? And by what authority do you call for a second meeting of the Vidaldmeet on this matter? Not even a monarch can do this. Furthermore your own supposed election as king still remains unclear as to its validity. In view of all this – '

'I thought I made clear, Lord Cadwalader,' Matthias interrupted sharply, 'that the liberation of Westrigonia is my priority. I entirely fail to see why it is not yours as well. Now I will answer your questions as follows. The value of Yolande's endorsement of my appointment is entirely symbolic. Those Westrigonians who continue to look to a Zoller-Abstein monarch as their preferred choice can accept me as Marechal accordingly and it will be easier for me to assert my authority. As for the second point, I accept that I have no authority to call a second meeting of the Vidaldmeet, whether I am monarch or not. However, I would suggest that it provides such an obvious solution to this difficulty that those who do have such authority will not hesitate to bring this to pass, whether they are numbered among my followers or Yolande's. The key point for me is that I am accepted as Marechal at a time when there is a need for military leadership to liberate the country from occupation. As to the validity of my election, well, you will have to discuss that with the Vidaldmeet itself. At this moment in time it must be accepted as valid.'

'If that is so, Lord Raspero, then you can take on the role of Marechal without the support of Her Majesty,' the Royal Councillor pronounced. 'Your own appointment will suffice.'

'You are the elected King of Westrigonia!' Lord Rayerfeld shouted, tugging at his black beard angrily. 'You have no need of this foreigner's support. Look at her: she doesn't even understand Westrigonian.'

Yolande was listening carefully to the translator talking in a low voice into her ear.

'Let me make this quite clear to everyone present, whether on my side or the side of the Zoller-Absteins,' Matthias said loudly, to silence the murmuring amongst his own followers. 'I am not going to become another Good King Justin.'

The silence which followed this pronouncement lasted so long that Yolande's translator finally caught up. '<Who was Good King Justin?>' Yolande asked.

Rayerfeld rolled his eyes at this foreigner's ignorance.

'Justin the Second,' Matthias replied. 'He came to the throne in circumstances very similar to this. A disputed election, a divided Vidaldmeet, a foreign threat. He was a talented guy with a lot of good ideas but he ended up being the worst tyrant Westrigonia has ever known. It was with his overthrow that the Zoller-Absteins came into Westrigonia in the first place.'

'Justin the Second was never as bad as all that,' Lord Rayerfeld objected. 'That is Zoller-Abstein propaganda, lies about the last great Westrigonian King.'

'Tell that to Lord Camdenshall,' Matthias observed.

'Justin was a very strict king,' Lord Rayerfeld said, not quite meeting Camdenshall's eyes.

'Your sentiments are admirable, Lord Raspero, but your argument fails to address the questions I have raised. Why should Her Majesty – '

Eleanor interrupted the Royal Councillor. 'What did Justin do to Lord Camdenshall?' she asked Matthias. She only knew of Justin the Second from the official transcripts, not from family gossip.

Cadwalader was too angry at having been interrupted to speak any further at that moment.

'Good King Justin had the entire family of the Camdenshalls slaughtered in front of the fifteen-year-old Erasted, the only remaining eligible heir to the Earldom of Camdenshall, and told him that if he, Erasted, failed to be loyal to King Justin the Second, the name of Camdenshall would no longer be heard in Westrigonia. Erasted was Camdenshall's great grandfather.'

'Erasted had his revenge. He helped overthrow Justin and bring the Zoller-Absteins into Westrigonia.' Lord Rayerfeld said this as if it made everything alright again.

'I see the issue you have raised of being Marechal is no longer of interest to you,' the Royal Councillor said spitefully, still in a temper from having been interrupted by Eleanor.

'Perhaps you could speak on this matter yourself, Yolande,' Matthias said. 'Will you agree to recognize me as Marechal of Westrigonia?'

He held up his hand to keep anyone from speaking until the translator had brought Yolande up to date with everything that had been said. To his surprise, this actually worked; though on due reflection he realized that he was, after all, a king. Matthias the Fourth, no less!

'<The circumstances of this proposal remain unclear, Lord Raspero,>' Yolande replied, '<so I cannot see how I can respond without further deliberation and consultation of this matter.>'

Matthias did not wait for the translator but replied straightaway. 'Stalling is frequently an excellent political tactic to adopt, Yolande, but it is misplaced in these circumstances. Westrigonia is under occupation. We have to fight back, and we have to fight back now.'

'What are your qualifications for this role, Lord Raspero?' the Royal Councillor asked abruptly. 'Surely a more suitable candidate than yourself can be found? Would you not agree that if this were so, then you should acknowledge that other candidate as Marechal, given the priority of liberating Westrigonia which you yourself have nominated?'

'It may have escaped your attention, Lord Cadwalader,' Matthias commented drily, 'but I have just taken down the entire Palace Guard. Consider that as my qualification to be Marechal.'

The Royal Councillor was entirely unimpressed by this. 'Your personal talent as a street-fighter is one thing, Lord Raspero,' he responded equally drily, 'but to preside over a national military strategy is quite another. If Her Majesty and yourself can agree on a suitable candidate to be Marechal then – '

'It's a trick to have a Zoller-Abstein Marechal,' Lord Rayerfeld shouted.

'Patience, Lord Rayerfeld,' Matthias said with a grin. 'Of course it's a trick to have a Zoller-Abstein Marechal. However – '

'The question to be resolved is that of the suitability of the Marechal,' the Royal Councillor interrupted. 'It is that which is at issue.'

'As King I have the authority to appoint myself Marechal,' Matthias said loudly. 'And I am King by election of the Vidaldmeet.'

There was a moment's silence; then: 'Do you challenge the authority of the Vidaldmeet to elect the Monarch of Westrigonia, Yolande?' Matthias asked bluntly, almost aggressively.

The Royal Councillor hastily took up the challenge of responding to this question in case Yolande said the wrong thing in front of witnesses. 'The authority of the Vidaldmeet is not in question, Lord Raspero. It is your attempt to gain Her Majesty's support for your appointment as Marechal that is at issue.'

'<I think it very unlikely that a flawed election will stand for long,>' Yolande declared, having just had Matthias's last question translated for her.

'Yolande, do you understand what is happening right now across the country?' Matthias asked in exasperation. 'Soldiers are kicking in people's front doors, looting and stealing, women are being raped and abducted, men are being beaten and killed, lives are being destroyed.' He paused to allow the translator to catch up with him. Cadwalader waited with narrowed eyes, listening while all the cogs and gears of his mind spun like a decoding machine. 'The longer this goes on the more damage is being done, every single day. And in the end the survival of Westrigonia is at stake. We might become swallowed up by our enemies, divided into two, eaten, chewed and digested. Baalbabak will take one half, Melisende will take the other. Westrigonia itself might cease to exist. It has happened before that countries have ceased to exist. And it will happen again. Countries can die just like people can die.' He paused again as the translator muttered away into Yolande's ear. 'I say again to you: we must liberate Westrigonia now. This must be our priority. There are those like you who will challenge my election. Very well, if you support me as Marechal they will follow me. We will liberate Westrigonia together. When this is done there will be a second Vidaldmeet to decide on the question of who is to be monarch. If we can agree on this, I am prepared to be bound by my word of honour to keep this agreement. Now do you agree to support my appointment as Marechal of Westrigonia?'

There was a deathly silence amongst all those present, which the muttering of the translator served only to emphasize. Matthias's companions looked at each other with faces aghast at how Matthias was throwing around his words-of-honour like confetti. A hard look and a raised hand from Matthias stopped the Royal Councillor from speaking. It was for Yolande to speak. She would have to decide.

'<Lord Raspero,>' Yolande replied, '<I say once again that your proposal remains unclear. We really must deliberate further on this matter before coming to a decision.>'

Matthias didn't wait for the translation but responded immediately. 'You do not have time to deliberate further, Yolande. You must decide right here and now. My proposal is only for this moment in time. If you fail to accept, it will not be offered to you again. Now I ask you again: do you accept my proposal or do you not?'

'<I will not be badgered by you, Lord Raspero,>' Yolande replied with a flash of temper. '<I have already made it clear that I cannot accept or refuse your proposal without further deliberation.>'

Matthias sighed. 'Then you have refused my proposal. It will not be offered again. Let it be understood that there is no agreement between us. I appoint myself Marechal by my authority as King of Westrigonia. That is all we have to say to each other at this moment in time.'

Matthias rose to his feet, waving to his followers to do likewise. He waved his wand to remove the mobile karns binding Yolande's wrists. He had set them so gently that she had entirely forgotten about them. He then set to work unbinding the members of the Palace Guard one by one from their antlered supports. They fell to the ground and rolled over and clambered to their feet groaning from the aches of having been suspended in the air. Only Romano landed neatly on his feet without a single groan, grim-faced and ready to kill someone. He was not the Captain of the Palace Guard for nothing. Matthias did not return their wands to them, but instead gave them a stern talking-to. 'You have raised your wands against the rightful King of Westrigonia, have you not? On this one occasion, and this one occasion only, I will overlook your treason. Let me remind you, however, that treason is punishable by death, and if you raise your wands against me again, I will have you executed. Is there any part of this simple statement of mine which any of you fail to understand?'

The soldiers of the Palace Guard gazed back at Matthias with expressionless faces. If they failed to understand anything, they were keeping it to themselves.

'Very well. Captain Romano, as I am Marechal of Westrigonia, you are under my orders. I therefore order you to take directions from the former Queen of Westrigonia. Queen Yolande retains the formal title of Queen despite no longer being the monarch, so you may continue to address her as Her Majesty while addressing me as Marechal, even though in actual fact I am King. Now, the North Quarter will continue to house the Queen and the Crown Princess and their retinue. The Queen may also continue to have authority over the West Quarter. You will guard this part of the Palace. For the time being you will also continue to guard the perimeter of the Palace as before, until I make other arrangements. The East Quarter will be taken up by myself and my followers, and I will also have authority over the South Quarter. That will be all for now. Is that clear?'

Romano said nothing in reply to this, but looked at Yolande. As far as a simple soldier such as Romano was concerned, it would take more than Matthias's bravado, and threats of execution, to disrupt the existing chain of command.

Matthias waited impassively while the translator finished translating all this into Yolande's ear. Yolande looked up to see that everyone was staring at her. The ball was in her court. Yolande raised her chin, determined to appear dignified, and nodded in a regal fashion at Romano. Everyone else present started breathing again.

'Come, Yolande, Eleanor, ladies and gentlemen,' Matthias said in his own regal fashion. 'Let us go.' He gestured to the Oberon Door with his left hand and set forth.

Matthias looked around him like a tourist on a sight-seeing tour as he walked along, chatting to Alaric or Rayerfeld as he pointed to this or that. When he arrived at the Sara Hall, he walked to the Mahsa Door and turned and waited for the entire company to arrive. Without needing to be told, the party of the Queen stood some distance away from Matthias and his followers, so that there was a space between them.

'Yolande, I bid you farewell for the time being. As Marechal of Westrigonia, I now go to strike at the obvious fault line of our enemies. I will split them in two along this fault line, and smash the two halves together and leave them broken in pieces on the ground. In the meantime, I ask you to keep to your part of the Palace, while I keep to mine. However, when I return to the palace, I invite you and Eleanor to have dinner with me so that we may further discuss the politics of our circumstances. Until then, farewell.' With that, Matthias waved his wand and sent all the wands of the Palace Guard wrapped by mobile karns in three bundles to lie at the floor at Romano's feet, followed by all the remaining mobile karns of the Palace Guards, wrapped up in their own bundles. Matthias then turned around and casually strolled through the Mahsa Door, timing his exit so expertly that by the time Romano had picked up a bundle of wands and untied it by hand, Matthias was gone. It was skilfully done: Matthias did not hang around, which might have raised the question of whether the Palace Guard should attack him now in circumstances in which he would certainly be captured by them; but nor had he bolted out of sight by dashing through the door, which might have encouraged a pursuit of him. He had left as if he had all the time in the world, while in fact disappearing out of sight in an instant. This nonchalance held even Romano back, plus of course Matthias's threat to execute any Palace Guard who attacked him.

And besides, he was the King of Westrigonia, after all, by election of the Vidaldmeet. The uncertainties of his opponents were fitted together like pieces of a jigsaw puzzle by Matthias to form his own apparent certainty. His followers left through the Mahsa Door with many a backward look at Yolande and her party standing in the middle of the hall, as if half-prepared to defend themselves against a last-minute attack; but Yolande watched them go without comment, and even Romano, truth to tell, was relieved to take the road of peace.

12:35 PM, Monday 13 April 1882 A. F.

Matthias walked briskly through various corridors and hallways until he came to the Cadeyrn Hall. There he set forth for the Qasaba Door at the side, which he opened with a wave of his wand, stepped through and promptly began descending the stone stairs immediately ahead. The others followed a little hesitantly, for these stone stairs were somewhat grim looking and the deeper they went the more the stone walls began to glisten with dampness. The gas lamps on the walls shed a light that seemed to push against the increasing darkness as if at something heavy. At the bottom of the stairs was a heavy wooden door reinforced with iron fastenings. Although there was a large and elaborate doorknocker that was the face of a gargoyle, Matthias knocked on the door loudly by kicking it repeatedly with his boot.

After some time there was a rattling sound and a panel in the door slid back. A squinty face with suspicious eyes peered out at the lords of Westrigonia standing on the stairs.

'Who are you? What you want? What's the meaning of this?' a voice asked querulously. The owner of the voice sounded like someone who was not used to being disturbed without prior notice, and did not like the experience.

'I am Matthias Raspero, King and Marechal of Westrigonia, and I command you to open this door and place yourself at my service.'

There was a silence while the guardian of the door gazed at Matthias with a wrinkled nose.

'You what?' he asked after a while.

Matthias lost his patience. He pulled his wand and moved into action, with the result that the locks of the door clicked open an instant before Matthias's boot connected with the door. Squinty-face spouted a shouted complaint as the door flew open and struck him with such an impact as to send him flying backwards. Matthias's mobile karns grabbed him and brought him back upright to stand before the Baron of Raspero, who by now was standing in the forcefully opened doorway.

'I am Matthias Raspero, King and Marechal of Westrigonia, and I command you to place yourself at my service. Is that understood, Dungeon Keeper Ferran?'

Dungeon Keeper Ferran took a while to process this new information. 'No one told me nothing about this,' he said eventually.

This was perfectly true. Ferran led by and large a solitary life down here in the dungeons. Gossip rarely came his way, and certainly the fast-moving pace of events of that day would have passed him by. He had only just heard of the invasion of Westrigonia itself the other day. No-one ever told Ferran anything, but it was really his own fault for keeping so much to himself all the time.

'Well, I am telling you now,' Matthias said firmly. 'Now, the question to be decided is this. Do I lock you up in your own dungeons or do you obey my commands?'

Ferran thought this over. 'How can you be King?' he asked after a while.

The lords of Westrigonia standing on the stairs shifted about impatiently. They seemed to feel that Ferran was holding them all up. Matthias, however, seemed to have all the time in the world. 'The Vidaldmeet elected me as King of Westrigonia yesterday afternoon. I have appointed myself to be Marechal as well. You may address me as Marechal.'

'If you're King, then what about His Majesty Frederick and Her Majesty Yolande?'

'Frederick is abroad and Yolande is upstairs. And I am here. Now, Ferran, make up your mind about what you are about. After all, if I am to lock you up in your own dungeons, I need to get a move on. Well?'

'This is very irregular.'

'Perhaps. But in what regular way would a transition as unexpected as this take place? Are there norms which we have failed to observe? And what do you know about it anyway, Ferran?'

There was a silence. A long silence.

'So, if you're King,' Ferran began to say, 'then-'

'And Marechal, don't forget. And you are to address me as Marechal. By my royal command.'

'So, if you're King, and Marechal too, then I got to speak to the Steward, and Romano, and Councillor Hannfyon. I mean, how do I know that you're really the King? You could be trying it on.'

It had to be admitted that Ferran's position was a reasonable one. But these were not reasonable times.

Matthias waved his wand, bringing Ferran to his knees and binding's Ferran's hands behind him. Matthias stepped forward in order to look down more vertically upon his prisoner. 'Listen to me, Ferran. Either you obey me or I lock you up. Now, I am giving you one last chance to make up your mind. What is it going to be, bozo?'

Ferran looked up into the implacable face of the Baron of Raspero.

'Well,' he said, 'alright then, this is very irregular, but who am I to say what's, ah, what's, ah, yes, alright, alright, Your Majesty, I-'

'Marechal!' Matthias snapped impatiently. 'How many times do I have to tell you? You are to address me as Marechal!'

'Yes, Your, ah, Marechal, alright, I'll obey you like you said.'

Matthias brought Ferran back to his feet and released him. 'Then bring all the prisoners forth from their cells, and bring them up to the Cadeyrn Hall. Do it now, Ferran. I will await you upstairs.'

1:15 PM, Monday 13 April 1882 A. F.

While they were waiting in the Cadeyrn Hall for Ferran and the prisoners to come up from the dungeons below Shyester asked: 'May I ask Your Majesty what we are doing?'

Matthias took a deep breath and let it out with a groan. 'How many times do I have to tell people to address me as Marechal? What is wrong with everyone? What is your problem, Shyester? Do you have a problem with obeying this royal command? Or is it your memory that is at fault?'

'Not at all, Marechal,' Shyester said smoothly. 'Far from it. And I am sure I will come to understand why at a later time. May I ask the Marechal what we are doing?'

'We are recruiting soldiers for the forthcoming battle to liberate Krastienst.'

'Soldiers, Your, ah, Marechal, did you say?'

'Right now I only have,' Matthias raised his hand in order to ostentatiously count everyone present, 'nine fighters, including myself. A few more will come in handy, very handy.'

'I beg your pardon, Your, ah, Marechal? Fighters, did you say?' asked Counsellor Waldemar.

'Fighters?' asked Counsellor Englebert, a little nervously. 'What does that mean, may I ask?'

'I am really more of a scholar,' Keeper Annora said in an apologetic manner.

Alaric lowered his head and turned away to hide his smile.

'Of course we'll fight,' said Cavalier Lyttleton grimly.

'Bring it on!' agreed Rayerfeld.

Camdenshall accepted this latest twist of fate with a philosophical air. He had become fairly philosophical in the past six years of being secretly in Matthias's service.

'What kind of fighting are we talking about, Marechal?' Shyester asked.

'Street fighting,' Matthias told him.

The esteemed dignitaries of the Kingdom of Westrigonia looked at Matthias in such disbelief that their mouths fell open.

Alaric turned away completely as if to study a painting on the wall. In fact, he was fighting off waves of laughter.

Ferran came up the stairs followed by five prisoners shuffling along behind, still in leg and arm chains. They all had shaven heads, as they had all been sentenced to death.

'Who have we here, Ferran?' Matthias asked.

'Well, Marechal,' Ferran said, 'this here is Gentian, what's in prison for burglary and killing a man and what not.'

Gentian glared at Matthias with a sneering expression on his face. He was tall, well built, with tattoos on his neck.

'Go on,' said Matthias to Ferran.

'This here is Leocadio, what has killed a man and his life is forfeit on account of what he done.'

Leocadio was tall and thin, with an ingratiating expression on his face. 'It's not true, Marechal,' he said insistently, 'not a word of it's true, I swear to you on the graves of all my fathers.'

Matthias nodded to Ferran to continue.

'This here is Eyike, what has killed beyond count, and whose crimes is heinous beyond what words can say.'

Eyike was blond and blue-eyed, with a baby-faced innocence to him. It was noticeable that the other prisoners kept their distance from him, as if even they were afraid of him. The lords of Westrigonia retreated a step on hearing his name. Everyone there had heard of his deeds, which were the stuff of nightmares. The rational thread, if any, of his activities, snapped when unwound through a mortal's jittery mind, leaving only fragmented images: sharp knives, severed limbs, bloody boiling cauldrons on deserted moonlit plateaus and bodily parts made into items of furniture. Eyike did nothing but smile at Matthias.

'This here is Bedrioch, who is what killed a man what he caught in bed with his fiance, killed him with a knife something cruel.'

Bedrioch was short and burly and stared at the ground with his shaven head lowered.

'And this here is Frankie the Villain,' Ferran said, 'what calls himself a poet, but is a thief and a murderer, and there's more blood than ink on his hands, for all his poetry.'

Everyone present looked with interest at the latest prisoner to be introduced. They had all heard of Frankie the Villain, a moderately known poet of the day and career criminal. His poetry was said to be impossible to translate out of the Westrigonian language. Most of his poetry had been composed in prison, which was also where he had formulated much of his philosophy. His philosophy of life was that the rich were no better than anyone else; in fact the rich were, according to Frankie, worse than everyone else, a lot worse. Frankie believed that the rich were to blame for everything that was wrong with his life, and so it followed that he had no scruples about robbing them whenever possible. He also had no scruples about cheating people. He believed that for the powerless, the world was rigged against them; and as cheating was a way of evening up the odds, cheating was really in the service of justice.

All of Frankie's philosophy issued from one root. Frankie had never been able to see any reason at all why the rich should have their privileged lifestyle while he had nothing. The logic of this inequality entirely escaped him. He did not believe for one moment that they were any better than he was. Why then should they have more? If their level of being was loftier than his, then it was only fair that their rewards should be greater than his. Being better than him went along with having more than him like the two sides of the same coin went along together with each other. But as far as he could see, and he believed that he could see very clearly indeed, the rich were greedy, stupid, arrogant, violent, crooked and lecherous, and if anything they were worse than he was, much worse, which was why he had decided to call himself Frankie the Villain. It was his way of being ironical.

The poet criminal had finally fallen in with a band of robbers who were all betrayed by a prostitute for the reward money, and Frankie was the last of their number still surviving, as the others had by now all been executed.

Frankie's (by now extensive) knowledge of the law had kept him alive thus far by instructing him in making up one legal excuse after another to delay his execution. He had, for example, when sentenced to be executed on 28 March, pointed out that legal provisions in the July 1675 Act of the Vidaldmeet ruled out all executions during the month preceding, and the month following, a solstice or an equinox on which an eclipse had fallen. The committee formed to investigate this matter had ruled in his favour, and the date of his execution had been changed to 21 April.

Frankie looked disdainfully around at the lords of Westrigonia, his nostrils wrinkling as if the insignia on their clothing was giving off bad smells. There was an indentation in the left side of his chin, whether left by nature or nurture was unclear; his few remaining teeth were yellow and crooked, the ungainly survivors of several collisions over the years between the stationary object of his jaw and the moving force of a fist or boot or rock. His skin was mottled with purplish streaks. He stood slightly hunched, as if the weight of his life had bent his body out of shape. This was the walled garden of his immortal soul.

Matthias had long heard of Frankie the Villain, and long detested him. To Matthias Raspero, born to a life of wealth and privilege, the egalitarian philosophy of Frankie the Villain was something to be stamped into the ground. Frankie was not a Leveller, not being an atheist, but to Matthias he was little better than such. His baronial soul was offended by Frankie's very existence.

'Welcome to you all,' said Matthias in a friendly fashion. But for now Matthias was all smiles and friendliness, and the proverb *Beware of barons bearing gifts* was not on anyone's mind right then, though perhaps it should have been. 'I am Baron Matthias Raspero, Marechal of Westrigonia. I have a proposition for you all. Our noble kingdom has been invaded by the Baalbabakans and the Melisendiens, and we are under occupation. As Marechal of Westrigonia I am authorized to offer you your freedom if you will fight for me. What do you say?'

The prisoners all looked at Matthias without saying anything. It was Frankie, of course, who eventually spoke first.

'I got something to say, Your Marechal Highness, but wait, do I need a public platform and an audience to speak my mind? Oh, yes, maybe I have to be dressed in furs first, your magnificence, isn't that right?'

'Not at all!' Matthias said with a forced friendliness that fooled no-one. 'Speak your mind just as you are.'

So Frankie spoke his mind as follows:

The Tale of Justin and the Bandit as told by Frankie the Villain

In the days of Good King Justin as he was, yes, king, just as he was then, as king, and a bandit was brought before him for sentencing and the King asked him, he said, well, what do you have to say for yourself, you're a man for hanging, I can see that straight away, but you can speak first, bandit though you are. And the bandit said, oh, I'm a bandit am I, that's what you say, but I tell you this, if I had an army and all the great lords bowed low to me, then I'd be a king like yourself, and no-one would say different, and that's how it is. And Good King Justin knew this to be the truth and so Justin said, the king said, you have spoken rightly, and he freed the bandit and made him a rich man, and the bandit, he lived as a lord lives till the end of his days.

Matthias had never before heard this story of Justin and the bandit but it was too obviously made up for him to accept it as being true. He didn't believe a word of it. So he said almost absently, as if his thoughts were elsewhere: 'The historical provenance of that story has been questioned.'

'Oh, of course, yes, questioned, that's how it goes, isn't it? Yes, yes, question it till it goes away and hides in the corner, sorry to have ever bothered your worship's greatness just for one single second! That's the fine way of things, isn't it? Yes, yes, it's all so fine, all so fine.'

There was a moment's silence. Matthias's thoughts might really have been elsewhere.

'Provenance,' Frankie the Villain said bitterly, looking around him at everyone else present and licking his lips, 'provenance.' It was as if he was daring anyone to say that word to him again.

Matthias's gaze re-focused on Frankie the Villain. 'I offer you freedom and money,' he said. 'I do not ask you to fight for me but to fight for your own freedom and riches.'

'Riches?' Leocadio repeated. There was an enormously pregnant question cradled in the round-bellied vowels of the word, as pregnant as a pregnant hippopotamous is pregnant.

'One hundred thousand strada, to each of you,' Matthias said firmly.

'Oh, it's a fine thing to be paid all that money,' Frankie the Villain said, but even his faith in his own skepticism was obviously shaken.

'I am making this pledge in the presence of witnesses,' Matthias continued, gesturing all about him with a vague wave of his left hand in order to take in the lords of Westrigonia who were present and obviously closely following all that was going on, 'and no-one can say otherwise. And do not forget your freedom for you walk out of here with me right now. Fight until Krastienst is liberated and you have earned your money.'

'And when is that?' Gentian asked.

'One week, perhaps longer,' Matthias replied, 'but I will hold your contract completed after no more than a year has elapsed if we are still under occupation. And when the time comes to be paid I will take you myself to the Treasury and you will be paid out in good coin and notes while you watch and given the money in leather satchels stamped with the golden insignia of the Treasury.'

There followed a silence while the meaning of the words spoken by Matthias filled the minds of the crooks he was recruiting with a rapid swelling motion like the heave of an ocean wave. The tassel-fringed curtains of a brothel could not have been as seductive as the tendril-snaked thoughts of this their vision: the Treasury awash with glittering money, and great handfuls of that money being counted out and handed over to them in leather satchels stamped with the golden insignia of the Treasury as if they were already lords of the land . . . Now that was a sight for them to behold with an imagination like the inflated crest of a cockatoo. That was a day-dream for you! It was even better than crime!

'But you must decide now,' Matthias said, moving restlessly to break the spell, 'for the time to fight has come upon us.'

It was obvious from the faces of all of them that their decision had already taken itself. Matthias took everything as read without further comment.

'Ferran, release them from their chains.'

From the expression on Dungeon Keeper Ferran's face, this was all a big mistake, but he obeyed the Marechal's order without comment.

'Let's go,' said Matthias. 'Follow me.'

Matthias led his group of noblemen and prisoners to the Ishtar Door of the Palace. Two of Romano's guards were there but they stood aside obediently as Matthias waved them away impatiently. Matthias drew his wand and threw the Ilbert Door open, displaying yet again either his knowledge of Palace security, however illegally it had been acquired, or a mastery of wandlore far beyond the ordinary. As they exited into Deforrest Street, Matthias waved his wand again and closed the Ilbert Door behind them.

Everyone of course had questions but Matthias was not waiting for anyone to speak. He strode along as if they were already running late, making his way directly towards a checkpoint of Melisendien soldiers on the street.

The war for the liberation of Westrigonia was about to begin.

CHAPTER TWENTY FOUR

All the guests at my dinner party,
They all wanted different foods.
I told them:
If you think you have been insulted,
Then think so.
I told them:
If you don't like it here,
Then go somewhere else.
Frankie the Villain.

1:55 PM, Monday 13 April 1882 A. F.

Deforrest Street was large and wide, with the Palace towering up to one side, and the other side taken up with shops, apartment blocks, semi-detached houses and a walled training ground for wand-fighting. It was utterly deserted except for the checkpoint of bored-looking Melisendien soldiers just before the junction with Dejan Street.

Matthias marched determinedly directly up to this checkpoint, whose soldiers stiffened in battle readiness at the sight of such a mismatched group of shaven headed prisoners and Westrigonian noblemen coming straight at them. Their battle readiness was almost reflexive, as such a group did not look as if they were about to launch an attack, given that the shaven-headed prisoners were unarmed, and the noblemen did not look much like fighters. Their battle readiness was, in short, not very ready.

<<'Halt! Where are you going?'>> asked the Melisendien sergeant in command of the checkpoint. He spoke in Melisendien, because it was the only language that he spoke.

This question sounded to the Westrigonians like: 'Ga-dra'hir elmfoy,' and no-one had any idea of what the sergeant, who after all was only doing his job, had said to them.

'What's it to you?' Matthias retorted rudely, pulling his wand and shouting 'Take them down!' as he threw himself at the enemy.

There were sixteen Melisendien soldiers at the checkpoint, who faced fourteen Westrigonian opponents. Five of these, the released prisoners, had no wands or weapons, which rendered them immediately unable to fight. Of the eight-strong Westrigonian delegation, there were really only Alaric, Camdenshall, Rayerfeld and Lyttleton who followed Matthias into battle, whilst the others drew their wands and stood there looking apprehensive while anxiously doing nothing. But Matthias, the inheritor of the wandlore secrets of the Rasperos, was the key figure.

The checkpoint was arranged in the usual configuration of being divided into halves on either side of the street, thus allowing people and goods to pass through while enabling the checkpoint to snap shut and bar the way to transgressors of the military code governing their noble occupation of a foreign country. But this was not all. Beside where the sergeant stood was a communication console consisting of portal-transportation materials that could be used to transport small weights which activated type-writer keys which enabled communication between the checkpoint and the military network of which it was part. Matthias knew all this as well as any of the soldiers he was fighting, which was why the first soldier he attacked was the one standing next to the sergeant with a red square on his upper left sleeve which identified him as the soldier in charge of operating the communication console. This unfortunate fellow, once so proud to have received this promotion, with its special rank and extra pay, was grabbed by Matthias's karns and whirled around in a cartwheel fashion that sent the sergeant to the ground while both their wands flew through the air to Gentian and Bedrioch. By now, Alaric had taken down his man, bound him and grabbed his wand, Camdenshall was parrying several blows, Rayerfeld had been taken down and Lyttleton was locked into battle with three opponents. The other soldiers were in an indecisive state of mind, half turning to help their sergeant, half facing in the other direction, and as Gentian and Bedrioch dived into the battle, Matthias took down three opponents at once in a spinning motion that sent karns around all their ankles and pulled them off their feet. Three more wands went flying through the air to Eyike, Leocadio and Frankie, as Matthias parried the mobile karns of four soldiers, who had all turned their attention on him at the same time, which was a mistake, given that they had other enemies moving on them from behind. Matthias flipped himself to one side and stood there, taking no further part in the battle while he evaluated the performance of his impromptu battle group. He pulled Eyike off the fallen soldier he had overwhelmed, given that Eyike was beginning to inflict sadistic pains on his victim, and ordered Eyike with an upraised finger to take no further part in the battle. Eyike looked back at Matthias with an innocent look and an appealing smile. Matthias turned away from the psychopath and continued to observe the battle, which by now was nearly over. Before long, the Melisendien soldiers were the prisoners of the Westrigonian band of rebels.

Matthias ordered everyone to come along. He led his little band along Deforrest Street and around the corner into Okeanos Street and into the Rayyan Tannery which stood on the corner.

The Rayyan Tannery had been making leather out of animal skins for three centuries. Matthias threw open the closed doors of the tannery and marched into the courtyard. To the right, where the beamhouse of the tannery was located, the journeymen and apprentices were hard at work using poles to push hides into troughs to soak, given that Garrick, the manager of the tannery, saw no reason for work to cease merely because of an occupation. Everyone turned around to gaze open-mouthed at the oddly-assorted bunch who had just arrived.

'I am Baron Matthias Raspero, the Marechal of Westrigonia, and I commandeer this tannery in the name of resistance to the occupation.'

Matthias had his Melisendien prisoners marched into the middle of the courtyard and stripped of their uniforms. He ordered Alaric and the dungeon prisoners to strip and put on the Melisendien uniforms, and made a start on doing this himself.

'Are you disguising yourself in those foreign uniforms?' asked Shyester.

'Well observed,' Matthias said shortly.

'This is contrary to the international treaties to which Westrigonia is a signatory.'

'Is it?'

'If you are captured in those uniforms, you are not protected by those international agreements. You will be summarily executed.'

'That's right,' Matthias agreed. 'Enough, Shyester! All of you, listen up. You are to wait here for our return. As for you, Garrick, send your employees to contact their families. That is an order from the Marechal of Westrigonia. I want everyone capable of taking part in the resistance to come here and report to me for duty.'

Matthias led his band of six fighters, dressed in their ill-fitting Melisendien uniforms, out of the door and into Okeanos Street.

3:45 PM, Monday 13 April 1882 A. F.

'Your Royal Highness, you must be very careful,' Lady Nina said breathlessly. 'I can guess what Lord Raspero plans to do.'

'Really? And what is that?' Eleanor asked, with a light yawn to conceal her interest in anything Matthias might be up to.

'He can become King if he forces you to marry him because you are the Crown Princess,' Nina said. Her eyes shone with barely concealed excitement at the prospect of such wickedness and depravity actually taking place in this very palace!

'I will never marry that man!' Eleanor shouted furiously. 'I absolutely refuse to marry him. He is faithless, despicable . . . ' she trailed away into silence while hunting more adjectives that were low enough to apply to Matthias.

'But what if he forced you to yield to him?' Nina asked eagerly. 'You are completely at his mercy.'

'Shut up, Nina!' Eleanor ordered.

Nina subsided into the required silence with a gleam in her eye.

Commentary by the Distinguished Palathar of Dezantebos on the liberation of Krastienst by Matthias the Fourth, as published in October 2082 AF:

Stand back, stand forth, I proclaim my news! Listen carefully! The tales we were told as children do not add up. And what is it that we are told? That King Matthias, followed by an ill-assorted collection of noblemen and prisoners from the dungeons, attacked the Melisendiens and took their uniforms, attacked the Baalabakans and took their uniforms, and attacked the Melisendiens in the Baalbabakan uniforms. And then what happened? Every school-child knows the rest. While being pursued by the Baalbabakans, Matthias and his band, disguised in their Melisendien uniforms, were given shelter by the Melisendien garrison at the buildings of the Ignac School, whereupon on the instant and most treacherously, as is permitted in times of the warfare of combatants, that is to say treachery is permitted, Matthias overcame the guards of the doors of the Ignac School and threw open the doors to the pursuing Baalbabakans, who stormed the garrison and took the Melisendiens prisoners, but not the King and his band, who had long since escaped by another door. But how did Matthias know of that other door? And what then transpired? Forty fighting men of the Kalidasa nation, who just happened to be transported to the Krastienst portal at the command of Matthias at that time, and no-one disputes this, stormed the Baalbabakan garrison at the Joonet Observatory, already under the command of their paymaster King Matthias, and took the Baalbabakans prisoner. These prisoners included amongst their number Oafstadt himself. And the Baalbakbakans themselves, in their chronicles of this time, state plainly that Kalidasan mercenaries took their Prince captive. What can be as clear as this statement from the Baalbabakans? And abruptly these Kalidasans disappear from the pages of history, but not as completely as some would hope, for there appear folk songs in the Kalidasan nations which refer to this time, and how the members of the Kalidasan band of mercenaries were so well paid by King Matthias for their efforts as to retire as wealthy men in their own nation. But historians refuse to accept these folk songs as true records of history, and instead insist that the tale of the Kalidasans is a myth, despite all the numerous eye-witness accounts. Yet I say this. If the Kalidasan mercenaries were in Krastienst fighting for King Matthias, then when did he hire them? There are mysteries here which the historians run from like the cowards they are. A plague on the House of the Historians! Where is the truth? I will tell you where it is. The truth is in the back pocket of King Matthias, grinning in his grave like an ape. He has made fools of us all. Well, I am not a fool, and this I say. The thirty-seventh Baron of Raspero, whose shadow was in the shape of a corkscrew, made his plans to liberate Krastienst before the invasion of Westrigonia took place. The evidence for this perfidy is plain.

8:40 PM, Monday 13 April 1882 A. F.

The noise of the fighting had increased during the day, until by now the city was wracked by full-fledged combat. Astrudel had earlier excitedly rushed up to Eleanor's Chambers to tell them that the Ballbabakans and Melisendiens were fighting each other full tilt.

Astrudel now rushed in again to say that the Marechal had made his headquarters at the Rayyan Tannery. She did not stay long after delivering this news, but soon enough rushed out again. With the city in such chaos, there was money to be made.

Eleanor sat in her high-backed chair, a much more optimistic figure now than she had been in the morning. How greatly could fortunes change in a single day! She fiddled absently with her bracelet while listening to the disparate sounds of combat across the city. Matthias had said that he would strike at the enemy on their obvious fault-line, which at the time had seemed an enigmatic statement to make. Like all riddles, however, once the answer was known it seemed as if it should have been easy to guess all along.

Eleanor's ladies-in-waiting, Nina, Mitzi and Georgette, sat nearby talking now and then in hushed voices that would not intrude upon the Crown Princess's contemplations. They had much to gossip about, what with the revelation that Matthias Raspero had once been Eleanor's boyfriend, as proven by the bracelet that Eleanor continually fiddled with as she sat with her thoughts far away. Mitzi, who was a cousin of Matthias's, was telling the others how Eleanor had made a special point of questioning her about her relationship with the Raspero family when interviewing her for the position of lady-in-waiting. Mitzi had been puzzled about this at the time, and had then later forgotten all about it. Well, her memories had now come back! She understood now that it was her family relationship with Matthias that had gotten her this position. Mitzi felt insulted, especially as she had never liked the foreign-born Princess anyway.

Georgette was quite definite in her observations that Matthias and Eleanor were now utterly unsuited for each other, whatever their prior relationship. She did not say that this was because she, Georgette, was much more suited to the wand-fighting baron, but this unspoken thought was very much present in her mind.

Nina thought everything was wonderfully romantic and love would triumph over all. She also commented that one of Matthias's companions, Alaric Niedbala, had kept on looking at her and she was wondering if she had done something wrong.

Sometime later, Eleanor arose and departed for her bedroom. Her ladies-in-waiting dutifully attended her and then retired to their own quarters. They talked excitedly until late, and fell asleep to the distant sounds of combat fading and flaring over the city like a continuous and complicated drum-roll.

The conspiracy theorists multiply like bacteria in an infected wound. What is it with these people? Why do they insist on these mysterious Kalidasans, long since disproved, regal murder of dungeon prisoners, long since disproved, regal foreknowledge of invasions, long since disproved, three hundred mercenaries from numerous nations, so varied in their origins that they were obliged to converse in Anglashian, long since disproved, and the supposed code books of the Melisendiens and Baalbabakans in the possession of Matthias the Fourth as seen in the Rayyan Tannery by an apprentice who told this story to his grandchildren . . . shall I say disproved? How does one disprove a waft of smoke? I say to all these nonsense peddlers: by improvisation and organizational brilliance, by inspired leadership and galvanized followers, King Matthias brought about the liberation of Krastienst entirely by improvised means upon materials supplied by the motives of the moment. There were no foreign mercenaries. There was nothing more, no prior planning and no secret foreknowledge of the invasion of Westrigonia. It was by nothing but an astonishingly adept weaving of the materials brought to his hand by chance that King Matthias did bring about this miracle.

3:55 PM, Tuesday 14 April 1882 A. F.

The Chambers of the Council of the Kingdom of Westrigonia were situated in the South Quarter of the Palace of Krastienst at ground level. The large windows, whose glass panes spanned the distance from about knee height to well above head height, looked out on a verandah that ran along Dejan Street. The fifteen-foot high ceiling was covered in frescoes illustrating themes and stories from the Book of the Herakrim, while seven bronze chandeliers hung down, each with five gas lamps at the ends of their curved arms. The Central Council Chamber Meeting Room was roughly one hundred feet in length, and was elliptical in shape, this being exactly the same geometrical ellipse as the city of Krastienst as a whole, and in the centre of this Room was an elliptical table that also replicated on a still smaller scale the same ellipse. The table was made of enormously thick and highly polished block of oaken wood joined together, with inset patterns of lapis lazuli and gold. Around the table were nine chairs, for the monarchs of Westrigonia and the seven Councillors. This Council was the highest governing body in the country. This was where the highest matters of state were discussed and this was where all important government policy was formulated. After the Vidaldmeet itself, the Council decided things.

There were Seven Councillors. The most important had come to be known as the Royal Councillor, and was the executive head of government who chaired the Council and reported directly to Their Majesties. The official name of this Councillor was the *Councillor for the Identity of the Nation,* and by the scheme of things as defined by the Constitution, the Councillor for Identity was charged with everything to do with what the nation was about, its reason for existing, its very being, its life-force, its creativity and power. The other Councillors were: the *Councillor for History and Tradition,* the *Councillor for Communication and Commerce,* the *Councillor for Relationships and Networks,* the *Councillor for the Defence of the Nation,* the *Councillor for Growth and Ceremony,* and the *Councillor for Law* (sometimes called the *First Councillor*). There were often quarrels about which Councillor should deal with which issue, given the inter-related nature of human affairs as seen in these terms. On occasion, the Star Chamber was required to provide arbitration in these matters. Because the judgments of the Star Chamber were infallible, they were always accepted, even when they made everything worse while adding to the general confusion. It was said that Counsellor Kane Ophelius, charged with the task of reporting to the Councillor of History and Tradition on whether public libraries should be primarily under the control of History or Communication or Networks, arose one day and banged his head into the wall in an attempt to steady its swirling, and then left his whole life behind him without another word. He went to the Kader of Dalibor and became an apple picker, married a milk-maid, fathered ten children and lived a long and happy life.

Yolande had called a meeting of the Council to discuss the latest developments. Cadwalader, the Royal Councillor, took his seat with an important air, as if only too well aware that the fate of the nation rested in his hands. The Councillor for History and Tradition, Lady Daphne Frieda, was not able to attend due to the occupation, and that seat was filled by her advisor Honourable Anne Ramsey, clever and ambitious and young. The Councillor for Communication and Commerce was there Magister August Raymond, with his shoulder-length long white hair and chest-length long white beard, looking like a sage who has descended from the mountain after having plumbed the secrets of the universe. (This appearance was entirely deceptive. The only mountain Magister Raymond had ever ascended was that of his ego, and he was very far from descending this mountain.) The Councillor for Relationships and Networks was there, Lady Maria Grestryne, a dark-haired red-lipped beauty with a mind like a razor. The Councillor for the Defence of the Nation was not there, being in Pentharborg, as would be noted by innumerable conspiracy theorists over the course of time, and that seat was filled by the nervous and un-warlike figure of Honourable Sachairi Tabean, his elegant fingers drumming a complicated rhythm as he waited, his shoulder-length hair framing a triangular face with deep set eyes. The Councillor for Growth and Ceremony was there, Lord Nadir Baard, in his ermine-trimmed dark blue robes, pulling at his fleshy jowls with his stumpy bulbous fingers, his bright blue eyes betraying his razor sharp intelligence. The Councillor for Law was also there, Lord Ringold Sacheverell, thin and gaunt, pulling on the lapels of his dark robes with long fingers, his hair made up in ringlets that framed his mournful face.

Yolande opened the proceedings. Her translator, seated behind her, translated her remarks into Westrigonian as she went along. '<Welcome to you all, and thank you for being here in these trying circumstances. Now to the first point of business without delay. I insist that no blow is to be launched against Lord Raspero or his followers. It has been brought to my attention that there are hotheads who have been reported as volunteering their services for armed actions up to and including the assassination of Matthias Raspero, the imposter monarch of Westrigonia. I rule any such action as inadmissible. You may express a contrary opinion if you wish, but please note that this is not a matter for debate. It is my royal decree that no such action can be permitted. Now, does anyone wish to speak on this matter?>'

Honourable Ramsey was first off the mark, eager to make an impression. 'Of course, given that he has pledged his word of honour not to hand you over to the invaders, it is possibly in our interests to leave him in place for the time being.'

'That is precisely why Raspero made that pledge,' Honourable Tabean commented. 'It now becomes in Her Majesty's own interest to leave him with enough power to enforce his order on his own followers, who can't be happy with this situation.' Sachairi was so subtle that it was not clear whether or not he approved or opposed Yolande's decree. Everyone had always thought that he would go far, given his talent for walking both sides of the street at the same time.

'It was an act of moral weakness on his part,' said Lady Grestryne. 'His backbone gave way when faced with the Queen of Westrigonia. Raspero is a weakling.'

'Far from it,' Lord Baard said, shaking his head in disagreement. 'Raspero has neutralized Her Majesty's capacity to act against him by this pledge. She is holding back all those who would act against him in consequence. It is an extremely clever move on his part. Let us not forget that this fugitive Baron has a track record that is, it has to be said, formidable.'

'He is a trickster who has gotten away with things up to date,' said Grestryne, not giving ground. 'That is all.'

Magister Raymond opined as follows. 'If the invaders are no longer a threat to Her Majesty, then Raspero's protection has become worthless. Besides, even if we openly fight him, he cannot hand us over to the enemy. He has pledged his word thus. This was the action of a naïve simpleton with little experience of politics. Did you see the expression on Shyester's face when Matthias made that pledge? Hah! Let observers legitimately laugh out loud! I vote that we assassinate him.'

The Royal Councillor Cadwalader began to speak at this moment for the first time. He knew when to make his opinion decisive. 'Raspero's blunder in making this pledge has weakened his position considerably. Yet we-'

'<This is not a vote!>' Yolande said sharply, having caught up via her translator with Raymond's belligerent proposal. '<I thought I made that clear. I have issued a royal decree on this matter. No action will be

taken against Lord Raspero. I will brook no argument. Is that clear to all of you?>'

Magister Raymond inclined his head with a courteous deference. He had quite deliberately mistaken the nature of the debate as a veiled insult to Queen Yolande, and no-one present had missed this insubordination.

Cadwalader flushed red. He did not like having been interrupted, but he could not make a protest about it, given that it was Her Majesty who had interrupted him on the grounds of Raymond's insolent 'mistake'. Cadwalader felt like a man jostled by rude passers-by. But the Royal Councillor, whose lumbering elephantine form was so clumsy in the physical world, had an adept mind on the dance-floor of committee meetings. He could change tempo in a heartbeat. 'It is indeed clear to us all, Your Majesty. Raspero is off limits. We have all examined your decree, and found it flawless. But as to the next item on the agenda, may I suggest the vote in the Krastienst by which Raspero has been elected King? Your Majesty.'

There was a silence of cold-eyed calculating looks, impassive faces, guarded expressions and folded hands. The fact was that at a time like this, Yolande's position as Queen was tenuous. *When the great fall, there is loot to be gathered.* Astrudel would have been happy to be at that Council meeting. It was a gathering of wolves.

'<We must gain a clear understanding of the Krastienst vote,>' Yolande declared. '<Is Lord Raspero the elected monarch or is he not?>'

Cadwalader replied on the instant, asserting his authority. 'It seems unfortunately beyond doubt that he has in fact been so chosen after the dethronement of yourself and Frederick,' he pronounced. 'All the reports indicate – '

'Then why has there been no public display of the relevant Acts as required by custom and law?' Magister Raymond interrupted.

Everyone had been asking that very question all day long and Cadwalader's patience was wearing thin. 'These are difficult times even for rebels and traitors,' he pointed out brusquely, 'and no doubt there is an explanation of this momentary oversight. The absence of these documents does not gainsay what all the reports indicate, including those of eye-witnesses who are on our side and have testified under oath as to what they have witnessed. We must proceed on the basis of these reports being true.'

'Raspero is a slippery eel who has pulled the wool over our eyes before,' Ramsey pointed out. 'Nothing concerning him can be trusted. I want something in writing.'

'The eye-witness testimony *is* in writing,' Cadwalader said as if trying not to shout. He was pained as much by Ramsey's mixed metaphor of an eel pulling wool over people's eyes as by anything else. Cadwalader cared about such things. 'Raspero has been elected King.'

'<And where is he now?>' Yolande asked in a tone of complaint. '<He simply disappears, and leaves us without a word of explanation. What kind of King is that? Courtesy is the province of princes, and where is *his* courtesy? I ask you, where is it?>'

'Nowhere to be seen, unlike in the days of our only true monarchs Frederick and Yolande,' Tabean said in his most sycophantic manner. 'Those days will soon return. Your second reign will be even greater than your first.' Tabean was grovelling to Yolande as a way of indicating to the others that if he was to turn against her, the price of his betrayal would be high. He would not sell himself cheaply. He expected a big pay-day if he plunged a knife into Yolande's back.

'There are rumours that Raspero has international allies, even in the depths of the Protectorate itself,' Scribe Ramsey commented by way of saying something. Ramsey felt overlooked.

'Rumours!' Cadwalader snapped contemptuously. 'The business of government requires firmer foundations than that.'

'There are certainly foreign mercenaries abroad in the city,' Raymond said. 'These are not rumours but first-hand reports. The first thing Raspero did when he seized the Public Portal was transport fighters for hire from a variety of countries, but none from the Protectorate, obviously, given that mercenaries are illegal there. But certainly from Kalidasa, Felicia, Sandford, and other places besides. Half the city is under Raspero's control now, but more importantly, King or no, Raspero is going to have his own power base when the dust settles, a power base that might be impervious to outside influence such as that which we can bring to bear ourselves. How can we bribe foreign mercenaries to come over to our side when we don't even know their names?'

'Yes, but how on earth did Raspero hire these foreign mercenaries so quickly?' Baard wanted to know. 'They must have been waiting to come at the time he sent for them.'

Sacheverell, the Councillor for Law, nodded. As he did not often speak, a nod from the great man contained as much meaning as the lengthiest of speeches from someone else.

After gravely inclining his head to acknowledge Sacheverell's important contribution to the debate, Raymond continued his comments. 'Raspero has liberated the Westrigonian prisoners of war and placed them under his command as the self-proclaimed Marechal of Westrigonia. He used these mercenaries to accomplish this. The initiative is clearly with Raspero for the moment.'

'But what support can he command in the Vidaldmeet?' Ramsey asked. 'Surely that will be decisive.' While her comment was relevant, she had said it at the wrong time. Honourable Ramsey was not destined for greatness.

'<The Vidaldmeet is a nest of snakes and traitors,>' Yolande observed.

There was an awkward silence. Even Cadwalader looked as if he was trying to think of a brand new topic of conversation. Raymond said nothing, but he memorized what Yolande had just said. Later he would write it down. It could be damaging.

And so the meeting of the Council of the Kingdom of Westrigonia proceeded. There were other points to discuss, but only one central axis around which all their deliberations turned. Would Matthias Raspero succeed in becoming King?

A Reluctant Verdict Handed Down on those Events made Infamous by Repeated Controversies as written by Counsellor Obrad Robbiesterfen in December 2132 A.F.:

From the very beginning of the reign of King Matthias there has come a

Controversy which has dogged all accounts of this glorious monarch by its refusal to go away. The facts are clear. Matthias the Fourth recruited from the dungeons of the Palace of Krastienst five prisoners as resistance fighters. At a key point in one of the battles to liberate Krastienst, in the afternoon of Tuesday the 14th of April 1882, after more than twenty-four hours of continuous fighting, while in retreat from a pursuing Melisendien battle group, Matthias ordered the gates of the Rada Gallery Courtyard closed before these five dungeon prisoners could pass through into a place of safety from the pursuing Melisendien soldiers. Four of the prisoners died then and there. And so the controversy began. Did Matthias knowingly and deliberately arrange matters so that the dungeon prisoners would be killed, thus relieving him both of paying the reward money he had promised them and of being saddled with the political problems of their future presence as heroes of Westrigonia? This is the suspicion and the accusation. After extensive investigations lasting a lifetime, I am now in a position to offer the definitive verdict on this vexatious issue. Matthias the Fourth is completely innocent of this charge which has been levelled against him. This I tell you so you know it.

12:05 PM, Wednesday 15 April 1882 A. F.

The fighting was still raging in the capital, but the Westrigonian forces under the command of Matthias were now in the ascendant, and the high commands of the Melisendians and Baalbabakans were desperately trying to regain their earlier co-operation, having realized by now that they had been duped into fighting each other. The situation in the Palace had much improved. Food supplies had been restored, Romano's guards were in contact with Matthias's fighters, much of the city was back in the hands of the Westrigonians, and while life had not entirely returned to normal, everything was a lot better.

Astrudel had come by Eleanor's Chambers with the latest news. The Marechal and his fighters had been escorting a group of captured Melisendien soldiers to their place of confinement, when a raging mob of Westrigonian citizens had demanded to lynch them. The Marechal had held them off and pointed out that Westrigonia was a signatory to international treaties regarding the safety of prisoners in uniform captured during battle. It had come to the point where the Marechal had been required to personally step forward, look at those in the front line of the mob directly in the eye, take out his disc and inform them that the first idiot to step forward would die. The mob had dissipated after that, and the Melisendien prisoners had been escorted to safety.

Eleanor had been profoundly unimpressed by this tale. 'Matthias can indulge his whimsicalities if he chooses,' she said. 'The Melisendiens can go hang as far as I am concerned.'

'Oh, you can talk of these whimsi-whats-you-call-its,' Astrudel snapped back. Eleanor had used a term of High Westrigonian that Astrudel could not even pronounce. 'Say what you want. My grandfather was Melisendien. What the Marechal did was noble. He's a nobleman, all right. The Rasperos have been around forever.'

Eleanor's eyes glinted as she noted a weakness in her overbearing nanny. 'Was your grandfather Melisendien? That explains, well, many things. But I will let it go. I am merely pointing out, nanny, that it is not the job of a Westrigonian Marechal to defend Melisendiens. I would be happy to see them all hanged.'

'Oh, we would all be happy to see some people hanged,' Astrudel said with a sneer. She was losing her temper. Eleanor, seeing this, and scenting blood, moved in for the kill.

'I was merely referring to the well-known propensity of Melisendiens to safeguard their own interests. Two Melisendiens were once walking along together when one of them said to the other: "If you can guess how many coins I have in my pocket, you can have them both." A remarkable people.'

Astrudel retreated from the fray with blinking red-rimmed eyes and changed the subject. Still on the Marechal, and with an eye on her own personal advantages, however things should turn out, she said: 'Oh, I've got no problem with Melisendien jokes. I've heard them all. Everyone's talking about how the Marechal is defending the law. But there's other things that people are saying about your boyfriend, Your Royal Highness.'

'And what are people saying?' Eleanor asked casually, as if not that much interested.

'He's leading them into every battle, always being the first to take on the enemy,' Astrudel said as proudly as if this had been her own idea.

'What? But how dare he?' Eleanor was enraged. 'How very common of him!'

'He might be killed and be a tragic hero,' Nina gasped, 'and we will always wonder what might have been if he had lived.' Her eyes shone.

'Shut up, Nina,' Eleanor ordered.

'Oh, he's a wily one, the Marechal,' Astrudel continued approvingly, as if honesty would have disappointed her. 'Even Death won't catch him so easily. Not until the appointed time and place. No-one can avoid that.' The rosy-cheeked Astrudel made fatalism sound like a healthy lifestyle.

'Well, he will most certainly have to cease and desist from this fighting with the common soldiers,' Eleanor said decisively. 'It is the common soldiers who go into battle first. This is because the people first into battle are most likely to be killed. No-one misses common people. That is why they get to die first. I will certainly have to speak to Matthias about this. I will not have this low behaviour on his part continue for a moment longer.'

'I wouldn't be going about saying that the Marechal shouldn't be fighting, if I were you,' said Astrudel with her usual impudence.

'Oh?' Eleanor raised her eyebrows. 'And why is that?'

'Because people will say that you're a foreigner and a traitor who is sabotaging the fight to liberate Westrigonia by opposing the Marechal fighting.'

'I see. So the Crown Princess of Westrigonia cannot, it seems, remind the Marechal of such minor claims on his attention as propriety.'

The massive sarcasm of Eleanor's comment was entirely lost on the low-bred Astrudel.

'It's not propriety that people care about right now, it's the occupation.'

'This is the difference between the common people and their rulers,' Eleanor observed with a detached air. 'The common people entirely fail to recognize the importance of propriety. But of course that is why they are common.'

'When your door's kicked in by the boot of the occupier,' Astrudel replied with her habitual bluntness, 'you've more to worry about than propriety.'

'I will not argue about this matter with an inferior,' Eleanor snapped. 'You are forgetting your place, nanny.'

'Oh, I'm forgetting my place, am I?' Astrudel replied, entirely unruffled by this reprimand. 'Well, that's told me, hasn't it?' As she left the room, she slammed the door hard enough to make the porcelain figurines rattle on their shelves.

An Impartial and Fair-Minded Account of Controversies and Bloody-Minded Foolishness arising from Considerations of Certain Issues from the early days of the reign of King Matthias the Fourth of Westrigonia, as Penned by the Noble and Nearly Infallible Hand of Knight of the Realm Sir Reginald Tahmasp in February 2178 A.F.:

I have seen rutting bulls on the Alsastriadan Plateau butt their horned heads against each other repeatedly until one withdraws from the fray, ceding the waiting trembling hot-blooded bovine maiden to the harder-headed victor. Good luck to that species! We laugh, but are we any better ourselves? I refer, of course, to the historians butting their heads against each other without a maiden in sight. Good luck to that species! But no no-one laughs. This is no joke. There are four hundred and thirty four separate documents relating to the employment of three hundred mercenaries in the employ of Matthias the Fourth in the Battle of Krastienst of 1882. For the sake of the heavens above written in micro-point! How much further does anything need to be proven to be accepted as fact? The arguments against these mercenaries largely centre on the impossibility of their recruitment subsequent to the invasion of Westrigonia. These arguments are left irrelevant if the Baron of Raspero could have been granted such foreknowledge of the invasion of Westrigonia as to have enabled him to lay his plans for the hiring of these mercenaries in advance. But it is precisely this foreknowledge that the advocates of orthodoxy refuse to accept as probable, or even possible. And so all this nonsense continues with no end in sight after nearly three centuries. Come, let us butt heads on this issue until someone's skull cracks! Isn't that the logical way to resolve this question?

12:25 PM, Thursday 16 April 1882 A. F.

Baron Matthias Raspero, King and Marechal of Westrigonia, made his way towards the Palace of Krastienst in a much-varied company. There was his personal bodyguard, under the command of the black-bearded and burly Captain Steindahl, a number of friends, several hangers-on and well-wishers, wide-eyed hero-worshipping children and a gaggle of assorted chattering laughing citizens of Westrigonia, too varied to be assigned any category other than that of "gaggle". The battle was over. The enemy had been defeated and taken prisoner. Krastienst was liberated.

Matthias had not slept for three days and nights, yet he felt not the least sleepy. It was true that he was clumsy in his movements, that he nearly tripped on crooked pavement stones, and that the sunlight was too bright and the shadows too dark and noises too sudden and loud. Things moved across his field of vision that were not there when he looked again. Logically, he was able to deduce that his sleep deprivation was such that he needed to sleep, which was why he was returning to the Palace, using the last of his energy to arrange this last matter. His friends Alaric, Acteon and Haris, seeing his condition, kept close by him. At the Ilbert Door, Matthias banged loudly on the door knocker. The Door was opened promptly, and the guards there stepped aside. Matthias turned around and pointed at all those who were to be granted admittance at the Palace, and said loudly, 'You can come in, goodbye to all the rest of you.' With a parting wave, he entered the Palace and made his way to the Mahsa Door and entered the Sara Hall. There were two of Romano's soldiers standing guard outside the Quinlan Door, which led to the North Quarter.

'Go and inform Her Majesty Queen Yolande that I wish to speak with her immediately,' Matthias told them.

They bowed, and one of them promptly departed.

Yolande was not long in coming. An earlier message from Matthias had informed her that he was on his way. Eleanor, alerted by Astrudel as to the latest developments, also turned up. Various others thronged the hallway behind them.

'Yolande, I wish to invite you and Eleanor to have dinner with me tomorrow night at seven. I will come for you at six o'clock. We may talk to each other, catch up with everything and hopefully work out what to do. What do you say?'

While Yolande's translator muttered into her ear, Cadwalader said: 'May I inform-'

He was cut short by Matthias raising his left finger and pointing it directly at the Royal Councillor and saying: 'Shut your face, Cadwalader, or I'll shut your face for you.'

Cadwalader obeyed this summons to silence, and the onlookers did not wonder why. It was not so much that such dialogue was not a commonplace occurrence in the rarefied heights of the Palace of Krastienst, given that people did not talk that way normally in these elevated environs. It was more that Matthias was quite a sight. His hair was sticking up, he was three days unshaven, his eyes were as red-rimmed as any devil from hell could wish for, his robes were ripped almost to rags, and there were splashes of blood over his person that were not his own blood. The Marechal looked like someone you would not wish to encounter in a dark alley. Furthermore, the way he had pointed his finger at Cadwalader was extremely thuggish. He was like a drunk in a bar looking for a fight. Whether or not Cadwalader still had the sense he was born with was a matter for debate, but he certainly had enough sense to shut up on the spot without another quibble.

'<You have been away from the Palace for three days, Lord Raspero, without a word as to your whereabouts, as to the progress of your –'

'<It is enough of the talk that is of such the multiplied concern,>' Matthias interrupted the Queen of Westrigonia with an upraised hand, like an official calming a multitude. He also glared at her with a certain fierceness, which caused Yolande, noting his alarming appearance, to nearly step backwards and the watching Romano to nearly draw his wand. '<It is that I am not sleep since I am last see you, and so for me now it is the short talk of this time as I am now to go sleep without the delay of this time or of any time.>' Matthias had run out of thoughts to express, and he paused at this time as much because he had forgotten what he was supposed to say next as for any other reason. His mind had gone blank.

Eleanor, who had not taken her eyes off Matthias for a single moment, noted this sudden weakness. 'Lord Raspero, did you say that you haven't slept for three days?' Eleanor asked sweetly.

'Yes, exactly,' Matthias said shortly, looking over at her.

'Have you had a bath or a shower in the past three days, Lord Raspero?' Eleanor asked even more sweetly than before.

'No.'

'Oh!' Eleanor paused and then sniffed loudly.

Matthias tried to gather his scattered thoughts. '<So, Yolande, it is now the goodbye as I am sleep now.>'

Eleanor sniffed loudly.

Yolande was catching up via her translator what Matthias and Eleanor had been saying to each other, while distractedly noting Matthias's Anglashian farewell. '<I understand that you are in need of rest, Lord Raspero. Please do not let me stand in your way. I accept your dinner invitation with pleasure, and look forward to the chance of conversing with you further on that occasion.>'

Eleanor sniffed loudly.

'<I thank you, Yolande, of this the what you are saying at this time, and->'

Eleanor sniffed loudly.

'Alright Eleanor I get it!' Matthias said, unable to stop grinning foolishly. 'I have strong body odour because I haven't washed for three days.'

Eleanor sniffed loudly. By now several people were laughing quietly.

'<It is all the decided thing, Yolande, as of now and so it is->'

Eleanor sniffed loudly. More people were laughing now. Matthias couldn't help chuckling himself.

'<It is of now only the dinner invitation of the morrow and it is the silence from you, Eleanor, of such other things as these. That is all. It is the goodbye of you from me at this time of now, and it is the goodnight also.>' With a bow, Matthias turned on his heel and was gone, followed by one last loud sniff from the Crown Princess of Westrigonia.

He left behind an amused Crown Princess, and a thoughtful Queen of Westrigonia. Yolande was far from being upset by Matthias's exceptional rudeness. Matthias had behaved no worse than several indelibly memorable drunks of Yolande's experience, and his passing comment that he had not slept since he had last seen her made up for much. Being so sleepless meant that he was not himself. He could be forgiven. Besides, the capital had been liberated, thanks to him, and there was now the prospect of clearing up some uncertainties at the forthcoming dinner which Matthias had confirmed was now being held on the morrow. Yolande turned away and made her way back to her Chambers with a sense that at least one thing had come into focus.

Eleanor, for her part, was also looking forward to the dinner tomorrow night.

A Lasting Judgment after all the Wearisome Debates and What-Have-Yous and In-Your-Faces-Westrigateses Babbledygook Topplety-talk by InMeister Sabine Page as written by his own hand in June 2578 A.F.:

And where will it end? We are told that King Matthias must have had foreknowledge of the invasion of Westrigonia, with all the consequences such an accusation implies. But on what basis do these accusations rest? On irrefutable documents and all the rest of such tiresome and trivial babbledygook do these accusations rest. It is tedious and pointless to list them all, so here are some of the most salient: the conquest of the Palace of Krastienst by Matthias on his arrival through the Portal requiring a prior sabotage; the three hundred mercenaries whose presence in Krastienst have been attested to by numerous evidences; the diaries of the Lady Lestrange; the various evidences concerning the pre-planning of the conquest of Krastienst by the forces under the command of Matthias the Fourth at the time of the

Battle of Krastienst in 1882; and a host of other historical perspectives besides. As against this mountain of evidence and argument I say this: 'Get lost, you mongrels!' A single word of truth is enough to refute this falsity. Did not Matthias himself say, 'What is enough is enough on any day of the year.' That alone is sufficient to destroy all back-biting calumnies on this most noble of monarchs. This my judgement will last through the ages.

CHAPTER TWENTY FIVE

The greatest criminal has never stood trial,
For the rich and powerful are his friends.
The name of that criminal is poverty.
He is master, tyrant, friend, lock-picker,
And he will never stand in the dock,
While his accomplice is king.
Frankie the Villain

11:05 AM, Friday 17 April 1882 A. F.

Matthias found a place to sleep, and woke twenty hours later with a foul taste in his mouth and an urgent call to nature sounding deep in his bodily organs. He sat up groggily and looked about him.

He was in the Rollo Chambers in the East Quarter of the Palace, reserved for visiting dignitaries of the highest rank. It was starting to come back to him that he had chosen this place the day before, made sure that it was empty, told everyone that he was now retiring until further notice, and closed the doors on them all. As a fugitive for these past seven years, Matthias's caution had become second-nature. He did not want to wake up to find his enemies standing over him. He therefore used his wand to place his own combinations on the doors and windows to make sure that no-one could enter while he was asleep. He then divested himself of his robes and boots and lay down on the enormous four-poster bed. He felt so wide-awake still that he realized that he might well lie there for some time before going to sleep. He wondered if he should use his wide-awakeness to have a wash. He noted that the light coming through the windows had somehow changed, and realized that he must have already been asleep without having realized it. Had someone been trying to open the door? What had awoken him? While contemplating this puzzling development, he must have fallen asleep again, because now he was awake all over again.

By looking at the clock and making arithmetical calculations, which were thankfully rudimentary in nature given that he had to perform them so soon after waking up, Matthias worked out that he had been asleep for twenty hours. The memories of the past few days came flooding back, and Matthias recalled that he was now King of Westrigonia, in theory at least. The thought brought him to his feet. This was not a time to be lazing about.

He showered and shaved and looked about for fresh clothes. He found a variety of robes and trousers and various undergarments that, while being perhaps somewhat old-fashioned, were undeniably Westrigonian. He was no longer dressed like an Anglashian gentleman. Matthias then marched to the doors of the Rollo Chambers and threw them open.

Numerous people standing about the hallway turned towards the King. A hubbub of voices broke over Matthias, in which questions could be discerned relating to matters of governance, missing people, palace protocol, complaints about precedence, complaints about perceived slights and requests about making requests. Matthias sent off someone to bring him the Steward of the Palace, Jervis Nereus, and began patiently to wade through the demands of his petitioners one by one. Eventually Nereus appeared.

'Although I am King by election of the Vidaldmeet, I am to be addressed as Marechal. Is that understood?'

'Yes, Marechal,' Nereus replied, demonstrating an immediate intelligence.

'Now, I am having dinner tonight with the Queen and Princess. Yes?'

Nereus paused. Matthias had touched on a matter that had consumed the Palace all day long, even overtaking the war as a matter of priority. These were uncharted waters, and no-one knew how to handle the protocol of such an unprecedented situation. No-one knew how many of the guests at the dinner would be of Matthias's party and so it could not be decided how many of Yolande's party were to go. This was related to the question of whether the members of Yolande's party should be one more in number than Matthias's in order to show the Queen's superiority, or one less in number in order to show her superiority in the opposite way, or exactly of the same number? An equality of numbers seemed dangerously, well, equal. Complex arguments had been raging over this issue all day. And this was only one of the issues involved.

Another was the vexed question of who should be chosen as the members of Yolande's party. Was this a social gathering or a working dinner? The question of seating arrangements was yet another complex equation to be solved, but it could not be solved until the terms of the variables, namely the identities of the people going to this dinner, had been assigned. And even on the basis of those who were certain to be there, which were only Yolande, Matthias and Eleanor, it was not clear how to proceed. Should Yolande and Matthias each be at the head of the table on opposite sides, or did this place them on too much of an equal footing? If only one of them were to be at the head of the table, it would certainly have to be Yolande; but would Matthias agree to this, given his claim to be King? Probably not. Nor had the dining venue yet been nominated, and that question was itself fraught with complexities. Just to make everything worse, it was not clear in the Yolande camp who they could negotiate with in the Matthias camp, which seemed to be a disorganized rabble. The Marechal himself had disappeared, and none of his followers were prepared to tell anyone where he was, if they even knew themselves. The forthcoming dinner constituted the biggest headache with regard to Palace protocol that the Palace functionaries had ever encountered in their lives. In later years they would laugh about it, but not now.

Steward Nereus paused, therefore, with good reason. He then said carefully: 'There are a number of issues with regard to protocol, Marechal, that remain to be decided concerning-'

'Enough!' Matthias cut him short. 'The soup will be Chorso, the main course Mitasam, the dessert Pejatos. Rehunda wine and sparkling water and other beverages as is convenient may be served. I give the chef a free hand to add anything else to this scheme of things. Now, I will meet Yolande and Eleanor and the other members of her party in the Sara Hall at six o'clock. From there we will go to the Veceslav Room where we will converse for one hour, and we will then go to the Sabina Dining Room. We will have dinner, and then proceed to the Hariman Room, where we will enjoy our after-dinner refreshments. After that, I will escort Yolande and Eleanor back to the Sara Hall. That is all. You have your instructions, Nereus. See to it.'

While Matthias proceeded with his day, Nereus returned to the Royal Chambers with this latest news. Yolande's advisors pounced on this information like starving people given food. Matthias's menu was clearly political. These were all national Westrigonian dishes. If Yolande opposed them, she would look unpatriotic in the eyes of her people. Yet was there anyone in the kitchens who knew how to cook these dishes? The chefs imported by Frederick and Yolande from Trentland, Anton and Ferdinand, would no doubt refuse, with many an eloquent wave of their meat cleavers, to provide such a repast. But what was to be done? A new complication had arisen. Sighs rose up into the air. An already long day had become longer.

6:00 PM, Friday 17 April 1882 A. F.

Matthias turned up at the Sara Hall at six o'clock, and waited for Yolande, who arrived a careful three minutes later. Cadwalader launched into a meticulously planned speech to the Marechal, addressing the essential concerns of Yolande with regard to this barbarously impromptu dinner. Matthias heard him out without a change of expression on his face, looked at his pocket watch when Cadwalader was done, noted that the time was now twelve minutes past six, and said: 'The only question you have not asked, Cadwalader, is how on earth all these issues can be resolved in time for dinner. <Yolande, you are come now, or the dinner is off.>' Matthias turned on his heel and walked off. Yolande followed after a moment's hesitation. It seemed that the dinner was still on.

Matthias had earlier made arrangements for the Veceslav Room to be made ready for his purposes. This room was often used for meetings between dignitaries. It was a hexagonal room seventy feet wide with an arched doorway embedded into each wall. The wall around each archway was decorated with reference to a great poet of the past: there were unfurled scrolls with excerpts of poems written in beautiful calligraphy, paintings and wooden carvings and the occasional bas-relief in bronze, with a marble bust of each poet at the top of each archway. The onion-shaped domed ceiling had a fresco showing the bare-breasted Goddess of Inspiration ignoring a multitude of suitors in order to bestow her favours on one lucky poet. The red cherry-wood parquetry floor had six long Ramudien carpets stretching from the doors deep into the room. In the centre was a small labyrinth with hexagonal sides made of black marble with inlaid mother-of-pearl fillings along the paths of the labyrinth. A number of chairs, but no tables, stood about the room. They were all identical Fifteenth Century oak chairs with green cushions and curved armrests. The point of the chairs being identical was that dignitaries could not fuss about any perceived slights to their standing by being made to sit in a chair inferior to someone else's.

Matthias went to his designated chair and stood there politely waiting for Yolande and Eleanor to arrive. He gestured to their chairs as they came along, and then sat down himself with them. There was a bustling and a rustling of dresses and fans and tailcoats as people found their seats. Eventually everything rattled to a standstill and there was silence.

'Yolande,' Matthias began, 'I would –'

'Might I interject in the briefest possible of all such interjections?' Cadwalader asked in his most melodious-tone-of-voice. 'You appear to be unaware of the most elementary diplomatic protocol of such occasions as those in which we are today engaged. This is not how such matters proceed. Let me be so bold as to explain this matter. First, we –'

Matthias's wand was upraised and with a smack a gagging karn flew through the air and incapacitated Cadwalader's speaking faculties. The great man made incoherent noises in protest at this treatment while clawing ineffectually at the gagging karn with his hands and a hopelessly waving wand. Matthias waited with a stern look on his face.

Eleanor was delighted by this happy sight, and nearly (nearly!) forgave Matthias the Fourth for all the offences he had caused her over the years. The Crown Princess hardened her heart. Matthias had stolen a kiss from her only to disappear without a word with his ill-gotten loot for all these years. He had also moved a motion of no confidence against Eleanor's parents in the Vidaldmeet. His villainy was of the darkest hue. He could not be forgiven quite so readily as all that. But it was good all the same, Eleanor had to admit, to see that toad Cadwalader gagged in this fashion. Eleanor's heart sang.

Yolande for her part looked sideways and did nothing. Truth to tell, she was not too unhappy at the prospect of Cadwalader being sidelined for a while. She often felt limited by Cadwalader. He was so helpful and knowledgeable, that it was difficult not to go along with what he wanted; and besides, much of the time, neither Yolande nor her husband wanted to be too much troubled with the problems of running the Kingdom. The day-to-day running of the government could always be delegated to people like Cadwalader. But now circumstances demanded the personal intervention of Yolande, and Cadwalader was getting in the way. Much of the time he undoubtedly knew what was best to be done, but today might well be different; it was certainly unprecedented. Yolande felt the need to take charge personally herself, and Cadwalader and his endless expertise was beginning to feel like a nuisance.

Matthias's calmness, good humour, and above all else, his immediate pledge not to subject Yolande to the status of being a bargaining chip with his enemies, had had their effect on Yolande. In the midst of the barbaric environs of war, the Westrigonian baron seemed civilized to the Anglashian lady. Yolande had the strong impression that she could deal with Matthias. If she had been twenty years younger, she could quite easily see how she would have liked to have had a candle-lit dinner with him in a secluded spot far from the tumult of the day. But that was not the issue. She had few allies, and paradoxical as it might otherwise have seemed, Matthias seemed to be an ally in these strange times. Yolande trusted Matthias more than Cadwalader would have thought wise. Cadwalader would have had a thing to say about the frailty of women had he known of Yolande's private thoughts. Rightly or wrongly, Yolande said nothing about Matthias's treatment of Cadwalader, although her intervention would have proved sufficient if it had been forthcoming, as Matthias would have been obliged out of courtesy to bow to her wishes.

Cadwalader grew quieter, although if his rolling eyes could have spoken, a torrent of words would have filled the air. Matthias withdrew his gagging karn with a wave of his wand. Cadwalader breathed in as if to speak but Matthias forestalled such an occurrence with a raised hand and a stern look which the cowed Cadwalader obeyed.

'I am the King of Westrigonia,' Matthias declared in his most portentous tone of voice, as if he had been practicing, 'and I will set my own rules. You will be quiet or you will not be present. Is that understood?'

'There are certain –' Cadwalader began to whine, looking to Yolande for help, but Matthias cut him off by gagging him again and waving at Steindahl and declaring peremptorily: 'Lord Cadwalader is to be imprisoned in the dungeons immediately! See to it, Captain Steindahl, without delay!'

Now that, Eleanor thought to herself, was the good thing about being a king. You could throw someone like Cadwalader into the dungeons just like that! She was half-reminded of all sorts of things which she had half-forgotten. She steeled her heart against liking Matthias all over again.

King or not, Matthias wanted his gagging karn back, and so it was that the departing Cadwalader's voice filled the air while Steindahl dragged him outside by his heels. Eleanor's happiness was now complete. Yolande said nothing. Neither did anyone else. The entire court sat back and watched the show. It was both expedient (in the sense of having to do nothing) and enjoyable (in the sense of being pleasurable) to go along with the whole thing. And so that was that for Cadwalader! The poor fellow would not be seen again for a while; and sad to say, he would not be missed.

Once there was silence in the room, and a semblance of continuity about the place, Matthias said: 'Yolande, I would like to begin by – '

'Lord Raspero!' Eleanor interrupted peremptorily. 'I have some concerns that must be addressed first.'

Matthias looked at her. 'Of course, Eleanor,' he said courteously.

'May I ask first if you have had some sleep?' Eleanor asked with her eyebrows raised.

'I slept twenty hours straight,' Matthias said.

'Good, because I want it to be quite clear that I will not tolerate any further rudeness from you!' Eleanor snapped fiercely, glaring at him. 'You were inexcusably rude yesterday and the fact that you had not slept is no excuse for your behaviour. Let it be quite clear that I expect better manners from you in future!'

Matthias inclined his head with perfect politeness and said: 'I am well aware of the requirements of courtesy, Eleanor, and you shall have no cause for complaint in this regard.'

'Precisely so!' Eleanor said and tapped her fan on the palm of her left hand. 'Now, I wish to make it quite clear that I will not go into exile. I refuse to leave Westrigonia. This is my home and you will not force me to leave. Is this understood?'

'I thought you didn't like it here in Westrigonia anyway. You preferred Troderent.'

'What?! That was . . . years ago. How stupid are you! What a thing to say! You – '

'Alright, alright, I get it. You now love Westrigonia and you don't want to live anywhere else. However, I can't make any commitment to you on this matter.'

'You can and you must and you will!' snapped Eleanor. 'How dare you threaten me with exile!'

'Eleanor, there are complicating factors – '

'I am not interested in your complicating factors – '

'Enough!' Matthias shouted and held up his left hand. 'Eleanor, this will end in one of three outcomes for me. I will become King of Westrigonia by the second Vidaldmeet, I will become Baron of Raspero under another monarch or I will return to Anglashia. What happens to you might not be my decision. However, I can promise you this. You may stay here in the Palace until the second Vidaldmeet takes place and no-one can force you to leave here against your will before that time. That is all I can say on this matter at this particular time.'

Eleanor considered this and said: 'Very well, that is acceptable.'

Matthias turned back to Yolande and said: 'Yolande – '

'Lord Raspero,' Eleanor interrupted sweetly, 'there is one further matter of importance I must discuss with you.'

'Of course, Eleanor,' Matthias said with impeccable courtesy. 'And what is that?'

'You appear to insist on addressing me by my first name. If you persist in this behaviour you will leave me no choice but to likewise address you by your first name. After all, I am the Crown Princess of Westrigonia and I cannot remain at a disadvantage in this matter.'

'Very well, Eleanor,' Matthias said equably. 'I have no objection to you addressing me by my first name.'

'Whether you have an objection or not is beside the point! It is what will happen if you persist in this course of action.'

'Ah!' Matthias nodded. 'That's very clear. Very well . . . Eleanor.'

'Very well . . . Matthias,' Eleanor said determinedly with a fierce glare in Matthias's direction.

Matthias turned back to Yolande. He waited courteously for her translator to finish translating his latest exchange with Eleanor before speaking.

'<It is out of the question for you to be on such familiar terms with Lord Raspero,>' Yolande protested, looking across at her outspoken daughter. '<I cannot allow this to continue.>'

'<Then you must insist that *Lord Raspero* addresses me more formally,>' Eleanor riposted without hesitation. '<Surely you cannot leave me at such a disadvantage as this? It is an affront to the dignity of our royal name.>'

'<Lord Raspero addresses me by my first name while I *choose* to refer to him as Lord Raspero,>' Yolande pointed out. '<You must make the same choice. After all, you are strangers to each other, are you not?>'

'<Far from it, Yolande,>' Lord Sakesheld said peaceably. He couldn't bear to see people quarrel, and so he made haste to repair this growing breach between mother and daughter. '<They were childhood sweethearts. That makes them old friends now and there's nothing improper about old friends being on first name terms.>'

'<Childhood sweethearts?>' Queen Yolande's mouth fell open. She turned to face Eleanor. '<Is this true, Eleanor?>'

'<Certainly *not*!>' Eleanor said emphatically, blushing bright red. '<It is most certainly *not* true!>'

'<Is this true, Lord Raspero?>' Yolande asked, turning to face Matthias.

Matthias looked puzzled, as if trying to remember. 'It kind of vaguely rings a bell,' he said.

'*It vaguely rings a bell*?!' Eleanor snapped furiously.

'Wait a moment, it's starting to come back to me,' Matthias said wide-eyed, as if in pretended alarm. 'Kissing you in the Rose Garden, giving you that bracelet, yes, I remember everything as if it happened yesterday.'

'And do you also remember,' Eleanor asked angrily, 'never coming to see me again and never even writing me a letter?! Not one letter?!'

'I've had a lot on, Eleanor.'

'Yes, and of course a letter takes such a long time to write, doesn't it? All of one hour.'

'Did you have time to read letters in between your various betrothals?' Matthias asked meaningfully with raised eyebrows.

Nina giggled.

While Eleanor tried to find a response that was savage enough, Queen Yolande interrupted her translator to ask: '<But how on earth could you two have even known each other?>'

'We met at your coronation,' Matthias replied, looking directly at Eleanor, 'over those three days. It was a whirlwind romance.'

Matthias smiled at Eleanor, who stared back at him stony-faced while his reply was translated to the Queen.

'<But Eleanor, how can you have said nothing of this to me?>' Yolande complained. '<After all the warnings I have given you to beware of adventurers and fortune hunters.>'

'<I was well aware, Mother, that Matthias Raspero was the fortune hunter,>' Eleanor said, openly giving Matthias a disdainful look. '<That's is why I paid his attentions such little regard that I did not even bother to tell you about his feeble attempts to romance me.>'

'<You let him kiss you!>' Yolande said in horror.

'<Did I?>' Eleanor asked out loud as if trying to remember. She blushed bright red again. '<I had completely forgotten that.>'

'<Did Lord Raspero really give you that bracelet?>' Yolande asked, gesturing towards the offending item.

'<This cheap thing?>' Eleanor said scornfully. '<In any case, it was stolen property.>'

'It was not stolen,' Matthias objected. 'Lieutenant Willselm Raspero of the 42nd Regiment was granted it along with other jewellery as legitimate war loot from the Treasury of Sashkind.'

'War loot!' Eleanor snapped scornfully. 'Yes, it would be that kind of present, wouldn't it, from a barbarian like you!'

'<Lord Raspero, how can you have done such a thing?>' Yolande protested. '<How can you have given such little thought to Eleanor's reputation?>'

At that Matthias laughed. 'Reputation? Get real, Your Majesty. We were both twelve years old. Don't tell me you never did anything similar when you were a girl.'

'<I most certainly did not,>' Yolande declared severely. '<Clearly you do not understand the requirements of a royal upbringing.>'

'Come off it,' Matthias said, shaking his head. 'You were not born a royal. You were raised to be the Countess of Koppany. It was Frederick who had the royal upbringing as the future Duke of Leland. Then your father beggared himself to put you and your husband on the throne of Westrigonia. He bid just about everything he had at the Monarchy of Westrigonia Auction of June 1872 and then retired to his estates in Sardenland which by then was all he had left.'

'And that is exactly why the Zoller-Abstein domination of Westrigonia must end!' shouted Lord Rayerfeld furiously. 'The outrageous sale of the throne in this manner is beyond all that is decent!'

'Well, you'll have plenty of opportunity to get outraged about this policy over the next few weeks,' Matthias said calmly. 'The forthcoming auction of the throne of Westrigonia by the Lord Protector will no doubt be widely publicized.'

There was a silence.

'The forthcoming auction?' Eleanor asked. 'What do you mean?'

'Well, the First Protector isn't going to sit back and just allow me to be king, is he?' Matthias replied. 'But my election means that Frederick and Yolande are no longer King and Queen of Westrigonia. So the way is clear for De'Asterides to have an auction. And given the fact that De'Asterides still wants to put some height between him and the other four dwarves, even after all this time, he's not going to let the opportunity slip by. Furthermore, the Mentortrems, which is your branch of the Zoller-Abstein family, opposed his election as First Protector, so Frederick and Yolande aren't exactly his favourite people right now anyway. So there'll be an auction coming up for the throne of Westrigonia. Trust me.'

'The other four dwarves?' asked Eleanor. 'What do you mean?'

'There were five candidates at the election for First Protector,' Matthias explained. 'They were nicknamed the Five Dwarves for obvious reasons. The election dragged on and on, the Great Assembly was divided, public opinion was indifferent, and, well, as you know, eventually a resolution was reached.'

'And how was that resolution reached?' Eleanor asked eagerly, forgetting in her eagerness that she was supposed to speak to Matthias with disdain. This was one of the great mysteries of the age.

'No-one knows except the Five Dwarves and their immediate circle,' Matthias said with a laugh that suggested that he himself did in fact know. 'There are only rumours. One rumour is that the Five gathered together at Perntharborg and played a game of cards, and the winner of the game remained a candidate while the other four withdrew their names from the election.'

'There are other rumours,' Counsellor Hanaeker-Erny said with a salacious giggle.

The rumours he was referring to could not be discussed in polite company, but mere propriety wasn't going to stop Baron Rayerfeld. 'The Zoller-Absteins-' Rayerfeld began to say with a puritanical fervour, but he was cut short by Matthias.

'*Have members of their family present.* Now, Yolande, it is time for us to discuss current events. Are you quite sure that it is out of the question for you to appoint me as Marechal?'

With Cadwalader out of the way, Yolande felt able to relax and consider the question properly. '<But why is it, Lord Raspero, that you are so insistent on this point when I supposedly no longer have the power to make such an appointment? And how can I make such an appointment in any case in these circumstances?>'

Matthias nodded understandingly, like a schoolmaster dealing with a bright pupil who had asked a reasonable question. 'As to how you are to perform this act, the answer to that is simple: in accordance with the Constitution. I can make all the necessary arrangements for witnesses, signed documents, and so on. Leave everything to me. You won't have to lift a finger with regard to setting anything up. All you have to do is say the appropriate words and sign the appropriate documents. This will take ten minutes. Now as to what it all means, well, naturally, the effect of your action is purely rhetorical. But it will mean that those in Westrigonia who follow the lead of the Zoller-Absteins will be obliged by this development to accept that I am Marechal, and in this way I can lead a unified resistance to this invasion of our country.'

Matthias spoke so smoothly that Eleanor nearly believed every word he said, yet the Witch of Trentland sensed somehow that Matthias was lying through his teeth. But how could he be lying when he was simply stating the truth as everyone knew it to be? Something did not add up.

'<That is all very well, Lord Raspero,>' Yolande said with a half-amused shake of the head, '<but I cannot act alone in such a matter. I must consult with others. You really must wait for my answer. I cannot speak now.>'

'The First Protector will tell you to give me nothing, and he will further command you to oppose and obstruct me at every turn by any means you have available. But he will not do this for your own good but for his. He will accept the decision of the Vidaldmeet ostensibly in order to keep the peace by respecting the rights of Westrigonia, but his real motive will be to have another auction for the throne of Krastienst in order to strengthen his hand amongst the various factions of the Zoller-Absteins by favouring one outcome over another, not to mention all the money he will receive from the winning bid. You and Frederick and Eleanor and Jason will be out on your ear before this is all over, trust me.'

Now this Eleanor found all too believable, and the Crown Princess of Westrigonia was not at all happy to hear that anyone might dare to challenge her status. Speaking in Anglashian so that her mother could understand but looking directly at Matthias, Eleanor said: '<Reference has been repeatedly made to the second Vidaldmeet by yourself, has it not, Matthias? Did you not say that you would yourself refuse to be king until then?>'

'Oh yes, let's all speak in Anglashian,' Rayerfeld grumbled. 'Let us settle the national affairs of Westrigonia in the *foreign* language of a bunch of *foreigners*.'

Eleanor decided then and there that she would stamp on Rayerfeld like a bug when the time came.

'My point about having a second Vidaldmeet is that everyone can unite around their decision, whatever that decision might be. Surely we can at least agree on this point, Yolande?'

Yolande listened to her translator with bowed head, and then looked up at Matthias to reply: '<But that still leaves open the question of what we are to do now.>'

'Ah!' Matthias said delightedly, holding both hands in the air as if about to catch a ball flying through the air. 'Exactly! You have put your finger precisely on the point which so bedevils us today. We must develop a working relationship, you and I, with regard to these national issues. But what is this working relationship to be? My suggestion is this: that I take on the role of Marechal, which after all is the next most senior position under the Constitution after the monarchs during wartime, which gives me undisputed military authority for the time being, which means that I can lead our armies in the national liberation of Westrigonia. Once that goal has been achieved, we will have the time and space needed to resolve these other issues. As to us getting along, well, you keep your half of the palace, I'll keep the other, we'll meet up for dinner now and then, for business meetings, networking and fact-finding and so on, and given that we bear each other no ill-will, things will work out as they will and we can all accept the outcome in a positive and constructive manner.'

Yolande laughed in a cheerful way on hearing this translated. '<Lord Raspero, if only things could be quite so simple.>'

'Things can indeed be this simple if we refrain from looking upon them in a complicated way.'

'<I can give you no answer at this time, I regret to say, Lord Raspero. But I will give careful consideration to everything you have said.>'

The Steward of the Palace, Jervis Nereus, who had been hovering discreetly in the background for some time, now saw his chance to dive into the conversation. Bending forward deferentially, he said in a grave way as if fully aware of the import of his words, 'Dinner is served, Marechal.'

'Excellent!' Matthias said loudly. 'I'm starving. Yolande, Eleanor, let's go eat.'

The party arose to their feet in a hubbub of discreetly muttered chit-chat as everyone shared their impressions in an excited fashion. There was a buzz in the air, even a sense of history being made, as the two monarchs of Westrigonia, the former one and the present one, set forth for the Sabina Dining Room with everyone else in tow.

The Sabina Dining Room was a long rectangular room eighty-one feet long and twenty-seven feet wide. It was painted white with gilded floral designs covering the walls and cornice, the gold and white colours combining in such a way as to almost dazzle the eyes. The ceiling overhead bore a fresco showing the Sage Arktos the Wanderer climbing a mountain path, his long white beard gleaming in the light of the yellow sun. One side of the room contained arched doorways leading onto a balcony overlooking the Palace Gardens, while numerous paintings of a variety of birds and animals, from peacocks and ducks to stags and rabbits, were hung along the other three sides of the room. A dazzlingly white damask tablecloth was spread out along the enormously long oaken table, with Seventeenth Century chairs painted bright gold along the sides of the table. The white and gold crockery shone in the bright light of the bronze chandeliers overhead, with its attendant silverware and crystal glasses lined up with a mathematical precision.

Matthias took his wand and used his mobile karns to tip up the chair at the head of the table so the back of the tilted chair rested on the rim of the table. Matthias then stepped to one side of the table, gestured to the seat opposite him and said: 'Yolande.' He gestured to the next seat further along and said: 'Eleanor.' With a general wave of his hand and the instruction to 'Seat yourselves!' to all the others present, he set forth a process somewhat analogous to the tumbling of lottery balls into a tube, after which everyone was seated hither and thither with smiles on their faces and an almost delirious sense of conventions flouted. These were heady times indeed at the Palace of Krastienst!

7:20 PM, Friday 17 April 1882 A. F.

An implacable fate had befallen Alaric. He had fallen in love with first sight with Nina Delwyn in the Room of Accomplishments when he had first arrived in the Palace in the company of the Marechal. The great matters of state being negotiated at that time and place had become a blur as he had tried not to stare too obviously at the object of his adoration. He had thrown himself into the Battle of Krastienst with an accentuated abandonment of the personal; or, to put it in plainer language, he had been so elated with the vision of the mysteries of the universe which he had experienced that he had not cared whether or not he lived or died. He was in a place beyond these polarities. Thus he had gained himself an immortal reputation in those three days. Even Matthias had looked at him sideways with raised eyebrows, as if wondering what was going on with his protégé. And now he found himself back in the presence of his beloved. Alaric had not held back, with his usual diffidence, from being pushy. He was not entirely himself. He was ready to conquer.

Alaric was of medium height, slim, with dark-brown hair that was fashionably shoulder-length, a straight nose, high cheek-bones, delicate lips and dark-blue eyes with long eyelashes. He looked like a poet, although truth to tell his only talent with a pen was as a forger.

From little acorns do great oak trees grow. Who knew what the most momentous events of that day might have been in the eyes of a prophet looking upon the past, present and future as one? Certainly, besides the obvious great doings of the day, there were other things going on that might have led who knows where in the unfathomable intricacies of the indefinite future. Such as, for example, the determined manoeuvring of young Alaric Niedbala, who would as a person be beaten into shape by the hammer blows of history in a future yet to take place but which a prophet could see as already *in* place. Not that young Alaric knew anything else other than the path laid down at his feet that he walked along by being obedient to the promptings of his heart.

In the Sara Hall, he had noted the positioning of Lady Nina Delwyn, and had unobtrusively, and with a strategic eye, departed in the general hubbub in such a way as to drift into her close proximity. But nothing had come of this, except perhaps an occasional sideways look from Lady Nina Delwyn in his direction, as if she were aware of his attentions. Once in the Veceslav Room, Alaric had sat in his chair, occasionally stealing a sideways glance at Lady Delwyn, who somehow seemed to always catch him at it with a slightly startled look. Was she looking at him as well? When the general departure for the Sabina Dining Room began, Alaric gathered all his courage together and made his move like a wandfighter in a street battle seizing the moment. He sidled across the room with sideways steps, looking all around as if inwardly debating where he was supposed to go, and then stepped directly in the path of Lady Nina Delwyn, bringing her to a halt.

'Lady Delwyn, allow me to escort you to the dining room.' With this abrupt declaration, Alaric stepped forward, took Nina's right hand in his, tucked it into his left elbow, and set forth, taking Nina along with him by the simple expedient of using his elbow as a means by which to clench Nina's hand in a pincer grip and pull her along. The wide-eyed Lady Nina Delwyn went along with this caveman behaviour without protest. She looked over to her side at her fellow ladies-in-waiting, who were openly laughing at her predicament. Nina felt not only that she had been abducted by a barbarian, but that no-one cared!

Her abductor had taken her into the Sabina Dining Room and waved her to a chair. Nina looked about her for help, but everyone seemed preoccupied with their own affairs. She looked to the Crown Princess of Westrigonia, her personal figurehead capable of forging through any adverse waves of life, only to see that Eleanor was preoccupied with Matthias to the exclusion of all else. Nina was both abducted and abandoned!

For his part, Alaric was trying to think of something new to say. Nothing was coming to mind, and time was running along.

It was not as if Alaric had not already provided conversation starters. He had asked Nina how long she had been resident in the Palace of Krastienst. Nina had squeaked in reply. Alaric had then said that the weather had been very mild of late. Nina had said nothing. *Did Lady Delwyn not agree,* Alaric asked insistently, *that the weather had been very mild of late?* Nina had still said nothing, but in a very panicked way. Alaric let it go. After all, the weather was neither here nor there. He just wanted to hear her speak. Was her voice high or low, placid or tempestuous, melodious or grating? But in a spirit of humility, Alaric understood that perhaps he had not yet hit upon the correct conversational topic. But what could he say next? The war was perhaps best avoided at that time. Should he say something cheerful? It was then, out of the blue, that young Niedbala said, almost as an act of desperation: 'As I am to pay court to you with a view to our future marriage, it would be as well if we were to become acquainted to a certain degree whenever possible.'

Nina noted that her abductor had abruptly told her that he was going to marry her. Her astonishment at this declaration must be gauged at her past experience in the ocean of romance.

Her first romantic experience had occurred at the age of fifteen when, a bottle having stopped with its snout in her direction, she had been kissed by a plump freckle-faced youth who bore an expression of disdain, and with cheers that were also jeers, the embarrassed girl had sat down feeling unworthy. Her second romantic experience had occurred when, at a solstice celebration, a youth selected by a lottery had been obliged to be her dinner companion for the evening. He had continuously insulted her girth, her complexion, her intelligence and her birth-date. He might well have been working his way to an attack on her mere existence, when the evening thankfully came to an end. Nina thus felt that true love, in the material realm, was not for her. And now a companion of the King, who had been making eyes at her, had declared his intention to marry her.

Anyone can be pushed only so far. Nina was not one to lose her temper. She had no temper. But she knew that there was a line to be drawn.

'You are not going to marry me,' she said.

'You don't like me?' Alaric replied.

'No, I don't like you.'

'Why not?'

Nina looked around her to see that the world had paused. It had simply stopped moving. Either that, or her perception of time had altered. 'I just don't,' she said. The world was moving again.

'Well, that's that,' Alaric said, apparently conceding defeat. But like any lover in history, he was only waiting his time.

Nina felt beleaguered, but, for some reason, surprisingly cheerful. She stole a look sideways at her lover, to see him calmly spooning soup into his mouth. Nina turned back to her own soup-bowl with an unexpected feeling of warmth stealing its way over her body from top to toe.

7:35 PM, Friday 17 April 1882 A. F.

Soup was served, bread rolls were provided, napkins were tucked into place and the diners bent to their labours. Little was said while they ate for everyone present was hungry. Having finished his bowl, and waved his refusal of more soup from the attentive servant hovering by his elbow, Matthias said: '<It is the most excellent necklace of your evening attire, I may say, Yolande.>'

'<My jewellery is not a topic for discussion,>' Yolande said severely.

'<Of course it isn't,>' Matthias agreed hastily. He picked up his wine glass and sipped his Rehunda wine, the finest of the finest straight from the royal cellars, no less! (Alas, it was wasted on Matthias, who was not much of a drinker.) But the wine glass gave Matthias another topic of conversation. '<This wine glass, it is the special of Fulguritium Glass, it is not so? It is the story from me of this glass, what it is that is happen,

this is the great-etc-uncle for me, his name Skyler Raspero, sixth son of baron so of course it is not for him the money, so it is *sink or swim* as the Anglashians say. Anyway, he is the great friend with Samstride Celestyn and it is that they are to go into mountains to look for the gold, because it is that Samstride Celestyn is know of rocks and metals and such things. And it is one day the lightning and it is the sand is glass from this lightning, and for them it is such the story that it is happen that they are say, it is sign from heavens! So they are say, now we are make glass. And so they begin the company Fulguritium Glass, and it is become famous glass making company. But it is that Samstride Celestyn and Skyler Raspero is one day it is big quarrel, over something or other, so it is that they are not to speak from the other, but it is that they are must work for company, so it is that they are only to write notes to each other if they are to say this thing to one or this thing to the other. And it is until they are die, it is only this way of things, that it is that one is walk up to the other, and is hand the other the note, and then it is that walk away, and the other is read note, and it is write the reply, and it is to walk to the other and give reply note, and so it is this way for forty years!>'

Matthias laughed to show that his story was done.

Yolande looked at him without expression and said nothing.

'They are excellent glasses at any rate,' Eleanor remarked. 'I have always thought so.'

'*There is only the best in the Palace of Krastienst,*' Matthias agreed, citing the well-known saying.

'Including the best people – usually,' Eleanor said a little acidly, swirling her own Rehunda wine in her glass and taking a measured sip.

Matthias sighed. 'At some point, Eleanor, you are going to have to let it go that I did not write to you.'

'But whatever do you mean, Matthias? I entirely fail to understand you.'

'There is something you fail at?' Matthias asked with a good-humoured smile. 'Well, don't blame me for it!'

'I often fail to understand my inferiors,' Eleanor confessed with her own good-humoured smile. 'It is their stupidity that is so puzzling. I am sure that you never experience this difficulty.'

'I remember when we were kids and I asked you: *Are you always like this?* After all these years, I think the answer is finally coming in.'

'And what do you mean by *always like this?*'

'Bossy and critical.'

'I am not bossy and critical.'

'You could write the book on *bossy and critical.*'

'How dare you be so rude?!'

'I took a deep breath first!'

Yolande, having closely followed this exchange via her translator with mounting alarm, intervened at this point. '<Might I ask you two to desist from continuing this conversation? Eleanor, it is most unseemly of you to engage in such badinage. It must end now! Lord Raspero, as you are speaking to my daughter I must ask you to respect those conventions which apply in these circumstances.>'

'Alright, Yolande,' Matthias agreed promptly. 'As you wish.'

Eleanor took a sip of her wine while staring up at the ceiling. Her nose could not have been higher.

Matthias looked so serious that it was obvious to those who knew him well that he was desperately trying not to laugh.

8:40 PM, Friday 17 April 1882 A. F.

Everyone had retired to the Hariman Room after dinner, where Matthias had courteously waved Yolande and Eleanor to their seats while sitting down himself. Attentive servants brought them cups of coffee or tea, or glasses of wine, with little chocolate biscuits.

After some general chit-chat, Matthias got straight back to business. 'Yolande, if only this delightful evening in each other's company could be extended indefinitely. Yet like all things good or bad it is drawing to an end. If there is anything you especially wish to discuss with me at this time, I am listening.'

'<Yes, Lord Raspero, there are several matters I wish to discuss, but first amongst them is the military situation. Just what is going on?>'

'Krastienst is liberated, all Westrigonian soldiers here in the capital are being organized as a fighting force, there are twelve hundred Baalbabakan prisoners of war, and nine hundred Melisendien prisoners of war.'

'What do you mean that Westrigonian soldiers are being organized as a fighting force?' asked Magister Raymond. He was trying to make his mark now that Cadwalader was no longer around.

'I mean that not all the officers accept my authority as Marechal, and so those officers who *do* accept me as Marechal are being put in charge of the soldiers. This requires re-organisation.'

The rumours that everyone had heard had just been confirmed by Matthias himself.

'<That is highly unacceptable,>' Yolande objected. '<Those officers who are still loyal to myself cannot simply be sidelined in such a way.>'

'How can I lead the fight against the enemy if my orders are not obeyed? I do not notice anyone complaining about Krastienst having been liberated. Yet this liberation was accomplished by that old-fashioned idea of troops obeying their commanders. But if you support me as Marechal, Yolande, then I will happily reinstate all these officers because then they will obey my orders.'

'<Time and again, you return to this issue. How many times must I tell you, Lord Raspero, that my response will be forthcoming at a later time?>'

'Well then, your officers will just have to wait for that later time, won't they?'

'Is it true, Lord Raspero,' Raymond asked, still out to make his mark, 'that these officers are still being held as prisoners as if they were still prisoners of war?'

'Absolutely. And please bear in mind, Magister Raymond, that there are serious questions to be addressed concerning the military strategy of Marechal Sabas. There have been accusations that the Zoller-Abstein faction here in Westrigonia sabotaged the war effort.'

'Hah!' Rayerfeld said delightedly. 'Now you're talking!'

'That is an outrageous and false accusation!' Raymond proclaimed. 'It is an absurdity.'

'How do we account for the utterly useless military strategy of the Marechal appointed by Frederick and Yolande?'

'It was not deliberate sabotage,' Raymond said heatedly. 'Your accusation is false.'

'The only way I can free those officers is if you appoint me Marechal so that they accept me as their commander-in-chief. Technically speaking, of course, the appointment by your hand, Yolande, is only rhetorical, having no force in law, but it will provide these officers with a rationale to accept my orders.'

Raymond pressed on. 'If your supposed election as King is confirmed by the public process proper to this development, those officers will accept you as Marechal. When will this take place?'

'Take the matter up with the Vidaldmeet. It is up to them to do this.'

'Why have they not yet done this?'

'I have no idea. *The Vidaldmeet is its own reason.* Your guess is as good as mine.'

'May I ask about these foreign mercenaries which you are employing?' Honourable Sachairi Tabean asked.

'What foreign mercenaries?' Matthias asked blandly.

After a moment's pause, Tabean said: 'There are widespread reports of foreign mercenaries fighting in the city.'

'Firstly, there is no fighting in the city,' Matthias pointed out, 'so there is one problem with your story right there. The city has been liberated. Secondly, there are bound to be wild rumours during wartime. Many of these rumours are born of the enemy and intended to mislead. Is there anyone here who would wish to facilitate the work of the enemy? There are no foreign mercenaries in Krastienst, nor have there been over the past few days.'

'But Condorcet saw them himself. Didn't you, Condorcet?' Tabean asked, turning to his fellow minister for support.

Condorcet nodded. 'Certainly. I saw the Kalidasa at Helion Street yesterday morning.'

Matthias gave him a very cold look. 'To those who choose to peddle falsities, I have this to say. I am King and Marechal of Westrigonia, and I might remain so. Those who incur my enmity in the meantime would do well to remember that. Do you have anything more to say, Condorcet, or can we be spared your babbling for the time being?'

The cold look Matthias gave him seemed to have frozen Condorcet's innards, for he sat immobile. (Later on Condorcet was to confess that he had been mistaken about his original claim. He had in fact seen a travelling theatre troupe on Helion Street, and mistaken them for Kalidasa mercenaries.) No-one else said a word, either. It is common sense not to make an enemy of a king.

Raymond turned the topic of conversation to mundane matters. The regulation of the city's food supplies, committees to look into this or that, confiscated materials that were being reclaimed by their supposed owners, urgent matters of governance that had to be attended to without delay, and many other such issues, were brought up by Yolande's ministers. Matthias said little more himself, but delegated all these questions to his subordinates; Yolande said nothing at all, and only vaguely paid attention to what her translator was saying; and the Witch of Trentland by and large ignored all these mundanities and, with eyes hooded, contemplated the King and Marechal of Westrigonia.

All around them was a low mutter of voices as the others chatted amongst themselves. Alaric had shepherded Nina to the side, where they had been joined by Mitzi and Georgette, who had come to check on Nina. Acteon, Haris, Darnell, Gerbern and Felim turned up and soon there was a merry conversation going on.

10:05 PM, Friday 17 April 1882 A. F.

Matthias stood up, held up his left hand commandingly and everyone fell silent. Being King had its advantages, Matthias thought to himself. Silence itself came in response to a royal command.

'Yolande, our evening together draws to a close. I leave early tomorrow morning. But as soon as I return I wish for us to meet again and discuss things further. And of course Eleanor. But in the meantime, during my absence, you may discuss issues with Acteon here. For now, please grant me the honour of escorting you back to your Chambers in farewell.'

Matthias waited for this to be translated to Yolande. Everyone rose to their feet, and they all set off together for the Sara Hall.

There was a sense in the air that something had been settled that night. Neither side would attack each other. Each would leave the other alone. And along with that accommodation came a sense of relief all around. People had been tense without even realizing it. A cheerful muttering of voices rose in the air as they walked along, mixed in with soft laughter, forming a muted revelry.

Matthias and Yolande bid each other goodnight with a regal nod of the head, Eleanor raised her chin and gave Matthias a superior look, and the two groups went their separate ways.

CHAPTER TWENTY SIX

Everyone has forgotten how rough it was before.
I made this road, but no-one thanks me.
Frankie the Villain.

9:50 AM, Saturday 18 April 1882 A. F.

Matthias completed his liberation of the township of Raspero by ten to ten, but it had been much hairier than he had anticipated. Having arranged a portal transportation from the Public Portal of Krastienst to the Public Portal at Raspero at just before seven o'clock in the morning for himself and nineteen Westrigonian soldiers, he expected that the Melisendien occupiers of Raspero would be suspicious and have the Portal well guarded, but he had not expected there to be several hundred Melisendien soldiers waiting for him. If he had not planted a Sabahudin Energy Structure at an earlier time, he would have been taken prisoner. As it was, he was able to seize the controls of the Portal and hold off the Melisendien soldiers while reinforcements were brought through from Krastienst. The tide of battle turned slowly in Matthias's favour. Over the next few hours Matthias took back his barony from the occupiers by street-to-street and house-to-house fighting until the battle was over.

For Matthias, having his barony back was all that he sought. As far as all his carefully laid plans were concerned, this was it. The barony of Raspero had preceded the creation of Westrigonia, and as far as he was concerned, it could succeed it as well. Saving Westrigonia was not his priority.

9:50 AM, Saturday 18 April 1882 A. F.

Yolande had summoned Eleanor to the Pearl Room for a nine o'clock meeting. There was mother-daughter business at hand. She had also called a meeting of the Council of the Kingdom for ten o'clock in the morning. Eleanor strolled in late at ten to ten, but as the Councillors were not, in the end, to all turn up until one o'clock in the afternoon, there wound up being time enough all around for everybody.

Yolande got straight to the point. She was too upset for small talk.

'<I shall not dwell on my disappointment at your behavior, Eleanor. I would never have suspected such a thing from you. You have always been remarkably well-behaved with regard to your relations with members of the opposite sex, and this has been a source of great reassurance to me. A misbehaving daughter can wreck the best-established of families. I simply cannot understand how you of all people can have behaved in this fashion.>'

'<Really, Mother, you are making an enormous fuss over nothing. It – >'

'<It is not *nothing* to kiss boys in the Rose Garden! It is not *nothing* at all! It is a scandal and an outrage!>'

'<Well, it has been my only indiscretion at any rate.>'

'<Yes, well, that is something. At least it is not a pattern of behavior on your part.>' Yolande paused there, as if preparing to move on, but then her self-control snapped. She couldn't let it go. '<My own daughter, luckily your reputation is intact, as is I am sure everything else, but what will people say? I am speechless! All this kissing in the Rose Garden! The world will say, no doubt, that I am a negligible mother. I mean negligent. But of course negligible as well! But I ask you, how on earth could I, how could anybody, should we entirely discontinue this business of Rose Gardens? Why do we have Rose Gardens in any case? The very name of *Rose Garden* is suspect in the eyes of propriety by combining the terms of *rose* and *garden*, from which nothing exemplary can arise! I am shocked shocked *shocked* by all this Rose Gardenery behavior on the part of my own daughter whose behavior, at least in this regard, has always been exemplary up till now as far as I have always known which clearly was not far enough! Did I go around being kissed in Rose Gardens as a young girl? No, I did not. Then why have you taken this path? And what will be the end of all this? Please bear in mind that it is not just anyone who has been my daughter's Rose Garden kisser. It is Matthias Raspero who merely

happens, by some infernal coincidence of a mocking world, of a world which wishes to trample all loving mothers underfoot, this Raspero of all people has been elected King by the traitorous Vidaldmeet, and it is *he* who has been the snake in the grass of the Vidaldmeet, I mean the Palace Rose Garden. I mean what I mean is perfectly clear, how could it be clearer than this, which it is in its entirety, an awful entirety, I am shocked, what is to be done, something must be done, how dare he, how dare you, this is a scandal and an outrage, I am speechless, as I have said before but will say again, I say to all, beware!, do not, very well, as it is, this is all I have to say on the matter, I will say nothing more!>'

Eleanor made no reply to this outburst, but gazed at her mother in a wide-eyed and innocent fashion. Outwardly she was trying to look thoughtful. Privately she was thinking that her mother had lost it.

Yolande changed her mind about saying nothing more. '<I have a good mind to place you in the custody of the Kindly Sisters.>'

From a mother to a daughter, this was a serious threat. The Kindly Sisters were chaperones for hire who were called in to watch over the virtue of young maidens, and they were battle-axes beyond compare. Their fanaticism in the service of the moral universe had gained these elderly and emaciated women a fearsome reputation that made the bravest of men and women shake in their shoes. The healthiest and most cheerful of plants were said to shrivel up and die when the Kindly Sisters passed by. No-one called in the Kindly Sisters except as a last resort.

Eleanor was as unmoved as if Yolande was a toddler throwing a tantrum. '<Really, mother, you are over-reacting. In any case, you could not do this without the approval of Matthias, so it is not entirely your decision to make.>'

'<I am sure Lord Raspero would respect the rights of a mother over her child.>'

'<Possibly. Am I to take it that our conversation is over?>'

'<No.>' Yolande took a deep breath, and then exhaled loudly as if with the exhalation of that breath all of the bad energy would go away and leave her level-headed, calm and happy. It didn't really work. '<But let us move on from these matters. It does seem to me that, regrettably as

it may have happened, your acquaintance with Lord Raspero, as utterly inappropriate as it might have been, might nevertheless have provided us today with some unintentional benefits, by which I mean of course that you are possibly in possession of an insight into Lord Raspero's mind and character that may well be of some use to your father and myself in these very turbulent and trying circumstances. Am I right in supposing that you have some understanding of Lord Raspero?>'

'<You still do not appear to understand the situation you are in, mother,>' Eleanor explained patiently. '<It is not Matthias you have to deal with. It is the Vidaldmeet.>'

'<Go on.>'

'<The Vidaldmeet have decided to remove you and father from the thrones of Westrigonia. Therefore you are no longer the monarchs. They have decided to elect Matthias as King. Therefore Matthias is King. Your strategy must be to persuade the Vidaldmeet to reverse this decision. You must deal with the Vidaldmeet.>'

'<And how should I do that?>'

Eleanor paused, staring into the distance as if organizing her thoughts. This was in fact exactly what she was doing. Eleanor was wondering to herself if she really wanted to help her mother defeat Matthias when her own interests might lie in helping Matthias instead. She was very far from having forgiven Matthias for his many offences, yet she did recognize that one could not be stuck in the past indefinitely.

'<I must deal with the Vidaldmeet?>' Yolande prompted her daughter.

'<You must make sure to win the second vote in the Vidaldmeet,>' Eleanor said. '<That is what this will come down to.>'

'<But if we have lost the first   vote, it is not at all certain that we will win the second.>'

'<The Vidaldmeet will not readily forgive father for signing away so much of Westrigonia when he was a prisoner in Rozneft.>'

'<Good heavens, child, do you know how much your father suffered in those infernal dungeons? I have been informed of this in a matter that is so confidential that you will not repeat what you have heard from me to another. Frederick was kept without food, and and given only an

occasional glass of water, by those insisting that he sign their treaty. The Baalbabakans carried savoury dishes past the windows of his prison cell in order that their appetizing smell might amplify the torments of his hunger. Naturally, after a day and a half of such torture, your father gave in and signed the treaty.>'

'<I doubt that this tale of woe will mollify the Vidaldmeet or public opinion.>'

'<Such a tale will not be told in public. It is demeaning to the dignity of a royal personage.>'

'<Demeaning is also a term that might well be applied to the recent war. There is much public anger at the mismanagement of our military strategy when faced with this invasion. It is very unlikely that the Vidaldmeet will vote to return you and father to the thrones of Westrigonia. Also, as Matthias pointed out, it is in De'Asterides's interests to have another auction for the Westrigonian monarchy. However, you do have one card to play.>'

'<And what is that?>'

'<De'Asterides will not want Matthias to become King. If that comes to seem likely, and if returning you and father to the throne is the only way of stopping that happening, then he will forego this auction and support you.>'

Yolande mulled this over, her fingers toying idly with a jewel-encrusted letter-opener. '<So the question is: how likely is Lord Raspero to become King, or to retain his position if he is indeed already King?>'

'<I would not underestimate Matthias if I were you. You are safest to assume a higher likelihood than not.>'

'<You appear to know him quite well. What do you suppose his strategy will be?>'

'<Misdirection, duplicity, trickery, and a sudden *fait accompli*.>'

'<What kind of *fait accompli*?>'

'<Now that I cannot foretell at present. I would need to be fully informed of all developments as they occur in order to be able to warn you in advance of what Matthias plans.>'

Eleanor was as much jockeying to be involved in decision-making as anything. Whether or not she would be on her mother's side when the time came, only that time would tell.

It seemed that Yolande, who was no fool, had guessed something of this from the way she contemplated her daughter for a moment before saying: '<Is it conceivable, in your view, that Lord Raspero may even consider an advantageous marriage to you as a stepping-stone to the throne?>'

'<As a Zoller-Abstein princess, the Westrigonian nationalists will be opposed to me becoming Queen. Their opposition might be decisive.>'

'<What about your own feelings on this matter?>' Yolande asked. '<Do you still retain any affection for Lord Raspero?>'

'<Certainly not,>' Eleanor said promptly. '<Of course not. Definitely not.>'

Yolande chose to accept this denial, even though she felt that it had been repeated too often to be entirely persuasive. '<Excellent. I am glad to hear it. Well, I thank you for your advice, Eleanor. Now, if you will excuse me, I have other matters to be attending to.>'

It was clear to both of them as Eleanor departed that things had changed. Eleanor was no longer as subject to her mother as she had been before.

7:00 PM, Sunday 19 April 1882 A. F.

It had been observed by Yolande's advisors that it was necessary for Yolande to have Matthias around for dinner in order to recalibrate the equilibrium of her own queenship. Matthias agreed to this, and so everything was held in reverse, but much more precisely. For example, name plates were provided for where everybody would sit, and the menu chosen by Yolande was of Anglashian dishes. Matthias, having lived so long in Anglashia, could hardly object, and nor did he. The dinner was held in the Obrad Dining Room of the Royal Chambers. An earlier meeting was held in the Jehanne Room at which Yolande and Matthias conversed with regard to the contemporary politics of Westrigonia. Every now and then Rayerfeld snorted his protests about foreigners, causing

Matthias's mouth to twitch in amusement and Yolande to all-but-roll-her-eyes. There was, in short, a developing rapport between the former and current monarchs of Westrigonia.

Alaric found himself separated from Nina, but he kept his eye on her, and she kept her eye on him, and so in a sense they felt a companionship born of such shared looks.

There was only one hiccup in the otherwise smooth proceedings of the evening. Eleanor, finding herself placed at the far end of the table from Matthias and Yolande, quite deliberately by Yolande's personal orders, kicked up such a fuss that Yolande was forced to agree to a change in the seating arrangements, given that Matthias was taking her daughter's side to the point of threatening to walk out of the dinner. With an air, not of triumph but of grim justice upheld, Eleanor took her seat next to her mother, who was opposite Matthias. So the dinner proceeded.

8:25 PM, Sunday 19 April 1882 A. F.

Towards the end of the dinner, as everyone was relaxing with their desserts and beverages, the topic arose of dinners that had been held at Pentharborg. It was then that Sakesheld, always the conciliator, sought to bring the Raspero baron into the circle of family around the dinner table.

'<You are of course related to Lord De'Asterides, are you not, Lord Raspero?>' Sakesheld commented in a scholarly fashion.

'<Oh it is the very vague happening not to be the really related, I think,>' Matthias replied, with a slightly puzzled frown, as if wondering how this was relevant to anything.

He didn't fool Eleanor for a moment. She immediately pounced. '<You are related to Lord De'Asterides, Matthias?>' she asked pointedly. '<How is that so?>'

'<Oh, it is very vaguely by some marriage that is the very long ago one,>' Matthias said dismissively.

'<Not quite so vaguely,>' Lord Sakesheld observed, holding a finger up in the air: a scholar making a point. '<Your great-etc-aunt was the great-etc-grandmother of Lord De'Asterides. So you are very distant cousins.>'

'<It is that it is something like that,>' Matthias said with a tempered impatient carelessness, as if this was of such little importance that he was wondering why he was even discussing such a non-issue. Eleanor smiled at this, her eyes on his face like a hawk in a spiral.

'<And how did that come to be so?>' Eleanor asked, enjoying every moment of Matthias's concealed discomfiture.

'<It is that I am not to remember exactly such a matter that is hardly so.>'

'<Do you remember, uncle?>' Eleanor asked, turning to Lord Sakesheld with a laugh. Matthias shot her a sideways look, which Eleanor ignored.

The scholar, challenged on a point, immediately straightened up in his chair, and said: '<Now, let us see, the great-etc-grandfather of Lord Raspero gave a daughter in marriage to Lord Yenifer, her name was . . . Karen – >'

'<Camryn,>' Matthias corrected him immediately.

'<Ah yes, I'm sure you're right,>' Lord Sakesheld said condescendingly, as if encouraging a bright pupil. '<And Camryn was the great-etc. grandmother of Lord De'Asterides.>'

'<But who was this great-etc-grandfather whose daughter Camryn was given in marriage?>' Eleanor asked, persisting in knowing every single detail of this matter.

Sakesheld puffed out his cheeks, momentarily at an impasse as he tried to remember. Eleanor looked across at Matthias with raised eyebrows.

Matthias sighed, as if exasperated by all this irrelevancy. '<Camryn is daughter of Sir Nicholas and Lady Isabel Grangeshield. Lord Yenifer is nephew, son of sister, of Mikhail Hunyadi.>'

The name of the legendary Mikhail Hunyadi brought a silence to the room. Everyone there looked at Matthias with an increased respect. No-one had known of this family relationship of his with one of the great figures of history.

'<But how did that happen?>' Eleanor asked, interested for the first time in doing more than merely provoking her ex-boyfriend.

Matthias paused, almost smiling, and then said: '<Hunyadi is send the assassination squad to kill Nicholas, but it is that Nicholas is capture

leader assassin and he is say, "Your boss is the dead one if it is not the peace now," and so it is that this is for Hunyadi and Nicholas are become the friends, and it is that they are in business together of Allied Portals.>'

'<An interesting tale,>' Sakesheld said with little of his usual good humour, '<but may I ask what the evidence is that any of this actually happened?>'

Matthias shrugged. '<It is the problem for you, not it is the problem for me. You are look records, Allied Portals, the founded of Hunyadi, then it is Sir Nicholas Grangeshield is Master Grangeshield Estate, it is flying carriages of Anglashia that is have license, so the portals are the invented new, so it is that the flying carriages, it is not now only fastest travel, so Hunyadi is buy license of Grangeshield Estate, but Nicholas is say no, he is liking the carriages, so Hunyadi is to kill Nicholas so to own all of new portals which they are the secret, but then it is Grangeshield Estate is give license in exchange five percent Allied Portals of Hunyadi, so it is Nicholas and Mikhail are the friends, and later it is the marriage of Camryn and Yenifer.>'

'<But how on earth do you know all this?>' Sakesheld insisted on knowing.

Eleanor knew straightaway that this was a question that Matthias was going to ignore, so she tactfully pushed the conversation along: '<Sir Nicholas must have made a lot of money from this deal, given how successful the portal system became.>'

Matthias nodded. '<It is very much the money for whole Allied Portals. Yes, Sir Nicholas is make the very money of deal, perhaps ninety million strada for Grangeshield Estate in next thirty years.>'

There was a momentary silence. A profit margin of that size commanded a certain respect from all those present. But then, the development and introduction of portals had been an earth-shaking event that had not so much changed history as changed the conditions in which history was made.

'<I have read no less than five biographies of Mikhail Hunyadi,>' Sakesheld declared, '<and at no time has there been any suspicion that Hunyadi sent out death squads. Not even his fiercest enemies suggested such a thing.>'

'<It is *off the books*,>' Matthias told Sakesheld in all seriousness. '<But Hunyadi is the dangerous one.>'

'<The man who was the first First Protector, the founder of the Protectorate, is not known to have ever engaged in such activities as those to which you refer!>' Sakesheld almost snapped.

Matthias looked hesitant, as if he was starting to have doubts about what he was saying. '<It is family gossip of Rasperos, it is the talk I am heard before, the story of the fireside on the dark night, but who is to say if truth or not told now of this?>'

'<Ah, family gossip, well, I had no idea that the provenance of such an allegation was of such a high order!>' Sakesheld commented in his most sarcastic tone of voice. '<Well, you will have to excuse us lesser mortals, Lord Raspero, but we require stronger evidence upon which to lean our frail bodies, much stronger evidence than malicious gossip told around the fireside in the guise of family reminiscences of nonsense that never happened!>'

Matthias now looked even more doubtful. '<If it is the so very unlikely thing happened, then it is not the evidence for this. Perhaps it is not the thing happened if it is that it is the made-up story. It is then not happened.>'

'<It most certainly never happened,>' Sakesheld said firmly, but he sounded mollified by Matthias's recantation of his error. '<One can place no reliance on gossip, even the family gossip of our near and dear ones. Gossip is by definition unreliable, and it is better, far better to simply assume all gossip to be false.>'

Matthias nodded slowly, as if the light of Sakesheld's assertion was piercing the darkness of his own ignorance. '<Yes, it is only the gossip. I am see this now.>'

'<So that is settled,>' Sakesheld said, his usual friendliness now returning. '<This allegation is unmerited, unfounded, thoroughly false, and we need not even refer to it again.>'

Matthias nodded with such a serious look on his face that Eleanor knew he was desperately trying not to laugh. '<It is so even as you have said.>'

It was at times like this that Eleanor felt sorry for her learned uncle.

Sakesheld gave every appearance of being a man who sought the truth, yet the truth could only approach him on his own terms or not at all; and on this occasion it was to be not at all. The Witch of Trentland knew without needing to be told that Matthias had learned of this tale directly from those family records which he had inherited, which perhaps contained writings by the hand of Sir Nicholas himself. The story which Matthias had told was completely true in every respect, and those five biographies which Sakesheld had read were simply incomplete. Furthermore, the Crown Princess of Westrigonia noted the subtlety of Matthias's response. To characterise bona fide historical records of unimpeachable authenticity as family gossip was to stretch the truth, but not impossibly so. Matthias had deflected Sakesheld's enquiry not by directly lying, which would have lessened the dignity of the Raspero family name, but by misdirection. Further furthermore, Her Royal Highness could tell that Matthias did not see such a story as in any way detracting from the renown of Mikhail Hunyadi, and neither had his ancestor Sir Nicholas. From the sound of it, Sir Nicholas had admired the energetic and focused nature of Hunyadi's business dealings, and had not only gone into business with Hunyadi but had even become connected through family marriage with the Troderent magnate.

Eleanor remembered as a child going to dinner to the very house in which Hunyadi had lived, and sitting at the very table at which Hunyadi had sat, and looking up at the portrait of Hunyadi on the wall. (She was, like Matthias, a distant relation.) Mikhail Hunyadi had stood for his portrait, a short, slightly rotund figure in his respectable sixteenth century clothing, almost blinking sleepily out at the viewer of his portrait. The most brilliant mind of his generation looked like a friendly greengrocer who would struggle to add up the cost of your purchases of his apples and oranges; and contrary to the determined denials of Lord Sakesheld, there were lots of dark rumours about the Sage of Troderent, which all his biographers studiously ignored. In the words of Frankie the Villain,

> *The first of the First Protectors,*
> *Did not have blood on his hands.*
> *That is why there are soap factories.*

Eleanor looked across at her mother and noticed that Yolande was not fooled by anything that was happening either. Everything that had been said would eventually come to the ear of the First Protector, in these wartime circumstances, and that might be in part why Matthias had been so forthcoming about his family history in the first place. He was sending a message to the First Protector that peace was always obtainable. Eleanor could see that Matthias, even in the midst of reaching for another bread-roll, was playing the game of politics like a piano.

'<But who was this father of Camryn, Sir Nicholas?>' Eleanor asked Matthias.

'<You are of this understand this matter, Eleanor,>' Matthias replied. '<It is that it is second son of twenty-fourth Baron of Raspero, Alexandre, is go Anglashia and marry the Anglashian lady, and it is his grandson who is Sir Nicholas. And then it is thirty-third Baron of Raspero who is not having the heir, and so it is great-etc grandson of Nicholas who is Oliver who is to come Westrigonia for to be thirty-fourth Baron of Raspero, and he is called the Anglashian Baron for this. And so it is Oliver who is great-grandfather of me. And this is so.>'

'<It must have been quite a challenge for an Anglashian gentleman like Oliver to have become a Westrigonian baron,>' Eleanor commented. She could not help thinking of her own story, that of an Anglashian girl who became a Westrigonian princess.

'<Yes, it is not only of me that it is the delegation of Westrigonia come to Anglashia and say, "It is the position for you in Westrigonia." For Oliver, it is Westrigonian delegation of barony who is come Anglashia and say, "It is Baron of Raspero for you, come and take in your hand of this time now." For me, it is Westrigonian delegation who is say, "It is throne of Westrigonia for you, come and take this time of now in your hand." And it is what is said, that the more things change, the more they stay the same.>'

'<It was not quite the same for you,>' Eleanor said argumentatively. '<Oliver had to learn the language and culture of another country. You just went back to how things had been before. Nearly.>'

'<It is in Raspero there are the three statues of town square, it is triangle

of these statues, and it is one that is of Daniel, with the sword held high, for it is many the stories of Daniel of the great warrior. And the second statue, it is of Etienne, and for him it is sitting with the scroll in his hand and pen in other hand for it is that Etienne is the great scholar. And then it is Oliver, and his hands, they are the empty ones, and so it is third statue in Raspero. And it is these three that are greatest barons of Raspero.>'

'<Why were his hands empty?>' asked Eleanor.

'<Yes, this is question,>' Matthias agreed. '<Why so? For Oliver's hands are the full ones, you understand, he is save Barony, he is give much. But it is not weapon or the scholarship in his hands, so it is he is beyond these things, or it is that he is yet to receive that which is greater, for when it is that in your hand is filled, it is that you are not to receive what is greater still. But Oliver, he is the one ready to receive this. But this is only the interpretation of who is to say is not the known one, you understand.>'

'<Who had these statues made?>' Eleanor asked.

'<Oliver.>'

'<An interesting man,>' Sakesheld commented. '<He greatly contributed to the economic development of the Westrigonia of his time.>'

'<He is save Westrigonia from the Zoller-Abstein Protectorate predator of this economic enslavement of that time, and for this he is called the traitor of the Anglashians.>'

'<Yes, that is what I said,>' Sakesheld said in an ironic tone, as if it was at times like this that he entirely gave up on the world.

'Really, the Anglashians, the Westrigonians, why on earth can it not be understood that to be human is a larger category that includes them both?>' Eleanor burst out.

'<It is not so simple the matter of this,>' Matthias replied, with a shake of his head.

'<Yes, it is exactly this simple,>' Eleanor insisted.

'<It is for me in Anglashia not always that I am the human when it is that I am speak the foreign broken Anglashian.>'

'<I speak fluent Westrigonian and for this I am called the Witch of Trentland,>' Eleanor snapped with a certain bitterness. '<Why have you

never troubled to properly learn Anglashian anyway? You have had time and opportunity enough.>'

'I look forward in later times to discussing with you many issues, even this one,' Matthias told her. He paused, so that the translator could finish muttering into Yolande's ear. '<But it is for now the time to be moving on.>'

They all moved from the Obrad Dining Room to the Pedrutian Room, where more political discussions were held. Shortly afterwards, the party broke up and the evening came to an end.

CHAPTER TWENTY SEVEN

Ten poems are not enough,
To say what one poem cannot.
Truth is always well-rounded.
(I don't mean by this what you think I do.
But your thought is more exciting.)
I was told all this by a sage.
He really said this to me,
I heard him as clearly as you hear me,
It was said to me in the light of day.
Frankie the Villain

11:25 AM, Tuesday 14 April 1882 A. F.

For twenty-four hours, with only two hours sleep, Frankie had fought at the behest of Matthias. Frankie's skills with a wand did not measure up to his skills with a fountain pen. He had blundered, tripped, parried and thrown what blows he could, in the company of his fellow dungeon prisoners, foreign mercenaries, Westrigonian soldiers freed from being prisoners of war and Westrigonian citizens fired up by reasons of patriotism or revenge. No-one seemed to know what was going on except the Marechal, who was directing events as if following a carefully laid-out plan.

And then had come the Betrayal. Ordered by the Marechal to stand at a checkpoint until the signal to retreat was made, Frankie and his fellow dungeon prisoners, Gentian, Leocadio, Eyike and Bedrioch had stood their ground in the midst of all the confusion. The situation was chaotic, discs and karns were flying through the air, and then the signal to retreat came. But as the dungeon prisoners ran towards the Cadell Gate of the Mikayla Botanical Gardens, pursued by homicidal Melisendien soldiers, the Cadell Gate closed in their faces and their retreat was cut off. They turned to face their pursuers, and were rapidly cut down by a hail of discs, all except for Frankie, who evaded being killed in the following manner. By throwing his wand into the air in a histrionic manner and leaving his arms held high and throwing himself on the ground and rolling about in an exaggeratedly expressive manner, as if his elbows had become adjectives, Frankie succeeded in making such a spectacle of himself that the pursuing Melisendien soldiers momentarily forgot to kill him. Fortuna spared him then as the Melisendien sergeant who came upon him took him prisoner by binding his limbs with mobile karns. So it was that Frankie the Villain became a prisoner of war. As he looked about him, he saw that Gentian, Leocadio, Eyike and Bedrioch were all dead, and it was then that the terrible truth dawned upon him: Matthias had deliberately engineered this situation in order that they should all, Frankie included, be killed in battle against the Melisendiens, now that Matthias no longer needed their service, thus sparing the Marechal having to pay them the reward money as heroes of Westrigonia. It had all been a trick on the part of the Raspero baron. Everything Frankie had ever believed about the villainy of the rich and powerful had been confirmed a hundred-fold.

Fortuna had not finished with Frankie. By some strange affinity that transcended their other differences, the Melisendien sergeant who had captured him understood him perfectly despite not speaking Westrigonian any more than Frankie spoke Melisendien. Their communication, primitive though it might have seemed to an outside observer, contained glints of the eye, sneering lips and suspicious squints which achieved a precision of communication far beyond the approximations of language. They understood each other perfectly. It was Frankie's luck to have been taken prisoner by a man just like him. The sergeant, whose name was Odalis, was already his best friend.

Frankie knew, he *knew*, beyond doubt, that Matthias had deliberately shut the Gate on him to bring about Frankie's death at the hands of the enemy. His latest best friend Odalis, having learned of this betrayal via a translator, also agreed that this must be so. They were both delighted to have identified such murderous treachery, such perfidy, in the highest places in the land. The sight of this dark villainy filled them with an exultant delight. Nothing could have made them happier than the sight of this evil wrong-doing. It proved them right about everything. Odalis agreed to help Frankie get his hundred thousand strada if he, Odalis, got half. Frankie haggled him down to twenty percent, and they were in business.

Fortuna, however, was still scribbling away like a child with a crayon. The Melisendiens were themselves taken prisoner, Frankie was freed, and with many a lying promise to his former benefactor, he walked away to get his money, having already decided to double-cross Odalis, who after all was in no position now to offer him anything. Odalis, who understood this decision as if he had taken it himself, watched Frankie go with a bitter expression. They each understood that honour was a concept of the rich and powerful designed to hoodwink the masses into being subservient to a scheme of things not in their favour. In the end, there was only the double-cross.

2:35 PM, Tuesday 21 April 1882 A. F.

The Treasury of the Kingdom of Westrigonia stood at the corner of Eadric Street and Yancy Street. Matthias had made a special point of capturing it early on in the Battle of Krastienst, and it was guarded by a battalion of soldiers hand-picked by Matthias and loyal to him personally. The Treasury contained reserves of seven hundred and twenty million strada, and the political figure who controlled that money controlled a lot more besides.

Among the stranger sights of history is this one: Matthias Raspero and Frankie the Villain walking down the marble staircase to the Strong-Room of the Treasury where the money was stored, and into the

Strong-Room itself, where one hundred thousand strada in bank-notes and coins were packed into a leather satchel stamped with the insignia of the Treasury of the Kingdom of Westrigonia, and handed ceremonially to Frankie by a Treasury official. By one reckoning, there were to be one hundred and fifty-seven paintings of this scene in existence by the end of the following century, not one of which ever hung in the Palace of Krastienst for the duration of the Raspero dynasty. Matthias's biographers either confirmed that this scene did in fact take place, or denied that anything of the sort had ever happened, or said that the evidence was not clear enough to pronounce a definitive verdict. All seventeen operas about Matthias Raspero composed over the centuries contained this episode, however, given all the singing and instrumental flourishing that such an occasion evoked.

Most accounts agree that Matthias, irritated by Frankie's accusations that he had tried to double-cross Frankie by having him killed in battle, made sure that it was known far and wide that the deal had been honoured and Frankie had been paid in full.

3:55 PM, Tuesday 21 April 1882 A. F.

Frankie left the Treasury in delight, humming to himself and skipping along as if he were a child again. He hugged the treasury satchel in his arms in such a way as to be certain in his mind that it wasn't going anywhere. After all, the satchel held all the happiness of the rest of his life in its leather casing, and he wanted to make sure that all this happiness was tightly secured. Otherwise it might roll down the road and be never seen again, and where would he be then, and what could he do about it? Frankie shivered at the coldness of this thought, and mumbled to himself as he walked along. But then a thought struck him. He would have to fall asleep at some point, and what then? Frankie stopped in his tracks in the middle of the street. Falling asleep was not something that could be avoided. It would happen eventually. Frankie felt trapped by the inevitability of this development.

All of a sudden, Frankie giggled as the wildest, craziest thought he had ever had in his life came to him. He could put the money in a bank for safe-keeping, and go and help himself to it whenever he wanted! How wild was that! He giggled madly to himself as he set off to find a bank, bent over the heavy bag clutched to his chest. The reason for his amusement was that he had spent much of his life trying to figure out ways by which to rob banks, and now here he was depositing his money in one!

But all the banks in the city had been closed an hour earlier by order of the Marechal.

Frankie chewed at his lower lip as he wondered what to do next. He set off once again, aware of the looks he was starting to attract as waves of recognition of who he was started to ripple through the streets around him. It dawned on Frankie then that his story was known and people just like he used to be would be looking for him, having heard that he had all this money with him. By now he was a frightened man. His mind recoiled at being where he was; yet the consciousness of all that money in his bag forced him to stay alert. His own perceptions frightened him; the world was becoming overwhelming. Waves of recognition of his predicament were washing over his brain, which was supported by a neck which had become a bendy stalk.

He realized that he needed to get off the street, and along with this realization came, as if providentially, the sight of the Tavern of the Bull on Cretan Street. He hurried there, took a room, hurried upstairs, locked himself into his room, and took stock of his surroundings.

The dark wooden table, the bed with its red bed-coverings, the wash-basin and arm-chair all seemed imbued with a glossy sheen that spoke of the inner magnificence of the world. His room seemed magical to him then, like the cabin of a magical ship taking him to a magical shore.

As evening came he lit the gas lamp on the wall and everything became even more magical.

He realized that he was in the mood to write something. And he had always wanted to write of how Ninelstadt had become Leader of Baalbabak.

The story of how Ninelstadt had become the first Leader of Baalbabak, as told to Frankie the Villain in prison by a fellow prisoner

There was a petty thief called Ninelstadt who one day stole a suitcase at a train station. He was caught red-handed after being furiously pursued by police and passers-by. The suitcase was opened and found to be full of revolutionary political pamphlets. The original owner of the suitcase having long since disappeared, Ninelstadt was prosecuted as a Leveller revolutionary and thrown into prison. He was not charged with the theft of the suitcase. Quite the opposite: he was now charged with being the rightful owner of the suitcase. Once in prison, his fellow Leveller prisoners took to him and made him their leader. The revolution came a year or two later and Ninelstadt left prison as the leader of the whole country.

10:05 PM, Tuesday 21 April 1882 A. F.

Frankie, who had an enormous capacity for belief, had believed this story straightaway as soon as he heard it. He had always wanted to write a poem about it. But time was passing, and nothing was coming.

Frankie's poetry was both a vehicle for his philosophy and a way for him to bind his thoughts with words before he lost sight of them. The poverty stricken poet had written graphic accounts of how he had shivered as he had thawed out frozen inkwells by clasping them in his armpits in order to write his poetry during winter. Frankie's literary career had had its ups and downs. Famous at one time, displaced the next, his life had been dogged by poverty and imprisonment. But whenever he felt inspired to write, he wrote.

He wrote *Provenance, by order of the Marechal,* then stopped to wonder what rhymed with Marechal. Ideas flooded his brain. There was a banging on the door of people shouting for him to come downstairs and have a drink. Frankie shouted at them to go away, and returned to his poem. For a moment, he was stuck, and then all of a sudden the next line came to him, and the next:

Provenance, by order of the Marechal.
Providence, give this order to that military misfit:

Bend over so I can kick your arse!
Let my foot be the measure of your downfall!
From the tips of my toes to the heel of my heel,
There is the unit which when multiplied,
By its own movement through the air,
Becomes the length of our precious Marechal,
Fallen flat on his face at our feet!

Frankie quivered with excitement over his still-unfolding poem, which lay beneath him like a giggling half-naked woman having her clothes pulled off. It was all going so well! There were perhaps too many exclamation marks, which was a common fault of his over-excitable character, but he could always change that later. The main point of the poem was that the Marechal was having his arse kicked, and the literary merit of this exposition was undeniable. Next would come a point about how fools thought that they were not fools, and he began to see how this could be expressed.

In the midst of his excitement something nudged him. Frankie started up and looked about him but there was nothing there. The room looked the same as ever. But his hearing had been heightened by this mysterious warning and so he heard stealthy movements in the corridor outside, movements that he was not intended to hear given that they were so obviously stealthy, now in the corridor outside the door of his room, just there and no further, and Frankie was frightened with a gushing fear in his chest which was like an eruption of cold vomit against his rib cage.

The door handle turned surreptitiously but the door did not open because he had locked it. But a key slid into the lock from the outside and turned and unlocked the door which promptly did open after all.

Suddenly it was as if Frankie had acquired intuitive powers of the higher mind such that he knew of what was hidden beneath the surface layer of his existence. He knew in this manner that the landlord had closed down the inn: the doors had been locked and bolted to separate those inside from those outside. And those inside were united in one compact concerning Frankie and his satchel of money, his official satchel with the seal of the treasury stamped on its gleaming leather exterior; namely, they plotted his murder in order to take his money for themselves.

All this Frankie somehow knew to be true beyond doubt even though he could not have said how he knew what he knew. His perceptions had become an immediate knowledge that could not be doubted because it was so immediate a knowledge: he knew then that the landlord had given the key to his room to those who wished to rob Frankie, and the landlord had done this for a promised share of the money which Frankie had in his satchel. The whole tavern had been closed down, locked up, and only those who were there would be present at this crime; everyone in the tavern, they were all in this together, they had made a pact, a pact that would be sealed in Frankie's blood, they plotted to murder him and steal his money. Frankie understood further that if he had been on the other side of the door, he would have been one of them because it was all a matter of deciding one way or the other and who was he to be different or better than the rest anyway? He had become one of the rich and that made him a target for the poor, and it was all so easy to understand that Frankie could no more turn away from his understanding than from his own shadow. But the door was opening, throwing its own shadow into the room, and the world itself was beginning to turn away from the unfortunate Frankie the Villain.

There were three or four figures in the doorway, with a sense in the air as if the whole corridor behind them was filled; it all looked like a painting by Bruschel: the harsh yellow light of the gas lamps in their wall brackets, a yellow that was almost dirty by fading at the edges into a brown that was the brown of aged paper; the figures standing in the doorway were casting shadows into the room like demons stepping out of hell. Poor Frankie couldn't speak for terror. There was a darkness in the right hand of one of the figures, a darkness that glinted with a metallic edge as if the darkness was itself a sharp blade opening up Frankie's throat; he clutched at the wetness drenching his chest but the wetness was a stickiness that was also a horror. The floor was coming at him at an angle but he could do nothing to avoid its crooked impact; figures were stepping over him and stooping over his satchel of money as the darkness spread to swallow Frankie the Villain.

If there is an afterlife, Frankie entered it then; if not, not. He was found dead in his room the next morning by his seemingly shocked and shaken landlord, who knew nothing of what could have happened; or so he said. Frankie's money had disappeared. There was no investigation. The authorities had more important things to concern them at that moment. (The Marechal pointed out somewhat impatiently that he had an ongoing national war of liberation to claim his attention). Frankie the Villain was thrown into a pauper's grave with not even the usual state-provided mourners.

In the end there is only sympathy, and a prayer that if there is a world of the dead, it would treat poor Frankie more kindly than had the world of the living.

CHAPTER TWENTY EIGHT

I ask for very little,
But my greed is never satisfied.
Frankie the Villain

9:15 AM, Thursday 23 April 1882 A. F.

The past week had not been kind to Yolande's nerves. Her informants brought her news of Matthias's battlefield victories while her servants brought her increasingly irate letters from a First Protector who had never liked Frederick and Yolande in the first place, given that they were members of a branch of the Zoller-Abstein family that was hostile to his political fortunes. No-one brought her news of what tomorrow would bring and Yolande could only guess.

The worst of it all was that she had never even wanted to be here in this country in the best of times. Queen Yolande of Westrigonia had never liked Westrigonia. Even on the sunniest of days, this foreign country seemed dark to her; the people and their culture frequently baffled her, while to learn their impossible language was a task she could never even approach. How on earth they even managed to produce such speech sounds was a puzzle. Every day was a temporary transition in the middle of nowhere. She knew full well how foreign she was here in Westrigonia. Her true home lay abroad in Trentland, the land of her forebears, the land of her childhood, the land of Anglashian civilisation.

It was clear that she needed to confer with Frederick, who had now been released from his Baalbabakan prison, and the First Protector. In order to do this, she needed to leave Krastienst through the Public Portal, and in order to to *that* she needed the permission of the so-called Marechal of Westrigonia, Baron Raspero, who was currently nowhere to be found. Yolande sighed to herself for the umpteenth time. She had to be patient and wait for Matthias to return to the Palace. But then a letter arrived from the First Protector which made at least the immediate future crystal clear. De'Asterides had summoned her and Eleanor to Pentharborg.

In consequence of this, Yolande summoned Eleanor to the Pearl Room.

'<How much fresher the air is today!>' Eleanor exclaimed with an appreciative sniff. '<I have no doubt that it is due to the absence of Lord Cadwalader.>'

'<Please sit down, my dear,>' Yolande said in her most affectionate tone of voice. Every syllable of her utterance was drenched by the warmth of her maternal affection.

Eleanor yawned lightly behind a discreetly raised fan, and sat down with an air of indifference.

'<How you have grown over the years!>' Yolande exclaimed. It was as if her pride was turning to joy. '<My clever and beautiful young daughter! The Jewel of Krastienst indeed! Truly, what a jewel!>'

Eleanor yawned again, much less delicately than before, and much more loudly, allowing the rounded potbellied sound of boredom to be made audible in a yawn. She was not impressed by the sudden appearance of maternal pride on the part of her mother. She could smell what made the flowers grow.

Yolande paused as if wondering whether to overlook this deliberate rudeness, or be offended. She decided to be the wise mother, understanding of the caprices of youth.

'<I have good news, daughter of mine. I have received an invitation from the First Protector for both of us to travel immediately to Pentharborg. As we leave tomorrow, we must make haste with our packing.>'

'<I am not going anywhere,>' Eleanor said immediately. '<And I would remind you that the King of Westrigonia has pledged that I may stay here in the Palace until the second Vidaldmeet debate. And I would remind you further that as the master of this household the King's word is law.>'

'<I am afraid that you really have no choice in the matter,>' Yolande said firmly. '<You are coming with me, and that is all that there is to it.>'

'<I will hold Matthias to his pledged word, and I will stay. I am not going anywhere, and that is final!>'

'<Lord Raspero cannot interfere with the authority of a mother over her daughter. Not in Westrigonia, not in Trentland, not in Anglashia, not anywhere, King or no.>'

'<A King's word cannot be countermanded here in the Palace of Krastienst. Matthias has said that I may stay until the second Vidaldmeet, and no-one can force me to leave against my will. I hope the translator properly translated this pledge that he made. I am not saying another word about a matter which is settled.>'

'<You are under my authority, and I command you to leave this place and accompany me to Pentharborg. I will say nothing more than this, for nothing more need be said.>'

'<Let me translate for you what Matthias said. He said that no-one can force me to leave the Palace of Krastienst against my will. Those were his exact words. I paid careful attention to them at the time. Well, it is my will that I stay here, and you cannot force me to leave. The King of Westrigonia has authority here in these walls, not you.>'

'<I am not continuing with this pointless argument, Eleanor. You are coming with me to Pentharborg.>'

'<I am not going anywhere with you. I am staying here.>'

'<Did you not hear what I said? An invitation from the First Protector is a command. You have no choice but to obey it. Neither do I.>'

Yolande had switched from arguing on the basis of her mother's authority over her daughter to arguing on the basis of the First Protector's authority over the subjects of the Protectorate, and the glint in Eleanor's eye showed she had noted this shifting of her opponent's position. Her mother had given up on her authority as a mother.

'<The authority of the First Protector here in Westrigonia is precisely what is at issue at this time. Wake up to yourself, mother! The Protectorate has lost the support of the Vidaldmeet. Westrigonia is on the edge of leaving the Protectorate.>'

'<But we are not on the edge of leaving our own family. The Zoller-Absteins are our family, and the First Protector is the head of our family. What he says has authority over us for this reason.>'

'<My choice in this matter is mine to make, and I make it as follows. I will stay here in Krastienst. You go if you wish. You will make your choice and I will make mine.>'

'<You should beware of such wilfulness as that which you display. For now, I will say nothing more. You are coming with me and that is that! You may leave this room now.>'

Eleanor rose and stamped over to the door. Once there, she turned and said: '<I am not coming with you and that is that!>' She left the room before her mother could reply so that she could be the one to have had the last word.

10:35 AM, Friday 24 April 1882 A. F.

The next summons from Yolande to Eleanor was refused by the Crown Princess. She insisted that Yolande come to the Chambers of the Crown Princess if she had anything to say.

Yolande was in a quandary about what to do. To accept this reversal of invitations was to accept being in the weaker position. She sent for Matthias, who, not being available, was represented by Acteon who, with a grave courtesy, promised to communicate immediately with the Marechal. He was as good as his word, reporting to Yolande within the hour that Matthias had sent a message saying no more than, "Princess Eleanor has my support." Yolande's ploy had failed.

The former Queen of Westrigonia set forth for her rebellious daughter's Chambers, breathing deeply as she strode along. Eleanor received her visitor with a calm demeanour that betrayed no sign of gloating. She waved her mother graciously to a seat in the Rose Room, and offered her refreshments in such a way as to emphasize that she was the hostess and her mother was the guest. Yolande bore this graciousness as if she were lying down on a bed of nails. On seeing this, Eleanor became even more gracious. After some preliminary chit-chat, Yolande came to the point.

'<As you know, we are leaving for Pentharborg. May I ask if you are progressed in your preparations for our departure?>'

'<I am not going to Pentharborg, mother. But I thought you would have already left by now. Why are you still here?>'

'<I am still here because of the difficulty I am having in getting you to come with me. Really, Eleanor, for how much longer is this absurdity to persist?>'

'<By this absurdity you must mean your desire that I accompany you.>'

'<As your mother, I must insist that you come with me.>'

'<Your parental concern is such a blessing as I have never received before,>' Eleanor replied acidly. '<Yet I must deny myself such a pleasure as your continued company on the grounds of my duty as Crown Princess.>'

'<Your duty is to your mother.>'

'<Please stop your pleading, mother, before my heart breaks in two.>'

Eleanor's ladies-in-waiting shrank back into their chairs. Their grasp of Anglashian might have been shaky, but their understanding of the Crown Princess was not. When Eleanor was in this vicious a mood, it was best to be as far away as possible.

Yolande pressed on. '<You are no longer the Crown Princess,>' she declared, in complete opposition to all previous government policy. However, there was an argument with her daughter to be won. '<The Vidaldmeet, in their wisdom, has elected Baron Matthias Raspero as King of Westrigonia. All the reports we have received have confirmed this. It is a fact that must be acknowledged.>'

It was a fact that Yolande had not acknowledged before, and would dispute again later. But now was now.

'<Matthias has only taken the title of Marechal.>'

'<Title or not, if Lord Raspero is indeed King in fact, then I am no longer Queen and you are no longer Crown Princess.>'

'<Whatever my title, this is still my country in any case. I have chosen it as such. I will not leave now while my country is in such danger. My duty is to serve my country and I will follow my duty no matter what you say.>'

Like a cross-country runner swerving around a pot-hole in her path,

Yolande changed direction. '<I have never understood your desire to be Westrigonian. However, as a loving mother I have never denied you any chance for you to grow, to explore the world, to achieve your full potential. When have I ever stood in your way to become all that you can be? But you were so young when you left Troderent. You largely fail to understand the choice you now face. You are still far younger than you realize. You are too young to understand how young you are.>'

'<I am also, it seems, too young to understand the point you are struggling to make.>'

'<Come with me, and we will go to stay in Troderent as soon as possible. You will be reminded of the values of civilization. Your affection for Westrigonia will wane, trust me. This is a barbaric country and I fear that as your mother I may have been negligent in not taking you back to your true home more often. Come to Troderent with me and observe the world anew. Afresh your perceptions shall lead you to new considerations of where to find peace, which can only persist in civilisation. In any case, you will at least be able to observe the outcome of these turbulent political events from a place of safety, and should you choose to return here it will obviously be in circumstances much different than these.>'

Eleanor laughed cheerfully and tapped her fan on her knee with an extravagant gesture as if bashing a cymbal with a club at a drunken party. '<You are making a fool of yourself, my dear most blessed mother, but it seems that you are too foolish to understand how foolish you are. I know I should thank you for your concern, but given that the basis of this concern is your foolishness, I will not.>'

'<Eleanor, you cannot remain here alone while I leave. Can you not understand this?>'

'<Then do not leave. I am not going anywhere, and the man you say is King of Westrigonia has given me his word I may stay if I choose, and I do so choose.>'

'<Eleanor, I command you as a mother commands her daughter to come with me!>'

'<No, I will not come with you. I refuse! I have a higher duty to obey than a foolish command, whether from a mother or not.>'

'<Beware of this defiance! I cannot protect you if you should be disowned, disinherited, cast out from the family who has loved and nurtured you only to meet with such ingratitude.>'

'<I refuse to leave! That is the last word I have to say on this matter!>'

And so their exchange continued, with Yolande's comments, exhortations, entreaties, pleadings and angry rebukes meeting unvaryingly with a wall of refusals from her high-spirited daughter. In the end Yolande left her daughter's Chambers in defeat.

She would have to go to Pentharborg without the Jewel of Krastienst at her side unless she could enlist the aid of the so-called Marechal of Westrigonia.

3:45 PM, Friday 24 April 1882 A. F.

By a process of drawing upon her full regal authority, Yolande had prevailed upon Acteon to prevail upon Matthias to come to the Veceslav Room. Yolande told her daughter about this forthcoming meeting by letter and cunningly added that it was up to her whether she chose to come or not; Eleanor, naturally, turned up on time. Matthias arrived not long after.

'<Lord Raspero,>' Yolande said with a welcoming smile. '<How wonderful to see you again. May I be allowed to congratulate you on your many victories? No-one talks of anything else, the length and breadth of the whole country.>'

Matthias replied in Anglashian, or rather, his version of that ancient and august language. '<It is that it is the too kind of you about this matter, which is the nothing much to speak of in all honesty.>'

'<You are much too modest, Lord Raspero. But such modesty is only to be expected from a nobleman such as yourself, born and bred from such ancient nobility.>'

Matthias inclined his head with an air of acceptance. '<It is that your kindness is without the extent that is the observable one.>'

Eleanor observed that Matthias understood that he was being buttered up by Yolande with some end in view. She sat there as calmly as she could, but truth to tell she was a bundle of nerves. She knew what Yolande was about, but she could not be as equally certain of what Matthias's response would be.

'<Alas, Lord Raspero, I have some bad news.>' Yolande had abruptly changed tack. She was getting down to business. '<Eleanor and I must leave for Pentharborg immediately. As you are in control of the Public Portal, and as we must travel by this Portal, I must ask your kindness to be extended even further and grant us permission to travel first thing tomorrow morning. But before we leave, I must ask if there is anything which we may do for you?>'

Eleanor gripped her fan tighter as a way of restraining her from speaking. She felt that her future was about to be decided irrevocably one way or the other. She reluctantly had to acknowledge that her mother had not handled the whole matter too badly up to this point.

Matthias said nothing for a moment, and then the whole world changed. He turned to Eleanor and said: 'Is this true, Eleanor? Are you leaving for Pentharborg with your mother?'

Yes! Eleanor exulted to herself. This was how it should be. Her point of view was being taken into account. There was something to be said after all for ex-boyfriends, however treacherous they may have proved in all other respects.

He had spoken in Westrigonian, and Eleanor replied in the same language. 'No, Matthias, it is most certainly *not* true. I have informed my mother that you have given your word that I am not to be made to leave against my will before the second Vidaldmeet, and that I am holding you to your word. I refuse point blank to leave the Palace! I am not going anywhere. My mother is simply trying it on.'

Matthias looked her in the eyes while listening to this, and then said to her directly: 'This Palace would be a poorer place without you. It would merely be a shell. You are its living heart.'

Eleanor had learned how to deal with ardent compliment-makers by that stage of her life. 'You may grovel all you please, Matthias, if you insist on humiliating yourself in public. Suit yourself. May I say in passing that we would all be richer without your incessant prattling? But perhaps I speak to no purpose if I hope to instruct you.'

To Eleanor's annoyance, her provocations merely evoked a grin on Matthias's part. The King of Westrigonia turned back to Yolande, who had not followed this exchange, as her translator was not present, and said: '<Yolande, it is that Eleanor is not go with you at this time. It is the decision of her, and it is that it is my word that she is stay until second Vidaldmeet if it is that she is choose so. You are understand this of this time.>'

Eleanor realized then that Matthias had grasped everything in a flash. He understood all the background quarrels and argumentation between mother and daughter over this issue, and why it was that Yolande was buttering him up in order to get him on her side. Eleanor let herself relax a little, but only a little. Who knew what might happen next?

'<You do not understand, *Mister* Raspero,>' Yolande said, emphasizing her demotion of Matthias's noble status, '<that I have ordered Eleanor as a mother commands her daughter in this matter. It is not for you, not even a king, if you are a king which you are not, but if you were you cannot anyway, it is not for you to intervene in this matter. The authority of a mother over her daughter is outside the authority of the state. Eleanor will come with me because I have commanded that it be so, and I trust that you possess sufficient breeding and education to recognize this without any further argument.>'

'<I am King, Yolande, and it is that my word is being the supreme one from this matter. Eleanor is stay.>'

'<It is not only that the authority of a mother over her daughter cannot be superseded by a representative of the state, but also that the rules of hospitality by which you are bound preclude you from acting against the interests of your guests.>' Yolande had shifted ground now to argue that as she was a guest of Matthias, he could not oppose her wishes.

As a Westrigonian born and bred, Matthias was used to argumentation, and he had grown up with the laws of hospitality drummed into his skull. He took this latest gambit in his stride, and spoke with a calmness that only emphasized his inflexibility. '<You are being these guests in this my house, Yolande, and it is that I am the master of this household. As she is being my guest Eleanor is not being forced against the will of her

expression to be departed if it is that she is the choose to stay of this time. So, Eleanor is stay as the guest of me.>'

'<So this is what my life has been reduced to.>' Yolande was beginning to lose her temper. '<To be at the mercy of a knuckle-dragging barbarian who cannot even speak Anglashian properly.>'

'<May I point out, mother,>' Eleanor said coolly, deciding to stick her oar in, '<that the king is not the *representative of the state* as you said earlier. His role in the constitution is very different. Are you really, ah, *unaware* of such an elementary matter as this?>'

Matthias nodded understandingly, thereby throwing more fuel on the flames. '<It is the very difficult position for such the esteemed lady as you to be within at this the one moment of time and no other.>'

There are times when sympathy makes everything worse and for Yolande this was one of those times. '<How dare you, how, you, you, a knuckle dragging barbarian such as yourself, no Westrigonian is worthy to be a monarch, what a primitive backward country this is, and here am I, a *mother*, denied that parental authority which is the basis of all civilisation. But what do you know of civilisation? It is a wonder that you have learned to eat with cutlery. How dare you? How dare you? You are so vastly my inferior that it is, I cannot, you, you grotesque creature, I command you as a creature in the form of a man to obey one who is set over you by the forces of nature and history and to do as I tell you to do as an inferior obeys his superior.>'

'<It is much the interesting point of view of it is that you are say these things, yet it is that I am not the one to agree of this point that you are say now. Eleanor is stay.>'

'<You are not well advised to so adamantly set aside that egalitarian ethos by which the Protectorate pretends to be run,>' Eleanor told her mother with an affected concern. She was delighted by her mother's intemperate outburst. She could use these words against her mother later if push came to shove. '<The fact that I have memorized your words for future reference is neither here nor there, as I am sure you will agree. But pray continue, mother. You were saying?>'

'<Are you aware of the consequences, Lord Raspero, of making an

enemy out of the First Protector in such a matter as this?>' Yolande had given Matthias his title back, in order that they could be friends again if the right agreement was reached. '<The First Protector has summoned Eleanor and I to Pentharborg, and it is not for you to oppose him.>'

Matthias laughed with such an unfeigned merriness that Yolande realized she had blundered in her choice of threat. '<It is the long time now that I am the hunted one of the big reward. It is already the torture and the execution of me from the Protectorate. It is not to be in the bigger trouble now for me of this matter.>'

Yolande collected herself, took a deep breath, and spoke very determinedly. '<Mr. Raspero, I am leaving for Pentharborg and Eleanor is coming with me. Is that understood?>'

Matthias raised his hand in the air, palm facing forward, as if setting himself in opposition to an angry mob, and spoke firmly to the mother of his ex-girlfriend. It was his stone-faced demeanour and hard, glass-like eyes that conveyed his inflexible refusal to budge on this issue as much as what he said. '<It is that Eleanor is stay here by her own choice, and it is my given word that this is so. It is the nearly thousand years that it is the Barons of Raspero, and it is not of me to be foresworn. It is not the other thing to say of this now. Enough!>' Matthias turned his palm-facing-out-hand around and chopped it through the air like an axe while saying *Enough!*

Yolande breathed heavily in her fury, but abruptly stood up, accepting defeat. '<Very well, Mr Raspero. I wish to leave at the earliest opportunity. I command you, by my royal order, to have the Public Portal ready for my departure first thing tomorrow morning. Eleanor, come with me.>' With that Yolande stormed out of the door in a temper. Eleanor followed her mother feeling more relaxed and cheerful than she had done for a long time.

The Marechal was informed later that afternoon that Yolande and Eleanor would not be dining with him that evening. Matthias took this snub with a smile.

It was all part of the grand scheme of things.

7:55 PM, Friday 24 April 1882 A. F.

Now that Matthias knew that Yolande had been summoned to Pentharborg, he knew that the next stage of the Protectorate's plan was about to be activated. He therefore arranged to have about seventy or so Baalbabakan prisoners brought before him in the Yulian Room of the Great Exhibition Hall on Fabricius Street. The prisoners were marched to their chairs and chained into place, watched over by Westrigonian soldiers under the command of Captain Steindahl. Matthias and his retinue sat in their own chairs facing their captive audience.

Matthias introduced himself to the Baalbabakans, pausing so that his translator could catch up every now and then. He spoke of the histories of their respective countries, their similarities and differences, their mutual respect and deep reciprocal admiration, their achievements in a glorious past that was only overshadowed by their even more glorious future. The Baalbabakans listened to all this with expressionless faces. Matthias ended his comments with the hope that the current unpleasantness would shortly come to an end, given its pointlessness.

There was a silence, and then a Baalbabakan prisoner shot to his feet and shouted a sequence of rapid-fire speech sounds, which Felioциus, Matthias's translator, translated as follows: 'I declare my loyalty to the 39th principle – Let us march on in the direction pointed out by the out-flung arm of our beloved leader!'

Matthias nodded thoughtfully. This might have been an error of judgement on his part because another prisoner, presumably mistaking Matthias's politeness for interest, also bolted upright and made his own contribution, which was translated for Matthias's benefit as follows: 'I declare my loyalty to the 45th principle – All inefficiencies have been abolished by the rightful decree of our leader!'

Matthias again nodded thoughtfully, and then said promptly and with a firm wave of his hand: 'The fame of these, the Eternal Glorious Principles of Incomparable Baalbabak, is such that we have already heard all about them here in Westrigonia. So there is no need for you to keep going.'

Three prisoners however were already on their feet, so Matthias's attempt to hold back the flood was in vain. The varying and overlapping pronouncements of these three were disentangled on the spot by Feliociius, who had an agile brain, and translated as follows:

Principle 73 – Together in a death-defying way we march onward with our feet firmly together! (Feliociius confessed to some difficulty in translating this principle, but this seemed to be the general idea of it.)

Principle 26 – Only by the wisdom of our joy-giving leader are we able to ride the horses across the plain!

Principle 57 – Our weapons in our hands, we go to our glorious deaths, and we ask only not to live in shame!

It seemed clear by now that all the Eternal Glorious Principles of Incomparable Baalbabak ended in exclamation marks!

'Admirable sentiments,' Matthias began to say, but by now all the Baalbabakan prisoners (except Oafstadt Cadfan-son) were on their feet and talking at once so Matthias, with a sigh, waved them to silence with an upraised hand and went through the assembled company one by one, pointing to each to speak in his turn so that everyone had a chance to have their say without anyone missing out, and thus it was that the walls of the Yulian Room of the Great Exhibition Hall had their chance to hear many of the 144 Eternal Glorious Principles of Incomparable Baalbabak.

Principle 35 – Always to be on the lookout without ever pausing is the only goal of the true hero!

Principle 49 – Go beyond all that is known of what can be done!

Principle 54 – Kill every enemy to the last man so there is no-one left to surrender!

Principle 38 – All the work of the humblest servants are the vital links in the chain of Baalbabakan integrity!

Principle 23 – We run towards our victory by keeping our faith to the death and beyond!

Principle 41 – Even when we learn our tasks we are in battle against the enemy which is everything that is not Baalbabakan!

Principle 17 – Keep the faith in Baalbabak even in the face of the hostility of those who do not understand!

And so the slogans continued. Matthias passed the time by wondering what the Baalbabakan prisoners really believed.

Oafstadt Cadfan-son of Baalbabak was a tall burly man with soft almost effeminate features, a small button nose and deep-set eyes. His most striking characteristic was his booming voice, which could rattle window-panes. As the last Baalbabakan soldier finished speaking, Oafstadt rose to his feet with a sneer and in his booming voice made his own contribution, which was not, as it turned out, one of the Eternal Glorious Principles of Incomparable Baalbabak. This is how the embarrassed translator put it:

'Last night I had intimate relations with your mother!'

'Did she notice?' Matthias promptly replied.

The Westrigonians had already begun to laugh before this comment was translated into Baalbabakan by the straight-faced translator, and while Oafstadt glowered furiously, his temper not helped by the gales of laughter coming from his Westrigonian opponents, his hapless Baalbabakan subordinates desperately tried not to laugh themselves even though the effort seemed to be coming close to claiming their lives.

Laughter can be a deadly thing. Traditionally tyrants have feared laughter above all else. Why should this be so? That is difficult to say. It is perhaps the removal of a restraining sobriety such that what remains must be true, being of intoxication. Or perhaps it is the implication that life is not such a serious business after all, which if true would make tyranny impossible to sustain for even a single day. But who really knows?

Matthias enjoyed the moment with a smile on his face, then raised his hand and waved everyone to silence.

'We have enjoyed this exchange of views, but now it is time to turn to business,' Matthias declared grandly, but he was interrupted by Oafstadt, who again rose to his feet to boom out another comment, which was translated as follows:

'A dog had intimate relations with a donkey and in this way you came into the world!'

Matthias lost patience. 'Steindahl, get this imbecile out of here,' he ordered with a wave of his Marechal's hand.

There was pandemonium. Steindahl led his guard into a seizure of Oafstadt that was brutal in its bloody-minded directness: Oafstadt was slammed to the ground, bound hand and foot and dragged out of the door while each and every Baalbabakan prisoner flung himself against his chains, shouting and gesticulating. It was not long after Oafstadt had disappeared that the Baalbabakan prisoners became quieter, flailing their chains every now and then almost as a matter of form. Their protests seemed to be a matter of playing a part.

'If none of you have any more intelligence than Oafstadt,' Matthias told the Baalbabakan captives, 'then the heavens help Baalbabakan.'

Matthias obviously could not know at the time that what he had just said would in time become a Baalbabakan proverb and an especially favoured saying among parents exasperated with their children. (Oafstadt Cadfan-son, already near the end of his short and unlamented life, would never know, luckily for those within reach of his temper.)

The Baalbabakan captives looked back at Matthias without expression, though not without feeling. Matthias, who had spent several years of his life on the run, understood them.

Baalbabak had had the misfortune of being the only country to fall to the Levellers back in the days when the Levellers were a going concern. It was inevitable that Ninelstadt, the leader of the Baalbabakan Levellers, should become as absolute a dictator as history could show. The once prosperous and cultured country had become a personality cult. Ninelstadt had sat down one evening, and with the help of a bottle or five of the finest Baalbabakan wine, and the additional help of one or five equally inebriated companions, had dreamed up the Eternal Glorious Principles of Incomparable Baalbabak and written them down in his own hand; needless to say, his drunken scrawls were now quasi-holy relics in one of the many Museums of the people dedicated to Ninelstadt, and there were many Baalbabakan "scholars" who performed acts of divination on the shaky lines of his poor handwriting.

'Let me spell out for you the circumstances in which we find ourselves,' Matthias continued, directing his remarks now towards General Hasdrubal. 'Baalbabakan is about to be invaded by the Protectorate.

This will happen tomorrow at dawn. It would seem, therefore, that your fighting capacities are best arranged with respect of the defense of your own country rather than the invasion of another. Don't you think?'

Hasdrubal might as well have not heard this observation, even though it had been translated into Baalbabakan.

Matthias, having lived by his wits for many years, was not fazed by this unresponsiveness. He knew where the insecurities of a Baalbabakan general were to be found. 'Of course, if the Great Cadfan were to learn that you had been forewarned of this invasion but had done nothing about it, things would not go well for you or your families. But perhaps you still intend to sit there like a dummy and continue to say nothing?'

Hasdrubal looked into the cold eyes of his Westrigonian opponent, and bowed his head slightly. His response was translated in this fashion: 'It is excellent, in the old-style form of manners, to be as equally and enjoyably prepared to talk about the latest topics of conversation that have been presented to us like freshly picked flowers still scented from the fresh fallen morning dew. This morning dew is fresh fallen not from heaven, which doesn't exist, but from the condensation of water molecules in the air by scientific principles as discovered by the leading minds of Baalbabak. How excellent! Would you not agree with this?'

'Tell me, General Hasdrubal, do you know anything of the characteristic features of plague outbreaks?'

'You are happy to consider the great wisdom of Incomparable Baalbabak because this great wisdom is sweeter than honey, more intoxicating than wine, more dazzling than the bare-bottomed beauty of the Lady of the Mountains. Yet do you thank us for these gifts we bring to you? No. We lay the treasures of the ages at your feet but all you do is complain. The day will come when you will fall on your knees and beg us to forgive you for your offenses. When that day comes, with a swift and surgical blow from the sharpest of our swords, we will cut the heads off your shoulders in such a way as to give you a painless death, and in this way, and in this way only, shall we show our mercy.'

'Plague outbreaks have the following characteristics. The origin of the outbreak is in a place such as a seaport or crossroads that is linked to at least a certain amount of traffic. There must be a certain threshold to the size of the population where the outbreak takes place. The population density of the affected area, the surrounding network of roads or rivers, all are relevant. Yet what do we see when we contemplate the recent plague outbreak at Ganbaatar? We see that not one of these characteristics applies. And so what shall we conclude from this, General Hasdrubal?'

Hasdrubal kept on ploughing his own furrow. 'Incomparable Baalbabak can hardly see the people of Westrigonia because you are as small as ants compared with us. You are so far below us as you scurry about gathering your blades of grass that we can hardly make you out. These blades of grass are enormous to you because you are so small, but to us they are tiny. We put these blades of grass between our thumbs and fingers and blow on them to make musical sounds that make children laugh. But you, you tiny Westrigonians, you live off this grass as your sustenance and for this we shake our heads in sorrow, and then we laugh!'

'All across the Protectorate, the brothels and taverns of those cities where the standing armies of the Protectorate are normally situated have the same complaint. They have no business. All the soldiers have disappeared. What do you make of this, Hasdrubal?'

The fable of the bag of gold and the hanging rope as told by General Hasdrubal to Baron Matthias Raspero

Once there was a man who hid a bag of gold by a tree. Another man came by the next day to hang himself, but on finding the gold, dropped the rope he had brought for this purpose and joyfully went on his way with the gold. The first man came back the next day, but on finding the gold gone, took up the rope lying on the ground and hanged himself in despair at his loss.

'Suppose that there has been no plague outbreak at Ganbaatar, which is just across the border from Baalbabak? Suppose that the armies of the Protectorate are there in secret. Suppose that the time has now come when they will invade Baalbabak, which has been largely emptied of its armies by the invasion of Westrigonia. This would mean that we are about to have a common enemy. The Protectorate is about to double-cross you, just as it has already double-crossed Westrigonia. I know that the Great Cadfan was promised the province of Steynrad in return for invading Westrigonia, but I also know that De'Asterides never had any intention of keeping this promise. He wanted all the Baalbabakan armies out of Baalbabak, and Westrigonia occupied. The Great Cadfan in Rozneft is always protected by a five thousand strong army, but with all the other armies of Baalbabak gone, this defense will not last long. Once De'Asterides has conquered Baalbabak, and Melisende also, and added their territories to the Protectorate, and taken back Westrigonia, he will be acclaimed as the author of the most successful foreign policy since Mikhail Hunyadi himself. But perhaps you think that no-one could ever behave so badly, given your precious Golden Rule? Well, Hasdrubal? Now what do you have to say? I can only hope that it is another fable.'

'The Great Cadfan will stamp on the invading army like an ant.'

'What is it with you and ants?' Matthias asked, half-amused and half-irritated. 'Never mind, I'm not really interested. You understand that the Protectorate has a sixty thousand strong army hidden in Ganbaatar. Thirty thousand for Baalbabak, thirty thousand for Melisende. Can you hear what I am saying to you?'

'The ears of Baalbabak are a thousand fold, multiplied like ears of corn in the summer fields of Incomparable Baalbabak. The squeak of a mouse is heard from ten miles away by our phenomenal hearing.'

'That's good. So I don't have to shout. I have told you, Hasdrubal, that your country, your Incomparable Baalbabak is about to be invaded and occupied by the Protectorate. This will be an encroachment of reality that your bluster cannot reverse, though I am sure you are about to say that one word from Incomparable Baalbabak can move mountains. But you have one chance at this time, and that is to be forewarned. If the Great Cadfan is warned today of this approaching adversity, then steps can be taken to save Baalbabak. But to seize this one chance that is offered to you, it is necessary that you first of all listen to me. But why don't you tell me again about the ears of corn in the summer fields of Incomparable Baalbabak?'

Another Baalbabak prisoner spoke up at this point. Although he officially bore the rank of Colonel, his lack of deference to his nominal superior General Hasdrubal, and the glassy glaze of his glossy black eyes, marked him out as a Leveller officer whose job it was to keep an eye on the regular soldiers on behalf of Incomparable Baalbabak. 'Your concern for the well-being of our country is commendable, Marechal. You no doubt have some sympathy for the Leveller plan to bring peace and prosperity to the whole wide world.'

'Far from it,' Matthias said with scarcely veiled hostility. 'I would be happy to see the infamy of Levellers such as yourself erased from the face of the earth. But as it is in my own interest for the Protectorate to fail to conquer Baalbabak, I am prepared to make a deal.'

'What kind of deal are you proposing, Marechal Raspero?' asked the Leveller Colonel.

'There are twelve hundred Baalbabakan prisoners here in the capital, five hundred and twenty prisoners in Fawnstone, seven hundred and thirty prisoners in Gaborton and eight hundred and seventy prisoners in Tamarille, making a total of three thousand three hundred and twenty Baalbabakan soldiers. You have something like twelve thousand soldiers still at large elsewhere in Westrigonia. Given that you will be withdrawing these anyway after the Protectorate's invasion, I have nothing more to say about them. But as to the prisoners of war in our custody, well, I shall require the payment of a thousand strada per soldier, which will come to a total of three million, three hundred and twenty thousand strada.'

'This is extortion! Incomparable Baalbabak will not pay a single strada!' the Leveller Colonel protested furiously.

'Then you must face the consequences of your policy. Because what I shall do in that case is hand all of you over to the Protectorate. After all, who is to say that many of your own men will not fight against your regime if given the chance? But time will tell.'

'Marechal Raspero, you are breaking the international treaties of the Protectorate in making this demand. Ransom demands of this nature have long been illegal under the international law of your own Protectorate.' A Baalbabakan Captain had made this point. No doubt he was a lawyer in civilian life.

'You're quite right,' Matthias agreed. 'If the Protectorate ever found out they would denounce me. Perhaps they would raise the price on my head from five million strada to an even higher sum. Oh well, I'll have to live with it, I suppose.'

Hasdrubal (who had been chosen by Fortuna to be the man who killed the Great Cadfan) covered his face with his hand to hide his smile.

The Leveller Colonel was far from smiling. 'Your demand is unacceptable and it is refused. Incomparable-'

'What are you saying, Colonel? That there is no need for the Great Cadfan to be informed of this offer? Are you prepared to take this decision on his behalf? Is that what you are saying?'

'Of course the Great Cadfan must be informed of your outrageous request,' said the Leveller Colonel, immediately backtracking. 'This is not-'

'If he is not informed of my proposed deal,' Matthias pointed out, 'he will not be forewarned of the Protectorate's imminent invasion. Even if he refuses to make this deal, he will at least get warned for free. But now the question arises as to which of you should bear this message?'

'The Great Cadfan will not listen to anyone but myself,' the Leveller Colonel said without hesitation. 'Only I can bear this message to the greatness of such a man. You do not understand this because of your ignorance, but now that I have told you the truth of the matter you have no excuse to fail to act accordingly.'

Matthias shook his head. 'No, definitely not you, Colonel. You have already presumed to speak in the place of the Great Cadfan when you refused my deal and called it unacceptable. No, I was thinking of you, General Hasdrubal. Will you be prepared to undertake this mission on behalf of the safety and well being of your own country?'

Hasdrubal gravely inclined his head and said: 'This is ordained, not by Fortuna, who does not exist, but by the implacable laws of history which are material in nature and which have decreed the triumph of Incomparable Baalbabak as a scientific outcome.'

'I see you have given up on telling fables,' Matthias said a little sarcastically. 'Very well. Now pay attention, Hasdrubal. Far be it for me to suggest your military strategy, but given that the goals of the Protectorate will be to seize Rozneft and the Great Cadfan at one swoop, it might be advisable for the Great Cadfan to withdraw to Yiannisberg, securing this as his base. All the Baalbabakan prisoners here can be sent to Yiannisberg by Portal, but only from the moment when you return here in person to convey the Great Cadfan's response to my message. By the way, I shall require payment in advance. That is all, Hasdrubal. I trust you are capable of conveying this message, and of bringing me the reply.'

'The Great Cadfan will keep his own counsel, and you will be informed of this, as an inferior, when it is your blessed good fortune to receive the benediction of the fine-tuned phrases of his beautiful speech. Until then you must be patient like a dog waiting to be fed by its master.' It seemed that Hasdrubal, after a short break, was back to his old self.

Matthias laughed. 'Alright, take your time. Given that the Protectorate will invade Baalbabak at dawn tomorrow with an invading force thirty thousand strong, what is there to be impatient about? The Protectorate will need eight flying hours to capture Rozneft and the Palace of the Great Cadfan, not to mention the Great Cadfan himself. After that, Baalbabak is theirs. But insult me again, why don't you, Hasdrubal?'

'It is excellent, in these times, to be amused by your child-like desire to have Baalbabak pat you on the head and praise you kindly. We can only thank you for the amusement which you have brought to us.'

'At last we can agree on something,' Matthias said, laughing as he rose to his feet. 'I can only thank you as well, Hasdrubal, for the amusement which you have given me.' With that Matthias turned away and gave orders for Hasdrubal to be taken to the Portal and the other prisoners to be returned to their makeshift prisoner-of-war barracks.

11:55 PM, Friday 24 April 1882 A. F.

It was nearly midnight by the time Matthias got back to the Rollo Chambers. After his meeting with the Baalbabakan prisoners, he had met with the Melisendien prisoners in order to set in motion a similar process, and then sent a Melisendien general back to Melisende. The Protectorate would now find, on attempting to bite and swallow Baalbabak and Melisende, that they would break a tooth or two. Baalbabak and Melisende would withdraw their armies to meet this threat while the Protectorate, having failed to score the knock-out blow they were counting on, would get bogged down in a protracted war, leaving Westrigonia able to deal with its current challenges free of the twin threats of war and occupation. Matthias's sabotage of the Protectorate's invasion plans would bring the entire project crashing to the ground.

That was the theory, at any rate.

CHAPTER TWENTY NINE

I have nothing to say,
Except that I have nothing to say.
Frankie the Villain

6:15 AM, Saturday 25 April 1882 A. F.

Two massive flotillas of several thousand flying carriages crossed the Baalbabakan border at sunrise, one flotilla on its way to various destinations in Baalbabak, the other flotilla on its way to various destinations in Melisende. The military high command of the Protectorate was counting on surprise to ensure the success of their military venture.

Alas for the pot-bellied generals of the Protectorate with their large moustaches! Surprise was the last thing they could expect now.

11:00 AM, Saturday 25 April 1882 A. F.

Matthias personally escorted Yolande to the Public Portal, accompanied by Eleanor and a crowd of others from the Palace who had come along to witness history. Everyone chatted merrily, laughing and joking. Yolande's mood did not lighten at all, given that her stomach had long ago turned to lead at the prospect of informing the First Protector that Eleanor had not come with her mother because the authority of the Protectorate had not been respected enough by her wayward daughter to command her obedience. Yolande had not been able to sleep all last night, lying awake as the hours tumbled past. It was now morning, and everything was too bright and loud for the former monarch of Westrigonia as they approached the Portal. Faces seemed slantwise in the sunlight, noises were too sudden and rounded and the looming imminence of her departure was like the inescapable destiny of a hapless figure in an opera. Yolande all-of-a-sudden didn't want to go. She wanted to stay here with Matthias, who she trusted a lot more than De'Asterides, and not move for a million years. And she knew quite clearly that she could stay if she wanted. Matthias would listen amusedly to her change of mind, and bow his head with his practised baronial courtesy, and the change of mind would be done. But Yolande knew that she would be failing in her duty if she did this, and she had never, *ever*, failed in her duty. It was this above all that had made her so angry with Eleanor in the past. It had been Eleanor's duty to be married in a way that was to everyone's benefit and look at how she had dragged her feet about that! And now it was Eleanor's duty to come to Pentharborg, and her not coming was again a failure to follow her duty. Yolande was all-but-ready to disown-her-daughter.

Yolande and Sakesheld and their immediate retinue stepped through the Portal gateway, with Yolande pointedly not saying farewell to either Matthias or Eleanor. Then they were gone.

The company returned to the Palace with Matthias and Eleanor at their head. Entering through the Ilbert Door into the Natasza Hall, Matthias turned to Romano.

'Captain Romano, you may continue as before,' he said. 'I place you under the direction of Her Royal Highness the Crown Princess Eleanor. Is that understood?'

'Yes, Marechal,' Romano replied.

'Eleanor, perhaps you would do me the honour of dining with me this evening?' Matthias asked.

'Very well, Matthias,' Eleanor said indifferently, folding her fan closed.

'Excellent. I now bid you farewell for-'

'No, Matthias, you do not bid me farewell for the time being, or any other time for that matter,' Eleanor said firmly. 'How do I know this? It is because you are not going anywhere. We have much to talk about.'

'Of course, and I look forward to our conversation. But I have ten or fifteen meetings that I am already late for and-'

'But what about our meeting right now? You can be on time for that, which will be in your favour. After all, why be late for yet another meeting?'

'Eleanor, I have a lot on-'

'You will find, Matthias, after speaking with me, that our conversation is part of what you have on. And I insist on speaking with you without delay.'

Matthias groaned. 'Alright. This afternoon at three o'clock we will meet. Until then, farewell.'

Eleanor watched him leave without further argument.

2:35 PM, Saturday 25 April 1882 A. F.

The day passed for Matthias in an episodic fashion, his forthcoming meeting with Eleanor never very far from his mind. The city was in chaos, everyone wanted to see the person in charge, who was none other than the self-appointed Marechal, and no-one knew what was going on. Matthias decided that his best policy was to make promises that everything would be seen to and give people a sympathetic ear. The rough outlines of administration that he had sketched out in the turbulent three days of the liberation of Krastienst seemed to be working moderately well. There were no riots, people were being supplied with food, the prisoners of war were securely guarded, and there was a sense in the air that order would soon return and life in the kingdom would be renewed. The appearance of Matthias with its attendant implication that someone was in charge, helped to reassure people as much as the detail of any proposed policy.

The time came when Matthias returned to the Palace, a baronial hand held up to thwart all residual attempts to claim his attention. The time had come to see Eleanor, and Matthias went to his rooms to tidy himself up and inspect his appearance in the mirror. He found himself feeling a little nervous, and so practised his breathing exercises to calm his nerves.

The kiss which Matthias had shared with Eleanor in the Rose Garden had lodged in his memory in such a way as to now be immovable. It was a kiss that was sweet and singular, lingering yet brief, passionate yet cool. Matthias could still feel how Eleanor's lips had felt pressed against his all those years ago, or at least, it seemed to him that he could still feel this, so vividly did he remember it. Matthias had shared other kisses with other girls in the years that followed, but not many. Matthias had felt too encumbered by his own fugitive status and the overpowering need to restore his family honour by regaining the barony of Raspero to allow himself such distractions as those of romantic dalliances. Besides, he felt unable to offer any assurances of a secure future to any beautiful girl who attracted his ardour. Obscurely or irrationally, he felt that any dishonourable behaviour on his part would alienate Fortuna's favour and separate him permanently from his homeland and his inheritance, and so he avoided those beautiful girls of his acquaintance over the years who might have driven him to lose his head. Furthermore, to have a five million strada reward on his head also rendered him greatly circumspect in the matter of who to trust with a knowledge of his true identity, which complicated matters still further. The beauty of a girl was not necessarily related in any way to her interest in collecting such a reward, and yet Matthias felt it to be dishonourable to court a girl without telling her who he really was. As the head of the family, he was able to keep his mother's match-making propensities in check. As for other possible activities, he was obliged to be restrained even there. Given that he had a morbid horror of contracting a venereal disease, he avoided women with generous hearts whose broad experience might have possibly exposed them to some kind of infection. It followed therefore that Matthias's love-life was lamentably (or commendably) absent for a healthy young man of twenty-two.

But all this, while true, was not the whole story. After going into exile, Matthias had set up his spy network which, naturally, had to include reports on the Royal Family. His spy in the Palace (Astrudel) had kept him fully informed of all the goings-on there, including everything that Eleanor was up to. Matthias was only too well aware that the malicious Astrudel would have been only too delighted, for a bonus payment of course, to have been able to provide tales of a scandalous nature on the behaviour, or misbehaviour, of the Crown Princess, but Eleanor's conduct was invariably exemplary. Matthias knew Eleanor to be a thoroughly trustworthy woman, and to an exiled nobleman constantly wrestling with questions about who to trust, this knowledge could not help but have an effect. To a young man of twenty-two whose romantic yearnings were so enormously unfulfilled, the knowledge that the Jewel of Krastienst, one of the most beautiful women in the world, was a lady of beauty and character, could not help but have an almost hallucinatory effect. Eleanor had come in Matthias's mind to be a figure of ideal womanhood.

Matthias's original plan assumed the safe departure of Yolande and Eleanor for Pentharborg at some time during the invasion. He would come go to the Raspero Portal, conquer Raspero, and then sit back and play his hand, always able to conquer the Palace at any time given the SES he had planted there. His election as King would be bartered away at a later date in return for the full restoration of his baronial inheritance. He had not foreseen the destruction of the exit portal by the departing Baalbabakan delegation which had left the Queen and Crown Princess trapped in Krastienst, but the knowledge that Eleanor had come to be in such danger had changed everything. Camdenshall had not at the time known what was going on, or why Matthias appeared to have so suddenly changed all their carefully made plans, but he must by now have decided that Matthias had deliberately deceived even his co-conspirators as to the nature of his real plans. Even if Matthias were to tell him the truth Camdenshall would not believe it. The truth was that Matthias had come to Krastienst to save Eleanor. This was, in part, because Matthias was, at least at one level of understanding, a young man of twenty-two who had not yet found his lady-love. It was not in Camdenshall's level-headed and pragmatic and dispassionate nature to understand this. (The stars had been too differently aligned at his birth.) It followed from Camdenshall's lack of understanding, therefore, that Camdenshall would never believe the truth of the matter. But that was how these things always go.

Awkwardly, though, that had left the Baron of Raspero stuck with the business of saving the country as its King and Marechal. Westrigonia's good luck was not necessarily Matthias's happiness. Matthias just wanted to go home more than anything. For many years now, the summation of happiness in his estimation had been to sink back into his ancestral castle and stay there. He was fed up with foreign places and wanted only his childhood home back again.

Matthias had much less of a starry-eyed vision of Westrigonia than Eleanor. His ancestor Etienne, the devious genius who had been the eleventh Baron of Raspero, had helped to invent Westrigonia in the Thirteenth Century, and Matthias was too well aware of this process to see the result, Westrigonia, as somehow God-given. Since gaining possession of the Great Library of Raspero seven years ago he had read the letters written by Etienne to his friends, and their letters to him, while the framing of the famed Westrigonian constitution was going on by the discussions as referred to by these very letters. He knew of all their doubts about all their certainties. The fact was that Matthias was much more a Baron of Raspero than a patriotic Westrigonian. His barony had preceded Westrigonia, and as far as he was concerned, it could just as well succeed it as well.

But this was far, far from being the extent of Matthias's problems. He had returned to the Palace of Krastienst, having not seen Eleanor for all these years, to find himself dazzled by the Jewel of Krastienst in person. Yet it was not only Eleanor's beauty that he had to deal with. Her poise and intelligence, her pride and sense of self, her eloquence and charm, continually made Matthias's stomach dissolve and his head divide into two separate and opposing halves. And now he was faced with the prospect of talking to her and he did not know what to say.

3:10 PM, Saturday 25 April 1882 A. F.

Eleanor was waiting at the Quinlan Door to the Sara Hall, seated to one side tapping her fan impatiently on the palm of her hand. She rose to her feet as Matthias approached with a disgruntled look. As it happened, she was secretly glad that Matthias was late because she, too, felt nervous at the prospect of their meeting.

'I will say nothing, Matthias, about you being much later than three o'clock.'

'That's good,' Matthias said cheerfully. 'I thought I'd get away with it.'

'Come with me,' Eleanor said peremptorily, and set off without a backward look. Matthias followed her while her ladies-in-waiting and Matthias's own clique followed them.

They all sat down in the Veceslav Room, deliberately chosen by Eleanor as their meeting place in order to emphasise that she sat now where her mother had sat earlier. She was now in charge of the Royal Chambers, and Matthias had to deal with her as the Crown Princess of Westrigonia, the most senior royal remaining in the land.

Eleanor noted that only Acteon, Alaric and Darnell were with Matthias. These three, then, were closest to Matthias as friends and advisors, being of the same age and background as the Baron of Raspero, performing functions for their employer comparable to those of her ladies-in-waiting. This was useful political information. They were pressure points of the body politic of the new King of Westrigonia. Eleanor noted further that Matthias had anticipated that the Crown Princess would turn up with only her ladies-in-waiting in tow, given that he had brought along only three attendants. It followed, therefore, that they could talk freely, given that the Rayerfelds and Camdenshalls of the world would not be present.

3:35 PM, Saturday 25 April 1882 A. F.

Eleanor, who had observed politics in action for so long that she had attained an almost instinctive grasp of its functioning, opened proceedings with a long and tedious speech. She discussed the context and highlights of the invasion of Westrigonia by Baalbabak and Melisende, managing to make this dramatic episode of history as boring as a recital of names and dates interspersed by cliches. Eleanor continued by noting Matthias's arrival in Krastienst and his spurious claims to the throne of Westrigonia. She concluded by noting that given the failure of the Vidaldmeet to publicly announce its election of Matthias as King, she was still the Crown Princess of Westrigonia until further notice. By now, everyone except the Marechal was half-asleep.

Matthias had appeared to listen attentively to Eleanor's speech, a grave and composed look on his face. He responded by saying how fortunate and blessed the Kingdom of Westrigonia was to have such a Crown Princess as Eleanor, and as far as he was concerned, she was still the Princess. But he was the King of Westrigonia by an election of the Vidaldmeet that no-one disputed had taken place. In summation of all these perplexities, all he had to say was that he hoped that the Crown Princess Eleanor would support the Baron of Raspero in his role as Marechal of Westrigonia. Matthias managed to make all this sound as deadly dull in his turn as Eleanor had in hers, largely by including plenty of pointless verbiage.

(Eleanor would later realise how big a clue she had just been given as to what was going on vis-a-vis the shenanigans of modern political Westrigonia, but at the time she missed it.)

Eleanor abruptly shifted gear, as if to catch Matthias off-guard. 'If you are Marechal, am I your prisoner?' she asked with a raised eyebrow.

Her ladies-in-waiting, and Matthias's followers, stirred themselves fully awake. Something interesting had just been said.

'Certainly not.'

'Then I may come and go as I please.'

Matthias hesitated. 'Yes, if you have sufficient protection, whether provided by myself or Romano.'

'Answer me plainly, Marechal. May I come and go as I please?'

'No. You may only come and go as I deem it to be safe.'

'Then I am your prisoner.'

'Oh, for heaven's sake, Eleanor,' Matthias said with a hint of genuine exasperation. 'Spare me your philosophical definitions. We are in the middle of a war. If your mother were still here, she would also insist on safeguards. But if you want to leave via the Portal for any destination you nominate, then go! Once out of the country, do what you want. But while you are here, you will act in accordance with the will of the King of Westrigonia.'

'And what is that will?'

'Right now? To liberate the country.'

'And when that is done?'

Matthias sat back in his chair, steepling his fingers and resting his chin on them. 'That's a lot to do, Eleanor. It's enough to be going on with for the time being.'

'Oh, stuff and nonsense!' Eleanor snapped, annoyed by what she saw as an insult to her intelligence. 'Don't tell me for one moment that you haven't made plans for more than *the time being*.'

'I might ask you, Eleanor, to address His Majesty Matthias the Fourth with a degree more respect than you have shown to date.'

'His Majesty Matthias the Fourth!' Eleanor sneered. 'That's a laugh!'

'Very well. Perhaps it will suffice if you address me as a gentleman.'

'You are not a gentleman. You are only a nobleman.'

Matthias was about to reply, then he paused. 'Wait a minute! I recognize that! Lena and her friends were giggling about that. It's a quote from some novel or other.'

'Oh yes,' Nina said breathlessly, leaning forward, 'that is from *The Kingdom of Happiness*. It's one of my very favourite books.'

'I have to say that I am insulted, Eleanor, that you choose to insult me by quoting from a novel rather than inventing your own insult. Your very laziness is itself insulting.'

'Good,' said Eleanor with satisfaction, 'I am glad to have insulted you properly then.'

'Yesterday you were a lottery prize, today you're the Queen of the Universe,' Matthias commented. 'What will you be tomorrow, may I ask?'

'Oh, you shouldn't make jokes like that, Marechal,' Nina said reprovingly. 'Her Royal Highness gave us all suicide pills in case the worst should happen.'

'It's just as well that I came along then to save everyone,' Matthias observed. 'Don't you think, Eleanor?'

'I expect nothing less than your service,' Eleanor replied grandly. 'I accept your gratitude at being able to be of such service, if that is what you are about.'

'You might not want to know what I am about,' Matthias said meaningfully, with a narrow-eyed look and a smirk.

'Of course I would not. It would be beneath me, being about you.'

'I can't tell you the truth then.'

'So I see. You don't trust me.'

'I trust you more than anyone, Eleanor,' said Matthias, 'because you're completely on my side.'

'That is your understanding.'

'We have always understood each other. Or perhaps my arrival at the Palace took you by surprise?'

'I said you would come immediately. I knew what you would do.'

Nina backed up Eleanor on the spot. 'Oh yes, she did. As soon as she heard you had been elected King she knew you were coming straight away.'

'I don't doubt it. I'm glad you're on my side, Eleanor. You would make a formidable opponent.'

Nina continued: 'And Her Royal Highness said the Baalbabakans and Melisendiens had better watch out when you come because you're so clever.'

'Did she now? I didn't know you had such a high opinion of me, Eleanor.'

Eleanor replied loftily: 'I do not have a high opinion of you. But I know that a street-fighter such as yourself, a brawler, might possibly be effective in street-fighting against other thugs like yourself.'

'Well, I was . . . effective. And, by the way, I'm still waiting for someone to say "Thank you, Matthias, for liberating Krastienst from enemy occupation." But all I get is ingratitude.'

'Because, Matthias, that is all you deserve to get.'

Eleanor was indifferent now to her earlier plight. Yesterday's terrors were today of no account. She saw no reason to be grateful to Matthias for having rescued her in the recent past given that she didn't need rescuing now.

Matthias said nothing but gazed at Eleanor in an amused silence.

The silence went on for long enough for Nina to decide that she was entitled to embark on her own questions. Truth to tell, Nina had no fear of Matthias and a burning desire to find out if her romantic suppositions were sound or not, as much for the sake of her diary as anything else. For whatever reason, Nina said to the Marechal, out of the blue: 'Is it true that you plan to marry Princess Eleanor?'

'Am I handsome?'

'In a country of handsome men, everyone would notice you most of all,' Nina replied with a very serious expression on her face.

Matthias smiled to acknowledge the double-edged nature of her reply. 'And why would I plan to marry Eleanor?'

'The man who marries the Crown Princess becomes the King.'

'But what if the Crown Princess refuses his suit?'

'You could ruin her so she has to marry you,' Nina said breathlessly. Her eyes shone with barely concealed excitement at the prospect of such wickedness and depravity actually taking place in this very palace!

'No, that's too complicated. But I like the way you think. Do you have any other ideas to put into my head?' Matthias asked with a grin.

'Matthias, I absolutely refuse to marry you,' said Eleanor.

'What am I supposed to do, Eleanor? Grab you by the hair and drag you to the altar and twist your arm until you say "I do"? That would be a nice way to begin a marriage.'

'Yes, this is all so funny, isn't it, Matthias?' snapped Eleanor. 'But I say to you again – I will not marry you under any circumstances.'

'As King of Westrigonia, I am a very eligible bachelor. Has this entirely escaped you?'

'As a bachelor, you must be looking for a wife. Is this not so?'

'My love-life is the least of my concerns right now.'

'But not the least of *my* concerns, apparently. Didn't you just say that I should have noted your eligibility as a bachelor?'

Matthias sighed as if acknowledging that Eleanor was ahead on debating points. 'Yes, I did.'

Eleanor decided to jump straight in and catch Matthias off guard. So she observed in an off-hand way: 'Your plan is to have the second Vidaldmeet elect you as King. As I am the Crown Princess, marrying me will strengthen your claim to be King, will it not? So. Do you plan to marry me?'

'Definitely,' Matthias said without hesitation.

This was not the answer Eleanor had expected. If anything, she had expected Matthias to beat about the bush and avoid the issue. The Crown Princess of Westrigonia contemplated the Marechal, who looked back at her directly in the eyes with a perfect equanimity.

'That is unfortunate,' Eleanor said at last, 'because I have no intention whatsoever of marrying you. Your suit is without hope.'

'Eleanor, if I never become King, but return to my estates as Baron of Raspero, would you consider coming with me?'

'What?' Eleanor was so genuinely astonished by this question that she could not think of anything to say but *What?* She was immediately angry at herself for such an inarticulate response, for which she saw straightaway that Matthias was to blame.

Matthias, for his part, could not help but feel that he was going about this the wrong way. He tried to get things straighter. 'I mean, would you marry me and become Baroness of Raspero if it meant giving everything else up, such as your own chances of becoming Queen?'

Eleanor stared at Matthias for a moment or two, and then asked: 'Matthias, are you proposing to me?'

'*No!*' Matthias said emphatically, then wondered if he had sounded *too* emphatic. 'No, I'm not proposing to you. But I will later. I mean, I plan to later. I mean, I hope to marry you, that's what I'm trying to say.' Matthias wondered to himself if he had ever in his life made such a mess of things as this attempt to talk things over with Eleanor. 'I might not be phrasing this very precisely. What I'm saying is that I definitely want to marry you. But I might not be King. Maybe I'm mixing up two separate points. Anyway, I'm just telling you how things are.'

'No, Matthias, you are not *telling me how things are*. Tell me this about *how things are*: do you plan to become King?'

'To tell the truth, Eleanor – '

'To start your reply in such a way is not encouraging. It leads me to believe the opposite. Just sit up straight like a man, if you are a man, and state things plainly.'

'If it is my duty to become King, then I will. If I can get out of it honourably, then I will.'

'*Get out of it*! Why would you *not* want to be King?'

'I think being Baron of Raspero would be enough. You have to understand, Eleanor, that the barony is a thousand years old, nearly, it's not such a bad place to live, all in all, it, well, I'm obviously biased, but it's a pretty amazing place to be.'

Eleanor's anger at Matthias now stood on new ground. She had become convinced that this was all some kind of trick. 'Oh, to be a baron is a finer thing than to be a king! I had not realised. Silly me! Thus, it would follow, I take it, that to be a baroness is a finer thing than to be a queen! I now see my indescribable folly in ever having thought otherwise. How can I thank you, Matthias, for opening my eyes in this way?'

'*Uneasy lies the head that wears the crown.*'

'A baron who a king saw as a potential future threat would lie his head down far more uneasily, believe me.'

'Yes, good point. The same thought has crossed my mind. Obviously the whole matter would have to be handled very delicately.'

'As delicately as you have handled talking to me? Why, you could give lessons in this kind of thing. Lessons in how not to do it. Now, I am trying to remember what we were originally talking about. Could you remind me?'

'I was telling you that I want to marry you.'

'Ah, yes! How wonderful to be romanced in this way, by a half-wit who might become a baron, but only if he can first escape being king! Now, let me see what my answer is to your question, which is of course not a proposal. Hummdy, dummdy, umm, ah! Here it is! Found it! Matthias, I do not want to marry you under any circumstances, whether you are king, baron, or the town fool. If you propose, I refuse. Can you grasp this statement?'

It was by now clear to Matthias that he had messed up everything. It was not that he had failed to plan out this conversation. It was just that all his carefully thought out points, the details of the whole situation, had never been given a chance to come forward given the starting point of his dialogue, which he now realised had been misconceived. 'Yes, Eleanor, your position is perfectly clear.'

Eleanor set out to make her position even more clear than perfectly clear. 'You are a shabby baron, if you are even a baron at all, which of course you are not. The thousand years you have referred to are obviously up. The barony of Raspero has rolled up its eyes, turned up its toes and given its last gasp at the mere sight of you. The universe itself would die at the sight of you, which is why the stars close their eyes in horror if you are ever out at night. I shall not refer to your past as an escaped prisoner, a man convicted in the eyes of the law of nefarious and illegal doings, a man sentenced to prison after having been found guilty of breaking the law.' Eleanor realised she was being less than completely fair, but she was too angry to stop now. 'How dare you suppose that I could ever marry you? Marry you? You are the last suitor that I could ever contemplate marrying. You are a nasty smell masquerading as a man. Marry you? Dream on, bozo!'

'Well, perhaps we can do a deal,' Matthias said peaceably. 'If you become Queen, married to someone else, you can support me returning to my estates as Baron of Raspero. Some other man can have the pleasure of being married to you. What do you say?'

'*Some other man*? But why not just put a chalk mark on the ground and marry me to that? Some other man indeed! Do you even bother to listen to yourself speak?'

'You are avoiding my point, no doubt intentionally. But perhaps I should make my own plans without reference to you. Is that what you are saying?'

'*Yes*, that is what I am saying,' Eleanor snapped, so angry now that she would have crumpled up the city of Krastienst into a paper ball and thrown it out the window, if she had had the power. 'Make your own plans, and leave me out of them. Do not ever talk to me about this subject again! Do you understand me?'

'No, Eleanor, I do not understand you,' Matthias said with something of a groan. 'I thought I was honouring you, in my own way, to the extent that I am capable, by saying that I wanted to marry you. I did not realise that you would take my declaration as such a mortal insult.'

'Oh, did you not? How then was I supposed to take your declaration?'

'As an honest, well, honest declaration.'

'Hah! Do you imagine I do not know the word you shied away from using? You were going to say, an honest *proposal*, then changed your phrasing, did you not?'

'Alright, I confess it. But I-'

'Do you know what I most despise about you, Matthias? It is your cowardice. You see, if you had proposed to me like an honest man, I would have thought more highly of you. But that is not the way you went about it. You wanted to know if I would accept your proposal if you made it, so that is why you adopted this crabbed crookwise tortuosity of sideways circumlocutions. It is precisely that craven avoidance of a potential refusal that marks you as a gutless two-faced coward.'

Matthias laughed and shook his head. 'You have certainly learned to speak Westrigonian, and no mistake. But if that is the point of contention, it is easily resolved. I can propose to you here and now as the Baron of Raspero. But before I do this, is there anything you want to say to me beforehand?'

Eleanor would have spoken had she not been rendered speechless by the sight of Matthias reaching into his robes and fishing out a diamond ring.

'You have told me already that you will refuse me if I propose. I will propose anyway if that is the point at issue. But that is not the point at issue. The point is, Eleanor, that I might not become King.' Matthias put the ring away in his robes and said: 'You have to understand that I am asking what is more important to you: to be my wife or to become Queen. If it is to become Queen, then I accept that without argument. What kind of conceit would I need to possess to argue with that? But is that your decision?'

'I think I begin to see what this is all about,' Eleanor said slowly. 'This is all some sort of test. Like in a fairy tale. Where does someone's affections truly lie? If I say that merely being a baroness is sufficient for me, then I am qualified thereby to be Queen. Is that so?'

'No, Eleanor, it is not so. When my father and brother were killed, it placed on my shoulders the burden of carrying on the family tradition. I never asked to be king.'

'So what? Being king is now within your reach. So reach out and take it.'

'But what if in the end I do not become King? I would still want to marry you anyway, but you might not want to marry me if you had the opportunity of going on to become Queen with someone else as your husband.'

'Matthias, have you not heard a word that I have said? I do not want to marry you under any circumstances. What is it about this simple statement that you have such difficulty in grasping?'

At that Matthias bowed his head and closed his eyes. He breathed in and out a few times, then opened his eyes and looked at Eleanor. 'I have something to attend to before dinner. Perhaps we should stop for today and continue this discussion on another occasion. What do you say?'

'Continue this discussion? But what on earth can you mean? Continue what discussion?'

'Believe it or not, I haven't given up on the idea of marrying you. You'll have to browbeat me a lot more than you have done already. Not that you haven't done a sterling job of browbeating me. You can be pleased with yourself. Trust me, I have been browbeaten. Congratulations. Yet I have not given up hope entirely.'

'Hope was the greatest evil in Pandora's box. That's why it stayed behind when all the others fled. To cause the greatest damage of all.'

'Interesting,' Matthias said, and yawned. 'Or not. Eleanor, let's go.'

Matthias stood up, and stretched out his hand courteously to help Eleanor arise. Eleanor ignored his outstretched hand, placed her hands on the armrests of her chair, pushed herself up and set forth without another look at Matthias. The two groups went their separate ways.

5:35 PM, Saturday 25 April 1882 A. F.

'So, did you observe? He wishes to propose to me, and he has declared his intentions accordingly,' Eleanor told her ladies-in-waiting, who had not been surprised by what they had witnessed. But then, they had seen the way Matthias looked at her.

'Play hard to get,' Georgette advised. 'Make him sweat. Otherwise he won't respect you.'

'Tell him you expect to have the freedom to have as many lovers as you want,' Mitzi suggested in her turn. 'He'll kick up a fuss but too bad for him. Give him indigestion at the thought of getting in your bad books.' If the truth were to be told, Mitzi's advice was intended more to sabotage any romance between the Marechal and the Crown Princess than to help her employer along. Mitzi's nationalist resentment of the Zoller-Abstein Princess, which had always smouldered, had by now burst into flames. Mitzi's favourite day-dream at the moment involved Eleanor being burned at the stake by a jeering and hostile mob of Westrigonian nationalists, her piteous pleas helping her not at all.

'Oh no, your Royal Highness,' Nina moaned in torment, 'don't listen to them. Tell the Marechal you will be his forever and ever and ever and there is no other man for you but him.'

'Yaaaah,' Mitzi yawned contemptuously, 'that'll work, Nina. Oh? Wait a moment. A question just occurred to me. What was it? Oh, I know. Has it ever worked for you? Well? Has it?'

Nina's mouth fell open, so she unfolded her fan and held it over her face so only her frightened eyes peeked out at Mitzi. Behind the fan she uttered some utterly undecipherable speech-sounds.

'That would be telling, wouldn't it?' Georgette laughed. 'Rampaging Nina, at it with who? Hah!'

Nina now raised her fan over her face so that not even her eyes could be seen. She was obscurely terrified that her secret would be guessed if anything of her face could be seen. Her secret, which was that Alaric had declared his intention to propose to her, was not exactly compromising to her reputation, but it troubled her nonetheless, being such a direct declaration. She believed that by completely hiding herself from everyone's gaze, they would see that she had nothing to hide.

The merits of Nina's strategy were irrelevant as the others simply ignored her anyway. Perhaps Nina's strategy was, in its full context, a brilliant one. It did, after all, achieve its goal. Her secret remained undetected.

Eleanor reflected that none of this advice was helping her at all. Not even her knowledge of Westrigonian metaphysics was of any use. She was on her own.

5:35 PM, Saturday 25 April 1882 A. F.

Matthias's claim of other business to attend to had been a ploy to withdraw his wounded pride from further savage attacks at the hands of the Crown Princess of Westrigonia. His mind was still on his wooing of Eleanor.

'That didn't go well, did it? Nonetheless, I am still thinking of proposing to Eleanor,' Matthias told his companions.

'Treat her like dirt. Otherwise she won't respect you,' said Haris.

'I have heard that sentiment,' Alaric said loftily, looking at Haris as if he were a beetle. 'I have never managed to believe it.'

'Wisdom from the horse's mouth,' Acteon said mockingly. 'Or from the other end of the animal.'

'Tell us of all your conquests!' jeered Haris.

'I hope to find happiness with the woman I love,' Alaric said stiffly. He felt that the others were driving him into playing the role of a stuck-up prude, which he did not want to do, but at the same time he felt that he had no choice but to go along with what the others wanted. Also, he was terrified that the others would find out that he was a virgin, at the age of twenty-two.

'Who understands women anyway?' asked Darnell.

'No-one ever understood women. Women don't understand women,' Haris declared, like a wise man instructing the multitudes.

'*Women don't understand women*,' Acteon repeated mockingly. 'What is that supposed to mean?'

'Hopefully our new king will bring back duels of final combat,' Haris said harshly, glaring all the while at Acteon. 'People will be much more courteous when that happens, won't they?'

'Not if people keep on talking nonsense,' Acteon shot back, entirely unintimidated by this implied threat.

Matthias reflected that his followers were not helping him much by their comments. Like every lover in history whose nerves were wound tight by a beloved, Matthias felt utterly alone. All advice was useless. He would have to figure this out by himself. As far as proposing to Eleanor went, he was on his own.

7:15 PM, Saturday 25 April 1882 A. F.

Matthias was late for dinner. Eleanor stood to one side of the dining room, with such a "don't-mess-with-me" look about her that her ladies-in-waiting had surreptitiously withdrawn to one side, where they felt safer. There they were joined over time by Alaric, Acteon, Haris, Felim, Darnell and Gerbern.

'That was very impressive how you identified that literary quote, Lady Delwyn,' Alaric said. 'The one about not being a gentleman but only a nobleman. You knew what book it came from straight away, without a moment's hesitation. It was pretty amazing, to tell the truth. You must be very well-read.'

Nina gazed wide-eyed at Alaric.

'What's this?' Acteon laughed. 'Boleyn's Law of Flattery!'

Alaric looked puzzled, then shook his head dismissively, as if he had no idea what Acteon was talking about, and no interest in finding out.

'Oh yeah, that's right,' Haris remembered. 'Boleyn was saying that if you want to chat up a pretty girl, pay her lots of compliments.'

Alaric looked even more puzzled. 'What are you talking about? I wasn't there.'

'Funny that I can remember you being there,' Acteon commented.

'I wasn't in Mara that time,' Alaric shot back. 'So I don't remember you being there. But you were there, weren't you?'

Acteon looked embarrassed and changed the subject. 'So, ah, how excellent it is that the war is going so well. Don't you think?'

No-one said anything for a moment, given Acteon's all-too-obvious embarrassment.

'Is it true that the Marechal has liberated Walburga?' Nina asked breathlessly.

'I believe so, Lady Delwyn,' Alaric said.

'Oh.' Nina gazed wide-eyed at Alaric and said nothing more.

Alaric's friends all looked at Alaric as well with smiles twitching at their mouths. They were waiting for him to move so that they could pounce.

Alaric grinned like a schoolboy and rose to the challenge. 'Do you have a connection with Walburga, Lady Delwyn?' he asked.

'I am from there.'

'Ah, I have, ah, visited Walburga,' Alaric commented. It was all he could think of to say.

'You've been to Walburga as well?' Felim asked, open-mouthed.

'What're the odds?' Haris asked in astonishment.

'That is spooky,' Gerbern said with mock-fearfulness.

Darnell was just giggling.

'It sends shivers down my spine,' Felim agreed.

'Which all goes to show how amazing you are, Lady Nina,' Haris said.

'Your literary pursuits inspire admiration,' Gerbern commented.

'And you are extremely beautiful,' Felim continued.

'Not bad cleavage,' Haris pointed out.

'Beauty *and* brains,' said Gerbern.

'You're amazing, Lady Nina,' said Haris.

'You're absolutely amazing, Lady Nina,' said Felim.

'You are incredibly absolutely amazing, the Lady of all Ladies Nina,' said Gerbern.

Nina just looked at them all wide-eyed without saying a word. The other ladies-in-waiting were giggling quietly.

'Just ignore them, Lady Delwyn,' says Alric. 'I always do.'

At this point Matthias showed up, coming in with Hayden and Kade. They were laughing merrily about something or other. Nina, Mitzi and Georgette returned to Eleanor's side, while Matthias's friends went to stand by him.

Eleanor was silently folding and unfolding her fan in such a way as to indicate that she was deep in thought while watching Matthias and his friends talking together. 'How very, very interesting,' she said out loud as if speaking to herself.

'What is interesting, Your Royal Highness?' Nina asked eagerly.

Eleanor ignored the question. Nina might as well have not spoken.

'How very, very interesting,' she said again, tapping her fan on the palm of her left hand with an air of triumph as if she had just found the solution to an historic geometrical problem.

The ladies-in-waiting looked at each other but said nothing further.

They did not have too long to wait before they learned what Eleanor had found so interesting.

'You appear blessed in friendships,' Eleanor told Matthias later that night at dinner. 'Would you not say so yourself?'

'Your friendship is an especial blessing, Eleanor,' Matthias said promptly.

'But you have not seen your friends for, oh, for how long has it been?' Eleanor raised her eyebrows.

'Oh, what is it now, seven years or something like that,' Matthias said vaguely, as if trying to remember the exact figure.

'*Seven years*,' Eleanor repeated as if to emphasise that it was too late now for Matthias to retract his estimate. 'And how you chatter among yourselves as if it was only yesterday that you were all happily together.'

'That's the magic of friendship,' Matthias said in all seriousness. 'Who can explain it?'

'*The magic of friendship*,' Eleanor intoned slowly. 'But how wonderful to encounter magic in this world of tears! How very, very wonderful!'

'Isn't it?' Matthias agreed.

'Silence!' Eleanor shouted and slapped her hand down on the table-top. 'You have not gone seven years without seeing each other. You have obviously been up to no good over all that time. Well? Do you deny this?'

'Up to no good?' Matthias repeated. It was his turn to raise his eyebrows. 'That's a bit of a hostile comment, isn't it?'

'Don't avoid the issue, Lord Raspero, or Marechal, or whatever you are calling yourself today. Answer the question!'

'Every now and then we may have met occasionally,' Matthias confessed.

'You are conspirators,' Eleanor accused him fiercely. 'Liars and deceivers, spending all your time together while pretending that you were not seeing each other. Isn't that so? Answer me!'

Matthias sighed. 'I'm glad you're on my side, Eleanor. You do have a habit of seeing through me on occasion.'

'On occasion?' Eleanor sneered. 'You mean to say all the time, do you not?'

'I have been on the run, with a price on my head, hunted, and it was all I could do to stay one step ahead of my pursuers. Of course if my old friends could help me out from time to time, naturally I accepted this help with gratitude.'

Matthias's friends seated around the table all nodded gravely on hearing this.

Eleanor realized immediately that she was being shepherded away from continuing along this line of enquiry she had opened up and her suspicions multiplied then and there on the spot. She chose to reverse everything Matthias was implying. 'Far from never having a moment's peace to stop and contemplate your affairs, you have had plenty of time to meet up with all your friends so that you could make all your secret plans, plotting and scheming in the dark, hiding in the shadows while you hatched your plots. Well? Do you deny any of this?'

'I don't deny we met up now and then,' Matthias conceded grudgingly. 'But really, Eleanor, there's no need for all your wild and unseemly comments. What have I done to deserve this kind of false accusation?'

Eyes narrowed as she looked closely at Matthias, Eleanor realized that Matthias was retreating along the lines of what she was saying only in order to steer her away from stumbling across . . . what? 'A man of your talents, Lord Raspero,' she said with a gentle smile, 'has spent the past seven years doing far more than merely avoid capture.'

While Matthias himself gave nothing away, there was a perceptible stiffening of posture amongst several of his companions, and Eleanor missed none of it. 'It was all I could do to avoid re-capture, Eleanor,' Matthias said with a slight air of embarrassment, as if to acknowledge that he should really have done better, 'given that I had a five million strada price tag on my head. Five million strada! That's a lot of money. There were people who did nothing but hunt me. I was like some kind of hidden treasure. Trust me, I had to look sharp to keep out of their clutches. I had no time to do anything else.'

The others all nodded on hearing this as if they were acknowledging a self-evident truth. It was then that Eleanor's intuition snatched the answer she was looking for out of the air. 'Ah!' she said, leaning back in her chair and picking up her wine-glass with a little smile on her lips, 'you did not have the time, then, to arrange for your election as king?'

Matthias looked amused at this absurd comment, but he was unfortunately undermined by his friends, who in their varying ways confirmed Eleanor's guess by shifting about in their seats in as guilty a fashion as any prosecutor could have desired. 'How on earth could I have done that?' he asked with a chuckle.

'You tell me!' Eleanor riposted. 'How *did* you do that?'

'It is an interesting academic question,' Matthias said politely, as if it wasn't really *that* interesting, 'but I am sure that you do not intend to be taken seriously.'

With a dismissive wave of her hand, as if she had lost all interest in the question, Eleanor returned to her meal with a certain air of satisfaction, as if she had just beaten Matthias at chess. Matthias ate in a peaceful silence, looking over at Eleanor now and then with a kind of amused respect; his friends ate in an uneasy silence as if they dared not say anything; while Nina exercised her mnemonic skills to ensure that she could remember all this when the time came for her to update her diary later that night.

11:25 PM, Saturday 25 April 1882 A. F.

Nina was not able to get to her diary until much later that night, given that Matthias and Eleanor were getting along so well that time passed, the evening lengthened, and still they were laughing and talking, piling on more and more moments-to-record onto Nina's memory. But now at last Nina was reunited with her diary.

Each lady-in-waiting had their own chambers, consisting of a good sized bedroom with an alcove with a desk and chair and bookshelves, plus a bathroom and a living room. Nina sat at her desk, bent over her diary, her fountain pen in hand, writing carefully in her beautifully rounded, perfectly formed handwriting all the doings of the day which she had witnessed. There was a lot to write, and so Nina was a busy girl.

Nina and Alaric would have seven children together, and their fourth child, a daughter named Mikayla, would inherit Nina's diaries by a special provision in Nina's will. Mikayla bequeathed Nina's diaries to her daughter Jaana, who bequeathed them to her daughter Gentiana, who bequeathed them to her daughter Harmonie. By now, one hundred and sixty seven years had passed since the year After the Fall 1882, which is to say it was the year After the Fall 2049. Harmonie, after some discussion with her husband, allowed her great-great grandmother's diaries to be published in full, or more accurately, largely in full. Nina, with her penchant for writing everything down with a truthful exactness, regardless of what it was about, had gathered together all the gossip of the day, whether proven or unfounded, and artlessly repeated it all. Much of her diaries had to be blacked out. Untold legal actions might have followed an unedited publication, given that Nina, as a leading member of Westrigonian society, being married to no less than an Earl, was privileged to the choicest gossip of the day. But what remained of Nina's diaries was explosive enough. Firstly, there was the natural fascination with the legendary figures of Matthias and Eleanor. Secondly, there were the revelations that no-one had hitherto suspected, such as Eleanor's accusation that Matthias had engineered his election as king by the Vidaldmeet. This made a splash across the whole of Westrigonia. People furiously talked of nothing else for weeks on end. Families fought over this issue, fathers threw their sons out of windows for having the "wrong opinion" of this matter, whether for or against, and taverns forbade the discussion of Nina's diaries alongside the consumption of the alcohol which they dispensed. The country shook from end to end as if in the grip of an earthquake.

The historians were thoroughly united in their rejection of Nina's testimony. Nothing like this could be found in their theories, therefore it had to be false. There was no other evidence to be found anywhere else. Nina's diaries alone contained this idea, and so therefore Nina's diaries were not to be believed.

After all, as against the sober-minded collective judgement of the historians of the day, there was to be weighed in the balance the eyewitness testimony of a large-breasted girl who kept a diary. Only one side could be right, and that side was not, according to the historians of the day, Lady Nina.

Time would pass, and the historians of the day would be seen for the clowns they were. Nina's diaries would be vindicated. But before that would happen, time would have to pass.

CHAPTER THIRTY

A cracked vase looks fine,
Until it is filled with water.
Are you completely sure,
You want to read my poetry?
Frankie the Villain

2:05 PM, Sunday 26 April 1882 A. F.

Matthias was gone the first thing next morning, so Eleanor had little to do but wander around inspecting her domains. She had Romano call out his guard for her to review, and directed them to tidy themselves up and stop looking so scruffy. She repeated this a couple of times during the morning, just to be difficult. No matter how shiny the boots of her guards, she wanted them shinier. She bossed around her ladies-in-waiting, the kitchen staff, Nereus and anyone else who happened to cross her path. By lunch-time, everyone who could hide from Eleanor was in hiding.

Eleanor had her lunch sent up to her Chambers, and then afterwards withdrew into the Rose Room and sat in her favourite high-backed winged chair. No-one else but her was ever allowed to sit in that chair. Now at last she had the time and space to think properly about what Matthias had said. She opened the door in her mind behind which his words had taken lodging, and carefully reviewed everything that spilled out of its confinement. Her feelings reared up inside her like weaving cobras readying for a fight at the sight of so much disorder in her usually well-ordered mind.

One of these feelings was one of alarm at the sincerity of his suit. Up till now, she had believed that he could not marry a Zoller-Abstein Princess for political reasons, and their flirtation was merely a matter of a shared amusement. She had seen him as an ex-boyfriend who was bound by his word not to cause her harm, but whose romantic intentions would surely be directed elsewhere. This was the basic of their shared amusement, or at least that she had considered to be their shared amusement. Now there was no longer anything to be amused about. This had all become deadly serious. But she could not see what to make of Matthias's declaration that he did not plan to become King, but only to regain his Raspero estates. She did not believe it for a moment, yet she could not see the point of making such a claim.

Another feeling that was spitting fire had to do with the sudden reversal of her own preconceptions. It had long been a complaint on her part that she should be free to choose her future husband, rather than having some arrangement imposed on her. Now she was no longer sure that this was in fact preferable after all. She was tempted to change her mind on this issue. Love somehow seemed much more dangerous than it had when it was a purely theoretical matter. An arranged marriage was at least a perfectly safe, civilised affair, calm and rational and ordered. Marrying for love seemed by contrast like being abducted by wild-eyed bandits. Her nerves were stretched tight for no reason at all that she could see, while her stomach hatched clouds of butterflies, these butterflies being incubated by a nameless apprehension irrationally seizing hold of her sense of self. And as she was perfectly free to refuse Matthias's suit if she chose, given that he was bound by his word not to harm her, it made no sense that she should feel so apprehensive. She had absolutely nothing to fear from Matthias. So why then was she so nervous?

Another of her feelings was all about how the future had changed its nature. What other future paths could she walk? As she looked back on her life, she realised that by becoming Westrigonian she had ceased to be Anglashian. She had told herself that to be human encompassed both, and she could be larger than a narrow nationalism, but now she doubted such a philosophy. If she was forced to leave Westrigonia, she would have to try to recapture a sense of being Anglashian that was by now largely foreign to her. The thought of being exiled from Westrigonia produced a feeling in Eleanor like that of being thrown over a high cliff onto sharp rocks far below. It was not a prospect she could contemplate with equanimity. In fact, as the Crown Princess of Westrigonia, she could enter into an arranged marriage with any male who had two legs and walked upright if she could be Queen of Westrigonia thereby, and even these two conditions were negotiable. But now she was being given the chance to remain in Westrigonia as the Baroness of Raspero (if she was being given that chance (if that was what Matthias was about (if she could trust Matthias))).

And here was yet another of her spitting-fire cobra-feelings on the warpath. Could she trust Matthias? What was he about? Matthias had boldly romanced her as a twelve-year old boy with an enormous confidence that had been somehow reassuring at the time; but now Eleanor felt far from reassured at Matthias's endless self-confidence. What was he really about? Eleanor felt that in one way she wanted Matthias to be completely ruthless in order to triumph over his enemies, while at the same time she did not want him to be completely ruthless as far as the future of a Zoller-Abstein Princess was concerned. In short, she wanted him to be completely ruthless and not completely ruthless at the same time, which was of course against elementary logic. And this infuriated her even more than she was already infuriated, and made her wonder if in some way Matthias was to blame for all this. Of course, he probably was. And she would crush him for this when the time came. If it did, which it would, when it did. But what was she to decide now?

4:25 PM, Sunday 26 April 1882 A. F.

A restlessness had come upon Eleanor, and after a while, she had left her Chambers to pace about the empty corridors, followed by her ladies-in-waiting. As she passed through the Kaelyn Gallery, she heard a low wolf whistle, followed by some muttered comments, and identified the source of this disturbance as being two of Romano's guards standing at the side, where a balcony railing provided a vantage point onto the Decebal Hall below. As Eleanor approached, she could hear the two palace guards exchanging comments on the object of their contemplations.

'Now that's something,' said the one. 'I think I'm in love.'

'Me too. She's something. Is she Raspero's girlfriend?'

Eleanor stopped in her tracks. A sudden chill had settled in the centre of her chest.

'Dunno, never seen her before. But I'll give Raspero this, he's got good taste. What a looker!'

Eleanor snapped her fan open in such a fashion as to announce her arrival as she stepped up to stand beside the guards. Matthias was standing in the Decebal Hall with the usual crowd of hangers-on attending him, and by his side was a blonde woman in a blue dress, with gauze-shrouded bare shoulders and elbow-length white gloves. She seemed to have just emerged from the velvet petal-folds of a delicately-scented flower, her limbs shaped and enfolded in a gossamer garment which revealed little and promised much. Her delicately shaped red-painted lips, tilted nose, high cheekbones and arched eyebrows over sapphire blue eyes formed a face sculpted so precisely that it was without flaw.

Eleanor's stomach was clenched into complicated sailor's knots. She couldn't remember when she'd last felt so upset. She was reminded again of how little she really knew Matthias, and these episodes formed the odd disjunctions to her usual evenly complacent feeling that she had Matthias completely figured out. She relieved her feelings by giving the guards such a tongue-lashing that they did not even dare to speak; they did not even dare to nod as if to even understand what she was saying would be an effrontery. Eleanor turned on her heel and walked away when she was done with them. She was still in a temper, and her ladies-in-waiting kept some distance away as they followed her along the empty corridors of the Palace of Krastienst.

6:05 PM, Sunday 26 April 1882 A. F.

Eleanor came along to the Veceslav Room with her ladies-in-waiting in tow, outwardly calm but inwardly seething with anger and anxiety.

Matthias and his friends and the blonde woman in the blue dress were waiting for them.

'Hello Eleanor, how are you?' Matthias asked pleasantly.

Eleanor said nothing, looking back at Matthias and tapping her fan on the palm of her left hand.

'Eleanor, have you met Lady Godelric?'

Silence.

'Eleanor, this is Lady Acantha Godelric of Stayrint. Lady Godelric, you have the honour of meeting Her Royal Highness the Princess Eleanor.'

Lady Godelric curtseyed very prettily and said: 'I am greatly honoured to meet your Royal Highness.'

Eleanor gazed at her contemptuously in a stony-faced silence, then looked away dismissively.

'Ladies-in-waiting, this is Lady Godelric. Lady Godelric, this is Lady Delwyn, Lady Philokrates and Lady Marjolaine.'

'I am so delighted to meet you,' Lady Godelric said gushingly.

Nina stared at Lady Godelric in a wide-eyed fashion. Mitzi and Georgiana looked around the room a little awkwardly. None of them said a single word. The tension in the room was rising.

'You can say "hello" to Lady Godelric if you like,' Matthias suggested.

The silence continued.

Matthias accepted defeat with a sigh. It had been a very different story earlier that day when Matthias had introduced Lady Godelric to his male friends.

'Delighted, Lady Godelric,' Acteon had said, grinning foolishly, and giving a little wave with his left hand. 'Delighted, and, um of course, honoured, very much so, charmed, ah, yes, charmed, and so on, which all goes without saying. I am saying what goes without saying, because, well, hah-hah-hah, that is the very latest style, is it not?'

Matthias sighed audibly, embarrassed by Acteon's babbling. But there was more babbling to come.

'I yield to no-one in my happiness at this meeting,' said Felim, with a chivalrous bow and a wave of his left hand that presumably also meant something. 'Lady Godelric, I am honoured, honoured and charmed, yes, and I have to say, standing here, I am just, well, there is nothing to be done, to be talking about such matters, yes, it is so.'

'Delighted to meet you, Lady Godelric,' Alaric said courteously, with a stiff bow of his head.

'Yes, of course, very precisely. But of course, as it happens, it happens to be like, as it is, so to say,' said Darnell in his turn. 'And that is so, Lady Godelric. Most definitely, as we can all agree.' Darnell made opening and closing gestures with his hands that made no sense at all.

'I am far beyond all others in my personal and unbounded happiness at this meeting,' said Gerbern, with a gesture of his hand that implied that Darnell was a fool. 'Lady Godelric, I am at your service. People often mock me because my family is so wealthy and has so many millions of strada, no, they don't mock me, no-one has ever mocked me, they would not dare, but my wealth, there is such envy, but I am at peace, no-one dares do a thing. Is it such a terrible thing to be rich? But I digress. What does mere money mean to a lady of such grace as yourself? Lady Godelric!' Gerbern ended his oratory with a gracious little bow.

'My family has so much more money than Gerbern's family that we look down on them as poor,' Haris said. 'But enough of that. I am honoured to meet you, Lady Godelric. Let us play cards when the time arises, not that it arises in that way, just that the arising is not necessarily that kind of rising, hah-hah-hah, up into the air, I am just saying, let us play cards and enjoy an evening together one day when the circumstances are propitious.'

That had been earlier in the day, and masculine sentience had not markedly increased since then. Matthias controlled his exasperation as best he could. Now it was dawning on the young monarch of Westrigonia that, given that the Crown Princess and her ladies-in-waiting were as hostile to his dinner guest as his male friends were slavishly admiring, he had blundered in inviting Lady Godelric to the Palace. Matthias had only been trying to be as stylish as a newly minted king should be, especially given Lady Godelric's undeniable beauty, which would adorn any palace. He could see that trench-lines were being dug by the women of the company for a prolonged bout of warfare that would not end amicably.

Matthias set his shoulders square and prepared to face the rest of the evening.

'Shall we sit, Eleanor?' Matthias asked, and held out his left hand to escort her to her chair.

Eleanor struck his hand down with her fan and stalked off to her chair.

Matthias tried to look calm and unsurprised, as if all was going well. He waved the rest of the assembled company to their respective seats and personally escorted Lady Godelric to the seat where she would be sitting. Eleanor glared at this common courtesy to a dinner guest as if at a textbook example of wrong doing.

'Lady Godelric has been in hiding,' Matthias said to the assembled company after taking his own seat. 'We have just liberated Waybridge, and so she has been enabled to come out of hiding.'

'I played a key role in the liberation of Waybridge,' Darnell said to Lady Godelric. 'How glad I am to see that I was thereby in service to you in this matter of you being enabled to come out of hiding.'

Eleanor folded her fan closed in such a way that it was clear that Darnell's life was in danger.

'I trust you are well, Eleanor,' Matthias said courteously.

'What did you say?' Eleanor asked, as if distracted.

'Everything alright?'

'No, Matthias, as it happens, everything is not alright,' Eleanor said firmly.

'What's up?'

'Perhaps I should ask *you* that question,' Eleanor said, tapping her fan restlessly. 'May I ask *you*, Matthias, what on earth you think you are doing bringing *that slut* here to the Palace?' Eleanor had raised her fan and pointed it at Lady Godelric while saying the words *that slut*; now she brought her fan back to tap into the palm of her left hand.

'Now you are not to treat my guest Lady Godelric in such a rude way,' Matthias said, trying to speak as firmly as a lion tamer. 'She is my guest and as such I expect you to be polite to her.'

'Do you know who she is?' Eleanor asked furiously.

'Of course I know what happened,' said Matthias. 'I didn't live in a cave. But that graveyard business was, what, seven years ago. And it was a controversial matter, opinion was divided –'

'No, Matthias, opinion was not divided!' Eleanor interrupted. 'She has not been received in polite society since that time.'

'Well, she's being received here now and you'll just have to live with it.'

'No, I do not just have to live with it!' Eleanor retorted. 'She can't stay here. She is not welcome here.'

'That is not for you to say,' Matthias stated firmly. 'She is my guest.'

'This is my home!' Eleanor said fiercely. 'This is my home and she is not welcome here!'

'Eleanor, you'll have to drop this,' Matthias said, a little impatiently. 'She is staying and I'm not arguing any more about it.'

'Either she goes or I do!' Eleanor declared. 'And if I am the one to go, I shall never speak to you again.'

Matthias sighed loudly and stood up. 'Eleanor, we'll talk in private over there. Come with me. Now!'

He held out his hand and gestured to the other side of the room. Eleanor struck down his hand with her fan and stood up and set off across the room with Matthias behind her.

When they were alone together on the other side of the room Matthias said: 'Eleanor, I can't tell her to go now after having invited her here. It's really out of the question.'

'It is out of the question for me to stay in the same room as that slut!' Eleanor snapped.

'Eleanor, why are you taking all this so seriously? She's an interesting person to have to dinner. She's even had an opera written about her. A bad opera, admittedly, but still – '

'Hah! A *bad* opera!' Eleanor interrupted emphatically.

'Alright Eleanor, I'll do a deal with you. You have to recognize that I can't turn her away now. Either you will return to your quarters or you will stay and be polite to her as my guest. If you agree to stay and be polite, then after dinner I'll see her to the door and she'll be escorted back to her place and I will never invite her again to the Palace. Are we agreed?'

Eleanor considered this for a moment. 'Very well. We are agreed.'

This time when Matthias held out his hand Eleanor placed her hand in his and allowed Matthias to escort her back to her chair, a triumphant smile playing about her lips. She sat down, still with a barely concealed air of triumph and unfurled her fan, studying the drawing on the fan as if she had never seen it before.

Matthias sat down and looked about him at everyone. They all looked back at him. There was a long awkward silence.

'So here we are,' Matthias said, slightly desperately. 'How is everyone anyway?'

Silence.

'Lady Godelric has been in hiding during the occupation,' Matthias told the assembled company. It was a feeble conversational opening as he had already said this before. 'Isn't that so, Lady Godelric?'

'Yes, that is so, Marechal,' Lady Godelric said in her slightly husky breathy voice. There was something fascinating about her voice, about the huskiness of the way she spoke, her breathiness, her shapely red-painted lips forming words that sounded almost doubled like an echo.

Eleanor's grip tightened on her fan but she did not look up.

'That must have been very hard for you,' Matthias said sympathetically.

The men all nodded, expressing their own sympathetic understandings of Lady Godelric's suffering. It was clear that from their point of view Lady Godelric need never suffer again. She only had to say the word and they would spring into action.

Eleanor's lips formed a thin line into which the fatness of the globular world itself could have disappeared without a trace.

There was something magical about the way Lady Godelric looked around at them all while she said: 'The Melisendiens put a price on my head of two million strada. Everyone was looking for me. I was in great fear of being betrayed. Who would not betray me for such a large sum of money?'

'You could have worked it off,' Eleanor said sharply, snapping her fan closed.

'A cryptic remark,' Matthias said briskly, and gave Eleanor a hard look. She chose not to look at him. Matthias took a deep breath, as if wondering what more to say to Eleanor, then decided to let it go.

'At least that is not insulting, Lady Godelric,' Matthias said with a friendly smile. 'When I first went on the run there was a price of twenty thousand strada put on my head. Twenty thousand strada! I was deeply insulted. Surely I was worth a lot more than that!'

Everyone chuckled. Matthias relaxed a little. The atmosphere seemed to be perceptibly lightening.

'But I don't understand,' Lady Godelric said huskily. 'Why did you have a price put on your head?'

'There was once a time, Lady Godelric, when I was nearly as famous as you,' Matthias replied. 'I was found guilty of treason and sent to Cayetano prison. I escaped from there and went on the run. It was then that I had the price of twenty thousand strada put on my head.'

'But it is impossible to escape from Cayetano prison,' Lady Godelric said in puzzlement.

'Yes, Lady Godelric, it is impossible to escape from Cayetano prison,' Matthias agreed. 'That is why I was nearly as famous as you.'

'But how did you escape from Cayetano prison?' Lady Godelric asked.

There was a silence in which everyone looked at Matthias. Even Eleanor looked up from her fan.

'That is a question which I have never answered, and which I never will answer,' Matthias said in a friendly tone. 'But enough of this! Later I had a price of five million strada put on my head by the First Protector himself. Now that was more like it. I felt that my worth was being more properly recognized!' Matthias chuckled, to show that this was a light-hearted comment intended to elicit humour, but absolutely no-one else laughed at all.

There was too much tension in the way Eleanor was grinding the point of her fan in the palm of her hand, resulting in a certain amount of nervousness all around. It was like waiting for a bolt of lightning to strike.

It was then that Nina, being Nina, had to abruptly make a comment that came out of nowhere. It must have made to sense to Nina that her contribution somehow followed from what was being said, but to everyone else, it seemed like a jarring disruption. 'Oh yes, what happened to Phelan and all his men?'

There was a silence all around. Once again everyone wanted to know the answer to this question. Eleanor looked up from her fan again.

'*Those who know do not speak, those who speak do not know,*' Matthias said with an unfailing cheerfulness. 'But this is all ancient history in any case.'

There was another silence as it became clear that Nina's question would go unanswered. Eleanor's gaze dropped back to her fan.

'Five million strada!' Lady Godelric exclaimed, having been forced by Nina's interruption to wait all this time before expressing her astonishment. This delay made her astonishment seem less spontaneous. 'But why was that?'

'It seems that Lady Godelric has been living in a cave,' Eleanor declared, straightening up in her chair and opening her fan. 'She appears to know nothing of what is going on in the world.'

'Living in a cave has its attractions when looking at some people,' Matthias said with a sharp edge to his voice, looking across at Eleanor. Eleanor folded her fan closed and tapped it absently on her knuckles, looking into the distance as if entirely unaware that Matthias had said anything to her. Matthias paused, took a deep breath, and sighed heavily. He turned back to Lady Godelric.

'You are a national figure, Lady Godelric,' Matthias said as sympathetically as before. Lady Godelric looked back at him wide-eyed, her red lips slightly parted. 'The Melisendiens understood this and thus they sought to undermine our national morale. If they had taken you prisoner it would have been a blow against Westrigonia itself.'

Eleanor giggled.

Matthias sent her another hard look, which she again ignored.

'You are a national figure, Lady Godelric,' Matthias repeated, looking at Eleanor all the while that he spoke, 'and thus it is that the Melisendiens tried to capture you.' He paused, looking at Eleanor as if willing her to look up at him but Eleanor's gaze was fixed on her fan. Matthias turned his attention back to Lady Godelric. 'After all, you have even had an opera written about you.'

'A bad opera,' Eleanor commented, unfolding her fan.

'Excuse me?' Lady Godelric said, leaning forward and looking closely at Eleanor. It appeared that she had decided to start to fight back. 'What did you say, your Royal Highness?'

'I said that the opera written about you was a bad opera,' Eleanor said loudly, straightening up and shooting Lady Godelric a nostril-flared disgusted look. 'A bad opera,' she repeated fiercely. 'Isn't that so, Matthias?'

'Yes, it is a bad opera,' Matthias agreed. 'But still, it is an interesting story, so perhaps one day a good opera will be written about you.'

'A bad opera?' Lady Godelric said, looking at Matthias as if he had struck her. 'Do you really think it is a bad opera?'

'I'm afraid so, Lady Godelric. I know that the closing song is a classic and people whistle the tune on the street. But even so, the treatment is clichéd, the themes lack originality and the structure is tedious. It is simply a bad opera and there is nothing to be said for it.'

'Oh!' Lady Godelric leaned back in her chair as if weakened by shock. 'I am sure that your opinion cannot be refuted.'

'Well, it's not just me,' Matthias said. 'It's the consensus opinion. But as it happens, if I did not have a price on my head, I could knock on the door of a school tomorrow and apply for the job of music teacher. Believe it or not, that is my one qualification. My schooling was interrupted by being arrested and then living as a fugitive, but by then I had already acquired the qualifications to teach music.'

'Matthias, you have never told me this,' Eleanor declared, looking over at him.

'Well, the subject has never arisen. Now you know,' Matthias said impatiently. 'I bet that at the end of my life, when I look back on everything, I'll say: I wish I had just been a music teacher.' He smiled to show that this was a joke, but no-one laughed, or even smiled. Everyone was on edge. Their gathering was like a war zone.

'Dinner is served, Marechal,' said Steward Nereus, who could spot a conversational opening when he saw one.

'That's good,' Matthias said, 'I'm starving.'

He stood up and held out his hand for Eleanor. She took his hand with a disdainful look that passed over Lady Godelric's head, like a boxer taking a swing at his opponent. Everyone but Nina felt the awkwardness of the occasion to be embarrassing. (Nina could not have been happier.) Matthias and Eleanor led the way into dinner in the Sabina Dining Room. Alaric made sure to be by Nina's side as they followed.

7:10 PM, Sunday 26 April 1882 A. F.

At first the dinner proceeded reasonably smoothly. The soup was served, the guests ate in a silence that was only broken by those occasional sounds that are made by people eating soup. No-one wanted to say anything. Nina's eyes gleamed as she memorized everything that had happened so far for her diary entry of that day. The more people suffered, the more exciting her diary became.

As they finished the soup, and the bowls were being cleared away, Lady Godelric turned towards Matthias and said: 'But surely, Marechal, on my next visit here, you will allow me to bring my own personal chef to advise your own chef on the correct proportion of pepper to pumpkin?'

'You shameless brazen hussy!' Eleanor yelled, and banged the table with her fist. 'How dare you criticize our pumpkin soup?'

No-one missed the real point of contention, which was Lady Godelric's passing reference to her *next visit here.*

'Chefs don't always take kindly to such instruction,' Matthias said peaceably, trying to navigate his way through this latest storm. 'Your chef may as well stay at home.'

'And you may as well stay there with him!' Eleanor snapped at Lady Godelric.

'Eleanor!' Matthias shouted. 'What did you fail to understand about the agreement we just reached?'

Eleanor said nothing but stared into the distance as if this remark had not been addressed to her. Matthias gave her a very long, very hard look, then turned back to his guest. 'But I thank you, of course, for your kindly offer of such assistance as this.'

'It is nothing, Matthias,' Lady Godelric said with a friendly smile.

'MATTHIAS!' Eleanor yelled. 'Oh! I did not realize that you were on first name terms. Is this so? *Matthias?*'

Matthias held up his left hand, palm facing outwards, towards Eleanor in a peace-making gesture as he said to Lady Godelric: 'It would be best if you were to address me as Marechal, Lady Godelric. We are not on first name terms.'

'But of course, Marechal,' Lady Godelric said as if deeply remorseful. 'How could I have been so foolish? Please forgive me for such a lapse of attention.'

'It is not a lapse of attention, Lady Godelric,' Eleanor said furiously, 'it is a lapse of manners. And let me assure you, to have good manners is necessary in the Palace of Krastienst. Being a slut might be enough where you come from but it is not enough here.'

'Eleanor,' Matthias said a little dangerously, 'if you fail to honour our agreement it is abrogated. But enough of this. The next course is served.'

There was a deadly silence as everyone tucked into to their steak and potatoes and roasted vegetables, topped by a delicious creamy gravy and accompanied by a side salad. Lady Godelric looked at peace with herself and the world as she daintily fed off the food on her plate, which was hardly enough to fill up a bird. Eleanor occasionally banged her cutlery against her plate in a way that put everyone's nerves on edge. Nina was dizzy with happiness as she employed a variety of mnemonic techniques that would help her record everything that had happened in the pages of her diary. Not a word was spoken by anyone, as by now everyone present was in survival mode.

8:45 PM, Sunday 26 April 1882 A. F.

As they arose from the dinner table Matthias said: 'I cannot thank you enough for having so honoured us by being our dinner guest tonight, Lady Godelric. I am sure that I speak for us all, when I say how regretful I am to say goodbye to you at this time. Please allow me to escort you to the front door, after which I will see to it that you are escorted safely back to your accommodation. Everyone, say your farewells to Lady Godelric. Alaric, you can come with us.'

Lady Godelric looked around in a state of some confusion. 'I am sure that I do not understand, Marechal.'

'Perhaps I should explain things to her,' Eleanor said maliciously. 'I will speak plainly enough to be understood, believe me.'

'You were invited here for dinner and we have had dinner, Lady Godelric,' Matthias said with a forced smile. 'Now it is time for you to leave. Ladies and gentlemen, you may say your goodbyes.'

The men all fell over themselves to say goodbye to Lady Godelric. With a deliberate rudeness, Eleanor did not say a word but turned her back and set forth for the door leading to the Hariman Room, followed by her ladies-in-waiting.

Matthias and Lady Godelric and Alaric set forth. Lady Godelric stole covert glances at Matthias as they walked along, but made no comment. Alaric strolled beside them in a debonair fashion, blissfully unaware of what lay in store for him. Time passed. Soon enough they came to the Ilbert Door.

'I must bid you farewell at this point, Lady Godelric. May I say how delighted I am to have had the pleasure of your company tonight. Unfortunately I cannot invite you here again, but this one occasion on which you have graced us with your presence is sufficiently memorable as to, well, ah, be remembered by us all.'

Matthias thought to himself that he could have phrased everything a bit more elegantly, but somehow his usual fluency of words and manner had deserted him.

Alaric was trying to think of something courteous to say in farewell for his part but his mind was a complete blank.

'You cannot invite me here again?' Lady Godelric queried.

'Exactly!' Matthias confirmed. 'But this one occasion, was, ah, enough.'

There was a silence during which it occurred to Matthias that the word *enough* didn't sound right, somehow.

'Enough, by which I mean of satisfaction, ah, yes, general happiness, um, what else can I say? Not enough as enough, no, I mean to speak of abundance, of the general overflowingness of, ah, yes, that kind of thing.'

'I am sorry to have been such a poor guest that you cannot bear to have me here again,' Lady Godelric said as if apologising.

'No, no, no, not at all,' the Marechal said hastily, 'you have been an excellent guest. Excellent! None better. But such are the circumstances we find ourselves in at this time.'

Lady Godelric bowed her head. She seemed to be fighting off tears.

'So!' Matthias said decisively. 'Once again, I say my farewells, Lady Godelric. But I leave you in good hands. Alaric will see you safely home.'

'I what?' said Alaric.

'I will not have my guest left at the door in such a manner as this,' Matthias said, giving Alaric a hard look as if to make clear that Alaric was not to argue. 'You will escort Lady Godelric home as the gentleman you are. So! That's settled! I bid you, once again, the fondest of farewells.'

With that, Matthias turned on his heel and set off walking at a brisk pace, abandoning Alaric to his fate.

Alaric was left with no choice but to offer his arm to Lady Godelric. She placed her white-gloved hand in the crook of his elbow and turned her delicate face up to look at him. The two set off through the Ilbert Door.

Matthias had not chosen Alaric at random. In fact, he had earlier noted that Alaric was the only male member of his party to have remained reasonably composed during his introduction to Lady Godelric. His failure to drool had also, unhappily for the luckless Alaric, drawn the attention of Lady Godelric, who was not one to take such indifference lightly. Alaric was now a man marked by Fortuna herself.

9:10 PM, Sunday 26 April 1882 A. F.

Matthias made his way to the Hariman Room, where everyone was lazily lounging around and chatting and munching on chocolates in between sips of Rehunda wine. Matthias surveyed the group, who had all fallen silent at his arrival, given that he was, after all, the King of Westrigonia. When a king walks into a room, people pay attention.

'Going back to war tomorrow will seem like a holiday after dinner at the Palace,' Matthias said as he sat down.

Everyone roared with laughter. Their laughter echoed off the walls around like ripples rebounding off planar surfaces and doubling by the simple laws of harmonics into the complicated turbulence of that unrestrained laughter. And still they laughed, their laughter swirling around their bodies as swiftly flowing water in a river swirls around rocks in the river-stream. Their laughter was the bursting of the tension of the day into laughter as a storm breaks into rain and lightning-thunder and hard-blowing weather. It was a fine thing to be young and in the Royal Palace of Krastienst on that day. It was one of the finest things which life had to offer, and it was happily taken into their greedy hands by all those present. And still they laughed, helplessly now, while the world waited outside. Life could begin again tomorrow, but for now they laughed as happily as if they were on holiday.

The world outside waited grimly for its time to come again. Laughter never lives too long. By its very nature it is succeeded by sobriety. But while laughter lives, there is no tomorrow.

CHAPTER THIRTY ONE

Desire does not rest, I do not rest.
Desire does not rest, I do not rest.
It is folly to expect justice from the unjust.
It is folly to expect justice from the unjust.
It is a good thing to say good things twice.
It is a good thing to say good things twice.
Frankie the Villain.

9:40 PM, Sunday 26 April 1882 A. F.

Alaric had commandeered a flying carriage in order to escort Lady Godelric back to the Hadewig Hotel. He was the personification of courteous companionship all the while, by this means assuring Lady Godelric that she was in safe hands. His failure to slaver over her, despite her immediate proximity, was a direct affront to the sensibilities of Lady Godelric. Alaric's indifference to the charms of his companion had an effect on Lady Godelric's mind analogous to angering a venomous snake. Alaric's offences were multiplying with each passing minute in Lady Godelric's eyes.

The Hadewig Hotel was a large imposing sandstone building with arched windows and balconies with white-painted iron railings. Matthias had commandeered the Hadewig Hotel by the simple expedient of paying the owner a large sum of money, taken directly from the Treasury, for the exclusive use of the Hadewig Hotel for the Marechal's purposes.

Thus it was that the Suite of Peace had been placed at the disposal of Lady Godelric.

Alaric escorted Lady Godelric to the Suite of Peace, which had a dove inlaid in white enamel in its wooden double-doors, and bowed to her. 'I now bid you farewell, Lady Godelric.'

Lady Godelric tilted her head as if alarmed and gasped: 'Did you hear that sound?'

'What sound?' asked the young and innocent Alaric.

'There was a sound of someone moving through my rooms. What if it is a masked man, who knows I am here alone and helpless?'

Alaric's wand was in his hand without him even being aware that he had drawn it. 'Perhaps I should take a look.' Alaric had received the normal wand-fighting training of any man of his background, but in addition to this, he had received specialist tuition from the Baron of Raspero himself. For thirty-seven generations, the Barons of Raspero had been renowned for their wand-fighting skills. Thus it was that Alaric had no fear of encountering any enemy on the other side of the doors of the Suite of Peace. He was brave and honourable, and ready to defend the innocent, and this was acknowledged by Lady Godelric's lips drawing back almost with a hiss, revealing teeth a little too sharp and eyes staring at an enemy a thousand yards away. This moment had passed by the time Alaric looked across at her. By then, she was suitably composed as a woman alarmed and alone.

'You are too brave and much too kind,' Lady Godelric said as she opened the door with a trembling hand.

Wand in outstretched hand, Alaric went through the rooms of Lady Godelric's suite like a warrior ready for battle. There was no-one to be found anywhere. Lady Godelric in the meantime waited with her back pressed up against the wall, with one white-gloved hand on her heart and another white-gloved hand to her mouth, the very picture of a vulnerable woman besieged by the wolves of a savage world.

Alaric informed Lady Godelric of his finding that she was safe and sound.

'You are my hero, my saviour, my guardian of the ages. Any woman would yearn for you to defend her.'

'Right,' Alaric said a little uneasily. 'Well, I'm off then. I bid you farewell, Lady Godelric.'

'But surely, you will not leave me all alone amidst the terrors of the night.'

'Well, of course I will inform Captain Ingramstadt of your concerns. But have no fear, given that the Hadewig Hotel is intended by Matthias for very important persons such as yourself, it is secure.' Alaric stepped to one side and eyed the open door as if preparing to make a run for it.

'But surely you will not leave me alone in the midst of my own personal terrors.'

'Well,' Alaric began cautiously, 'your own-'

'Oh please, stay for five minutes, and no more. I do not ask for too much. Five minutes!'

'Five minutes?' Alaric queried. But he was already on the back-foot, and this was only a delaying gambit.

'If I ask for too much, then *go* and do not spare my unworthy presence even a backward glance!'

'Right, five minutes,' Alaric conceded reluctantly. He felt as if a cliff was at his feet, given that the consequent gossip would be unconquerably rampant if he were to be more than five minutes in Lady Godelric's private rooms. What would Nina think? Alaric would often look back on that moment of time. He would later feel that he could have left at that point, given Lady Godelric's entirely insincere entreaties.

'Oh, you are much too kind,' Lady Godelric quavered. 'And so brave! Please follow me.'

Alaric followed her into the next room, where she waved him into a nearby chair.

Lady Godelric went to the side, where she busied herself mixing their drinks. Alaric felt a certain uneasiness at the sight of her back bent over her labours. He dismissed his concern as irrational.

Lady Godelric brought him a golden goblet, ornately engraved and studded with rubies. She sat down in her own chair with a silver goblet, ornately engraved and studded with emeralds. 'Skull!' she said and raised her own goblet, and drank deeply.

'Cheers,' Alaric said in reply, and drank cautiously from his own goblet. The liquid it contained tasted smoky and sweet. 'What is this drink?'

'It is a cocktail of my own devising. As I am the hostess, please allow me my prerogatives. We must drain our drinks with a single swallow, in celebration of the Marechal. Come! Skull!' With this proclamation, Lady Godelric emptied her goblet.

'Skull!' Alaric followed suit, and found himself nearly gagging a short time later later. By then, his goblet had been snatched from his hand, refilled and returned by a swiftly-moving Lady Godelric. It now had a measure of Rehundan wine, which Alaric used to swill his mouth clear of its foul taste.

Alaric wrestled with his feelings of nausea. When he was at last able to speak, he said: 'What was that drink?'

'It is akdov and blackcurrant juice, with a silver Melisendien teaspoon of Satu Sable Potion.'

'Of what Potion?'

'Satu Sable Potion. It is a potion which mounts the animal spirits in the bloodstream, and thereby rises up through the ventricles and openings of the body into the brain, after which it deranges the senses and plunges the mind into insanity.'

'And why does it do that?'

'Because it seizes hold of all the appertures of the senses and locks them into a particular rhythmic pattern. If the person becomes involved within the hour in physical love-making, then this pattern is disrupted and their sanity is saved. But if not, there is no hope for them. They will go mad within the hour.'

'What are you saying?' asked Alaric. 'That I will go mad within the next hour if I do not have sex?'

'Self-administered pleasure will not do. It is the polarities of the male and female bodies in the act of physical love-making that is required to recalibrate the equilibrium.'

'The equilibrium of what?'

'The body under the influence of the Satu Sable Potion becomes a love-making machine capable of ascending the heights of pleasure, after which there follows an easy descent onto the plains of enormous satisfaction. But if this release is not obtained, then there is nothing else to be done on their behalf.'

'There's no antidote?'

'You have drunk the Satu Sable Potion. The consequences will follow.'

Alaric contemplated his situation with his head tilted to one side.

'So what kind of potion is this exactly?' he asked eventually.

'The naked witch must pick three mandrake apples at moonrise, crush them to squeeze out their juice, add to this juice the blood of a small male bird bled by the left wing, add to this a thumb-size of ambergris and the same of olive oil, and then three dried and crushed suckers from the tentacles of an octopus preserved in honey. Heat this mixture in a glass vessel containing a cup of Melisendien red wine, stirring all the while with a silver spoon until reduced to the height of three fingers, then take off the heat, add a thumb-size of cinnamon and a stick of aloe wood, and seal in a silver flask. Then the flask must be placed beneath the mattress of working prostitutes in a busy brothel for three days and nights to absorb the elemental spirits associated with the act of fornication. The surface of the flask must be covered with the appropriate sigils, so that once these elemental spirits have entered the flask they are trapped and cannot leave.'

'Ah.' Alaric nodded as if he had this kind of conversation every day. 'An interesting recipe, quite the procedure. Did you do all this yourself, may I ask?'

'There are those from whom such a potion can be procured for the necessary sum, which is very steep.'

'I'm sure it must be. I mean, that's a lot of work, not to mention the danger of working with, um, trapping these elemental spirits which, I would assume, has to be done just right.'

There followed a short silence which Alaric found uncomfortable.

'So how did you get into this kind of thing?' he asked, more to say something, anything, than because he wanted to know. In point of fact, deep down, he really *didn't* want to know.

Lady Godelric leaned back into her chair, pushing herself against the backrest in such a way as to suggestively suggest her dress sliding up her thighs with the merest of motions. 'You must understand, I am a woman who is all alone, at the mercy of those who would . . . ' Her blue eyes seemed to become larger and larger, while her red lips receded in Alaric's vision like the red shoes of a ballerina with longer and longer legs. Her very gaze, so long and hard as it was, seemed to penetrate him somehow, sideways so to speak.

Alaric realized his thoughts, or perhaps his perceptions, were becoming disordered. If there had been a difference between the two before, there was now a distinction without a difference between them, or to put it another way, the potion which he had unwittingly imbibed was beginning to have its effect.

'And what happens if, um, due to an over-seizure of a misapprehension of his circumstantial circumstances, the poor devil is unable to perform?'

'There are always ways and means towards any end.'

'Such as what?'

'There are lap-dogs trained to lick one's private parts, after which anyone will subsequently perform.'

Alaric shifted in his seat. 'I had no idea. In fact, to tell the truth, that is already far more than I wished to know. But I am sure that you must think me hopelessly, um, unacquainted with such a world as that to which you refer.'

Alaric wanted nothing more than to simply leave in safety and in peace. But it was much too late for that.

Lady Godelric's red lips parted in reply, and her dress slid up her thighs even more suggestively than before.

'Perhaps you would be so kind, Lady Godelric, as to be my means of deliverance from this fate.'

'Are you suggesting, Honourable Niedbala, that I should surrender my virtue to your probing male demands right now?'

'Yes, exactly,' Alaric said, 'but please, ah, call me Alaric.'

'But you will call me Acantha in return if I am to surrender to your insistent demands, will you not?'

'Definitely, Acantha.'

Lady Godelric looked away as if mulling all this over. Archly she looked back at Alaric with her chin drawn inwards and said: 'How can any woman refuse a gallant lover such as yourself? I can only surrender to the commands of your masterful ascendancy.' She stood up and extended her hand. 'Come! Take my hand.'

Alaric stood up in his turn and took her hand, whereupon she led him to the bedroom.

10:50 PM, Sunday 26 April 1882 A. F.

Lady Godelric had not misled her latest lover. Alaric had indeed become a love-making machine capable of ascending the heights of physical pleasure, after which he had descended gently to the plains of enormous satisfaction, animated by the potion infused into his bloodstream and led every step of the way by his experienced mistress. It was now over and Alaric lay exhausted, turning over in his mind how to leave as soon as possible. How long did he have to wait so as not to seem discourteous?

He wondered if he had really been in the danger claimed by Lady Godelric, or if it had been a trick. He had certainly been drugged, that was for sure, but she could have been bluffing about its effects.

'So I take it that I am past the danger of that infernal potion?'

'You have alchemically transformed the potion into sexual energy and consumed it all. You are perfectly safe now.'

'Well, that's good. So. Acantha, I had better return to the Palace shortly.'

'But of course you must. But first we shall have a glass of wine together.'

'I think not,' Alaric said with a little laugh. He was trying to come up with a witty comment about his acquired aversion to Acantha Godelric's beverages, but found himself distracted by the sight of a naked Lady Godelric walking across the bedroom to the drinks cabinet, and pouring them each a crystal-glass goblet of red wine, and then returning to the bed and handing Alaric his wine. Reluctantly, Alaric took the goblet and drank from it. He had never felt less in control of his own life.

'You must certainly return to the Palace,' Lady Godelric said, agreeing again with what he had said earlier. 'You are in the service of the Marechal and he shall expect your return. I can only hope to rely on your discretion as to our dalliance.'

'Definitely!' Alaric said emphatically.

Lady Godelric's lips thinned as if she felt affronted by Alaric's eagerness for no-one to learn of what had happened. A more gallant lover would have wanted the whole world to know.

'You will continue to serve the Marechal as before. You do live in the Palace, do you not?'

'For the time being, while the war's on,' Alaric said evasively. He felt his temper stirring. He had had little time to think about what was happening to him, given the suddenness of Lady Godelric's ambush, but he felt that he was being pushed about.

Lady Godelric read all this in a moment and coquettishly snuggled up to him. 'If you ever need a place to stay, you may always come to me. Your gallantry has won my heart.'

'Thanks,' Alaric said shortly. 'That is very kind of you.'

'It is not kindness. It is womanly feeling. How bravely you faced danger on my behalf. And yet there was no danger, thankfully, on this occasion. Yet earlier tonight, I also felt threatened.'

'Earlier tonight?' Alaric asked a little dully. He really didn't care. He wanted to be gone.

'I have seen the Witch face to face, and yet I have escaped the darkness,' Lady Godelric said as sonorously as if she were reciting poetry.

'The Witch?'

'Do not suppose me not to know of the Witch of Trentland.'

'Who? No, I've never heard of, ah, anyone like that. Does she live in Trentland?'

'She lives in the Palace calling herself Her Royal Highness the Princess Eleanor, and she is known to practice witchcraft.'

'Really?' Alaric tried to look as if he had never heard anything like this before. 'Well, who would have thought that? Of course, it must be slander.'

'She is a witch who now seeks the throne of Westrigonia,' Lady Godelric continued, as if the thought of doing the same thing had never crossed her own mind, 'and what will happen if she succeeds? I fear for Matthias. Surely you must share my concerns.'

'Not really,' Alaric said firmly, 'Matthias is pretty good at taking care of himself. Besides, witchcraft might even help us out right now, given the odds against us!' He laughed, to show that this was merely a light-hearted comment rather than a serious remark.

'Would you stoop to such measures even for such a noble end?' Lady Godelric asked him in all seriousness. She appeared not to have a sense of humour.

Alaric tried to find an exit from this conversation. He felt he was on stage as a puppet in a puppet show, playing a role that would inevitably end in him being clubbed over the head. 'What, you mean like summon demons or something? That kind of thing?'

'Demons are easier summoned than banished,' Lady Godelric said as if she knew what she was talking about. 'But who does a foreign witch really serve?'

Alaric shifted uncomfortably in his chair. He felt that this kind of talk was going to get him into trouble somehow. 'There are of course all sorts of political uncertainties, generalized shibboleths of undetermined, um, improbabilities, all in their varying ways interconnecting to form the interstices of the day, if you see what I mean, to put the matter simply.'

Lady Godelric threw back her head and laughed. She had astonishingly white teeth, and her laugh was surprisingly melodious. 'The matter may have been put simply for a man of such keen intellect as yourself, but you must forgive me for failing to understand what you have said.' She laughed again, even more merrily than before. It seemed that she did have a sense of humour, after all.

Alaric found himself, reluctantly, laughing a little in response despite himself. 'Well, all I was saying is that none of us know what is really going on right now, what with the fog of war and all that.'

'But surely, my fine Alaric, a clever young man as yourself, and such a good friend of our Marechal, must know of the highest counsels of the land.'

It was becoming clearer and clearer to poor Alaric what this seductress from hell wanted with him. He was her entry into the Palace where the young Marechal had so recently taken up residence.

Alaric felt that he would be damned whatever he said, so he tried to say nothing meaningful. 'My apologies, Lady Godelric, but I really cannot discuss such matters as these.' He straightened up a little as if preparing to leave, but it was difficult to seem decisive in Lady Godelric's four-poster bed.

'But of course you cannot,' Lady Godelric agreed immediately. 'But how is it that such a gallant young man as yourself, brave and handsome, became such good friends with the Marechal? Surely this is not a secret of state?'

'Oh, we're not really *that* good friends,' Alaric said dismissively, 'I mean, we just sort of knew each other as kids, that's all, family connections, that kind of thing.'

Alaric's failure to brag of how he and the Marechal were like *that* had the opposite effect than he intended on his companion. Lady Godelric concluded, perfectly correctly, that only a close friend of the monarch of Westrigonia would deny being a close friend.

The story Alaric was not telling Lady Godelric was as follows:

The day Matthias and Alaric became friends

Matthias and his distant cousin Alaric had been standing on the walls of Castle Niedbala, the ancestral home of the Niedbalas, on a hot summer's day, watching the peasant boys swimming in the river below. The clothes of the noble-born youngsters were sticking to their skin like a coat of paint, so oppressive was the heat. They yearned to be swimming in the river themselves.

'Don't you wish you were swimming in the river right now?' Matthias asked Alaric.

'Definitely!' Alaric replied.

Matthias laughed. 'All over the country right now the noble kids are looking down at the peasant kids swimming in the river, wishing they were peasant kids, while all the peasant kids are looking up at the castle wishing they were noble kids,' Matthias commented, and laughed again. 'Makes you think, doesn't it?'

Alaric's elbow twitched and his head jumped up. He started to laugh wildly. He'd never heard such a thing said before! It struck him as a revelation and it was so curious that it didn't even matter if it were true or not. It was such an amazing thought! He could see in his mind's eye, as if in a painting, precisely the scene that Matthias had described happening across the whole country at that particular moment in time: all the peasant boys, swimming in all the rivers of the country, gazing up at the castle walls of their masters and yearning to be standing on those walls, while all the noble children of the land were gazing down yearning to be swimming in all the rivers. He laughed so helplessly that he ended up lying down across the castle wall like a sock draped over a railing. Matthias held his hand out over Alaric's back, ready to grab him if he overbalanced, laughing in his turn at Alaric's laughter.

From that moment onward Alaric had followed Matthias as a disciple follows his master.

It took him some time, but eventually Alaric managed to get away from the Suite of Peace. He fled into the night, taking with him the terrifying memory of the greatest romantic triumph of his young life. He would be forever scarred by this happiness.

6:10 PM, Monday 27 April 1882 A. F.

'So how did your evening with Lady Godelric go?' Matthias asked Alaric cheerfully. 'You didn't get back until twenty past two in the morning.'

Matthias knew this because by now he had organised the Palace sufficiently for all arrivals and departures to be logged.

'Oh God, I couldn't get away,' Alaric replied, rolling his eyes, 'she wouldn't stop talking. Anyway . . . ' Alaric trailed off with a shrug.

'Oh God, you couldn't get away,' Eleanor repeated mockingly. 'Yes, you must have suffered, with your male member like an erect pole and your brain shrunk to a pea.'

'Well, that sounds alright,' Alaric commented with a little laugh. The good humour of this response was supposed to be like a shield which deflected the gladiatorial aggression of Eleanor's deliberate savagery, but Eleanor was already unleashing another gladiatorial blow.

'But you couldn't get away, despite all your no doubt valiant attempts to escape. Perhaps you put your arms around her as part of your escape plan?'

'Hah, far from it,' Alaric said in a jocular fashion, as if he was out having a drink with the boys and this kind of talk was perfectly normal, 'although I don't deny she has a superficial glamour. Although really – '

'A superficial glamour?' Eleanor interrupted him. 'But that is nothing more than lipstick on a snake. But perhaps snakes excite you?'

'No, not at all, in fact – '

'Twenty past two in the morning!' Eleanor suddenly exclaimed, as if the import of this statement had only just now sunk home. 'And what did you say you were doing all that time? Talking? Yes, I have heard that Lady Godelric is famous for her . . . conversation.'

Even in the rising tension generated by Eleanor's hostile treatment of poor Alaric, there was a general laugh at this witticism.

'Well, of course we were only talking,' Alaric said as casually as he could, 'I mean, I'd only just met the girl so really, I mean, no, yes, of course we only talked, it was nothing like that.'

'So this is how you repay our hospitality,' Eleanor continued, with the grimness of a prosecutor listing all the faults of the accused. 'It is not enough to take shelter under our roof, to break our bread which we have freely offered you, to be our guest according to the tradition by which you are thereby honoured, but you will bring disgrace upon our name by your scandalous behaviour. You will no doubt come and go as you please, and if any of us dare to object, you will no doubt be outraged at seeing a limit placed on your lust.' Eleanor's voice had risen throughout all this, until by the end she was nearly shouting.

Alaric looked to Matthias as if for help, but Matthias was watching Eleanor with his lips twitching, as if amused. Alaric could feel Nina's hurt eyes looking at him from the side.

'Not at all,' Alaric said a little helplessly, 'far from it, it's really not like –'

'You spend your nights in the company of loose women and your days here in the Palace. Is this what is to be said about you? Well? Is it? Is it? But we are of course supposed to praise you, I am sure. Is that not so?'

'I assure you, your Royal Highness,' Alaric said as composedly as he could, beginning now to recover from the shock of being so suddenly under attack and starting to feel his temper rising, 'nothing at all happened that was immoral. As I keep on saying, I only just met the girl.'

Eleanor noted that Alaric was ready to start to fight back, and so like a shrewd tactician, she called off hostilities in order to retain control of the ground she had gained.

'Very well,' Eleanor said, folding up her fan as if she had finished with Alaric (for now) and was ready to move on, 'I see no reason not to accept your version of events. Nor do I see any reason to doubt your loyalty to the Palace. But perhaps you choose to object?'

'No, I'm completely loyal to the Palace,' Alaric said in his most level tone of voice.

There followed an uncomfortable silence. Everyone present understood what had just happened. Eleanor had bullied Alaric; Matthias had sat by and done nothing; Alaric had not dared to fight back; and so in the environs of the Palace, it would be a brave man or woman who dared to even mention the name of Lady Godelric within Eleanor's hearing.

Eleanor understood that if she were to become Queen of Westrigonia, she must be as much feared as loved, and preferably feared.

CHAPTER THIRTY TWO

A man who knows himself,
Rules the world.
A man who does not know himself,
Is ruled even by a dog.
I once believed this,
And I hope to believe it again.
Frankie the Villain

11:30 AM, Tuesday 28 April 1882 A. F.

Mitzi and Georgette had decided that they wanted to know what Alaric had meant by his passing reference to Acteon in Mara. They had deputed Nina to the task of finding out, given that they had noted Alaric's interest in her. Having sent a note to Alaric asking him to escort Nina to the laundry room, they then used questionable strong-arm tactics to place Nina in a dress showing plenty of cleavage. By each girl grabbing onto an arm, they marched Nina along with them and pushed her out of the Quinlan Door into the Sara Hall, where Alaric was already waiting.

Nina had been nicknamed Moon Face as a child, having a large round white face. Her extremely large breasts were counter-balanced by a large rounded posterior. From the side she looked like a sea-going ship of old, jutting bow and stern. Her warm brown eyes gazed at Alaric with a mixture of alarm and fascination. Alaric stepped forward, and with a little bow, took her hand and placed it in the crook of his elbow, and they set forth. On arriving at the laundry room, Alaric released her arm and stepped away.

Alaric had rehearsed more than one way to tell a pack of lies to Nina about how nothing had happened during his evening with Lady Godelric, but as it happened he never needed to say a word. Nina had already decided that Alaric was a completely innocent man, and so the subject was never brought up.

Nina remembered her instructions, and went to work.

'Do you like my Makynli?' she asked.

The Makynli in question was a piece of jewellery in the form of a circle of a snake made of gold biting its tail; this gold snake-circlet was quartered with a cross of silver, the end-points of the cross being fastened onto the gold circle by emerald gem-stones. On the centre-piece of the cross was fixed a square piece of lapis lazuli. The whole thing was about two inches in diameter.

It was a strikingly beautiful ornament, but this was not what struck Alaric most forcibly at the time. Nina was standing demurely with her eyes downcast with the Makynli on a chain around her neck. She was wearing a low-cut strapless dress, while her Makynli rested on her smooth warm skin just above her cleavage. It was this cleavage that drew Alaric's gaze far more than the jewellery. The warmth of its softness was almost visible. Alaric was fascinated by the question of how far down Nina's cleavage he could look at that moment in time.

Nina looked up at Alaric, who roused himself sufficiently to say: 'Ah, yes, that is amazing, very much so, yes, definitely!'

Nina giggled on hearing this, holding her hand over her mouth, her shining eyes turned up to the hapless Alaric.

Alaric wondered why the universe was suddenly throwing beautiful women at him. His luck with women up till now had been like anyone else's: a girlfriend here and there, even a sweetheart with whom he had exchanged the traditional pledges of eternal love; that romance had lasted a whole two months! Still, others could say the same. It was true that he was good-looking and rich, but he lacked the smooth talk and the predatory instincts of the playboy. Alaric was too much of a romantic at heart to be a predator, believing as he did in the One. This made him look soft in the eyes of the unsatisfied girls he respected too much to conquer. Alaric was nothing out of the ordinary in love; such was his life.

And now here was Lady Delwyn offering up her half-unclothed breasts to his lustful gaze. But given that the said Lady Delwyn was the lady-in-waiting to the Crown Princess of Westrigonia, Alaric knew enough to tread warily. Eleanor's attack on him had had its intended effect. He had a healthy respect for Eleanor now.

'I have to go,' Alaric pronounced. 'I have serious and important affairs of state to attend to.' Alaric tried to look dignified. 'Goodbye.'

'But don't you like my Makynli?' Nina asked plaintively.

'I absolutely love your Makynli,' Alaric said, taking another good look at her cleavage.

Nina giggled again.

Exasperated by all this giggling, and with a sense of being provoked by the very universe itself, Alaric grabbed Nina and kissed her.

The sweetness of her lips, and the softness of her body in his arms, affected Alaric as much as his boldness affected Nina: the two lovers flowed into each other's arms as if melted by this moment of passion.

Alaric let go of Nina and stepped back.

'I really have to go and see to important matters of state,' Alaric said, as much as if he was trying to convince himself as much as Nina. 'I bid you farewell.'

Seeing him turn away Nina burst out: 'Wait! You can't go.'

She had never had such a kiss, and besides, she had to find out what she had been sent to find out; but which was which she could not have said right then.

'Well, of course I wouldn't go, if my business wasn't so important,' Alaric said, lying through his teeth, such was the state to which he had been reduced.

'But you have to tell me what happened to Acteon in Mara!'

'What? I have to tell you what?'

Let it be understood from the outset that Alaric was initially outraged at the ice-cold crystal realization that Nina's flirtatious friendliness had been directed to only this point, namely to acquire a story from him concerning a question which had recently arisen. Let it also be understood, for Alaric was certainly no saint, that Alaric's second thought was to wonder if he could now look further down Nina's cleavage from this understanding of her perfidy. But thirdly, Alaric had kissed Nina already, and this kiss had lodged in his soul, or at least in his memory of what his soul had experienced, and thus it was that he forgave her everything on the spot. As for the next point (by now Alaric had lost count) it seemed that he could kiss Nina again whenever he wanted to, given that she had to accept it as the price for hearing the story which she wanted to hear; or so at least was the conclusion reached by Alaric.

It was clear to Alaric at this stage of his contemplations that there was only one thing to be done at that moment, so without a single further thought he pulled Nina into his arms a second time and kissed her thoroughly. The rights and wrongs of everything disappeared into the air with their kiss.

It was sometime later, when they came up for air, that Alaric asked reprovingly, 'Why do I have to tell you about Acteon in Mara?'

'Because you have to,' Nina said breathlessly.

Dazzled by her beauty and swallowed by their shared kiss, Alaric had no defense against this argument. But such is the force of love: to lose is to win; to give the beloved what they want is to gain the world.

'Alright,' he agreed, 'so be it. You want the story: here it is.'

The Tale of Acteon and the Body Snatchers as told by Alaric

Matthias and Acteon Quattroy had arrived at the river-town of Mara early in the morning. After having a bite to eat, they had strolled around the town like travellers with time to spare. They were pretending to be brothers from Netis, here in town to visit their 'uncle', who in fact was their local criminal contact. They lingered unobtrusively by the bridge near the water-mill in order to read the graffiti on the stone-work.

Matthias had devised a code for communication among his network that used graffiti symbols that were meaningless to the uninitiated eye but which were very meaningful to his merry band of Westrigonian acolytes and their various associates. Symbols for hands, feet, eyes, houses, arrows and various other items, along with shapes vaguely like letters, said what they had to say just as readily as normal writing. On this occasion, Matthias's 'uncle' had said, by leaving a message that looked like a fish balanced across the prongs of a 'Y' surrounded by eleven dots, in the form of a graffiti made by a water-soluble paint that would wash off in the next rainfall, 'Come see me at eleven o'clock.'

The two 'brothers' wandered along to the town-square, where Matthias left Acteon at a few minutes before eleven o'clock with a stern farewell warning to be careful and stay alert. Acteon was a look-out for Matthias during his meeting.

Various people were coming and going in the square, but one arrival in particular caught Acteon's attention. She was a busty leather-clad young woman, her hair striped blond and black and falling to her shoulders as if blown there by the wind. Her bare mid-riff was just as provocative as her cleavage and her long legs in their leather mini-skirt, and while doing his best not to look at her, Acteon nonetheless felt that by bad luck, every time he looked in her direction, she caught him at it. The time came when she came over directly towards him and spoke to him in a friendly fashion.

'Do you like me?' she asked.

Acteon could hardly deny having ogled her earlier, so he was stuck. 'I have a girlfriend,' he lied.

'That isn't an answer.' She ran the tip of her tongue suggestively along her upper lip.

'It is courtesy, whichever way you look at it,' Acteon said smoothly.

He had attended the prestigious (and expensive) school of Ramhart but all of his education was of little help now. She was smiling at him with her head turned a little sideways, as if observing every thought that was slithering across his mind. Her red lips were warm like blood, her white teeth were almost painfully sharp, her eyes were highly intelligent but distinctly predatory.

Ignoring all common-sense (and abandoning his post!) Acteon went back with her to her place. The kindest explanation of his behaviour was that he wasn't thinking clearly; on the other end of the same explanatory scale was that he was being a complete fool. Anyway, the Body Snatchers (for such they were) ambushed Acteon with a brutal skill that not only took him unawares but made him piss his pants.

In all fairness to Acteon, it must be pointed out that the version of events as recounted by Acteon himself made no mention of any such detail as this one of Acteon pissing his pants. To put it plainly, Alaric had completely made up this detail of the story.

In any case, Acteon's pants, pissed in or not, did not remain on his body after the aforesaid ambush because before long he was lying naked, tied up on a table, while three or four people examined him. One of them was marking the skin of his naked body with an ink brush while declaiming out loud, with a lascivious interest, the names of the body parts in question and their alleged nutritional and medicinal properties.

Acteon realized that he had fallen into the hands of the Body Snatchers, a notorious group of cannibals who sold human body parts for consumption to other cannibals.

One of these cannibals examining Acteon was the busty woman from the town square, and it was now, much too late to do him any good, that Acteon remembered Matthias's warnings against the honey trap. The honey trap was when a beautiful woman enticed a man to a place where he could be ambushed.

'You know which body part I want to eat,' said the honey trap woman. She curled her lips over her sharp white teeth as if she was ready to eat right now!

Nina gasped out loud.

It seemed for a moment to Acteon that the skin of her face was like a sock beneath which bulged a reptilian head. Every organ of his body, internal and external, shrank away from her hungry gaze.

'Now, now, steady on, the customer comes first,' one of the other figures said with a laugh.

'The customer is always right,' said another figure with another laugh.

'But we get to eat the left-overs,' the honey trap woman whined like a child insisting on her promised treat, 'and to lick the bones and crunch them and eat the marrow.'

Nina's mouth fell open.

Acteon tried to speak but all that came out was 'Yammeryadrigbliud', such was the state of complete terror to which he had been reduced.

According to Alaric.

So the merry scene of cannibal medical science continued, worthy of a Dark painting by the later Goyevsky: the cannibals gathered around their pinioned prey, their heads lowered so as to pay close attention to all that his naked body had to offer them. A voice broke in the air above their bowed heads at that moment.

'What's going on?' asked Matthias.

There were four figures standing around the table on which Acteon lay, and all their heads turned around as one to the door like a wolf-pack alerted to a sudden arrival; but it was much too late for any of them. Matthias was already moving. Acteon could follow little of the fight from his prone position on the table, but it was not long, fifteen seconds or so, before Matthias was standing by the table looking down at him.

'What did I tell you about being careful?' asked Matthias.

'You did tell me, I just slipped up,' Acteon replied. 'Are you going to untie me or what?'

'Why I should bother, I don't know,' Matthias said as he untied Acteon. 'Just remember that you owe me one.'

'Definitely,' Acteon agreed as he sat up as a free man and no longer a restaurant meal, 'you got it. I'll owe you two if you like.'

Alaric ceased talking, having ended his tale, and contemplated Nina.

Nina looked wide-eyed at Alaric.

'That is the tale which you requested,' Alaric said, 'so be it.'

It occurred to Alaric at that point that he could kiss Nina again with perfect immunity from objection, and so he did exactly that. He felt in command of the situation but it might be argued that the submissive Nina had become a riverbed down which all his waters flowed, and so who was in charge of what in an ultimate sense had become debatable.

9:30 PM, Tuesday 28 April 1882 A. F.

Lady Godelric had sent for Alaric to join her that evening, and so it was that Alaric found himself back in the Suite of Peace. He declined her offer of a drink with such brusqueness that Lady Godelric did not press the matter.

Alaric's love-life had gone from non-existent to unbelievably complicated literally overnight, and that was without taking into account all the possible political implications, given that he was already being targeted by all and sundry as a confidant of the new King. Alaric knew he had to reduce the sum of his lovers to the arithmetical remainder of one, and that remainder of one could not be Lady Godelric.

Yet Lady Godelric was not to be denied quite so easily. It would never be clear to Alaric how it had happened that he had gone to bed with Lady Godelric again. He did remember that Lady Godelric had raised her hand to stroke his face, and a scented dust had made him sneeze. After that, things became hazy.

After their love-making, an exhausted Alaric fell asleep, and that night he had the following dream.

Alaric's dream about Lady Godelric

There was a rustle by the windowsill, below the open window. Alaric opened his eyes. By the virtue of a divine providence that was taking care of him for no apparent reason, he was already facing the window and so the opening of his eyes made no sound and no visible movement and so remained undetected by the fox standing under the open window.

Alaric could see the fox quite clearly in the diffused moonlight reflecting off the brass wall outside. The fox had its head tilted as if listening for something. Then it moved, and with a flicker, which was a blink of a worldly eye, it transformed into Lady Godelric, walking toward the bed as naked as the day she was born. Alaric's eyes closed in an instinctive terror. He sensed rather than felt the deft-footed weight of the vixen lady climbing onto the bed like a small animal, nimble and quick and agile. His senses shuddered at their sensing.

He then could feel his companion looming over him and nuzzling his shoulder. Somehow he was already awake. He pretended to awaken by rolling over in a sleepy fashion, pretended to smile at the sight of the sharp face inches from his own, pretended to be reluctantly delighted at receiving the insistent expression of her furry desires, and by forsaking heaven and earth gave her everything she wanted from him and more besides.

He must have fallen asleep afterwards, because he awoke in the morning to find sunlight streaming over his face. He knew then that it had all been a dream; a vivid dream, admittedly, but a dream nonetheless. It had obviously not happened for real. There could be no doubt whatsoever on this point.

For the rest of his life, however, Alaric was never able to hear the phrase *she's a foxy lady* without a shudder.

CHAPTER THIRTY THREE

Ilk all-alike, said the observer of all the observed.
I just laughed. Who was he to say such a thing?
There is ilk, and this I do not dispute.
There is certainly ilk, and it is there to be seen.
Ilk aplenty abounds like leaping gazelles,
And it is there in all their likenesses.
But ilk that is unalike, ah! Yo! Yay!
There is the poem no-one has yet written.
Frankie the Villain

9:30 AM, Wednesday 29 April 1882 A. F.

There was a knock on the door of the Rose Room and Master Maurice Cadenula, the Epistolary Servant, entered with a bow that proffered the silver tray he was carrying in the direction of Her Royal Highness the Crown Princess Eleanor. 'I bear an epistolary communication from the First Protector, marked as urgent and for your eyes only, Your Royal Highness.'

'Why not call it a *letter*?' Georgette called out at Cadenula. 'Epistolary communication! What nonsense!'

Georgette had been raised in a household that detested diversion.

Eleanor sent her rebellious lady-in-waiting a silencing look and reached out her hand for the *epistolary communication*.

Cadenula retired from the room with the required bows and backward shuffling. His obsequiousness was not even noticed by the Crown Princess, who was busy studying the letter she held in her hand with its red embossed wax seal showing a spider rampant, which was the insignia of the Realm as chosen by Mikhail Hundayi, the first of the First Protectors. It might have been that Hundayi had liked spiders or it might equally have been that he had, as a matter of indifference, adopted the epithet thrown at him by his many enemies as his own badge of pride. Be that as it may, the spider was the emblem of the Protectorate.

Eleanor felt a tremendous sense of importance, especially given the covert glances being directed at her by her ladies-in-waiting. Here she was, in the centre of things, about to read a letter (which was an *epistolary communication* no less!) that had been sent to her by the most powerful person in the world.

With a sense that at last she was receiving the recognition she deserved, Eleanor eagerly opened the letter, and began to read.

The Epistolary Communication from Lord De'Asterides to Princess Eleanor

To Her Royal Highness the Crown Princess Eleanor of Westrigonia, and dare I also add, to this your proper title, that title of far more significance than that of officialdom, the Jewel of Krastienst. You will not take offence at my familiarity with you, given the depth of your generous heart, of whose nature you have given me more than a glimpse on several occasions.

Eleanor felt a chiaroscuro chill in the depths of the vein-channels of her bloodstream on reading this offensively familiar opening to the First Protector's letter. This shock to her nervous system was followed by a slight feeling of nauseousness. A woman who had a *generous heart* was very often pregnant and unmarried and socially dead, and so she was far from being paid a compliment by the obverse meaning of the convex lens of this phrase. Furthermore, what would anyone else think of De'Asterides's claim to have been given by Eleanor *more than a glimpse* of her generous heart? De'Asterides's overt lecherousness and outright ogling of her had made her uncomfortable on many an occasion, but he had done no more than be creepy. He had once, at the famous Ball of Pentharborg at which Eleanor had been nicknamed the Jewel of Krastienst, when kissing her gloved hand, taken the opportunity to sniff her glove, which the young and naïve Eleanor had taken at the time to be an off-colour joke. Now he was implying that his interest had been rewarded in kind. The Crown Princess of Westrigonia was suddenly profoundly thankful that she had not gone to Pentharborg the week before where even her mother would not have been able to protect her against a glove-sniffing man all-powerful in his own domain. She sensed that she had avoided something dark and dangerous by not going to Pentharborg. Eleanor now found that she was shaking. With a shudder, she reluctantly returned to reading the letter like someone obliged to handle a snake.

Alas to my dearest and most distant cousin, but I must to business without delay (though delay is so sweet and amplifies the pleasure to come! Do we not both know this?)

Eleanor paused to take a steadying breath. The thought crossed her mind that De'Asterides had had copies made of this letter for others to read in order to destroy her social reputation. Certainly no-one reading this letter could have failed to note its immoral implications, which were entirely false. This letter was not only a lie, but it was a vicious lie intended to poison her bloodstream with its venom.

The matter is too urgent to delay for even the moment required by the courtesy of these our troubled times.

Eleanor had to re-read the last sentence, which made little sense. How could *troubled times* have *courtesy*? She realised De'Asterides was deliberately trying to confuse her to make her more vulnerable to his epistolary assault, and with that recognition she all-of-a-sudden found her nerves steadying at the understanding that she was in a fight, and she had the skill and training to deal with this kind of attack.

I must write to you of this Raspero.

Eleanor straightened up in her chair and continued reading.

Raspero is not to be trusted. He is duplicitous in the extreme, a criminal, a fanged beast of the night.

Eleanor re-read this last phrase in some puzzlement. Did De'Asterides see her as a nine-year-old girl to be terrified by talk such as this? Whatever Matthias, in all his annoyingness, ultimately was, to call him a *fanged beast of the night* was absurd. For the first time, the thought crossed Eleanor's mind that the most powerful person in the world might be a buffoon; or of course this might be some kind of act. Eleanor resumed reading.

Raspero has run from my justice like a fugitive coward for so long that I have come to despise him as a gutter-crawling man, as not even a man, this ruffian with no pretence to civilisation, this detestable rebel who would not stand still long enough for me to arrest him, this fleet-footed crook who now has the effrontery to claim that he is the King of Westrigonia. But enough of Raspero's failings. A bright, clever and intelligent girl such as yourself has seen them all for herself by now, have you not?

Eleanor bristled. It was not only De'Asterides's elephantine attempts at flattery that annoyed her, but more especially the redundancy of calling her *bright* and *clever* and *intelligent* in the same phrase. De'Asterides's stupidity was starting to annoy her. The man needed to work on his prose style.

We all have some concern for your safety in the hands of a ruffian such as Raspero, a man with no decency, no civilising qualities, a barbarous brute who is known to us for his dark deeds. If possible you must leave Westrigonia at the earliest opportunity. Come to Pentharborg where you will be safe. But should this prove difficult, or should you be obliged to remain in the midst of the barbarities of Raspero and his company, then you are hereby required and commanded by the order of the First Protector to observe on all the sayings and doings of Raspero and report all your observations to myself without delay. Any information you may provide us may be useful. Tell us what you can. We shall judge of its value.

Eleanor could not help but be infuriated by this latest comment. It was not so much that she was being asked to be a spy that annoyed her, although that was in fact an outrageous imposition on her noble nature. It was more the supercilious assumption on the part of De'Asterides that she would be a brainless spy incapable of understanding what was going on.

What your mother has told me gives me great concern. It is understandable that you should be so impressionable at your age, but the essence of this matter is clear beyond dispute. This supposed king is a fraud, he is nothing but an imposter. If Raspero has any claim to being a king it is only to that of being the monkey king. I cannot emphasize enough how far short his claim to the throne of Westrigonia will fall when the day of his reckoning shall come. There are matters of which I cannot speak yet, but I say this: if Raspero becomes King of Westrigonia, then I am not the First Protector of the Protectorate.

Eleanor paused here and re-read this passage. She was struck not only by the vehemence of De'Asterides's tone, but his certainty that Matthias would fail to become King. He was hinting at having a secret knowledge of current affairs that guaranteed this outcome, and Eleanor had the uneasy feeling that De'Asterides was not bluffing. De'Asterides knew something, that was clear. There was a plot to deal with Matthias of which De'Asterides was supremely confident.

It is all to easy to see how an impressionable young woman such as yourself, even the Jewel of Krastienst, might lack proper judgement in such circumstances, regardless of where such behaviour might leave your public reputation, which up till now has been spotless, given what the world knows of the Princess Eleanor.

Eleanor noted the implicit threat in the phrase *given what the world knows* and noted further that De'Asterides had obviously been informed that she and Matthias had a history. The gossip machine of Pentharborg must be in over-drive, Eleanor reflected to herself.

It must be forcibly brought to your attention that your whole future is at stake. One careless misstep on your part may imperil more than your reputation. The penalty of treason is death. You cannot in any way, shape or form assist Raspero in his plots against the well-being of your own family. I say this not because Westrigonia is important. Far from it. The municipal finances of the city of Troderent alone is a larger figure than Westrigonia's whole budget. Westrigonia is a backward, provincial country of negligible international importance. In any case, you must be very clear that Raspero will not, cannot, marry you under any circumstances. His nationalist followers will not stand for it. To them you are a foreigner, a Zoller-Abstein to boot, which makes you unacceptable to those who are so steeped in the nationalist tradition that they can think in no other terms but those of nationalism. To them you are a foreigner, and there is nothing you can say or do that will remove or re-direct their antagonism. Raspero, who knows this far better than you, will use you for his own ends. Do not trust him. Under no circumstances believe his lies. I repeat, do not trust Raspero under any circumstances. He is your enemy.

Eleanor took several steadying breaths, and continued reading.

I say again, come to Pentharborg if you can. If not, then remember that you are of the Zoller-Abstein family. I have nothing more to say to you than this: always bear in mind where your true loyalties lie.

I remain your true friend as always,

Braeden De'Asterides

Eleanor laid the letter down, and stared into the distance. After a while, she came to herself and realised that her ladies-in-waiting were all looking at her sideways while ostensibly contemplating their own distances.

'That man is a snake,' Eleanor declared, folding up the letter with a certain vehemence and stuffing it back into its envelope.

'But what did he say?' asked Nina.

'You do not want to know,' Eleanor replied, knowing full well of course that Nina *did* want to know.

'Well, of course I don't want to know,' Nina agreed. 'But how is he a snake?'

Eleanor felt her foreignness weigh on her at that moment. How could she tell her Westrigonian ladies-in-waiting that her Anglashian family wanted her to spy on Westrigonia? Did they suspect any such thing? And what would happen to them or their families if De'Asterides succeeded in his plans? They would have to come to Eleanor for protection against the First Protector. But what would Eleanor herself do? What would she have to do for the First Protector in order to be able to provide them with that protection? She would rather die than give him her supposedly generous heart, that was for sure.

'I will speak to the Marechal about this matter,' Eleanor declared in a tone of voice that made clear that her ladies-in-waiting were to enquire no further. 'That will be all.'

Eleanor felt completely alone.

And nothing more was said in the Chambers of the Crown Princess of Westrigonia.

4:40 PM, Wednesday 29 April 1882 A. F.

Having received a summons in the late morning from Lady Godelric to come and see her immediately, Alaric squared his shoulders, braced himself for battle, and went to the Hadewig Hotel much later in the day. Alaric was fed up with everything, and was determined to put an end to this situation without delay. It was not even clear to him how he had managed to wind up in such a mess, but recriminations would have to wait until he had accomplished his mission.

He spoke for some time with courtesy and consideration to a very attentive, if perhaps slightly amused, Lady Godelric. Fully aware of the sensitivities of the moment, he gave this matter his full attention in order to spare the feelings of the fair lady in front of him. He explained to Lady

Godelric, with references to history, mythology, the importance of family and the unfathomable intricacies of the human heart, that it would be best if they ceased to see each other. Alaric concluded by saying: 'It is not that I am not appreciative of how you have bestowed your affections on me. I am enormously flattered. Just about any man in the world would give anything to be where I am now. You are one of the great beauties of the age. But alas, it is time for us to go our separate ways bearing our precious memories of the times we have spent with each other.'

Lady Godelric threw back her head and laughed, her lips pulled back over her exceptionally white teeth like a yawning fox. Her laughter was surprisingly melodious and so pleasant to listen to that Alaric felt partly hypnotised by its modulated peals. This laughter, far from adding to Alaric's cheerfulness, subtracted even what little good humour he had left. Alaric had a sense of foreboding that things were not going well. Lady Godelric's laughter was, if listened to in the right way, like the bell tolling the news of doom.

'Who is she, my gallant Alaric?' Lady Godelric asked when she had at last stopped laughing.

'Who is who?' Alaric asked in genuine puzzlement.

'The lady whose charms have stolen your heart away like a thief in the night from all the rest of us lovelorn women dressed only in the cotton shift of our contemplations and shorn of your affections like a sheep shorn of its wool.'

Lady Godelric's metaphors made no sense to Alaric, but the general trend of her questioning seemed worryingly clear. 'What do you mean?'

'You are in love with someone. Who is it?' Lady Godelric was no longer being pleasant. Her face had become hard, and her eyes hostile.

'No, not at all, you are mistaken. There is no-one of this sort, absolutely not.' Alaric might have been one of the top forgers in the world, but he was hopeless at lying.

'Does she have brothers? An elderly father, not of good health? A family upon whom misfortune may fall like savage wolves on a child in the woods? Well?'

'I don't follow you,' Alaric said quite truthfully.

Lady Godelric leaned back in her chair and shifted around as if erotically stirred by everything that was happening. 'My gallant Alaric, *you* have stolen *my* heart, and what am I to do now, how can I stop you so heartlessly spurning me and walking out of the door after having taken from me what I should not have given you? Yet you were so overpowering, so demanding, that I yielded to your imperial mastery. Yet now that you have taken from me what I should not have given to you, it is incumbent on you as a gentleman, as a man of honour, to remain as my paramour. A gentleman would not spurn me in this manner. Are you not a gentleman?'

'Ah, affairs of the heart do happen, this kind of situation is regrettable and of course frowned on by society but still, between the two of us we can agree to move on without recriminations. I assure you I would like us to remain friends and on the best of terms.'

Alaric had little hope that what he had just said would make any difference to how things were going, and he was not wrong.

'My gallant Alaric, I cannot remain silent about your brutal treatment of me. You have taken advantage of a vulnerable woman, and in a moment of weakness I allowed you to make me mine. As I say, I cannot remain silent about this. I have many admirers, among whom are the best wandfighters in the country. I shall insist that you yourself are left alone. But as for your father, your two brothers, the husband of your sister, I cannot promise that they may not face challenges. There are men who will seek to avenge my dishonour at your hands, and as I say, they will spare you because of my great love for you, but your family, alas, cannot be spared likewise. And as for the girl to whom your affections have been bestowed, I assure you, that once it becomes known far and wide how you have used me, she will have nothing to do with you, especially with the body count mounting up. And I shall keep my eyes and ears open for a girl weeping her eyes out, perhaps in the Palace, and when I have learned of such a one, I shall see to it that her family is destroyed along with your own. Now tell me, my gallant young Alaric, are you still quite so determined to discard me like a glove of yesterday?'

'Surely you are not making quite such open threats,' Alaric said disbelievingly.

Lady Godelric rose to her feet and walked slowly with swaying hips to the bedroom door. There she stopped and looked back at Alaric. 'I do not make threats, my gallant lover. I only draw conclusions. Now I offer you this choice. You may leave and become my enemy, or you may follow me and remain my lover. Make your choice, my beloved Alaric.'

Lady Godelric stepped through the bedroom door. Alaric stayed where he was for some moments, as if thinking; but there was nothing to think about. He was not able to act as if for himself alone. After a while, Alaric rose to his feet and strode forward and, with a silent inward groan, passed over the threshold into the bedroom beyond.

CHAPTER THIRTY FOUR

I am Shakespeare today,
So pay attention. There are:
5 chaffinches singing in the garden,
2 lizards slow-moving on the desert rock,
5 horses galloping through the arched city gate,
6 fiances standing in line for the Crown Princess,
And one deep bow to the difference.
Frankie the Villain

2:30 PM, Wednesday 29 April 1882 A. F.

Eleanor's long black hair was braided and coiled around her head, and wrapped with a gold wire netting threaded with green and white gemstones, while diamond earrings sparkled high above her bare shoulders. Her strapless low-cut dark green dress, pulled in tight around her narrow waist, gleamed with velvety hues up and down the length of her slim, long-legged figure. As always when alone with the Jewel of Krastienst, Matthias had to make a special effort not to stare.

Matthias and Eleanor were walking towards the Clearing of Apparent Conduct in the centre of the Palace Gardens, next to the Rose Garden. Eleanor had taken it upon herself to lecture Matthias about this place as they strolled along: its history, the plants and trees, the dietary habits of the occasional wandering peacock, as if to emphasize her long association with this place was in effect to establish her credentials as the proprietor of the Palace of Krastienst. She was the gracious hostess, and Matthias was her guest. Matthias nodded as if listening attentively, while stealing the occasional glance at her cleavage and barely hearing a word. Eleanor's beauty was having an almost hypnotic effect on Matthias, who felt like a leaf being swept along by a swift-flowing stream. The thirty-seventh Baron of Raspero took a deep breath and looked into the distance in order to gather his scattered faculties.

'Shall we sit down here?' Eleanor asked. It was an instruction rather than a question, as Eleanor promptly settled down comfortably on a nearby carved wrought-iron chair, waving Matthias to do likewise.

They sat there in silence while Matthias gazed with an open admiration at his companion. Luckily Eleanor was used to being stared at and so bore his scrutiny with equanimity.

'I have received a letter from the First Protector,' Eleanor remarked.

'That is only to be expected,' Matthias replied casually.

His insouciance infuriated Her Royal Highness the Crown Princess Eleanor. 'Perhaps the contents of the letter are also *only to be expected*.'

Matthias shrugged. 'No doubt he told you not to trust me but to trust him instead.'

'And can I trust you?'

'I am not yet corrupted by power.'

'Not *yet*.'

'Exactly, not *yet*. So you can trust me for the time being.'

Eleanor smiled politely as if in appreciation of this witty response, while privately contemplating how she would like to cut off Matthias's head and boil it in a vat. 'I cannot tell you how reassured I am by your courtesy and consideration at this time.' She spoke evenly and calmly with the utmost consideration.

'What are you in such a temper about?' Matthias asked cautiously. He was surprised by all this, having been under the impression that for once they were taking things easy.

'I am *not*,' Eleanor said, breathing deeply to control her temper, 'in a temper.'

Matthias groaned as if in surrender. 'Alright, fine, this letter from

De'Asterides. I am utterly untrustworthy, a dodgy Westrigonian whose character can never measure up to the Anglashian standards of the Zoller-Abstein clan, is that right? If you sign up with his Eminence the First Protector, all you wish for will be granted you, but if you choose otherwise you will be disowned and disinherited and cast out from the circle of civilisation. Is that it or have I missed anything out?'

'That is essentially it,' Eleanor replied, careful not to let her voice shake. 'And what do you have to say for yourself?'

Matthias paused, and contemplated this question as if it were a fierce dog that would bite if it were not fed. 'Believe it or not, you do have your good points.'

'Such as my beauty, no doubt.'

'Now that you mention it, yes.'

'But there are other ways for you to slake your thirst for my beauty short of marriage, are there not?'

'Relax, Eleanor. I'm not going to lift a finger against you. You have my word.'

'Your baronial word.'

'I increasingly can't see how I'm going to get out of being king. Every move I make to defend myself against my enemies defines another step on my path to the throne. Some people mock the idea that Fortuna rules the world because they believe in free will. But right now where's my freedom, I ask you?'

'Perhaps it is in the same place as my sympathy for your whining complaints, sobbing on its shoulder.'

'I am reminded yet again why I want to marry you,' Matthias said with an impish grin.

'And I am reminded yet again of why I do not.'

Matthias groaned theatrically. 'Well, I obviously have to improve my courting game. If I bend the knee and swing from the shoulder, that might do it.'

'Matthias, why do you want to marry me?'

'Believe it or not, you do have some good points other than your beauty.'

'Such as?'

'You could probably carry off the business of being either baroness or queen quite well.'

'*Probably?*'

'Alright, *definitely*. You over-react to the least thing I say nowadays. How am I to court you in a warm-hearted, spontaneous yet carefully considered fashion if my every step is on eggshells?'

'I will give some thought to your predicament once you have given some thought to mine.'

'Eleanor, you're over-reacting to this letter from De'Asterides. No doubt he also wants you to spy on me as well. This is precisely what the nationalists will accuse you of in due course anyway, whatever you do. What do you want me to say anyway? Welcome to the world of politics! If you continue on in public life, you'd better get used to secret letters and double-dealing and the like.'

'Is there any double-dealing in this instance?'

'You can't trust De'Asterides, believe me. He will use you to get what he wants, and discard you if necessary.'

'That is precisely what he says of you.'

'Then you have to make a choice, don't you?'

'Do you doubt the choice I will make?'

'Look, you are old enough to make your own choice, but if you are so determined to get my advice, then fine, here it is. Write De'Asterides a letter making it clear that your loyalty is with Westrigonia. Burn your boats behind you by telling him to get lost in so plain a fashion that there can be no mistaking your allegiances.'

Eleanor felt her heart become lighter on hearing this. She had already known all this herself, but had allowed this clear knowledge to become shrouded in a fog of personal doubts. To hear things stated so plainly dispelled the fog. Everything was much clearer. She found herself looking forward to writing De'Asterides a letter that would burn his ears. She titled her chin upwards and replied, 'So, that is your advice. Others would advocate prevarication.'

'Prevarication will do you little good in these fast-moving circumstances. You have to make a choice now.'

'As do you. Why is it exactly that you want to marry me?'

For once, Matthias did not take refuge in humour but looked steadily at her. Eleanor met his gaze, but she felt her stomach turn over with trepidation at the seriousness of his gaze. She was reminded of how apprehensive she was deep down that Matthias might be perfectly sincere in his courtship of her; and while she of course wanted to know if this was so, she also did not want to know.

Matthias was struck by how green her eyes were as she looked at him. It was not just that: her lips were as red as a rose moistened with the early morning dew, her skin as pale and clean as the snow fresh-fallen during the night, her hair as black as the blackness of the night between the glittering ice-white brightness of the stars, and he could even smell the freshness of her scent as if she were in his arms at that very moment. Her beauty tilted the plane of Matthias's mind like a boat on the slope of a deepening oceanic swell.

'I could list all the reasons in your favour, but that would merely be dissembling. The truth is that I love you.'

'But how can you love me? You do not know me.'

'Of course I know you. How can I not know you? I knew you from the moment I first met you. Surely you can say the same of me?'

'Far from it. But what do you know of me then?'

'I know you well enough, believe me. We understood each other from the very beginning. I trust you completely even though you make my head spin around in six different directions. What is that if not love?'

'It might well be your mental feebleness.'

'From the way you insult me, we might as well be married already.'

'Matthias, you still have not answered the question I originally asked you. I asked you: why do you want to marry me? Well? What is the answer to that question?'

Matthias contemplated this question for a moment, then replied: 'You are very beautiful, Eleanor. Any man would want to marry you.'

'And?'

'Well, you are of good character, you are intelligent, well brought-up, well spoken, observant, strong-willed and decisive, so I think all in all you are quite an amazing catch for any man.'

'And?'

'And what? Am I supposed to continue? What else is there to say? You are the complete package, Eleanor. You are a beautiful princess straight out of a fairy tale. No-one asks the hero of a fairy tale *why* he wants to marry the princess. He just does. That's just how it is. And if you stop to think about it, that is exactly how it should be. The laws of the story-telling universe demand no less. Surely someone as sophisticated and educated as yourself does not need to be told this?'

Eleanor was unmoved by Matthias's transparent flattery, and equally unmoved by his literary equivocations. She spoke in Anglashian as if to make her point sideways to an Westrigonian baron directly in line for the throne. '<Matthias, I am not out of a fairy tale. Regrettably, or not, I am out of Anglashia. Yes, I am beautiful, but so are many other women. Yes, I am praiseworthy in all the ways which you mentioned, but the question as to *why you want to marry me* remains unanswered. Please answer it, if you can.>'

'But I have answered it! Very well, you consider my answer incomplete. But what should I do? I have settled upon you as the summation of all my queries on the nature of womanhood. You are the One, Eleanor. What else can I say?'

'You do realise, do you not, that I do not like you at all?'

Matthias groaned and rolled his eyes skyward. 'And what am I supposed to say now? Alright, I'll bite on your obvious bait. Please tell me, oh Jewel of Krastienst, why it is that you do not like me at all?'

'Shall I start with the seventy two obvious points, or proceed immediately to the two hundred and sixteen less obvious points?'

'You liked me at one point. You did let me kiss you, after all.'

'No, Matthias, I did not *let* you kiss me. You stole that kiss. It was an act of theft, and I have never forgiven you for it.'

'Ah, in any case, we were kids. So – '

'You have not changed since then, so you are still guilty, being unchanged.'

'My point is that you did like me when we were kids. Did you not?'

There was a pause while they looked at each other.

'Yes,' Eleanor conceded grudgingly. 'I did like you when we were kids. Happy now?'

'Ecstatic! But if you liked me then, why are you so opposed to any chance of liking me now?'

'Because you betrayed me then, that is why. What am I supposed to do now, wait for you to betray me again?'

'I did not betray you. My father forbade me to ever contact you again.'

'What?'

'You heard me.'

'Why did he do that?'

'He said he would cut my balls off if I ever tried to contact you again.'

'Thank you, Matthias, for that definition of the verb *forbade*. But my question remains unanswered. *Why* did he forbid you to contact me again?'

Matthias looked away from Eleanor and contemplated the garden for a while. 'There are a lot of things that I do not know exactly.'

Eleanor noted how Matthias was avoiding eye contact and commented: 'But I suspect that you do know some things approximately, do you not?'

'Are we to deal with approximations? That's fine, as long as I am not to be held *exactly* accountable for them.'

Eleanor sighed. 'Matthias, I already know that your father was of the faction opposed to the Zoller-Abstein monarchy. But perhaps I have said too much already.'

'I am sure that you know more than me about everything. In any case, what is past is past. Is that not so?'

'Do you suspect my parents of having a hand in your father's death?'

'No. I know who killed him, and it had nothing to do with Frederick and Yolande.'

'Who was behind it?'

'The First Protector, with Phelan as his instrument.'

'Why did you not try to get my help when your father was killed? We could have become allies then. Why have you ignored me all this time?'

'I have not ignored you all this time. I have followed events in Westrigonia closely all this time. You have often been in my thoughts. I never thought that we would meet again, but I have never ignored you.'

'Did you have a spy report on me?'

'Definitely not,' Matthias lied with perfect fluency.

'So when was it that you decided to marry me?'

'The idea has been growing on me over the past few days. Had you left for Pentharborg with your mother, I would have given up on it. But you stayed here, and that was when I decided to marry you if you would have me.'

'Well, I will not marry you, so that is that.'

'But I will not argue with you if you reject my suit either because you do not want to marry me or because you choose to become Queen instead. After all, I will return to Raspero if I do not become king. To tell the truth, I would prefer not to be king if possible.'

'Stop right there! You plotted and schemed to put yourself where you are now. And don't deny it.'

'I don't deny it. But my endgame is not necessarily to be king. But in any case, my plotting and scheming, as you put it, was not to put myself exactly where I am now. Things were not supposed to turn out this way. You and Yolande were supposed to withdraw to Pentharborg. I was going to go to Raspero from where I could barter away my kingship for the full restoration of my inheritance. Whether or not Frederick and Yolande returned to the thrones or whether or not a new set of monarchs were chosen, was an incidental matter as far as I was concerned. Whether or not Westrigonia itself survived was not my concern. The barony of Raspero preceded Westrigonia, and it could just as well succeed it as well. Who knows? You have to understand, Eleanor, that for seven years I have thought of nothing else but returning to my ancestral lands. But I was forced to change my plans when I heard of your predicament. As the saying goes, no battle plan survives contact with the enemy. When the Baalbabakan delegation burned out the exit portal of the Palace, thus leaving you and Yolande trapped here, I changed my plan and came straight here to the capital. I had made arrangements in the Waiting Room of the Portal by which to capture the Palace if that became necessary in the long run, only to find that I had to activate that plan straightaway. I came here to save you. I give you my word of honour that this is the truth.'

Eleanor looked away from Matthias and looked into the distance and said nothing. Matthias had the good sense not to say anything. After a while Eleanor said, sidestepping all the issues which Matthias had raised, 'But now that you are here, changed plans or no, you can actually become king rather than bargaining the opportunity away. Given that your plans have changed once, they can be changed again.'

'It is a possibility, Eleanor, and I am not ruling it out. But for now, my original plan remains as it was. Now that you are safe, as soon as I can I will go to Raspero and follow my original game-plan.'

'But why stop at being a baron when you could be a king?'

'You don't understand, Eleanor, because you still have something of the Anglashian mentality. If you pride yourself so much on being Westrigonian, then try to understand this: to be Baron of Raspero is a magnificent thing. Believe me.'

'But of course it is. But take this from the Crown Princess of Westrigonia who calls the Palace of Krastienst home. To be King is much more magnificent. Believe me.'

'You have never even been to Raspero.'

'Yes, I am sure that means that I haven't lived. Excuse me for my royal provincial backwardness. Merely to have seen the greatest palaces in the world, including Pentharborg, which could fit the Palace of Krastienst in the servants' quarters, and your castle in the stables, is not enough to prepare me for the magnificence of Raspero. Shall I hang my head in shame?'

'Eleanor, you have still not answered my question. Would becoming Queen preclude you from becoming the Baroness of Raspero?'

'Why should one preclude the other? Being king would not stop you from being Baron of Raspero as well. All kings have other titles, various estates, sundry honours and recognitions. I could just as easily be Queen and Baroness and Countess and whatever else I could manage to grab. But surely you understand these elementary issues? What if marrying me helped you win the vote in the second Vidaldmeet? If you become king, being baron as well will be merely a formality.'

'Eleanor, I have repeatedly referred to the second Vidaldmeet. This does not mean that it will happen.'

'What do you mean?'

'Exactly what I say.'

'But what is it that you *are* saying?'

'I am saying that when everyone's eyes are fixed on one side of the stage, the other side can be put into play.'

'What does *that* mean?'

Matthias sighed. 'Eleanor, there is not going to be a second Vidaldmeet until certain conditions have been fulfilled. Unfortunately for you, the Zoller-Abstein faction in Westrigonia are on the way out. Nothing personal. This is only business, nothing more.'

'You plan to kill them, or dispossess them?'

'No, nothing so drastic. I am not cutting anyone's head off, trust me. I am not going to be a second Justin the Second. No, once they realise that their titles and estates will still be theirs once they change allegiances, then they will change allegiances.'

'And if they don't?'

'Then what must be done will be done. But these are all speculations.'

Matthias was about to say more, but the crunching of gravel of running footsteps approaching their grotto made him turn his head and slide the handle of his wand into the palm of his hand. The alertness of his wandfighter's demeanour reminded Eleanor that they were still at war, and the lassitude of peace was a luxury which only tomorrow could promise to lay at their feet.

A messenger came into view in his red-and-gold uniform. He ran up to Matthias, sank onto one knee and said: 'Marechal, there is a request from Pentharborg for a delegation to come immediately to the Palace.'

'Ah,' Matthias said with a little smile, 'so we are come to that so soon. Go and tell Steindahl to call the Palace Guard to the Portal. Tell Wright that he may inform the delegation that they may come as soon as we signal them that we are ready.'

'Yes, Marechal,' the messenger replied with an obedient bow of his head, and stood up and promptly ran off.

'We must return, Eleanor,' Matthias said, standing up and offering her his hand.

Eleanor ignored his hand and stood up by her own devices. Matthias hardly noticed, so distracted was the look on his face.

They set off for the Portal. Eleanor's sideways look told her that Matthias's mind was back in the labyrinth of worldly politics. She was free now to consider her feelings about what Matthias had just told her, yet once again she avoided opening that door. She needed the complete privacy and seclusion of her Chambers in order to shut out the world entirely for such an important moment of introspection. Besides, she had to keep her wits about her and pay attention to this forthcoming visit of the delegation from Pentharborg.

'When you say, Matthias, that *we are come to that so soon*, what is it that we are come to?'

'You will get hysterical if I tell you, so I will not.'

'I will now get angry if you don't tell me, given what you have just said.'

'You want to be Queen, Eleanor? Very well. Let us see if you have the nerve. But first, what would you suppose yourself to be the point of such a delegation?'

Eleanor thought about this. 'To explore the possibility of negotiations, try to gain some sort of rapport, a kind of fishing expedition, among other things.'

'Good. That is what this is supposedly about on the surface. But what is the real point of this visit?'

Eleanor thought for a while, then gave up. 'You tell me.'

'It is to assassinate me.'

'Matthias, you are not serious.'

'And I will allow the visit to proceed, but don't worry. I will take precautions to safeguard my life. Trust me, this is something that I have become adept at over the years.'

'You cannot possibly allow this delegation to even enter the Palace Portal if this is what they are about! I will not allow it! This is my home too.'

Matthias stopped and turned to face her. There was an implacable look about him that reminded her of the stone-faced government officials who had informed her parents of the necessity of some hard-hearted government policy or other. 'If you wish to be Queen, Eleanor, then be prepared for days such as this. Either you can take it or you cannot. But perhaps you wish to whine that you are not yet ready.'

Eleanor said nothing, taken aback by the suddenness of Matthias's attack and forced further on the back-foot by the seriousness of his demeanour.

'Come with me or go to your room and hide from today's troubles,' Matthias said as if speaking to a child, 'but do not distract me more than you have already. Your hysterical reaction is not helping me. If you persist in pestering me, I will have you escorted away until this is all over. Now, if you will excuse me, I have to focus very carefully on what is about to unfold.'

With that, Matthias turned on his heel and strode onwards, his mind already elsewhere. Eleanor followed, biting her lower lip to keep her from speaking further. She could tell from the set of Matthias's shoulders that he meant what he had said, so she said nothing more.

CHAPTER THIRTY FIVE

Why do women cry at weddings?
Frankie the Villain

4:45 PM, Wednesday 29 April 1882 A. F.

Matthias disposed his forces in the Waiting Room of the Portal with a strategic care that did something to soothe Eleanor's nerves. She found that her heart was beating rapidly, like a captive bird held gently immobile in a strong pair of hands. Her ladies-in-waiting stood anxiously by her side, as if somehow aware of her state of nerves. Eleanor wondered to herself for a moment if being Queen would really include days such as this. She had not seen her parents have to endure such uncertainty, but then, their circumstances would not necessarily be hers. She was struck all of a sudden by the thought that the blood-soaked days of the past, so securely wrapped up in the pages of history and separated from the present, might well abruptly resurface. She had herself been personally threatened by the invaders in a manner beyond the circle of civilisation by having been made the object of a lottery. Now her own family wished to assassinate Matthias. For a moment, it occurred to her that to be the Baroness of Raspero might not be quite the demotion she had at first supposed.

Captain Steindahl and the Palace Guard had received their instructions from the Marechal. 'Very likely, the assassins will be four in number. They will almost certainly be Force Nine soldiers. Look for those amongst the visitors who look like well-trained solders. You are not to use discs. You are only to use karns.'

The air shimmered, and suddenly there were twenty number of people standing in the Portal, which were the maximum number allowed. Matthias identified the four assassins straightaway. Although dressed in the robes of noblemen, they wore the black boots with silver buckles that only Force Nine soldiers were allowed to wear. Amongst the other members of the delegation from Pentharborg were Frederick, Yolande and Jason. Camdenshall was also amongst their number.

The leader of the delegation was Lord Augustus Sandalio, who was short and fat and had a monocle on a golden chain dangling on his breast. He came towards Matthias, halted and bowed and said: 'Lord Raspero, we thank you for receiving us. It is really very kind of you.'

'Sit down,' Matthias said briefly, waving with his left hand to the chairs facing him. It sounded as if he was being rude, but truth to tell, even Matthias, who had nerves of steel, was having to remember to breathe. He was so hyped up that sounds seemed louder than usual, and colours seemed brighter. Sandalio sat in the chair facing Matthias, while one assassin sat beside Sandalio, and the other three sat further away.

Matthias knew that the signal to attack would be given by Sandalio, but he wasn't sure what the signal would be, or how long Sandalio would wait before issuing the order to attack. It would not come straight away, because everyone, especially Matthias the target, would have to relax by listening to the hypnotic cadences of Sandalio's opening speech. Matthias guessed that the attack would come when Sandalio finished speaking, and it became Matthias's turn to speak. That seemed logical.

Sandalio droned on for some time about Westrigonia, which he praised to the skies, and the Protectorate, which he acknowledged had been at fault in not coming to Westrigonia's assistance earlier. He made a passing reference to the invasions of Baalbabak and Melisende by the forces of the Protectorate, and then concluded his remarks by saying that he looked forward to hearing what Lord Raspero now had to say, even concluding his speech by using the phrase *over to you*.

Everything happened faster than all-at-once. Suddenly Matthias was not sitting in his chair as four discs slammed into its oaken backing with a multiple impact that echoed around the Waiting Room of the Portal, burying themselves a third of their length into the wood, such was the ferocity of their velocity. Simultaneously with the flight of the discs came four figures flying through the air, wand-hands moving forward and then down to their feet to govern their motion. They were in a Y-shaped formation, straight out of the textbook.

Unluckily for them, Matthias had read that textbook.

5:05 PM, Wednesday 29 April 1882 A. F.

Matthias had tracked the sudden surge of wand-energy just before the attack, and rose on the instant into the air while the discs whizzed past underneath him to whack into the back of the chair he had just been sitting on. Matthias knew that the Force 9 assassins knew that their target had an SES force field at his disposal. Their strategy would be to rely on surprise and speed. Yet having missed their target, their mission had already failed. It would now be the pleasure of the Marechal of Westrigonia to spell out the word m-i-s-s-e-d. He had made sure to make plenty of eye-contact with his would-be assassins during Sandalio's speech, thus ensuring a loss of confidence on their part even before they had jumped into action. With the SES force-field at his disposal, he could now deal with them at his leisure.

Matthias had nick-named his opponents Curly, Flat-nose, Impatient and Edgy. He took hold of Curly by his own mobile karns and threw him against Impatient, while taking both their wands off them. Flat-nose and Edgy were thrown against each other and their wands were taken. Matthias then bound them all in mid-air with their own mobile karns in motions so fast that they looked like one seamless continuous motion. After this, the Marechal of Westrigonia let them all fall from the air onto the ground with painful, bruising thuds.

By now, Steindahl and the Palace guards were in action, binding all the members of the Pentharborg delegation to their chairs with mobile karns. Steindahl himself was lashing out in all directions with his wand out-stretched, like a maddened wasp-nest in human form.

Seeing that it was over and that Matthias was safe, Eleanor lowered her chin to her chest with a moan.

Matthias then made a statement which his biographers would make famous through the ages. 'Your attempted assassination of me has brought this meeting to an end. After all, you would have not have tried to kill me if you had anything left to say.' (The precise phrasing which Matthias himself had used was never to be recorded for posterity with any degree of certainty. The state of shock which everyone was in was to blame for this. No less than fifty-four paraphrases were eventually to compete for public acceptance. The surviving witnesses to this event could only agree that none of these paraphrases was the exact phrasing used by Matthias the Fourth himself, which had been immeasurably superior. Matthias had, in the words of one of these witnesses, "absolutely nailed the whole situation in such an evocative and poetic expression as to leave us all laughing." This particular witness, while not remembering the exact words used, insisted that Matthias had said something like: 'I can only say goodbye to men who have just this very minute tried to kill me. So goodbye!' Translations into other languages such as Anglashian were only to complicate this matter beyond all hope of a simple resolution.)

'<I had absolutely no idea that this would happen,>' Sandalio said, attempting to sound as convincing as he could. '<I am shocked and outraged at the behaviour of these mavericks, these assassins whose presence in our midst is due to subterfuge and imposture.>' He opened his eyes as wide as he could as if that would make him look *shocked and outraged*.

'Ah!' Matthias exclaimed, nodding in a perfectly mocking understanding. 'Of course you didn't know. The phrase <over to you> with which you concluded your opening remarks was without doubt not the signal for these assassins to attack me. By the way, the next time Force Nine soldiers go undercover to assassinate someone, might I suggest that they do not wear their distinctive boots which only Force Nine soldiers are allowed to wear? It's just a thought. I'm only saying. In any case, I will respect the safe conduct which you requested and received. My understanding of this matter is that even the assassins themselves must be allowed to go free, given that all of you received safe conduct. But I will say this. From this day forth, we will know in Westrigonia what to make of the Protectorate. You have shamed yourself in the eyes of the world, and all you can do now is whine. Worst of all, you have shown yourself incompetent not only at invading other countries, but at such a simple matter as killing a single person standing in front of you. Just how pathetically inept are you?'

Every Westrigonian present thoroughly enjoyed watching the expressions on the faces of their Anglashian opponents as Matthias's statement was translated to them. But then Yolande spoke out so as to re-direct proceedings into another direction entirely.

'<I would speak with you alone, if I may, Marechal,>' Yolande asked loudly.

She had spoken more loudly than she intended, out of a fear of not being heard. She seemed to have more shouted than anything else; but she did not care. She could not care less about anything except saying goodbye to all this. She was ready to trample upon anything that stood in her way, including good manners.

'<Of course,>' Matthias said, inclining his head with his usual courtesy. He turned aside, and with a few hand gestures and accompanying words, conveyed the instructions to Captain Steindahl that Yolande was to be allowed to approach him while the remaining members of the delegation would be confined in their current places as prisoners.

Eleanor rose to her feet to follow Matthias and Yolande. Her ladies-in-waiting made ready to follow *her*, and several other members of the court made ready to follow *them*. 'Only Eleanor!' Matthias ordered, waving everyone else back. The disgruntled ladies-in-waiting settled back in their chairs, along with everyone else.

Matthias led the two women to the side and gestured them to chairs while he sat down himself and stretched out with his feet on a footstool.

Yolande sat straight-backed and calm, her hands folded in her lap. Eleanor knew her mother well enough to tell how nervous she was under her carefully composed demeanour. Matthias she could not yet read as easily, but this she did know, whether as a matter of insight or deduction: he saw this meeting as a move in a game of chess, and he already knew what pieces he wanted to move. Eleanor readied herself to pay attention.

'<How it is that I am help you, Yolande?>' Matthias asked in a friendly manner.

Eleanor noted how Matthias was already treating Yolande as a supplicant. Yolande had had to all but beg for this meeting, and Matthias was driving that point home by being so friendly.

Yolande might not have noticed this snobbish condescension on the part of Matthias, so intent was she on her next statement. '<I have decided that I will support your claim to be King of Westrigonia,>' she declared.

Matthias nodded to show that he had heard her. '<And it is in return you are want what?>'

Eleanor almost winced at the bluntness with which this was spoken. It was almost contemptuous on Matthias's part, yet Matthias was not a contemptuous person. Eleanor saw what this was really about: it was what Matthias wanted that was the key point, and Matthias would get what he wanted or else!

There was another level of subtlety on Matthias's part, Eleanor noted; Yolande's support, so highly prized as it might be in other circumstances, was being treated as merely a bauble.

'<I wish to go directly to Troderent when I leave Krastienst, from the portal here under your control to that of my home country.>'

Matthias paused at this, and Eleanor could see that he had not seen this coming. '<It is also question what it is of your husband to this matter?>'

Yolande shrugged. '<What of him? He can go back to the First Protector and the latest woman with whom he shares his bed.>'

Such plain speaking made Matthias pause before replying.

'<If it is that Frederick is say, oh no, it is that you are return with delegation, then it is the difficult situation of the diplomatic protocol, you are understand this, it is, well, the multifarious aspects of such matters like to these of the difficult diplomacy, so if it is that he is to kick up the fuss then what it is that I say of him for this matter?>'

'<They just tried to kill you!>' Yolande pointed out. '<You don't have to pay them any attention at all. Let them say what they want!>'

Matthias shook his head. '<I wish only that it is that things are being so simple. They are owe me now, you are understand me, it is the ground

that is high, the negotiating advantage of such bargainings, because from what they try do it is that First Protector has the lot to explain. But now if it is from me the diplomatic controversy, it is that it is the confuse the issue, so it is from they have done this thing wrong and now I also am the guilty one as well so it is not the high ground of my feet after this change.>'

'<But surely you cannot mean that!>' Yolande sounded desperate.

'<Mother,>' Eleanor said gently, '<ask Matthias what he wants from you in return for this favour.>'

Yolande looked at her daughter briefly, then turned back to Matthias. '<What do you want from me in return for this favour?>' she asked as meekly as if obeying orders.

Matthias looked at Eleanor as if trying to remember what she was doing there, then said: '<Well, if it is that I am incur such the incubating detraction as it is of this, the uninvited and unwelcome one of not the other moment, then it is the compensation that is the meet one, when it is that all things considered for this time.>' Matthias paused, as if to lengthen the looks they were giving him, then made his demand: '<Very well. If it is that you are appoint me as Marechal of Westrigonia after it is that delegation is go from this place, then it is that I am say yes, that it is you are go from here Troderent and it is not person to stop you, not husband Frederick nor the other person of any place here now.>'

Eleanor's brain almost leaped out of her skull with its acrobatic somersaulting. Matthias was already King, so he was already Marechal by his own appointment of himself as Marechal. He did not need Yolande's appointment; yet he did! Otherwise he wouldn't be making such a big deal of this. Eleanor could see very clearly, with crystal clear clarity, that this was what Matthias had wanted all along. Yet why should he want this when he already had it? This did not make sense. It made no sense at all. But if Eleanor knew anything at all, it was that Matthias was making a play for something that he needed to have; and now that she came to think of it, Matthias had wanted this from the beginning, right from when he had first arrived in the Palace of Krastienst.

'<There is no need to involve my husband in my future travel plans,>'

Yolande said hastily. '<He need only be told that I will not be leaving with him today, but staying here in Krastienst. After all, I – >'

'<Alright,>' Matthias agreed, nodding as if to emphasize that his interruption was only the extension of his agreement with what she was saying, '<you are stay here, others go, it is not for them know more than this, only that you are stay here. Tomorrow morning, you are appoint me Marechal of Westrigonia with due legality and in full accordance with the constitution of Westrigonia, and when it is you are do this, you are leave Krastienst portal and are go Troderent portal. On this I give you my word.>'

Of everything that Matthias had just said Eleanor had heard, emphasized above all else, the phrase: *in full accordance with the constitution of Westrigonia*; this had to be the central point to Matthias's political manoeuvring. It had even for once been phrased in correct Anglashian grammar, as if Matthias had made the effort of at least getting this particular statement exactly right by memorizing it. Eleanor thought to herself that if she could understand this, she could understand everything that Matthias was up to at the present moment. But Yolande's appointment could only be meaningful if – Ah! Everything snapped into focus and Eleanor all-of-a-sudden understood what Matthias was about.

Yolande, for her part, seemed to have just heard what related to her desire: '<I appoint you Marechal, you allow me to go home to Troderent. That is what you are saying?>'

Matthias nodded. Then he said, almost as if taking a break from his demanding regal duties to talk like a normal human being, '<You are say Troderent is home of you but I wish that it is that here of Krastienst, that it is home of you here.>' Matthias spoke with perfect seriousness, as if he wished that this was so; and with another flash of insight, Eleanor saw that this was nothing less than the truth. Matthias, she realised with an abrupt focus of her mind that was so acute that she could have counted the flappings of a fly's wings, wanted still to be the second son of the Baron of Raspero, with Frederick and Yolande on the throne and a world of undeclared potential at his feet. So much more than this might have happened in his life that becoming King was almost a demotion, or, if not quite that, at least a less varied life than what might have conceivably been. In short, Matthias was still a boy at heart who would rather be a pirate than a king.

Yolande looked at Matthias, as if she had never seen him before, and said: '<No-one will miss me here.>'

It was an oblique response, but Matthias understood her perfectly. '<I will miss you here.>'

He said nothing more but looked directly at Yolande, who looked away, as if confused by what might be being asked of her. '<I am surprised that you should say such a thing. After all, your own father wished me gone.>'

Matthias looked away from Yolande, and bowed his head to his chest. He reflected a moment, and then said without looking up again: '<So it is agreement for us, yes, it is so? I allow you go Troderent after you are appoint me Marechal. Yes?>'

Yolande was silent a moment, as if the questions she would have liked to ask were delaying her ready acceptance of all that she yearned for, but then she turned to Eleanor, as if only then remembering the presence of her daughter, and asked: '<And what of you, Eleanor? We must now make arrangements for you to come home with me.>'

'<I am home, Mother. I am the Crown Princess of Westrigonia, and when I marry, I will be Queen of Westrigonia. This Palace where we are now talking is my home. I wish you well in your own travels.>'

Yolande breathed deeply in and out, looking at her daughter as if not knowing what to say, almost envious of another's certainty.

At the thought of returning home to the family estates in Troderent, Yolande had all the feelings of a prisoner about to be released from her confinement. Among these there were feelings of guilt, of not doing her duty as she should. She had only come to Westrigonia to be Queen out of a sense of duty. She had not wanted to leave behind all that she knew and loved, all that was familiar to her, the life that she was happy with, but she was a wife and daughter and daughter-in-law and mother and so she accepted her new role as Queen. From the moment she had arrived in Westrigonia, she had not liked anything about this strange and foreign country. It was with a certain feeling of resentment that she would sit through security briefings which explained how Westrigonians animated with nationalist sentiments could prove a danger to the well-being of her and her family; if her resentment had taken the form of words, those words would have been: "Do you really think I want to live in this God-awful country in the first place?"

But naturally she had not said anything like that out loud, not even privately to her husband, who she could see had his own difficulties to surmount, and needed all the encouragement he could get; it was obvious to her that his spirits were hanging by a thread in any case.

Now she could go home. She would go up to the Long Room, curl up on her favourite sofa and have the servants bring her cups of sweet tea while she read the latest novels or looked out over the East Garden; she would have nothing whatsoever to do except what she lazily chose to pencil into her calendar.

There was freedom, the freedom of complete idleness, but the feelings of a prisoner being released are not as simple as those of merely anticipating a freedom to be enjoyed. There is also the prison that is being left behind to consider. She would leave her daughter behind, and her husband, and her duty. As for her husband and her duty, those she felt she had served well enough, but there remained her daughter. She looked at Eleanor as if wondering how well she knew her.

'<Once I leave here tomorrow I cannot protect you.>'

'<I am the Crown Princess of Westrigonia, here in my own country. Where else can I be better protected than here?>'

'<Lord Raspero will safeguard your well-being, without doubt, but if you return home with me, I will see to it that you are well taken care of in all respects, including that of choosing your own husband.>'

'<But why would you do this for me now, Mother, when you have never even suggested such a thing before?>'

'<Because times have changed, and you need no longer continue as a Crown Princess.>'

'<The times may have changed, Mother, but my status as the Crown Princess of Westrigonia has not.> You do agree with me, Matthias,' Eleanor continued in Westrigonian, turning to the would-be Marechal of Westrigonia, 'do you not, that I am Crown Princess of Westrigonia in full accordance with the constitution of Westrigonia?'

Matthias might not have noticed her use of the phrase *in full accordance with the constitution of Westrigonia* as he smiled and said in all seriousness: 'Yes, I do.' He said this as if they were already at the altar.

Eleanor turned back to her mother. '<There, you see, I am already in my estates. Now you return to yours.>' She spoke with a certain authority, that of a hostess to her guest.

But Yolande's mother's instinct was already in full bloom. '<Do you plan to marry this man?>' she asked her daughter, with a mother's disregard of convention, as if Matthias was not there.

'<My marriage has always been a political affair,>' Eleanor replied, as if observing the seasonal fluctuations of shellfish. '<Never mind that.>'

Yolande turned to Matthias. '<Do you plan to marry my daughter?>'

Matthias looked amused, which Eleanor had long ago recognised as one of his defences against telling the truth. '<Naturally, I am marry one day, it is way of things, and it is that your daughter is the great catch, but also it is the politics so who it is to say is not the known person. But why it is that you ask?>'

'<I am her mother,>' Yolande said. Much of her poise seemed to have returned to her. '<That is why I ask.>' She sent a challenging searching look at Matthias. '<You have avoided my question.>'

'<It is that I am only having the one plan at this time of now, Yolande, and it is the secret one, you are understand.>'

'And I will help you keep that secret, Marechal,' Eleanor said helpfully in Westrigonian, leaning forward to tap Matthias on the knee with her fan in a friendly fashion. 'When Mother leaves tomorrow, you will be the most senior official in Westrigonia, with power *plenipotentiary extraordinarias* to be wielded as you choose.'

Eleanor could see that it took all of Matthias's self-control to keep from looking rattled on hearing this. 'Thank you, Eleanor,' he said courteously. '<But it is not known the future for any of persons, but for you it is clear that this is so, that you are return home to life you choose for future.>'

'<And this . . . payment . . . you have demanded from me for this favour,

namely that I appoint you Marechal, even though I am no longer Queen
. . . >' Yolande sounded too bewildered to finish her sentence. She had
resolutely held back all this time from looking this particular gift-horse
in the mouth.

'<It is that it is the purely theoretical appointment, it is this merely
nominal of not the substance, it is the rhetorical point of view of rhetoric,>'
Matthias said airily, waving his hand through the air even more airily,
'<but the symbolism is matter for the politics at the time like this one of
now. You are obvious get better of deal, but perhaps it is to haggle from
you now?>'

'<Not at all,>' Yolande said in alarm, '<far from it, not at all, I was merely
. . . well, yes, we are in agreement then, and you have given me your word
on the matter have you not?>'

'<Yes, I have,>' Matthias said gravely, '<it is absolutely so and done and
dusted!>'

Matthias stood up and waved his companions to their feet. '<Let
us return to others from this place of now and it is concluded these
negotiations, such it is as they have been!>'

Matthias had declared this as grandly as any king of old, but Eleanor
now knew exactly how thin the ice was beneath his feet, and despite
her faith in his ability, she had to focus on her breathing to maintain a
semblance of self-control as they returned to join the others. Even to
say that Matthias was standing on thin ice was an exaggeration in the
circumstances; it would be more accurate to say that all this time he had
been standing on nothing but thin air.

Eleanor grudgingly had to give Matthias full credit for sheer nerve.

5:40 PM, Wednesday 29 April 1882 A. F.

The others were far from an equable group. The disastrous outcome of
their earlier adventuring was by now merely an embarrassment, and they
wished to move on. Their confinement was an irksome irrelevancy that
they required to be removed without delay. The rich and powerful never
expect to suffer for their wrong-doing. After all, why should they?

Matthias missed none of this, and it was with a stately deliberation intended, at least in part, to annoy his prisoners by prolonging their arrested motion that he announced to his unwelcome guests the following Proclamation: '<It is now that you are the gone guests of this place, from where you are not now the welcome ones. So it is that Yolande, our only welcome guest of this the throng of you, it is that she is stay now as guest in palace by my royal invitation, which it is that she is accepted now, and it is that remainder of peoples, that is to say, you in this person, is go from here now without delay. This I have said so that you know it.>'

'<This is an outrage,>' King Frederick protested, striving in vain to rise to his feet. '<How dare you detain my wife in such a manner?>'

'<I am not being detained, Frederick,>' Yolande told him with a deliberate malicious coolness. '<I have asked to remain here and my request has been granted by the new King of Westrigonia, Matthias the Fourth.>'

Frederick looked bewildered by this sudden turn of events. His mouth opened and then closed without Frederick the First actually managing to say anything.

'<It is quite alright,>' Sandalio said in his most soothing tone of voice, as if talking to a madwoman, '<to speak your mind without fear of duress or coercion from those,>' his eyes shifted sideways to silently indicate Matthias, '<who would divert such a gracious personage as yourself from her true inclinations.>'

'<Let me be perfectly understood by all present,>' Yolande said loudly, '<I am staying here of my own free will. I choose not to return with you. And if the First Protector should ask you why, you may tell him from me that it is because I consider him to be a fool, an imposter, a clown and a miscreant.>'

There was a silence while those present reflected upon the political implications of this list of epithets. It was clear to them all that Yolande was burning her bridges behind her, but it was not clear why.

'<Yolande, I cannot allow you to do this,>' Frederick said firmly. '<I am afraid that I must insist that you return to Pentharborg with us.>'

'<Frederick, go back to Pentharborg and the latest woman with whom you share your bed. I will stay here.>'

Jason looked sideways at his father on hearing his mother's embarrassingly public revelation. Jason himself, at the tender age of twenty-one, already had three mistresses of different nationalities in different parts of the civilised world, which suited what he thought of as his cosmopolitan sensibilities. He had mistresses because it seemed like the thing to do.

Nina's grasp of Anglashian, while basic, was sufficient for her to have gathered the general gist of what had just been said. Her eyes gleamed and her nostrils flared while she carefully memorised this scandalous quarrel. She was a girl who had a date with her diary that very night!

'<Your behaviour is not that of a prince and gentleman,>' said Sandalio, who seemed to have recovered his spirits now that it had become clear that Matthias would after all honour his pledge of safe-conduct.

'Considering you just tried to kill me, I'm a blasted saint if you ask me.'

'<Two wrongs don't make a right,>' Sandalio pontificated in his most sanctimonious manner. '<You cannot kidnap Queen Yolande in this fashion, when we have come here as guests protected by the sacred obligations of hospitality. I ask you to reconsider this path, which is that of a bandit, on which you have embarked.>'

'I see what you are about,' Matthias said in a resigned manner. 'You want to cancel out your own bad behavior by pretending that I have done something equally wrong. Well, that is not for either of us to judge.'

'<You will certainly be judged for the manner in which you have detained Queen Yolande,>' Sandalio said in a sorrowful tone, as if he regretted seeing Matthias do this to himself.

'<*Our revels now are ended,*>' said Matthias, who by now was in a philosophical mood. '<*These our actors were all spirits and are melted into air, into thin air.*>'

'<*We are such stuff as dreams are made on,*>' Frederick said in reply, '<*and our little life is rounded with a sleep.*>'

The rival monarchs of Westrigonia looked at each other in an amicable fashion. With a bow of his head, Matthias said: 'Let me have the honour of escorting you all to the Public Portal.'

Steindahl released his prisoners, with an air of reluctance, as if he had plenty of energy left with which to have whipped them. The Pentharborg delegation was shepherded out of the Palace and along to the Portal. Matthias, Eleanor and Yolande kept them company, along with a detachment of Westrigonian soldiers. Little more was said by any of those present. The Anglashians looked glad enough to be going still in one piece, and while Matthias was cheerful enough, Eleanor was still in a state of shock and Yolande seemed impatient to say goodbye and be done with it.

The Pentharborg delegation left through the Public Portal and Matthias, Eleanor and Yolande returned to the Palace. There they all said their goodbyes and the day was done.

CHAPTER THIRTY SIX

King Justin suspected that every man,
Who came near him meant to do him harm.
Some men fall sick at the sight of a woman.
Frankie the Villain

9:05 AM, Thursday 30 April 1882 A. F.

Matthias had chosen the Paunayloron Room for his rendezvous with destiny. The Paunayloron Room was square-shaped, each side being one-hundred and twenty feet long, with a bell-shaped ceiling covered with dazzlingly brilliant frescoes of many of the great battles of history. In the centre of the room was a gold-plated fountain from which issued not water, but a gold plated candelabra with wedding-cake layers of candles reaching high into the air. On one side of the room was a theatre stage, with chairs with red cushions set before it for the audience to sit in, while scattered all around the room were tables and chairs. Enormous golden Melisendien carpets covered the red cherry-wood floor-boards, while yellow velvet tapestries hung from the walls, suffusing the room in a golden glow.

Matthias arrived at six-thirty in the morning, perhaps betraying his nerves by repeatedly sending messengers from seven o'clock onwards to find out when Yolande would be arriving. Yolande was not to be rushed, especially in the morning. Matthias had insisted the night before that she arrive for their appointment at seven o'clock in the morning, and Yolande had agreed to this only out of politeness. She had no intention whatsoever of actually fulfilling this pledge. No lady of distinction arrived at any kind of appointment at seven o'clock in the morning, let alone a former monarch.

The other strolling players of Matthias's drama had not turned up either. Matthias had sent for Ibtisamade, Deemer, Yakimire, Zhirayr and Abbey, the Justices of the Star Chamber. He had also sent for all the Councillors and their stand-ins. By seven-thirty no one had turned up and the Marechal was pacing up and down the room placing guards to keep away the usual crowd of petitioners. Time was passing, and Matthias's plans coming to pass depended on whether or not time was Matthias's friend.

Eventually Fortuna relented and started dealing out the winning cards of Matthias's hands. Magister Raymond, lured forth by an ambiguously worded letter, turned up. The Law Lord Ringold Sacheverell came along. Justices Deemer, Abbey and Yalimire came along. By eight forty-five Matthias had his witnesses. Explaining to them that Yolande was appointing him Marechal, he produced his scribes and already written-out documents, accompanied by his legal argumentation.

Then at last Yolande and Eleanor turned up and they were in business. Matthias had promised Yolande that it would take no more than ten minutes and indeed, by twenty past nine they were done. Yolande had formally pronounced Matthias Raspero the Marechal of Westrigonia in full accordance with the constitution of Westrigonia.

Instructing his witnesses to remain where they were, and backing up these instructions by further fierce iron-clad instructions to Steindahl that no-one was to leave, Matthias departed the Paunayloron Room and the Palace of Krastienst in the company of Yolande and Eleanor, and escorted Yolande to the Public Portal. There he bid farewell to Yolande and returned to the Palace, and went directly to the Paunayloron Room. History recorded how calm and composed the Marechal looked throughout all this, but history did not record the tumult of emotions in Matthias's chest. Only Matthias would ever know of his nerves on that day. His rendezvous with destiny had not yet run its course.

Matthias summoned all the witnesses, who were still present, and rather disgruntled, given that they had earlier tried to leave and been restrained by Steindahl, and informed them that as he was Marechal of Westrigonia, and as both the monarchs of Westrigonia were out of the country, he would exercise those constitutional powers of *plenipotentiary extraordinarias* which he possessed in order to activate Clause Twenty-Seven of the Constitution of Westrigonia.

The thunderous silence by which his legal witnesses mutely shouted their dismay on hearing this proclamation moved the Marechal not at all. With a grim faced fierceness, the Marechal of Westrigonia exercised his powers of *plenipotentiary extraordinarias* on the spot and history was made. When it was done, and the documents were signed, Matthias looked at the time of day as written down and now unchangeable for all time. It was quarter to eleven in the morning. Matthias hoped it would do. Either time was on his side or it was not. Only time itself would tell.

10:45 AM, Thursday 30 April 1882 A. F.

Matthias now declared to his witnesses that they could leave or stay as they chose. Sensing history in the making, they chose to stay, their earlier impatience forgotten.

Matthias then informed his followers that they were going to play a game of Piccolet. The table was set up, they all sat down, and the stage was set. Numerous painters over history were to take that scene as their subject. *Card players on the Edge of the Abyss* by Oryon, *Piccolet players on the Morning of Doomsday* by Yaridne and *The Last Game* by Plough were to be among the best known of these paintings.

Little was said as they played their game. But then Steindahl came to announce the arrival of a delegation from the Vidaldmeet.

'Ah, we are come to that so soon,' Matthias said with a smile. 'Bring them on.'

The card game was adjourned. Matthias and Eleanor and all their followers took their seats. A new stage was set, onto which came the delegation from the Vidaldmeet.

12:05 PM, Thursday 30 April 1882 A. F.

First of all came Shyester, striding along proudly with his chest puffed out like a songbird. Behind him came Lord Taalay Oana, Lord Eadgar Nandor, Counsellor Jannik Patrizio and Lord Camdenshall.

Shyester spoke first. 'Miscreant Raspero, the Vidaldmeet has decreed that you are to be placed under arrest. The charge is treason. If you throw yourself on our mercy, this will be duly noted and taken into account and we may, or may not, be merciful. If you are obstinate and proud, wilfully disobedient, if you are a rebel and a renegade, there will be no mercy shown to you. Now, Miscreant Raspero, surrender yourself to the officers of the law who stand before you.'

'I hope you will excuse my slowness in following everything you are saying,' Matthias said politely, 'but as King of Westrigonia I cannot be guilty of treason. The very charge is an absurdity. I refer you, friend Shyester, to those rules of elementary logic which we studied as children at school. Perhaps you could be so kind as to explain what you are about.'

Shyester turned about in a showy way and said: 'Camdenshall, I wish to minimise my interaction with this creature of the dark, so perhaps you would be so kind as to explain to him that his imposture is now at an ignominious and inglorious end.'

Camdenshall stepped forward with a grave air. No-one missed the significance of Camdenshall's current role. He had been the leader and spokesman of the delegation that had gone to Anglashia to inform Matthias that he had been elected King. Now Shyester stood in his place and Camdenshall took his directions. 'Miscreant Raspero, there was a procedural irregularity in the use of the proxy votes by which you were elected King of Westrigonia by the Vidaldmeet. This came to light when the sources of these votes were contacted to confirm that their votes had been properly registered. They have all denied ever intending to vote for you. Therefore their proxy votes are now null and void. Your election as King is invalid. Yet suspicion has fallen on you as the author of a fraudulent vote in the Vidaldmeet, which means that you are suspected of having committed treason, as the imposture of pretending to be a king counts as treason.'

'If what you say is true,' Matthias said reflectively, 'then I was never King at all.'

Shyester stepped back into the fray. 'What we say is true,' Shyester said with a little smile. 'Your conclusion does follow.' His lawyer's soul quivered.

'Other conclusions also follow,' Matthias continued as reflectively as ever, 'such as that Frederick and Yolande have continued to be the lawful monarchs of Westrigonia throughout. You do agree with this, do you not?'

'Of course. The issue is self-evident.'

'In which case, my appointment as Marechal by Queen Yolande at twenty past nine this morning in the presence of these witnesses' (Matthias waved vaguely with his left hand towards *these witnesses*) 'had the full force of constitutional law. You do agree with this also, do you not?'

Shyester's eyes flickered. 'You are dissembling, Miscreant Raspero. The arrest warrant issued by the Vidaldmeet is for Baron Matthias Raspero. What of the appointment as Marechal which you claim? It changes nothing. You are under arrest, Miscreant Raspero, Marechal or no.'

'*Pay attention, bozo!*' Matthias shouted rudely. 'I am establishing certain conclusions as premises from which further conclusions can be drawn. Now, I am bringing to your attention the fact that I was appointed Marechal by Queen Yolande. Now, given that Queen Yolande left Westrigonia shortly afterwards, it therefore follows that as Marechal of Westrigonia I have powers of *plenipotentiary extraordinarias* in the absence from the realm of the King and Queen, so at the moment Yolande left through the Portal I had these powers. Do you dispute this interpretation of constitutional law?'

Shyester's eyes flickered again. 'Such powers do not protect you against the arrest warrant as issued by the Vidaldmeet.'

'I did not say that they did,' Matthias replied with a lazy smile. 'But shall I continue?'

'Miscreant Raspero, time presses and I really must refer to the arrest warrant issued by the Vidaldmeet. I ask you to come quietly or face the full consequences of defying the express will of the Vidaldmeet. I hold here your arrest warrant.' Shyester held a scroll up into the air as if it were able to deal out thunderbolts.

Shyester's confidence was waning. He had no armed force with which to back up his arrest, which was rapidly becoming an attempted arrest which seemed to be going nowhere. His assumption from the start had been that if Matthias resisted arrest, the Vidaldmeet could call upon the full armed force of the entire country to prosecute the case, whose end would be inevitable if delayed. But Matthias's argumentation was beginning to wear him down.

'Ah, yes, the arrest warrant issued by the Vidaldmeet. May I inspect this arrest warrant?' Matthias asked meekly. 'I believe it is my right under law to do so.'

'Of course you may,' Shyester assured him, as if eager to soothe any worries Matthias might have on that score. 'Come, you may approach me and take it.'

'I will give you a choice, Lord Shyester,' Matthias said with a hint of steel in his voice. 'You may bring me that warrant or I will have Steindahl bring you to me. Is that clear?'

'Miscreant Raspero,' Shyester said with a frown, 'I am allowing you to inspect this warrant. Do not exercise my patience further!'

Matthias sighed. 'So, what I said was not clear. Steindahl, bring this fellow to me. If he resists, use force. If any of his companions attempt to intervene, use force on them as well. Now, Steindahl, snap to it!'

Steindahl did not, as it happened, need any prodding. He really didn't even need telling twice. He had resented the rich and powerful all his life because he was not rich and powerful himself. The burly and bearded Captain was never happier than when bringing down the high and mighty. Now that he had a position of authority from which to humble mighty figures such as Shyester, he relished any pain he could inflict on them. Although Matthias had supposedly noted his fighting qualities during the Battle of Krastienst and thereby become his patron, in fact, Steindahl had been working secretly for Matthias for three years as a bodyguard and undercover agent.

Steindahl and five of his guards marched forward. Steindahl grabbed

Shyester with mobile karns, lifted him up into the air, slammed him to the ground with a brutality that made everyone grasp, and dragged him head first along the ground, his arm holding the arrest warrant still outstretched until they reached Matthias, who reached down, took the arrest warrant from Shyester's grasp, and motioned to Steindahl to return his captive to his former position. Steindahl waved his wand and flung Shyester along the ground to where he had been standing before. A groaning Shyester clambered to his feet. None of Shyester's companions had dared move a muscle while all this was happening.

'This is an outrage!' Shyester protested. 'How dare you treat me in such a manner!'

'I am concerned that you are attempting to arrest me with an invalid arrest warrant. Surely a man who would sink to such depths as this cannot be expected to be treated other than as a wretch and a renegade, a lawless man outside the proper bounds of society.'

'The arrest warrant is valid, valid, sound and whole and clean, Miscreant Raspero. Do not poison the air with your foul lies!'

'Ah, well, it is time for me to inspect this arrest warrant and pronounce upon its validity.' In a showy manner, Matthias unrolled the scroll, inspected it, and then declared: 'This arrest warrant is invalid. Do you understand, Lord Shyester, that your warrant, being *invalid*, cannot be enforced? Or must I explain this to you?'

'The arrest warrant is not invalid, Miscreant Raspero. It cannot possibly be invalid. Must I explain to you the full legality of all the details of this document which I bear?' Shyester completely believed every word he was saying, given that the best legal minds in the country had hammered out every detail of this arrest warrant, which therefore couldn't possibly be invalid, yet Matthias, the monkey king sitting before him, had a mocking smile on his lips which was giving Shyester butterflies in his stomach.

'There is no need for that. Allow me to explain to you why your arrest warrant is invalid, to save us the needless trouble of such a conversational exchange. Unless of course you are desperate to demonstrate your legal expertise in front of us all. Well, what of it, Slippery Shyester? Do you want to go first?'

'I must ask you to address me correctly.'

'Then *you* must address *me* correctly as well. Stop calling me Miscreant Raspero. The correct form of address is Lord Raspero or Marechal. Now, shall I go first?'

There was a long silence. This whole business was starting to get on Shyester's nerves. Yet it was clear, surrounded by a Palace guard who took orders from Matthias, that he could not resolve this issue by force.

'Please do,' Shyester said as calmly as he could manage.

'Let us begin,' Matthias began in a peaceable manner, 'by noting the time of day as listed on the arrest warrant. No doubt you will say that this detail is one of those that make this document a correctly drawn up arrest warrant. All well and good, this is true. But we note nonetheless that the time of day when this arrest warrant was made was that of ten to eleven this morning. Do you wish, Lord Shyester, to dispute this point?'

Matthias had said *Lord Shyester* as if by being so polite he was doing Shyester a favour.

Shyester made no response. He had no idea at all where Matthias was going with all this, but it was obvious that Matthias was going somewhere, and that Shyester was not going to like being there when the travellers finally arrived at their destination. The butterflies in Shyester's stomach were, impossibly, turning back into caterpillars, which were now munching on the leaves of his intestines.

Matthias said nothing for a moment, as if to emphasize Shyester's silence; then the King of Westrigonia, or rather, more accurately the Marechal of Westrigonia, continued his exposition like a professor of logic demonstrating the proof of a theorem.

'However, at a quarter to eleven this morning, at a time *prior* to the issuing of your arrest warrant, I invoked Clause Twenty-Seven of the Constitution and abolished the Vidaldmeet. I did this in accordance with my powers of *plenipotentiary extraordinarias* as Marechal. It follows, therefore, that at the time the Vidaldmeet issued this arrest warrant the Vidalmeet did not exist. Therefore your arrest warrant is invalid.'

Matthias gave Shyester a level stare and said nothing more.

'Clause Twenty-Seven?' Shyester queried. It was all he could think of to say.

'My ancestor Etienne helped write that clause, so it is a clause of the constitution I understand well. Do you require me to explain it to you, Lord Shyester, or do you understand what I have done?'

'You have taken a drastic step, m-uh, um, Lord Raspero.' Shyester was beginning to feel that he was in a waking nightmare. He wanted to go home and lie down and wake up to find that this had all been a bad dream.

'Well, *so have you*,' Matthias shouted. 'Or was arresting me just another day's work for all the *merry* members of the *merry* club of the Vidaldmeet? Not *drastic* at all, was it, to have me arrested? Well? Say something! Answer me! Or has the cat got your tongue?' Matthias surveyed the remaining members of the Vidaldmeet delegation with a certain grimness. 'And what do the rest of this party have to say? Are you all imposters, here to parade under false documents and make false claims of arresting people? I should have you all thrown into the dungeons!'

There was a silence all around. Matthias let the silence drag out just this far, and no further, like a musician measuring out a pause in a concerto, before speaking again: 'Lord Shyester, or rather, *Slippery Shyester*, we now enter into a strange interregnum where none of us have titles, where the law does not apply, where all that we have known and loved is gone. What claim have you to your land and title by right of law when there is no law? Come, feel free to call me Miscreant Raspero if you choose. Naturally, I can have you beaten or whipped if I so choose, and what can you do about it? Names or broken bones, take your pick. Or are you going to be polite to me now out of a fear of the consequences of being rude, a fear you did not have before? Well? Answer me, you pompous slippery self-important fool. *If* you still have the courage to speak.'

There was a silence. Shyester looked as if his brain had stopped working. The other members of the Vidaldmeet delegation looked as if someone had just clubbed them over the head. The significance of what as going on was dawning on them despite their determined attempts to avoid what stared them in the face. The entire rationale of their existence had gone. The Vidaldmeet had ceased to exist.

Matthias waited like a hunter about to fire an arrow at a moving deer, then spoke again. 'In the absence of the rule of law, might has become right. The only law now is that of the jungle, which is no law at all. Obviously, what must happen next is the resurrection of Westrigonia, or to put the matter another way, just as the Constitution of Westrigonia was written by a process in the thirteenth century by our forefathers, so a new constitution, a Westrigonia the Second so to speak, must be written now. This means that everything such as lands, titles, and so on, must be reformulated. This means that many who are wealthy now might well be dispossessed in the future. Speaking for myself, I would quite happily see you, for example, Shyester, a turncoat and a traitor, rendered penniless and turned out on the streets to beg for food for the rest of your miserable life. But perhaps you will whine that I am being too harsh?'

Matthias's face had turned bleak, and he looked as pitiless as the man who had poured the Sweet Drink down Phelan's throat. Shyester swallowed audibly.

'It is of course an ontological question concerning the Vidaldmeet,' Lord Taalay Oana said, speaking out for the first time, 'and so as for the legality of this decision of yours, the possible madness of, ah, Yolande, rendering such a decision problematic, all this remains to be seen, Lord Raspero, does it not? Perhaps the matter is far from being as clear cut as you claim.'

There were nods all around from the Vidaldmeet delegation, each separate nod being the clutching at a straw of a drowning man.

'Well spoken, Oana,' Matthias said approvingly, like a schoolmaster welcoming a contribution from his favourite pupil. 'That is quite right. In fact, let me make plain that I have no intention of hindering your exit from this place. You may return to the Vidaldmeet and inform them of what has happened. I will in any case publicly proclaim my decision. And then you may deliberate on the matter, and decide that it has not happened at all, or if it has happened, it does not apply. One way or the other, you will decree that the Vidaldmeet still exists. Perhaps you will pass an Act of the Vidaldmeet to this effect. And then everything can continue as it always has done, can it not? Well, Oana? Is that the import of your comment?'

Oana's only response was a thin smile.

'But what will happen next, Oana? Have you properly considered the future? What of the armies of the First Protector, currently engaged in Baalbabak and Melisendia? If they are successful, perhaps they may arrive in Westrigonia and empower the Zoller-Abstein faction to take control of the situation once again. But what are the chances of that? West Baalbabak is armed to the teeth and fighting like wolves, as are also Southern Melisende, and De'Asterides may well have found that he has bitten off more than he can chew. The longer he fights there, the longer it will take him to arrive here. And time is precisely what you do not have. So your faith in the Zoller-Absteins may well be misplaced.'

Oana kept his thin smile in place, but only with an effort.

'And what else can we say of the future, Oana? You see, there is a big question mark over just how much support the Vidaldmeet may find among those who we like to refer to as the *common people*. You see, Oana, when it comes down to it, just how much are the pompous self-important fools of the Vidaldmeet such as yourself actually loved by the people? Normally, this does not matter. Life continues as normal regardless of public opinion. People shrug and accept yet another indignity, yet another absurdity, yet more eye-rolling stupidity, because it is the way that things are, and what can anyone do? But once it becomes known right across the length and breadth of Westrigonia that the Vidaldmeet has been abolished, it will become clear to everyone that they do not have to pay taxes, that they do not have to obey the law, that they may take matters into their own hands, that everything is up for grabs. And what plans have you, Oana, to deal with such a national breakdown of law-and-order? Well? Will you call out the army? What if they refuse your order? Technically speaking, as Marechal at the end of the existence of Westrigonia, I am still in charge. The army might well obey me, not you. Or if they answer your call, to what ends will you direct them? To the arrest and imprisonment of their own family and friends? To my own arrest? I am the one public figure in Westrigonia who is known the length and breadth of our land for actually fighting the enemy and liberating our country. I would like to think that this would give me some claim on the public's affection. I ask you directly, Oana, if you fully comprehend all the possible consequences that may follow from what has happened here today? Well? What do you have to say for yourself?'

Oana's thin smile had by now completely disappeared.

'It is clear, Lord Raspero,' Lord Eadgar Nandor said ingratiatingly, taking up the burden of being the Vidaldmeet's spokesman, 'that the decision to place you under arrest was ill-advised. Naturally this decision must be revoked. In view of recent developments, I am sure, in fact I have no doubt at all, that the Vidaldmeet will reconsider this matter in your favour. I trust that such a change of heart may have the effect of altering this sequence of events to which you refer.'

'You do not appear to understand, Nandor, that Clause Twenty-Seven cannot be reversed. It so happens, by one of those curious coincidences that make us marvel about what life is all about, that I was asked about Clause Twenty-Seven at my Ceremony of Recognition. I was able to successfully deal with this question. It would appear, Nandor, that you would fail such an examination. There no longer exists a Vidaldmeet to reverse its decision, just as the Vidaldmeet did not exist at the time it made this decision in the first place. Strictly speaking, no decision was ever made. A non-existent entity cannot act. I cannot put the matter more simply than this. You will excuse me, Nandor, I am sure, from explaining these legal matters to you. Ask your friends what it all means. But enough of this. Let me tell you how things stand. We are simply back at square one. We are now in those ruder times to which we habitually refer to as *the past*. We have the task of forming another Westrigonia. Now I do not know if I shall have the honour of being King under those new conditions. But I do know this. If I should see any of you present here today kneeling before me on my throne and asking if I recognise you, my answer will be a simple *No*. So you had all better start praying, and praying hard, that I am not the new King of a new Westrigonia. Because you are my enemies and I do not believe in forgiving my enemies. I believe in destroying them. But perhaps you will whine that I am treating you all unfairly?'

There was a long silence. The Vidaldmeet delegation, to a man, were white-faced and sick-to-their-stomach-looking.

Not by chance, there were several lawyers amongst the Vidaldmeet delegation. Amongst these were Counsellor Jannik Patrizio, who, after thinking-on-his-feet then and there in the exigencies of the moment, spoke as follows: 'Lord Raspero, given that you are bound by your oath to the Vidaldmeet to take no action contrary to the well-being of the Vidaldmeet, it follows therefore that you cannot abolish it. Let us be clear about what you have said yourself. You were never king, so therefore you have always been the Baron of Raspero, so therefore you cannot have have abolished the Vidaldmeet without breaking your oath to the Vidaldmeet. If you have broken your oath you are foresworn, and by this criterion Queen Yolande's appointment of you as Marechal is invalidated, because being foresworn acts retrospectively on everything you have ever done, in which case you were never Marechal and could never have activated Clause Twenty- Seven. What do you have to say?'

There was a general stir all around, and not only on the part of the Vidaldmeet delegation. Matthias's own followers were gasping for breath. Like the spectators at a public chess match observing a breathtaking bishop-check-King, everyone was on the edge of their seats.

Matthias waited his moment, smiling a superior kind of smile, before speaking out like a highly paid lawyer playing to the gallery in front of the jury: 'Let us break down your argument into its component parts. First of all, this oath you refer to: when did I swear it?'

There was a long silence, during which Patrizio felt himself becoming a ticking clock. To break the spell of this hallucination, he said: 'But of course you did swear such an oath. Otherwise you were never a member of the Vidaldmeet.'

'As it happened, I didn't swear such an oath,' Matthias said. 'I know what you must be thinking. In order to have addressed the Vidaldmeet, in order to have activated Clause Seven, in order to have been anything at all, I must have sworn this oath. But as it happened, I never got around to it. You must remember, Patrizio, the exigencies of the moment to which you refer. I became Baron by a ceremony presided over by Justice Deemer, and during this ceremony I stood by the open coffins of my father and my elder brother. My formal oath-taking to the Vidaldmeet never took place. Yes, I went to the Speaker and told him that as a member of the Vidaldmeet I wished to activate Clause Seven, and he took my motion and tabled it, even though technically I was not a member of the Vidaldmeet as I had not yet sworn an oath. You must address any relevant questions about this to the Speaker. Why he overlooked this procedural requirement I have no idea. I did indeed become Baron of Raspero in a ceremony of Proclamation presided over by Justice Deemer, but as that is a separate legal matter to being a member of the Vidaldmeet, it means that technically I am the Baron of Raspero who never became a member of the Vidaldmeet, even though by constitutional law the one automatically follows from the other. It therefore follows that I am not foresworn, so therefore my appointment as Marechal was valid, given that the Baron of Raspero was thereby appointed such, not a member of the Vidaldmeet, and so therefore my abolition of the Vidaldmeet must stand as read.'

There was a general chuckling and muttering amongst his supporters as it became clear that the ever-elusive Matthias had slipped away yet again from a legal seizure of his temporal being.

'In which case,' Patrizio said, fighting on regardless of this set-back, 'not having been a member of the Vidaldmeet, your motion of Clause Seven should never have been allowed. This was a clear transgression of the rules of the Vidaldmeet.'

'You are quite right,' Matthias agreed with a nod of his head. 'You will have to take up the matter with the relevant historians and the Speaker of the Vidaldmeet, Lord Zelimir. Perhaps a committee can be formed to look into the matter and pronounce upon it. In the meantime, you will have to excuse me. I have other matters to attend to.'

'But this matter is not so readily resolved as all that,' Patrizio said, grasping now at whatever he could think of. 'Surely you accept that you must be taken into custody while such a transgression is investigated in a fair and thorough manner?'

At that Matthias threw back his head and laughed. As the merry peals of his laughter rang through the room, the other members of the court joined in, until the Vidaldmeet delegation alone stood not laughing in the laughter, which was not at all pleasant for them.

Matthias eventually brought his laughter under control, and waited until the general laughter had subsided. 'You must excuse me, Patrizio,' he said calmly. 'I have no intention whatsoever of being taken into custody by anyone. I am the thirty-seventh Baron of Raspero, and I am returning to my ancestral domains. My barony existed before Westrigonia, and we shall see what happens next. The kingdom of Lachtna existed when Daniel declared himself to be Daniel of Sacramento, but it no longer existed at a later date because Westrigonia followed and swallowed it up. Who knows what there will be in the future? You talk of such a transgression of the Vidaldmeet's rules as if this meant anything of import, but this betrays your failure to understand what is going on. You see, the Vidaldmeet, as mighty and unchallenged as it was, no longer exists. When it existed, it naturally followed from the very greatness of its existence that a transgression of its rules was a matter of the greatest import. The whole national army could be called out on such a matter. But as it no longer exists, such a transgression no longer matters. Or to put the matter another way: try calling out the army now for a procedural transgression that occurred seven years ago and observe the results. You see my point?'

It seemed that not one of the Vidaldmeet delegation had anything to say.

Matthias therefore resumed speaking. 'Before you leave, let me tell you something of my future plans. I intend to return to the barony of Raspero, where Daniel ruled long before Westrigonia even existed. I am still the thirty-seventh Baron of Raspero, whether there is a Westrigonia or not. You may all likewise return to your own estates, or to the Vidaldmeet, or wherever you choose. It is your choice, and I cannot say that I am interested one way or the other. And in Raspero, I will receive those visitors who care to come to see me, as Etienne received those visitors who came to see him, and in time a new Westrigonia shall arise, as it did before. You see, this has all happened before. Etienne and his friends wrote the Constitution of Westrigonia, and stop and think for a moment of what this means. The Constitution is not something given, like an atlas. Or rather, it is an atlas in the sense that it gives a map of an immaterial country, but it is not provable or disprovable in the same way as a geographical atlas of material countries. But enough of philosophical pleasantries. I say only this to you: there will be a new Westrigonia, and you will have no place in it, if I have anything to say about it. Well? Have you anything to say? Explain yourselves! What are you about? You look like a likely gang of rogues to me, ripe for hanging, the lot of you. But perhaps you will protest?'

Shock can only last for so long, which is why it is called *shock*, and so it was that the shocked Shyester had by now begun to recover the use of his formidable faculties. 'Not at all,' Shyester said smoothly, 'it is understandable that you should resent our entirely innocent advent into these hallowed halls given the incidental allocation of our initial intentions. May I ask if we may peruse the relevant documents as to the invocation of Clause Twenty-Seven?'

This request was echoed by the vigorous nods and exclamations of the rest of the Vidaldmeet delegation. The brutal treatment of Shyester, who had been all but clubbed to the ground right in front of them, had had its intended effect on these nobles. They had a healthy respect for Matthias now. Besides, the dissolution of the Vidaldmeet was an event unprecedented in history. They all gathered around the documents clucking like chickens in the presence of a wolf. They questioned the Law Lords, conferred amongst themselves, while Matthias and Eleanor and their courtiers watched with a certain malicious amusement.

Eventually the Vidaldmeet delegation turned to face Matthias and Shyester declared with something like a bold servility: 'By the force of custom, if even of law despite these unfortunate developments, we depart hence from this place to inform the members of the Vidaldmeet of this most unprecedented development. We bid thee farewell, Marechal Raspero, and may we meet again under much more pleasant circumstances.'

'Of course you may leave,' Matthias informed his guests in a kindly fashion.

For a moment no-one moved, no-one said anything; it was as

if everyone were inside a dream in which everything had become disconnected while making a non-waking kind of sense that could not be re-assembled upon awakening.

'Now!' Matthias shouted. 'Steindahl, get these ruffians out of here.'

Seeing the gleaming eyes of the Captain of the Palace Guard moving towards them, followed by his wand-wielding troops, the Vidaldmeet delegation, like clucking hens faced by a fanged foe, shuffled their feet towards the door while vociferously protesting their fate. The room was cleared of the Vidaldmeet enemy in a trice.

History had been made. Painters, playwrights, novelists, composers, lawyers, historians and philosophers would debate the events of that day for centuries to come. The day that Matthias Raspero abolished the Vidaldmeet would be long-remembered. But there was yet more drama to come. This day was not yet done.

CHAPTER THIRTY SEVEN

Folly bangs on heaven's door,
Demanding admittance on important business.
And Lady Godelric is in bed this morning.
Frankie the Villain

1:35 PM, Thursday 30 April 1882 A. F.

Her Royal Highness the Princess Eleanor rose to her feet and paced with a deliberate staginess to stand in front of Matthias. 'Lord Raspero,' she said, 'we will speak together in private. Now!'

With that, she turned on her heel and marched toward the Adamus Door. Matthias rose to his feet and said: 'Acteon, take charge of these documents, and stay here for the time being,' after which he followed Eleanor.

Mitzi, Georgette and Nina were already on their way after the Crown Princess. Gerbern, Felim, Haris, Darnell and Alaric followed Matthias.

Eleanor walked briskly through the corridors, turning only to check that Matthias was following, until eventually entering the Kaelyn Gallery. She walked up to an alcove by the side, wheeled around, and stood there grim-facedly watching Matthias crossing the Gallery in her direction.

Eleanor was a storm about to arrive. Ever since the assassination attempt she had been in a state of shock, but that shock was now wearing off. She was now ready to respond to what had happened yesterday. Eleanor's ears still echoed with the sickening thuds of the assassins' bolts sinking into the wooden back of Matthias's empty chair. She kept hearing those sounds over and over.

Matthias came up to Eleanor and said, 'Eleanor,' in a friendly but guarded fashion.

'You are not, you are no longer to address me by my first name. I refuse you that right. You are to address me by my full title. Is that clear?'

'Eleanor, I can see that you are upset, but-'

'No, you cannot see anything. You are a fool. What can you see? Nothing! Now, which part of my refusal to allow you to address me by my first name do you fail to understand?'

'Eleanor, why don't you tell me what I have done wrong?'

'Hmm, let me think. Oh, I know! Allowing an assassination attempt on your life to take place here in the Palace. *This* Palace, which is *my home*.'

'Eleanor, we've been over this-'

'No, we have not *been over this*. You simply charged ahead into this situation without any consultation and –'

'Wait a minute! I told you it was about to happen.'

'That was not a consultation! It was a decree.'

'Well, it's done now-'

'And so are you, Marechal. Done! You are done now! You will stay away from me from now on, do you understand me? Your conduct is beyond anything, it is beyond all the words I have to say. Bringing whores back to the Palace to slake your lust –'

'No!' Matthias said so determinedly that even an angry Eleanor was forced to stop for a moment. 'The Barons of Raspero do not behave in this fashion. I cannot allow such a comment to stand.'

'The Barons of Raspero this, the Barons of Raspero that. Do you ever talk about anything else?'

'Eleanor, I understand that- '

'No, you do not. You understand nothing. *Nothing!*'

'You're in a state of shock – '

'No, no, far from it, Matthias. I have never felt more serene in my life. Discs flying through the air, assassins, murder attempts, *in my own house*, what is there to be shocked about? This is normal, is it not, for a Raspero monarchy? Nothing like this happened in my parents' time, but you plan to live life like this everyday, don't you?'

'Eleanor, this was much less risky than it might have seemed on the surface of things. I don't mean to boast, but I was ahead of them every step of the way. It was-'

'Oh, you don't mean to boast, but you will go ahead and do it anyway. Oh, Matthias, you have invented a new logic. One that does not work.'

'Their strategy relied on a surprise that was not there. That was-'

'As a criminal on the run, a hunted fugitive wanted for law-breaking, an outlaw with every decent person's hand turned against you, obviously you no longer remember how normal life works anymore. Your understanding has become corrupt, your perceptions deranged, your character that of the gutter in which you have lived for all this time. Do you understand, Matthias, that assassination attempts *are not normal*? Do you at least understand this?'

'Why don't you tell the First Protector this? Has he been a fugitive? What is his excuse for behaving like this? Why –'

'Oh, I see, this has nothing to do with you. It is all the First Protector's fault. I have lived here in the Palace for ten years without a single assassination attempt happening, not one, but now that you are here things have changed but, and let me note this carefully, this change has nothing to do with *you*.'

'Eleanor, you are failing to observe the desperation of De'Asterides in taking such a step. Stop and think-'

'No, *you* stop and think. Everywhere you go murder and mayhem follow. And why is that? Are you saying that it is a complete coincidence that murderers fly through the air whenever you sit down for a moment? Why don't you go somewhere else –'

'No, why don't *you* go somewhere else?' Matthias snapped. 'Westrigonia has been invaded by Baalbabak and Melisende, now the First Protector is sending assassins, and all I am doing is trying to regain my inheritance, but tell me again how all this is my fault. I did not ask for this to happen.'

'No, but you foresaw it.'

'I know how they think. They are very predictable.'

'You could have avoided being in such danger by not allowing events to proceed.'

'Yes, I could have. But they would have tried again in a manner that I might not have foreseen. They cannot try again to kill me now. I have gained that benefit. And look at all the other benefits I gained. The Zoller-Abstein faction in Westrigonia will have to answer for what has happened. Rayerfeld will not let it go. The First Protector is starting to look like a man who can get nothing right, and he has plenty of enemies who are just waiting the right moment to stab him in the back. I gained a lot of political credit yesterday. I don't deny there was risk, but oftentimes there is no reward without risk.'

'Very well, Matthias. It seems that I am entirely in the wrong to seek to live in a home where assassins do not attack its residents every other day. I wonder now what I was thinking.'

'No. Eleanor, you are entirely in the right to seek to live in peace. That is what I want as well. So,' Matthias spread his hands wide with an air of acceptance, 'we are entirely of one mind on this issue.'

'How very excellent!' Eleanor snapped her fan shut. 'I hope we can be of one mind also on the question of never being married.'

'Well, obviously, now would not be the right time to-'

'There will never be the right time to present your case. May I point out that being pursued daily by assassins is hardly a recommendation to a suitor in a civilized society? You have spent so much of your life as a fugitive that you may well consider yesterday to be just another day of being pursued. Are you aware, even vestigially, that a civilized woman seeks other qualities in a suitor than that of being able to dodge the discs of assassins? I am sure that you must wonder why this is so, do you not?'

'You are fully entitled to be in a temper but if-'

'Oh, am I? How very gracious of you to be so understanding. It must be the near brush with death you have just experienced. It has woken you up and animated your faculties of comprehension.'

It was perhaps unwise of Matthias to sigh and roll his eyes at this moment. This was fuel to the flames of Eleanor's temper, and so what followed was perhaps inevitable given that Eleanor, turning her back on Matthias, chanced to look down and see the Dalmalym Pig.

The porcelain figurine of the pig standing on the alcove table was widely disliked. Eleanor was not alone in considering the figurine to be unbelievably ugly and an offence to aesthetic sensibilities, but no-one had taken action against its presence up till now for two reasons. One was that it had been a gift from the Vice-Regent of Dalmalym, and thus a matter of international diplomacy; the other was that it was priceless, being one of only two such works by the master Atrecatcullaria. Diplomacy and money have never been lightly disregarded at any time in history. The pig's day had come, however. Nothing was going to save it now. Eleanor had never liked that pig. Something about its snout, its bottom sticking up into the air, its greedy thrusting-forwardness, had always grated on her nerves. Eleanor pulled her wand like a wandfighter going in to battle. Her grasp of wandlore was as awkward as Matthias's grasp of the Anglashian language, but even so she was well-versed enough in the appropriate combinations as to seize the pig figurine by mobile karns and throw it furiously against the wall with a force which sufficed to smash the pig into a satisfying multitude of scattered fragments. The pig figurine had been destroyed beyond repair.

Matthias cast an anxious glance at a nearby porcelain figurine of a shepherdess playing her flute, but he needn't have worried. Eleanor had always liked *that* one.

'Was there a point to that action?' Matthias asked peaceably.

'Why? Did you plan on taking it with you to the barony of Raspero when you return there?'

Eleanor was brandishing her wand in the air so wildly that Matthias, fearing that she would poke her own eye out with it, gently took hold of her wrist, slid the wand out of her hand and returned it to her pocket. This brought the two of them so close together that Matthias could feel Eleanor's breath against his cheek.

They could each feel the presence of the other as a physical force.

'Lord Raspero, you are standing much too close.'

'That sounds all right to me,' Matthias said, taking her hand in his and placing his other hand gently on her waist. 'Anyway, it's only to stop you breaking something else.'

'You will stand further away,' Eleanor said as firmly as she could manage.

'Any moment now I'll do exactly that,' Matthias agreed. He was by now almost speaking into her ear. 'But what's the rush?'

Eleanor raised her arms to push Matthias away, but they were somehow going around Matthias's neck and they were kissing. Eleanor was so astonished at this turn of events that she decided to stop it at once. But the resolve to act seemed to be just out of reach, and they were kissing each other more and more passionately. Eleanor decided to defer her disapproval of what Matthias was about for the time being. She would get around to it later.

2:05 PM, Thursday 30 April 1882 A. F.

'So there's our next Queen,' Gerbern commented, looking over at Matthias and Eleanor embracing and kissing.

'Matthias could do better,' Haris commented.

'Really? How?' Darnell asked.

'He could get someone with bigger tits,' Haris replied.

'You're such a romantic, Haris,' said Felim.

'Yes, you should write poetry to express your finer romantic sensibilities,' Mitzi observed. Mitzi herself had moderately sized breasts.

Haris sneered. 'You know I'm right. You just don't have the guts to admit it.'

'Yes, it takes so much courage to drool over cleavage,' Gerbern observed.

Haris sneered again.

4:25 PM, Thursday 30 April 1882 A. F.

Astrudel came barging into the Chambers of the Crown Princess. 'Your Royal Highness! It's all over the Palace! Everyone's talking about it! You and the Marechal. You're back together. He's your boyfriend again. Congratulations!'

Eleanor tried not to look pleased, but the truth of the matter was that she looked like any other girl in history who had found her man. 'I see. People are gossiping, are they? Well, so be it.'

'Oh, you're no fool, Your Royal Highness, this one isn't getting away, is he? You've got a throne waiting for you, and a handsome husband. And when you're sitting on your throne with your handsome husband, you'll forget about all those what have served you so loyally over the years.'

'You are such a pessimist, Astrudel,' Eleanor said blandly, as if unaware that Astrudel wanted an immediate assurance as to her prospects of future security.

'Aye, with good reason,' Astrudel muttered darkly. 'It's a harsh world we live in, when folk forget those what have sacrificed their all for them what have prospered. To the death I've been loyal to you, stood by your side I have when I could have run for it like others I won't name.' (Given that Astrudel had already and repeatedly named these deserters-from-their-duty on numerous earlier occasions, her forbearance was less impressive than it sounded.)

11:15 PM, Thursday 30 April 1882 A. F.

To the Lord De'Assterides, First Protector of the Protectorate, and flagpole-bearer of many upright and valiant titles, I bid you greetings. May I also add to these, your proper titles, that title of far more significance, namely that of the Fool of Pentharborg. You will not take offence at my familiarity with you, given the shallowness of your imbecilic mind, of whose nature the whole world has rolled its eyes on more than one occasion.

Eleanor looked over what she had written so far. She wondered if her deliberate misspelling of De'Asterides's name was too obvious an insult, then decided to let it stand.

You will no doubt excuse my peremptoriness in proceeding without a moment's delay to the business of this letter. But I must write to you of Westrigonia, of which I am the Crown Princess. We are at present under a foreign threat from which only the forces of Westrigonia under the command of Baron Raspero can hope to save us. But I must especially reply to your request, no, your purported command, that I spy on the Westrigonians for your benefit. You say that the penalty of treason is death while asking me to engage in treason. Where is your logic? I will not behave traitorously to my own country, Westrigonia, on your behalf, no matter how many clumsily written letters you choose to send to me.

Eleanor reflected on the dual nature of her audience before proceeding with her letter. She was writing not so much to De'Asterides as to those to whom he would have shown copies of the letter he had written to her.

I say to you directly, De'Assterides, that your letter to me was offensive not only because of its inherent stupidity as because of its plainly misrepresentative nature. I have never given you a glimpse of anything, let alone a generous heart which I do not possess. But why have you chosen to be such a liar? I am not enough interested to even bother to try to guess. You are a fool, and that is sufficient explanation.

Eleanor's fingers performed a drumroll on her writing desk as she attempted to summon up more insults. But then she gave up and changed direction. There were times when you had to know when to let go.

Let me explain something to you. I am not just the Crown Princess of Westrigonia. I am a Westrigonian. You are the enemy of my country, which means that I am the enemy of you. There is nothing more to say on this matter. If you should ever choose to write to me in future, please bear this in mind. I look in vain amidst the verbiage of your letter for anything relevant to anything, so I say only this. The sovereignty of Westrigonia is absolute and pure. A foreigner like you can simply get lost. I tell you this so that you know it.

Signed,

Her Royal Highness,

The Crown Princess of Westrigonia,

Eleanor.

11:59 PM, Thursday 30 April 1882 A. F.

It was the last tick of the clock before the end of the day. By this time, everyone in Krastienst knew of the re-ignited romance of Matthias and Eleanor. Agendas hidden and visible stirred, tongues wagged and factions flexed their fingers.

CHAPTER THIRTY EIGHT

He stooped to pick up a crown,
To place upon his head,
And make him important.
That was how his troubles began.
Frankie the Villain

The month of May entered Westrigonia like a bull bellowing its way through a gate now that its time had come. Lambs jumped skittishly and ran madly through the pastures and learned of the daily delights of chlorophyll-flavoured grass. Calves slavishly followed their mothers through pastures strewn with yellow and blue five-petalled wild flowers. Ducklings happily followed their mothers out of the river and back again, through purple sage flowers and green nettles. A variety of birds were courting and mating and nesting. Roses appeared in the midst of all the verdant profusion of late spring. Forces stirred in the earth as if its surface was a tablecloth that was being tugged on.

10:35 AM, Friday 1 May 1882 A. F.

It had taken some time for Alaric to corner Matthias and insist on a personal one-to-one conversation, and now all Alaric had to do was to say his piece.

'Well, Matthias, what I want to say is, in a manner of speaking, well, how can I put this, I've decided to be a suitor for the hand of Nina Delwyn, if you understand me.'

'Good for you,' Matthias said, nodding in approval. 'She's very, ah, statuesque.'

'She's an angel of beauty and goodness brought to earth by the stars themselves,' Alaric said fervently.

'That too,' Matthias agreed absently, his thoughts already turning elsewhere. He had more important things to think about than Alaric's love-life. 'Well, let me know when to offer you my congratulations, or commiserations, of course, if your suit is refused.'

'Ah, well, it's only in public that I have to be a suitor because I have already proposed and been accepted, secretly, so there is the consent of her parents to be obtained. Fingers crossed!'

'Good for you, congratulations! I am very pleased for you, Alaric, and your happiness to come.'

'Yes, well, about that, there's a slight, I mean, so to say, what's the word, difficulty, if that's the right word, or obstacle, if you see what I mean.'

'What kind of difficulty?'

'Well, I've been having, it was a complete accident, um, an affair, well, a fling really, except it keeps on going, but anyway, as it happens, with, um, Acantha Godelric.'

'Lady Godelric?'

'Exactly. Her.'

'And this is your difficulty? You're worried that Lady Delwyn might find out about it, is that it?'

'No, well, yes, that would be another difficulty, but it's not the difficulty that I face right now.'

'What is the difficulty which you face right now?'

'Acantha sort of won't exactly let me go. I keep trying to end it but she won't let me go my own way. She makes me keep on seeing her. I don't know why exactly. Part of it might be that she sees me as a way to get to you, but apart from that, I don't think I mean that much to her. I'm a kind of trapped animal, a pet or something. She's very malicious, forget the sweet exterior, she's as tough as nails.'

'Well, just break up with her and call it quits so it's done,' Matthias said a little impatiently, as if Alaric was being annoyingly feeble.

'Well, I've tried to, but she won't have it. And she knows how to make all these potions, like stuff that'll make your private parts wither away.'

'Seriously?'

'Seriously. I have to break up with her without her hating me and being my enemy.'

'Hmm.'

'So what do you think?'

'No girlfriend in the whole of history is not going to become your enemy after you reject her. Look at it from her point of view.'

'Acantha isn't my girlfriend. She just wants to get to you. Plus she's vicious and depraved and enjoys enslaving me. Matthias, I really need your help on this one.'

'If Eleanor is asked – '

'No!' An alarmed Alaric interrupted the monarch of Westrigonia. 'Not El-, er, the Princess, no, when it comes to Acantha she becomes utterly deranged.'

'Deranged?' Matthias queried a little dangerously. He reserved this kind of talk about Eleanor for himself alone.

'Not deranged, no,' Alaric corrected himself hastily. 'That's the wrong word entirely. It's just that she wouldn't think twice about destroying me in order to get at Acantha.'

'Hmm,' Matthias responded, as if he wasn't entirely convinced.

'Matthias, if I've ever helped you out, well, if you can help me out just this one time, I'll never ask anything from you ever again.'

'You never have asked anything from me,' Matthias conceded grudgingly. 'I'll give you that. Alright, Eleanor stays out of this. But what is it exactly that I'm expected to do on your behalf? What's your plan of action?'

'Umm, plan of action.' Alaric tried to sound as decisive as he could. 'Ah, yes, that. Any ideas?'

Matthias groaned and shook his head like a schoolmaster feigning despair. 'Alaric, always reason from first principles. Now, given that people always act from self-interest, what do we do?'

After some thought, Alaric suggested tentatively: 'Make Acantha an offer that she likes.' He felt a bit resentful that he was expected to actually take part in the decision making. He wanted Matthias to have his usual brilliant ideas and solve the problem.

Matthias, who understood this, had just been emphasizing Alaric's dependence on him. Having made his point, he let it go. 'Alright, I'll give the matter some thought. It will be dealt with. In return, I demand one thing from you. Alright?'

'And what's that?' Alaric asked cautiously.

'That you be a good and faithful husband to Lady Nina Delwyn.'

'Absolutely, yes,' Alaric agreed. 'Completely agreed.'

2:15 PM, Saturday 2 May 1882 A. F.

'Eleanor is a human being,' Matthias said. 'This at least I know, and this at least is good.'

Eleanor sniffed loudly. 'I am being complimented, and by what a compliment! I am a *human being*! No fiance has ever praised me so highly! Tell me, Matthias, did you really conceive of such adulation on your own behalf, or has this phrase been scripted for you?'

'It is neither adulation nor mimicry,' Matthias replied promptly, 'but a truth, it seems, beyond your knowledge. Or do you suppose that your days in the Palace Library have taught you all that needs to be known?'

There were times like this when Matthias's comments about Eleanor's life in the Palace seemed too detailed to be a matter of happenstance, guesswork or inference. He must have had a spy in the palace. While thinking about this, Eleanor paused long enough for Alaric to charge in. 'Are there human beings in appearance who are not, um, human beings? So what's going on? And do they change? What do you mean by this, Matthias?'

Everyone stared at Matthias. As it happened, Alaric was not the only one present who was wondering what Matthias knew, but the Barons of Raspero have ever guarded their knowledge.

'Appearance?' asked Matthias in a baffled manner. 'If you are talking about appearance and reality, what do I know of such things? We are all here in appearance, are we not? I might as well ask *you*, friend Alaric, what do *you* mean by this?'

Everyone now stared at Alaric. After a while, the young man cracked. 'Oh, well, nothing, I mean you know, legends and stuff. Ghost stories. The Mountains of Weiden, that kind of thing. That's all.'

'Oh, I am not from the Mountains of Weiden!' Eleanor said sarcastically. She was in fact probing. This was like a cautious pawn move in a chess game. Eleanor could sense that there was something behind what Matthias had said. There were more pawns to be moved. 'And I am a human being as well! Oh, Matthias, you must no doubt have fallen in love with me for these very reasons! Or will you deny this out of cowardice?'

'I am definitely not a coward,' Matthias said with the easy laugh of someone who has proved his courage on the battlefield, 'and so I deny only this accusation.' He laughed again even more merrily than before. No-one else laughed, however, so his merriment fell short. Eleanor's silent gaze was both present and future: Eleanor planned to be around, and she would take careful note of her enemies. Even a future king found himself alone in the midst of such devilish-eyed scrutiny.

4:00 PM, Sunday 3 May 1882 A. F.

'That reminds me of a story,' said Alaric.

'What story?' asked Acteon. He was getting ready to throw Alaric off his story-telling rhythm by making inappropriate interruptions.

'About King Haruldine, and the archer and the tomb in Yajnuacetal,' Alaric replied with the utmost seriousness. 'But of course everyone will say, obviously, how they have heard this story already.'

Alaric only said this because he knew everyone, obviously, would have heard this story already.

'Oh no,' Nina said breathlessly, 'no-one has heard this story.'

Ever since he had kissed her, she had been obsessed with Alaric. In her diary-writing world, he was the One, and they would have twelve children together and live in a great castle on the top of a mountain at the centre of the world.

Mitzi looked at Georgette and rolled her eyes.

'King Haruldine,' Alaric said, beginning his story in a tone of voice that made clear that it was way too late to stop him now, 'invaded Yajualuner in the year of such-and-such, the precise date of which escapes my attention now, which is why I refer to this year as the year of such-and-such.'

Alaric looked sternly around at everyone, as if to check that they were listening. His very carelessness with dates was, his look implied, all part of his mastery of the tale he would tell. Of course he knew the exact date of these events. He was just pretending not to in order to make a point, the point being that it did not matter when this had happened given that they were now outside of history and in the realm of myth.

His listeners all nodded with varying degrees of enthusiasm. Acteon cast about in his mind for something to say that could derail all this success Alaric was having with his story-telling, but he was already too late: Alaric was continuing his tale.

The tale of King Haruldine and the archer

Haruldine razed the capital city of Yajualuner to the ground. This city was called Yajnuacetal, which meant City of the Rose and Purple Flowers in their now extinct language. But a Yajuax archer managed at the end to shoot Haruldine with an arrow, despite Haruldine's extreme cowardice in hiding from all the fighting in his fortified tent, due to Haruldine, at the very end, having been assured that all was over, emerging from his protective seclusion to boastfully survey his new dominion. This Yajuax archer, rising to his feet and by some combination of luck and skill and the merely fortuitious similitude of an entirely contingent moment, fired off an arrow that pierced through Haruldine's neck and felled the cowardly king on the spot. The archer was immediately hacked to death by a dozen or so outraged warriors but the damage had been done. Haruldine lay dying, and his last words were that his tomb should be erected on the place where he had been felled, with its epitaph being: "Look around you and behold what I have wrought." The city all around should remain a destroyed ruin, Haruldine went on to say, because that would be the legacy which he would bequeath to the world. So to this day, the ruined city of Yajualuner and Haruldine's tomb have remained wedded together in the eyes of heaven and earth.

There was a silence while everyone looked at Alaric, who for his part gazed into the distance as if communing with the spirit of eternity. Nina gazed adoringly at the love of her life.

'That's not the story I heard,' Acteon said argumentatively. 'Haruldine was betrayed by his top general Ukbecistran, murdered in his tent, and left there in his tomb with this inscription as an ironic commentary on the failure of his reign and the end of his dynasty. The archer was just a cover story for these political shenanigans.'

'How did Haruldine manage to say all those things with an arrow sticking through his neck?' Haris asked.

Everyone chuckled. Haris looked pleased with himself.

11:10 AM, Monday 4 May 1882 A. F.

'But of course I should say nothing given that you are fully conversant with all that need be said,' Eleanor remarked while studying her fan as if reminding herself of how fans were made.

'No, Eleanor, not at all, say what you want to.'

Eleanor looked up at Matthias with a momentary fierceness, as if to emphasize that she was overlooking his many failings. 'But why should I say a single thing? You need nothing but yourself, is this not so?'

'Believe it or not, I need you more than anything else,' he said, and he meant every word he said at that moment.

'Oh, then I can speak after all,' Eleanor said, with a definitive sarcasm, as if only just then solving a mathematical riddle. 'I had not known this was so.'

Matthias sighed, as if he was a saint ready to turn sinner. 'I have a lot on, Eleanor. But I am listening.'

'Then listen! Do you know anything of Westrigonia? Let me explain to you what is going on here. Many of the laws and shibboleths and commonplace babblings of what passes for thoughts in this our land are based on fallacies. For example, do you know that women are hollow logs through which pass the children they bear? But this is so by analogy! You see, when seeds are pressed into the earth, they germinate and send down roots and grow forth into mighty trees and plants and vegetables. All well and good! Now, when a man's seed enters into the womb of a woman this seed germinates and grows by various stages into the baby that is born and so it is that a woman is a hollow log because the baby passes through her. And so it is that the woman has no rights over the children she bears, because these children have issued from the male seed just as the fruit of the tree provide the seeds for the next tree. The man owns the children as an extension of himself. This is the basis of the laws of Westrigonia regarding the rights of the parents over the children. But the facts are completely wrong. The woman provides the egg which the seed inseminates. She is therefore the co-creator of the child. We know this now due to our modern knowledge. So we can no longer say that the male sperm impregnates the woman just as a seed pushed into the ground germinates into the next tree. What has happened is that our law is derived from a supposed metaphysical truth which is derived from a mistaken physical fact.'

'What's your point?' asked Matthias.

'We should change the law,' Eleanor said firmly. 'That is my point. Let us get with the times.'

'Perhaps I should have a committee formed to look into all this,' Matthias said thoughtfully.

Eleanor slapped the arm of her chair furiously, 'How dare you be so rude!'

'What am I supposed to say to any of this?'

'You are supposed to say something intelligent!'

'Do you really imagine that you are the first person to have suggested this kind of reform? Justin the Second said many similar things, but as I keep on saying, I will not be another Good King Justin. Try to grasp this simple statement.'

'You are hiding behind this never-ending refusal of being like Good King Justin,' Eleanor said furiously. 'It is nothing but your excuse to do nothing.'

'Justin made changes that he had to enforce by suppressing dissent, and everything went from bad to worse.'

'Justin did not have me with him,' Eleanor said firmly.

Matthias laughed. 'That's a good point. But even so, change is not so simple as you propose. Remember how King Cayman the Learned attempted to bring back some of the more commendable sinecures of earlier times that had been abolished by the hasty and intemperate actions of zealots. He suggested, as innocently as anyone could have suggested, that it was not necessarily a bad thing to be paid for doing nothing. And what was the result? He was overthrown and killed. He was found hiding under a bed dressed in women's clothes, dragged out and beaten to death with a broomstick.'

'So said his enemies!' Eleanor said reprovingly. 'That story is widely thought to have been made up.'

'And is Cayman around to say different? No! History is written by the winners. In any case, the issue of sinecures is more complicated than Cayman's enemies made allowances for. After all, when you stop to think about it, why shouldn't people be paid for doing nothing? What is it with the fanatical ferocity of these social reformers? Their real complaint is that no-one has given *them* a sinecure. They are driven by envy. Name me one person in the whole of history who had a sinecure and complained about it!'

'And so this will be the length and breadth, without depth, of your reign,' Eleanor said almost peaceably, as if she were now resigned to the inevitable. 'You intend to be just another fool with a crown on your head.'

Matthias took a deep breath and sighed moodily. 'And what is the measure of success of a monarch, Eleanor? Being alive is not a bad starting point, if you ask me, which of course you are not, given that you are the one lecturing me. But in any case, once we have a complete knowledge of what is to be done, then we can get on with it; but what is to be done? Those who say that they know what is to be done have to date invariably been those who have made everything even worse than it was before. But of course you know better! So tell me: what is to be done?'

'We say that as women are co-creators of children, they have co-equal rights with the fathers. And we write that as a law.'

'But why stop there? Why not give women all the rights over the children and write men out of the picture altogether?'

'Because that would be only to repeat the current error in its opposite form. But perhaps you prefer to ignore the truth?'

Matthias took another deep breath, even deeper than before, and again sighed even more moodily than before. 'I understand what you are saying, Eleanor. But to change this one law would have knock-on effects which would change other laws, which would change others, and by the end of it all what would remain of the original situation?'

'So what you are saying is that you choose to do nothing because you cannot foresee all things? But doing nothing may well destroy everything just as effectively because leaving the system of laws as a whole to remain as they are will mean that in the long run the laws will become the widespread object of mockery and contempt, and they will be overthrown by a revolution. The law has its bare buttocks hanging out of its trousers, and the longer this remains so the greater the mockery which will arise. To do nothing in order to save everything is ultimately to endanger everything! But of course, please ignore everything I am saying because I am only lecturing you after all!'

Matthias sighed again, and this time it wasn't for show. 'Alright, I will support *some* changes if I become King. But that is far from certain as things stand at present.'

'Will you bring back sinecures?' Gherardo asked eagerly. He was all in favour of this project.

'Monarchy itself has been called a sinecure,' said Topher. He was against sinecures.

'*Time tells all things,*' Matthias said evasively.

3:20 PM, Tuesday 5 May 1882 A. F.

Matthias had arranged to meet Lady Godelric in the lobby of the Hadewig Hotel. He had made sure that there were witnesses to their meeting in the form of Westrigonian military officers standing nearby, out of earshot, but able to see what was going on.

Lady Godelric was all smiles and attentive small talk as they settled into their chairs and conversed upon the great doings of the day.

'Lady Godelric,' Matthias said in a pleasant manner, 'can I thank you for being so kind as to see me today?'

'No, Marechal,' Lady Godelric said breathlessly, 'it is *you* who *I* must thank for such a kindness.'

'That being done,' Matthias said with an urbaneness that encompassed even such a pleasing disagreement as this, 'I must proceed to a less happy conversational exchange.'

After a pause, Lady Godelric, who was indefinitely subtle, said: 'But whatever can you mean by *less happy*, my gallant Marechal, the lord of my heart and loins?'

'I am not the lord of your loins,' Matthias said on the instant, knowing full well that he could not let this pass by unchallenged. 'Or your heart. But never mind that. I want to talk about Alaric, who is not the lord of your loins either, despite your recent intimacy.'

'But whatever can you mean, Matthias?' Lady Godelric asked.

Matthias knew enough to reinforce this red line. 'Lady Godelric, you will refer to me as "Marechal" or you will not refer to me at all. Is that clear?'

Lady Godelric's opened mouth and leaning-forward-posture might have been indicative of anything.

'Now, as to Alaric, he is not only my protégé, but he has a certain value for me with regard to an arranged marriage which I have in mind and which has a certain political value for me. It is necessary that his public reputation is spotless. Therefore your dalliance with him must end. Do you understand what I am saying?'

'But to whom will my precious, my beloved, my one-and-only-love-of-my-life Alaric be married to, like a prize bull in a meat market?'

'Never mind. My point is that this marriage will have political dimensions that are to my advantage. Therefore, you have to let Alaric go. But let me make plain, I understand that you are not to be left empty-handed. You are perfectly correct to refer to a market. We are now in that market, and so let us haggle. What is your price for letting Alaric go?'

Lady Godelric's red-painted lips were opened as if in disbelief at the heartlessness of the world into which she had been born. 'But what are you saying, Marechal? That the Alaric who has conquered my heart, and my body, is to be sold by me like a slave-boy in a market?'

'Metaphors come and go, Lady Godelric. Never mind slaves in a market. I am only talking about accepting a parting of ways between the two of you. That is all. And let me be more plain spoken than before: when I refer to price, I do not necessarily mean money, although that can of course be included. I just mean an agreed settlement.'

'Young Alaric is of enormous value to such an esteemed personage such as yourself,' Lady Godelric gushed in the friendliest of fashions. 'You will do anything on his behalf.'

Matthias made sure not only that he had full eye-contact with Lady Godelric, but that his memories were of nothing but snow-drifts while he said the following to Lady Godelric: 'Alaric is dispensable, as are you. Furthermore, over the years I have become acquainted with a variety of disreputable acquaintances, who would happily take a lady such as you, even with her tongue cut out, as a lady able to provide services to the multitude of men who compose their clientele. But perhaps you will protest that I am talking to no purpose.'

For a moment nothing was said. But as their eyes locked, everything was made clear. Lady Godelric could see what he was capable of while looking into his cold eyes. So she backtracked.

'But no-one can say this, that the Marechal, that the Baron of Raspero himself, could talk to no purpose. No, no, I protest, it is not so, it is not true. Everything you say is to the point.'

Matthias took her point. She was ready to make a deal. 'Indeed this is so. May I congratulate the Lady of Stayrint herself on her swift acumen? Let Alaric go and we are in business. Fail to concede this point, and there is nothing to be said. I reason from political and sentimental axioms, but I reason nonetheless. Now, what are your conditions?'

'What are my conditions?' Lady Godelric bowed her head, as if about to burst into tears. 'Conditions? But whatever can you mean?'

'What can I mean? Alright: point number one. You will stay away from Alaric. If I ever hear of you coming near him again, I will see to it that you are removed from any place that can do him harm. Do you understand me, or are you going to whine that I am speaking a language that you don't understand?'

Lady Godelric's lowered gaze and her still posture showed that she had heard every word that Matthias had said.

'Point number two: you will leave Krastienst tomorrow and go back to Stayrint. You are very ill-advised to ever cross my path again. Point number three: there is no point number three at this time. That remains to be defined. Now: I am willing to hear your objections at this time. You may speak, and I will listen.'

Lady Godelric was a fox who knew the precise limits of her realm. Matthias, due to his years of discipline of being on the run, was immune to her charms, and he was as ruthless as he had hinted. Lady Godelric knew this without needing to be told. So she reserved her energies to achieving what could be done.

'But Alaric, who has conquered my body and my heart, why is he not here today? Surely he has not forsaken me at this time?'

'Alaric has already tried to break up with you, as we both know. But you are perfectly correct. He would oppose you being too harshly treated.'

'Oh, blessed Alaric,' Lady Godelric said automatically, 'he will defend me against the dangers of this world.'

'Only up to a point.' Matthias had in fact being playing his own little game. It was unlikely that Alaric would oppose any harsh measure being taken against Lady Godelric. 'But it is not Alaric you have to deal with. It is the Marechal of Westrigonia, who wishes you to go back to Stayrint at this time, without delay. You leave tomorrow. I have spoken. That is all.'

With that parting comment, Matthias rose to his feet and departed without a backward glance, waving the attentive Captain Ingramstadt to see Lady Godelric safely back to her rooms.

5:10 PM, Wednesday 6 May 1882 A. F.

'She's a witch,' said Rayerfeld. '*And* she's a foreigner. She can't be Queen.'

Matthias nodded understandingly. Another man might have lost his temper on hearing his girlfriend called a witch, but not a man who had been chased by the police forces of five continents. 'I am thinking, my good friend the Baron of Rayerfeld, of making you Postmaster General. Would you be prepared to take on such a commitment?'

Rayerfeld's first thought was to wonder about the identity of the witches abroad in Westrigonia at that hour. It had always been his childhood dream to be Postmaster General, but how on earth could Matthias have known about it? What was going on? He stared at Matthias, but the look of polite enquiry on the Marechal's face was as uninformative as a brick wall. Perhaps the Marechal had not known, and this was all some kind of coincidence, or Fortuna was being playful.

'Why on earth would you do such a thing, Marechal?'

Matthias had no intention of answering this question properly by saying that the public library records of Rayerfeld's borrowings as a child had disclosed the likelihood of such an ambition. (By now, Matthias had the resources of the government at his disposal.) Instead, he dissembled on the spot. 'My offer has nothing to do with the widespread nature of the ambition amongst our youth, past and present, to be Postmaster General.' He paused while Rayerfeld blinked as this entirely made-up statement sank into the Rayerfeld brain. Rayerfeld now felt like part of an hitherto-unsuspected movement amongst the youth, past and present, of the nation. Matthias pressed home his advantage. 'The point is, my good Rayerfeld, that the position of Postmaster General is beyond politics, which is why it is so widely respected. Naturally, as Postmaster General, you cannot make political comments. For example, if Princess Eleanor was to become Queen of Westrigonia, you would have to accept this outcome without opposition. But of course, you understand this already without needing to be told in so many words. I'm just saying, given what you were saying.'

Rayerfeld's mind was reeling, but one suspicion stood out from the crowd of thoughts. 'You are bribing me with this appointment!' he snapped in outrage.

'Certainly not!' Matthias said immediately, wondering inwardly if he had overplayed his hand. 'Far from it. No-one can bribe you. This is well-known.' (Rayerfeld's honesty was indeed well known. He was one of the few honest public figures in Westrigonia.) 'But just think of what a figure you would cut as Postmaster General. Your beard, your air of defiance, your bristling belligerence, well, people will say that you can't make this up! I am not talking about the statues of you that will be raised by public subscription and so forth. I am just talking about how amazing you would be as Postmaster General, that is all. That position is *you* down to a crossed t and a dotted i. I am amazed just thinking about it. The prospect is astonishing by its very precision, its exactness, and I do not choose these words lightly.' (Matthias in fact was choosing these words lightly. He had found by experience that this was how to go about the business of bamboozlement.) 'When the news is voiced abroad that the Baron of Rayerfeld has been made Postmaster General, everyone will say: "But of course! Who else could it be?" '

Matthias had been careful not to repeat his earlier comment that Rayerfeld would have to accept Eleanor as Queen if he were made Postmaster General. Such a point could only be made once. Rayerfeld would only be antagonized by being pushed. It could be nothing but carrots and encouraging words all the way from now on.

Rayerfeld looked grumpy, as if Matthias was stepping on his daffodils. 'That is all very well, Marechal, but, well, I mean to say, what if, I mean, people will say, I mean, well, all well and good, but, but why do you want to have me as Postmaster General?'

'I wish to have a *Ministry of all the Talents*,' Matthias said without hesitation, dragging forth from memory a phrase from a history essay he had written as a schoolboy. 'Let everyone be in their rightful place. You cannot yourself, my good friend Rayerfeld, doubt for one moment that you would be an excellent Postmaster General. Well?'

Rayerfeld stared long and hard at the Marechal and then asked: 'Is this a bribe to help get the witch Eleanor on the throne?'

I know when to tell the truth, and when not to tell the truth.

'Of course it is,' Matthias said on the instant, reversing his earlier denial, 'but Eleanor will become Queen one way or another, even if I have to run you over in the meantime. I am merely suggesting a civilized way to accomplish the inevitable.'

Rayerfeld half-snorted as if in disbelief, and Matthias knew that he had won. Rayerfeld had come around to his side. Honest people are always swayed by a display of honesty. It hits them where they live. 'Inevitable?' Rayerfeld queried. 'Says who?' Yet all the fight had gone out of the man.

There were only the formalities of concluding hostilities left to be done.

'Listen to me, Rayerfeld,' Matthias said insistently, leaning forward as if to be even more insistent with his every word. 'Your nationalism is correct but narrow. We can't ignore the whole of the rest of the world. There's more to life, more to our country, more to everything than banging this one drum over and over. If I become King, trust me, I will see to it that this country will be properly governed. And if I become King then Eleanor will become Queen. The two go together. But Westrigonia will take its place amongst the nations of the world. They will not be shut out. And even you, in time, will acknowledge the value, at least in part, of foreignness. Without the foreign, there is not even the possibility of being ourselves. Westrigonia is also, by definition, what is not Westrigonia.'

'Spare me your philosophical nonsense,' Rayerfeld said abruptly. He was obviously avoiding using stronger language. 'But I will grant you one thing. You have your wits about you. You could be King. And you are Westrigonian, despite all your babbling about the wonderful foreigners. And so Eleanor –'

'*Princess* Eleanor,' Matthias interrupted, with an edge to his tone of voice.

Rayerfeld hesitated, but then conceded the point. 'And so Princess Eleanor would be, well, limited in her Zoller-Abstein aspirations. You would be a Westrigonian king, would you not?'

Matthias sighed. 'You talk as if you knew what it meant to be Westrigonian, Rayerfeld. My ancestor Etienne was amongst those who all but *invented* Westrigonia. I say that hesitantly. A culture is more than the constellation of its political, economic and social systems. Music, language, religion, poetry, mythology, novels, painting, the theatre, technology, and so on, must all emerge and interact over time. And time is key. Without time, nothing. And we are still in time today, here and now, carrying on as if we know what is what and who is who. But of course I am talking to one who knows everything already. Go on, Rayerfeld, lecture me some more. What were you saying?'

After a long silence, Rayerfeld said: 'I believe in our way of life. Is that so very wrong? Well, Marechal? Is that what you are saying?'

'Listen to me, Rayerfeld. Westrigonia will remain Westrigonia. I promise you this. But tomorrow's Westrigonia will be as different from today's Westrigonia as we are different from our parents. And they will remember Eleanor as Queen and you as Postmaster General.'

'And Matthias the Fourth as King.'

'That too.'

Rayerfeld tried to look grumpy, but he was all too obviously secretly delighted. 'I will give careful thought to your proposition, Marechal. Perhaps I shall accept your offer. And very well, if I must be non-political as Postmaster General, I will refrain from opposing Princess Eleanor as Queen. You are buying me off, are you not?'

'Believe it or not, Rayerfeld, I am trying to secure the best outcome all around. Is that such a bad thing?'

Rayerfeld tugged at his beard. 'I will give you my answer tomorrow.'

'I await your answer with great anticipation,' Matthias said with a certain formality, but by then of course, they both knew what the answer would be.

Matthias had rolled Rayerfeld with an expertise that was mathematical in its precision. And best of all, they both knew what had happened and that knowledge was itself the acceptance of what had happened.

It was done.

10:20 PM, Wednesday 6 May 1882 A. F.

Lady Godelric departed Krastienst in a flying carriage provided to Lieutenant Gustav Saranna by the Marechal. The stars glittered brightly overhead as she poked her head out of the flying carriage like a child, calling to Lieutenant Saranna to come and see how beautiful they were. Lieutenant Saranna came over and looked for himself, his arm pressing lightly against her side.

Earlier that day, Captain Ingramstadt and Major Ubertostyne had fought a duel of final combat. Ubertostyne had been killed and Ingramstadt badly wounded, perhaps fatally wounded. He now lay on his sick-bed, hovering between life and death. Lady Godelric visited him, and kneeled by his bed in a flood of tears, and even licked his blood-soaked bandages, such was her sympathy for the fallen man. It turned out that the duel had been fought over which of the two men would remain as Lady Godelric's lover. The Marechal, on the news being brought to him, lost his temper and shouted that it was long past time for Lady Godelric to leave Krastienst. The task of seeing this done was appointed to Lieutenant Saranna, a brave and honourable man from a good family who had distinguished himself fighting under Matthias during the Battle of Krastienst.

So it was that Lieutenant Saranna escorted Lady Godelric back to her estates in Stayrint. The gallant soldier did not return to Krastienst the next day. Indeed, there was some confusion about where he was and where he was supposed to be. Some days later, it emerged that he was living with Lady Godelric as her lover. He was dishonourably discharged from the army, and some weeks later turned up at the family home, with a wild look in his eyes, and having lost weight. His sleep was these days disturbed, and he jumped at sudden noises. He was never the same man again. By then, Captain Ingramstadt had been long dead.

Lady Godelric was not one to go home quietly.

7:20 PM, *Thursday 7 May 1882 A. F.*

Then everything went into reverse and the world moved backwards.

Matthias and Eleanor had a quarrel. The ostensible cause of the quarrel was a disagreement about the correct manner of handling bread rolls at dinner, but of course, as always in such matters, this was merely appearance only. All quarrels have hidden roots.

What had happened is that Eleanor, after putting up with Matthias's misbehavior without complaint for some time in a saintly and forbearing manner, found that she simply could not put up with these daily outrages any more. Matthias dealt with his bread rolls at dinner by seizing them in his hands and tearing them in two, and then tearing them again into bite sized pieces to be an accompaniment to the food on his plate.

This was not how things were done in the Palace of Krastienst, Eleanor informed the Marechal. Bread rolls were not torn apart as if by wild animals in the forest in such a fashion. Bread rolls were cut by the sharp knifes supplied for such a task and placed conveniently and neatly to the side of the plate upon which the bread rolls rested.

Matthias replied that in the barony of Raspero where he had grown up, bread rolls had always been dealt with in such a fashion as he dealt with them. His good humour was much shorter than usual, a clue that the Crown Princess of Westrigonia failed to pay attention to at that moment in time. (But then quarrels are always, upon prolonged inspection, found to have been based on particular moments in time.)

Eleanor pointed out that Matthias was not in the Castle of Raspero but in the Palace of Krastienst. She reminded Matthias of the saying *when in Malta, do as the Maltese do*, and for Matthias's benefit, spelled out that what that meant in these circumstances was that Matthias should behave in the Palace of Krastienst as is appropriate in such environs.

Volcanoes tremble the ground in fair warning before blowing their top, and so did the Marechal, who lost his temper with a fair amount of preamble in the way of increasingly vexed statements.

Matthias pointed out that a) he didn't have to sit at the same table as the Princess Eleanor in any case, and b) he could always go to Castle Raspero where as the thirty-seventh Baron he could break his bread rolls precisely as he blessed well chose to break his bread rolls.

Eleanor stood her ground in the midst of these molten lava flows all around her. She had stated the facts, and the facts only, in the interests of civilisation and morality, and while she did not expect Matthias to thank her, she did expect Matthias to at least acknowledge that there were standards to be adhered to by even those merely visiting the Palace.

Rising to his feet, Matthias shouted that he did not consider Eleanor to be a suitable dining companion, that he had no intention of dining with her again, and that he had had enough of her insufferable petty mindedness. With that, the Marechal of Westrigonia turned on his heel and stormed out of the dining room.

7:45 PM, Thursday 7 May 1882 A. F.

Matthias did not cool down or calm down after returning to his rooms, the Rollo Chambers. He paced up and down like a lion in his cage, his whole being heating up as if fed by raging flames. His very solitude amplified his anger. He was fed up with everything. Was it his fault that half his family had been killed and he had been driven, what with one thing and another, into taking such steps as destroying Phelan and sabotaging the expansion of an empire? No, it was not his fault. Why was he even here in this blasted blessed Palace of Krastienst where everything had to be just so anyway? He was supposed to be in Castle Raspero at this very moment, and why was he not there? Matthias saw then very clearly, and with such a crystal clear clarity that he could have in an instant counted the petals of a cherry tree in full bloom, that he was only here in the Palace of Krastienst because of Eleanor. If it were not for her, he would have been long gone. And that led ineluctably to the obvious question of why on earth he should stay for one moment longer here in the Palace on behalf of that stuck-up self-serving self-righteous Crown Princess, given that he had after all already saved her from her enemies (and not even been thanked for it!) and was now being press-ganged into being the monarch of Westrigonia by forces of history acting as the lackeys of Fortuna.

It was as if a shout had shattered window panes. There was a feeling of space, of freedom, of being able to stretch out with luxurious abandon, of vastness unfettered. Matthias saw all-of-a-sudden that it was time to leave the Palace of Krastienst and go home. For seven long years he had yearned to return home and now he could do it. What was he waiting for? What was he doing here anyway?

Matthias decided, then and there, with a sense of finality, that this whole business of fooling around with matters of high state was best left to the ship of fools who normally sailed these waters. He would manage his allotted portion, and to blazes with everything else. Let the world burn! He would safeguard what was his, and all would be well.

8:55 AM, Friday 8 May 1882 A. F.

Matthias stepped into the Public Portal of Krastienst and stepped out of the Public Portal of Raspero. He was home!

Since recapturing Raspero from the Melisendiens, Matthias had done what he could to catch up with his barony and his people. But in between fending off the Protectorate and the Vidaldmeet, he had had little time for what was for him the most important issue of all: his baronial inheritance.

Now he had time, and he spent it freely. He moved back to Castle Raspero, and began re-furnishing it. All that had been hidden in the caves of the Mountains of Lochfric and overseas were brought back. Lady Jimena Raspero came back. Lena and her fiancé, Lord Hallvard Obradsean, a Zoller-Abstein Marquis from Troderent came visiting. Castle Raspero was its old self in a very short time. The Lord of Raspero had returned to his domains after his exile, and all was well.

11:45 AM, Sunday 10 May 1882 A. F.

Eleanor was not able to put up with Matthias's absence for more than two days. She stepped through the Public Portal of Raspero with her retinue behind her and a certain runaway monarch ahead of her.

Matthias had left Eleanor a letter explaining that he was abdicating any claim to the throne, that he was returning to his ancestral heartland, and that she could count on his support in any of her future political undertakings. The play on words between *undertakings,* as in things that you do, and *undertakers,* as in the buriers of the dead, was even more deadly in Westrigonian than in Anglashian. Eleanor crumpled up his letter in her hands, but that didn't change the fact that Matthias was gone.

No matter! Eleanor received her visitors, read her letters, and made her political calculations; but there was something missing.

Eleanor found, surprisingly, that she missed the presence of Matthias.

His absence was a continual emptiness in her stomach. When he had taken her in his arms and kissed her, she had felt his presence from the top of her head to the tips of her toes. Even when they were apart in separate rooms, she could feel that he was present in the Palace. It had felt reassuring to have her boyfriend so close by. It was not just that Matthias was a renowned wand fighter, or that his cleverness and endless resourcefulness were also reassuring. It was also that he had a certain prestige due to his chequered career that gave him a political authority in these uncertain times. But above all else, supremely above all else, was that Eleanor knew, she knew in her heart, that Matthias loved her and would defend her against her enemies. But now Matthias was gone, but her enemies were still there.

It was this latter point that pressed upon Eleanor. She observed, in the veiled looks and sideways statements of those politicians who discussed the latest developments with the Crown Princess, the same destructive venality that had made of her a lottery prize not long before, and would no doubt treat her as viciously again. It was not the first time in her life that Eleanor was forced to realise that the very attributes of her life that raised her up were the same attributes that dragged her down. She was a titled beauty, and that made her both an object of praise and a target for destruction.

Eleanor understood that her beauty was a force that acted on Matthias just as it did on others. Yet Matthias, like all other gentlemen of honour of Eleanor's acquaintance, was prepared to bow to Eleanor's rejection of his attentions, and move on. But alas for Eleanor, and all other ladies in her situation, there were those for whom honour was merely a façade behind which their lusts fermented. Eleanor felt not only besieged, but undefended. Romano and the Palace Guard still protected her, but for how much longer? Who was in charge? Apparently, no-one. The Anglashian ascendancy was in retreat. The Protectorate was in disarray. And in these circumstances, the Marechal of Westrigonia had disappeared.

So it was that Eleanor went to the Public Portal of Krastienst and travelled to Raspero with her ladies-in-waiting. With a peremptory courtesy she requested an audience with the Baron of Raspero in accordance with the ancient principles of hospitality which still obtained in Westrigonia, if not always elsewhere.

Matthias received her in the Room of the Globe, his mother and sister and her fiancé in attendance. By the time she reached there, Eleanor had been struck anew by doubts about her presumptions. Castle Raspero was an astonishing symphony of wood and marble, plaster and brickwork, paintings and statuary and furnishings, and this was only of what she had seen on her journey from the door to the Room of the Globe. Eleanor was reminded that Castle Raspero had been called *a vision of taste and beauty allied with the world's resources* by Magister Iagan Hachirousan.

The Steward of Raspero escorted Eleanor to a place before the chair occupied by Matthias, where he gestured her to a standstill, bowed to the Baron, and retreated a number of steps to a place of standing-still-and-waiting. Eleanor approved the pageantry.

Time passed, the silence continued and Eleanor, standing before the stern gaze of the Baron of Raspero, chose to speak. 'Matthias', she began, 'I-'

With an upraised forefinger, Matthias silenced her and said: 'You will address me correctly, or you will leave these premises. I am addressed as Lord Raspero.' His face was like a mask.

Eleanor was suddenly reminded of when Matthias had arrived at the Palace of Krastienst and she had made the same, but reversed, complaint. Along with this comparison, came the observation of how their circumstances had differed between then and now. Along with that additionally came a sense of how much distance there was between the two of them. Matthias had taken her in his arms and kissed her every chance he could over the past few days, only to now glare at her as if she had broken the law.

Eleanor could see that the situation she was in was too complicated for logic and reason. If she clashed with Matthias and insisted that she could call him by his first name, he would have her thrown out. If she accepted his decree, then she would always be at arms distance from the Baron of Raspero. Eleanor understood then for the first time since Matthias had left the Palace how serious all this was. It was not just the look on his face. It was also that she stood in Castle Raspero itself, and she began to understand the claims that his ancestral homelands had on Matthias's heart. Eleanor was struck forcibly by the truth: Matthias had no intention of ever returning to the Palace of Krastienst. It would take a good deal of skill and misdirection to turn him around.

'Do you accept me as being Westrigonian?' Eleanor asked. After a long pause, she added: 'Lord Raspero.'

Matthias considered this question like a stone statue contemplating eternity. After a while, he said: 'Yes, I do.'

'Good. Then you are not rejecting me as a foreigner, are you?'

'Your Royal Highness, why have you come here?'

'Why? I have come here because you left me. I have come her to ask *you* the questions. And my question number one is this: why do you always take me in your arms and kiss me if all you ever do is leave me?'

Eleanor noted in her peripheral vision that Matthias's sister and mother stirred on hearing this, while Lena's fiancé, who did not speak a word of Westrigonian, looked on in compete ignorance of the drama unfolding before him. (Although Lena, who spoke fluent Anglashian like a native, would enlighten him later.)

'That is rather a biased and incomplete accounts of events,' Matthias said like a judge on his bench rejecting a procedural plea, 'but in any case it does not answer my question. Why are you here, Your Royal Highness?'

'To ask you why you are not *there*,' Eleanor snapped, even though she understood that snapping at Matthias and bossing him about was not in her interests. She therefore proceeded less snappily, and more pleasantly: 'I have come here to ask you why you are not in the Palace of Krastienst governing the defence of the realm.'

'The defence of what realm?' asked the thirty-seventh Baron of Raspero.

'You see? How can you even say that? You act as if you are not even Westrigonian. The defence of what realm? The defence of the realm of Westrigonia, that is what realm.'

'What does Westrigonia have to do with me?' asked Matthias.

Eleanor stopped then, as if her whole life had come to a pause. There it was: what did Westrigonia have to do with anyone? What did it have to do with her? Why could she not just leave?

'Are you a clever person, Lord Raspero?'

'Up to a point,' Matthias replied, as evasively as a clever person would.

'Up to a point,' Eleanor repeated, as if aware of the ambiguities which bracketed the phrase. 'Then answer me this: who else could govern the realm as effectively as you?'

'I am sure that you could answer this question much better than anyone else.'

'Have you any idea at all of the danger I am in now that you are gone? Romano and the guards protect me for now, but how long will that last? Not long. You have only been gone three days, but already I can watch the sands running out of the glass.'

'Then run home to Trentland,' Matthias said with a certain measure of contempt.

'Trentland is not my home, nor has it been for quite some time. But where is your home? The barony of Raspero, you will cry. All well and good. But I say this to you, Matthias the Fourth. Yes, Matthias, that is your name, is it not? If you turn your back on your chance of being King of Westrigonia, you are dishonourable, and there is nothing to be said for you. But come, why don't you whine about how badly you have been treated and how that makes you not liable to follow your duty?'

'You talk about my duty as if you know all about it,' said the Baron of Raspero.

Eleanor could tell that Matthias was weakening. How she knew this she could not tell exactly. The Witch of Trentland somehow sensed the shift of emotions in Matthias's chest. 'I do know all about it. Ask me if you choose, or I will tell you anyway. Your duty is to your country, Westrigonia, to which you owe everything that you are. Is that not so?'

'No, that is not so,' answered the Baron of Raspero. 'I owe everything to my Raspero bloodline.'

'And where would that bloodline be today without the Westrigonian veins through which it runs? The country cries out for a king, but you have run away. Fine, you do not want me by your side. Then choose someone else to be your Queen. But I will say this to you. If you ask me to marry you as your baroness, I will accept your proposal.'

It was not only Matthias that was silent at that moment in time. The world itself was stopped still. But then Matthias spoke, and the world started moving again. 'Eleanor, sit down.'

With a gesture of his hand, Matthias waved the Steward into action. Chairs were brought forth and Eleanor and her ladies-in-waiting were seated.

'I am surprised by your decision, Eleanor,' Matthias said. 'You seemed so determined to be the Queen of Westrigonia.'

'Even determinations can change.'

'Then they can never have been very determined.'

'Then it is just as well that you were never determined to really marry me.'

Matthias laughed, to Eleanor's relief. This was more like his old self. 'Well, being married tends to last for longer than a change of mind. That's something to bear in mind.'

'What about being in love, Matthias? How long does that last for?'

'A lifetime,' said Matthias implacably.

'And are you in love with me?'

'Eleanor, why are you here? Yes, I know, I heard you. Your authority is undermined without me there. But apart from that?'

'Matthias, are you in love with me? Yes or no?'

After a long pause, the Baron of Raspero, despite being implacable in his own domains, said: 'Yes.'

'Then why are you not by my side in the Palace of Krastienst?'

'Because I cannot be sure of you. What are you about? You bang on and on about what to feed peacocks and how to cut bread rolls, and that is all I can tell of your character.'

'Matthias, that is unfair.'

'Then run back to Krastienst, or Troderent, and whine about what *is* fair.'

'If you truly love me, you would judge me more reasonably.'

'Love has nothing to do with being reasonable.'

'You do not need to prove your love for me by being unreasonable.'

'I do not need to prove my love for you at all.'

'Yes, you do. You left me all alone in the midst of my enemies.'

'I made sure that Romano would protect you. I made arrangements before I left the Palace.'

'And how long were those arrangements supposed to last for? Well? How long?'

'You tell me. At some point, continuity must be managed.'

'Fine. But look at me, Matthias. Look at me directly and tell me that you don't care what happens to me.'

Matthias paused and then said: 'As the Baroness of Raspero, I care about you more than anything else.'

'But I am not the Baroness of Raspero. I am the Crown Princess of Westrigonia. And what then?'

Matthias laughed. 'Eleanor, I see what you are about. You are pointing out that I have not proposed to you yet. But not so fast. Why don't you move here for a while so we can talk more about what is to be done? After all, I understand that I do have to propose to you properly if we are to be engaged.'

Eleanor tilted her chin and said: 'Very well.'

3:25 PM, Sunday 10 May 1882 A. F.

Matthias lost no time in proposing to Eleanor. He was not going to hang about in this matter. He had the most beautiful girl in the world at his mercy, and he was not going to fail to grab her while the grabbing was good. After lunch he took her on a guided tour of Castle Raspero. He figured that even a snobbish princess would be impressed by its magnificence, and he was not wrong. Oliver's riches and aesthetic sensibility had conjured up a setting not unworthy of a fairy-tale.

At last Eleanor felt that she understood Matthias. He had never been due to inherit all this, being the second son. Stefan had been due to be the thirty-seventh Baron of Raspero. But the deaths of his father and older brother had left Matthias not only as Baron, but had saddled him with the responsibility of seeing to it that the family title and estates were restored to him. He had plotted and schemed for nothing else for seven years, only to find that the machinery he had set in motion to achieve this goal had acquired a life of its own and swerved direction in order to aim at the end of putting Matthias not back in his barony but on the throne of Westrigonia itself. Fortuna was playing her usual tricks. But now, walking through Castle Raspero, Eleanor finally understood why it was that Matthias had sought nothing more than his return to his own inherited domains. Castle Raspero was indeed special, and to be the baron of these domains, with unchallenged authority in your own sphere, could indeed compete with the splendour of monarchy.

Matthias's guided tour ended on the castle walls overlooking the township of Raspero and the countryside all around. The castle walls were so wide that an old-fashioned horse-and-carriage could have driven around their square circuit. From their commanding height, there was a view over the township below with its river flowing through the middle of it; lifting the gaze higher led to the sweeping vista of the valley beyond, stretching all the way to the Rohesia mountains in the blue-tinged distance. Behind Castle Raspero towered the Mountains of Lochfric, gaunt and severe, where green forests found haven in the midst of giant outcroppings of bare rock.

The golden sun shone down from a pure blue sky. A breeze blew gently, ruffling the clothes of the procession emerging onto the castle walls and moving along to the corner overlooking the township. At their head were the figures of Matthias and Eleanor, and following along behind was the watchful figure of Lady Jimena, who was now their self-appointed chaperone, and behind her followed Lena and Hallvard.

Matthias stood beside Eleanor by the castle wall overlooking the town and chatted to her about the view, still in his guided tour mode. Just as Eleanor had seen fit to lecture Matthias all about the Palace of Krastienst, so it was that Matthias now chose to lecture her about the Barony of Raspero. Matthias then turned and looked at Eleanor with such a serious air that she knew that something was up. She did not have to wait long to find out what it was. Matthias fished out a diamond ring from his robes and sank down on one knee, holding the ring up in the air for it to glitter in the sunlight. Eleanor gripped a nearby stone of the castle wall to keep herself standing.

'Eleanor, there has never been anyone but you for me since the day we met each other as children. You have been in my thoughts and in my heart from that day to this. You are the love of my life. Your dignity and sense of self, your beauty and pride and intelligence, your poise and charm and elegance have completely won my heart. There has never been anyone else but you for me, and there never will be anyone else but you. I want to marry you and be a good and faithful husband to you and a good father to our children. Eleanor Leland, will you marry me?'

'Yes, Matthias, I will marry you,' Eleanor said as steadily as she could manage given how unexpectedly close she was to tears. Her emotions had grabbed her like a wild-eyed bandit deaf to reason.

Matthias stood up and slid the diamond ring onto her finger. He then took Eleanor into his arms and her arms went around his neck and they kissed each other on the castle walls under the blue skies of the barony of Raspero.

CHAPTER THIRTY NINE

It is clear enough what the fault lines of the world are.
Frankie the Villain

The news of the engagement of Matthias and Eleanor spread across Westrigonia and abroad in a matter of days. The male admirers of the Jewel of Krastienst cursed the stars under which they had been born for failing to have granted them Matthias's good fortune. Westrigonian nationalists were shocked, and took the news as a blow. Their latest hero had turned out looking dodgy, as all their heroes always did. Most subjects of the realm accepted this development as being positive. No-one talked of anything else.

It had been an unusual year for politics in Westrigonia, and this was just the latest twist in a complicated tale that had involved nothing less than the stunning abolition of the Vidaldmeet. People joked that the country had never been governed so well as now that the Vidaldmeet no longer existed. The members of the Vidaldmeet laughed along with everyone else, but not nearly so heartily.

But things were not quite this simple. It was a matter of opinion as to whether or not the Vidaldmeet in actual fact did not exist. The Vidaldmeet had, in their wisdom, decided to ignore their own abolition and continue as if nothing out of the ordinary had happened. It was a bluff that might or might not work. Taxes were still being collected, law and order still applied, the country had not descended into anarchy, but no-one knew for certain how much this was due to an inertia that might not last.

As far as Westrigonian politics was concerned, Matthias's withdrawal to the barony of Raspero was seen as a masterstroke. Nothing could have emphasized his essential centrality to the political process of continuing with the nation of Westrigonia. It dawned on everyone that nothing could be done without him. He was the one public figure who commanded nearly universal respect. Even the Zoller-Abstein faction, while publicly saying that his youth and inexperience and criminal background rendered him unfit for any kind of public office, let alone the monarchy itself, privately conceded that he was a man to be reckoned with. His romance with Eleanor had opened up the possibility of a rapprochement between Westrigonian nationalism and the Zoller-Abstein faction which no-one had overlooked, least of all those who wanted no such reconciliation. No-one believed for one moment that Matthias had withdrawn to Raspero because of a quarrel with Eleanor. She was only, after all, a woman. It was all a breathtakingly clever trick. Justin the Second had pulled off a similar stunt on his way to the throne. The nobles of Westrigonia began beating a path to Raspero to see the Marechal and implore him to return to Krastienst and take up the reins of government.

11:05 AM, Monday 18 May 1882 A. F.

Matthias and Eleanor returned to the Palace of Krastienst arm in arm. Eleanor returned to the Chambers of the Crown Princess of Westrigonia, while Matthias moved into the King's Chambers. Lady Jimena came along as well, having appointed herself as their chaperone. Lena and her fiancé by then had returned to Trentland.

Matthias set two books by his bed for his bed-time reading. One was an admiring biography of King Justin the Second called *The Life of Justin the Second: the last great King of Westrigonia*. The other was a strongly disapproving biography of King Justin the Second called *The Life of the Imposter Monarch Justin the Second: Usurper and Tyrant of Westrigonia*.

It had occurred to Matthias that if he carefully studied everything Justin had done, he could avoid becoming like him. Matthias was determined to avoid being dragged along the same path as Good King Justin.

12:30 PM, Wednesday 20 May 1882 A. F.

Matthias called up a force of seven thousand soldiers, and went to Aldbach. Of all the absentee landlords who had acquired estates in Westrigonia after the downfall of Justin the Second, Lord Faye of Aldbach was one of the most notorious. He spent his days, and especially nights, in the fleshpots of the Protectorate, and on the rare occasions he visited his Westrigonian estates, it was in the company of his Anglashian friends to whom he pointed out the features of Westrigonian life as if they were visitors to a zoo. For Westrigonian nationalists, he was among the most hated of all the foreigners that plagued them.

Matthias issued an arrest warrant for the absent Lord Faye as a way of making sure that he stayed absent, stripped him of his estates, and conferred those estates and the title of Earl on Alaric, who took the name of Aldbach as his new name. Alaric also publicly announced his engagement to Lady Nina Delwyn.

All this set the political circles of Westrigonia to chattering about who was who and what was what. Matthias obviously did not have the legal authority to behave like this (although was there such a thing as legality without a country within which it existed?) but he did have control of the army, and he was on course to become King, which meant that in the long run he would be able to push this measure through anyway, which made it accepted without opposition now. But what was most interesting was that Alaric, as Matthias's protégé, was to marry a member of the Delwyn family, given that the Delwyn family were amongst the most prominent of the Zoller-Abstein faction, which was how they had managed to get Nina the position of lady-in-waiting to Eleanor in the first place. (Eleanor's appointment of Mitzi had raised eyebrows.) By this move Matthias was sending an obvious signal to the Zoller-Abstein faction that he was willing to make a deal. And by now, with everyone's nerves run so ragged with all the political uncertainty of the times, a deal was precisely what everyone wanted.

The question, of course, was what kind of deal exactly?

3:20 PM, Monday 15 June 1882 A. F.

They finally brought Matthias his Letter of Declaration. It was written on lambskin in eight differently coloured inks – forest green, royal purple, scarlet red, a shining iridescent blue, a dark blue, a jet black, a burnt yellow and a mahogany brown, the colours of each letter being chosen with regard to the morphology and phonology of the words as they related to the esoteric dimensions of monarchical rule. There were delicate black-ink line drawings in the margins of Matthias and Eleanor, the Royal Palace, the Crown and the Throne.

Matthias was suitably appreciative. 'It is a document worthy of the greatest of kingdoms, which is our Westrigonia.'

The monarch is not monarch until served with papers. Qismat the Unready had evaded his pursuers for months. Westrigonia had had to do without a monarch while he hid from the pursuing officers of the law with his mistress. Eventually they caught up with him, bound him hand and foot, pressed the Letter of Declaration into his hands, and Qismat had no choice but to accept his monarchical duties.

In the end, it had been decided that Westrigonia had been recreated by universal agreement and it would remain as it always had been while being reborn. Not a finger needed to be lifted anywhere. Everything was new while remaining as it always had been. The deal was that no deal was necessary. Matthias was elected King by the Vidaldmeet with 43 votes in favour, two against and four abstentions. The Vidaldmeet approved his marriage to Eleanor. The barony of Raspero had been returned to Baron Matthias Raspero. Westrigonia had left the Protectorate and was now an independent sovereign nation once again.

The Protectorate itself was in turmoil. Baalbabak had in the end been conquered. The Great Cadfan was in hiding, but it was only a matter of time before he was found. The turning point had been the role played by the Baalbabakan prisoners which the Great Cadfan had refused to ransom, having decided that he didn't need them. Matthias had offered them to the Protectorate, with Camdenshall as the mediator, and the Protectorate had acquired custody of them after the payment of ten million strada to the Westrigonian Treasury. (This was an illegal move for De'Asterides to make, but he got away with it because it helped him win the war.) Those Baalbabakan prisoners of war who had turned against the Great Cadfan and fought for the Protectorate had formed networks amongst the Baalbabakans which had decisively undermined the Leveller regime and brought it crashing down. This was less of a victory for the First Protector than might have at first been thought, because Baalbabak was in such a parlous state that it would require large sums invested by the Protectorate to bring it back into the circle of civilisation. Tax-payers were grumbling about their glorious victory.

Melisende, however, was a different kettle of fish. Not only had they paid the ransom Matthias had demanded, but they had sent messengers to the Marechal to cultivate good neighbourly relations. An immediate friendship had been formed between all concerned in the negotiations. In consequence of this, Matthias had provided them with key strategic resources and the prospect of a permanent alliance. In consequence of *this*, the Protectorate's forces in Melisende, despite being much larger, had been soundly beaten and driven out. De'Asterides had been forced to pay large ransoms to the Melisendiens for the release of Protectorate prisoners-of-war, even though this was illegal under international law as devised by the Protectorate. Given his failure to conquer Melisende, this breaking of the law might well not be overlooked by the Supreme Council. Increasingly, the talk in the Protectorate was that De'Asterides had to go.

6:35 PM, Friday 17 April 1882 A. F.

On the day (and at the exact time) that Cadwalader was imprisoned, he knew the world he lived in and what would happen next. He was dragged by Captain Steindahl down to the dungeons, and delivered into the malignant hands of Dungeon Keeper Ferran, but Cadwalader was not flummoxed. Yolande would send for him, he would be released, and normal service would resume.

But Yolande did not send for him, and normal service was not resumed.

And the blasted and blighted figure of Ferran remained in Cadwalader's eyes-forced-open vision like a deliberately ugly sculpture of the late Orange period of the master Atrecatcullaria. Cadwalader gave Ferran a piece of his mind, and Ferran responded by "forgetting" to give Cadwalader his rations for a whole day. Cadwalader's hunger pains were such that he, in his turn, "forgot" to rebuke and insult and denigrate his captor, and his rations, such as they were, having been restored, kept on coming, meagre though they were. It dawned on Cadwalader, with regard to the world he had formerly lived in, that he was now a denizen of a different world.

Cadwalader consoled himself with thoughts of how posterity would lament his incarceration. Poets would pull out their pens, balladeers would tune their instruments; there would be paintings which showed the great man as either mournful or bravely defiant while hanging from his chains in his dungeon. Social reformers would refer to this most shameful episode of Westrigonian history as a way of bolstering their arguments.

Such was the magnitude of Cadwalder's egoistic self-appraisal that Cadwalader never doubted his own continued importance for a moment. He struck poses for painters to later immortalise while composing his own brave words on how he had dealt with his ordeal. All this helped him bear his sufferings without actually having to suffer.

After a while, however, a gnawing doubt, like a worm in an apple, began to work its way through his brain. Perhaps the truth of the matter was that no-one would ever pay this event of his imprisonment the least attention. No poem or ballad or painting or political speech would ever refer to it. It would be seen, if it would be seen at all, which it would not be, as an event of such trivial unimportance as not to be worth mentioning. Cadwalader groaned out loud. Now he really *was* suffering. He tried to rally his spirits by earnest refutations of these negative thoughts, but his refutations somehow failed to refute.

It occurred to him that he could always get the ball rolling by commissioning a poem or two, a painting here and there, and in such a way bring about the witnessing of his sufferings which was all that gave them meaning. This restored his spirits for a while.

But still his incarceration continued. It was the sheer remorselessness of remaining in that infernal dungeon that began to grind him down. Day after day his imprisonment continued. What of the world outside? What was happening? Why had he not been freed?

Cadwalader's path through life had been one of a succession of stepping stones provided by Fortuna herself. If Cadwalader sat down in a public flying carriage, the seat next to him had already been taken by Y, who was on his way to such-and-such a conference; given that Cadwalader had been to school with Z, whose support Y needed, it seemed only natural to Y to invite Cadwalader to come along with him to the conference. This naturally led to his next stroke of fortune. Cadwalader's journey through life was that of a rudderless boat on a mighty river being borne along by powerful currents which could not be opposed. Patronage, proteges, marriages, appointments, strokes of luck and fated events all took their appointed place along the pageantry parade of his charmed life.

But there was one pebble in the great man's shoe, and that was his insatiable lust for Her Royal Highness the Crown Princess Eleanor of Westrigonia. His enmity towards Eleanor was because of her beauty. He wanted her more than he had ever wanted anything. Yet somewhere in the bloated carcass of his egoistic self-regard, there was a shred of rational objectivity marooned in time and space, otherwise known as his intellect, which told him that Eleanor would choose to throw herself out of a flying carriage rather than submit to his advances. He knew this without needing to be told. As Eleanor's maturing years brought her up to greater and still greater heights of beauty, she became known as the Jewel of Krastienst, and Lord Augustus Cadwalader watched it all happen with an immeasurable sense of loss. Cadwalader in fact was agonised at the sight of the Princess's growing beauty, and the knowledge that he could never have her. The older she became, and the more lusted after by her admirers, the more agonised Cadwalader became and the worse his bullying of her. And so it was that whenever Eleanor spoke, Cadwalader rolled his eyes at the suggestion that Her Royal Highness the Princess Eleanor could say anything worth listening to.

And now Cadwalader, the Royal Councillor of Westrigonia, was a prisoner in the dungeons of the Palace of Krastienst, abandoned by the monarch whom he had served so faithfully, in his own estimation at least, notwithstanding all the bribes he had taken for less than perfect governance. He was a prisoner in the dungeons!

At first Cadwalader *denied* what he was going through, on the very reasonable grounds that before long someone would come along to free him and he would be restored to his earlier freedom and, more importantly, to his earlier importance; but this did not happen. Cadwalader subsequently felt a certain *anger* that he was being treated so shabbily, given that it was such an injustice. After this, he turned his attention to how to *bargain* his way out of imprisonment, but as time passed and still no-one even came to visit him he began to visibly sag in his chains and to look gloomier and gloomier. But then came a time when he *accepted* his predicament, and neither enjoyed it nor resented it. It was true that his time was his own more than it had ever been during his busy and productive life. He had always complained that he had never had time to himself due to the demands of his political career; well, now time was all he had. He allowed himself to enjoy a certain laziness, lolling about in his chains; he started to talk to the Dungeon Keeper, and found poor old Ferran to be, far from a mean-minded tyrant, an anxious father with money-worries and disreputable relatives. Cadwalader and Ferran struck up an unlikely friendship.

Cadwalader was now more appreciative of the simpler things in life. He yearned to see the blue sky and the yellow sun. Prison had done him a world of good. He was a much better man than the narrow-minded politician he had once been. Cadwalader had once memorized as a young man a plethora of Zen proverbs and wise sayings. Cadwalader had completely forgotten about that time of his life, when he had been an idealistic young man; now, to his surprise, he found that the sayings were still all there in his memory. He revisited them, hanging from the walls in his chains, and as he did so, his chains became merely a fashion accessory rather than a hindrance. Cadwalader felt like a free man in constrained circumstances.

Cadwalader had long ago given up all hope of ever getting out of the dungeons. But Fortuna, who governs all things in this world, was about to spin her wheel once more.

10:30 AM, Wednesday 24 June 1882 A. F.

'May I ask your Majesty what is to be done about Lord Cadwalader?' Royal Councillor Lawrence Oanez asked deferentially.

'Who's Cadwalader?' Matthias asked. The name seemed vaguely familiar.

'He was the Royal Councillor to Frederick and Yolande.'

'Ah yes, I remember him. What about him?'

'Is he to remain in the dungeons, your Majesty?' Oanez queried. 'I ask only with regard to the relevant paperwork.' As it happened, Oanez had accepted a hefty bribe from Lady Cadwalader to raise this issue with Matthias. (Lady Cadwalader was dealing with numerous legal and financial issues that required the freedom of her spouse. If it had not been for that, harsh as this sounds, she would have been only too happy to leave Lord Cadwalader where he was.)

'Why is he in the dungeons?'

'Your Majesty had him imprisoned some time ago.'

'Ah yes,' Matthias nodded. 'I remember now. Why did I imprison him?'

'I am afraid that I have not been informed as to this matter.'

Matthias stared at Oanez for a moment, as if to silently urge him to change his answer, but Oanez, his head bowed, remained mute. As far as Oanez was concerned, he had earned his bribe by honestly doing the work required of him. Cadwalader was now on his own. Oanez was done.

'Why did I throw Cadwalader into the dungeons?' Matthias asked, looking about him for help. 'Does anyone remember?'

There were head-shakings all around and muttered uncertainties. No-one else seemed to remember either. It was yet another indignity heaped upon Cadwalader's head.

Matthias could remember having had Cadwalader thrown into the dungeons, but for the life of him he could not remember why he had done it.

'Why did I throw Cadwalader into the dungeons?' he asked everyone within earshot again.

Silence.

'Does anyone remember?'

More silence.

Matthias bowed to the inevitable. 'Oanez, have Cadwalader brought before me this afternoon.'

4:45 PM, Wednesday 24 June 1882 A. F.

Cadwalader waddled awkwardly in his leg chains, which did not permit the fully extended stride of his legs, while his arms bound in their own chains added to the impression of an amphibious creature clumsily in motion on land. Steindahl brought the captive in front of Matthias and then stepped backwards.

Matthias and Eleanor and their retinue sat in the Reception Area of the Throne Room and gazed at their visitor.

'I am trying to remember why I threw you into the dungeons,' Matthias said. 'Perhaps you could be so kind as to remind me. Why *did* I throw you in the dungeons?'

'*Care about what other people think, and you will always be their prisoner.*'

'Just as you say,' Matthias said a little warily. He wasn't sure what kind of trick the former Royal Councillor was playing now. 'But this is a simple question about the past, and of course the present and future, with regard to what is to be done with you. So? What have you to say?'

'*If you are depressed, you are living in the past. If you are anxious, you are living in the future. If you are at peace, you are living in the present.*'

'I do not understand you, Cadwalader. What are you about?'

'*If you understand, things are just as they are; if you do not understand, things are just as they are.*'

'Not for you,' Matthias said with a smile, 'unless you think the dungeons are no different to being here. Why were you imprisoned again?'

'*I sold water by the river,*' Cadwalader said with a smile.

'Could you be a bit more specific?' Matthias asked quizzically.

'*In this one falling leaf is the whole autumn.*'

'That's being more specific?'

'*The Way is this everyday life.*'

Matthias laughed out loud at this, but he was the only one who did. Everyone else stared at Cadwalader as if he had gone nuts. 'And what's everyday life?'

'*We buy the cauldron, but it is the emptiness inside that counts.*'

'So the cauldron is everyday life?'

'*While we sit peacefully, the grass grows by itself.*'

'Surely it is time to execute Cadwalader while the grass is growing?' Eleanor suggested to Matthias. 'Perhaps he has a choice saying concerning this occasion!'

'*You will not be punished for your anger, you will be punished by your anger.*'

'There we go, I knew it!' Eleanor cried out. 'Once this fat toad is dead and buried, we will feel bad about having killed him! Oh well, let's do it anyway.'

'*When you realize how perfect everything is you will tilt your head back and laugh at the sky.*'

'That does it!' Eleanor said, somewhat savagely. 'What is perfect is this toad's execution.'

'*Three things cannot be long hidden: the sun, the moon and the truth.*'

Matthias laughed yet again. The King of Westrigonia was enjoying this.

'We must be in the presence of a saint,' Eleanor said with a wide-eyed sarcasm. She was growing still more angry. 'I do believe I can even smell the flowers of his holy aura.' Eleanor would always detest Cadwalader, and nothing would ever raise her low opinion of this man. He had ridden roughshod over her sensitive feelings for as long as she had known him and nothing he could do now, absolutely *nothing*, could earn her royal forgiveness for the offense he had caused her by his low insolence.

The others present stirred uneasily and kept quiet. Politics could be a risky business, and no-one wanted to be remembered for having responded inappropriately on this occasion.

'What is it that you are about, Lord Cadwalader?' Matthias said, sounding as if he was not sure whether to be exasperated or laugh a third time. 'If you have a penchant for quotes, why don't you consider quoting Oedipus? Have you seen the play by Sophocles? Oedipus is wandering the world alone, blinded and destitute, and what does he say?'

The former Royal Councillor said nothing.

'What does he say?' Matthias asked again.

Still the former Royal Councillor said nothing.

'Shall I say it for you?' Matthias offered.

At this the former Royal Councillor stirred, looked up at the King of Westrigonia, and said: '*Notwithstanding the extremity of my suffering, I am led in my old age and in the greatness of my soul to judge that all is well.*'

The former weasel-politician turned human being and the former baronial-fugitive turned King looked at each other for a moment of shared understanding and then Matthias the Fourth declared: 'Guards, release this man from his chains! He is free to go!'

Eleanor stirred a little rebelliously, but said nothing. (Although she tapped her fan in a manner that was eloquent enough!) Nina got ready to write all this down in her diary. Mitzi was wondering if she could use any of this for her hoped-for political career. All those present were, as is the custom in a court, contemplating their own personal advancement in the grand scheme of things.

Alack, alas, *besorrow and besplains*, Cadwalader's reformed character did not last. He was soon enough swallowed up by his wife's complaints, his children's demands about his grandchildren's needs, and the earnest solicitations of his large retinue. Before long, his earlier anxiety returned in the form of pride in all of his accomplishments, and he was as bad as ever. He would go to his grave in this mortal condition, which is to say still believing in the illusion of his importance. His last chance of redemption ended up slipping through his fingers.

10:45 PM, Friday 26 June 1882 A. F.

Matthias was in the King's Chambers preparing for bed. He strolled hither and thither in his pyjamas, looking about and not even acknowledging to himself that he was avoiding another excursion into Justin's biographies, and further evidence that he was doing everything in exactly the same manner as the demon king. Matthias did not know if he was battling Fortuna herself in his attempts to avoid turning out like Justin the Second, but he did know this: he would not go down without a fight. And maybe that was all that counted in the end.

There was a painting in the King's Chambers which he returned to again and again. It showed certain key members of the Vidaldmeet visiting the King of Westrigonia after a decisive vote. And amongst them was a well dressed figure with a large R on his chest. The R was shaped like three or four R-shaped figures interlaced amongst themselves. It was Oliver Raspero, called in his own day the Anglashian Baron.

Oliver had been his father's grandfather, and Matthias had caught the tremor of awe in his father's tone of voice whenever he referred to him. There was something magical about Oliver, something special, something that made people proudly say *I knew him*. Long ago, the thirty-third Baron of Raspero had died without heir, and so the Steward of Raspero and his assistant had set out for Anglashia to seek a rumoured descendant of the Barons of Raspero. There they had encountered Oliver Raspero, a thief of such skill that he had stolen the entire barony of Raspero and taken it for himself. But that secret was hidden safely away among all the other secrets of the Great Library of Raspero, the story written in Anglashian in Oliver's own hand telling of what Oliver had once done long ago when he was young.

But that is a story for another day.

CHAPTER FORTY

Everything is governed by Fortuna.
Frankie the Villain

5:35 AM, Tuesday 30 June 1882 A. F.

The sun rose on the long appointed day. All preparations had been made and there was nothing left to do but do the deed itself. Like Mikhail Hunyadi who, on the day his armies marched off to war, famously sat down to read a novel, the authorities had nothing but their nerves to deal with. Today would witness both a wedding and a coronation. All going well, it would signal the beginning of nothing less than a dynasty.

8:40 AM, Tuesday 30 June 1882 A. F.

Eleanor was a bundle of nerves in the Dressing Room of her Chambers. Constantly having to remember to breathe, she was attired in her wedding dress by several Royal Dressers overseen by Lady Farley, the Dresser to the Crown Princess.

The wedding dress was made of sparkling white lace interwoven with dazzling white pure-silk charmeuse and overlaid with more white pure-silk satin. Eleanor's bare shoulders were overlaid with layers of transparent chiffon. Her hair was pulled up and bound by a netting studded with emeralds and rubies and amethysts.

Eleanor spoke little, did not seem to hear what was said to her until it had been repeated two or three times, and looked pale. She was trembling very slightly. All the women present were understanding of her nerves. Even the hard-hearted Mitzi was being nice for once.

All her life, Eleanor had wanted only two things: to choose her own husband; and to become Queen of Westrigonia. Now, on the day when both of her wishes were about to come true, she found herself having second thoughts about everything. She was reminded of the saying *beware of what you wish for in case it comes true.*

It was true that her second thoughts were due, at least in part, to being nervous. This was, after all, her wedding day. Everyone is nervous on their wedding day. It was also her coronation day, which was something else to be nervous about. She would be married to Matthias at one o'clock and crowned at three o'clock. The usual three days of coronation rituals would follow their wedding night, which would be tonight. So Eleanor was, not unexpectedly, contemplating closely the path she was on, given such a workload as this.

She wondered if enough time had elapsed during their courtship for her to be completely sure that she was doing the right thing. Had it even *been* a courtship? It had all been very informal, without even a chaperone in attendance. Certainly it should have gone on for longer. Now all of a sudden she was getting married! How had she agreed to this schedule? Well, she had agreed, and it was too late to back out now.

There was, of course, the unavoidable consummation of the marriage to come. Like a tongue probing a loose tooth to explore a sense of impending loss, Eleanor's mind kept returning to this approaching experience looming over her like a masked man. She felt paralysed by nerves at the prospect. It would be much more reassuring if her wedding night did not have to be tonight. Obviously, it would have to come eventually. It was just that tonight was too soon. And secondly, now that she came to think of it, it would be easier to consummate the marriage with a husband for whom she had no feelings. She wondered how she could ever have thought that it was the other way around. Far from it: a wedding night with a man for whom she had no feelings could be dealt with like a medical operation, a form of invasive surgery. It would be unpleasant, but she could grit her teeth and bear it. Her mother had been right all along after all. A wedding night with Matthias, her very own good-looking-rebel-turned-king, her very own Matthias who she had known all her Westrigonian life, was a hundred times, no, a thousand times scarier. Why this should be so made no sense, yet it was so. She was in love with Matthias and she was marrying him and it was terrifying.

And then she would become Queen. If being a titled beauty had made her an object of lust and a target for destruction, being a young and beautiful Queen would both protect her and make her even more prominent.

Eleanor wondered if she would ever feel safe again.

8:40 AM, Tuesday 30 June 1882 A. F.

Matthias for his part was also a bundle of nerves. He would have preferred to be facing a battle to the death against a fierce opponent rather than get married and become King. It was not that he did not want to marry Eleanor; far from it. It was just that he was wondering if today was too soon. Perhaps they should have waited for longer. All the calculations earlier, both esoteric and political, had pointed to seizing the moment at this time and no later, but now Matthias was not so sure.

Matthias stood in his Dressing Room saying little, with such a distant expression on his face that he had to be spoken to more than once before he heard what was being said to him. There were several people in attendance, being supervised by Lord Garsea, the Dresser to the King.

Matthias was being attired in a sleeveless red leather jerkin; his hose was coloured a bright green. His robes were purple, open in a V-shape at the front and hanging down in four triangular sections from the waist down. His knee-length black leather boots were so highly polished that they gleamed.

Matthias's mind continually returned to one question, which was whether or not today was too soon to get married. He could identify the key problem. It was that he was in love with Eleanor. This changed everything. Matthias found himself in a position to observe that an arranged marriage was, in some respects, a lot easier than marrying for love. Provided that the girl was not mad or bad, and most weren't, things would work out one way or another. Love might well be over-rated, the King of Westrigonia reflected to himself. After all, when it came down to it, everyone could surely get by without it. Despite what the poets said, the world would in fact keep turning around without love pushing it along.

And then there was the business of becoming King. Historically, Westrigonians had either loved their King or killed him. The advent of the Protectorate had smoothed out this cycle of creation and destruction, but Westrigonia had now left the Protectorate. (For the nationalists, this had been the condition without which not.) Everyone, except the absent Lord Faye, had kept their estates and their titles, and so, with their cards still in their hands, had everything still to play for. The Zoller-Abstein faction had pinned their hopes on an eventual return to the Protectorate, via the mediation of a Zoller-Abstein Queen, and so had given way on this issue for now, which is to say only for the present, not for all of the indefinite future.

Time, as always, was everything.

11:20 AM, Tuesday 30 June 1882 A. F.

Krastienst had been settled in times that were ancient even before the Fall. At varying times a fort, a trading settlement and a market town, it had struggled along through the ages as largely a straggle of buildings surrounded by falling down chicken coops and archery ranges. Then the tip of Fortuna's finger had descended on this locale and everything had changed in a heartbeat.

The great walled cities of Odellburg and Yimaston had been slugging it out over the prestige of being the new capital of the forthcoming Kingdom of Westrigonia, and as a compromise, Krastienst had been proposed instead, being midway between Odellburg and Yimaston. Much to everyone's surprise, this proposal had been accepted, and the new capital was overnight a going concern.

The design of the city as being an ellipse with the two focal points taken by the Palace and the Vidaldmeet was the idea of Etienne, the eleventh Baron of Raspero. His good friend the well-travelled Magister Farley had taken over with regard to the internal design. He had taken the Cretan Labyrinth, ancient in times even before the Fall, and laid out this labyrinthine circuit by stone paved paths within the elliptical walls, which at that stage were represented by ropes suspended between stakes driven into the ground. He had then overlaid this path with a more normal network of square and rectangular grids of roads connected by angled alleys and crescent-shaped paths. Thus it was that the original labyrinth was hidden in its setting of the roads of the city. At two ends of the labyrinthine path were placed the Palace and the Vidaldmeet, and south of them was where the paths crossed, and there was placed the Temple of the Herakrim.

On this day, the path of the labyrinth had been marked out and cordoned off and guarded by soldiers. Eleanor left the Palace via the North Door. Her wedding dress had such a long train it was carried by no fewer than fourteen nine year-olds, seven of them female and seven of them male. She strode slowly along the path of the labyrinth, which went north, curved around to go south, and then looped around. Eventually she would reach the Temple of the Herakrim.

It was the longest walk of Eleanor's life. Although it took thirty minutes, it seemed like half-a-lifetime: the cheering crowds, the sea of red, white and black (the national colours of Westrigonia) all around, the measured tread of the armed escort before and behind her, all combined to overwhelm her senses and float her mind into a dream-like sense of unreality.

Behind her strode Matthias, at a carefully measured distance from Eleanor which meant that his future bride came in and out of sight as they wound their way along their path.

The weather was perfect. The sky was blue, with puffy white clouds. The cheerful bright sunshine flooded its golden glow across the city. Gentle breezes ruffled the brightly coloured clothing of the populace, who thronged the streets, waving flags and shouting excitedly. The soldiers patrolled the streets, laughing and taking flowers from the people to tuck into their lapels; important-looking officials strode about as if they alone knew what was what; children gazed avidly at the sights to be seen, which would fill their memories for a lifetime. Here were the monarchs of Westrigonia, resplendent in the streets. Even the polished white stone seemed alive, basking in the sunlight of this blue-skyed day. Those who were there on that special day would always speak of it as if it had been an experience that defined them.

Eleanor arrived at the Temple of the Herakrim and stood there waiting for Matthias to catch up. They then entered the Temple of the Herakrim together.

11:50 AM, Tuesday 30 June 1882 A. F.

The Temple of the Herakrim had a gabled curving roof made of blue tiles. The curvature of the roof was in order to ward off evil spirits, which could only move in straight lines. Underneath the roof was a square shaped building of red sandstone with only one entrance, which faced south. This one entrance was reached by ascending a staircase of one hundred and eight steps made of black granite stone. The entire temple was on a raised platform made of the same black granite. Like a temple of the ancient world that had demanded human sacrifices, the Temple of the Herakrim towered majestically above the multitude. Historically it had exerted a similar authority, although in its defense, it had to be said that it had never demanded human sacrifices.

The square shaped floor was inlaid with a circle that touched its sides, and was divided into four by a cross. The circle was glossed with gold and the cross with silver. The quartered segments made of marble inside the circle were differently coloured, being turquoise, purple, yellow and black. The four sections of flooring outside the gold circle were all of sky-blue marble.

Above was a pyramid shaped ceiling which displayed frescoes showing various scenes from the Book of the Herakrim.

In the middle was an altar between two pillars which towered up high into the air surmounted by golden and silver crowns, respectively. At this altar waited the Sealer of Bargains. He was a tall, thin imposing figure in a silver-and-black robe, with a headdress made of painted wooden boards with multi-coloured ribbons hanging off them.

Matthias and Eleanor made their way along the central silver line of the cross hand–in-hand, passing through the congregation. Yolande and Frederick and Jason were there, and Lord Sakesheld, Lady Jimena Raspero, Lena and Hallvard, Alaric and Nina, Acteon standing awkwardly in between Mitzi and Georgette, both of whom were after him, and many other relatives and family friends and dignitaries besides. Matthias and Eleanor came to a halt in front of the Sealer of Bargains. There they made their vows, and exchanged rings, and there they were formally married as husband-and-wife. It was all done by ten past one.

1:10 PM, Tuesday 30 June 1882 A. F.

Matthias and Eleanor emerged from the Temple of the Herakrim and took their places in the flying carriage waiting for them at the foot of the one hundred and eight steps leading down from the entrance to the Temple of the Herakrim. The flying carriage set off at walking speed and at only four feet above the ground through the cheering multitudes of the streets of Krastienst. The flying carriage traced out the remaining path of the labyrinth before arriving back at the Palace of Krastienst. There Matthias and Eleanor descended, and entered back into the Palace. They were now a married couple, but their day was far from over. They still had their coronation ahead of them.

They entered the Palace and walked along the corridors which had been cordoned off with red rope until they came to the Corridor of Approaching leading to the Throne Room. The corridor was lined with household staff of the Palace, among them Astrudel and Nereus, courtiers, dignitaries, ambassadors and a variety of functionaries, who all bowed as the newly-weds passed by. Hand-in-hand, they walked steadily along this corridor to face their fate in the Throne Room itself.

A Commentary on our great monarchs of old Matthias and Eleanor by Styrenius the Truthful in the year 2349 AF:

The King who was called Matthias the Just and his Queen Eleanor the

Wise ruled with the extremest of excellence in such long ago days that we term them among the ancients. For surely it was none amongst any of the kings and queens of Westrigonia who knew so well the governance of their country. It was said that if a pin was missing from a pin-cushion, that Their Majesties would remark upon it. Never was the Kingdom of Westrigonia so prosperous and peaceful as in this time, for it was said that nothing was amiss in the best-governed of kingdoms. Indeed, many have observed that these monarchs, having achieved such fame in their own lifetimes and beyond, became immortal by become nothing less than playing cards, for Matthias became the King of Swords and Eleanor the Queen of Diamonds in the immortal Halstedt Deck. But others have said that even this is not the true measure of their fame, for it was notable that His Majesty Matthias the Fourth, upon his second son Stefan reaching the age of twenty-one, abdicated the Barony of Raspero in order that Stefan (who Matthias said was his reincarnated brother) should ascend thereby as the thirty-eighth Baron of Raspero. And so Matthias's eldest son Oliver the First became King of Westrigonia after Matthias, and his eldest son Adal the Third became King in his turn, and then after him came the next King of Westrigonia, Kalin the First. And with him came an end to the Raspero dynasty, for Kalin fell from the throne. And many have said that these four generations of the Raspero dynasty saw the heights of Westrigonia. And so it came to be that even these generations passed by. Yet the Barony of Raspero endures, and exists still to this day. And so many believe, as the songs do attest, that in the time of the greatest troubles of what shall remain of Westrigonia, a saviour shall arise from the Barony of Raspero, as a saviour had once arisen in times of old.

3:00 PM, Tuesday 30 June 1882 A. F.

Matthias and Eleanor entered the Throne Room hand in hand. Many of those who had attended their wedding were there again to witness this second ceremony: Alaric and Nina, Acteon still in between Mitzi and Georgette, Lady Jimena and Lena and Hallvard and many other others besides. The Councillors were there, and a guest of the Protectorate as an observer, and many others besides. Beside two red cushions placed by the thrones stood the Keeper of Keys. Matthias and Eleanor sedately approached the thrones, mounted the three steps and kneeled down on the red cushions. The Keeper of Keys took forth a large heavy crown made of solid gold and placed it on the head of Matthias the Fourth, proclaiming the ceremonial statements by which he was now King of Westrigonia. He took forth a large heavy crown made of solid silver and placed it on Eleanor's head, proclaiming the ceremonial statements by which she was now Queen of Westrigonia.

It was done.

Matthias and Eleanor arose, stepped to their Thrones, turned around to face the room, and took their seats in a slow steady stately manner. As they became seated, everyone in the room sank onto one knee and bowed their heads to the new monarchs.

And so it came to be that at that time and in that place, they raised up Matthias and Eleanor to be King and Queen of Westrigonia.